RIVER OF SAND

By

Sam J. Pisciotta

RIVER OF SAND

ISBN 978-0-9915496-4-1

Printed in the United States

Lupo Publishing, Sam J. Pisciotta, Pueblo, Colorado

RIVER OF SAND

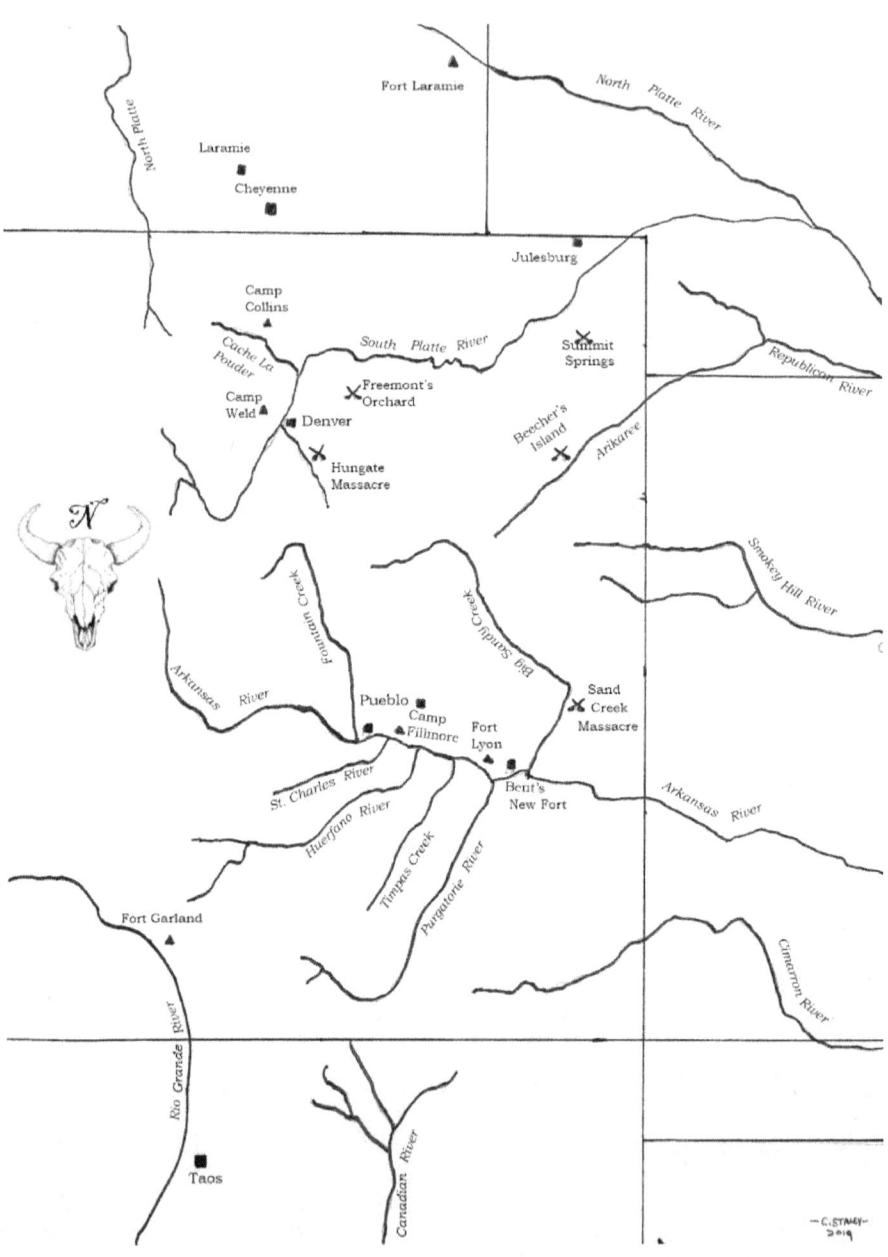

COLORADO INDIAN WARS
1850-1869

PROLOGUE

June 1869 – Fattening Up Moon

A dust devil whipped up and blew past the spot where Whitney Voss lay on his stomach, looking out from the cover of the fallen cottonwood tree onto the dry prairie grass and sage brush that surrounded his place of refuge. His lips were dry and cracked, and his mouth felt sticky. Water was within reach, less than a hundred yards away, but it might as well have been a hundred miles. For the past eighteen hours, he and his companions had been pinned down behind the aged cottonwood trunk that lay at the head of a wash leading down to the river. The tree had probably once thrived, judging by its size, and offered shade and shelter, but it had long ago fell victim to either old age or one of the violent storms that plague the open prairies.

Now, the downed giant offered protection on one side of a fortified stronghold for Whitney and his companions. The slight depression at the head of the drainage behind the fallen tree offered cover from the other side and had been deepened by the men themselves using their knives and hands to dig and block the downstream approach.

Though safe from their Indian adversaries, they all felt the possibility of death, some from the wounds they suffered, all of them from thirst. None had a drop of water since they had been jumped the previous day by the Cheyenne war party, and to make their suffering even worse was the availability of water in the nearby river.

Whit adjusted his position, and with the movement, the pain of his own wound returned. It shot around from his back, and down his right hip and leg. He could also feel the pull of the dried blood on his shirt where it had stuck to his back. Like his companions, he suffered in silence. Six of twelve men from their party were injured, and one, Private Knowles had been killed. Knowles had been the first one hit when the shots rang out near mid-afternoon the previous day. He had been struck in the chest by an arrow that tore through his lung. He had stayed in the saddle until cover of the cottonwood had been reached. His companions then helped him into the wash and made him as comfortable as possible while they fought off the Indians.

Doctor Craigavon tended to the trooper, but there was little he could do. His medical bag had been attached to the cantle of his saddle and had been lost when the horses were stampeded by the Indians. Whit, as well as two of the other soldiers, had also received their wounds before forting up behind the tree. The doctor himself had received a flesh wound as he went to the aid of the soldiers who had been holding the horses, pulling the wounded trooper to the safety of the wash. Craigavon ignored his injury and saw to the welfare of the others before settling down with rifle in hand to help drive back the attackers.

Whit wondered if Knowles had not been the lucky one to have died quickly with little suffering. He now thought about the possibility of being captured, and with that in mind, he calculated saving the last bullet in his pistol for himself.

As the hours dragged on into the afternoon, the Cheyenne only made half-hearted attempts to attack. They knew that, sooner or later, the whites would either run out of ammunition or become too weak to fight. Whit also knew this, and though he fought it, he found himself drifting off, losing his concentration and doubting what was real. He contemplated what had brought him here, to this lonely spot in the middle of nowhere. What were the choices he had made that lead to his dying here, his scalp to be a trophy on some Dog Soldier's belt?

Through the haze of heat that floated above the ground, Whit thought he saw a figure approaching, it was blurry and seemed to walk straight toward him, not seeking to hide or conceal its advance. As the form drew closer, Whit determined that it was a woman. Her long, raven hair drifted in the hot breeze, and the fringe of her buckskin dress swaying with each step. She stretched out her hand, softly calling out his name and he knew who she was.

CHAPTER ONE
THE CHANGING SEASON

May 1851 - Bright Moon

Powdery rooster-tails of dust rose in from the wheels of the wagons as they made their way westward, following the well-worn Santa Fe Trail along the Arkansas River. The hot still air allowed the fine powder to rise slightly, then fall almost where it was picked up by the iron tires. The teamsters cursed and their whips cracked like gunshots in the dry air, mixing with the creaking of the wagons and bellowing of the oxen. Every sound seemed to melt into a single monotonous pattern, until there was one long droning that felt never-ending.

In advance of the caravan rolling along the dusty road, Whitney Voss rode in search of cooler air and relief from the noise behind him. At the distance of almost a half mile, the pandemonium of freight wagons was faint, but still audible. He could turn in the saddle and see the freight wagons belonging to William Bent moving slowly; and though only just within earshot of the noise, he was certain if there were any sign of danger he would hear or see it in time to react.

Whit adjusted the balance of the Deringer rifle that lay across his thighs, between his hips and the saddle horn, reassured by its weight. He was confident in the security it offered in either the procurement of meat or in keeping an adversary at bay. The .50 caliber, muzzle-loader could throw a 180-grain lead ball toward a target over two hundred yards with deadly consequences. For close-in defense, Whit carried a single shot, .54 caliber Aston pistol, tucked into his belt next to a large-bladed hunting knife. Of the three weapons, the knife held more sentiment. It had belonged to his grandfather, Benjamin Voss. When the old man gave the blade to Whit, he had told him, "Take care of this knife, Son. It was given to me by General George Rodgers Clark, and it was my constant companion when I lived in the wilds of the Stoney Mountains. I have kept it all these years as a reminder of those times." He had smiled at his grandson and added, "I know that staying here, and working in a wagon shop is not what you are made for. I was much the same as you when I was young. But I came back, and am happy with the life I have led. You, Whit, are the only one of my children who seems to want to see what is on the other side of the river, and I wish you well."

Whit's father, Zebulun, had not been happy with his son's choice of leaving the family business for the unknown of the western frontier. In his mind, the west offered nothing but danger, and he had wanted his youngest son to stay in Pittsburgh and continue in the family business. It had taken both Benjamin and Whitney's namesake, his uncle, to persuade Zebulun that Whitney would never be happy as a craftsman.

"Would you let your son go off into the wilderness?" Zebulun asked his brother.

"If Ben wanted too, I would give him my blessing," his brother replied. "Whit isn't like my son, or like his own brother, Aaron. He'll never be happy working at the forge," he paused then added, "Funny how you seem to forget you were born out in that wilderness, big brother."

Zebulun shook his head and then replied, "He's only 19 years old, not quite a grown man. I only want the best for my son, that's all."

"He's a man in more ways than you know, Brother."

With reluctance, Zebulun gave his blessing and Whitney left home to drift down river to St. Louis in the spring of 1849. There, he fell prey to the lure of the gold rush drawing thousands to California. Traveling along the Santa Fe Trail, he viewed the new western frontier and was instantly attracted to its rugged beauty. By the time he had reached the trading post of Bent/St. Vrain & Company on the Arkansas River, he decided that digging for gold might be more work than it was worth.

Whit wasn't prepared for the sight of the adobe "castle". Though he had grown up around the buildings and factories of Pittsburg, and had seen the cities of Cincinnati, Louisville, and St Louis, he was awed by the sight of structure standing on the plains north of the Arkansas River. Though its dimensions were only one hundred and forty feet by one hundred and eighty feet, there was nothing like it west of the Mississippi.

The fort faced just a little off true north, its walls thirty inches thick and fourteen feet high. At the northeastern and southwestern corners stood round towers eighteen feet tall and seventeen feet in diameter. The main entry faced north and lay tunnel-like between two rooms, a gate at both ends. It was large enough to pass freight wagons through, nine feet wide by seven high, and its outer gate was stoutly made of iron-sheathed planks.

Above the entry, and forming its roof, rose a watchtower with a belfry holding an iron bell; and rising above the belfry was a flagpole from which Whit could see the Stars and Stripes floating in the breeze.

He entered the front gate passageway coming out into the inner courtyard, called a "placita" by the locals, in the center of which stood a large fur press for packing buffalo robes. Moving about the placita were laborers, hunters and traders employed by the Company.

Rooms were set around the entire placita, facing inward. There were over two dozen of these. The trading and storage rooms along the eastern side were somewhat larger than the others. Outside their doors, which fronted the courtyard ran a timber-supported veranda.

Whit noted what appeared to be a carpenter and blacksmith shop at the back wall. The sounds emanating from the work in progress brought to mind the memories of the wagon yard and home. For the first time since he had left Pittsburg, Whit felt a small pang of homesickness. But this soon passed as his gaze fell upon the domestics working around a large fire.

This was the first time he had seen the women of Nuevo México. These dusky-skinned women from Mexico were enticing with their coal-black eyes, and their bare, tawny shoulders bronzed by exposure to the sun. His eyes widened as he saw their skirts, with a hemline that stopped at mid-calf, exposing their ankles and their dainty feet shod in slipper-like moccasins.

Whit couldn't keep his eyes off of these Spanish beauties, and he barely noticed the few Cheyenne Indians that were present at the fort. The Cheyenne were the main customers and were often at the fort to trade buffalo robes and other furs for the goods offered in the trade room.

Unknown to Whit, a set of brown eyes sparkled at the sight of his lean body and blond hair. They were those of a young

Cheyenne girl, Little Bird. She was seventeen years old and though Whit had no idea, she was entranced by his pale blue eyes and blond locks. He was far from the only fair one among the Whites, but the brief sight of Whit left an impression on the girl that she would never forget. From her place behind her father, she watched Whit as he moved around the placita. When Whit disappeared into the darkness of one of the fort's rooms, it was if someone had extinguished a light, and she ached for him to emerge and bring back the light.

She was to be disappointed as her father, finished with his business of trading buffalo robes, signaled with a nod of his head that it was time to leave. She was crushed, and as she walked out of the gate, she glanced back in hopes she could capture one last glimpse of the young Whiteman.

In the midst of the fort's hustle and bustle, Whit decided that California was not the place to go. Here, among these people of the new American territory, was where he wanted to be. Rather than move on with the tide of emigrants, he entered the main trade room to inquire about the possibility of employment. The head clerk, Charles Goodall, was pointed out to him and he approached Goodall, introducing himself. He assured the clerk that he was earnest in his desire to stay and work at whatever task was required of him.

The adobe fort was the center of the Bent/St. Vrain & Company's trade empire which included other posts; to the north on the South Platte River was Fort St. Vrain, to the south, Fort Adobe on the Canadian River, along with company stores in New Mexico at Taos and Santa Fe. The primary trade was with the Southern Cheyenne and Arapaho Indians along the Arkansas River and with the Mexicans of the new territory south of the river in New Mexico.

Goodall told Whit there was no need of additional help in the blacksmith shop, nor with the carpenter, but there was always a need for a strong and intelligent young man. Whit soon found himself engaged as a hunter, earning $300 a year, and credit for any buffalo hides, skulls and tongues he brought in.

Over the next few days, Whit witnessed the true scope of the unbelievable surge of Americans sweeping westward, as they passed by the fort on the Arkansas. Word also reached the post on the Arkansas, that unknown to these emigrants and gold seekers, they brought with them the dreaded disease, cholera.

From St. Louis, it had moved upriver to Independence and Westport, and then westward with the California bound travelers. By the time they were aware of its presence, they had dotted the trail with graves at almost every mile.

Once out in the clean air of the western prairies, these immigrants thought the plague had burned itself out, but this assumption turned out to be false. A village of Cheyenne camped with a group of the westward bound Americans on the Oregon Trail, and when they left for the south, they carried what they called "the Big Cramps" with them, infecting other Cheyenne bands as well as some Kiowa. Within weeks, almost half of the Southern Cheyenne were dead.

After further examination of these modern pilgrims, Whit was certain he had made the right choice. He had signed on for employment in June and was just settling into the routine of life at the post when he was ordered to helped load all the goods contained inside the adobe fort into twenty of the large freight wagons, each pulled by six yoke of oxen.

After seventeen years of business in the adobe castle, William Bent had decided to abandon the trading post, and move his business east to Big Timbers. The partnership of William, his brothers and Ceran St. Vrain, had come to an end. The cost of building the company's empire had been too much for William to bear, losing his first Cheyenne wife, Owl Woman, and then his three brothers in its creation.

Moving down river some forty miles to Big Timbers, William, his second wife, Yellow Woman, and his children, moved into the new post. It was a modest structure of three log cabins joined to form a U-shape, the open end facing the river, and all enclosed with a picket stockade. It was not long before William was settled down and began doing the only business he knew, that which he had perfected over the past three decades, trading with the Indians.

Whit spent the next two years working for William Bent, hunting meat and making the trips between Westport and the new trading post at Big Timbers. His job was to guide the wagons and supply the teamsters with fresh meat as needed. This work gave him the stability of permanent employment, with a feeling of freedom, a luxury in his mind. With this feeling, came loyalty and a sense of duty toward William Bent, who reminded him somewhat of his grandfather, Benjamin. Benjamin was the patriarch of the Voss family, overseeing the family business of building wagons, much like those that now trudged along behind Whit. He often wondered if some of those wagons had not been made by his family, and at times he would look for some sign that the craftsmen from that shop had left their mark on the large vehicles.

It was not fair to say that Whit had lost his wanderlust; he had only placed it in a holding pattern while he had a job he loved. His admiration of William Bent and the love of the new territory had left him content. That was until he caught sight of a particular Cheyenne woman. She had captured not only his attention but had instilled a feeling in him that stirred him to his very core.

Right after the new post was built at Big Timbers, Whit made his first trip accompanying William Bent into the Cheyenne camps to trade and spread the word about the new post's location. Though he had seen some of the Cheyenne around the trading post, he was excited to see his first big camp. But the excitement of the Cheyenne camps was eclipsed when he caught his first glimpse of a Cheyenne maiden in the village of Chief Crow Horse. Though he had only caught a glimpse of her, Whit was captured by her doe-like eyes, lost in her gaze, leaving him breathless and his heart pounding in his chest. He had no idea that this maiden of the prairie had herself cast her gaze on him months earlier, and only now their eyes had met and a deep yearning was shared by both. Whit could hardly wait until his next chance to see this beauty named Little Bird, daughter of Black Dog and Prairie Grass Woman, and he found himself searching for her when she was out of sight.

Little Bird had thought constantly over the past months of the pale-eyed young man with hair the color of the sun. She had seen him again, and she had dared to cast more than a glance his way, catching his attention and delighting in the obvious reaction she had caused. His entire continence had changed; she had won his heart without even half trying. When Little Whiteman, the name William had been given by the Cheyenne, left the camp taking Whit with him, Little Bird was not as dejected as the first time she had lost sight of Whit. This time she knew that he would be back.

After leaving the village in search of another group of Cheyenne, Whit informed his employer of his infatuation with the girl. At first Bent shrugged it off, but after Whit continued to pester William for knowledge pertaining how one went about courting a Cheyenne girl, Bent reluctantly gave in, and offered to help broker at least the first steps in getting Whit and the girl together.

The girl was in the prime of her life and sought after by several young Cheyenne men, but guided by William Bent, Whit had a leg up on these lords of the prairie.

"Don't get in too big of a hurry," William advised, "The Cheyenne take special care and put a lot of value on the chastity of their young women. You can't go bulling your way in like you're after some harlot, or even some white gal from Westport. You have to gain the trust and respect of the gal's father, her mother, uncles and the like. Courting among these people can take a year or more. And remember, anything you do with that gal reflects on me, and I won't let what's in your pants get in the way of the trust that has taken me thirty years to build." Whit promised and from that day on worked hard to not only secure his future with the girl, but make William Bent proud of him.

Within a month of spreading the news about the new post built at Big Timbers, William and Whit were back in the village of Crow Horse, and William helped Whit by introducing him to Black Dog, the reason for the introduction not lost on either Black Dog or his extended family. After the formalities of smoking a pipe and eating, Whit offered presents to Black Dog consisting of a green English point-blanket, a Sheffield knife, some blue beads, coffee, sugar and packets of vermillion. The Cheyenne was only then willing to discuss the subject of his daughter's availability.

There was talk of Whit's lack of prowess as either a hunter or a warrior, and doubt as to the number of horses Whit would bring to offer Black Dog over the course of the courtship. It was also contingent on whether the girl herself had any desire to be courted by a vé'ho'e, a White man.

It was at this critical time that another problem arose. Black Dog told his wife to go out of the lodge and ask their daughter what she thought of the arrangement. When the woman returned, she was followed into the lodge by another young woman, not Little Bird.

Whit felt that he had been the victim of a trick and that some form of switch had been arranged. When he expressed his concerns to William, and William passed them on to Black Dog, it was discovered that Black Dog believed that Whit wanted to court his oldest daughter, Sees Far Woman. When the misunderstanding was cleared up, Whit's fears were calmed, but turmoil erupted in the Black Dog household. Black Dog and Prairie Grass Woman, were disappointed that the white man had not come for the older daughter. They had hoped that they could marry off the daughter who had been the more disappointing of the two. Though as beautiful as her younger sister, she had a hard look about her and had proven herself too strong-willed, difficult to deal with and somewhat touched by spirits. This had made Sees Far Woman undesirable to most of the young Cheyenne men.

As it was now clear that Whit was seeking permission to court Little Bird, she was told and informed her mother that she would return the interest shown by Whit and was more than willing to let the blue-eyed man court her. Black Dog, his wife and Sees Far Woman were not as happy. Prairie Grass Woman bent forward from where she sat behind her husband and whispered into his ear. He smiled and proposed a solution that would benefit, in his wife's mind, everyone.

"It would be good if Sky Eyes were to take both daughters into his lodge as wives," he suggested. The idea seemed to be more than welcome by everyone concerned, except for Whit. When this was translated to Whit by Bent, the look of shock that crossed his face was clear to everyone.

"I can't do that, Mr. Bent. I don't want that other gal, I'm looking to marry just Little Bird," Whit's rejection of the idea was plain without any translation. Bent attempted to relay the message in a fashion that would soothe any hurt feelings.

"My friend is a young man, and though he would be honored to take both of your daughters, he has a heart for only your youngest," he said. This left Black Dog and Prairie Grass disappointed, but Sees Far was crushed, her pride beyond wounded. She thought herself made a fool of, and immediately came to hate the white man with the pale eyes and hair the color of the sun.

An agreement was soon reached on the number of horses that Whit would bring his prospective father-in-law over the next few months, as well as an unspecified number of gifts for the rest of the family, and the process of courting began, much to the mixed joy and angst of both Whit and Little Bird. It was soon evident that neither would let much more time than was necessary go by before they were wed.

Whit soon found that he could buy the worn-out stock of the travelers headed west, and after a few weeks of fattening them up on the sweet prairie grass, he built a small herd of horses. Within a short six months, Whit had provided over a dozen horses, as well as the other required gifts to Black Dog and his fiancée's extended family. This gained him respect and expedited by the desire of the two young people, Whit and Little Bird became man and wife before the winter snows began to fall.

The first months of the marriage were like any honeymoon, the new couple being completely consumed with each other's company, and everyone seemed to have accepted Whit except for Sees Far Woman and Bear Voice. It became evident that Bear Voice had no fondness for Whit, nor any white man for that matter. It was also known that he had held an infatuation for his niece, and he made no effort to hide his jealousy. Most people ignored Bear Voice's obsession, and the gossip soon changed when Sees Far Woman moved into the lodge of Bear Voice and his wife, Buffalo Cow Woman.

As for Whit and Little Bird, they gave little thought to Sees Far Woman or to Bear Voice. Their love grew stronger and through the winter months they shared their own lodge, enjoying each other's company with the excitement and passion of newlyweds.

They spent hours talking and learning about each other's families, people and cultures. Little Bird learned to speak some English from Whit, and in turn she taught Whit to speak Southern Cheyenne and more important, she schooled him in the sign language employed by all the plains tribes to communicate with one another.

Little Bird never tired of Whit's stories about the east and where he had grown up. When he described the cities and the number of people, she doubted him, and accused him of weaving a tale. Whit swore to her that what he said was true, and convinced her that in the spring he would take her with him on his trip to Westport for William Bent. This excited Little Bird and she made Whit promise to purchase her some fine material to make a dress for the trip. She also started on a new pair of moccasins and leggings for the journey, beading them with intricate patterns in red, white, sky blue and cobalt blue beads.

It was in mid-winter, during the Big Hard Face Moon when Little Bird surprised Whit with the news that she was pregnant. At first, she was apprehensive, fearful of telling him. She had heard many stories of Whiteman who came from the east and took a "Mountain Bride" to keep him warm during the winter months, only to leave her when spring came. "Would Whit leave her when she grew fat with a child?" she wondered. But what choice did she have but to tell him and go on from that point.

When Whit heard the news, he became ecstatic. He thought his life was complete with Little Bird as his wife, and now he was to be a father and he knew nothing more could make him happier.

Little Bird also confided the news that she was with child to her mother and, of course, her sister. Both women seemed happy for her and construction of items for the coming baby was started. Her sister, Sees Far, began to make the cradleboard that would serve the child as a safe place to sleep, and provided the child physical protection when the family was traveling, either carried like a backpack, attached to the travois or suspended from a horse's saddle. It was also a symbol of spiritual protection and wishes for a long, healthy life.

Sees Far was not surprised by her sister's news as she had experienced a dream where a young man had emerged from her sister's lodge. He had shone as bright as the sun and it was not possible to look at him. When people did cast their eyes in his direction, they fell to the ground and died. All suffered except for Sees Far, who he placed his arms around and called "Mother."

To hang on the cradleboard, Sees Far fashioned a fetish in the shape of a turtle. The child's umbilical cord would be placed in the amulet as added protection. Also in the amulet, Sees Far, secretly placed her own special medicine, in hopes that it would make her dream come true and she would someday have the child as her own. To extend control over Little Bird, Sees Far told her that she had a dream where she saw harm coming to the child if Little Bird took it away from the People. She stressed that Little Bird should not travel to where the sun rose when the grass turned green. If she did, she risked the death of her child.

With the fear for her child's safety, Little Bird told Whit that she would not go with him to Westport in the spring. She did not tell him about her sister's dream, she only stated that she felt she would be too far in her pregnancy to travel such a distance. Though he was disappointed, he understood.

"Maybe we can go next spring, and I can show off not only my beautiful wife but my child," Whit said.

"It may be safe then," Little Bird said.

***

Whit accompanied William Bent back to Westport in the spring and the time away from Little Bird created an ache in his heart. He longed to be back with her, to hold her in his arms and he feared that he would not be with her when the child was born.

William assured him that Indian women were a hardy breed, and that even in the worst of conditions, the child would be born healthy and strong. This helped somewhat, but Whit still worried and couldn't wait to get back to the west.

It was at the end of June when Whit returned to the camp of the Cheyenne and was anxious to find his wife. He did not have to search long, as he found her in front of their lodge, scrapping a buffalo hide staked out on the ground.

"What are you doing?" he blurted out the question, thinking that she was doing work that could harm her or the baby. Little Bird looked up, and seeing Whit, sprang to her feet and threw herself into his arms.

It was only when she was enfolded in his embrace that he noticed that she was as slim now as she had been when they first met.

"The child," he said, *"Is everything well?"*

"Yes, my love," she said, and letting go of him she turned, stepped over to the lodge and removed the child from the cradleboard that had been leaning against the hide cover.

"Here, greet your son." She smiled and handed the child to Whit.

Tenderly, Whit took the small bundle up and could not believe how small the child felt in his powerful arms.

"I thought you weren't to have him until later?" he questioned.

"He decided to come early, but he is healthy and strong." She paused, and then added *"I have named him Yellow Horse because he has the light skin of his father."*

That is a good name, but we will have to give him a Whiteman's name also," he said. *"I have always liked Zachariah. Can we name him that also?"* he asked.

"Yes. Does it have a meaning for your people?"

"If I remember my mother's holy book teaching, he was a wise man, a prophet, a medicine man. We can call him Zachary, as is the custom of my people to shorten a name."

Life throughout that summer seemed idyllic to the young couple and they were inseparable, except for the times that Whit made the trips to other Indian camps to trade with William Bent. If it were a Cheyenne camp, Little Bird and Zachary would sometimes join them, but if it were with a different tribe Little Bird hesitated to accompany them.

After a time, Whit noticed a melancholy began to settle over Little Bird. At first, Whit noticed that her sleeping patterns were erratic; her restless nights caused by unsettling dreams, and at times, nightmares.

Whit attempted to comfort her, but she rebuffed him, saying that she would be well in a few days or so. At other times, when she seemed her old self, Whit made the mistake of becoming amorous with her. She rejected his advances, claiming she was either exhausted or that she felt no desire. She, at one time, told him that she could not stand to be touched in any manner. She became increasingly sorrowful, with mood swings and showed a temper Whit had never seen before. She would turn on Whit, criticizing his words or actions, finding fault in almost anything he did or complaining about those things she felt he failed to do.

Her ill treatment was not saved for Whit alone. She started to avoid contact with her family and friends. Ultimately, she lost interest in their child, surrendering the majority of Zachary's care to her mother, sister-in-law, or worse yet, her sister. Little Bird began to speak less and less, and Whit spent more and more time away from the Cheyenne camp and his wife.

Summer passed with the band moving from camp site to camp site in its annual trek across the prairie, following the buffalo and making raids on the horse herds of the Pawnee or Comanche. After a successful fall hunt, the band of Crow Horse's Cheyenne made their winter camp again upriver not far from the trading post and returned to Bent's post to trade their surplus buffalo hides.

RIVER OF SAND

Whit could not understand what had happened to his wife and it was hard to stay away from her. But, Whit could not avoid the situation forever, and needed to take trade goods to the Indian camp and barter for the buffalo. With cautious reluctance, he approached his in-laws hoping to see his son and possibly Little Bird. His visit turned happy when he saw Zachary and the child clung to him, cooing with contentment.

When Little Bird appeared, she was polite but not overly friendly. Whit waited until he had a chance to speak with her alone, and only then did she seem to respond to him in a softer and more friendly manner.

"I have missed you," she said, surprising Whit.

"My heart has been sad without you," Whit replied.

"I am made to think you should come back to my lodge," she said, her eyes looking away from him.

"I would like that," Whit said, and he opened his arms inviting her into his embrace. She stepped forward and slowly pushed herself against him nestling her face against his chest. Whit wrapped his arms around her and held her, feeling her body shaking. He wondered what could cause her to shiver but passed it off.

Whit went to the fort and unloaded the buffalo robes he had traded for, then took more items for trade and returned to the Cheyenne camp to spend the winter.

As the snow blew in from the north and camp life fell into the routines of winter, Whit, Little Bird and Zachary settled into a life together. This second winter of their marriage was not the same as the first. Less time was spent in simple chatter, and the fire of passion had cooled to a mild flame. Though Whit tried to be romantic and to please Little Bird, she was at best passive and at most cool. Whit thought it may be due to the confines of the lodge for such a long period during the cold weather. The only time either of them left was to visit other lodges, and Little Bird seemed to make those visits longer than was necessary, especially those to her sister, Sees Far. He had hopes that when spring came her mood would change, and their relationship could be repaired.

***

With the spring winds blowing softly along the plains, and the greening of the grass, Whit brought up the subject of a trip to

19

the east. Little Bird informed him that she no longer had a desire to see the big villages of the white men and told Whit that she felt he should go on his own.

"I will stay with my people," she said. *"Several of the bands will gather together and I would like to see this. My sister will be moving to the band of the Dog Men, along with our uncle, Bear Voice and I may go with her for a time."*

He reluctantly accepted her decision and promised to come back as soon as possible. To his surprise Little Bird told him, *"We will see if you return. Many of your kind take a wife among the people, and when they no longer desire the woman, they never return."*

"You know that I desire you more than any other, and I will always return to you," he replied in Cheyenne. *"You and our son are my life. I could not live without you."*

"We will see," was her only reply.

That had been almost three months ago, and Whit hoped that the time they had spent apart would have softened Little Bird's heart and made her miss him as much as he had missed her. His heart ached for his wife, and he longed to hold her in his arms. Only a day or two separated them, and Whit vowed he would make things right between them.

He looked back at the wagons and wished he could leave them behind and race in search of her. He knew though it would be some time before he would be anywhere close to Big Timbers and the possible location of his family. In the wagons were not only the trade goods but a wagonload of gifts from the Government meant to appease the Indians along the Arkansas. Indian Agent, Thomas Fitzpatrick, and William Bent rode with the wagon train, and their destination was the newly built Army post of Fort Atkinson, one hundred and fifty miles east of Bent's Fort. For Whit, it felt like a thousand miles.

***

Bear Voice, his body covered with perspiration, sat cross-legged, alone, peering eastward into the darkness. He looked with unseeing eyes at the point where the sun would rise on the eastern rim of the world. He waited for that moment when the horizon would turn a soft yellow, pale white, then to bright blue and finally the sun would push itself up into the sky. The day would start, and his four days of fasting would end.

Around him in the darkness, the only living creatures that moved were those whose warm blood allowed them to scurry about in search of food, the night sheltering them from the heat of the day and keeping them safe from most predators. Some of these nocturnal voyagers, barely taking notice of him, came close to Bear Voice, crossing into the sacred circle of tobacco ties he sat inside, and then they scurried away when discovering his presence.

As he had done the past few mornings, Bear Voice would greet the sun by singing a prayer. This fourth morning would end his time alone, searching for a vision, for answers and guidance from the spirits. He had prayed and sang during almost every minute of the past four days, save for the previous day. The Sun had been at its zenith when Bear Voice broke his singing and had slipped into the vision he had sought. When he awoke from the dream-state, it was past sundown. He quenched his thirst with water and spent the remaining time in an attempt to unravel the meaning of what he had seen.

This was not the first time Bear Voice had made a quest for a vision. His first time had been over twenty-five winters ago, when he had barely entered manhood. During that first quest, the hours had passed by slowly and thoughts of discomfort and selfish wants filled his head. There had been no vision, no spirit guide had come to him. No signs at all from the spirits who had failed to manifest themselves. There was no guidance for someone, like him, who hoped to leave the ways of childhood and become the leader of his band. Bear Voice wanted more than anything to take the place of Heavy Hand, as chief of the Hairy Rope Band. He had felt leadership was not only his duty, but his right. But the mantle and honors went to Crow Horse, the son of Heavy Hand, who led the band to this day.

After coming down from the hill that first time, Bear Voice reasoned that he had not been granted a vision because he had not looked in the right direction for his future. He concluded that real power to lead the People came from the medicine man, not the chief, and it was power that Bear Voice wanted, power to punish those who had taken from him the things he loved most. The chief of a band led only as long as the people were willing to follow, and it was the words of the holy men that the people truly listened to. It was they who dictated customs and laws. His disappointments filled him with an anger that had turned him sullen and bitter. It was at this time he turned to look at the old healer, Little Wolf with an eye of understanding.

In Bear Voice's mind, Little Wolf was not the amiable and wise consoler everyone thought he was, but a sly, conniving manipulator. Bear Voice also surmised that the old holy man was far smarter than he let on. In this last assessment, Bear Voice was correct. At first, Bear Voice began to follow Little Wolf and pester him with questions about the power possessed by the healers of the People. In his quest for knowledge, Bear Voice consistently overstepped the boundaries of good manners and decorum accepted by the People as common courtesy. His persistence finally paid off, and Little Wolf had agreed to accept Bear Voice as a student, as an apprentice to the arts of a holy man.

"It is not good for the People to have everything they want," Bear remembered Little Wolf saying, as the old man drew a breath of smoke from his pipe. Then, pausing, he added, *"These pale-skinned ones have a medicine that is so different from that of the People, that I believe that the two cannot live together without one of them choking. Those relying on the gifts of the Vé'ho'e, the White man, will perish."*

Bear Voice knew what Little Wolf had said was true, but he also thought the old medicine man was a hypocrite. Though he preached against the medicine of the Whites, he had taken the Whites into his heart, even to the point of letting his daughter, Walks Straight Woman, marry one. This had angered Bear Voice, she should have married another Cheyenne, or one of the allies of the People like the Arapaho or even the Lakota. In Bear Voice's mind there had been a price paid by Little Wolf, as the girl had died of the Whiteman's sickness soon after her marriage.

When Bear Voice voiced his opinions to Little Wolf, the healer told him that he did not have the heart of a healer, that he would never use his power for the good of the people but would be constantly tempted to throw out bad medicine and do harm. He told Bear Voice that harm always came back. Bear Voice was not the only one that Little Wolf had taken as a student and when the time came for Little Wolf to pass on the mantle of his position as healer among the People, he had chosen the other young man, called Carries the Shield, rather than Bear Voice.

Little Wolf was wrong, thought Bear Voice. How can it but help the people to wish harm on those who are their enemies. After his disagreement with his teacher, Bear left the band and joined one of military societies of the Cheyenne, the Dog Soldier, called Dog Men in the People's tongue. This militant group was more aligned to his way of thinking. With the knowledge of medicine that he had already learned, and his natural way of influencing people, Bear Voice soon became accepted as a holy man.

From that time on, Bear Voice had tried everything in his power to hinder the Whites. He used his medicine to stop them from building their trading posts in the territory of the People. He fasted and offered his own suffering by cutting forty pieces of flesh from his arms. But this selfless act had produced nothing like the sicknesses brought to the People by the Whites. Nothing like the Whiteman's sickness, that ate the flesh on their face or the one that turns the inside of the body to water.

Bear remembered the last time this Whiteman's sickness had attacked the People. Many of the Cheyenne had gotten sick and one of them, Little Old Man, had donned his war shirt, mounted his best horse and rode through the camp with a lance in his hand.

"If I could see this evil thing, if I knew where it came from, I would go there and fight it!" he shouted. The words had barely left his lips when he was seized with cramps, fell from his horse, and died. From that day forward, Bear Voice refused to touch any item made by white hands. He cursed the Whites with every waking breath, with every prayer he uttered.

As his power grew, so did the respect he received. Soon people came to him in want of revenge, to seek harm on others, or to create bad medicine out of spite, jealousy or outright hatred.

Bear Voice knew he must have someone of like mind to share his secrets with, someone to pass on his knowledge of these dark arts. No young man among the people added up to his expectations and he decided that a woman would be a better choice. In his opinion, his wife Buffalo Cow Woman was dull witted and of little use to him, other than to keep his bed warm and cook him meals. So, Bear Voice took as an apprentice, his niece, Sees Far Woman. Taking a woman related to him into his lodge was frowned upon. Some men had more than one wife, but

Sees Far Woman would not be a wife to Bear Voice, she would become, his protégée.

There were other reasons that he had chosen her. She held a special power, one that would enhance those of Bear Voice. Her dreams were vivid and whatever she dreamt had a way of coming to pass. She had also had her heart broken by a Whiteman. The man had taken Sees Far Woman's younger sister Little Bird as his wife, rejecting Looks Far, and Bear Voice had lost the woman he desired. So it was that both Bear Voice and Sees Far Woman held a special hatred for not only all Whites, but this one. Bear Voice hated this man so intensely that the man invaded Bear Voice's thoughts constantly, and more destressing, was into his prayers over the past four days.

This man had come among the Hairy-Rope Band of the People, was taken in as a brother, and had courted and won the hand of Little Bird. After the two were married, Bear had worked his medicine against this man and had turned to Sees Far Woman for the use of her special medicine. He had taught her the arts of conjuring up accidents and illness, and the two of them aimed this at Whitney Voss.

Its outcome, though, was similar to that of Little's Wolf's daughter. Rather than the Whiteman turning sick, Little Bird was affected. She had begun to show symptoms. First, she had become depressed and confused. Then, she began to suffer from nightmares, and visions of ghosts or evil spirits.

Waiting for the sun to rise, Bear Voice pushed back the thoughts of those disappointments. He concentrated on his people and their future plight. The last two winters had rolled out of the north with little moisture but carried a deadly cold that took the lives of the old and very young. These frigid dry winters had left the grasses short and brittle, begging for water the poor spring rains refused to offer. The parched grass drove the great buffalo herds east from their normal migration patterns in search of food. This compelled the People of the plains to range further in search of their own sustenance. It had also made the People dependent on the Whites for the meager handouts of goods, promised them if they would not make war on their enemies or on the Whites.

Thoughts of the first time he had been granted a vision crossed his mind. The vision of his spirit guide, the Bear That Walks Like a Man, had come to him and he had changed his name to reflect that spirit. The spirit of the great bear, the silver tipped grizzly, had spoken a warning to him of the dangers in taking too strong a hold on the ways of the Whites. He blamed them for every evil that befell the People

"Do not covet the medicine of these pale-skinned ones," the grizzly said in its deep voice, shaking his head. *"The way of the People points in another direction. Following the way of the Vé'ho'e is the same as drinking from a river of sand."* Drinking from a river of sand, these words had stayed with Bear Voice.

And now, Bear Voice contemplated his most recent vision. He had found himself standing on the open prairie, a thick, cold mist hanging low to the ground. Through the haze, his spirit helper had again come to him, this time gaunt and older. The great bear walked with a limp and had trouble rising onto its hind legs to stand upright. Though weakened, the sound of its words had been strong and sent a chill through Bear Voice.

"The People have not listened. They have sat by and let the pale-skinned ones come into their country. They will stand by while others, the Lakota, Comanche and the Kiowa rise up and fight the Whites." The bear shook its head as if not believing what he himself was saying.

"How can you allow this to happen? Do not let the weak, old men who always talk of peace send the People to their death. Do not let them drink from a river of sand." The bear then dropped to all four feet, turned and slowly walked away, fading into the mist.

Bear Voice moved these thoughts around in his mind. He was sure the change in the weather, and the patterns of the buffalo's movements were a punishment sent to the People for putting so much value in the goods that the Whites brought to trade. Their acceptance of the Whiteman's medicine had caused the Maker of All to turn his face from the People. Bear believed the Dog Soldiers had been sent to save the People from the Whiteman's medicine. Bear pondered this and rising to his feet, he began to pray again, his voice piercing the early morning air.

"Grandfather, have pity on me. I stand here alone. I need your help to destroy those who would take the food from the mouths of your People. Those who would close the eyes of the People to the gifts you offer in favor of those the Vé'ho'e offer. Help me destroy those who would turn the People away from you. Open the ears of the People to my words."

The sun began to peek over the rim of world, and it was clear to Bear Voice that there would be no relief from the coming day's heat. He sang out, calling on the Creator of All for aid. He called on the buffalo to return. His singing rose in prayer matching with the rhythm of his small hand-held drum that he beat. As the sky became lighter, dust floated in the dry summer air creating an orange-red haze on the eastern horizon.

Bear Voice knew the dust in the eastern sky was created by the slow moving Vé'ho'e wagons. These wagons were so large that it took twelve of the Vé'ho'e's spotted buffalo to pull them, rolling on large wooden wheels. Each wheel reminded Bear Voice of the sacred medicine wheel, but how could something bringing so much evil be supported by medicine wheels?

These wagons were on their way to the new White Soldier House. There, the White Chiefs would give out gifts to the People, and talk, speaking words that were like honey to the ear, but in truth were like the venom of the snake with rattles on its tail. Bear Voice knew that the White Chief, Broken Hand Fitzpatrick and Little White Man Bent would be at Soldiers House, and they would be the ones offering the gifts and the poison words. With them, Bear thought, would also be Yellow Hair. Bear Voice looked forward to seeing him. He hoped there would be some excuse to kill him, and wipe away any further thoughts of him and of Little Bird.

If he could only use his medicine to kill all the Whites, things might change and return to the ways of the past, before the evil gifts of the Whites came among the People and seduced them into losing their way. The People traded with Little White Man Bent for those evil goods, giving up the precious buffalo robes and the tongues of the great beasts. Some of the buffalo had been killed by the People solely for their hides and their tongues, adding to the sins of the people.

So much had changed for the People since the coming of the Vé'ho'e. When Bear was young, he himself had enjoyed the wondrous goods they brought, items such as steel knives, cotton clothing, wool blankets, metal cooking pots and mirrors. These wondrous things were now commonplace among the People. Most valuable of all the white medicine items brought to the people were the firearms. The introduction of guns to the People had changed their lives almost as drastically as when they had first obtained horses.

The People had long ago begun to trade horses stolen from the Comanche for guns, first from the Pawnee then the Mandan. Then came the French traders from the north, the Spanish from the south, and finally the Long Knives from the where the sun rose. All of these foreigners brought the guns, powder and lead to the People, asking to trade for the skins of the beaver and of the buffalo. In the past years, all the bands of the People had traded buffalo robes and tongues to Little White Man Bent, many more robes than the People would normally have taken for their own use and more robes than any man could count.

The acquisition of guns had also helped the growth of the Dog Soldier Society. Bear remembered that when he was but nineteen winters old, the first chief of the Dog Soldiers named Porcupine Bear had become crazy from the Whiteman's fire water and killed another Cheyenne named Little Creek. For this crime, Porcupine Bear was exiled, and many Cheyenne as well as some Lakota warriors joined him to form a new band. Porcupine Bear's band of outcasts had grown into a separate division of the Cheyenne nation and became famous for the bravery and enterprise of its leaders and warriors. The Dog Soldiers camped mainly on the Red Shield and Bunch of Trees Rivers and were closely associated and related to the Ogallala and Brule Lakota.

Bear Voice had lived with this warrior society for many years and he knew it would eclipse all the old societies, such as the Kit Fox, Bow String or Red Shields. Most of these old societies were influenced by old men, the Peace Chiefs, such as Lean Bear and Black Kettle. One day, the Dog Soldiers would rise up and take over all the bands of the People, and that day would begin the end of the Whiteman in the country of the Cheyenne.

It was close to the end of the day before Bear Voice made his way back to the village along the Flint Arrow River. Approaching it from the plain that gently eased down toward the river bottom, Bear Voice felt a slight breeze against his face. Looking toward the west he saw the gathering of dark clouds and he smiled at the possibility that the blue-gray billows might bring the rain he had prayed for.

***

The wagons pulled up to Fort Atkinson on the bluff overlooking the Arkansas River, just after noon. The new fort was the first regular army post to be built on the Santa Fe Trail, in the heart of Indian Country. There were forts at both ends of the trail, Fort Leavenworth on the Missouri River to the east and Fort Marcy at Santa Fe New Mexico in the west. The fort was built of sod, its roofs covered with poles, brush, sod and canvas. Therefore, the soldiers quartered there gave it the name of "Fort Sod."

It was a miserable establishment compared to Bent's trading post, but it would have to do until funds and manpower could be allocated for improvements. The Fort was shaped like an elongated hexagon, almost coffin like. The north wall was one hundred and fifty feet long, the east and west walls, three hundred and fifty feet in length, with the south wall a mere sixty feet that extended out another twenty feet past the east. This was where the location of the gate, and only entrance, was located. Along the west wall inside the fort, from the south to the north there was a building for storage, a blacksmith, a wheelwright and barracks. On the north wall was the Officers' Quarters. There were also buildings along the east wall. The bluffs around it were low, and the country on all sides was unbroken prairie, and there was no timber even on the river bottom. The one thing it did not lack was water supplied by the river. Firewood and sufficient grass for the horses would have to be found further away for the fort and Whit shook his head when he thought of the poor logistics from this location.

The objective of stopping at Fort Atkinson was to gather the tribes along the Arkansas and relay the news from the Great White Father. Thomas Fitzpatrick would ask them to spread the word that a large gathering of many nations would be held in a few months at Fort Laramie to discuss a treaty.

Congress had held up a treaty until early in the year, and Fitzpatrick hoped that giving out some gifts now to these Indians would convince them to go north and meet with other tribes of the west. His intention was to establish a lasting peace between the Government and the Native tribes, as well as among traditional Indian enemies. If Fitzpatrick could secure safe passage for the emigrants through Indian country, and stop the different tribes from waring against each other, there was a possibility that life in the west could be ideal.

As an added incentive, the Army would impress the tribes along the Arkansas, and they would see the might of the Americans. With this in mind, Fitzpatrick sent out runners to gather the Arkansas Indians. Whit was more than happy to be one of those runners and headed west in search of Crow Horse's Cheyenne.

The Army consisted of both Infantry and Dragoons, commanded by Colonel E. V. Sumner. Some of the troops would stay at the fort with Colonel Sumner and the bulk would go on to New Mexico. Accompanying some of the army officers were their wives, a sight that would also surprise the Indians.

With a bundle of gifts tied to the cantle of his saddle, Whit whipped his horse into a ground-eating lope, hoping to find the Cheyenne camp before nightfall. His heart pounded with the hoof beats as the distance grew shorter between him and his family. He looked toward the west, where gathering over the western horizon was a growing bank of blue-black clouds. The sun was now completely hidden behind the darkening shroud when the village came into his sight.

Whit slowed his horse as he approached the crescent of lodges, and several warriors came racing out to meet him at full speed. He stopped his mount and waited for them to reach him, their ponies kicking up dust, their shouts piercing the air as they circled around him.

"Ho, Pale Eyes," cried out White Badger, Whit's brother-in-law. *"It was thought you had gone under,"* joking that Whit had been thought dead.

"No, I have not given up my hair yet," Whit replied in Cheyenne.

"This is a good thing. I would not want someone else to have it." Whit knew that this was only a half joke as White Badger had no real love for him and would just as soon scalp him, if they had not been family.

"Come to my lodge and eat," White Badger offered.

"Thank you, Brother, I would find my wife and son first," Whit said.

"Ahhh...she is with my wife, as is your son," White Badger said. *"Come, I will race you,"* and he kicked his heels to his pony's flanks while reaching over and slapping Whit's horse on the rump with his quart.

They trotted toward the lodges, slowing their speed as they came to the outer line of teepees, stopping when they reached the lodge of White Badger. Like the others around it, the front and side had been rolled up to allow the air to flow through and cool the interior. Sitting on a buffalo robe in front of the lodge was White Badger's wife, Red Willow Woman, playing with Whit's son, Zachariah.

Whit vaulted from his horse, and going down on one knee held his arms out to the child, who recognizing his father, toddled over to him on his short legs. "Gawd Zach, your papa sure did miss you," Whit said, squeezing the toddler, and receiving a warm hug and giggles as a reward.

"Yellow Horse has grown in the past two moons," said Willow, using Zachary's Cheyenne name. *"If you had been gone longer, he would be a grown man."* Her attempts at humor were genuine, because in her own way, she liked Whit.

"Yes, I have been gone too long," Whit replied, speaking in Cheyenne. *"Where is Little Bird?"* Whit looked around, not seeing his wife. A change passed over Willow and her eyes dropped. She hesitated to speak, but answered him.

"She has not been well. Spirits visit her dreams, and she seeks solitude by herself along the river," Willow said. What Willow did not add was that Bear Voice, and Sees Far Woman had been coming around and filling Little Bird's head with thoughts of hopelessness, dread and fear.

"She is there now," Willow pointed to where the river flowed through the stand of giant cottonwoods.

Whit remounted his horse and moved off to find his wife, all hopes of her change of heart questionable now. These hopes were dashed even further by the sight of Sees Far Woman, standing outside the lodge of Bear Voice. Her gaze seemed to bore into him as he passed by her.

The rumble of thunder echoed from the growing overhead darkness moving toward the village. Without thought, Whit dropped his eyes to avoid Sees Far Woman's look of malice. He had never really understood why she had held on to her burning hatred of him. He had attempted to develop some kind of friendship with all of his wife's family, but it seemed no kind act by him could soften the heart of Sees Far Woman.

He put thoughts of Sees Far behind him as the moved deep into the canopy of the cottonwoods, the sound of raindrops bouncing off the leaves. As he made his way through the trees, the rain intensified. The growing wind, rustling the leaves, mixed with the increasing thunder and gave the river bottom an atmosphere of its own. The aroma of the light rain falling on the carpet of dry leaves filled the air, and though the moisture was badly needed, Whit thought it almost unpleasant.

After searching for some time, Whit sighted his wife's pony nuzzling the carpet of the dead leaves and branches aside to reach the grass below. He looked around thinking Little Bird could not be far from the pony. Dismounting his own horse, he continued his search on foot, calling out her name in Cheyenne as he made his way through the trees. He found her standing under a giant cottonwood, where she was looking up into the branches that stretched out over her.

"*Little Bird,*" he called her name again. She seemed not to hear him, and he walked up, placed a hand on her shoulder, which startled her and she turned around. He thought he had frightened her, but her face was blank of emotion and she stood looking at him as if there was no surprise in his appearance.

"*I called to you. Did you not hear me?*" he asked.

"*I was thinking...*" she started to speak, and her voice trailed off.

"*Are you well?*" he asked.

"*Yes, I was not sure that it was truly you who was calling, or that it was a spirit who was trying to play a trick on me,*" she said, tilting her head, her face now showing that she was confused.

"*I have returned to you as I promised,*" Whit said. To his surprise, she threw her arms around his neck and pulled him close to her, just as she had done in the past.

"*I have missed you, Husband, I dreamed that you had gone over to the other side and that you were calling me to join you there,*" she sobbed as she spoke to him. Whit squeezed her tightly and kissed the top of her head, the familiar, sweet scent of her filling his nostrils, and he smiled. She had returned to him, her heart had softened and she loved him again.

Following a night in the lodge of White Badger, Whit and Little Bird rode to Fort Atkinson accompanying the entire village of Crow Horse's band. Visiting the band were a few Dog Soldiers, which included Bear Voice, but Whit never gave a thought about the medicine man. Again, he took notice of the looks cast his way by Sees Far Woman, and for a brief moment a shiver ran through his body.

Whit still couldn't understand why she had stayed so cold toward him. He had attempted to mend any hurt feelings with

Little Bird's family, bringing presents for each of them. Everyone except Sees Far and Bear Voice had accepted these gifts with appreciation and grace. Sees Far and Bear Voice had refused to even touch the items.

Little Bird explained to Whit that her sister and uncle's medicine would not allow them to handle or own anything from the White world. She told him that there were many among the Cheyenne that had rejected the medicine offered from the east.

"Why?" he asked.

"They see no good in the Whiteman's medicine," she replied.

"It is not medicine; they are only things that make life easier, like the knife on your belt, or the brass kettle to cook meals in." He shook his head. *"I do not understand."*

"No. You will never understand, my husband," she said. *"That is the problem your people have. They believe their way is the only way to live."*

"And Bear Voice does not think the same about the old ways of the people?" Whit asked.

This had never occurred to Little Bird. Who was right, she thought to herself. The life of the People was changing, and with each season, came a different wind from the east. As she had been told by her husband, were there actually more Whites than there were stars in the sky?

It took almost a full day from the band to arrive and set up camp near the fort, and within a few days other bands of Cheyenne, Arapaho, Comanche, Apache, and Kiowa began to gather at Fort Atkinson. They were given many gifts by Fitzpatrick and treated to bread, coffee, and pork.

He thanked the head men from the gathered Indians for coming to talk to him and hear what he had to say. Among other things he discussed with them was the big gathering planned for July at Fort Laramie, at the confluence of the Goose and the Moon Shell Rivers, the Laramie and the North Platte. The Cheyenne and Arapaho agreed to attend, but the Comanche, Apache, and Kiowa were uneasy to attend.

"You would have us travel to the land of our many enemies," Bull's Tail of the Comanche said, "If we go far into that land, our women and children will not be safe. All of our horses will be stolen." The Kiowa and the Apache agreed.

"There will be a great peace talk," Fitzpatrick insisted. "No one will fight. You and your people will be safe." But no amount of assurances from him could convince them.

What they did agree on before leaving was one last feast. The atmosphere was the culmination of what had been brewing for several days. The familiarity of such close contact broke down the barriers between the two races. To the whites who had never seen the Indians of the plains, they were a genuine curiosity. The braves in their feathered head-dress, and beaded buck-skin war shirts and leggings along with their women bedecked in their fringed dresses piqued their interest. And their counterparts, the Indians, found the White soldiers and their women just as interesting.

Fitzpatrick and Bent had spent most of their lives among the Indians of the plains, and knew how important it was to maintain a certain amount of detachment and decorum when dealing with them. It was dangerous to be too familiar, and Fitzpatrick voiced his apprehension to Sumner.

"It is not wise to allow the soldiers and their women to engage in unrestrained fraternization with the Indians and their squaws."

"I see no problem with the situation, Mr. Fitzpatrick. If trouble were to arise, my Dragoons can quell it."

No sooner had these words been exchanged between the two, when a young Cheyenne warrior spied a ring on the finger of one of the officer's wives. Without a word, he strode forward and pulled it from her finger to examine it. The woman screamed, and her husband, taking up a buggy whip, began to lash the young Cheyenne across the face. Fitzpatrick and Bent moved in to stop the incident from going further, but as fast a prairie fire driven by the wind, word spread through the Cheyenne camp.

The insult inflicted on the lone Cheyenne was taken by many as one toward the entire camp. Bear Voice saw an opportunity to punish the Whites. He painted his face white and green and put on his bearskin robe, with its massive scalp, made of the ears, face and upper jaw of the grizzly forming a head piece. Mounting his horse, he rode through the camp calling all the warriors to prepare themselves to do battle.

"Paint your faces! Gather up your best war horses!' he shouted, "String your bows and prepare for war!"

Before long, the Cheyenne had drawn up ready for battle, yelling taunts, encouraged by Bear Voice and a few Dog Soldiers. In response, Sumner ordered his dragoons into line, forming up with loaded rifles to repulse any assault. Fitzpatrick and Bent quickly went to Crow Horse and two of the chiefs with cooler heads. With their help, Bear Voice and his agitators were separated, and their tempers eased. More presents were offered, and the Cheyenne who had been whipped was offered a fine horse to ease his pride. The fuse burning toward a powder keg had been snuffed out.

The following day, the Indians began to break camp and move off in different directions, the Cheyenne and Arapaho, westward up the Arkansas. They would split up, but had decided to go slowly north to be in the area of the Laramie River in two moons. It seemed that incident of the whipping had been forgotten by most, but Bear Voice would not forget, and he vowed that one day he would get revenge on all White men, especially Sky Eyes Voss.

CHAPTER TWO
WIND IN THE COTTONWOODS

July 1851 –Moon of the Ripening Chokeberries

Moving slowly along the Moon Shell River, Crow Horse's band of Southern Cheyenne made their way across the plain. Though it appeared to be an unorganized group, there was a well-regulated system for the movement of a village. Far out in front were scouts, who were on the constant lookout for enemies, game or water. Behind them were assembled the majority of the warriors, forming a front and side buffer between the outside world and the women, children and older people assembled in the middle. Behind, or to one side, came the vast horse herd driven by young boys, and finally more men of warrior age, to act as a rear guard.

Mixed in with the advance and flanking warriors were Dog Soldiers, their concern not only of outside danger, but keeping the younger men under control. The young hot-blooded warriors, if not restrained, could go on their own, possibly engage an enemy, or spook game before an organized effort by the main group could be executed. This was especially important when a war party went out, or a large buffalo hunt was planned.

The wagons of William Bent paralleled the route of the moving village as it followed the North Platte River, the wagons navigating a course requiring them to seek the more even ground of the well-worn Oregon Trail. This was not necessary for the Indian travois as they adapted to the change in terrain easily, going almost anywhere a horse could travel.

Whit rode close to the wagons, with Little Bird at his side. Attached to her saddle was a travois trailing along behind her horse. Secured to the travois was a small lodge cover, her meager personal possessions, and atop this baggage was a cradleboard containing Zachariah. The cradleboard was larger than the one that had been used for him as an infant, he was not swaddled, and his arms were free so that he may hold or play with a toy. From the top of the cradleboard dangled the fetish that See Far had made for the child.

William Bent also rode close to the wagons and was anticipating the unprecedented trade opportunity that the gathering of tribes at Fort Laramie would offer. One the headquarters of the American Fur Company, Bent's chief rival in the west, the fort was now a military post. Located at the confluence of the Laramie River and the North Platte River in the upper Platte River Valley, it was in a perfect place in the heart of the northern buffalo range. It was also the primary stopping point along the Oregon Trail, sitting at the bottom of the long climb leading to the Western slope of the Rockies, via South Pass. In 1849, it had been purchased and its operations were taken over by the Army, with the purpose of protecting the wagon trains on the Oregon Trail.

Fort Laramie came into sight, sitting on a slight rise above the Laramie River, and the Cheyenne picked up their pace as the excitement among them mounted. A few of the young men wanted to rush forward but were held in check by the Dog Soldiers who were maintaining the movement of the village. Reaching the point where the Laramie flowed into the Platte, the entire village spread out along the south side of the river and began to make camp, unpacking and setting up their lodges.

The camp was set up, according to custom, in a circle open on one end. As it was summer, most of the women had replaced their year-old and worn-out lodge covers. These new ones stood out fresh and white against the surrounding landscape. Once normal life had commenced in the village, preparations were made to go to the fort and see what new wonders the Whites had on hand.

William Bent's wagons took advantage of the well-used crossing east of the fort, and found a place a little over a mile away. There they would be close enough to do business with both the Military at the fort, and the expected Indians. The location also gave the availability of forage for his stock. Tents and awnings were soon erected, and Little Bird placed her lodge a few yards away. It wasn't long before the little camp had become "home" for the small group, and Whit, Little Bird and little Zachariah accompanied William Bent to visit the fort.

The forts, Fort William and then Fort John, had once been owned by William Bent's biggest rival in the fur trade, the

American Fur Company. In fact, Thomas Fitzpatrick had once been a partner in the operation of the AFC prior to his being appointed Indian Agent of the Upper Platte and Arkansas in 1847.

Fort John was purchased by the Government from the American Fur Company, for $4,000 in June of 1849, and was officially renamed Fort Laramie. Three companies of dragoons arrived at the fort that same month, and Company 'G' of the 6th Infantry, arrived in August to become the post's permanent garrison. The objective of the Army was to protect and supply emigrants along the emigrant trails.

Aware of the mounting tension between the Natives and the Americans, Fitzpatrick had urged, from the outset of his appointment, a treaty council to ensure peace.

By early 1851, Fitzpatrick's efforts had borne fruit and the U. S. Congress appropriated $100,000 for the purpose of establishing a treaty. He wasted no time in getting the word out and the meeting on the Arkansas at Fort Atkinson had been his first stop.

In front of Whit, sat Zachariah, nestled between his father and the saddle pommel, his chubby little hands holding onto the saddle horn, his eyes wide with amazement at everything he saw. Little Bird and Whit rode down to the sutler's store located a few hundred yards north of the post. Fort Laramie reminded Little Bird and Whit in many ways of Bent's old trading establishment. The feel of the surrounding area was much the same, and Whit became very comfortable, but Little Bird, seeing the adobe walls, hesitated.

They crossed the area where Fort William had stood, its timbers cannibalized for building the newer establishment just a few years ago, and just shy of the sutler's store, she stopped her horse.

Whit had gone several steps before he turned to speak to her and found she was not with him. He looked back and found her looking about as if she were searching for some unseen danger. He turned his horse around, and moved back to her side, speaking to her.

"Little Bird, are you unwell?" he asked, but she acted as if she had not heard him. He repeated his question, this time in Cheyenne and reached out to place his hand on hers. She pulled it back, as if she did not recognize him, her eyes wide with fear.

"Little Bird, my love, are you ill?" he asked, concerned that she was showing symptoms of the malady that had griped her in the past.

Her gaze cleared a bit as if she had just woken up from a deep sleep, and she gave an unconvincing smile saying, *"I am well. I was thinking of something far away, and was startled for a moment. I believe that a shadow passed over me."* This puzzled Whit, but he passed it off as she seemed to be back to her old self.

"Come, let us see if they have something special to make you smile."

They rode on to the store, and tied their horses outside, and Whit with his son entered the wooden building. Little Bird made it as far as the doorway, and hesitated just outside. As if to summon up some form of courage, she stepped through the doorway into the semi-darkness. The smell inside was almost stifling to her and she fought back the bile that rose in her throat. The man behind the counter was removing goods from a box and placing them on the shelves.

The items in the store were meant to supplement the rations that the soldiers received, and the sutler took advantage of their cravings for such things as tobacco, chocolate and of course whiskey.

A soldier's pay was only $8.00 a month, but before he received it, any debts he owed either for the laundress or the sutler were taken out. If he were short, that wasn't a problem, for the sutler would extend credit up to one-third of the soldier's wages. This situation led to constant problems with soldiers being in debt. With whiskey at 50¢ a quart, most soldiers were always short of funds.

Whit scanned the goods lined up on the shelves looking for something that was out of the ordinary, something that William Bent did not carry in his stock of goods. What caught his eye was box marked "Parkinson's Celebrated Royal Doncaster Butter-Scotch." He smiled and asked for a handful. The storekeeper wrapped up the sweets in brown paper and handed them to Whit who handed him a Spanish silver dollar. The clerk looked at the unexpected silver and smiled, asking Whit if he would like credit for the remaining amount.

"Sure," said Whit. "I suspect that I'll be back for one thing or another."

"What name may I put down in the ledger for you?' the clerk asked as he opened the ledger book.

"Whitney Voss," said Whit.

The sound of his name drew the attention of a gray-haired and bearded man sitting in the corner of the store. Pulling the pipe from his mouth, he watched as Whit handed one of the small pieces of candy to his son and his wife.

"Do not swallow," Whit warned, *"Let it melt on your tongue."*

Little Bird and Zachariah had both tasted stick candy and Mexican chocolate, but the taste of butterscotch was an unimagined treat. The child's eyes widened, and he moved the sweet around in his mouth, giggling. Little Bird's mood changed, and she smiled, her eyes brightening as she looked at Whit in surprise. Seeing her and his son smile made Whit happy and it promised hope for the future.

As they left the sutler's store, the gray-haired man followed them, keeping a short distance behind as he scrutinized Whit. Finally, he quickened his pace to catch up and when he was a few steps away, called out to Whit.

"You are a Voss, No," he asked, speaking with a heavy French accent.

Whit stopped, and turning around looked at the old man that had addressed him.

"Yes, Whitney Voss," he answered.

"You are the son to Benjamin Voss, maybe?" the man asked.

"Who are you and why do you ask about Benjamin Voss?"

"I am Antoine Martin," the little man said, "I was a good friend to Benjamin Voss, long time ago!"

"You knew him from where?" Whit asked.

"He and I, we fought the Black Foots and we trapped the beaver."

"Benjamin is my grandfather."

"Then he is still alive, yes," a smile broke across Martin's face. "C'est une bonne nouvelle! I have not heard of him for many, many winters, but have often thought of him and his beautiful femme," He paused and rubbing his beard, he looked back at the store and added, "Come let us go back to the store and you can buy me whiskey, no?"

"It would be better if we did that at another time," Whit said. "Will you be here for some time?"

"Oui. I 'ave a Brule woman, and will be a translator in the série de négociations, 'ow you say, the talks between the Americans and the Lakota."

"Tomorrow then. You can come to my camp, there along the river," Whit pointed out the wagons. "You are also welcome to join us for a meal."

As they were riding slowly back to the camp, Whit asked Little Bird if she would rather take a short journey away from the camps to spend some time alone, just the three of them.

"*I would like that,*" she said, and they turned north-west following the North Platte.

The heat of the open plain around the post was left behind as they entered the canopy of trees along the river. The air became cooler, refreshing to breathe and the water flowing along became tempting.

"*It would be nice to go swimming in the river, would it not?*" Whit suggested with his question.

"*Yes, I would wish to bathe,*" answered Little Bird.

"*Let us find a place suitable,*" said Whit, and he began to scan the banks for a secluded place, where they would have some privacy and be hidden if someone happened to come along.

It was not long before they found such a place and leaving the horses to graze on the sweet grass next to the riverbank, they removed their clothing and slipped into the cold water of the river. Whit held Zachariah in his arms and the child squealed with delight as he and his father splashed around.

Little Bird eased herself into the refreshing water, lying back, and let her entire body slip below the surface. She emerged slowly, her wet hair trailing back behind her shoulders as she stood, wiping the water from her face.

"*I have missed this,*" she said. Like all Cheyenne, she enjoyed the habit of bathing at every chance, even in cold weather it was not uncommon to clear the ice on a river in order to bathe.

Whit looked at his wife, her flawless bronzed skin, shiny from the water. He was mesmerized by her beauty and could not keep his eyes away from her. "She must be the most beautiful women in the whole world," thought Whit.

"*Do you know I love you more than anything?*" he asked her.

She turned to look directly at him, and for a brief moment she smiled, then she shook her head thinking, "*You have no idea what you are saying.*"

They finished bathing and Whit spread out a blanket on the riverbank where they could lay and dry off. Soon Zachariah was fast asleep, and Whit lay on his side still looking at his wife, on her back gazing up into the branches of the trees above them.

"I would live like this for ever if I could," Whit said, but Little Bird seemed not to hear him. *"Would you stay like this if it was possible?"* he asked.

She didn't answer but turned to look at him, paused a moment, and then moving Zachariah to one side of the blanket, she moved to Whit's side. She placed her hand on his bare chest and ran her fingers up to caress his cheek in her hand.

Whit leaned over, hesitating inches from her face, and then he kissed her gently on the lips. To his surprise, she responded, and they were soon entwined in a passionate embrace, and there in the coolness along the river they made love.

When they separated, Little Bird lay on her back again staring up into the leafy branches above them.

"I do not like the man with the white hair on his face," she said.

"Do you mean the Frenchman?"

"He has a way about him that I do not trust."

"We have only just met him. We should wait until we know him better in order to decide if we can trust him."

"He said that he will speak to the Cuts Throats the words of the White Father."

"Yes, he is one who does that. There are many here who will do this type of talking; Little White Man Bent, Broken Hand, and Blackfoot Smith will also speak the words at these talks."

"None of them can be trusted," she finally said, and a visible change came over her. She was gone into that place where she retreated away from him and the rest of the world.

When it was time to head back to the camp, Whit had to call her name several times before she acknowledged him, rose up from the blanket, dressed and mounted her horse. The remainder of the day, and on into the next morning, she did not speak.

The next morning, Antoine Martin and his Brule wife, Elk Woman, showed up at the camp. With them was another man as old as Martin, but where Martin's hair was a dirty gray, this man's was snowy white. Where Antoine was heavy set, this man was lean, and looked more the part of an old trapper. Though lean, he looked strong with broad shoulders and muscular arms. His complexion was dark from years of exposure to the sun, and his bright blue eyes stood out.

The Lakota woman was more than half the old Frenchman's age, and though tall, was heavy built, with a round face. Her dress was made of fine, red trade wool and she wore several pairs of silver earnings, brass and silver rings on almost every finger, and several strands of Venetian glass beads around her neck. Her leggings and moccasins were also heavily decorated with glass beads in intricate patterns. Around her ample waist, was a wide leather belt, with brass conchos, and brass tacks. Like many Indian women, from her belt hung a knife in a case, an awl case and a bag holding a flint and steel. All these beaded in the same patterns as her moccasins. Everything about Elk Woman said she belonged to a wealthy man, but Martin himself looked as poor as any of the old trappers that frequented the forts along the Oregon Trail.

"Bonjour, mes amis!" Martin shouted as he slid down from his horse. "And we 'ave come to share breakfast with you! We 'ave brought you gifts and a guest that will surprise you." The other man slowly dismounted; his movements slowed by age.

Elk Woman dismounted her horse and pulled a bag from the pommel of her saddle where it had hung. She stepped forward and handed the bag to Little Bird who accepted it with a polite *"Thank you,"* and the hand sign that expressed the same.

"Good morning, Monsieur Martin," said Whit. "Come and sit down. Breakfast will be ready soon and we will eat."

"Merci, you must not call me monsieur, I am a friend of your grand-père. You call me Antoine, no. You have whiskey, yes?" he smiled showing strong white teeth, uncommon among most men his age.

"It is a bit early for me," said Whit, "But I can find some." and Whit moved off to search through his belongings. He returned with a bottle and handed it over to Martin.

The other man reached out his hand and introduced himself to Whit, "It's a pleasure to meet you, Mr. Voss," he said his voice clear and strong.

"Thank you, Mr.?"

"Scott, Silas Scott. I understand that like this ol' coon, I knew your grandfather."

Whit was astonished that these two men both knew his grandfather, and recalling Little Bird's intuition he became suspicious for a moment.

"Come, let's sit and have some breakfast," he offered, and to Silas he said, "Monsieur Martin, I mean, Antoine, seems satisfied with whiskey, would you like the same or can I offer coffee?"

"Ah, coffees, please, and sugar if you have it. I have a taste for sweet things." The men then found a place to sit; Antoine and Silas eased themselves down to sit Indian style on the ground.

Whit brought Silas a cup of coffee, and Little Bird soon brought the men plates of cured ham and fried bread. As the men sat and talked, the two women made an attempt to talk to one another in sign language, as neither spoke the language of the other.

As the men ate and talked, Elk Woman attempted to get acquainted with Little Bird.

"Have you been with your man long?" asked Elk woman.

"Three winters," answered Little Bird.

"Does he treat you well?"

"Yes, well enough."

"I had another man before my little fat one. He was killed by the Black Feet. All who know this one call him Broken Nose. I call him White Turtle, for he moves slowly like the turtle. He takes his time with everything, especially under the blankets." She giggled and then added, *"He makes the sound like a buffalo bull when he sleeps because of his crooked nose. I do not mind so much that or that he is old, as he makes up for it with his generosity, and as I said, he is good under the blankets. Is your man good in the blankets? He looks like he has muscles made of stone, and I would think that was a good thing for making you happy."* Again, she giggled.

Little Bird cared little to know any of what Elk Woman had told her, and did not want to answer Elk Woman's questions about Whit's sexual prowess. She believed that is was not something she wished to share, especially when she herself thought about it very little. Yes, Whit had always pleased her, but she no longer had those feelings, she no longer had the desire to be intimate. That part of Little Bird was dead.

Little Zachariah toddled over and crawled into his father's lap, and sat looking at the stranger across from him talking with words he did not quite understand.

"And this little one, what is he called?" Martin asked.

"His name is Zachariah," Whit said.

"Zacharie in français, no?"

"I guess so, sometimes I call him Zachary."

The boy responded to his name and looking up said, "Papa."

"He is a strong looking little loup," said Antoine, "Is your père named Zacharie?"

"No, my father is Zebulun."

"Ah! Now I remember. Your père was a baby when I knew your grand-père, Benjamin. I used to call him, 'Mon petit loup' and this one takes after him. The Frenchman laughed and took a healthy swig from the bottle.

"Who do you work for Antoine?" Whit asked.

"I work for Antoine!" the Frenchman said. "I was a company man for the American Fur, before them I was with Ashley and when I was with your grand-père I worked for that bastard Manuel Lisa. I 'ave spent my life putting profits into the pockets of other men."

"And you Silas, are you employed?" Whit was sorry the moment he had asked, it had almost been a rude way to pose the question to Silas.

"I come up here to make sure the Cheyenne get a fair shake." Then he asked, "And you, who do your work for?"

"Captain Bent," Whit pointed over to the wagon camp not far away.

"You have been with him a long time?"

"A few years."

"I worked for Bent & St. Vrain for a long time. Think the world of William. I'll have to go over and palaver with him a bit." He shook his head and then said, "Like'd William's brothers too. Shame they died. Never took a liking to Ceran though." He spoke of Ceran St. Vrain. He looked over at Little Bird and asked, "Your wife is Cheyenne, isn't she?"

"Yes," said Whit, "Her name is Little Bird, daughter of Black Dog."

"I know Black Dog. He can be a mean som-bitch. Had me a Cheyenne wife. Lost her a few years back, best woman that ever took a breath." Silas looked down and then added, "Lost me a daughter a long time back, before my wife. I have a son and a grandson that are living with the Cheyenne."

"Oui, your boy, he is with the Dog Soldiers, no?" asked Antoine.

"That's what I've been told," said Silas.

"I've spent some time around the Dog Soldiers. Don't think many of them have much use fer Whites other than for guns and powder," Whit said.

"True, if this peace conference works though, they may be out of business, other than as camp police so to speak."

"Well, I guess there's good and bad in every race of people."

"Ah, then you 'ave much to learn. I 'ave seen things done by the Indians that no white man would do. Is that not so, Silas?" Antoine did not expect an answer, and took another swig from the bottle and then added, "You come to the talks with the Indians, and you will learn that what men say and agree to, is not always what is to take place."

"You mean the treaty? You don't think the Government will live up to their promises?"

"It is not the nature of either the American's or the Indians to keep the promise. They will do only what is best for them at the time. When it does not befit them, they will do as they wish." He looked at the bottle in his hand and shaking his head said, "This is empty, do you 'ave another?"

Over the course of the next few days, Whit learned much of his grandparent's exploits in the Rocky Mountains. Martin and Scott told him stories that placed a new light on the way he looked at Benjamin and Katherine Voss. Though he had imagined some of their past, he had never known the extent of what they had experienced. This also brought him to a new understanding of their relationship, their love. He now understood why the bond between them was so strong, and for a brief moment, he was jealous. He wondered why he and Little Bird were not like them.

Whit also took advantage of Martin's knowledge of the Ogallala and Brule Lakota, who were beginning to gather near the fort for the treaty talks. They had once been enemies of the Cheyenne, but for some time now they had been allies fighting common foes. There were even a few of the Lakota who had joined the Cheyenne Dog Soldiers, and took Cheyenne women as wives.

Though the conference was not scheduled to begin until September 1st, by the end of July a few bands of Arapaho had joined the Cheyenne and the Lakota near the fort, as well as more traders who saw the same opportunity as William Bent. A brisk business of trading filled the atmosphere around Fort Laramie. Also adding to growing local population and the garrison, was the arrival of one hundred and ninety-five dragoons to give a show of the might possessed by the Great White Father.

Captain William Ketchum, was the commander at Fort Laramie and the addition of new troops pleased him. The number of Indians arriving was exceeding the estimate he had been given to expect, and though Fitzpatrick assured him that it would be a peaceful gathering it was his confidence in his troops that kept his apprehension at bay. The interpreters; Fitzpatrick, his father-in-law, John Poisal, Blackfoot John Smith, Silas Scott and Antoine Martin kept communications with the Indians open and the peace was maintained.

The hot days of July drifted by into August, the Moon of Ripening Plums, and more dragoons arrived, escorting carriages loaded with White dignitaries, most of all Superintendent of Indian Affairs, David Mitchell, a former American Fur Company trader. Mitchell informed Ketchum and Fitzpatrick that the wagons of presents for the Indians would not arrive for several days. He blamed the Army, saying they had mishandled the shipment at Westport Landing. Fitzpatrick was frustrated. He had promised the gathered bands that he would have presents for them and counted on those gifts to maintain the peace. He now had to go out to their camps and explain the delay.

So far, the assembled bands had kept their word and there was peace. But word arrived that a large group of Shoshoni gathered by Jim Bridger, were approaching for the talks. Bear Voice, not sure if he could undermine the efforts of the Whites, spoke in private with a few of the young Cheyenne.

"Is it not the way of the White man to talk how he is a friend to the People, and then he gives our enemies guns and powder to kill us?" He waited until some of the gathered warriors expressed their thoughts, then added, *"Look, now the Snake approach, the Whites are happy to see them."* He called the age-old Shoshoni by their Cheyenne name. *"Are we to let the Snakes come to*

where they can steal our horses, our women and kill our children and old ones?"

The effects of his words were like a spark to dry tinder and a fire was lit in the blood of the young men. A dozen of the hot-headed youths slipped out of the village, and headed in the direction of the Shoshoni. Within a few miles, they came across two lone Shoshoni riding far in advance of their approaching brethren. With war whoops, the Cheyenne rode down the two, killed them and took their scalps.

When the bodies were found, the entire Shoshoni camp became enraged, halted and prepared for battle. Jim Bridger rode on ahead to warn Fitzpatrick, and the two of them with William Bent, quickly went to the chiefs of both nations and negotiated a solution to avoid an all-out war. The Cheyenne headmen promised reparations, and the anger in the Shoshoni camp simmered down.

Bear Voice was one of the few who spoke out against this, again stating that the Snakes were the enemy of the people and could not be trusted. But he was over-ridden, and the Shoshoni found a place to set their lodges and they too began to feast and trade as they waited for the promised gifts of the White man.

The days of August passed, and joining the conference with the Cheyenne, Lakota, Arapaho, and Shoshoni was the Minatare, Crow, Assiniboine, Mandan, Hidatsa, and Arikara. Over ten thousand Indians were gathered around the fort. All had not only their personal horses, but had brought extra horses for trading, and the herds roamed for miles and the grass began to disappear. The camps had remained in their original spots and the air soon began to stink due to the waste and garbage that had accumulated.

David Mitchell and the other commissioners decided the villages would have to move eastward to Horse Creek. There, Mitchell decided to start the negotiations. A large tent and awning were set up, and a tall lodge pole pine was erected as a flagpole.

The prominent headmen of each tribe were gathered under the shade of the awning, and though unconventional by Indian etiquette, negations were started without presents.

After discussion that seemed to go non-stop, by the men who knew the country, tribal boundaries were set. The largest portion of the west went to the Lakota and the Cheyenne. Most agreed to the boundaries, but in their own way of thinking those boundaries were flexible and they each claimed portions of areas set aside for another tribe. An example was the Black Hills that was seeded to the Lakota, but was also claimed by the Cheyenne and the Arapaho. Also, a large portion of the grassland recently taken and ceded to the Lakota was rich in buffalo, and was traditionally Crow land, but the Lakota had control. The Crow were given the right to the disputed area, according to the treaty. Holding any type of peace between the different tribes would be difficult, but Fitzpatrick held out hope.

To the white emigrants, travel rights across Indian territories were given and the government received permission to build forts. The government guaranteed annuities to the tribes, and a delegation of head men from the tribes was chosen to visit the Great White Father, President Fillmore in Washington.

Still, no wagons arrived, and as supplies ran out, the Indians began to slaughter a countless number of dogs to keep the festivities going. By September 20th, the situation looked as if the negotiations would fall apart, and the treaty come to nothing, but then the wagons appeared. With relief, Mitchell and Fitzpatrick handed the presents to the Chiefs who supervised their distribution, and took two full days to accomplish.

Once the gifts were given out, each group of Indians pulled down their lodges and slowly dissolved in different directions. Along with the Cheyenne and the Arapaho, went William Bent and his wagons filled with buffalo robes.

Whit had his fill of the closeness of so many people, and the clean air of the open trail felt good in his lungs. His spirits began to lighten, and he looked forward to preparations for winter and the solitude it would offer him and his family.

As he rode, he spoke to Little Bird, saying nothing in particular, but merely attempting to enjoy a conversation with her and exchange thoughts about the coming cold weather. Little Bird, though, had again become quarrelsome and agitated by Whit. It was as though their time together along the river had never happened. Her comments were curt, and condescending.

She finally reverted to making no comments and refusing to answer, or rather ignoring, any questions or comments from Whit. After a few days, he too stopped talking to her, and his only words were those to his son or to William Bent and the other employees of William.

The trip south grew tiresome, and the only relief from the torture of Whit's loneliness was the occasional chance to hunt buffalo with some of the Cheyenne. At least the killing of the shaggy beasts somewhat allowed him to vent his frustration, it gave him purpose.

His other outlet was the new friendship that had developed with Silas Scott. The old man had decided to go back south to the Arkansas with William Bent, and then return to his home upriver near the little adobe post of El Pueblo, located at the junction of the Arkansas and Fountain Creek.

Though Whit never expressed what he was going through with Little Bird, Silas felt the sadness in his new young friend. Rather than attempt to offer advice, he spent the time telling Whit about his life and his adventures in the fur trade, the Mexican War, and mostly the time he had with his Cheyenne wife, Red Calf Woman.

"Most of all, Son," he told Whit, "I have found that life here in the west is filled with uncertainties. The only thing we can count on is that life can be short, and you have to make the best of what time you have."

***

October 1851 - Moon When Thin Ice Begins to Form on Rivers

When the group of Cheyenne and Bent's wagons had reached the Arkansas, the Cheyenne broke up into small bands and headed for their favorite winter camping sites, and Little Bird with Zachary went on with her family. Whit went on to the trading post to help with the unloading of the buffalo robes that had been traded for, pack them into one hundred-pound bales and put them in the storehouse to wait until spring.

With all of the bales of hides stored away, Whit took a few days to hunt meat to fill the fort's larder for the coming lean months. He took his time hunting and seemed in no hurry to get back to his wife who he assumed was still with her family camped upriver. There seemed no reason to get back to her, other than his heart ached, a pain burned in his chest and he decided he had to be with her even if she had no desire to be with him. His duties completed at the post, Whit left to find the Cheyenne.

As the sun was just above the western horizon, Whit found the Cheyenne winter camp settled among the cottonwoods along the Arkansas near the Purgatory River. Most of the men were out taking advantage of the mild weather, hunting for more meat to put up for the winter, but a few moved among the lodges making preparations for the coming cold days. There were still racks for drying meat scattered among the lodges, and the few women who were working outside took little notice of Whit as he slowly made his way through camp. He sought out the lodge of his brother-in-law and found White Badger sitting on a buffalo robe outside of his lodge, working on a saddle.

"Hello, White Badger," Whit said, "I have come seeking my wife.

"She is not here," Badger said not looking up from his work. As he was speaking, Red Willow Woman and Zachary came out of the lodge.

"Papa!" yelled Zachary and he toddled toward Whit, who jumped down from his horse and scooped the boy up in his arms.

"Zachary, I have missed you so much!" He squeezed the child and Zachary hugged his father back.

"*What have you come for, Sky Eyes?*" asked Red Willow.

"*I have come to be with my wife and son,*" said Whit.

"*I am not sure that she wishes to be with you,*" quipped Badger.

"*I know that,*" said Whit, "*A woman should be with her husband, a child with his father.*" He looked at Red Willow and asked, "*Do you know where Little Bird is?*"

"*Where she is always. Down along the river among the trees alone.*"

"*Thank you,*" Whit put Zachary down and moved off into the trees along the riverbank.

He rode searching for his wife until the village was far behind him. The wind picked up and there was the smell of moisture in the air. The temperature would soon drop, Whit thought, and he wished he had brought a blanket with him. Small drops of icy rain began to sting his face as he moved along the leaf carpeted floor of the river bottom. He thought he spied tracks in the disturbed leaves on the ground and dismounted his horse.

Coming around a massive cottonwood, Whit spied a moccasin lying among the kicked-up forest debris. He bent down to retrieve it and as he began to stand, the creaking of the tree branch above him drew his attention upwards. There, suspended by a rawhide rope around her neck, was Little Bird, swinging gently from an outstretched branch. A flash of lighting, followed almost instantly by the crack of thunder, eliminated the river bottom and cast a white light on the lifeless body of Little Bird.

At first, Whit couldn't believe what he was seeing, and he stood looking up into the pale face of his wife, her eyes open and glazed over in death. He cut the rope and gently lowered her to the ground where he sat cradling her in his arms, the mounting sleet battering the two of them. There he held her, until the following morning, when he could finally work up the mental strength to take her back into the village.

As Whit entered the camp with the body of his wife, the first to see them was a young woman and she let out a wail of grief, soon joined in by other women as they began to gather. Whit took the body to the lodge of his brother-in-law and there lowered it from the horse to lie on a blanket.

People gathered around them and some accused Whit of killing his wife, White Badger was the first to reach out and strike Whit across the face, knocking him to the ground. Several other men added their own blows, then took hold of Whit and drug him to his feet. Whit was within a hairs breath of being killed when Red Willow Woman's cries stopped the beating.

"He did not kill my husband's sister! She has taken her own life! Look..." she pointed out the rope marks angling up from Little Bird's neck following her jaw line behind her ear. The mood instantly changed from anger to shock and then fright.

"She took her own life with a rope," a woman said.

"Her spirit could not escape and will be trapped!" another exclaimed. With this, many of those gathered around moved away not wanting to be near the body of a suicide.

"Take her away," White Badger demanded, looking at Whit. *"Take her far away. It is your fault that she has done this, and now her spirit will cling to you and bring nothing but evil."*

Slowly, Whit rose and moved back over to his wife's body. He rolled the blanket around her and then placed her back across the saddle of her pony. He then went to where Red Willow Woman stood and took his son from her arms.

"Do not take the boy," she pleaded. But Whit paid no attention to her, and mounting his horse turned and left the village. All watched silently as he rode away, among them, Sees Far Woman.

Whit rode down river, back to Bent's new post. He left Zachary with one of the Mexican women and borrowed a shovel. He then found a quiet place on the low bluff overlooking the river and dug a grave for Little Bird. Once he had placed the last shovelful of dirt over her, he piled up rocks to form a large cairn. He then sat down and spent the rest of that day staring out onto the plains, not sure what he would do now that he had lost her.

***

The mood in the Hairy Rope Band of the Southern Cheyenne was apprehensive and somewhat fearful after the suicide of little Bird. The fear grew from the report that a ghost, or restless spirit, had been witnessed walking through the camp at night. That, and the actions of the medicine man, Bear Voice, prompted the decision to move the camp further west where the Quarreling River ran into the Flint Arrow River. So within two, strenuous days, the Band followed the Flint Arrow River upstream from Big Timbers to wait out the winter months.

Bear Voice had been grooming his favorite horse when Sees Far Woman came to tell him of her sister's death. With an anguished cry, he had lost all composure and in a fit of madness pulled his knife from its sheath, and ran the flint blade across the animal's throat! The horse reared back, screamed for a brief moment and then fell to the ground thrashing in pain. Bear, the horses' blood splattered across him, stood enraged and his anger grew with every second. He turned and strode to his lodge where he began to take up items and throw them about.

He stood in the middle of his lodge, smoke from the disturbed fire mixed with dust floated in the air. He had finally taken control of his rage, but he still shook with the surge of hot blood that had coursed through his veins. Buffalo Cow Woman knew better than to attempt to stop him, and as soon as she could she slipped out of the doorway and moved off to a safe distance. Only Sees Far dare go near the lodge, while the tempest played out inside. After the sound of destruction inside the lodge died down and it was quiet for several minutes, she dared to go in.

Sees Far found her uncle standing in the center of the lodge, his head bowed, his shoulders shaking with what at first she thought was grief, until he turned and raised his eyes to look at her. For the first time in her life, she was frightened of him. She had never seen in any man what was reflected in his face. It was pure hatred, hatred so deep that it made her step back, her own deep hatred pale in comparison.

When he seemed to gain awareness of what he had done, he stared at Sees Far and screamed at her.

"You! You, are the one who made the bad medicine that took her life!"

Sees Far backed away and in her haste to retreat caught her foot on the bottom of the doorway, stumbled and fell to the ground. She began to crawl away, but before she could move out of his reach, Bear Voice had picked up his bow, and swinging it began to strike her.

"NO!" she cried, *"I loved my sister. The medicine was meant to kill Sky Eyes,"* she sobbed, *"My dream only saw a shadow across him, and I thought that it was he who was to die. I loved my sister."*

Bear Voice stopped his assault and took a step back. The bow fell from his hand, and as if awakening from a dream, he looked down at Sees Far and then around at other people from the village looking in his direction.

"She meant more to me than anyone else. You have no idea what she was to me," he said in a tone so low that Sees Far could not hear the words clearly and thought he might be talking to the spirits.

Bear Voice left the camp and walked out onto the prairie, and Sees Far helped Buffalo Cow Woman place the interior of the lodge back into somewhat order. Bear Voice returned long after the sun had fallen, and without speaking to anyone, went straight to his bed. The women slept close to the doorway, leaving Bear Voice to spend the night in fitful sleep. It was that same night that the ghost walked through the village.

At first, Sees Far thought the noise outside the lodge was that of a dog, or possibly a coyote, hunting for food. The scuffling of movement was soon joined by the low moan of a woman sobbing. Though for the most part fearless of all but Bear Voice, Sees Far began to shake with the thought that her sister's spirit was roaming the camp. Sees knew that her sister had died with a rawhide rope around her throat, and that her spirit could not escape this world and be free.

It was believed the spirit of the dead would follow the road of the departed, finding the trail where the footprints only pointed in one direction, up into the sky, following the Milky Way to arrive at a camp in the stars where it would meet the friends and relatives who had passed on before it. The spirit of a suicide could not follow that path, it would roam instead looking for some comfort among the living.

Sees Far was more than happy that the camp had moved, hoping in doing so she would leave her sister's spirit behind. Somewhere in the back of her mind she feared that her sister's death was her fault. The thought that she may have been jealous of her sister and maybe hated her more than she did Sky Eyes crossed her mind more than once.

She attempted to push these thoughts from her mind, to occupy it with the tasks of everyday life, such as tanning hides, cooking or even gathering wood. It was in doing this last task that she wandered among the trees along the river, her arms filled with pieces of cottonwood, that she heard her name called. She stopped and turned to see who it was that might be calling her and saw no one.

She called out, *"Who is there?"* but there was no answer. Though she did not hear the call again, she felt a presence. She walked back toward the camp, and before leaving the river bottom she turned to look back. There among the trees she thought she saw a woman, the fringe on her dress and her long black hair drifting slowly in the wind, but there was no wind. Sees Far felt a scream rising in her throat, but it would not escape her lips. The cry was choked off as the woman seemed to fade away like the morning mist burned away by the heat of the sun.

Sees Far spoke of this to no one. She feared that if she mentioned it, it would somehow make it true.

***

November 1851 – Hard Faced

Magdalena Lucía watched the child playing on the hard-packed dirt floor at her feet. His chubby little hands moved the small carved, wooden horse along, rocking it back and forth as if it were running. Her eyes slipped back to the shirt in her lap that she was mending with needle and thread, and almost as if the child had sensed her attention was no longer on him, he rose to his feet and took off running toward the door.

"Come back here, you rascal!" she called after him in the Spanish of New Mexico. She leaped to her feet and caught him, scooping him up in her arms. Squeezing him, she kissed his cheek and received mischievous giggles in return from the boy.

"Now stay by my side until I finish mending your Papa's shirt." She placed him back on the floor where she had been working near the fireplace, and returned to sewing the button on the shirts sleeve. Whitney Voss had lost the button and she had offered to replace it as soon as she could get him to surrender the garment. He had only one other shirt, the one he wore now. It was threadbare and worn so thin that no amount of mending could save it. Replacing the button on the shirt in her lap was not her only goal.

She took every advantage to be close to him, here not truly him but his scent. The smell of this well-worn garment held a trace of Whitney that sent a slight shiver through her. It was almost with reluctance that she had washed it before the button had been replaced and hung it to dry in front of the fireplace. The clean cotton material felt soft under her hands and she took the opportunity to make mental measurements. When time allowed, she planned on making him a new shirt and hoped that it could be a Christmas gift.

She had first laid eyes on the blonde-headed hunter more than a year ago, when she had first come to work for Señor Bent, at his trading post on the Rio Nepesta called Arkansas by the Americans. Magdalena fell instantly in love with the man, though he had a Cheyenne wife and a newborn child. Now he was a widower, and she was taking care of the child, Zachariah. Though Whitney paid her little attention, her heart leaped every time he was around her, and at seventeen years old, she felt her life would be perfect if she were his woman. She knew that he need only work through the grief of losing his wife, and sooner or later, he would come around to loving her. In the meantime, she would fawn on the child and cement the bond between the boy and herself. He already acted like she was his mother, and she would call him, "Mi'jito," the endearing term for "my son."

Yes, she thought, life was good here on the Nepesta, much better than her hometown of Abiquiú, on the Rio Chama, in New Mexico. She was paid a good wage, given a warm, dry place to sleep and the chance to see many different types of people, especially the Americans. Until she had come to work as a domestic for Bent, the only Americans she had seen were the old trappers and the rough Missourians, who had come into northern New Mexico. The trappers she remembered as being common among the people of New Mexico. She had known many of them, and they had always treated the people with respect, and many had married into the families of New Mexico, some becoming Mexican citizens themselves. As a child she had been exposed to the company of these American trappers and had even danced with some of them at fandangos.

The soldiers, who came from Missouri after the war, were of a different sort than the men who had dealt in the fur trade. These course and unmannered ruffians had scared her. She was barely in her teens when they had come to her village, and they treated the people with contempt. Her mother had more than once hid her so she would be safe from the lecherous eyes of the "invaders." These men, Magdalena feared, were the true Americans, until she had come to the trading post here in the north and met Whitney Voss.

Inside the walls, she heard not only her native Spanish, but French, Cheyenne, Delaware, Arapaho, and of course English spoken. Being intelligent, and quick to learn, Magdalena picked up on these languages and was soon able to speak and translate some of these with only a few mistakes. Her linguistic talents did not go unnoticed, and when no male translator was available, she found herself invaluable as the go-between for daily activities and at times for trade.

William Bent and those working at the post, soon referred to her as Maggie, taking the play on words and her given name. The Cheyenne, impressed by her skill called her "Mo'e'ha", Magpie, liking her to the chattering little bird. In Cheyenne tradition, it was considered a sacred messenger of the Creator and Magdalena was in their eyes a gift from the Creator.

The only one who did not use the nickname for her was Whit. If he addressed her, he used Magdalena, or spoke to her without the use of her name at all. To almost anyone it would appear that he held no respect for her, but in reality, it was not disrespect, but the lack of empathy he had begun to feel toward everyone. Whit had become increasingly bitter, and his treatment of the girl was no reflection on her, but on his growing self-hatred.

The one person he showed feelings for was his son, and then they were a mixture of emotions. Whit would take the boy gently into his arms, and his demeanor would soften, his anger drained away, but only for the short time the boy was with him. Whitney was a different man when he was with Zachary and as if to shield himself from this softness, this weakness, Whit left his son in the care of Magdalena.

Satisfied with the work she had done on Whitney's shirt, she stood, and reaching down picked up the child and walked the short distance across the post's plaza to the main trade room. The post was newly constructed, made of stone not adobe like its predecessor. Magdalena had never seen the old post, but she had been told it was much larger than this new one. She could not imagine what it had looked like. The establishment she now worked in was almost two hundred feet long and one hundred and fifty wide with walls sixteen feet high, surrounding a dozen rooms and the large central plaza. Along one wall was the long warehouse, where the buffalo hides were stored while waiting shipment. Although it had no bastions, like the old post, it retained the small swivel guns of the earlier fort and these were mounted on the corners of the roof.

"Pardon me, Señor," Magdalena said as she peeked into the doorway of the trade room. William Bent and Charles Goodall looked up from the ledger the two were scrutinizing. Without a word, Bent acknowledged Magdalena's presence and gave her unspoken permission to enter and state the nature of her presence.

Magdalena was not afraid of Bent, but her respect for him was the product of employer and employee. She also saw him as a man who could be austere and dangerous, patient but prone to quick anger and though he showed deep loyalty toward his friends, he could be stubbornly self-reliant. Magdalena understood all this and her respect was tempered by a bit of fear. This man could, if displeased with her, set her out to fend for herself. More than two hundred miles away from home, there would be nothing between her and that home, but the wilderness filled with Indians. She stepped into the semi-darkness of the trade room.

"I would like to purchase cloth," she said, her voice quiet but steady.

"What kind of cloth and how much?" asked Goodall as he stepped over to the shelves where the bolts of cloth were stacked.

"I would like the English flannel, azul añil, indigo, please," said pointing to the warm dark blue wool-flannel. She knew it would make a warm shirt without being too heavy.

"How much do you want?" Goodall asked again.

"I will need three yards, American yards, please," she said, referring the difference between the thirty-six inches measured out by the Americans rather than the "vara", or Spanish measurement, which was almost a one tenth shorter in length.

Goodall smiled, appreciating her intelligence. He measured out the cotton cloth using the marks on the countertop as a rule. Before cutting the length of the material, he advised her of the cost.

"That will be forty-five cents. Do you understand that?" he asked, reminding her that she made not much more than that for a month's wages.

"Si, I understand, and I have the," she stopped searching her mind for the correct word, "credit." She smiled. "I would also like six buttons, those," she pointed to the cards of buttons.

"Three yards, and six buttons," Goodall said, then added, "Not enough for a dress Maggie."

"No, Señor Goodall, it is not for a dress. It is for a shirt." She blushed.

"Ah, I see. You have your eye on someone in particular?" he asked knowing full well, the affection she held for Whitney Voss.

Magdalena smiled and gathering up the material, she turned to leave, but Goodall stopped her.

"Here, take a stick of hard candy for the boy, and one for yourself, a gift from me."

She took the red and white striped sticks, thanked him and went back to her quarters adjacent to the kitchen. She laid out the material and carefully cut it into the needed squares and rectangles required to make the shirt and began to sew.

She would have the shirt done soon but would wait until Christmas to give it to Whitney. She would sew each stitch with care, and when the shirt was finished, she would embroider a small flower on one of the cuffs, a yellow cactus flower, a sign of her love for him.

SAM J. PISCIOTTA

CHAPTER THREE
THE NEW WIND

March 1852 – Dusty Moon

Winter did its best to hold onto the plains, with icy, frigid nights and at times deep, wet snow with blowing winds. But spring fought back with longer days that also grew warmer and warmer. The snows that had fallen were replaced by rains.

The milder temperatures and life-giving moisture, aided by the winds that blew across the plains, brought back the grass that poked its tiny heads out from the ground. Soon, the buffalo would appear migrating north, crossing the Arkansas River, following the sweet, rich foliage.

Like the buffalo, and all other creatures of the west, Whit was ready to break free of his winter quarters at the post. William Bent spent his winter days with his wife and her people, leaving the operation of the post during the cold months of winter in the capable hands of Charlie Goodall and a few traders and hunters. There had been a necessity for Whit to provide meat for the post, and the few times he could get away, he would spend time with his son and Maggie.

Whit had grown accustomed to the presence of the Mexican girl, and as a matter of convenience he had moved her into his quarters to care for Zachary, her sharing a bed with the child. He had accepted her care for him also. Though she was fair to look at, and in the bloom of womanhood, Whit had yet to look at her as other than a caretaker. She cooked, cleaned and mended clothing as needed, and the new flannel shirt that she had made him was seen as a kind gesture, only that.

Zachary grew fast and strong, and, his intelligence evident by how fast he began to speak not only English, but Spanish and the Cheyenne of his mother's people, with Maggie's teaching. His short sentences were a mixture of all three, and at times it was hard to follow what he was saying. Whit showed his appreciation to Maggie by giving her small items such as brass bracelets, some German silver jewelry, and treasured most by her, a small silver crucifix inlaid with the body of Christ in gold.

Maggie also told the child bible stories, and Whit had no objection to her telling these tales to him. But, raised in a Protestant home, he took a dim view of her Papist faith. He found it superstitious and told her as much.

"Don't fill his head with nonsense," he told her. "It will only set him up for disappointment when he is older."

"There is much to hope for," Maggie told him, "If we do not have hope and faith, what reason is there to live?"

"Man's meant to struggle, live hard and take what he needs to survive. It's the way things are."

"And, what of love?" she asked.

"Love is for fools," he said and that ended the conversation, but both of them thought long and hard about love. Whit was sure that he could never love another woman as he had loved Little Bird. He still thought she had loved him, but couldn't understand why she had seen fit to punish him by taking her own life.

Maggie had a different idea of love. She had been raised in the belief that love was a gift that had to be cherished and nourished. She felt also that it was a blessing to be able to give unconditional love, like that she felt toward Zachary and Whit. The only thing she could not work out in her mind was why it should hurt so much. This pain was the only thing she and Whit had in common when it came to love.

Preparations for the first caravan to bring hides back to Westport were soon underway, and William Bent decided that he would take his wife and family east with him. He offered Whit the chance to take his son and Maggie, if he wanted. William, like so many others, had begun to think of the girl as Whit's "mountain wife". Maggie was among those who thought of herself in this manner. Though there was no consummation of this marriage. She inclined to wait until Whit was a willing partner, and there could be a proper blessing by a priest.

In the areas of New Mexico where a priest only visited a village once every few years, there was some leeway in when a couple would receive that blessing. At times, a priest would marry a man and woman, and baptize their children all in the same day, with no stigma attached. Maggie would be patient.

Whit agreed to take Maggie only so Zachary would have someone to look after him, and she would be company to William's wife, Yellow Woman.

"We will be going to the east soon," Whit told Maggie, "Mr. Bent has said that I may take my son."

Maggie's heart sank. She had become used to the idea that Whit would leave now and then, but Zachary had been with her constantly since the day Whit brought him to her. She wasn't sure, if Whit took the boy that she would ever see either of them again.

"Oh, please Señor Whit, don't take Zachary from me. Leave him. I promise I will care for him as my own son," she pleaded.

"No Maggie, the boy will go with me, and so will you." It was the first time he had addressed her by Maggie, and she was choked with emotion. Tears filled her eyes and without thought she threw her arms around Whit and hugged him. This startled Whit and he wasn't sure how to react, but gently pushed her away.

Maggie, realizing she had overstepped the boundary between them stepped back and dropped her eyes to the ground. She started to apologize, "I am sorry, I did not mean..." She was stopped by Whit, who smiled for the first time since she had been with him. The smile was small and lasted only the briefest of moments, but that small gesture brought more tears of happiness to her.

"The boy must have new clothes for the trip," Whit said, in an attempt to break the awkwardness, he felt. "I will purchase the material for that purpose from the company, and you will make him a pair of pants, a coat and a new shirt. There will also be material for you to make a proper dress for yourself. These will do until we get to Westport, and once there we will purchase ready-made clothing if we go on to St. Louis."

By the end of the month, buffalo hides and other furs were loaded onto the wagons and the caravan set out for the east. By April, the ground was in dry enough condition to travel and the wagons made good time following the Santa Fe Trail. A few stops were made along the way, such as Fort Atkinson, and Fort Leavenworth before they finally reached Westport.

Situated just before the Missouri River's northward bend, Westport Landing had become the main departure point for west-bound travelers headed for Oregon, California and Santa

Fe. Starting in 1821, with the opening of the Santa Fe Trail, traders had brought their goods west departing from St. Louis, and as time passed steamboats moved as far up the Missouri River as possible where travelers departed on foot and wagon for Santa Fe. Landings continued to move farther and farther west along the river until the late 1830's when Westport Landing displaced both St. Louis and Independence as the primary jumping-off point for trade and emigration west.

After the bales of buffalo hides were unloaded from the wagons, and readied for shipping down river by steamboat, Whit, Maggie and Zachary went with the Bents to their farm. Everything was new to Maggie, and Yellow Woman was kind enough to share with the girl her own knowledge of Westport. Yellow Woman was Bent's second wife, the sister of his first, and she had made many trips to the Bent farm, something her elder sister had done rarely.

William would spend only two nights at the farm before going on to St. Louis. The first day was be taken up with business arrangements in Westport, for the shipping by steamboat to and from St. Louis, and then the following day he would travel with the buffalo hides down to St. Louis. There he would negotiate the sale of the hides, arrange for the purchase of trade goods, and the Indian annuities he would take back west with him.

Whit sat at the table to William's right-hand side. There they waited for the women who would soon bring out the last evening meal at the farm before William and Whit left the following morning. As they sat, they talked, and William spoke of his apprehensions concerning the treaty signed at Fort Laramie.

"I fear that the Cheyenne will find it hard to become farmers," he paused. "I have heard stories from the old people that they were once tillers of the soil, but as soon as they obtained horses, they followed the buffalo, taking from them what they needed to survive. I fear also that they would find it hard to give up warring against other plains tribes. Their conflicts with others, such as the Pawnee, will be difficult to relinquish. What value is a Cheyenne brave if he has no war deeds to boast about, has no horse herd, and how can he obtain these if not by raiding other tribes?"

"You have lived among them since before I was born," Whit said, "You more than anyone would know. I have seen both good and bad among them in the short time I have known them. Do you not believe there may be good men among them who do not want war?"

"Yes, like you, I have lost that which was good, that which I loved." William spoke of his first Cheyenne wife, Owl Woman. He dare not mention Little Bird by name. It was obvious that Whit still hurt from his loss. But being a practical and not overly sentimental man, William began to speak of his second wife, Yellow Woman.

"It was only natural for me to take Owl's sister as my wife and mother to my children. She loves them as if they were hers, and I have had no complaints about her. She, too, is a part of the good." Though hinting that Whit should move on, William would not push the subject further as he felt what he had already said bordered on overstepping good manners.

His concerns were of little matter as Whit had no idea what William was suggesting, and would not have grasped the idea if Maggie had not entered the room at that moment, with the evening's meal.

Many women of the southwest had long since begun wearing the fashions of the east. Seldom did you see a woman of all but the lower class, walk down the streets of Santa Fe still wearing the Spanish Colonial styles. But, Maggie was not born to the upper class, nor was she from the lowest. She had traveled the entire distance from the Arkansas post in her usual attire; a cotton blouse over a blue wool-flannel skirt, bound at the waist by a sash, and about her shoulders she wore a rebozo that served as both overcoat and bonnet. She had saved the new dress for the occasion of arriving in Westport, and this she now wore.

Whit was surprised at the difference. The dress was made from the material that she had chosen before leaving the post on the Arkansas River. She had worked diligently it, keeping any sight of it secret from Whit until now. The material was of printed cotton paisley in soft, red and brown earth tones. The fan-shaped bodice was piped and came down to a point in front and the attached cartridge-pleated skirt flattered her slim figure. The dresses' long sleeves had a puff in them near the elbow, then narrowed back to cover her arms down to her wrists. From her waist, the skirt material flowed down to her ankles, and the well starched petticoats she wore gave it an almost bell shape from her hips.

In place of hard-soled moccasins, on her feet she wore a pair of black leather shoes that laced on the inside of her ankles. Between the top of her shoes and her hemline of the dress, she wore clocked silk stockings, the fancy embroidered pattern peeking out.

The most notable change in Maggie's appearance was her hair. Whit was accustomed to seeing her hair pulled back to hang in a single braid at the nape of her neck. Now, her long raven locks had been parted in the center and drawn down over her ears and back into a braded bun, interwoven with yellow ribbon. Around her neck she wore the gold chain and small, silver crucifix he had given her almost a year ago.

For the first time, Whit saw her not just as Maggie, the girl and caretaker of his son, but as Magdalena Lucía, a beautiful young woman. He was speechless, and for the briefest of moments thought it was someone else. He found himself smiling at her and upon seeing his smile, Maggie blushed. The warmth between them lasted only a few moments as a wave of guilt washed over Whit. It had been only six months since he had lost his wife, and though she had abandoned him and their son, he felt he was being unfaithful to her.

Maggie noticed the slight change in his demeanor, and she had seen a spark that could grow into a flame if Whit allowed it. She was now more than ever resigned that someday he would love her.

The men sat and ate quietly, what conversation they did make concerned business, but William had taken notice of Whit's reaction to Maggie's appearance. He said nothing of it, but he could see it was time for Whit's heart to heal, and Maggie might be the one to do it.

Whit gave Maggie more thought now. He knew she was intelligent, and when he returned from St. Louis with Bent, he gave her three small books. When he handed them to her, her first reaction was confusion.

"Thank you, Señor Voss," she said, "But, I do not know how to read." She was embarrassed, but Whit explained the reason he had given her the books.

"Maggie, these books will help you learn how to read, and when Zachary is older you can teach him." He took the first book from her and read the cover and described its contents. "This book is entitled the 'Eclectic Primer,' it has drawings in it and next to these drawings are the words. See." He opened the book and showed her a picture of a chicken, and next to the picture was the word "HEN" and the letter "H".

Taking up another book he said, "This volume is called 'The Eclectic Primer; for Young Children.' In its pages are the letters of the alphabet, the symbols that when combined, such as in the other book, make up words.

"The last book is another primer, and also has pictures with words in it, but the words are joined together to form sentences." He took the final book and showed her its contents. "You will also learn to write in a proper hand, not only print."

With the explanation Maggie's eyes grew wide and for the second time since she had known Whit, she threw her arms around him and gave him a hug. This time though, Whit returned the show of affection and hugged her back, but only slightly.

Once she had obtained pen and paper, she dove into the books devouring the information on each page, and though she did not have the aid of a teacher, her thirst for knowledge was not dampened, and as with the spoken languages, she learned fast.

***

July 1852 - Moon of Ripening Chokeberries

For Whit, the return trip west seemed to pass a bit faster than the eastbound one. His thoughts were not only on the caravan of wagons, but he had found thoughts of Maggie crossing his mind more often than in the past, and this made him feel a bit uneasy. His thoughts weren't like those he had experienced for Little Bird. There wasn't the hot-blooded beating of his heart, but there was a calm feeling of warmth. He began to treat her a bit different also, making an effort talk to her, to learn more about her. He was surprised that even after he had spent most of the past year in her company, he knew very little about her, and she was constantly surprising him.

As he thought more about Maggie, he found himself also thinking more of Little Bird. He had tried to push thoughts about his wife out of his mind, hoping that if he thought less about her, he would not grieve over the loss of her, that there would be less pain. But now he felt not only the pain of her loss, but started to feel guilty in that he was being unfaithful, and that angered him. The anger was not so much at himself but at little Bird. Until now, he had blamed himself, he had believed that it was his fault, that he had done something wrong. Now, with his feelings for Maggie growing, he realized that it was Little Bird who was to blame. Something had been wrong with her. She had abandoned him and their son.

By the time the caravan of wagons was close to Fort Atkinson, Maggie had gone through each of the books page by page, several times and had memorized the contents, associating the words with the pictures. Her skill with pen and paper would improve with time, but she had become adept at writing short sentences.

She had questioned the validity of some of the pictures though. Some in particular had bothered her, and she had asked Whit about them.

"This word is elk, but the picture does not look like an elk, it has a face like a mule," she said.

"True, it looks more like a moose to me," Whit said.

"What is a Moose?" she asked.

"It is like an elk only much bigger and found further north."

"And, what are these last two, a Yak and a Zebra? One looks like a hairy cow and the other a horse with stripes."

"I'm not sure," said Whit, "But, I suspect they have them someplace, as they are in your book."

"I would like to see a horse with stripes," she said. "Why are some words in American not spoken like they are spelled?"

"I don't know," Whit said, "I don't know. I would imagine that it is that way with any language. Spanish is much the same with words spelled different from how they are spoken." Maggie had not thought about learning to read in Spanish and she made a new goal for herself.

"Give me an example," she said to Whit.

"That is simple, in Spanish a "j" is sometimes pronounced with the sound of an "h", such as *jarro*," he said, pointing to a tin cup that hung near the water-barrel on the wagon. "If I pronounced it in American, I would say jar-ro." He let out a soft laugh.

"You are telling a tale!" she said thinking that he was making a fool out of her.

"No, Maggie, I am telling you the truth."

She would have many days to think about this, and she wondered if William McGuffey had written a set of books on Spanish.

She sat next to Yellow Woman in one of the two Dearborn carriages that carried them and the children; Zachary and the Bent offspring. As the light wagon moved along, she talked to the Cheyenne woman, excited about what she was learning in the books, but Yellow Woman seemed merely amused rather than interested.

"I do not see a reason to learn the words of my husband's people in their talking leaves," she said. *"It is better to know how to keep a lodge in order, and to bear children."*

This last remark stung Maggie, as she had hoped that someday she and Whit would have children of their own. She loved Zachary as if he was hers, but it was not the same. She was tempted to tell Yellow Woman that having children was important but not the only measure of a woman when Yellow woman spoke again.

"You are still young and there is plenty of time for you to give Sky Eyes more sons." She gave a knowing smile, and patted Maggie on the leg.

Fort Atkinson came into sight and it was not long before the wagons were pulled up and the teams of oxen were being unyoked. They had barely set the oxen out to graze when a rider came in at a dead run, his horse lathered with sweat.

"Indians!" he shouted. "Indians are attacking King's wagons back down the trail." A trader by the name of Hyrum King, with nine wagons of goods had followed Bent's train from Westport. If there were trouble with the Indians, the peace treaty would fall apart, and all the effort William Bent had put forth to reestablish his business would have been for nothing. All it would take is a single shot, and a full-scale war could erupt.

"Mount up," he called out to his men, and they raced back down the trail.

King had formed his wagons into a square, but his loose stock was being harassed by the Indians who turned out to be Kiowa and Comanche. The Indians were loitering in the area for the presents they had grown accustomed to expecting from the whites. When they saw an opportunity to run off some of the stock presented to them by chance, they couldn't resist.

The Indians were charging at the stock, waving blankets and shouting in an attempt to stampede the animals, cutting them off. Whit rode, following William and the rest of the men, to form a line between the stock and the Indians, all the time Bent shouting and calling at the Indians to back off.

In return, several of the Comanche rode directly at the whites in mock charges, pulling off within a hair's breadth of ramming into Bent's men. With the majority of the Indians backing off, the wagons were escorted to the Fort. When two companies of troopers for the Fort appeared, the Indians retreated to their camps, took down their lodges, crossed over to the south side of the river and were soon out of sight.

"I had hoped that we would be able to establish a better rapport with the Kiowa and the Comanche, but after all these years I should have expected nothing less," said William, shaking his head in resignation. He then turned to Whit, "None the less, we will still send someone to trade down on the Canadian. But, for the present, construction of the new structure must begin."

He spoke of his plans for the near future. A trading party would go south to the Canadian River and attempt to resume trade at the site of the adobe structure that had been built in 1843. Trade with the Comanche and Kiowa was more than tenuous, in that all the livestock belonging to the company had been killed by the Indians, and the traders harassed to the point of retreating all the way back to the Arkansas River. William had tried again a few years later, with the same results. The past failures didn't dissuade him though, and he had hopes for the future. He also knew that Tom Fitzpatrick planned to come out in the spring and add the Comanche and Kiowa to the signatories of the peace treaty of 1851.

Hopes for the future included the building of a real structure to replace the three small log cabins. Stone would be hewn out of the bluffs on the north side of the Arkansas River near the present post. Once this work was started Bent left for Westport, returning in the spring with stone masons and carpenters. More impressive was his plan to bring items the old fort never had, building hardware, ready-made doors, window frames, and glass.

As Peter Goodall would more than likely supervise the quarry work, and the trading expedition to the Canadian would not be until spring, Whit wondered if he would be returning to Westport with William. He waited until they arrived back at the post at Big Timber to ask.

"No, you will not be going back to Westport with me. I have another chore for you Whitney," Bent said, "You have proven yourself and I trust your judgment. In past years, when forage around the post was scarce, we purchased corn from the El Pueblo, Greenhorn or Hardscrabble. For the most part, all three have been close to abandoned. I've had news that Ceran St. Vrain, has sent Charlie Autobees up to establish a settlement at the mount of the Huerfano. This will help Ceran secure the land grant given him by the Mexicans. The American Government will soon be looking at those grants and my old partner, Ceran, doesn't want to lose all that land." Whit was not sure he understood what William wanted him to do, and he feared that his boss would ask him to take up farming.

Sensing Whit's uncertainty, William went on, "I'd like you to head up to the Huerfano and talk to Charlie. See if he would be willing to plant enough extra corn, wheat, beans and such to sell."

"You said El Pueblo was pretty much deserted? I though old Silas Scott was living near El Pueblo?" Whit asked.

"I know Silas had a place up the river, but as far as I know, he spends most of his time with one band of the Cheyenne or the other. He only goes back to his place on the river to plant a bit of crops in the spring, leaves them to tend for themselves and comes back in the fall to reap what nature has left him. You can go that far if you think he may be around, and it would be nice to know Silas' take on the mood of the other Cheyenne bands."

Whit left the following morning and was at the junction of the Huerfano and Arkansas River the day after. He traveled up stream for over five miles and found no sign of human activity. He did find though the river bottom was broad and thickly wooded with willow and cottonwoods, and there were wild grape vines and roses, and the grass covered bottomland was almost carpet-like.

Turning west, Whit moved on toward what had been the location of the little adobe settlement called El Pueblo. El Pueblo had been built by the partnership of five "ex" Bent/St. Vrain & Company employees: Robert Fisher, Mathew Kinkead, Joseph Mantz, and Edmond Conn, and George Simpson. The very existence of El Pueblo was illegal according to the Trade and Intercourse Act of 1843. It stated that whites without a proper license were not allowed to "hunt, range stock, nor make settlements, bring to the Indians such goods as he could sell..." Fines were $100 each for persons responsible for starting a settlement, $500 each for trading without a license, and $1,000 for each foreign (Mexican) resident entering Indian country without a passport. Whiskey sellers were subject to arrest by the military, and could be taken to Missouri for trial with 50% of their goods going to the Government and 50% to the informer, if there was one. Pueblo violated all the provisions of the Intercourse Act, but there was no one to enforce this law.

Its location was at the junction of the Fountain-qui-bouille, or Fountain Creek as it was called by most, and the Arkansas River. It was situated on a broad river bottom much like that of the Huerfano, only wider, stretching out almost a mile at one point. From its headwaters, the Arkansas runs as a steep fast-flowing river in narrow valleys, dropping over 4,000 feet in a little more than one hundred miles. West of its junction with Fountain Creek, the Arkansas River's bottom land was enclosed on each side by high bluffs, was about a quarter of a mile across, and timbered with a heavy growth of cottonwoods, some of these trees being of great size. Back toward the mountains, on each side of the river, the vast rolling prairie stretched away north and south for hundreds of miles, gradually ascending toward the mountains in the west. At El Pueblo, the valley widened and flattened markedly as it entered the Great Plains. For the reminder of its length, the Arkansas was wide, with shallow banks. But at El Pueblo, the river bordered only on the south by a high mesa, meandered back and forth like a snake, changing its flow and bends as the soft banks eroded during floods.

The flooding of the Upper Arkansas Valley left the soil rich, and all that was needed was to divert the same waters out into a tilled field and almost any form of produce could be grown. The attraction of the location had not gone unnoticed by the Plains Indians, who for generations had wintered in the area.

El Pueblo had been a thriving business for several years; its first year's profits rivaled that of Bent/St. Vrain. But El Pueblo's main source of income was as a transient point for whiskey, brought up from Taos and bound for the area north of the Platte.

For though Bent/St. Vrain did not trade in whiskey, and had a gentleman's agreement with the American Fur Company to stay south of the North Platte River, El Pueblo did not, and it dipped into the customer base of that company trading in the northern plains and the mountains.

With the massacre of most Americans in Taos and the destruction of Turley's Mill by El Pueblo Indians in 1847, the whiskey trade slowed to a trickle. The incentive to do business out of the little adobe settlement faded away, and the occupants drifting off to more profitable pursuits. Some, like Robert Fisher, returned to work for William Bent.

Just east of the Fountain Creek, Whit rode by what remained of the cabins that had sheltered the Mormon Battalion during the Mexican War, noting that within a few more years there would be no sign that they had ever been there. The roofs had caved in, the walls sagged to one side, and small cottonwoods had already begun to grow inside the structures. Whit pondered the frailty of what men leave in their passing.

He crossed Fountain Creek, taking care to avoid the areas of quicksand that were common to that area, and passed between the low bluffs that sat between the junction of that creek and the Arkansas River. Staying on the left bank of the Arkansas, he moved a few hundred yards above the mouth of the Fountain, and soon came in sight of El Pueblo.

As William Bent had surmised, it appeared deserted. It was nothing more than a large square enclosure, surrounded by a wall of adobe, miserably cracked and dilapidated. The slender pickets that surmounted it were broken down. Whit rode up to the gate that stood half open was dangling on its wooden hinges so loosely that he feared the slightest touch would surely knock to the ground. He eased himself through the opening and found no sign of recent habitation, the only movement was that of a few hens that had been left behind and gone feral. What had been a corral sat just to the left of the entrance, and what appeared to be a blacksmith shop next to that, the two taking up the entire western wall. There was half a dozen connected rooms along the northern and eastern walls, ending back at the gate. Like Bent's old fort, there was a low bastion at opposite corners of the small post.

"This wouldn't be a bad place if it had some care given it," Whit said aloud to himself. He moved over to where the blacksmith's arbor stood and eyed what was left of the forge. On the ground were the remnants of a broken wagon wheel, and Whit bent down picking up one of the spokes. Its feel in his hand brought back memories of working next to his brother Aaron, his cousin Benjamin, and his father and uncle at the wagon shop in Pittsburg. He tossed the wagon spoke aside and then peered into each of the rooms surrounding the little courtyard.

"Ought to keep your nose to the wind." A voice from behind him startled Whit and he turned bringing up his rifle to face a possible foe.

"Easy now, Son. You won't be needin' the firearm," it was Silas Scott who had walked up behind Whit with little more noise than a faint breeze blowing through the grass.

"Christ, Silas! You scared the hell outa' me," Whit said, relieved that it wasn't someone out after his scalp.

"You were pretty deep in thought there, weren't you?" Silas said, "Can't be too careful you know, many a varmint would have cut your liver out."

"You're right there. I don't know what I was thinkin' about."

"What you doin' poking around here?" Silas asked.

"Mr. Bent asked me to come up here and have a look-see. Thought Charlie Autobees was settling in down at the Huerfano, but I didn't find nothing down there. Thought I'd come this way and see if there was anyone here, or if I might run into you."

"Run into me, eh?" Silas scratched his beard with an unconscious motion. "What would William want with an old man?" Not expecting an answer, he quickly waved one off with a hand and continued, "Never mind. You come with me out to the cabin and we'll have a cup of coffee and palaver." He turned and headed out the gate to where their two horses were grazing on the sweet grass.

They rode west following the river for about four miles, passing old fields where corn stubble still poked up from the ground, and finally a small well-tended plot came into sight. Beyond it sat a squat log cabin, the eaves of the low roof almost touching the ground on the sides. The front of the cabin faced east, and attached to the cabin was a jacal style corral. Silas rode up to the gate in the corral and dismounted, as did Whit.

"Might as well pull your saddle off and make your horse comfortable," Silas said as he loosened the cinch on his own mount and pulled off the saddle. He then turned his horse loose to graze, assured by his knowledge of the animal that it wouldn't wander far. Whit, not as confident, drove a picket pin into the ground and tied his horses' front hoof to it with a long rope.

They entered the darkness of the cabin, Silas stopping past the doorway, lay his rifle against the wall just inside and waited a moment to let his eyes adjust to the semidarkness. Whit followed him in, setting his rifle to rest next to Silas'. When his own eyes adjusted to the light, he was surprised that the interior was unlike that of other cabins. It was spacious, but not overly huge, being about twelve to fourteen feet square. Unlike other cabins, there was no sense of the stuffiness, no closed-in feeling. The cabin had a rear window that allowed air to flow through from the open front door, and a proper fireplace, hearth and chimney, built from the rock of the surrounding area. This stone structure took up most of the north wall. Another thing Whit noted was that the inside was not cluttered; it seemed neat and well organized. Above a raised pallet that served as a bed, was a shelf with several books. In the center of the cabin sat a wooden table carefully made to sit level, accompanied by a low bench and a single armchair.

"Seat yourself while I heat up the water. Then we'll go outside and sit in the shade to talk," Silas said to Whit and pointed over to the bench. He then went to the hearth, and with flint and steel struck a spark to some tinder and set that under kindling. Within a few minutes, the water inside a small, wide-bottomed pot was boiling. Silas took up the pot and moved over to the table setting it down and then retrieved a small tin, and two tin cups, placing them next to the pot.

"Decided against coffee," Silas said, "How does a bit of good English tea, sound?"

"I think it sounds fine," Whit said, thinking he couldn't remember the last time he had drank tea. They each placed a generous pinch of the tea leaves in the cup and poured the hot water over them. They then went out of the cabin and sat on a fallen cottonwood that seemed to have conveniently missed the cabin.

"Now, tell me what William is up to," Silas said as he took out his pipe and tobacco. He filled the bowl, and striking a spark to a small piece of charred cloth, set it atop the tobacco. He puffed on the pipe as Whit explained to him the reason for his visit and caught him up on the news from the east and the events taking place around the trading post at Big Timbers.

"Well, William was right about Autobees," Silas said. "But, last I heard Charlie isn't coming up to the Huerfano until next spring. Two of our old friends are plannin' to give it a try here-a-bouts too. Joseph Doyle and Marcelino Baca been talkin' about moving into El Pueblo, or down on the Fountain."

"Any talk of Indian trouble?" Whit asked.

"Always talk," Silas chuckled. "Yep, a' course the Apache are still raiding down south, the Ute been stirred up a bunch, and there's the constant fightin' between them all. I remember..." Silas stopped in mid-sentence; his attention drawn to movement the other side of the corn filed.

Whit, seeing the change in Silas' countenance followed his gaze to the east. There he saw a dozen horsemen moving through the corn stalks heading for the cabin. When they cleared the field, they spread out and Whit recognized them as Cheyenne and a few Arapaho. Though both these tribes were friendly, he cursed himself, that his rifle was inside the cabin next to that of Silas. For a feeling of security, he placed his hand on the Aston pistol tucked in his belt.

Without glancing in Whit's direction, Silas instinctively knew what Whit was doing and in a low voice warned him, "You won't need that horse pistol. I know these fellows."

The riders came forward and stopped, some dismounting and letting their horses graze. One large warrior with a pockmarked face moved to Silas, and the old man stood up to meet him. They threw their arms around each other and hugged.

"It is good to see you father," the Cheyenne said.

"My heart is happy also, my son," returned Silas. Releasing the grip on his son, Silas turned to Whit and introduced the Cheyenne.

"This is my son, Richard. Called Little Gun by the Cheyenne, or Pistol," he said in English to Whit, and to Pistol, "This is Whitney Voss. His wife is from the band of Crow Horse, daughter of Black Dog."

Pistol looked Whit up and down and only nodded. Whit looked over Pistol, the two men sizing each other up. There was an instant uneasiness between them. This was only intensified when one of the Cheyenne pushed his way through the others and Whit recognized him as Bear Voice.

"*I know who this man is,*" Pistol said to Silas, "*Some of Crow Horses' band ride with me now.*" Silas looked over those with his son, the medicine man first catching his eye. Silas took a disliking to Bear Voice. The rest were a mixture of Dog Soldiers and some Arapaho.

Whit felt Bear Voice's gaze of hatred, and he returned a look of cool disregard, angering the medicine man.

"*Where do you go, my son?*" Silas asked.

"*There is word that some of the Ute tribe is camped west of here. We are led to understand they have many horses.*" Pistol made the hand sign for "black Indian," as he talked. "*We have some young men with us who need the experience of stealing horses, and taking scalps.*"

Silas was sorry to hear his son speak in this manner, but Pistol had long ago turned away from the ways of the white world, and the only Whiteman who held his respect was his father.

"*Stay, smoke and eat with me,*" Silas offered.

"*No, the blood in in the young men of my party is hot. Many have bad hearts toward the Whiteman, and I would not have one of these tempted to try their hand against you.*"

"Smart move," Silas switched to English, "I'd hate to kill such fine young men." Whit saw a change in Silas. His steel-gray eyes took on a fire that showed a power that hid deep inside the older man. "Yep, I'd end up eatin' someone's liver fer dinner."

"*I am made to think this old man has a wish to see his hair hanging from the belt of a warrior,*" for the first time Bear Voice spoke.

"*It would have to be a great warrior,*" Silas switched back to Cheyenne, "*But I see only one here among this pack of women, and that is Little Gun, my son.*"

Bear Voice's anger flared, and Silas smiled, knowing that the medicine man was already beaten if it came to a fight. He could tell Bear was all talk, and that was only when he had an audience.

"*White Hair has taken more scalps than there are leaves on that tree,*" Pistol said, pointing to the tree they stood beneath, "*The Blackfeet know his name and they shake with fear at the sound of it. I know of no warrior that could count coup on him and live to boast about it around the campfire.*" He shook his head and for the first time smiled, then spoke in English.

"Pa, you still surprise me. But, I fear that there is a great war coming and it would be best if you did not live here alone. Consider going down to Taos or Santa Fe where you have friends."

"You know I won't go too far from your mother, least not for very long," Silas said, looking off toward the small mound of rocks that marked the grave of his wife.

"She'd understand Pa," Pistol said, then he vaulted into the saddle and whipping his horse's flanks with a quart, he sped off followed by the rest of his war party. They crossed to the south side of the river and were soon on top of the bluff headed west.

"So, that was your son?" Whit asked as they watched the war party disappear over the rise of the bluff.

"Yep," Silas replied, "He's been runnin' with the Dog Soldiers for a long time."

"Seems that you have some history with the shit-eater Bear Voice?" Silas looked over at Whit.

"Yep, he never forgave me fer takin' Little Bird as my wife. Got worse when she died."

Silas hadn't known that Little Bird had died. His next words were cautious but meant as condolence.

"Sorry to hear that Son, she sure was a prize. When did you lose her?"

"Last fall, right after we got back from Fort Laramie." Whit didn't want to offer what had happened and Silas had better manners than to ask.

"How's the boy?" Silas finally asked.

"Zachary is doin' fine. Got a Mexican gal takin' care of him, me too I guess."

"That's good. Where they at?"

"Livin' down at Big Timber, but I'm thinkin' of sending them someplace safer for the winter. Not sure where."

"Not sure where that would be, except maybe back in Westport," Silas scratched his beard.

"You feel safe here?" Whit asked.

"Sure, most Indians know me, and no matter what my son thinks, I can take care of myself. Anyways, I'm not always alone. My daughter stays with me most of the time, when she's not with her mother's people. The small bunch she's with usually place their winter camp here-a-bouts. Makes things a bit handy, and another reason I'm not frettin' about trouble with the Cheyenne."

"Not sure Westport would be right for Maggie and the boy. It's a long ways off too."

"Maggie?"

"Magdalena Lucía. She's the gal takin' care of Zachary."

"Oh, I see." Silas smiled.

"Silas," Whit paused, "You think all those fellows will come up here to settle?"

"You mean Barclay and Baca? I believe there is a good chance of it."

"If there will be a bunch of people here, might be a safe place for my son and the gal."

"Seems logical," Silas said.

"I could fix up one of them rooms down in El Pueblo for them. Get them stocked up with meat fer the winter."

"Not sure it isn't too soon, Whit. Like I said, they aren't headed this way until spring."

"You'd be close though," Whit pointed out.

"Not sure of that, they'd still be miles away, and anything could happen," Silas thought for a moment and then added, "They could winter here with me. The gal would be company for my daughter, an' it'd be like having one of my grandsons here with me. I could teach your little fella a thing or two."

"That would be too much to ask of you Silas."

"Na, wouldn't be anything at all," Silas assured him.

"Then I'll bring them upriver soon as I can. What would you like in the way of supplies? I have to do that much for you."

"Well now, I won't begrudge you the pleasure of bringing me a few things. Let's see; tobacco, coffee, sugar, flour, beans, black pepper, powder, lead and flints. And if you're feelin' extra generous, see if William has some of that lemon powder. Another thing, the main spring on my Henry rifle is feeling a bit weak. See if you can scare up one that will fit."

Whit was surprised at how fast Silas had come up with such a long list, but for what he was asking of Silas, the cost would be minimal.

***

SAM J. PISCIOTTA

September 1852 - The Moon of Ripe Plums

The river bottom was covered with a think carpet of yellow-brown leaves from the cotton wood trees, and the scant foliage that clung to the willows and scrub-oak, waved in the slight breeze. There had been a few early snowstorms, but the snow that fell lasted only a few days before the warmth of the September sun melted it. Whit, accompanied by Maggie and Zachary, left the cover of the trees and entered the clearing along the river bottom. The corn field was bare except for the short stubble that poked through from the late growing weeds. Whit, with Maggie and Zachary, rode straight toward Silas Scott's cabin in the river bottom, and their attention went from the log structure nearby to where, set a half dozen lodges. These were evidently Cheyenne by the shape of the smoke flaps and the door covering.

Whit's approach was noticed and some of the occupants of the small camp came out to watch them pass, curious and wondering if the Whiteman had come to trade as behind him and the woman were three pack horses.

Whit eyed them as well, his right hand resting on the rifle that lay across his lap. He was certain they were Cheyenne, but not if they were Dog Soldiers. The hair on the back of his neck prickled and a slight chill ran through him at the thought that he had brought Maggie and Zachary into the jaws of danger. In a low voice he called back to Maggie,

"Might want to pull up next to me." She had anticipated the move and was already at his side, opposite of the Indians.

"If there's a problem, cut loose the packs, take care of yourself and the boy," he said.

"Ho, Voss!" A call came from the direction of the cabin and Whit's attention was drawn to the voice. It was Silas Scott, calling him. Whit put his heels to the horses' flanks, and it quickened its pace to the cabin.

"Hello Silas," Whit said as he dismounted his horse

"I was thinkin' you changed your mind about bringin' the gal and child here," Silas said as he walked forward and extended his had to Whit, who took it and could feel the strength that still existed in the older man's hand. Silas' grip was firm, and he did not need to squeeze another man's hand overly hard to prove his prowess.

"This must be the Maggie you were talkin' about." Silas turned to Maggie and took one of her hands in both of his rough, callused paws, squeezing it much gentler than he had Whit's.

"It is my pleasure to meet you, Magdalena Lucía," he said in Spanish. Maggie was surprised, not only by his proper Spanish, but by the use of her given name.

"Muchas gracias, Señor Scott," she replied.

"Is this Zachary?" Silas asked, "My how he has grown!" He watched the child, who once set free on the ground, went straight to his father and reached out to be lifted up. "Same as last time I saw him. He reminds me of your Pa when he was a sprout."

"I can't imagine my Pa as a sprout, but he does have his grandfather's stubbornness, and he's a handful," said Whit.

Maggie smiled as she watched Whit, who had in the past months started showing more affection toward the child and to her. Her gaze though went past them to the Indian woman standing in the doorway of the cabin.

Silas noticed the direction of her sight and offered an introduction.

"Let me introduce you all to my daughter." He led them toward the cabin and said, "This is Willow, my daughter. Willow, these are the folks I told you about, Whitney Voss, Zachary and Magdalena Lucía."

Maggie reached out her hand to Willow and in Cheyenne said, *"My heart is glad to meet you Willow. If you like, you may call me Maggie or Magpie, as do some of your people."*

"I believe that Maggie will be fine," Willow said in perfect English, but her words were not as warm as Maggie had wished. Like her brother, Willow's face was terrible scared, pockmarked from the effects of smallpox that had infected her many years back. Maggie, being naturally empathetic, did her best to hide the initial shock she had felt.

"Come and eat, then we will find a place for you to sleep," Willow said, and she turned back into the cabin. As if she had anticipated their arrival, Willow had fried cakes of corn meal and a stew made from venison ready for them. Though Maggie offered to help, Willow insisted she was a guest and should enjoy the meal.

When they had finished eating, Willow helped Maggie open the packs of goods and personal belongings and moved them into the cabin. Whit had brought everything Silas had asked for including the special luxury of tinned, smoked oysters and two bottles of Bordeaux wine.

"Been a long time since I've et' oysters," said Silas. "Thank you. I believe we'll save these for a Christmas treat."

"I hoped you'd like them," said Whit.

"Oh, I sure do," said Silas, "I do believe though, we'll break open one of them bottles and have a sip before we turn in. I'll save the other to enjoy with the oysters."

Whit and Silas sat outside the cabin enjoying the last of the day's warmth while they sipped the wine out of tin cups. Silas puffed on his pipe between sips of the Bordeaux, and asked Whit about his plans for the coming winter.

"Not sure what I'm gonna do," said Whit, "I was thinking of heading down and helping out on the Canadian with Bent's boys. But, they need help makin' meat for those cuttin' stone to be used in the new buildings at Big Timbers." He sounded disappointed. "Of course, Big Timbers is a lot closer to here, an' I think I don't want to be away from the boy for too long."

"Just the boy?" Silas asked.

"Well..." Whit started and paused, "I guess I've gotten use to havin' Maggie around."

"Just her bein' around, huh?"

"I'm not sure about it. I feel, well, guilty when I look at the gal."

"Guilty? Why? She ain't a child."

"No, it's only been a year since Little Bird..." He looked down at his cup not sure if he wanted to tell Silas the circumstances of Little Bird's death. "Silas, she killed herself. For a time, I thought it was somethin' I had done, but I realize there wasn't nothin' I could have done. She was just unhappy. I like that gal in there," he pointed over his shoulder to the cabin, "I'm just not sure if I'm good enough for her. Not sure I could give her the love she deserves."

"Hell Son, ain't none of us good enough for a decent woman. At first they see us and think, 'that there man is perfect for me.' And then after they got you for a while they think, 'Sure do wish I could change that man to the way he oughta' be.' There ain't no pleasing them." He chuckled.

"Was it that way with you and your wife?"

Silas smiled, and then said, "We had history before we married. She knew me right off, knew she couldn't change me. Wasn't so much the heated passion of young lovers as it was a real knowledge of each other. Some people live their whole lives together and never really know the other one. Red Calf Woman and I, we went through Hell and back. Took a special woman to put up with me.

"You just might have a special woman there, Whit. Yep, she is some."

Whit stayed a few more days, wanting to spend as much time with his son as possible, and without admitting it to himself, Maggie also. His worry about the presence of the Cheyenne camp close by was relieved when Silas introduced him to the small groups' leader, Crow Eyes.

Crow Eyes was a powerful built man, somewhere in his late thirties, his complexion was darker than most of the Cheyenne that Whit had met, and Silas explained to him that Crow Eyes was half Black. He did not go into the details of his linage, but told Whit that when the Smallpox hit the band of Little Wolf in 1845, Crow Eyes had lost his wife and two of his three children. In the same outbreak, Pistol and Willow had been infected, but had survived. Crow Eyes had not turned his sorrow into hatred, but many who had been afflicted did so, like Pistol and Crow Eyes' son Little Bear who now both rode with the Dog Soldiers.

"As long as Crow Eyes and me are around, your son and Maggie will be safe." Silas assured Whit.

When Whit left, Maggie watched him ride off until he disappeared among the trees along the river. Even after he was no longer in sight she stood looking at where he had vanished. She then turned and began her stay with Silas and Willow.

Once the cold weather and the snows of winter descended on the little valley, Maggie spent more time practicing her reading and writing, and Silas was impressed by her eagerness to learn. Maggie was soon looking through the few books that Silas kept on his shelf; "Robinson Crusoe", "The Odyssey of Homer", "The Raven and Other Poems" by Edgar Allan Poe, "Rob Roy", a volume containing some of the works of William Shakespeare, and a copy in Spanish of "El Ingenioso Hidalgo Don Quijote de la Mancha".

Maggie dove into the books but soon found herself bogged down in the language and prose. To her surprise and delight she found that Willow could read and write, not only English but Spanish and French, and had done so since she was a child. With Willow's assistance, Maggie soon made her way though some of the books on the shelf, and more important, mastered the art of writing in cursive, and her handwriting was fluid and graceful.

The book that caught her attention the most was "Don Quixote," for it was not only an interesting and amusing story, but written in Spanish. She told Willow and Silas she wished that she had a better understanding of the written word in that language, as Willow had to read most of the book for her.

On the evening that Silas calculated was Christmas Eve, Willow gave Maggie a small book, entitled "Cuaderno de Ortografia," a Spanish spelling book, published in1834, by Padre Antonio Jose Martinez. Maggie was surprised and thrilled.

"Where did this come from?" she asked Willow.

"My father gave it to me when I was little. He figured that I should learn words not only in English books. I suppose I should have given it to you before we tried to read Cervantes' book, but I had forgotten I had it among my belongings," Willow related.

"How is it that you know so much?" Maggie asked Silas.

"He is tight lipped about his past," Willow started, "My father was trained to be a priest as a young man. He knows English, French, Spanish and Latin."

"That was a long time ago, in another world," Silas brushed off more talk of his past.

"Thank you, Willow, Thank you, Señor Scott."

"Don't you think it's about time you called me Silas?" he asked.

"Yes, thank you, Silas."

The snows fell, and the area around the cabin descended into a peaceful haven for the four who soon began to consider each other as family. Maggie thought of Whit each day, and often talked to Zachary about his father, and Silas took to doting on the boy as if he were his own grandson.

CHAPTER FOUR
THE SETTLERS

July 1853 – Moon of Ripening Chokeberries

Winter passed with only three visits by Whit to the little cabin on the Arkansas. When he did show up, he brought more supplies and for a few days life was almost ideal for him and Maggie. As space was limited in the cabin, Whit was obliged to share a bed with her and Zachary. The first night was awkward, Maggie shaking with a mixture of fear and excitement at the closeness of Whit. Whit mistaking this as a sign of her being cold willingly offered to place his arms around her and share his body's warmth. The young woman found herself even more excited with the feeling of his arms around her, with the smell of him so close and she became engulfed with a desire for him like she had never felt before.

After the second night spent as the first, Maggie found herself searching for the now comforting place in Whit's arms. The feeling was not lost to Whit, and his desire for her grew. He found the nearness of her intoxicating and the feeling of her next to him arousing. He had to remind himself that it didn't seem right, and it took an almost herculean effort not to act on his desire and make love to her. He no longer thought of being unfaithful to Little Bird, it now never entered his mind. It was out of respect for Maggie that he held back. He didn't want to compromise what he thought was growing into more than a friendship. He feared losing her. But like her, he ached with that carnal desire that overpowers logic, becomes consuming if allowed.

Each time they parted, both were frustrated by that desire. For Maggie it seemed unbearable. His third and last visit marked the turning point in their relationship and the surrender to their passion.

It was a warn day in February that allowed them to take a short walk along the river and they talked about the coming months. They had decided that if Silas would allow it, Maggie and Zachary would stay at the cabin through the following spring and summer. Whit also promised he would try to spend more time there.

They walked under the outstretched, bare limbs of the cottonwoods and soon found themselves out of sight of the cabin. Maggie stood, with Whit directly behind her, looking out at the ice that covered a calm part of the river. A cool breeze kicked up wisps of snow and blowing them toward the couple brought a shiver to Maggie. Whit instinctively wrapped his arms around her and pulled her close, and enjoyed the feeling of her slender figure under the blanket-coat she wore. He held her for a short time and then turned her around, pulling her close again. She looked up into his eyes and he leaned forward and kissed her. The world around them melted away and they stood enfolded in each other's arms.

Whit's next visit in early spring, found them taking more walks together, though these took up little time in talking. They searched out a secluded place among the willows and tall grass, where they finally surrendered to their passion. Maggie had pushed back the fear of losing her chastity, her modesty acting as a shield in saving her self-respect. She did not completely abandon herself to the experience, holding back a bit of her passion, but yielding to Whit's touch. Whit, found himself holding back also, his touch applied gently. They reserved their lust for the rendezvouses that would come in the following days.

They spoke of the future and what it might hold for them. Maggie thinking in terms no further than a life with Whit and Zachary, Whit thinking of one in which he would better himself rather than work for someone else. He knew that times were changing in New Mexico, and there were rumors that the railroad may be coming west following the Arkansas River and then through the mountains and eventually to California. Whit saw an opportunity, and falling prey to the lure of adventure, left Maggie and Zachary promising to return soon.

This had been in the spring, and now the wind blew through the leaves in the cottonwoods, the breeze cooling the hot summer air. Maggie and Willow walked up and down the rows with a hoe, cutting the weeds that invaded between the corn stalks. They were careful not to damage the shallow roots and while keeping their eye on their work, they also watched Zachary as he ran up and down the rows playing. Now, in the middle of July, the corn in the little field had grown straight and tall.

Maggie had helped Silas and Willow plant the corn in the spring, waiting two weeks after the last frost to till up the soil and place the seed corn in the ground. She had also shared with her new friends the knowledge of gardening, passed down by generations of farmers in New Mexico.

Until this year, Silas had planted the corn and then wondered off to follow the Cheyenne hunt out on the plains or visit Taos and Santa Fe. He returned in the fall and accepted what had grown and been left to him by chance. Maggie was surprised that he had harvested anything at all.

First, they started digging an irrigation ditch to divert water from the Arkansas River. Of the three of them though, Silas was the only one who complained about the task of taking a shovel in hand for such a tedious task. Maggie ignored his complaints and soon water was ready to flow toward the field. In the meantime, Maggie and Willow prepared the field for planting. They were careful to plant the seeds four to six inches deep, and at least thirty inches apart. Maggie had also convinced Silas to plant blocks of several short rows rather than a few long ones. She said this would help the plants "marry".

When the plants were about four inches tall, she strode through the field and thinned it out, increasing the space between them from eight to twelve inches. Finally, she convinced them to plant beans and squash around the corn.

"Corn is one of the three sisters," she said. "They thrive when they are together. And if you plant the squash around the field, it will help keep the little banditos away."

"Banditos?" Willow asked.

"Yes, raccoons. Haven't you seen their little footprints in the mud and wondered how much of your corn they have stolen?"

"Little critters have to eat too," Silas quipped.

With Maggie's help, the anticipated harvest for this year looked good enough that Silas was compelled to build a corn crib next to the cabin. In a few months, they would start harvesting the fruits of their labor.

The fertility of the little valley had not gone unnoticed by others. Before the weather closed the mountain passes, and right after Whit's visit in February, Charles Autobees had arrived at the mouth of the Huerfano River with as many settlers as he could bring with him. A few miles upstream, he chose an area about one mile wide and started building an enclosure, a plaza, to include living quarters and a place to keep stock. With the coming of spring, fields were planted, and the little settlement of Huerfano was started.

Soon after, Marcelino Baca arrived at El Pueblo from the Greenhorn settlement, about twenty-five miles away. Baca moved into El Pueblo bringing with him his Pawnee wife and family. Like Silas, he planted a field of corn, but the plot he chose, close to the old trading post, was close to the slough that existed in a bend of the river. His efforts were rewarded with the river flooding the area, its waters swollen by the spring rains, and the snowmelt in the high country. Frustrated and without more seed corn, he returned to the Greenhorn settlement, but vowed to return and make a fresh start.

Whit rode past Baca's flooded fields and up the valley to the cabin. His first sight was the flourishing fields that spread out in front of the log structure. In the rows, he spied Maggie and Willow tending to the plants, Silas somewhat further away was working on the ditch. Whit was barely out of the tree line when the older man saw him and Silas set his shovel aside, taking up his rifle. He stood, with the firearm resting easily in his arms as he scrutinized who was approaching. Though his eyesight had diminished with age, objects at a distance were still clear and he soon figured it was a Whiteman who was coming closer. Just because it wasn't an Indian didn't mean there wasn't some risk. In Silas' mind, there was no skin color associated with good or evil, they both existed in every man.

The women had also seen him. Willow who was closest to Zachary, gathered him up into her arms and the three were already headed back to the safety of the cabin. Whit let out a yelp, and raised his rifle above his head as a signal that he was a friend.

"Hello the cabin," he called out.

This brought the women's attention back to his direction and they stopped their retreat, finally making out who it was. Maggie broke into a run in Whit's direction calling his name, and Zachary, set free by Willow, toddled after her.

Whit slid from his saddle, just as Maggie reached him and he lifted her off the ground, his arms encircling her in a bear hug, and with her arms around his neck, she hugged him back.

"I have missed you so much!" She said, almost squealing with delight.

"I missed you too," Whit said.

"Papa! Papa!" Zachary's small voice broke in.

"Zachary!" Whit exclaimed, releasing his hold on Maggie. Taking the child into his hands, he raised him into the air and swung him around, the child laughing with the excitement.

"Let's go up to the cabin," Whit said, and threw the child over his shoulder, Zachary still giggling. Silas and Willow were also happy to see Whit.

"Thought you'd forgotten all about us," Silas said.

"Na, just been busy. Things are changing pretty fast."

"Well, come on an' tell us all the news," Silas said leading the way to the cabin. They sat in the shade of the large cottonwood next to the cabin, and Whit shared what news he had.

"There's talk of the railroad coming out this way," Whit started. "All the way out to Salt Lake City and even on to California."

"Don't see them findin' a path through the Stoneys," Silas said, his knowledge of the Rocky Mountains serving as a basis of his opinion.

"Some seem to think it can be done," Whit said, Silas shaking his head.

"Well, if they find a way through, they're better path finders than I am."

"A lot of people are bettin' on it, Silas. Word is that Congress authorized spendin' money to do a survey, lookin' for routes in the north, through here an' maybe down south too."

"Might be able to cross over the divide at South Pass up north, an' Sangre de Cristo Pass down here, but that don't get them over the backbone of the Stoneys, the Cascades or the Sierras."

"A lot of people are banking on it." Whit added. "Word from New Mexico is that Kit Carson, Lucien Maxwell Dick Wootton, John Hatcher, and some others have put together herds of sheep and are taking them across the mountains to California. They say there's a lot of money to be made out in California as people out there crying for fresh meat."

"And, you're thinkin' about headin' out to California?" Silas asked.

"No, well, maybe," Whit said, the uncertainty in his voice clear.

"You know, I never was one to stay put in one place for very long," Silas said, "There was always something on the other side of the next mountain, a new valley to see. Been wondering for most my life, until I built this cabin, and then I only stayed here for short periods. At least that was until Red Calf passed away."

His voice cracked slightly as he thought about his wife, and Whit noted the change in Silas' speech. He no long spoke with the inflections of his peers; his words were pronounced properly, like a gentleman, a man of learning. Silas continued, "I found her sitting right here, under this tree. She had some sewing in her hands, and at first I thought she was just leaning back, enjoying the sun on her face, because she was smiling. I figure she must have been thinking about something beautiful that made her happy. There wasn't any pain in the look of her, just peace. I buried her over there, and I find it harder and harder leaving her for more than a few days. It broke my heart, losing her.

"Point is, Son, I've been all over, and I was always searching for something I never did find," Silas gave a little chuckle as if to clear the melancholy away and his speech changed back to that of the back-woodsman, "Ain't no use lookin' at the back trail, Son, best ta keep your eye on the skyline."

Whit was astonished by Silas. He thought he had the older man figured out but now realized that there was far more to the man than he could ever imagine. His admiration for him grew even more.

"How old are you, Silas?" the question came out without Whit meaning it to and he quickly added, "I'm sorry, I shouldn't have asked."

Silas chuckled again, "Truth be told, Son, I have to give that some thought. This here is 1853, so come Christmas time, I'll be...seventy-four years young."

"You've already told me about your time spent trappin' with my grandpa up on the Missouri, and about when you fought in the Creek War, and about the uprising down in Taos. But, you never did tell me where you hail from Silas."

"I was born in Scotland, left there as a lad, spent some time in France 'afore I ended up down in Georgia, where I learned ta hunt an' trap with the Cherokee."

"I guess I thought I'd seen a bunch just leavin' Pittsburgh," Whit said.

"Again, Son, it ain't always where you been that's the most important, it's what you did. A man's got to be able to hold his head up. I done a lot of things that most Christians would say will send me to Hell, I've kilt men, but never one's that didn't deserve it or weren't tryin' to kill me."

Whit thought for a moment and then said, "I have to go back down to Bent's place. I'll settle up what I need to and then look at coming back here, maybe make a try at ranchin' here-a-bouts."

"Maybe," Silas said, knowing that Whit was like him at that age, like so many of the men that Silas had known over the years. Whit would say he wanted to settle down, and in his heart mean it. But, the reality was there would always be that call from the other side of the mountain.

***

August 1853 – Breeding Moon

William Bent's new fort stood on the elevated ground above the river, positioned so that it could be approached from only one direction. The structure was somewhat smaller than its predecessor in outside dimensions, but it was still extensive. Inside were twelve rooms surrounding a central plaza, each room ten feet high and ranging in size from two apartments fourteen by fifteen and a half feet to a warehouse fifty-five feet long. There were arrow-shaped parapets on each corner of the structure, but unlike the old fort, no bastions. On a crystal-clear day, the dim line of the mountains in the west could be seen from the top of the sixteen-foot high walls.

Whit was still thinking about ending his employment with Bent, but he still had doubts. He had witnessed a change in the past few years that made him uneasy. William had returned from the east to the fort with the agency goods and he had worked out a method of distribution. Runners, Whit among them, were sent out to summon the different bands of Indians. Soon, hundreds of lodges, Cheyenne, Arapaho and Kiowa, covered both sides of the river, up and downstream from the fort. Celebrations, with feasting, dancing and the exchange of gifts went on for days. Whit watched as the different soldier societies of the tribes danced in the fort's plaza, and William hosted his own feasts for the chiefs in the main dining room of the fort.

The entire celebration concluded with the distribution of the annuity goods. The wagon loads of boxes containing the promised government goods were set out on the prairie and the Indians gathered in a large circle around them. The head man of each group chose members of their soldier societies to fairly distribute the food, clothing, gun powder and lead.

Among those who were present were the Dog Soldiers of the Cheyenne, and with them was Bear Voice and Looks Far Woman. Whit noticed that when the annuity goods were being distributed, Bear Voice refused his share and Looks Far Woman received a rebuking look from Bear Voice when she started to reach out for a bolt of cloth that had been offered her. Whit almost pitied the woman, she looked ragged and poor compared to the other women, and old for her age.

Whit felt he had to do something, for though he had no feelings for her, she deserved at least the minimum of what had been offered. He took his own blanket and searching her out, walked up to her.

He spoke her name and she turned to look at him, a look of surprise in her eyes. Whit then held out the blanket to her and she took a step back from him. Her eyes widened, and the look on her face changed from surprise to hatred.

"Get away from me!" she cried, this drawing the attention of those around them. The first to react was Bear Voice who rushed forward and with a quart struck Whit across the face. Dropping the blanket, Whit reached for the pistol in his belt with the intent of dropping Bear Voice where he stood. But cooler heads were present, among them Pistol, who stepped in between the two, his back to Whit, and he spoke to Bear Voice.

"This is not the time to draw blood," he said.

Whit felt a hand on his shoulder and found Crow Eyes standing next to him.

"I do not think this is the place to have a confrontation with Bear Voice," he said.

"Hell, I just offered her a blanket, she was my wife's sister," Whit said, his voice shaking with disbelief. "Why'd that sombitch hit me?"

"You evidently overstepped some boundary," Crow Eyes offered.

"Shit, I'll step up and have his liver if he ever hits me again!" Now Whit's anger was aroused.

"Come," Crow Eyes said, *"Come away and let us talk while the blood cools,"* and he led Whit away to his lodge. He knew that getting the Whiteman into his lodge and establishing him as a guest would help quiet things down. He also knew Bear Voice would hold it against him.

They sat in Crow Eye's lodge; one he shared with a woman called Meets the Enemy. Like Crow Eyes, she had lost her spouse, and the two had taken each other for lack of other relatives. Crow Eyes did have a son, Little Bear, but he disapproved of his father's "peace chief" attitude towards the whites and had taken up with the Dog Soldiers. Pistol and Meets were the soul occupants of the lodge except for those times when Silas Scott's daughter Willow stayed with them. Meets welcomed Whit as a guest and her grace and warmth eased Whit's tension.

"I will never understand why they cannot let it go," Whit said, switching to Cheyenne as a matter of respect to his host.

"Some people hold things for a long time. I believe that there is more than your history with them."

"I tried. You see how poor Looks Far is? She looks like she has not eaten. She is wearing clothes that most would throw away," He shook his head at the thought of her condition.

"She is in a poor state, but she does not go without. She stays like that because it is the way she has chosen. She is a holy woman. She is touched by spirits."

"A holy woman?" Whit couldn't believe what he heard. *"When did she become Holy?"*

"She has always been that way. She is a dreamer, a seer of the future," Crow eyes said. *"I know that you may not believe in these things, at times I do not myself. But, the half of my blood that is Cheyenne feels there is something special about her."* He paused for a short time and then added, *"A time has come among the Cheyenne when there is a need for a belief in more than what has been given to us."*

93

"*I am made to think the* annuities *are good for the People,*" Whit commented, not knowing what word in Cheyenne to use for annuities, as gifts didn't seem right.

"*Do you not see that Whites who travel along the roads drive away the buffalo or force them to move in a different way from that of the past? They now follow a narrower path. The goods given to the people do not last through the cold moons. If you look closely, you will see that the bands can no longer support themselves, more and more they depend on the 'Great White Father's' charity. When the cold months come the children cry with hunger. We must then raid other tribes like the Pawnee and the Utes.*

"*Soon though, I believe these tribes will come to the whites and complain. There is a difference between what we Cheyenne receive from the 'Great White Father,' and what is given such people as the Ute and the Apache. I do not complain, they do not receive gun powder and lead like we do.*" He said the words "Great White Father," with a tinge of sarcasm.

"*You do not think a time will come for the People to settle down and farm?*"

"*Would you be happy to be a farmer?*" Crow Eyes asked, not wanting or expecting Whit to answer.

As for Whit, he wondered if the plans he had made with Maggie to settle down was what he really wanted. He knew it was the right thing to do, after all he did have feelings for her, she was a good woman and she was caring for Zachary as if he were her own child. He just wasn't sure if he could settle down and be a rancher any more than he could have settled down and been in the wagon business.

***

September 1853 - The Moon of Plums Ripe

Silas rode along the bluff, south of the Arkansas River, his eyes scanning the prairie to the south-east, where the fringe of trees along the San Carlos River poked up dark against the dry, brown grassland in the pre-dawn light. He hadn't hunted the San Carlos for some time, but knew that there were usually mule deer to be found there and he had a hunger for fresh venison. He had seen some big bucks in the little canyons created by the waters that flow from Wet Mountains north of the peak called Green Horn Mountain, known as Cuerno Verde by the Mexicans.

The mountain was named after the Comanche war Chief Tabivo Naritgant, "Dangerous Man" in the Comanche tongue, but he was called "Green Horn" because of the green tinted horns that he wore on his buffalo head-dress in battle. Cuerno Verde was killed in a battle near the mountain by forces of the Spanish Governor Juan Bautista de Anza in 1779. Tired of the Comanche raiding down into Mexico every winter, de Anza led a mixed force of eight-hundred Spanish troops and Ute, Apache, and Pueblo auxiliaries on an expedition against them. The Comanche always returned to their home territory in the Black Hills each spring, and de Anza circling around in front of them, caught them just north of the Arkansas River. In a running-battle that lasted for several days, Green Horn was killed, making his final stand near that mountain named after him.

As always, Silas thought about where he was, and what he was doing, but a bit of the past still rolled around in his head. Though he had advised Whit not to dwell on the past, at his age Silas found himself thinking more about it. He thought of friends that had died, and wondered about those he hadn't seen for a while.

Movement on the east side of the San Carlos drew his attention, and in the light of the early dawn, he thought he saw a group of buffalo moving to the north. He sat in the saddle straining his eyes, hoping the brightness of the rising sun would illuminate them. He waited, patiently watching. The figures didn't move like buffalo, they traveled more in a straight line, "possibly Indians," he thought. No, they were wagons and what appeared to be cattle and sheep. Thinking they might be traders either coming up from the Green Horn settlement or from Santa Fe. He kicked his heels to his horse's flanks and urged it into a trot in the direction of the river and the caravan of wagons.

Coming up out of the small river bottom, Silas almost ran directly into the wagons, and his sudden appearance drew alarm, some of the men on horseback turning their mounts in his direction to cut him off. Silas raised his rifle over his head signaling them and rode forward. When he was close enough, he recognized Levin Mitchell and William Kroenig, both men were well-known to him, being brought up in the fur trade so to speak, and veterans of life in the mountains.

"Silas Scott!" Called out Mitchell, the big red-headed ex-trapper.

"How do, Levin," Silas answered. "Mornin' Bill," he said to Kroenig.

"Good to see you're still upright," Mitchell jested, "where you headed'?

"Out lookin' fer some venison, an' I spotted you. Mistook you for Indians at first. Where you all goin'?"

"We're takin' advantage of Ceran St. Vrain's offer to settle on some of his land grant. We're headed for the Huerfano, Charlie Autobees is already there," said Mitchell.

"Didn't you hear? They're talkin' about bringin' the railroad out this way and the Huerfano is bound to make a good stopping place," Kroenig added.

"I heard somethin' like that, but think I'll wait to see if it happens," Silas said.

"Ride a bit with us, and when we noon we'll treat you to a cup of coffee and some fresh beef." Mitchell offered.

"Much obliged," Silas said and fell in to ride alongside the small caravan.

As they rode, they talked more, and Mitchell caught Silas up on the news from New Mexico and the Greenhorn settlement.

Marcelino Baca had experienced a successful harvest of both corn and wheat at the Greenhorn settlement, and was now planning to return to the area around El Pueblo before winter. Joseph Doyle, another seasoned citizen of the mountain trade, was also packing up his family, and with a few others, moving to El Pueblo and to the mouth of the San Carlos.

"Looks like it's gonna' be a might crowded," Silas thought to himself. He left the group after they had "nooned", rested their stock at mid-day, and headed back to his cabin. He had much to think about. He had to admit to himself that a time was coming when civilization would overtake the west. The railroad would make its way west. With it would come settlers, farmers by trade, and soon, Silas thought, there would be church steeples, court houses and outhouses dotting the countryside. He was not so much worried about himself and those men like him, but wondered if there would be a place in this new west for the Indians.

**

RIVER OF SAND

October 1853 – Moon When Thin Ice Begins to Form on Rivers

As Levin Mitchell had said, Marcelino Baca had returned to the Arkansas, but rather than move into the old El Pueblo, he chose a spot about a mile away on the east side of Fountain Creek, and there he started his rancho. He began by building a house for his family, a substantial log structure; and for his hired hands, he built thirteen jacal and log houses. With these was also built a large corral to hold his herd of fifty horses. As the houses were being constructed, Baca also put his help to digging an irrigation ditch from the junction of Fountain Creek and the Arkansas River. This would supply water to his fields, and he could grow a sufficient amount of fodder to feed the five hundred head of beef that he had also brought with him.

The proximity of the Baca rancho gave Silas worry. That large amount of beef and horses would be a temptation to every Indian within a hundred miles, and he was sure that stock would start to disappear sooner or later. It was only a matter of time, and when this happened there was bound to be trouble in the little valley of El Pueblo.

Silas' worry was equaled by Maggie's excitement. Though she had been content with the company of Silas and Willow, Baca's family and hired help were New Mexicans, her people. She lost no time in making acquaintances at the ranch, especially the little daughter Elena, of Baca and his Pawnee wife, who became a playmate to Zachary.

Willow would go with Maggie and Zachary to visit the Bacas, but she never felt comfortable in the presence of Baca's wife, Tomasa, the Pawnee being traditional enemies to the Cheyenne. This uneasy situation seemed to bother Tomasa more than Willow, as she made it clear when she remarked to Maggie that she would rather see her child dead than in the hands of another tribe.

After a daylong visit to the Baca ranch, Maggie and Willow rode toward their own home, Zachary nestled in between Maggie and the pommel of her saddle. The women talked and Willow confided that she considered Maggie to be like a sister. They used a mixture of Spanish, English and Cheyenne, all known by both women. All three languages easily understood by the two.

"I do not find it easy to be close to other people," she started, "I see the way they look at me, and it does not matter if they are Red or White, they only see my face."

"There is much more to you than that," Maggie said. "You are a good and kind person."

"You do not understand," said Willow, "I once loved a man and I thought he would be my husband, but after the sickness, I hid myself from him. I would not let him see me, and soon he married another woman."

"Was he a Cheyenne?" Maggie asked.

"No, he was a friend of my father's. What made it worse is that he was a healer, what you would call a doctor among the Whiteman. When he came to visit me, I told my father that I did not want him to see me. I said that I was dead to him."

"I am sorry," Maggie said.

"Why should you be sorry? It is no fault of yours. I have chosen my life the way it is now, and I have no regrets, even when I see you and Sky Eyes together it makes my heart happy."

"I love you, my sister," Maggie said, "I know that someday a man will come along that deserves you."

They crossed the Fountain and moved through the low spot in the hill that separated the Fountain Creek and the Arkansas River just before their junction. The new inhabitants had begun to use this natural low spot as a passage from Baca's ranch to El Pueblo, and they called it the "puertocito", as it offered a passage that was almost a straight line of travel between the two. Willow reached over and took hold of the reins on Maggie's horse and softly warned, "Shhhh!" She then pointed toward the direction of the old adobe post. From that direction came the sound of voices, the braying of mules and whinny of horses. The two women moved forward slowly, and around the old post they saw several people and wagons gathered there. Among them, they saw Silas.

Riding up to the people gathered around the wagons, they found that Benito Sandoval was moving his family and several others into the adobe structure. Benito and others in the party were old acquaintance of Silas' from the past. These included; Joseph Doyle, George Simpson, who was an ex-Bent\ St. Vrain Employee and one of the original partners at El Pueblo in1842, Ben Ryder, who was once a carpenter at Bent's Fort, the half-Cherokee, Charlie McIntosh, Maurice LeDuc, Charles Pray,

Tanislado de Luna, Juan Ignacio Valencia and a new immigrant to the west, August Klausen, a tall, strongly built Dane.

Most of these men had brought their wives and children as well as hired help. Sandoval brought his wife Maria Espinosa and their four sons. With Joseph Doyle was his wife, Cruz Suaso, their children, James and Fannie, and Cruz's mother, Terestia Suaso, and her son Tomas Suaso.

The little fort was far too small for all the people that had come in the party, and some of the families, such as Doyle's, would stay only long enough to cut lumber to build homes of their own. But first, repairs had to be made on the little trading post before winter set in.

Benito Sandoval and his hands repaired the rooms inside the adobe post. They replaced the roof beams, called "vigas", that were broken or had fallen. And on these, they placed a new latticework of willow branches, called "latias", and finally a layer of sod and adobe mud over it all. With the roofs repaired, the rooms were cleaned, then the inside walls plastered with a new coat of adobe and whitewashed. Finally, the dirt floors were sprinkled with water and swept until they were smooth and as hard as rock.

When the work on El Pueblo was close to complete, Sandoval, and his help, fetched timber and cut planks for Doyle's new house. It was to be built six miles downriver at the mouth of the St. Charles, as most of the Americans were now calling the San Carlos River.

Maggie and Willow helped the women of El Pueblo, enjoying the change in routine, and taking pleasure in the women's company. Many of them were much the same age as Maggie, a few like Benito Sandoval's wife Maria Espinosa, a bit older. Among the younger inhabitants was Bob Rice, a fourteen-year-old boy, who Doyle had found living with the Cheyenne a few years back and had taken in.

Soon, Maggie and Willow became favorite visitors at El Pueblo, and the Baca ranch. The teenage boys especially found the presence Maggie exciting. Bob Rice, Pedro Sandoval, Benito Pais and Felipe Cisneros, all found excuses to be near her when she was at either El Pueblo or the ranch, their enthusiasm dulled only by Whit's arrival. Whit arrived during the last week of December, as usual, with supplies and gifts, and he announced that he had plans to stay through spring, or at least until the weather warmed up.

Whit settled in at Silas' cabin again, and his relationship with Maggie warmed further, their bond becoming stronger. Whit treated her with respect, and at times, he would call her Magdalena. Their clandestine rendezvous became fewer, but they were still intimate, enjoying the more carnal portion of their time together.

The excitement and the passion had not lost its intensity for Maggie, but it had been tempered by her growing maturity, her almost intuitive reaction to their lovemaking. Whit easily slipped into this new relationship with Maggie giving little thought to it. Like Maggie, he enjoyed their intimacy, but it seemed not to be a tie between them, it was a shared pleasure, though one not to be taken lightly. The two became a couple, not merely lovers, but something more. They were comfortable with each other, but not as husband and wife.

Willow was happy for Maggie, but as it had before, Whit and Maggie's relationship brought feelings of loneliness to Willow. In the past, she had been able to relieve the ache she felt by visiting the camps of the Cheyenne, and thought there were no suitors among those camps, she had found the companionship of other Cheyenne women comforting. It was now late in the year and no band of Cheyenne had arrived in the little valley to winter near the cabin, and Willow feared it would be a lonely winter. In her self-consciousness, she failed to notice she had caught the eye of August Klausen, the big, shy and modest man.

***

For the first time in many years, no band of the Cheyenne or Arapaho wintered at the confluence of the Arkansas and the Fountain. Nor did they find a winter camp site near the Huerfano or St. Charles River. The lack of small game and the search for buffalo took the bands further east, choosing sites near the Republican River in the north and the Washita and Cimarron in the south. But, the availability of food was not the only reason the Cheyenne and Arapaho had wintered near the Wet Mountains. This small range in front of the Sangre de Cristos was the edge of the territory belonging to the Ute, and the Ute were always in possession of horses.

Skirting well north, the little raiding party of Cheyenne crossed the Fountain Creek some three or four miles north of the Baca's ranch. They traveled west and then turned to the south, following the terrain from the upper prairie down into the valley of the Arkansas. The sun was just over the eastern horizon when they rode off the ridge composed of layers of blue-gray shale rock that crumbled under the hooves of their ponies.

Crow Eyes and Pistol were co-leaders of the two dozen warriors that descended into the little valley. Those under Crow Eyes, were a mixture of members from the Swift Fox and the Red Shield Societies, the latter, a group that was getting smaller and smaller among the Southern Cheyenne. The remaining ten warriors were under the leadership of Pistol, or as he was called by the Cheyenne, Little Gun, and were Dog Soldiers. All but five of the twenty-four men were unexperienced warriors and on either their first or second raid.

The group was held together only under the common goal of a proposed raid on the Ute in the valley west of the Sangre de Christos Mountains. The stop at the cabin of Silas Scott was not planned, but only a convenience, one prompted by Pistol and Crow Eyes. Little did they know that Whitney Voss would be at the cabin. Pistol knew the history between Voss and Bear Voice, who was among the Dog Soldiers on this raid. There were also others familiar with Whit, including his brother-in-law, White Badger.

More important to Crow Eyes was the presence of his son Little Bear, who was on the cusp of joining one of the warrior societies, and Crow Eyes hoped that he would not choose the Crazy Dogs. As he rode next to Pistol, they spoke quietly between themselves. Crow Eyes was the older of the two, both were half-breeds. They had grown up together, and both had suffered from the smallpox that had hit their band in 1845. The families of the two men were also inter-twined through marriage and close friendships. Crow Eyes had lost his first wife, and three of his four children. Pistol, sometimes called Little Gun, had lost one of his sisters, and nephew. He and his remaining sister, Willow, were left scared form the sickness. It would have made more sense that of the two, Crow Eyes would have been the most bitter. But, Crow Eyes, though a fierce warrior was still a man of peace when it came to the Whites.

As they crossed the river bottom, they were spotted by Pedro Sandoval who had just left Silas' cabin, where he had delivered fresh milk. At the sight of the Indians, he wasn't sure whether to turn back to Silas' or head for El Pueblo. He choose the latter, and kicking his heels to the flanks of the mule, he sped off to warn the families in the adobe post.

Silas stood in the doorway and watched the boy as he rode away. When Pedro spurred the mule into a run, Silas spied the advancing war party. Over his shoulder, he called back to those inside.

"Riders comin' in, an' I'm not sure they're friendly."

Whit came up behind him, rifles in hand, and he passed Silas' on to him. "Who you figure it might be?" he asked.

"Can't rightly tell in this light," Silas said, squinting his eyes in an attempt to make out the riders in the early morning light, the sun now behind them.

"Indians, for sure, but can't tell Crow from Comanche," he said, not meaning literally that they were of either tribe. "Might be Cheyenne. Maybe," he added, a slight tinge of hope in his words. If they were Cheyenne, there was more than likely nothing to worry about. If they were not, there could be blood spilled.

As the Indians came closer, Silas recognized his son in the front of the group, as well as Crow Eyes who rode next to Pistol, and he was relieved. He turned slightly and lay his rifle against the cabin wall, then turned back toward the riders. Whit retained his firearm but laid it across the crook of his left arm to rest.

Silas took out his pipe and filled the bowl with tobacco, tamping it down with his thumb. He then placed the stem between his teeth and took out flint, steel and char-cloth to start an ember. The spark took and Silas set it in the pipes bowl and drew a deep breath, setting the tobacco alight. A cloud of tobacco smoke encircled his head when he exhaled, and he seemed to relax.

Whit was always amazed how calm Silas could be. The older man seemed to have nerves made of steel, and Whit wondered if Silas would blink even if confronted by a Grizzly bear. Silas calmly puffed on his pipe as the riders pulled up, and Pistol slid from the saddle.

"Good mornin' Pa," he said.

"Mornin'," Silas said, and reached out a hand to his son. They shook hands and Silas greeted Crow Eyes in Cheyenne, *"My heart is glad to see you friend."*

"As is mine, Uncle" Crow Eyes said, using the term of respect.

"Come sit, and we will smoke," Silas offered.

"It is good," said Crow Eyes and he slid from the saddle, followed by the rest of the group.

Looking over the group Silas noticed Sitting Hawk, who had been married to, Corn Woman, the daughter Silas lost to the smallpox. It was clear that like Pistol, Sitting Hawk was bitter towards the Whites, for not only had he lost his wife, but his son. Thought of that child came instantly to Silas, and it pained him to think about the loss of his only grandchild.

Also, among those who in the group, was White Badger, brother-in-law to Whit and Whit went to him and held out his hand, saying in Cheyenne, *"My heart is happy to see you Brother."*

White Badger reluctantly took Whit's hand and with little emotion said, *"I see you Sky Eyes."*

Before they had released their grip, Zachary came out of the cabin door and toddled over to his father, wrapping his arms around Whit's leg.

"Is this my sister's son?" White Badger asked.

"Yes. This is Yellow Horse," said Whit as he picked up his son. And then to the child he said, *"This is your uncle, White Badger."*

Badger looked the child over. *"He has the eyes of his mother."*

Their conversation was interrupted by Maggie, who came and reached out for the child saying, "I am sorry, he got away from me." Whit handed Zachary to her and she turned and took him into the cabin.

"Soon he will be old enough that you must tell him about the People," White Badger advised.

"I think someday, his uncle will tell him about the People," Whit said, offering hope that there could come a time when any bad feelings between him and White Badger would be resolved.

Blankets and buffalo robes were spread out on the ground in front of the cabin, and all but a few of the Indians were seated. Bear Voice was among those few who chose to stay with the horses some distance off. He had seen Whit and his first thought was to start a confrontation, but he had no desire to go against the authority of Pistol or Crow Eyes. So, he stood sullenly staring at the seated group, occasionally making snide remarks under his breath, just loud enough for those standing near him to hear.

As Bear Voice watched, Maggie and Willow came out of the cabin carrying a large pot of coffee and a platter of fried bread in their hands. They passed out the bread and poured tin cups of the hot brew for the warriors. As Maggie handed Whit a cup, Bear Voice was quick to note the look that passed between the two. A mixture of emotions raced through the medicine man. The hate he felt for Whit was now fueled by the obvious bond between the two. Bear Voice now had another person to add on his list in revenge against the white man.

"What brings you out this late in the year?" Silas asked, speaking in English.

"The People need a small victory to boost their spirits. Have you heard of the losses suffered at the hands of the Pawnee these past two years?"

"I heard some," said Silas.

"Last year, Iron Shirt and many other warriors were killed by the Pawnee. This past spring, the pipe was passed around and many of the soldier societies took it up. After the proper medicine was made, the People with some of our Kiowa and Araphoe allies went against the Pawnee again, this time with the sacred Arrow Bundle and the sacred Buffalo Hat. A big camp of the Pawnee was found and although there were hundreds of them, we thought there would be a big victory, with many scalps."

"I hear it didn't go that way," Silas said.

"No, among the Pawnee were many Săvănē' hunters armed with their American rifles." He used the Cheyenne name given to the "Civilized" tribes of the Shawnee, Delaware, Potawatomi, Sac Fox and Iroquois lumping them all together. "During the battle, one of the Săvănē' went to for reinforcements and over two dozen of the White Indians joined in the battle. They were deadly with their rifles and turned the tide of battle and though the People stood their ground and fought bravely, we were driven back. The Săvănē' rushed out onto the battlefield and cut the hearts out of the warriors of the people who had fallen. Seventeen of the People and four Arapaho were killed, but we killed many of the Pawnee and four of the Săvănē'."

"So there gonna' be another campaign against the Pawnee come next spring?" Silas asked.

"There is already talk as those who lost family are calling for vengeance."

"Well, that don't explain what you're doin' here."

"We have had a good fall hunt. The lodges are full of meat, and there is plenty of grass to see our ponies through the winter," Pistol said. "We have heard that the Ute again have many more horses than they need."

"You need more horses?" Silas asked Crow Eyes.

"No, Uncle," said Crow Eyes "I ride with my son, Little Bear." He pointed out the young man. "He is of an age where he should start his own herd, and he needs the experience if he is to become a warrior. The People have many enemies."

Silas eyed Little Bear, and said in Cheyenne, *"If Little Bear has a heart as strong as that of his father, he will be a great man among the People."*

The young man took the comment as a complement but one that he figured as obvious. Of course, he would be great among the People, he thought.

"Pa, I still advise that this is not a safe place for you," said Pistol.

"What you figure I have to worry about?" Silas asked. His voice was clear and steady. When Pistol did not answer, Silas turned to Crow Eyes and asked, "You see something that I haven't?"

"Times are changing," said Pistol, speaking in Cheyenne, his seldom used English feeling uncomfortable at times. *"A storm is coming. There is an evil wind blowing across the land."*

"I have been among the People for many years. I have seen many changes. What could change now that would make a difference?" Silas posed the question to his son.

"More and more Whites come to the land of the People. Their numbers swell with the change of each season. Do you remember when I was a child and you took me to St. Louis? I was astonished by the buildings and all the people. You told me that what I saw there was nothing to compare with what lay further to the east." Pistol paused, looking off to the where the sun had now cleared the treetops, then spoke to his father in English. "Do you truly believe that there is room for both the Cheyenne and the Whites?"

"Yes, times change, Son," Silas said, "And, people have to change with them. I remember the stories told to me by your mother, stories about the Cheyenne and their past. She said in the time of her grandfather, the Cheyenne lived near the Great Lakes, east of the Missouri. When they grew strong, they crossed over the river, moved out onto the plains, and they drove other tribes, like the Comanche and the Crow out of the Black Hills. They took that land away from them. Many of the Cheyenne have said that it was the Creator who gave them the right to take that land from the other tribes."

Silas paused to let the two men think about what he had just said; "Now you ask me if I think there is room for both the Cheyenne and the Whites. No, not if we don't find a way to live together. The whites are coming, as sure as that sun rose this morning, and I tell you that among the Whites there are those who think the Creator has given this land to them."

Both Pistol and Crow Eyes remained silent for a moment, neither knowing what exactly to say. Pistol rose from where he sat and took a few steps away. He stopped and looking at the field where Silas had grown his crops, he made a decision and turned back to face his father.

"If what you say is true Father, I must choose of which world I belong," said Pistol, *"We have both seen the way I am looked upon by your people; I am a "Breed" and they will not let me live in peace, to hunt and move as I have been raised. I am Little Gun of the People. From this day on I will fight to keep this land."* He turned and walked over to where the horses waited, all the Cheyenne but Crow Eyes following him.

Crow Eyes, stood next to Whit and Silas. He reached out and shook each of their hands, and said to Silas, *"You and Little Gun have both spoken the truth. I believe that he will take up the pipe and go to war. I will attempt to make peace, but I do not think we will ever see peace again. Take care of yourself Uncle."* He went to his horse, mounted it and the group of warriors rode away.

Silas watched his son as he left, and a feeling of loss washed over him as powerful as when he had lost his wife. Deep down inside he feared that he would never see him again. He swallowed the lump that was growing in his throat and blinked a few times to force back the tears welling up in his eyes. He felt a hand on his shoulder and turned to see his daughter. In a gesture of affection, she rarely showed, she threw her arms around her father and hugged him.

"We best clean this up," Silas said referring to the blankets and buffalo robes spread on the ground, and giving Willow a slight smile, bent down to pick up one. A somber mood seemed to settle on Silas, Willow, Maggie and Whit, as they folded the blankets. Willow cast her gaze in the direction of the departing Cheyenne, and wondered where her place in this changing wolrd would be.

The Indians had barely gotten out of sight when a rider came from the direction of El Pueblo, at a dead run. Silas and Whit watched the man as he grew closer, and it was obvious that he was not accustomed to being in the saddle. He rode a large, gray mule, about seventeen hands high, but the rider's size made the animal look small. The man held a rifle in his right hand and barely had control of the animal with the reins he held in his left. For a reason unknown to Silas, the sight brought to his mind Cervantes' Don Quixote, and it made him smile to himself. It would not have surprised Silas, if the rider didn't fall from the saddle before reaching him and Whit.

As he got closer, Whit recognized him and said to Silas, "Looks like that fella' Klausen."

"Yep, seems to be in a hurry too," said Silas.

Klausen brought the mule to a sudden stop by yanking back on the reins, the big gray, digging its hooves into the ground and rearing up, almost spilling him from the saddle.

"What's the trouble?" Silas asked as he reached out and took hold of the reins close to the mule's head, in an attempt to help calm it down.

"They said der vas Indian attacking you!" Klausen, short of breath and his English a bit rough, spit out.

"No, not at the moment," Silas said. "You look all lathered up. You better get down and catch your wind."

Klausen, somewhat less than graceful, dismounted the mule that was still wild-eyed and a bit skittish from the hurried ride from El Pueblo. When on the ground, the big Dane stood taller than Whit and towered over Silas by well over a full head.

"Who said we were being attacked," Whit asked.

"The boy, Pedro San-do-vals," he pronounced the last name carefully, but adding the "s" at the end.

"There was some Cheyenne here, but they moved on," Silas told him. "There's nothing to worry about with the Cheyenne." Whit glanced at Silas hearing this last statement. "Come in the cabin an' have a cup of coffee, and some fried bread," Silas offered.

The cabin, built by Silas, had a doorway that allowed Silas to walk straight in, while Whit ducked slightly, but August had to bend forward at an awkward angle that made the others marvel at his size. Not only was Klausen tall, he was powerfully built, echoing the stature of his Nordic ancestors.

He sat on the bench and Willow brought him a cup of coffee and pieces of the fry bread they had made for their earlier visitors. As she handed the coffee cup on to him, Silas could see that Klausen couldn't keep his eyes off Willow, and at first, he thought Klausen was staring at the scars on his daughter's face. Silas' anger began to rise until he realized that Klausen was shaking slightly, nervous, almost afraid. Was he afraid that Willow still carried the pox? Silas thought. This angered him further until he heard the Dane speak.

"Thank you, Ma'am," he stammered out. Silas was close enough to see something different in the eyes of the Dane, not fear. Klausen was smitten with Willow.

"Well, I'll be damned," Silas thought to himself, then out loud, "Mighty brave thing you did, runnin' down here to fight Indians." this brought August's attention away from Willow.

"It vas nothing," he said. "I vould have done the same for anyone," He looked down at the coffee cup in his big hands.

"I bet you would, Klausen."

"Please call me August, my friends call me August."

"Alright then, August it is." They chatted and Silas asked August to tell him a bit about himself. August, said he was from Alborg, in Denmark. He had work as a sailor and fisherman for most of his life, until war broke out in 1848. Denmark, her Swedish and Norwegian allies, had declared war against Germany, Prussia and Duchies of Schleswig and Holstein. August said he served on a Danish warship, where he made a friend who convinced him that there was a fortune to be made in the Americas. When the war appeared over, he was released from service and with that friend signed on to a merchant ship headed for the Caribbean. From Cuba, he went to Mexico, where his friend was killed. August then made his way north to Santa Fe and there he met Joseph Doyle over a year ago.

"I have not found wealth," said August, "But I see a great opportunity to settle here along the Arkansas, start a farm and a family." Unconsciously, he glanced at Willow with this final statement.

"For not being from this part of the world, you speak mighty good American," said Silas.

"I have found that I must learn, or I will not be successful," said August. Then after a moment he continued. "Mr. Scott, I would like to talk to you in private."

"There isn't anything you can't say to me in private that can't be said here."

"I wish to speak of your daughter," August said almost under his breath, leaning close to Silas.

"Oh, and what do you have to say about her?" Silas thought the Dane was getting a bit ahead of himself.

"I would like your permission to court her."

"You don't even know Willow, only seen her couple of times," Silas said, then added, "And what makes you think she's wanting to be courted?"

With this Willow stepped closer, and said, "You two sound like you're making some kind of trade. I'm not a horse to be bargained for." She turned and left the cabin, a mixture of emotions confusing and angering her.

"You best go talk to the gal yourself," Silas advised August.

August rose and stooping exited the cabin and went to Willow who stood a few yards away.

"I am sorry," August started, which turned Willow around. "I don't know what the right way is to ask for an Indian woman."

"You're as ignorant as you are big," she said. "I'm not just some squaw to be bought for a string of ponies, so that you can have a slave to wash your socks and warm your bed."

"No, no, you don't understand," August stammered. "I am looking for a wife, a good woman to share my life with. I knew it was you when I first saw you."

"Why me?" Willow asked, her voice softening a bit, thinking about her scared face. "There are many beautiful women among the Cheyenne or the Mexicans that you could court."

"I think you are beautiful. You have dignity and I can see you have a strong character. I am sorry I do not know the right words to use."

Willow looked at the big man standing in front of her, and she believed he was sincere, and her heart melted.

"We will see how strong your heart is. You can tell my father that I have given you permission to come visit me. If by the spring you have proven that you will not take off for whatever is over the horizon, we will talk about marriage. My Cheyenne name is Willow, but I have a white name also, Katherine. You can call me by either."

***

CHAPTER FIVE
NEW FRIENDS

December 1853 – Big Freeze Moon

The smell of simmering chili verde mixed with the fragrance of fresh grilled tortillas, and the pinon wood burning in the fireplace. To Maggie these smells were the closest she had been to home in almost four years. She happily busied herself alongside Willow and the mistress of the house, Mary Craigavon.

The previous month, Silas announced that he was restless at the cabin on the Arkansas River, and had "a hankerin' ta head south," in his words. It had been some time since he and Willow had visited friends in New Mexico, and he told Maggie and Whit they were more than welcome to come along. Though content with life at the cabin, Maggie grew excited at the possibility of a visit to the place of her birth.

"Where do your friends live?" she had asked Silas.

"They have themselves a rancho down at Rayado. Shouldn't take us more than five or six days to get down there depending on how deep the snow is on Raton Pass."

"Rayado," thought Maggie. That would take her within one hundred and fifty miles of Abiquiú, but even being that close was too far for her to see her family. For the first time in the past few years, this thought made her home-sick and she experienced mixed emotions when they left.

During the trip south, Maggie put her melancholy aside when she noticed a change in Willow as she spoke of Mary Craigavon. The change was subtle; as if Willow slowly became a different person. Her usual reserve and shyness melted away. Willow had known Mary her entire life, and while they rode side-by-side, Willow told Maggie about the older woman.

Mary was Cherokee, born in Georgia, and as a young girl she had been kidnapped and taken out to the west where she eventually found herself among the Cheyenne. It was while she lived with the People, that her first child Crow Eyes, was born.

At about the same time, Thomas Craigavon, who had been searching for Mary since her abduction, found her and took her for his wife. The Craigavons settled down in New Mexico, raising their children and now their grandchildren. Willow also told Maggie that Mary was a strong independent woman. She was well educated, and she was also a *"curandera,"* a practitioner of folk medicine; an herb doctor and mid-wife.

When Willow spoke of Mary, she glowed in the same way as when she spoke of her own mother, Red Calf Woman. She said that Mary and Red Calf were so close it was if they were of the same blood. The more Willow spoke about the Craigavons, the more depressed Maggie became.

Maggie's depression melted away though when they arrived at Rancho Escondido, the home of the Craigavons. The main house sat between the Cimarron and the Rio Rayado, not far from the trail that crossed over the Sangre de Cristo Mountains to Taos. Built like a small fortress, it was like the Mexican country houses, with a large number of rooms surrounding an inner courtyard. In size it rivaled El Pueblo, but was better kept. The white-washed adobe structure was U-shaped, with the open end of the "U" closed off by a wall that contained a wooden gate, large enough to pull a careta or a Red River cart through. In the gate was a smaller door barely five feet tall, which would allow entrance to only a single person at a time without opening the larger gate. Like a small passage between hills, this door was also called a "puertecito."

Within a few hundred yards from the main house, were the living quarters of the hired hands. These small adobe and jacal houses, most comprised of a single room, were set in a neat row facing east, some with a coyote fence enclosure next to them for chickens, and other small livestock. Behind these structures, stood a hay barn and a jacal corral.

There was no period of settling in as the visitors from the north were made to feel like family from the moment they arrived. They had been met by one of the ranch-hands well north of the rancho and were escorted up to the main house where at the gate they were met by Mary who was happy to see them. Though near fifty years old, Mary seemed much younger, for she had retained her slim figure and stood straight, but relaxed, her hands resting on her hips. There were a few strands of gray in her raven-black hair, and radiance and grace in her beauty. In addition to her physical appearance there was also an inner strength and resolve that was evident in her bearing. At meeting Mary, Maggie instantly understood Willow's affection for the woman. Maggie was taken with Mary the moment they met, the woman making her feel at home.

With little reserve, Mary threw her arms around Silas' neck and gave him a kiss.

"Careful, Gal. You're libel to make me ferget you're a married woman," Silas said in jest.

"Silas Scott, you know you had my heart the first time I laid eyes on you and I only took up with Tom to make you jealous," Mary joked back.

"Where is the scoundrel?" Silas ask looking around for Tom Craigavon.

"We'll talk about him later," she said obviously wanting to change the subject. She then turned her attention to Willow and took the girl in her arms hugging her as if she was a long-lost daughter, and speaking in Cheyenne welcomed her, *"My heart is filled with happiness to see you daughter."*

"I have missed you also, Mother," Willow had always called Mary Mother, even when her own was still alive, as this these women had both cared for, and loved her.

"And who is this?" Mary asked looking at Maggie.

"This is Maggie," said Willow in English.

"Maggie? Is that your given name?" Mary asked.

"No, Señora, my given name is Magdalena Lucía Garza Valdez."

"She is called "Mo'e'ha", by the People," Willow said referring to Maggie's name in Cheyenne.

"Magpie? Are you a chatterbox?"

"No, I have a talent for language. I learn very fast and can speak several tongues almost as well as Willow."

"Well, that is splendid." She said, and then added, "But to me, you will be Magdalena." She smiled at the young woman and gave her a warm hug. She now looked at Zachary and asked, "Is this your little man?"

"No, Señora, he is the son of Señor Whit." She motioned with a nod of her head in Whit's direction. Whit, removing his hat stepped forward and extended his hand to Mary.

"Pleased to meet you Ma'am, I'm Whitney Voss," Whit said. Mary shook his hand and eyed Whit recognizing something in the charming young man. It took her only a moment to get past his good looks, and she realized what it was. He reminded her of her husband, Tom. In Whit's eyes were the same sparkle, that look of adventure, the same wanderlust that possessed Thomas Craigavon.

"It is a pleasure to meet you Mr. Voss," Mary replied.

"Please call me Whit," He said.

Mary nodded her head and to everyone she said, "Supper is almost ready and I could use more help in the kitchen."

It was unspoken that this comment was meant for the women, as the men would naturally need to care for the horses. Maggie and Willow followed her into the house and back to the kitchen. There Mary's daughters, Molly and Elizabeth, were working in the kitchen. The older daughter's real name was also Mary, but everyone called the Molly so as not to confuse her with her mother in conversation. The sisters were surprised and delighted to see Willow and when introduced to Maggie, greeted her with an embrace like their mother.

Molly had a daughter Judith, who was the same age as Zachary and the two were soon playing with one another, and Elizabeth was expecting her first child, in the spring. The husbands of the two sisters were out searching for two of the ranch's herders who had been missing since the day before and they were hopefully expected to return with them by evening.

While making more flour tortillas and tending the chili, they chatted, and the Craigavon women bombarded the two visitors about news from the north. First, they asked about the growing population on the Arkansas, and who had moved up there. Then they turned their questions, to more personal aspects of life in the north, careful not to press Willow, knowing she was sensitive about her status as an unmarried maiden.

Molly, the older of the two sisters, seemed to have a moderate amount of tact, and asked, "Are there many single men worth noticing, up there?"

Willow lowered her head and at first Molly feared she had hurt her friend, but Willow raised her eyes and smiling said, "There might be one or two."

"There is one in particular," Maggie blurted out, and received a half-reproaching look from Willow.

"Oh," said Molly, "And who might he be?"

"His name is August," said Willow, "And, he has asked me to be his wife."

"That's wonderful," Mary said. "Tell him that if he does not treat you right, he will have to answer to me." She turned her attention to Maggie and with an understanding smile asked, "How long have you been carrying your man?" She used the word "carrying", a term usually applied to men keeping a mountain bride. This was an arrangement, with no real attachment or intent of a permanent commitment.

"Momma!" Molly said, surprised that her mother would be so indelicate with someone she had only just met.

"I have been caring for Zachary since Señor Whit's wife died, two years ago." Maggie spoke openly, with no tone of defense in her words.

"I do not mean to hurt you child, but I have taken a liking to you and would see you treated well. So, there are no feelings between the two of you?"

"We are very close," Maggie blushed a bit and looked down for a brief moment. "We have lived together, and he has shown that he cares for me."

"He cares for you, as you care for the child?" Mary asked.

"I am not sure, but I love the child," Maggie said with true conviction.

"Ah, you love the child. Do you love the man?"

"I am happy with him, as his..." She stopped as she had no idea what she was to Whit.

Again, Molly spoke out, "Momma, you're embarrassing her?"

Mary moved over to Maggie and took her in her arms, resting her cheek against the smaller woman's head. "I promise you, Magdalena that before the grass turns green, you will be married." She pulled back, kissed Maggie on the forehead, and turned back to the pot of chili on the hearth.

While talking to the other women, Maggie learned the house had not always been so large but had been added onto after the Taos uprising in 1847. The small graveyard near the house, stood as evidence to the need for protection from the ever-present danger of raiding Indians. But this danger had not hampered the prosperity of the Craigavons in amassing a sizeable herd of cattle, sheep and horses.

The kitchen and the main room were what had once been the first house. Rooms on each side of this large space had been added, making living quarters, this gave each of the Craigavon children their own rooms. Molly and her family had one, Elizabeth and her husband another, and Mary her own. A final room, empty at the present belonged to the middle son, Sean who was away at school in the East. The oldest son, William, lived in Santa Fe with his wife and children.

Due to the size of the house, Maggie had expected to see servants or domestics when she first arrived, but soon found that management of the rancho and household fell into Mary's capable hands, with the help of her daughters, their husbands; James Duncan and Barrett Canfield, and over a dozen herders, that comprised the ranch's inhabitants.

Before sundown, Mary's sons-in-law returned with one of the lost Pueblo Indian herders, and the sad new that the other boy had been killed.

"We followed cattle tracks and found Santiago with an arrow in his leg," said Molly's husband, James Duncan, "He said he and Mateo had tracked the cattle most of yesterday and found them and a half dozen Apache. The Indians had stopped to kill and roast meat from one of the cows they killed. The boys thought they could scare them off if they surprised them even though they were armed only with bows and arrows. They killed one of the thieves and wounded two, but the Apaches fired back killing Mateo and wounding Santiago. He managed to take cover fighting them off and they then fled, taking their dead with them. We brought Mateo's body back with us and figured we would bury him here. Santiago is with his folks."

"I know we have spoken of this before," said Barrett, "But I feel we need to talk about arming the herders, at least with muskets."

"Thank you. We'll talk about that later," said Mary, "For now, we'll take care of the burial tomorrow. Wash up, and we'll sit down for dinner."

James and Barrett took their place on the right-hand side of the large table next to their wives, with the guests sitting on the left. Mary sat at one end of the long table, and at the opposite end sat an empty chair, obviously the place usually occupied by of Thomas Craigavon.

As they ate, they first shared the news from the settlement on the Arkansas, the events in Santa Fe and Taos, and of course the actions of the Indians both in the north and in the south.

"How have things been going?" Silas asked.

Mary answered him, "The Apache and the Kiowa, have taken a liking to our stock, but until yesterday, we haven't had a loss we couldn't live with. We can handle the thieves. For a short time, we thought there might be a problem with the ownership of the land, as the ranch is sitting on the Beaubien-Miranda Land Grant. It has been Lucien Maxwell's ever since he married Luz Beaubien in '42. Last spring, Tom spoke with him and they came to an arrangement. It seems that we have an indefinite lease, and can transfer it or sell it depending on the circumstances and Lucien's approval." She seemed concerned but determined.

"What is Lucien asking for in return?"

"I'm sure more than what was written in the contract. He shook hands with Tom and then put it all in writing. We have the land from the Little Cimarron south, but on the north side Maxwell is planning on building a mill on the Cimarron this coming year. I'm sure Tom will be happy when he finds out that Kit Carson is planning to settle nearby also. Are there any problems in the north?""

"The Cheyenne, Kiowa and Apache have been holding up to the treaty they signed back in '51," said Silas, "But, they figure that only counts concerning the whites and themselves. They're still sending out war parties and horse raids against the Pawnee and the Ute. Of course, I'd feel sorry for any tender-footed "Judy" who found himself on the prairie. There isn't a piece of paper signed by all the chiefs and government clerks that would save his hair."

"I can't see how those thick heads in the east think they can ever get all the tribes to live in peace with one another," James Duncan said, shaking his head.

"They've been killin' each other as far back as anyone can remember," added his brother-in-law, Barrett.

"Well, it has caused a lot of unrest and it's sure to spill over on top of us," said James.

"Can't expect them to change the way they've lived since the dawn of time," said Silas, "They were killing each other when the Pilgrims landed on Plymouth Rock."

"It's not just them fighting each other," said Barrett, "You hear what happened up on the Minnesota River Valley just last year? The Lakota killed over eight-hundred white men, women and children."

"Yep, I heard, and they got whipped for it, and three dozen of them swung on a rope," Silas said.

"Not enough of 'em," James said, "That man let two-hundred and sixty of them go free." He spoke of President Lincoln commuting the sentence of those Lakota prisoners.

"You'll find it doesn't always come down one on one, when dealing with the tribes. You can look at the Territories and see what happens to a people who lose a war." This came from Mary, and her statement also reminded her son-in-law that he was married into a family with Cherokee blood.

"Talk back in Missouri isn't about trouble with Indians," Whit said, "More conversations are going on about slavery, and if the territory here bout's will be with or without 'em."

"Texas still claims everything north up to Santa Fe," said Barrett, and they're a slave state."

"I can see us haven' our own state someday, and slavery will never hold here," said Molly, "I never did hold much for slavery. Just doesn't seem right, not natural."

"Natural for some," said her husband.

"Not that I approve of it, but there's always been slaves, way back before the Hebrews were makin' mud bricks for the pharaohs of Egypt," said Silas, "And, we all know many of the tribes keep slaves now."

"And look at what God brought down on Pharaoh and his people," said Mary, "They paid with their blood and their first born."

"I can see blood being spilled over slavery," said James.

"Let's hope not," said Mary.

"Times are changing, and if we're not careful, they'll change right over the top of us," Silas chuckled.

When dinner was finished, the table cleared, and the dishes washed, everyone kept their seats at the table, and they continued their conversation. All, except Mary and Silas, who took a seat near the fireplace to speak of things more personal. Mary poured her old friend a cup of hot tea and they chatted. Alone with a woman that had known him for almost thirty years, Silas dropped the slang of the west, and spoke as the educated man he was.

"How have you been, Darling," Silas asked.

"I'm feeling old, Silas."

"Hell, you're far from getting old."

"I guess I'm only tired, but I know I can't stop, someone needs to make sure what we've built here survives."

"How's William doing?"

"He has a good medical practice in Santa Fe. He and Roseanne have four children and they're all doing fine."

"Four! Didn't they just have their third?"

"That was twins, two years ago. The new baby came this fall. It was another boy."

"They name this one after me?" Silas chuckled.

"No, they named him Tobias, after Rosie's brother."

I suspect they're happy," said Silas.

"You'd think so, but I believe rumors of the railroad coming have him thinking of a fresh start up there. In fact, Tom and I talked about investing in something up that way if the land is as good as you say."

"What's Will's wife think of picking up and leaving her home?"

"Rosie is a good woman; she'll go wherever Will goes. I believe she might be happy to leave the bad memories of that place behind her."

"Hard to let go of the past sometimes."

"We have both lost so much Silas, but I can't let that define me, I have to move on for the children and grandchildren I still have." She now asked the question that had been on her mind since Silas had shown up earlier in the day. "Have you seen my son?" Silas knew she was asking about Crow Eyes.

"Yes, he has visited my place on the Arkansas a few times."

"Is he well?"

"Looked well to me. He has taken up another wife; Cheyenne woman named Meets the Enemy."

"Is she a good woman?"

"Don't know, he didn't talk much about her. He had other things on his mind."

"My grandson?"

"Crow is a bit worried about Little Bear choosing a society to join. The boy's thinking about being a Dog Soldier. That worries Crow some."

"The boy is smart, like his father. I'm sure he'll make the right choice when the time comes."

Silas didn't want to offer too much of what he thought was taking place on the plains. He didn't see any reason in adding to the worries that Mary already harbored. He decided to change the subject and ask about the absence of Tom.

"Where is he?"

"Tom? California," Mary answered with a slight tinge of resignation in her voice. "He went out there to do some trading in horses. The gold fever made a market for horse flesh, and Tom saw a profit to be made."

"How long since you've heard from him?" Silas' voice softened.

"He left early in the spring. As soon as the season changed, he got restless. I received a letter through the Army about mid-summer. He said he had made a good amount of money and was building up some breeding stock that he intended to drive back here and improve our horse herd. He hopes to be home by this coming spring."

"Can't sit still for long, can he?"

"No, Silas, I had hopes at one time that he would settle down, but it would be easier to rope the wind." Mary gave a soft laugh. "You know him as well as I do, and he'll always be looking off in the distance if he sits still too long. I saw that in him when we were children."

"I guess that could be my fault," Silas apologized; I'm the one that brought him out here to the west."

"Maybe you are part to blame, you two are cut from the same cloth. But, I knew from the time he came west looking for me that no matter what happens, he'll always come home." She paused a bit and then continued, "I see the same look in this new young man you brought with you."

"Whitney?" Silas asked.

"Yes, he has that feel about him, but I am determined that before he leaves this house in the spring, he will have given that girl his name."

"Maggie?"

"Yes," Mary said, with the certainty that left no doubt. Silas laughed and Mary smiled at him.

"How do you intend to get that done?"

"I have my ways Silas Scott, I have my ways."

Mary had already devised a plan that would steer Whitney to the altar. When it came time to retire for the evening, Mary took her first step. There were two empty rooms, one in each wing of the house; one near Mary's room on one side and the one belonging to her son Sean on the other.

"Silas, you and Whit can sleep in Sean's room and the girls and Zachary can sleep in the spare room next to mine," Mary was pleased with the effect this had on Whit. She could see he was disappointed that he and Maggie would be separated. Mary knew that putting that small distance between them would make him want to be near her all that much more.

The weather remained mild for the next few days and just before Christmas Bill Craigavon and his family made the trip from Santa Fe. With their arrival, the sleeping arrangements were shifted only slightly. Willow, Maggie and Zachary moved in with Mary. This final step seemed not only to keep the two young lovers separate, but with Mary sleeping in the same room, it almost created an impassable wall.

The household was in constant motion, with the increase of occupants, especially with the addition of four more children. William and Roseanne were thrilled to see Silas and Willow, and they took to Whit and Maggie instantly. Willow was somewhat reserved when she received Bill's greeting and Maggie noticed that Roseanne made a special effort to show Willow she was happy to see her.

When Maggie had a chance to take Willow aside, she quietly asked her, "Are you well, Sister?"

"Yes, I am good," Willow said, but Maggie knew better.

"There is something troubling you."

Willow looked toward Bill and speaking in a lower tone said, "He is the one I told you about. The one who I would not let see me after the sickness. He is the one I drove away. Now I do not know if he has bad feelings for me."

"It does not seem so," said Maggie looking at Bill, "and his wife seems to hold you in high regard."

"I do not know," Maggie said. They were drawn back into the talk among the others and Maggie decided to keep an eye on Bill and Roseanne to note any ill behavior toward Willow. Maggie intended to protect her friend even if it caused problems with the Craigavon family.

As everyone settled in, Bill and Roseanne answered questions about the news from Santa Fe, but Bill was most interested in talking about the conditions along the Arkansas. He was definitely enthused with the prospects of moving there.

His wife seemed neutral about it, but she admitted that she was willing to relocate, as long as her family stayed together.

"Do you think there is a chance the railroad will come out here?" he asked Silas.

"Not sure," said the older man, "I can see it making it as far as the Front Range, but I doubt they'll find a way through the mountains.

"Baca and Doyle seem be making a go of it though," Whit added.

"You really thinking about moving, Bill?" Silas asked.

"We have been discussing relocating for some time," Bill said.

"It's been hard for me," Rosanne said, "Seems that the past keeps coming back, I'd like a fresh start too." She spoke thinking about the murders of her mother, brother and their hired hands not half a dozen years back.

"I understand that. But why not just move into town?" asked Silas.

"It's still too close, and the changes that have taken place haven't made it any better."

"What all has changed?"

"It seems the new breed of Americans that are moving in have a feeling that the folks who have been here before them are somewhat inferior. The attitude is changing American against Mexican, Mexicans against American," Bill said.

"There is the new bishop too," said Roseanne.

"Bishop?"

"Yes, the year before last they sent a Frenchman named Jean Baptiste Lamy, to Santa Fe. Padre Ortiz told him that he had no authority to take over administration of the church in New Mexico, and most of the local priests backed him up, saying Bishop Zubiría, of the Diocese of Durango was their spiritual leader and superior. Lamy went down to Durango and had a chat with Zubiría, showing him the papal document that appointed Lamy to the Vicariate of New Mexico. Bishop Zubiría had to agree and wrote to the local clergy, supporting Lamy, and now Padre Lamy is Bishop."

"What about my old friend Padre Martinez?"

"He seems to be getting along with the Bishop. So far, the bishop has done some things Padre Martinez agrees with. Bishop Lamy has proposed the building of more churches in the territory, the creation of new parishes, and the establishment of schools. I am not sure how Padre Martinez feels about the bishop's intentions to suppress the *Hermandad,* and end the practice of the people living together without the sanction of the church. The Bishop feels that with the availability of more clergy there is no need of these practices," Bill said.

"Padre Martinez has always been a supporter of the *Hermandad,* the Penitentes," Mary said, speaking of the Penitent Brotherhood of *Nuestro Padre Jesús Nazareno.* "The Bishop believes the practices of the Brotherhood to be barbaric. But they serve a practical purpose. Where there are no priests, they fill in as spiritual examples, and even perform baptisms and marriages," she added.

Whit listened closely and when the talk of marriage came up he looked over to where Maggie sat with the children, and then he glanced at Mary and saw that she was looking in his direction. This made him feel uneasy and he looked away.

"The Bishop is twenty years younger than the Padre. I believe that sooner or later, something such as their different views on the brotherhood will come up that will cause a problem between them," Roseanne added.

The days became colder and snow fell off and on for the next week leading up to Christmas, and the turn in the weather forced everyone to spend more time indoors. The house, though spacious, soon became confining, and if not for the addition of the two new personalities of Whit and Maggie, life might have become boring. The women were kept busy and their numbers allowed them all time to enjoy making preparations for the Holiday.

There were still chores that needed to be performed outside the house, such as care for the horses, and the men welcomed the chance to break up the monotony. Whit's skills and experience from his families' wagon business was put to work at making repairs to the ranch's wagons and red river cart. The first wagon that he worked on was that owned by William.

Bill and Whit had become fast friends, and the more they talked the more Bill was certain that moving his family up to the Arkansas was a good idea. The land north of the river was outside any of the Spanish land grants and Whit reassured him that the land there was fertile and only needed water. Bill had been to the Arkansas River Valley several times with his father and Silas when he was younger. He remembered the trips there as some of his fondest memories. He shared some of these memories with Whit as they worked on the wagon, with Silas standing by, in his words, "to supervise," or interject his particular recollection of a certain event in the past.

"I'm thinking we could make a go of it up there," Bill said, speaking of the Arkansas Valley.

"What of your doctoring?" asked Silas.

"If the railroad comes, people will come. If I'm established with a good hold on the land, then I have an investment that can bring me profit there as well."

"Sounds like you have it all figured out," Silas said.

"I've given it a lot of thought. And I see a real future up there. It's already growing with Baca, Doyle, Autobees and Sandoval staking a claim and building things up. I'll bet within a few years there'll be a proper town at El Pueblo. Whit here can settle down and open up a wagon shop, be a pillar of the community." With this said Whit stopped his work, and with a look of surprise stared at Bill. Silas, seeing this, let out a soft chuckle.

Gaining his composure, Silas said, "You two better quit jawin', Mary will have our hides if we hold up dinner, especially as its Christmas Eve."

When everyone was gathered for dinner, the aroma of the Christmas feast filled the inside of the cabin. Every item on the menu was considered special. The main course was a smoked ham, taken from the larder and baked with a glaze of Mexican sugar. Accompanying the ham was a dry soup, made of vermicelli, dried tomatoes, onions and chili. Added to the holiday fare was goat cheese and fresh baked white bread. For everyone's sweet tooth, there was champurrado, a thin cornmeal gruel mixed with Mexican chocolate, sugar and cinnamon. Finally, to finish the feast, there were the tasty little pumpkin pies called empanadas, which fit neatly into the hand.

After dinner, a small jug of rye whiskey was brought out by Bill and everyone was poured a small dram. At this point, everyone received some small gift, making the day that much more special. Not to be out shined, Silas produced his contribution to the festivities, the tin of smoked oysters and bottle of Bordeaux wine that he had hoarded for months.

Most notable was the present Whit produced for Maggie. With little fanfare, he told her that though it wasn't as grand as other gifts she had received from him, he hoped that this small token would find favor with her. He handed her a small bundle of cloth, and when she unfolded it, she found a ring made from a horseshoe nail.

"I hope that'll do until I get you a proper wedding ring." It seemed that everyone except for Mary was surprised. Maggie had not been expecting the offer, and at first she hesitated, not knowing if what Whit offered was to acknowledge her as his mountain bride, or a real wedding with a priest. Either way, she leaped at the chance to have him declare his love for her and to have a hold on him.

"I would love to be your wife," she finally said, and she threw her arms around his neck and they hugged.

Everyone wished the two congratulations, Mary being the last to walk up and embrace Maggie, saying, "In the morning I will send someone to see if the pass is open to Taos. If it is open, we can send word to Padre Martinez and ask if he can arrange for someone to come here to perform the ceremony, possibly a brother." She was referring to a member of the Penitente Brotherhood.

"You don't have to go to all that trouble," said Whit.

"Oh, there is nothing I wouldn't do for Magdalena," Mary gave Whit a knowing smile.

"You think Padre Martinez would come?" Bill asked.

"Padre Martinez is the only priest for all three churches in Taos valley, and too old for the journey," Mary said. "I think he would more than likely send someone in his proxy."

"Too old!" Silas scoffed. "The man's younger than I am by over a dozen years."

"True Silas, but then again, virtue has a way of taking its toll on a man. Something you wouldn't know about," Mary joked.

"If the good Padre had consumed as much whiskey as you, he'd be better preserved," added Bill.

"I ain't too old to whip you," Silas said.

"The Padre Martinez isn't in the best health," Mary told Silas, "I'm sure he will find a way to make sure Magdalena and Whit's union will be blessed." She paused, and looking at Silas, she added, "Of course if someone cannot be sent from Taos, I would think there could be someone else who might say the words in God's name, to bless these two children." Silas seemed to ignore this comment.

To Whit, it seemed that the entire affair had been taken out of his hands. He felt that now he had no choice in what would happen, and for the briefest moment he held this against Mary. "Who did she think she was?" he thought. He pulled Maggie aside and just out of earshot, he spoke to her in a quiet voice, "We don't need all this," he said, "We don't need some priest sayin' words over us to make us a couple."

In the past few minutes since she had considered Whit's offer, and her willingness to accept whatever he offered, Maggie had changed her mind. The prospect of a real marriage, blessed by the church was what she now wanted.

"You would not do this for me?" she asked Whit. This took him back a bit.

"Well...I...I guess it ain't that big a deal to wait until you get your priest here." But, what Whit said was not what he felt, as the excitement of the proposal had diminished in his mind.

"It appears that we opened that bottle of wine a bit early," Silas said.

"Even if we're out of Silas' wine," said James Duncan, "We still have Bill's rye whiskey to toast the betrothed."

The jug was produced, cups filled, and the group took turns in voicing their good wishes for the couple.

Maggie sat next to Mary, and she leaned close and said, "Thank you." Mary replied with only a squeeze of the young woman's hand. Maggie then asked, "If I were to write a letter to my family in Abiquiú, might it be sent along with your man? I would very much like to let them know that I have been married."

"Of course, we can get a letter to your family," Mary assured her, "Do you think they might want to come to the wedding?"

"No, it would be too much trouble for my parents. They have no one to take care of their little farm. It is enough that they know. Someone will have to read the letter to them anyway."

The rest of the evening was spent in a good humor by all, and the jug of whiskey diminished in proportion to the rise in mood. It seemed the only one who had little to say was the groom to be, who had more than his share to drink.

On the day after Christmas, one of the hands from the ranch took the trail west over the Sangre De Cristo Mountains to Taos. The snows had not been overly deep, and by January 5th, 1864 the hand returned to the ranch alone. In his possession he carried a letter for Mary. The letter explained that there was no one to send to perform a marriage of the couple, not even a member of the Brotherhood. Padre Martinez also said if the couple professed their intentions in front of a witness, who was willing to say a blessing over the them, this would suffice until a real marriage ceremony could be performed by a priest. He suggested that Mary, speak with Silas Scott for this purpose.

When Silas was informed of the letter's contents by Mary he protested.

"You put him up to that, didn't you?" he asked Mary.

"I only suggested it in my letter to him," she said.

"You had no right. I don't talk to Him anymore, other than to say a few words over a grave. You know, I gave all that up." He was upset, but not truly angry at Mary.

"Silas, all you have to do is say the words. It isn't about you talking to God; it's those two being married."

"Damn you, Mary Craigavon, you keep trying to make me out to be something I'm not."

"You're a good man, Silas, that's all I have ever asked you to be."

"I don't have my book with me." He was still looking for a reason not to do what she had asked.

"You don't need the book, Silas, just ask them if they want to be man and wife in the eyes of God, and bless them in his name."

"Not sure He'll see it that way."

Silas consented, and when the time came to join the two together, he blessed the marriage saying, "O God, who created all things and set in place the beginnings of the universe, formed man and woman, making the woman a helpmate to man, that they might be one flesh, bless these two children." At times the words came hesitantly, as if Silas was attempting to remember something long lost. There was a pause after he had said these words, and looking out at those gathered around the couple, he finished by saying to Whit, "Well, kiss the gal!" Only then did he smile.

Whit turned to Maggie and she smiled at him, and not waiting for him, leaned up and kissed him.

As with tradition, Maggie took on Whit's name adding it to her own. She was now Magdalena Lucía Garza Valdez de Voss. The entire name seemed unnecessary to Whit but he figured he would never have to remember the entire thing, as he would still call her Maggie.

Willow went to her father as she could see that he had struggled with saying the words for the marriage. She had never seen him so hesitant to speak, and she worried that there was something deeply wrong.

"Your words were beautiful, Father," she said. "I would like you to say those for me on the day I marry."

Silas smiled at his daughter, and pulling her into his arms said, "Darling, I'll do better for you. I'll have those words and more for you."

In celebration, Mary had three yearling sheep killed for the wedding feast, and the beginning of 1854 started off with the promise of prosperity and hope.

After the feast, Roseanne found an empty space next to Willow who was sitting on a bench against the wall. Without hesitation, she sat down beside her, and laid a hand gently on one of Willows. Willow tensed, but showed no outward sign of apprehension.

"I understand that you are to be married soon?" Roseanne asked.

"Yes, he is waiting for me to return to the Arkansas," Willow answered.

"That is good," Roseanne smiled, and added, "Bill is very happy to hear that. He has always held you in high regard, and for that reason I also have good feelings toward you. I hope that if we move to the north that you and I can become good friends."

Willow turned to look at Roseanne and felt that the woman's offer of friendship was genuine. She returned the smile, and said, "I would like that very much."

***

January 1854 - Moon of Frost on the Lodge

Moonlight sifted through the trees onto the muddy road leading out of Etowah, dimly lighting the half-dozen men who rode to the ferry crossing on the Hightower River. When they reached the ferry at the river's edge, the full moon made the surroundings bright and clear and the river reflected images like a mirror. Here, the faces of the mounted men could be seen clearly, and the features of each distinguished from the other. With the men on horseback was a single man on foot who had been pulled behind them, a rope tied around his neck, his hands bound behind his back. More than once, the man had fallen, and the rider, who held the lead rope around his neck, had to stop his horse so the man would not be dragged.

They stopped in the clearing at the ferry crossing, and the man leading the prisoner gave a quick tug on the rope pulling the prisoner off his feet and face down into the mud.

"Get up, you son-of-a-bitch!" the rider growled, and the reluctant prisoner stumbled again.

"Quit jerking on the rope, Arron," Eli Thornton reprimanded the rider. Thornton had ridden next to the prisoner, Azariah Bolt, a man he had considered a friend his entire life, and now Bolt hoped his friend could save his life.

"Why? We're just gonna tie a big rock 'round his feet and toss him in the river," Arron Carter said over his shoulder.

"There'll be no further talk of killin'," said Hammond Burchfield, the leader of the small party and Bolt's father-in-law.

Azariah rolled onto his side, and by pulling his knees up and rolling over, struggled into a kneeling position. Then, with more effort, he shakily gained his feet. His clothes were torn and covered with red clay mud where he had been dragged behind the horse. Mixed with the mud on his face was blood that had flowed from his broken nose and split lip. His left eye was swollen, and most likely there were bruises hidden beneath the mud, that would be visible long after the sticky soil was washed away. Azariah looked like some macabre effigy of a man, not quite human, not quite clay.

"Untie him." Burchfield order. Eli Thornton and Arron Carter slipped from their saddles to unbind Azariah. Eli untying Azariah's hands as Arron slipped the rope over his head.

"Someday, I'm gonna cut your throat, you piece of shit," Arron whispered into Azariah's ear.

Azariah rubbed his sore wrists, his one un-swollen eye peering white out from his muddied face. He glared at Arron with that good eye for several moments, then moved his gaze from man to man, resting it on Thornton.

As if knowing what Azariah was thinking, Eli spoke to him, "I did the best I could Tiah." He called Azariah by the nickname he had grown up with. "Moses Carter and his sons wanted to cut your balls off first, and then hang you." Azariah turned his gaze toward Moses Carter and his sons, Josiah and Arron. They were still not happy that Azariah would be set free with little more than a beating to pay for the death of their daughter and sister. They knew, everyone knew, that Azariah had murdered the girl, or in the least drove her to killing herself. Suicide was the official version of the girl's death, but only Azariah knew for sure what had truly happened.

How had Azariah ended up here on the banks of the river, his fate close to the end of a rope? He had worked a piece of land left to him by his father, barely turning a profit on the crops raised. It took only two years for him to lose that land, and adding to his burdens, he had a young wife and two children to support. Thus homeless, he was forced to go hat in hand to his father-in-law, Hammond Burchfield, to ask for work, and was given a position in Burchfiled's fields, working beside the man's slaves. His pay amounted to little more than shelter for his wife and children. He wasn't sure who he hated more, his father-in-law, or the wife and children who were like a millstone dragging him down.

He found some solace in the company of his friends, who gathered at the tavern, Eli Thornton among them. There with his friends, Azariah was well liked, generous in their eyes, always buying drinks on credit. This credit was based solely on respect for his father-in-law. Azariah was also well-liked by the women, and though he was married, he had a certain charm that could melt a woman's better judgement.

What little respect he had faded away with the discovery of Belinda Carter's lifeless body in the Hightower River. Most people believed it was a tragic accident, while others believed the prevalent rumor that she had found herself pregnant and drowned herself in despair. Rumors also persisted that Azariah was the child's father and that he had helped end the girl's life.

When Azariah's womanizing became a topic of constant gossip, Hammond Burchfield threatened to whip him if he didn't change his habits. When the Carter girl was found dead, Moses, Josiah and Arron Carter went to Burchfield seeking justice.

Hammond sympathized with the Carter's and was convinced of Azariah's complicity in the girl's death. With little compassion for his philandering son-in-law, Hammond was willing to turn him over to the Carters. If not for the intervention of Eli

Thornton and Hammonds son, Harlon, Azariah would have already been swinging from a tree branch.

"You. You waste of human flesh," Hammond started, "You will cross that river, and you put as much distance behind you as fast as you can until you reach the Mississippi, and when you reach it, you cross over and keep going. If your wretched face turns up around here again, you'll wish I had let the Carter's hang you."

"What about my family? My wife, and youngin's?" Azariah asked, hoping for some kind of reprieve.

"You lost them a long time ago," Hammond said.

"What you gonna tell them when they ask where I am?"

"They will know what I tell them. You stole money from me and then slipped away in the night, just like any common trash. I'll give the story credence by offering a reward for you sorry carcass." With this said, Hammond told Harlon to wake the ferryman, and have him take Azariah across the river.

***

February 1854 – Big Hoop Moon

The wind coming out of the south had carried the storm out onto the eastern plains, and growing in intensity, then turned back to the west toward the mountains. It brought with it heavy, wet snow blowing in an almost horizontal direction. For two days, it had plunged the inside of the little cabin into complete darkness, and August Klausen huddled next to the small fireplace, its flames his only source of light and heat. He was not afraid, as he had survived many storms such as this in his homeland of Denmark, both on land and at sea.

It had taken six months of back-breaking work for August Klausen to erect a small cabin, and clear the few acres he had chosen to start his farm and ranch. From the cabin belonging to Silas, he had moved upstream on the Arkansas and found what he wanted about two miles away. Here the Arkansas flowed out from between high bluffs composed of layers of sandstone, blue shale, and limestone. The southern bluff in the little valley was somewhat lower on the south, being made of the same material. The prairie stretching out from these bluff tops was covered in short grass cactus, sage and piñon trees, the soil thin and poor for growing crops. In contrast, the valley floor was rich and dark, fed by the waters of the Arkansas.

The snow had built up against any obstacle that stood in its path, and a huge drift had built up against the east side of the cabin where the door was located. As soon as the sound of the wind had died down, August dug himself out of the white tomb that had encased the entire side of the house reaching the roof. As he emerged from his burrowing into the daylight, he was temporary blinded by the intense sunlight from the clear sky reflecting off the glistening landscape around the cabin. The icy fresh air filled his lungs, stinging for a moment, but it was refreshing and exhilarating him at the same time.

In clearing the land, he had left standing two giant cottonwoods near the cabin. He intended them to offer shade to the cabin in the hot summer months ahead, and he was disappointed that one of these trees had been blown over by the storm. He was grateful that its massive branches had missed the cabin when the tree fell. An added piece of luck was that tree would offer firewood close at hand for some time.

He looked out over the valley and above the tree line in the distance he could see smoke curling up in to the pristine, pale blue sky. It came from the direction of El Pueblo and further to the east, smoke rose from the other side of the small hills that hid the Baca ranch. "It looks like they have survived the storm also," August thought to himself. "Now, it is time for me to see if the horses and my mule have also survived."

He made his way around to the south side of the cabin, where he had built a shelter for the stock, and found one of the horses missing. He scanned the surrounding area and found a dark shape sticking out from a mound of snow. There was no doubt that the horse had somehow gotten loose of its headstall and wandered out into the freezing storm. August felt himself lucky that he still had the big mule and the little mare with the white blaze that ran almost the entire length of her face. August had chosen this horse for Willow for its even temperament and solid built. Loss of the mare would have caused him disappointment as he knew it was a gift prized by the Cheyenne and would prove his love for Willow.

He fed the horse and the mule, and then made his way to the roof of the cabin, easily walking up the hardened snow drift, and cleared away snow that was close to covering the chimney. He then came down and going over to the dead horse, brushed away the snow and cut meat from the rump. He found no reason to waste sustenance offered by fate. He returned to the cabin, and built up the fire in fireplace, and set the semi-frozen meat on a spit to roast. The young geldings' flesh was lean, and relatively tender. When it had reached a point where August thought it had been cooked enough, he sat down and cut slices from the roast as it hung from the spit. He found the taste to his liking, a bit sweet, something like a blend between beef and venison.

As the warm fresh meat sated his hunger, he thought of Willow and he was warmed even further. He had honorable intentions toward her, but he had been alone for the past months, and his love for her had also awakened his passion for her. For the first time since he had met her, he thought of what it would be like to share his bed with her. His longing for her made his heart ache, and he was determined that the time that passed before she returned from New Mexico would be torture for him. He was now even more determined to make a home for her, to have something that would be worthy of her love, worthy of the woman she was.

***

SAM J. PISCIOTTA

CHAPTER SIX
OLD ENIMIES

March 1854 – Dusty Moon

The winter snows had melted with the coming of spring and its warmer days and dry winds. Though the temperatures during the day were pleasant, the nights were still cold and winter, as if refusing to loosen its grip on the land, sent one last cold, wet storm to batter the Front Range. This storm caught Silas and his party when they had reached Greenhorn Creek, and they were forced to divert to the little settlement nestled against the mountains. The trip up from Rayado had been uneventful until this point, and it seemed to Willow that Silas who had been in no hurry to return to the Arkansas, had almost certainly conjured up the storm to delay them further. She became ill-humored and quarrelsome as the days passed.

As soon as the storm blew over and the skies cleared, Willow was anxious to resume the trip north, and Silas protested saying the snow was still too deep to travel. Unwilling to accept this, Willow said that if the entire party was not ready to leave the following day, she would go on her own. With little surprise, Silas reluctantly announced the following morning they would head out for the Arkansas, only some twenty miles away.

Bill Craigavon had left Rayado, accompanying Silas and the others, with the intent to look over the area near El Pueblo and choose a suitable place where he could start his own enterprise. He was not enthused to start farming, but rather looked for the prospect of ranging cattle and raising horses. He also envisioned the growth of the area if the railroad did come through. Those settled on the Huerfano believed they held the ideal spot, but Bill had a feeling that the junction of the Arkansas and the Fountain was superior.

By the time they reached the edge of the mesa overlooking the valley, Bill was sure he could convince his wife to sell the Santa Fe ranch and relocate to the new unspoiled land near El

Pueblo. Looking out to the north, Bill watched as Silas pointed out the lay of the land, using his pipe stem as a pointing stick. A trail of smoke, hanging low in the treetops on the other side of the river marked the location of Baca's ranch and of El Pueblo. Silas motioned further to the west, where his own cabin was and that of August Klausen. No smoke rose from that direction, and it crossed Silas' mind that August may have given up and left for warmer climates, or worse, had not made it through the winter. This he did not speak out loud, not wanting to alarm Willow.

"We just might want to stop by and see if Sandoval made it through the winter alright," he said.

"Shouldn't we go home first and get a fire going to warm things up?" Willow asked, not really concerned about that, but rather the welfare and whereabouts of August. She too had noticed the sky in the direction of his cabin was clear and blue, void of smoke.

"We'll get there shortly," Silas said, "The crossing is closer to El Pueblo and we'd have to go that direction anyway."

They moved down the small drainage called Salt Creek, and then followed the south bank of the Arkansas as it turned north and then back to the west. There, close to the adobe post, they crossed the river.

As if to grant August his wish, the storm had rolled in from the east and blanketed the valley. As the weather turned for the better, the trees had begun to show buds, and the new grass started to poke its blades up out of the drab-yellow remnants of the previous year's growth. The wet snow that had been an irritation for Willow had been a blessing to August. He had tilled up the soil on his small acreage, exposing the turned-up ground to catch any moisture nature offered, and the snow had provided that moisture.

August saddled up his mule and rode downstream toward El Pueblo, making a stop at Silas' cabin to check on its condition. The empty structure only made his heart ache that much more for Willow and he hoped that she would return soon. In hope of easing his loneliness, he moved further down the valley to the little adobe fort.

Smoke curled up from the several chimneys carrying with it the smell of cottonwood burning in the fireplaces. As August came around to the front of the post, he found the fort gate standing open. He dismounted and walked into the little courtyard, surprising Benito Sandoval's wife, Maria Espinosa, who was taking fresh baked bread out of the beehive shaped horno. The adobe oven's heat had baked the loaves to a golden brown, and the aroma drifted in the morning breeze to make August's mouth water.

"Oh, you scared me, Dutchy," Maria said, and smiled with relief. *"I thought you were an Indian!"*

Though August still had not mastered the New Mexican Spanish language, he recognized the word *indeo-dia,* meaning Indian, and the nickname Dutchy, that some of the fort inhabitants had begun to use when referring to him and it was shorter that the Spanish version of his name, Augustine. In his own polite way, he refrained from correcting their assumption that everyone who came from his part of the world was Dutch.

"Good morning, Mrs. Sandoval," he said, his words a bit hesitant, but void of the accent that plagued his English. His Spanish was proficient enough to please Maria.

"Come. Come, have some fresh bread and coffee," she invited him over also motioning with a free hand. He followed her into one of the living quarters and there found Benito and his four sons, waiting patiently for the hot crusty loaves. The youngest son, Juan Andre sat in his father's lap, with Pedro, Felix and Juan Isidro sitting next to the patriarch of the family.

Sandoval was considered the headman at El Pueblo, for at forty years old, he had become a man of property. For most of his life he had worked for others, but his relocation to El Pueblo would allow him to raise profitable crops and increase his small herd of cattle.

"Buenos días, Señor August," Benito greeted him, "Come in. Come in and sit down. You are just in time to have some of my wife's bread."

August thanked him, and like his host he took a seat on a rolled up sleeping mat against the wall. Maria soon served plates of steaming beans and slices of bread to each of the men, serving August first. She followed that with cups of hot, rich coffee laced with Mexican sugar.

Between bites of the delicious food, Benito spoke to August, "You should have spent the winter here at El Pueblo, rather than all alone down on the river."

"It vas good enough for me," August assured him.

"It was much warmer here than in your cabin. Summertime is fine for a log house. I intend to build one on Baca's ranch and farm with him. After the fall harvest, I will either move back here or maybe go to Mora for the winter." He paused as if thinking about his plans, then added, "Of course if my cattle herd has grown large enough, I may stay here. We will see. Speaking of my cattle, the cows should be calving anytime now. I have Felix and Juan Isidro to help me but if you lend a hand, I would be very grateful and of course make it worth your while."

"I think I would like to help," said August. "It would give me a better knowledge about cattle, and that can only be good."

"Are you going to marry the Cheyenne woman?" Maria asked, and Benito translated, not waiting to see if August understood.

"Ja, I plan to marry Wi...Willow as soon as I can." He pronounced her name carefully, forcing the "W" across his lips.

"You would do better if you were to marry a Spanish woman," she said, and Benito changed this to, "She will make a very good wife, just like a Spanish woman."

August suspected that there was something different in the translation but felt it had been done out of expedience rather than to hide some insult.

When his visit was over and August was ready to leave, Maria gave him a loaf of bread to take with him, and again Benito stressed his request for help when the calving began.

He led his mule out of the fort's enclosure and was met by Silas and his party as they approached. Startled, as if he was not sure what he saw was real, August stood unable to move. He said a short prayer hoping this was not a vision but in truth it was Willow who rode next to her father.

"Hello there, August!" called out Silas, assuring August of the reality of what was in front of him.

"Hello, Silas Scott," he called back as the group stopped only a few yards away. Willow not waiting longer than she had to, slipped down from her horse and ran to August throwing her arms around him.

"I have missed you very much, August Klausen," she said and with no reservation, kissed him.

Like everyone else, August was taken aback, and though pleased, had no idea how to react for the briefest moment. He hesitated and pulled the young woman closer to him and squeezed, feeling the warmth of her body against his. At that moment, August was the happiest man in the valley.

"I have missed you too, Wi...Willow," he said, the pronouncement of her name coming easer to him, and sounding sweet to her ears.

Two weeks later, on a clear spring morning, people from El Pueblo, the Baca Ranch, the St Charles and the Huerfano settlements, gathered at Silas Scott's cabin for the wedding of August Klausen and Willow Katherine Scott. The day before, a pit had been dug and a fire set in it to burn down to a large bed of coals. Then a yearling heifer from Sandoval's herd was butchered and the entire beef set inside the pit, covered with the excavated soil and left to roast until the wedding.

The couple was married, under the cottonwood trees, with Silas giving his blessing, and Maggie and Whit as witnesses. August wore his four-button sack coat, brushed out as best he could, his best shirt, and a black silk scarf borrowed from Whit. Willow wore a deer-skin dress tanned a creamy white, decorated with strips of glass beadwork, in cobalt blue, pink, black and yellow. On her feet were matching moccasins, and covering her calves were leggings that matched her dress.

Silas appeared, still wearing his buckskin pants and moccasins, but had cast aside his flannel shirt in favor of a new boiled white shirt, with a blue silk cravat, a black wool waist coat and a matching black frock. In his hand, he carried a small leather-bound volume which was not familiar even to those who knew him, as it had never had a place on his bookshelf.

He took a position under the shade of the giant cottonwood tree near the house, looking out on those gathered for the celebration, the wedding couple in place facing him.

Silas smiled and in clear words devoid of the slang he usually used, he spoke softly, but loud enough for all to hear, "I do wish your mother had lived to be with you today," he said to Willow. "But, I know she is here and that she will bless you today."

He then asked the two to exchange their consent to become man and wife, and both voiced their wishes, August stammering his words slightly and Willow voicing hers almost so quiet that only those close at hand could hear. Then, Silas brought out a small book, a Roman Missal, opened it and read, at times closing his eyes as if he knew the words by heart. He started in much the same way as he had for Whit and Maggie's' wedding, but with the Missal at hand, he said far more.

"O God, who by your mighty power created all things out of nothing, and, when you had set in place the beginnings of the universe, formed man and woman in your own image, making the woman an inseparable helpmate to the man, that they might be no longer two, but one flesh, and taught that what you were pleased to make one must never be divided;

Oh God, look now with favor on these your children, joined together in Marriage, who ask to be strengthened by your blessing. Send down on them the grace of the Holy Spirit and pour your love into their hearts, that they may remain faithful in the Marriage covenant.

May the grace of love and peace abide in your daughter Katherine,

May her husband August, entrust his heart to her, so that, acknowledging her as his equal and his joint heir to the life of grace, he may show her due honor and cherish her always with the love that you have for us.

May they be blessed with children, and prove themselves virtuous parents, who live to see their children's children.

And grant that, reaching at last together the fullness of years for which they hope, they may come to the life of the blessed in the Kingdom of Heaven.

In nomine Patris, et Filii, et Spiritus Sancti. Amen." He formed the sign of the cross over the newlyweds.

Silas then reached into his waistcoat pocket and pulled out a ring that he handed to August and Willow, saying "This belonged to my wife and I know she would want her daughter to have it." August took the ring and slipped it onto Willow's finger, they embraced each other, and then kissed. Before they could separate, Silas took up a new red four-point, English blanket and wrapped it around the couple.

There remained a hush over the crowd, for though many of the New Mexicans did not understand the words Silas had spoken, they felt the presence like that of a priest in Silas. None of those gathered there had ever heard him speak with such grace save for Bill Craigavon who knew a bit more about Silas' past.

Whit whispered to Maggie, "Them sound like the same words that fellow said over us down in Rayado."

"Yes, Señor Scott, speaks the words of a padre," she said, herself surprised at the difference in Silas.

August extended out his hand to Silas and shaking it said, "I promise that I will care for her for the rest of my life."

"Just give her your respect, and the rest will follow, Son," Silas said.

Willow leaned up to her father and kissed him on the cheek, saying "Thank you Father. You promised that you would say the words for my wedding, and you did more than I had hoped for."

***

April 1854 – Moon of Budding Trees

August Klausen and Willow planted the field he had cleared upriver, while Whit and Maggie helped Silas with the planting near his cabin. When the seeds were safely in the ground, the two families sat down to discuss what would be prudent for the future. The informal partnership between Silas and Whit in farming would now include August. The fields were not that far apart, but the cabin of Silas, made of cottonwood, was showing its age, and the structure August called a cabin, might not last another winter.

It was decided that if they were to make a real go of it, they would have to build a better structure to house them all. Thinking of both El Pueblo, and of the Craigavon rancho, they decided that adobe would be the best option. They decided to speak with Sandoval and Baca and make a deal in obtaining labor to build the new structure once the current year's crops were close to harvest. If there wasn't sufficient labor available, they would make the trip to Mora or Taos and hire men to come back in the spring and start construction.

The thought of a trip to Taos pleased Maggie. If it was a possibility, she would convince Whit to go and take her. A side trip from Taos to Abiquiú' would be convenient. She could then introduce her husband to her family and possibly convince some of her extended relatives to move to the Arkansas.

Life on the Arkansas seemed full of promise and the future looked hopeful. Everyone in the settlements believed this, and they placed their trust in it. Benito Sandoval's hard work finally paid off, he now owned a herd of about fifty cattle, and right after the wedding of Willow and August, he moved his family into a log cabin on Baca's ranch where he helped Baca farm the cornfield.

Doyle was prospering in the Indian Trade and Dick Wootton was doing a brisk business in raising stock. Cattle, mules and horses were needed New Mexico, and Wootton took advantage of the free pastureland along the Arkansas and the Saint Charles Rivers. Charlie Autobees and Bill Kroenig profited in raising stock also as well as corn and other vegetables. These men had worked out the difficulties of life on the Arkansas River and had become experts. When the railroad arrived, they would be the well-established, men of property.

With the change of the seasons, life on the Arkansas moved forward. Bill Craigavon scouted up and down both the Arkansas River and the Fountain Creek. The land was everything he had remembered and more. A fresh start in the area would be the best for him and his family. He then visited both the Huerfano and the Saint Charles settlements, and after visiting these and speaking with Doyle, Autobees, Kroennig and Dick Wooten, he held no doubts and more than ever he was convinced to move.

As a trader, Joseph Doyle was an excellent source of information. Bill asked if the Hairy Rope band of the Cheyenne had been recent customers, and Joseph said they had.

"Was Crow Eyes with them?" Bill asked.

"Yes, he was," said Doyle, "Carrying a new squaw too. He bought her some fine foo-fa-raw." Doyle used the old mountain man term for fancy clothing, or anything fancy on clothing, beads, silk ribbon, brass bells or tin cones.

"Any idea where they might be now?" Bill asked.

"They're more than likely headed up toward the Smokey Hills to hunt buffalo. The women will be needin' cow hides for new lodge covers," said Doyle. Spring buffalo cow hides were the best for making lodge covers, especially those of the older cows. These were the easiest to tan, because by April or May, the old cows were thin in flesh, and their hides thick.

"Thanks. I think I'll try to find them. Can you sell me some trade goods, gifts to take with me."

"Sure, probably have everything you'd want right here."

Bill left Doyle's place with a bag of gifts tied to the cantle of his saddle and headed northeast in the direction of the Smokey Hills River, called the Bunch of Trees or Cherry River by the Cheyenne. This had been the first time that Bill had crossed the prairie alone in many years. And though it had been some time, he was familiar with the territory, having spent some of his early years among the Cheyenne with his mother and his father. It had only been when the family had started to grow that Tom and Mary Craigavon moved to Taos and finally Rayado. Following in his mother's footsteps as a healer, Bill had learned much of her herbal craft as a youngster, and when he was older, he showed the desire to learn the medicine of American doctors, especially surgery. With this in mind, his parents sent him to school in the east. First to Saint Louis, and then with glowing recommendations from his teachers, to Baltimore where he was accepted at the University of Maryland School of Medicine.

Bill was bright and quick to learn, but once he left Saint Louis and arrived in Baltimore, his dark complexion made him stand out from his classmates. He carried his father's features, but the Cherokee blood he inherited from both parents could not be overlooked by many. When his teachers found that he was three quarters Cherokee and had been schooled in the art of "Indian cures," Bill faced ridicule and had to work twice as hard as the other students.

"You understand, Mr. Craigavon," one teacher admonished, "that Native techniques are uncivilized compared to our own practices and are far inferior." It had been over ten years since Bill had heard those words and they still lay heavy on him. He remembered that he wanted to lash out at the teacher, but the temperament he had inherited from his mother prevailed and he sought to vent his frustration elsewhere.

There was only one person in Baltimore that Bill could confide in, Father William Scott, Silas' brother, who lived at St. Mary's Seminary. Father William was older than Silas by a dozen years, and his life of self-sacrifice as a priest and a physician had taken its toll on him physically, but not mentally. Bill had been named by his father after Father Scott. The good man had tended to Tom Craigavon when he was a youth and brought back to health under the priest's care. Tom had never forgotten that kindness.

"I don't understand why they are so ignorant?" Bill complained. "They think they know everything about medicine, and there isn't a single one of them that can hold a candle to my mother and her ability to heal. There is a lot to be learned from the use of herbs."

Father William laughed softly, and said, "You can't expect them to see themselves as less than those who they consider savages." A hint of a Scottish brogue colored his words. "This would require them to admit that there is a deficiency in what they know. For my entire life, I have tried in vain to prove there is a connection with the infection of blood and the lack of cleanliness. I always found that washing my hands with clean water provided a better outcome in my patients' recovery."

"Why are they so obstinate when it comes to some Native ways?"

"They seem to be blind to it unless they can put their own name on an herbal remedy. What are called *Indian cures*, are very popular with the general public, but on the label the term must be prefaced by the name of a name of a physician. *Doctor Thumb's Indian Tonic*, and such," he said. "Try to discipline yourself. Take what knowledge you can from these men at Davidge Hall. Though you may think them ignorant at some things, they are fine surgeons, and you couldn't be in a better school to learn that skill."

Bill finished school and returned home just as the war with Mexico was starting. New Mexico was calm for the most part, the turmoil coming only after the war's end with the Revolt in Taos and some of the lawlessness that followed. It was during this time that Bill's little brother Thomas, and Roseanne's mother and brother were killed.

When it seemed that the troubles of war had passed, Bill and Roseanne rekindled their friendship and it soon blossomed into romance. The two settled in on the ranch she owned, and Bill attempted to establish his medical practice. Even with the increased number of Americans in the area, most people relied and trusted the old medicine, the type that Bill's mother offered. In fact, his sister Elizabeth and his mother outshined him in the arts of herbal healing. A fresh start in the north, where more Americans would be coming was the answer.

A meadowlark warbled its sweet, flute-like call and as Bill moved along, the bird flew from its nest on the ground. Bill loved where he was, the air of the prairie was clean, and it energized him. Here was where he took after his father, his love of the openness, of the wild, and its freshness. Sure, he thought, some of this would change, but not so much as to spoil it. He rode on, confident in his situation, assured by the weight of the rifle that balanced across his lap. The rifle was a Henry, made by J. Henry & Son, the same people who had made Silas' trusted weapon. Bill's, like Silas', was a big .50 caliber, but a bit heaver, weighing almost nine and a half pounds with a 1 1/8-inch-wide barrel, thirty-four inches long, set into a half stock.

His only other weapon was a sturdy hunting knife hanging from his belt. The knife had been a gift from his father's friend Ransom Carter, who had been killed by renegades. Bill had never quite understood what Ransom's words had meant when he gave him the knife, and he had never thought to ask either his father or Silas. Ransom handed Bill the blade and said, "Here, you take good care of this for me, and remember that gators like boys, so stay outta the river." Bill could only guess that it had something to do with the man's early days in Alabama. He smiled when he thought about the days when his father, Silas and Ransom would sit around and spin tales about their past, trapping, living among the Cheyenne and fighting Blackfeet or Comanches.

Like so many others, Bill had dropped his vigilance, and before he knew it a group of Indians were riding up on him, and he had no time to react other than to stand his ground. He pulled back on the reins and brought his horse to a stop as the warriors milled around him, yelling and attempting to spook him, or provoke him into rash action.

***

Nestled along the southern branch of the Smokey Hills River, lodges of the Hairy Rope band of the Cheyenne seemed to blend into the foliage of thickets of wild plumbs, and chokecherry, shaded by small bunches of ash, cedar or cottonwood trees. The prairies, consisting of mixed grass, stretched out in all directions from the river, in an unending carpet of rolling hills. The Smokey Hills was given its name by the first explorers to the area for its hazy, blue appearance at sunrise and sunset. Starting in the high plains, the waters of the two branches of the Smokey Hills River and their tributaries ran for over five hundred miles until their waters emptied into the Republican River. The richness along its course supported the immense herds of buffalo herds, deer, elk, antelope and smaller game such as rabbits and sage grouse.

The amount of game available could last the Cheyenne well into the next hunting season, and the racks of drying meat stood between the lodges, tempting small children and the camp's dogs. Guarded by the women, more than one child was scolded for this, and a dog was more than likely to be the recipient of a well-thrown rock or stick.

Bill Craigavon sat in the shade of the lodge belonging to Crow Eyes, its sides rolled up allowing the free flow of air to cool the inside. Crow Eyes was not only his host, but Bill's half-brother. With them was Little Gun, and another old acquaintance and longtime friend, the medicine man, Lone Wolf. Lone Wolf and Bill's father were as close as brothers, having known each other for most of their lives. The three men ate while they chatted. For the most part, Little Gun was quiet but was cordial to Bill having known him since they were children.

Bill looked over at Lone Wolf, and though he was the same age as Bill's father Tom, the Cheyenne looked much older. His hair was far grayer than Bill remembered, and his once robust body and powerful arms, were thin, frail and appearing weak. But when he spoke, Lone Wolf's voice was still clear and strong.

"My heart is glad to see you my son," he said, *"It has been many winters since you have last visited the people. You have grown to be a strong man."*

"It is good to see you also Uncle," Bill said, *"Though I have been away, I have held my Cheyenne family in my heart."*

"It is well that Little Bear was with the young men who found you," said Crow Eyes in English. "The blood in many of the younger men is hot, and there is constant talk of the war path." He glanced over at Little Gun, who placed no weight on the comment.

"You are lucky that you still have that lovely head of hair!" Lone Wolf half-joked, also speaking in English, a language he used infrequently.

"There is a lot of talk among some of the more militant among us, especially the Dog Soldiers," said Crow.

For the first time in the conversation, Little Gun spoke up, "Yes, a single man not of the People could very well loose his life at times like this."

"I knew I was taking a chance coming by myself, but it has been too long since I have seen my Cheyenne family," said Bill.

"How is Speaks With Her Hands?" Lone Wolf asked, speaking of Mary Craigavon.

"My Mother is well," he answered, "She thinks about you and her children all of the time." He looked over to Crow.

"Tell her we are well," said Crow, "And, let her know I think of her often. I hope that someday I will see her again."

Meets the Enemy Woman took the bowl from Bill's hand and refilled it with fresh roasted buffalo. As she handed it back to him, she gave him a warm smile.

"Thank you," Bill said. Then, to Crow he said, "Your new wife has a pleasant way about her."

"She likes everyone," Crow looked across to the lodge not far away and added, "Most people that is." He motioned with a nod of his head in the direction of that lodge and there sat Sees Far Woman and Buffalo Calf Woman scraping a buffalo hide staked to the ground. Every now and then, Sees Far would glance back, her eyes filled with hatred.

"Is there a problem with the neighbors?" Bill asked half joking.

"Let us say that is was good that Bear Voice was not with the group that found you," Crow said.

As if the mention of his name conjured him up, Bears Voice walked around his lodge. He stopped long enough to make some comment or complaint to his wife and then noticed the presence of Bill at Crow's lodge. With no hesitation, he strode to them and with an obvious lack of manners, addressed Crow.

"Where did this man come from?" he asked.

"He is my brother, and my guest," Crow said, not bothering to introduce Bill. Bear Voice scowled and turning, walked away, disappearing around his lodge.

"When you leave Billy, I will go aways with you," said Crow.

"As will I," said Little Gun.

"I too will ride with you young men," said Lone Wolf. "Now, I see you brought gifts. Is there some tobacco in that bag of yours for me?" He smiled and gave Bill a wink.

Bear Voice was incensed and needed to vent his rage that the very presence of a Whiteman caused. He went directly to the lodge of a fellow Dog Soldier, Whirlwind.

"Do you not see that there is a Whiteman in the camp?" he asked Whirlwind.

"I am not blind," Whirlwind said, *"He is the guest of Crow Eyes."*

"It is as should be expected from one who is not really one of the People. Everyone knows that Crow's blood is half Black-Whiteman and half Săvănē'." He spoke referring to the fact that Crow, being Mary Craigavon's son, was half Black and Half Cherokee with no Cheyenne blood in him.

"He has lived among the People his entire life," said Whirlwind, *"And, his actions are more those of one of the People than many I can name."* With this, he all but dismissed any further conversation with Bear Voice.

***

July 1854 Moon of the Ripening Cherries

In the days when the Cheyenne were living near the Great Lakes, they were a weak tribe and they were easy prey for those tribes who had already obtained firearms. They were pushed further and further west until they reached the Missouri River where for a few generations, they grew crops and ranged on foot onto the plains to hunt buffalo.

Two major changes occurred in the lifestyle of the Cheyenne, they obtained horses and firearms. Traded from other tribes along the great river, the horse gave the People mobility unlike any they had ever had before. They moved faster and further out onto the plains toward the Black Hills.

Oral tradition of the People said they obtained their first guns by the killing of a group of Assiniboinee. These guns were the smooth bore type, better suited for close in fighting or hunting, but like the horse it made the Cheyenne powerful compared to other tribes. Almost five generations had passed, and life was very different for them now.

As they had been for the most part victims in that past time, the People took on the attitude that strangers and enemies were one in the same. Many times, a lone man, or a party not instantly recognized as friends, was attacked. Thus, the People had many enemies, and only a few allies such as the Lakota and the Arapaho, though the Lakota had not always been allies. The Kiowa too had been an enemy for as far back as the People remembered, but since the treaty in 1851, peace between them and these two warrior tribes had held.

It was in this way that some Kiowa, along with Comanche and a small amount of Lakota, would accompany the Cheyenne on their war path against the Pawnee, with the intent to avenge the losses of the previous year and to wipe out the Pawnee. With these three tribes were also some Arapaho, Prairie Apache, and Osage. When the different tribes gathered together on the Pawnee Fork, there were over fifteen-hundred lodges, and the herds of horses and mules covered the prairie for miles around. The hatred for the Pawnee extended to what the Cheyenne considered "White" Indians, some of these being the Sac, Fox, Potawatomi, Shawnee and Delaware. These were all lumped into one group called Săvănē'.

Somewhere near the Kansas River, the Cheyenne and their allies came across a large group of Sac and Fox hunters. The hunters were far outnumbered, but as in the fight the previous year with the Potawatomi, the Sac and Fox hunters were well armed with rifles. Of the allied plains Indians most were armed with bows, and those armed with firearms had only smooth-bore trade guns.

The Săvănē' retreated to a ridge, taking the high ground, and there they dismounted. With their expert marksmanship, their superior rifles, and firing in relays, they keep the attackers at bay, charge after charge. Under withering fire from the ridge, the plains tribes could not get in close enough to use either their smooth-bore guns or their bows.

Again, the plains Indians were defeated, and their thirst for revenge was broken like their spirit. The different bands broke up and retreated back to their home territories. Among the Cheyenne was Bear Voice, and his anger grew with the shame he felt. The outcome could have been better, he thought, if the Cheyenne had possession of the same type of firearms as their enemies'. But, he chided himself as these were of the Whiteman's medicine, and that medicine was only harmful to the People.

The more he pondered this, he came to another conclusion. If the Whiteman was eliminated, the Săvănē' and others like them would no longer receive these weapons and the Cheyenne and their allies could eventually overcome them. The answer was to wipe out the whites. The question was how to start this, and who would be the first to draw blood. Would it be the People, one of their allies, or would it be the Whiteman?

SAM J. PISCIOTTA

***

September 1854 - Moon of Plums Ripening

Though small in number, not more than a thousand strong, the Muache Utes were one of the six bands that made up the Ute Nation. And, for as long as the Muache Utes could remember, their territory, consisted of the San Luis Valley, the Wet Mountain Valley and the plains of northeastern New Mexico up to the Arkansas River where they hunted buffalo and Arapaho scalps. This they considered their domain, and they imposed a tribute from travelers passing through it or those they considered trespassers. Though they practiced this form of "taxation", they were relatively peaceful compared to the Comanche, Kiowa and Arapaho who had raided along the Santa Fe trail, and the Apaches and Navajos who had recently killed over fifty citizens from the Rio Grande valley.

They stood at a disadvantage compared to the other tribes. The treaties signed with the U.S. Government did not allow them firearms as part of their annuities, even when those annuities were issued. In the spring of 1849, they were badly defeated in a battle with the Arapahos near the Hardscrabble. The victors took not only the lives of Ute warriors, but most of their stock. This left the Ute in a starving condition, and they had little choice but to start stealing stock from near the Rio Colorado.

In retaliation, fifty soldiers under Lieutenant J. H. Whittlesey were sent out to punish the Utes, using Charles Autobees and others as guides. The soldiers destroyed fifty Ute lodges with all the provisions and camp equipage. This devastated them even further and they sued for a formal peace, signing another treaty where they promised a cessation of hostilities, and restoration of captives and stolen property.

For the next few years, the Utes kept their side of the treaty. But, peace with the white man did not help the Utes situation. While the Ute grew poorer, the more hostile Indians thrived by raiding in New Mexico. There were also frequent forays by the Arapahos, Cheyenne and Kiowa into the San Luis Valley to rob and kill Utes, and this only added to their poor condition. By terms of two treaties made in 1851 and 1853 with the Arapahos, Cheyenne, Kiowa, Comanche and Kiowa-Apaches, the United

States guaranteed these Plains tribes a specified annuity including guns, lead and powder.

The Utes complained again to the Americans that they were not being protected from the plain's tribes. Not truly understanding the problem, and in an attempt to prevent problems, The United States agreed to establish military posts in the Ute territory and to give the Ute further annuities as the government deemed proper, but still no firearms. The government-built Fort Massachusetts at the east end of the San Luis Valley. The intent was to protect both the settlers and the Ute. The plains tribes simply ignored the fort and went on raiding the Ute.

More complaints by the Ute finally brought about a meeting in November of 1852. The Government invited some five hundred Ute to meet near Abiquiú and gave them $3,000 worth of flour and small trade goods accompanied by a feast of roasted mutton. This seemed to please the Ute and then Chief Coniache addressed the American hosts.

"Listen to me," he said, "My people have always lived by the hunt and do not know how to live in houses or to farm. The prairie Indians have committed many depredations upon our people, and we are told we must not make war. We do not wish to have our hands bound together when our enemies are permitted to steal our stock and murder our wives and children. If we are not to make war, we shall expect the Americans at the fort to protect us and our property." His voice held no animosity or threat. "We ask for very little. Give us guns, powder and lead and protection to hunt and protect ourselves."

Governor Bill Lane was sympathetic, but until February of the next year, he had no idea as to the scope of the situation faced by the Ute. Forty Ute families were found in the area of the Costilla and Culebra rivers starving. They suffered from raids by the Arapaho and Cheyenne, with many of their number killed, and their horses stolen. Lane decided that the answer was to move the Ute west of the Rio Grande, and that notice would be given to the plain's tribes forbidding them to enter Ute Territory. Before this could happen, the Governor was replaced by the less sympathetic Governor David Meriwether.

So it was that for five years after signing a treaty with the United States, the Utes maintained peace, and the Government did little for them except build a poorly positioned military post, distribute on a single occasion some flour, meat, and only briefly prevent New Mexican settlement in the San Luis Valley. Thus, the temperament of the Ute was close to breaking, and it would take little for them to lash out against a convenient target, one that would enrich them with little chance of danger.

In these years, the principle chief Among the Mauche Ute, was Chico Velasquez, and he kept his people, for the most part, peaceful. But, he contracted smallpox, and was soon dead. His replacement was a man named Ciniache, who unlike his predecessor, was too mild-mannered and held little control over his people. With little effort, his sub-chief, Tierra Blanca held more influence. Blanco, as he was called by some, stood out among his fellows. He was also distinguished by his red woolen shirt, and with a single eye set in his smallpox scarred face, he was a foreboding and terrible figure. He was of a different temperament than Ciniache, being shrewd and cunning.

Blanco soon began to gather about him trusted friends and warriors. He also courted his people's allies, the Jicarilla Apache. Embittered by the past few years, Blanco began his plan for retribution.

By October, called the Moon of long Hair by the Ute, they were looking ahead to a winter of starvation. Their frustration boiled over into rage and they began a series of actions that should have been warnings to the settlers along the Arkansas.

Near the Huerfano settlement, Tom Whittlesey's wife Marfa was out riding horseback with her two children when she was surprised by a band of Utes. She barely had time to tie her youngest to her with her reboso, and with the other child holding on from behind, managed to outrun the Utes who pursued her almost to her doorstep.

Only a few days later, Charlie Autobees started out from his home with a wagonload of flour and corn, intent on going to the divide between the Arkansas and the Platte to trade with Arapaho who were in that area. With him, traveled four men from the Saint Charles settlement and some Arapaho with their women and children. They were still south of the Arkansas River when they were surprised by a group of two dozen Ute. They spoke to Charlie in Spanish saying that if he handed over the Arapaho, they would not harm him. He refused, saying that the Arapaho were under his protection as customers, and before he had said his last word the Ute opened fire on the him and his companions, Charlie was immediately wounded, but the Utes were driven back and only four horses from Charlies group were lost.

Both of these incidents were considered a normal part of doing business in the west, and so there was no general alarm on the part of the settlements along the river. The fall harvest came in and the hard work of the valley's inhabitants paid off. Benito Sandoval ended up with ninety bushels of corn, and a herd of over fifty cattle. As he had planned, his wife and their youngest son went to Mora to visit family, and he moved back into El Pueblo temporarily with his other three sons. The visit in Mora was to be short, as his wife was to return after Christmas, and they would all move to the Huerfano village.

His friend, Baca had also prospered. His herds had increased over the summer, and his granary was filled with corn. He was in his own mind, now a "rico", a man of property. He was happy and felt secure in his home with his family and employees around him.

The season's harvest had also been good to August, Silas and Whit. Their harvest brought them more than enough corn and vegetables to last through the winter. The extra corn was loaded into a wagon that Whit and August would take down river to Bent's, trading for other goods, and possibly some silver. Silas would remain with the women and Zachary, and if the men made it back before Christmas everyone would go south to spend another winter with the Craigavons.

***

SAM J. PISCIOTTA

CHAPTER SEVEN
FIRST BLOOD

October 1854 - Moon When Thin Ice Begins to Form on Rivers

Whit and August rode along in the empty wagon, bouncing along the trail, its contents a fraction in weight compared to the load of corn they had taken to William Bent to trade. In return, they were bringing not only the staples such as flour, sugar and coffee needed to get them through the winter, but also a few luxuries. For Silas, they had procured a bottle of Scottish whiskey, a rarity in the west. And for the women, they had found two bolts of good English woolen cloth. In his coat pocket, Whit kept a small paper wrapped package of stick candy for his son.

At any other time, their spirits would have been good, but the news that they had heard at Bent's left them in a solemn mood. Disturbing news had reached the Arkansas, traveling from Fort Laramie to Fort Kearny and Fort Riley. In August, thirty U. S. soldiers were killed by Lakota Lakota not far from Fort Laramie. The details were not quite clear, but it seemed the incident had been caused over the theft of a cow belonging to a Mormon immigrant. The soldiers had killed a Brulé chief named Conquering Bear and the Lakota responded by wiping out all the soldiers present.

"Does this mean trouble here?" August asked Whit.

"Not sure," Whit said, "The Lakota and the Cheyenne are friends, but I would guess it all depends on how far it spreads up north."

"I vould not like a war to start. Especially now that I have a wife and a home." August shook his head.

"Well, from what I have learned about Indians, they don't usually take on the troubles of other Indians. They tend to take things personally, or as none of their business. That does change though when someone brings around the war pipe and ask their friends and family to smoke it and go on the war path."

"Did you see the looks those Indians at Bent's gave to us?"

"That's just their way. They like to intimidate a fellow. You know, size him up, see if they can rattle him."

"I will still feel better when I am home with Willow."

They hurried westward; the journey back more apprehensive than fearful. Both men were well armed, Whit with his Deringer rifle and August with a .54 caliber Tryon Rifle he had purchased from Joseph Doyle. Both men were excellent marksmen and had no doubt they could hold their own if the need arose. Their first stop was at the Huerfano settlement to share the news about the killing of Lieutenant John Grattan and his men at Fort Laramie.

Doyle, Bob Rice, George McDougal and Dick Wootton all listened to the news with interest, but none of them could see any reason to be alarmed.

Doyle said, "The trouble is too far north and it's with the Lakota anyway. I doubt it will matter much down here with the Cheyenne and the Arapaho."

"I don't know," said Wooten, "Them Lakota have a way of stirring up mischief."

"I would bet that everything will get smoothed over with a few gifts and a horse or two given up," added Bob Rice.

"The way we heard it," said Whit, "Was the Lakota offered the Mormon his choice of any horse he wanted out of the Lakota herd to make up for the cow, and he turned it down, wanting $25 in silver."

"I'd like to get that for a single cow," quipped Doyle, "And, I'll wager that Mormon cow wasn't prime beef! Hell, a good Indian pony's worth five times that."

"I'd keep my nose to the wind," said Wootton, "Can't really trust any Injin. I been around 'em for almost twenty years and I know 'em. I tell you, I've lived among 'em, traded with 'em, and..." He went on and on, really not saying much, but his attitude as far as Indians were concerned bordered on contempt.

This offended August, and Whit noticed his friend tense with a growing anger. He placed a hand on August's arm, and the two of them seemed to be the only ones who noticed Wootton's remarks had hit a cord with the big Dane. But, August restrained himself, and was silent for almost an hour after they had left the Huerfano settlement.

"You know, I was close to giving that Dick Vootton a good licking," he said to Whit.

"Lucky for him you didn't," said Whit, "I'm not too impressed with him either."

"I just don't want no trouble, but he riled me some. Good thing for him he didn't say nothing about my Willow, 'cause I don't know what I would have done."

Whit looked over at his friend and smiled. The only advantage August would have had in a confrontation with Dick was August was younger by at least ten years. Wootton was well muscled, as tall as August, but slightly heavier, and probably a bit less civilized when it came to a fight.

"Yep, you'd probably have scalped him right there and then," Whit said, adding a slight chuckle. August saw the joke and he started to laugh.

When they reached the Saint Charles Settlement, they shared the news about the Grattan fight with Levin Mitchell and Charlie Autobees. They were concerned, but not enough to change the way they went about their business. At El Pueblo no one was worried at all. It seemed the consensus of the inhabitants of the valley was that the trouble would either stay in the north or blow over and soon be forgotten.

Silas, on the other hand, listened with more interest, wondering how things could have gotten out of hand so fast as to become deadly. He voiced an opinion, "The soldiers must have underestimated the Lakota. Pride and arrogance will get a man killed every time."

"The way it was told to us, the soldiers even had a cannon, but they was up against some four-thousand Lakota," said Whit.

"Well now, they should have brought two cannons," Silas smirked. "Seems like the Lakota forgot what happened two years ago in Minnesota though. This killing at Laramie might have been a victory, but if a real war gets started, a whole lot of them will be on the losing side. They keep their women and children with them when they go to war."

"You think what Bill Craigavon said after his visit with the Cheyenne, is true then?" Whit asked.

"Yep, I've seen a change in the Cheyenne. The old groups like the Red Shields and Kit Fox are dying off and are being replaced by the Dog Soldiers. And, they ain't called Crazy Dog Men for nothing. There's some with them that would like to see a war now." Silas' comment made Whit think about the Cheyenne and this brought Bear Voice to mind. "Yes," he thought, "Some of them would like take a scalp or two."

"What do you think we should do?" he asked.

"We best be on our guard, no matter what. I understand a trader got killed down on Apache Creek near the Greenhorn. More than likely it was Ute that done it."

"You know who it was?" asked August.

"Nope, only that it was a white man. Right now, I believe we should get things ready for winter here, close up the cabin. Then, head to Rayado, maybe while we're at it, look in Mora or Taos for laborers to come back with us in the spring. We had better get started on building a decent place to live. Something a bit more secure, like we've talked about." Silas said. Then he added, "You boys with Billy Craigavon, can handle any business in New Mexico. I'm thinking I want to make a trip down to Bent's and talk to William. If the weather isn't too bad, I'll come south after that, or I just might spend the winter here. I'd like to be on my own for a bit."

By the end of November, Silas' and August's cabins were all but emptied, except for a few items that Silas felt he would need for the coming months. Everything else of value had been packed in anticipation of a long stay in New Mexico. Traveling with them would be Benito Sandoval's wife Maria Espinosa, and her youngest son. Maria would go as far as Mora, where she would visit her family and spend Christmas, the rest of the party would travel on to Rayado. The women would stay at Rayado, while Whit and August went on to Santa Fe where they would make contact with Bill Craigavon. The three would spend the winter making arrangements for the move to the Arkansas. This would include the sale of Bill and Roseanne's ranch, and contracting labor from Taos and Mora to come back north with them in the spring.

Silas had no qualms about Whit and August handling the business end of the proposed enterprise as he had other things in mind. He thought about how successful Joseph Doyle had been with his trading on the Huerfano, and Silas figured that his own experience with the Cheyenne and the Arapaho was far better than Doyle's, and there was room for competition on the Arkansas. Anyway, Silas thought, he really wasn't cut out to be a farmer.

RIVER OF SAND

After a short stop at both the St. Charles and the Huerfano settlements, Silas headed down stream towards Bent's New Fort. He made several camps on the way, one being at the site of the old fort. For the most part, it was now in ruins, save for a few rooms that had survived the destruction William Bent had planned for it. Silas sifted through the debris a bit and found nothing that was of value; some old harness, broken bottles, and a few empty boxes.

He spent the night in the room with the best roof, and in front of a fire, ate a light meal of tea and buffalo jerky. As he sat there, amid the ghosts of the fort's past, his mind wondered over all the effort that had went into the building of the Bent's empire over the past thirty some years. William had lost a wife, and three brothers during that time and Silas tried to understand what kept William Bent going. It might have been for the wife he now had, and the children that he had fathered. How much different was William's life than Silas' own?

They had both lost in much the same way. Silas had lost Red Calf, the only woman that he had every truly loved, and a daughter, Corn Woman. The family he still had was mostly centered on Willow. His son, Little Gun, roamed somewhere out on the plains with a wife and children that Silas had never met. He hoped there would be a time when he could see those children.

Silas' thoughts drifted back on those friends and comrades he had lost over the years, especially those he considered his brothers, men he had fought alongside. Men he had buried, and the words he had said over their graves.

"What was that boy's name?' he thought to himself, "The one killed by the Blackfeet, or am I thinking of that young Cherokee killed at Horseshoe Bend?" The faces weren't as clear as they once were, and the names seemed to have completely disappeared from Silas' memories. Then, two of faces came back to him and so did their names, Ethan Green Corn and Andy Gilmore. Both young men had followed him into the Rockies to trap beaver in Blackfoot country. Both young men had trusted Silas and he felt he had let them down. They had been captured by the Blackfeet and tortured over a period of two days. Silas shook his head and tried not to think about their suffering, attempting to concentrate on something else, anything else. He finally drifted off into a fitful sleep, and in the darkness of that

159

slumber he heard the cries of Ethan and Andy, along with the laughter of the Blackfeet warrior. As he had done that night almost forty years ago, he felt himself crawling through the brush toward the Blackfoot camp, the fire flickering in the blackness. Silas felt his way forward, stopping just outside the firelight and waited until all two dozen of the Indians were asleep. Then he made his way to where the young men were tied to stakes driven in the ground. He laid there next to Andy, listening to the labored breathing of the poor boy, his body and his face beaten, burned, mutilated beyond help. Silas felt the knife in his hand, and slowly reached over, at first thinking of cutting Andy loose. Then realizing the boy had no chance of living, he moved the knife to his throat. With the nightmare of what he had done so many years ago, Silas woke startled and drenched in sweat.

"Damn!" he said out loud. "Why you boys comin' back to haunt me now? I did what I thought was best, stopped you from suffering. Them Blackfoot devils would have kept at it another day or so. I couldn't let you go through that." He looked around in the darkness of the room; the light of the moon shining through the open doorway.

As he looked out through the opening something passed by quickly. Silas got to his feet, and rifle in hand, moved out into the night. His horse, Rocinante, was still hobbled nearby, and he went to the mare and whispered softly in her ear, "You see anything girl?" He ran a hand over the horse's neck and then moved away to survey the ruins of the trading post. Out of the corner of his eye, he caught a movement and he slowly made his way over the adobe rubble in that direction.

The prairie surrounding the old fort was illuminated by the full moon's brightness, and Silas could see only the stillness of the night. He watched for a few minutes and then turned to go back to the room where he had made his bed. He stumbled a bit as he made his way over the broken adobe bricks, just catching his balance and had to look down to see where he was going. When he looked back up into the courtyard, there stood a woman, with the moonlight at her back. Her long hair and the fringes of the Indian dress she wore were flowing in the slight breeze. Her face hidden in the shadow of her hair couldn't be seen, but Silas saw she was holding out her hand toward him.

He almost spoke his wife's name, but his common sense told him it couldn't be Red Calf. She lay in the ground under the pile of stones he placed over her body years ago. He moved forward and stumbled again, this time falling to one knee, pain shooting up his leg and into his hip. He rose up on to his feet, a bit shaken, and looking back to where the woman had stood, he found her gone.

With the nightmare about Ethan and Andy still fresh in his mind, Silas began to wonder if the appearance of the woman had been nothing more than the product of his imagination. He cussed himself, and with the sore knee and hip limped back to his bedding. He rekindled the fire and made himself another cup of tea, wishing it was something stronger. "A sip of whiskey would go good right now," he thought, for it had been a long time since his nerves had been rattled so badly, but then again, he reconsidered, it could just have been the cold night air.

Silas sat in front of the small fire for the next hour thinking about the past, wondering what he would have done different in his life. If he hadn't chosen the path he was still on, so many things might have been different. He shook his head and talking to himself out loud, said, "You know Ol' Coon, you did the best you could for the time, and if there is a price to pay when you go under, hold your head up and take what St. Peter says you have coming."

Calculating it was close to daylight, he packed up and saddled his horse. Before getting in the saddle, he pulled out his pipe and tobacco, filled the pipe's bowl, and struck a spark to a piece of char-cloth. He placed the small burning ember onto the tobacco in the pipe and sucked on the pipe steam, bringing the ember to a rich glow and setting the tobacco alight. He then placed his foot in the stirrup and started to get in the saddle. His sore knee and hip caused him to lose his balance and step back. He made a second attempt, this time pulling himself up with a bit more effort than it had ever taken in the past. He didn't have the strength he used to, and this was just one more reminder that he was reaching that time of reckoning.

"Not so fast," he again spoke to himself, "You aren't done in yet." He chuckled a bit, adjusted his seating and then kicked his heels to the horse's flanks.

As the sun climbed into the eastern sky, the day warmed up and with that soothing feeling of the sunlight's rays on his face, Silas' apprehension melted away.

Thoughts of the specter came back to his now clear mind, and he shook them off, replacing them with those of his dead wife, and the love he still felt for her. This warmed him further.

***

December 1854 – Big Freeze Moon

All was quiet along the upper Arkansas valley by Christmas, or so it seemed. Everyone had settled into the security that prosperity offers. Joseph Doyle and Bob Rice headed north to the Platte-Arkansas divide with two cart loads of goods to trade with the Arapaho camped there. Benito Sandoval moved back into El Pueblo temporarily with his oldest three sons awaiting the return of his wife from Mora sometime after Christmas. When she returned, they would begin the construction of their new home at the Huerfano settlement.

Having ordered trade goods from William Bent to be delivered in the spring, Silas returned to the valley. Silas had also decided that he would spend the rest of the winter at his cabin rather than go south to Rayado. The memory of his nightmare and the vision of the woman still bothered him. They had left him with a foreboding that he could not shake. He decided to busy himself, and with the need to stock up for the coming months, Silas joined Dick Wootton and four other men from the Huerfano village to do some hunting along the upper Arkansas.

Their hunt had been fairly successful, bagging four deer and two turkeys. They then considered extending their time out as this was in their opinion only a good start. Silas paired off with George McDougal, and Wootton with the other three men, expecting to cover more territory and improve their chances at find more game.

They had worked their way almost thirty miles upriver from El Pueblo when Silas drew McDougal's attention to a lone figure moving through the piñon and cedar trees.

"Look there," he said pointing.

"Elk?" George guessed.

"No, Indian," said Silas.

"Should we cut him off, see what he's up too?"

162

"No, he's probably huntin', just like us," Silas assured him, but the hairs on the back of Silas' neck bristled, and a feeling of apprehension came over him. He looked over at George and then suggested they go to where they had agreed to rendezvous with Wootton.

"Sun's gettin' low and I'm hankering for a hot cup of tea," Silas said. The two men rode in the direction of a creek that emptied into the Arkansas from the south that they had begun to call Coal Creek for the deposits of low-grade coal that could be found in the area.

As they made their way along the creek, they soon saw a faint column of smoke rising into the air and then heard the sound of voices. Slowly advancing, they soon found it to be Wootton and the other hunters.

'Hello, the camp!" McDougal called out.

"Hello," Wootton answered.

"Is that coffee I smell?" McDougal said as he and Silas rode in.

"Sure is," said Wootton, "Come on and have a cup. We got some news to discuss."

Silas and McDougal, dismounted, unsaddled their horses and joined the others.

"You seen any sign?" Wootton asked.

"Some, think we caught a glimpse of a lone Indian back a ways," said Silas.

"Well, there's more than one lone Injun," said Wootton, "We ran across sign of a big war party, not too far from here. Ute to my reckoning."

"Why you think they're Ute?" McDougal asked.

"Cause I can tell!" Wootton seemed annoyed that anyone would doubt him, "Twas Ute that killed that trader down by the Greenhorn last month."

"Large enough party to worry about?" Silas asked.

"Sure 'nough. More than I'd want to tangle with."

"Well, we had best keep our wit's about us," Silas added.

"They're headed east, and I'm thinkin' we best head back to the Huerfano, let folks know something might be up."

"Probably right," Silas said, "No sense in wasting time, we got a few hours of daylight left, might as well head out now."

They doused the fire then mounted their horses and headed back down valley, hoping they could beat the war party back to the little settlement.

Reaching El Pueblo the following day, they warned the inhabitants. Wootton, stressed that the gates should be kept closed and no Indians allowed in. He and his friends then left for the Huerfano village, and Silas turned back to his cabin.

Arriving back at his home, Silas looked about, contemplating the action he should now take. Leaving for Rayado on his own was not a journey he would once have thought twice about, he had always been self-reliant, and able to handle any situation. But, at this time of year when the weather could be deadly in the mountains, coupled with his recent self-doubts, Silas decided to stay. The only question was should he holed up in his cabin, stay at El Pueblo, Baca's ranch, the Huerfano or the St. Charles settlements?

Again, he took his own council, "You get'in all spooky in your old age?" he asked himself. "Hell, I may not be as good as I once was, but by Gawd, I'll be damned if I let a few Ute bastards drive me from my own home."

He took stock of what provisions he had on hand. There was plenty of gun powder and lead, and an ample quantity of dried buffalo meat and the fresh venison that was his share from the hunt with Wootton. Silas also had a large tin of English tea, several cones of Mexican sugar and tucked away above one of the roof's rafters was the bottle of Scotch whiskey Whit had given him.

The next few days passed quietly, and Silas spent the time cleaning his rifle and pistols, grooming his horse, cleaning her tack and when the light allowed him, he read. He grazed Rocinante only when he could be outside with her, otherwise he kept the mare inside the lean-to attached to the cabin. As he had advised so many of the young men he had taken under his wing over the years, it was better to count ribs than tracks when dealing with horses. On Christmas Eve, Felix Sandoval rode up to the cabin and called out, "Señor Scott, are you there?"

Silas opened the cabin door, squinting to adjust his eyes to the light, and then recognized the boy.

"*Felix, why you making such a racket?*"

"*Me padre sent me to ask if you would like to come to the fort and celebrate Christmas with us today. We will have plenty to* eat, some música and Jose Francisco has a deck of cards, we can play Monte'.'"

"You're too young to be gambling," Silas joked. "Let me saddle up Rocinante and we'll ride back together."

As they rode, they talked, Felix chattering on and on. He said his father had sent his brother Pedro with two wagons down the Arkansas, one filled with corn for Levin Mitchell at the St. Charles Settlement, and the other with the family's household good and furniture to the Huerfano. Felix was excited about the move, and the prospect of living in a proper house. He was also proud of his father Benito, and he reminded Silas that now his father was a "rico", a man of property.

Christmas Eve was the big day of celebration with the New Mexicans, and a feast was laid out at El Pueblo with many of the residents from Baca's ranch attending, partying through the day. By dusk, most of the residents from Baca's returned to their homes, but three of the men decided to stay at El Pueblo to play cards and drink on into the night. Their wives, preferring to sleep in their own beds, left their husbands to enjoy the free time. The only woman who did not leave was Chepita Miera Martin, who decided to stay with her husband Juan Blas. These fifteen people at El Pueblo celebrated well into the night with little care for the future.

Silas had left with the people from Baca's Ranch, going there at Marcelino's invitation. They spent the evening talking about the coming year, and their individual plans. Baca supported Silas' ambition to open a trading house either at El Pueblo, or at least closer to it than the St. Charles Settlement.

"I like you better than Doyle," Baca told Silas in Spanish, "I think you would be a better man to trade with. And, you are friends with the Cheyenne."

"I am not sure who is a friend with the Cheyenne anymore, Marcelino. But I'd like to give it a try. I think it's time that I settle down."

"Now that your daughter is married, you should think about getting yourself a woman," Baca's Pawnee wife said. "A man needs a woman to take care of him."

"Tomasa," Baca chided her, "Silas will take a wife if he wants one, until then it is no one else's business." He turned back to Silas, "I apologize, my friend. Sometimes, she had a sharp tongue."

"Do not worry, Marcelino, I am not offended," Silas said. The two talked long into the night. Weary, both men went to bed, Marcelino with his wife and their little girl Elena, and Silas curled up in a blanket next to the fireplace.

The eastern sky was just turning a dull yellow on Christmas morning, when young Benito Pais, riding bareback with an empty bucket in his hand, left El Pueblo to fetch milk from Baca's. He went through the puertecito, between the two small hills that sat on the western bank of Fountain Creek and crossed the Fountain at the gravely ford. As he made his way toward Baca's house, he heard a noise that drew his attention to the loma north of the pasture. There, outlined against the pale predawn sky, he saw a group of mounted Indians. Benito dropped the bucket he was carrying and grasped the horses' mane with his now freed hand to hold himself on the saddleless horse. He kicked the animal into a dead run and slid from the horses back as it reached the ranch house.

"Indios, indios bárbaros!" he shouted, bringing Baca to the door followed by Silas.

"Where?" asked Baca.

"There, on the loma." the boy pointed.

"Quickly, go to the cabins and wake everyone else." the boy headed to the jacal cabins behind Baca's house and pounded on the doors to spread the alarm. As Baca and Silas watched the Indians slowly make their way down off the loma, Benito returned with the old man, Jose Barela and the wives of Jose Ignacio Valencia, Tanislado de Luna and Rumaldo Cordóva.

"Get into the house," Baca said to the women, *"And you also Benito."* Then he, Silas and Barela moved forward standing just behind a short adobe wall that was in front of the house. The wall continued around to the back where the saddle horses, the milk cows and calf were kept.

Silas stood with his pipe held between his teeth and looked down at his rifle cradled across his arm. He flipped the frizzen forward, and removing the pipe from his mouth, blew the gun powder out of the pan. He then replaced his pipe in his mouth and re-primed the lock, snapping the frizzen back. He was now satisfied that if it was needed, his rifle had dry powder in the pan and would fire. He took a long draw on his pipe, exhaling a small cloud of grayish smoke that rose above his head in the cold morning air.

"They could be friendly," said Baca, more to convince himself than stating a fact.

"Not too sure, Marcelino. That looks an awful like your horse that big fellow in front is riding," Silas said. *"It would be wise to keep your guns ready."*

"Be careful," Barela said, *"Remember the Utes killed that man on Apache Creek. These are Ute and they will kill us."* From his place next to Baca and Silas, he also eyed the Indians as they moved closer.

Mounted on Baca's white mare, the Ute chief Blanco rode up to within fifty yards of the men. With him were over a hundred Ute warriors and a few Apache.

Silas moved several feet to Baca's right and Barela copied him moving an equal distance to the left. Spreading out made them harder targets, and all three men pointed their rifles in the direction of Blanco.

"¿Cómo estás, Amigo?" said Blanco, a smile on his pockmarked face, his single eye, squinting in the early morning light. *"Is this the way you greet a friend?"* he continued to speak in Spanish. The sound of the women crying inside the house could be heard and Blanco looked in that direction with his single eye.

"A friend does not come in the way you have, taking what you wish." Baca, pointed with the barrel of his rifle at the horse Blanco rode, then raised it to point at Blanco's head. *"If you come closer, I will take your head from your shoulders with a single shot."*

Blanco scowled. Whipping the horses' reins to one side, he turned the animal, and with by his warriors sped off in the direction of El Pueblo.

The three men watched the Indians retreat all knowing that there was no way to warn the people at the little adobe post.

"Hope they have the gates closed," Silas said.

"Look!" Barela said, pointing to the loma. There more Ute were driving off Baca's cattle and horses, leaving Baca a poor man. Baca only thought of this for a brief moment until he remembered Felipe Cisneros had gone up on the loma to bring the horses in.

"Ay, Dios Mío," he said. *"Felipe was out on the loma this morning.*

"What should we do?" asked Barela.

"Like I said, with luck, the gates at the fort are closed, and they will be safe." said Silas, "There is nothing we can do to help them."

"Should we warn those who are at the Saint Charles and the Huerfano?" Baca asked.

"Probably a good idea," said Silas, "Barela can saddle up and head down that way, maybe bring some help up here, and then we'll go over to El Pueblo."

"I will go up on the loma to look for Felipe," said Baca.

"No, it would be best if you stayed with your family. I'll go up there and see if I can find the boy."

As Silas had suggested, Barela rode east to the St. Charles settlement, and Silas on Rocinante, made his way in a circular path to the top of the hills above Baca's ranch. Silas hoped he would find the boy unharmed, but the Ute were unpredictable. There was the chance that the Ute wouldn't kill him but take him prisoner. They did a brisk business selling young boys to the Navajos and other tribes in the south, where they were a valuable commodity.

Just as Silas reached the top of the loma, a few hundred yards from Baca's house, he was hailed by Felipe Cisneros who had hidden among the sage brush. Silas pulled the frightened boy up onto the horse behind him. They turned to head back to Baca's house, when the sound of gunfire from the direction of El Pueblo drifted in the clear morning air. Though higher in elevation than the ranch by a hundred feet, the hill north of the puertecito was higher still and El Pueblo a mile away, was not visible.

"Hope they're givin' them bastards hell," Silas said out loud.

"¿Qué es lo que dicen?" Felipe asked.

"I said I hope the people at El Pueblo are safe." He turned the horses' head and with a slight nudge of his heels urged her forward and back down to Baca's house.

They waited for several hours and help hadn't arrived from the two settlements downstream and Barela hadn't returned either. Everyone at Baca's house was anxious to know what had happened at the fort, especially the wives of the men who had stayed the night at El Pueblo. It had been almost five hours since the Ute had left Baca's, and the usually patient Silas decided that it was time to go to the fort.

Baca and Cisneros decided to go with him, and just as they were leaving, Barela arrived. The old man was winded, and his horse lathered from the hard ride to the St. Charles and the Huerfano.

"Are they coming?" Baca asked of the men from the two settlements.

"Yes, but it will be awhile, I came back without waiting for them," said Barela.

"It has been quiet for some time now," said Silas, *"I would think it is safe to go and see what has happened."*

The four moved off in the direction of the gravel ford on the Fountain. As they neared it, they spotted someone lying on the east bank. It was Jose Ignacio Valencia. He had evidently been caught by the Utes trying to escape to Baca's and was killed not a quarter of a mile from the house.

They left Valencia where he lay and crossed the Fountain, cautious as there was a possibility that the Indians may still be around. Baca saw something and he raised his rifle, prepared to shoot, but Silas put a hand on the barrel and said, *"It's not an Indian."*

Staggering towards them was Juan Medina. He held his hands to a large gash across his stomach, attempting to prevent his intestines from spilling out.

"Water," he gasped as he fell to the ground. The men slid from their horses and went to Juan. Baca cradled the man's head as Felipe ran back to the river to scoop up some cold water in his hands, bringing it back for Juan who choked as he tried to drink.

"What of the people at the Fort?" asked Baca.

"All...are...dead," the words gurgling from his lips. *"Water,"* he begged, and before Felipe could give him another drink, Juan closed his eyes and was gone.

As they had with Valencia, they left Medina where they had found him and moved cautiously on through the puertecito. They had not gone but halfway through the gap when they found another victim, Guadalupe Vigil, his back pierced with arrows, and one piercing his right hand, as if he had held it up to protect himself. Like Median, he had probably tried to run from the fort and was killed. They left him also where they found him, and the prospect of finding anyone alive grew even dimmer.

As they neared the fort, they spotted a wagon sitting in front of the open gate and near it the bodies of two dead Ute. Sitting against one of the gate posts was Rumaldo Cordova, his head down, his chest covered with blood.

He was still alive but barely conscious, he lifted his head to look in the direction of the men approaching. His eyes filled with fear, and his own wounds became visible to them. Rumaldo had an arrow piercing his throat, and had a gunshot wound to his jaw.

"Rumaldo," Baca asked, "Can you speak?"

Rumaldo attempted to answer but his injuries were too severe, and he resorted to sign language.

"Ute..came..killed..all. Stole..my..wife's..sister. Stole..boys." he signed.

His sister-in-law was Chepita Miera, wife of Juan Blas Martin, and the only woman at El Pueblo that morning. As to whom the boys were, they asked Rumaldo if it was Sandoval's children, seven-year-old Juan Isidro and twelve-year-old Felix. He signed that it was.

Silas moved on into the courtyard of the little fort and the carnage that lay before him made him step back a pace. Instinctively, he pulled back the cock on his rifle. Though he knew the danger had passed, it was a subconscious comfort knowing the rifle was ready to fire.

He took a few steps forward and surveyed the scene in front of him. The ground was stained with blood around the bodies of Juan Blas Martin, Francisco Mestas and Manuel Lucero. In Lucero's hand was clutched a flatiron that he had used as a weapon to beat off his attackers, one of them lay close by, the mark of the flatiron on his shattered face.

A search of the rooms came up empty, but entering the northwest bastion, Silas found the body of Benito Sandoval, his body riddled with bullet holes. Sunlight streamed into the bastion from above and Silas looked up to see the roof had been torn open and the body of another Ute lay partially hanging through it. Another dead Ute lay next to Benito.

"Well, at least he took two of them with him," Silas thought. He heard a noise behind him and found Felipe standing there, his face white with the terror.

"Señor Silas..." He could speak no further.

"Come on son, we have graves to dig," Silas placed a hand on the boy's shoulder and led him back out to the gate.

As they went back out to where Baca and Cisneros were tending to Rumaldo, Joseph Doyle with men from the St. Charles and the Huerfano settlements arrived. They carried the body of Joaquin Pacheco with them. His body had been found next to the Arkansas about a half mile from the fort, and it had been mutilated to the point where he was hardly recognizable.

Outside the front gate, they dug a large common grave and in it placed the bodies of Mestas, Martin, Lucero, Sandoval and Pacheco. They dug it deep, placing logs from the fort over the bodies, and covering them with the soil.

After this was completed; they hitched a horse to the wagon and placed the wounded Rumaldo in it and headed to Baca's ranch. As a testament to the dead, they left six bodies of the fallen Ute for wolves.

On the way back to Baca's, they stopped and retrieved the bodies of Juan Rafael Medina and Jose' Ignacio Valencia so they could be buried at the ranch. The body of Guadalupe Vigil, they buried in the puertecito where he had been killed.

On arriving at the ranch, the women came out to see if their husbands had returned to them. All but Rumaldo Cordova's wife were heartbroken; most of all, the wives of Juan Aragon and Tanislado de Luna whose bodies couldn't be found.

After the burial, Silas left for his cabin. There would be mourning at the Baca ranch through the night and into the next day and Silas wanted to distance himself from the death and the grief that followed. He rode up onto the loma and followed the Fountain a few miles before crossing to the west side and then out across the piñon, juniper and cedar covered prairie to swing around and come at his cabin and August's from the north. He was not surprised at what he found, both small structures had been ransacked of what little had been left in them. Silas' books had been thrown about, but mostly undamaged. His tin of tea had been taken, its contents emptied on the floor and the small cones of sugar were missing, along with the small kettle that he cooked in. The other items missing were his dried and fresh meat, and the two blankets and buffalo robe that had made up his bed.

"No great loss," Silas thought to himself. "At least they didn't burn the place down, and I've done alright with a lot less." He turned his attention to the spot where his wife was buried and went to inspect the grave. He was relieved that it had not been desecrated. If that had happened, he might have done something rash like go after the Ute.

Silas returned to the cabin, made a fire and then carefully scooping up some of the spilled tea, placed it in his pint cup and brewed a cup of the rich, black beverage. He could do without the sugar but had to somewhat sift the tea through his teeth to cull out the grains of sand. As he drank his tea, he remembered the bottle of Scotch hidden above the rafter and was pleased to see the Utes had missed it. He smiled and pulling the cork from the bottle took a sip, and then another.

This was how Silas Scott spent the Christmas of 1854, in his own mind counting his blessings, or his luck. As well he might, for the following day the Ute returned to the valley, striking seven miles away at the St. Charles settlement. Some of the inhabitants had left Christmas day going down river for safety but sent nine Cherokee teamsters back to pack up their goods. In the early morning, they were surprised and all nine were killed by the Ute.

Emboldened by their success, the Ute stayed in the area. On December the 27th, they caught Baca's brother Benito and two traders from Bent's about two miles from the ranch and murdered them. In the same day, they moved another ten miles downstream to the St. Charles, and ran off forty-head of Levin Mitchell's cattle, but not before they had killed one of his herders and severely wounded another. In the following days Baca moved his entire family and those of his employees down to the St. Charles settlement, leaving Silas as the sole occupant in the area of El Pueblo.

The thoughts of many battles that he had taken part in ran through the mind of Silas Scott as he stood over the grave of his wife, Red Calf. The two of them had been happy on their little plot of land near the Fountain, and even when Calf had died, Silas still considered it his home. Now, with the pall of death hanging over the little valley he was not sure he could stay. There was a need for some sort of purification, some redemption of the site. It was possible that if left to nature's hand, the land could be cleansed. Now, at Red Calf's grave, he said his goodbyes then saddled up Rocinante and headed south for Rayado.

CHAPTER EIGHT
THE PATH TO WAR

January 1855 – MOON OF FROST ON THE LODGES

Silas Scott had made it as far as Apache Creek when the sun began to drop behind Greenhorn Mountain. Inside the ever-growing shadow of that Comanche Chief's namesake, he searched for a secure place to spend the night, not looking forward to a cold camp. A man alone had to be cautious, and the comfort of even a small fire could be a beacon leading hostiles to his location. He thought he had spied a good place to rest for the night when he was hailed by three riders' coming up from behind him. Instinctively, he pulled back the hammer on his rifle as he turned Rocinante to face the approaching men. Silas' vision had become somewhat diminished in the past year and as in the early morning twilight, dusk made distinguishing details at a distance questionable. Still not sure if it was friends or foes who had called out to him, Silas rested the rifle across his left arm, his right hand on the firearm's wrist, his finger on its trigger, and its barrel pointed at the riders approaching.

"*Hola,* Silas Scott!" he heard one of the men call out, and his apprehension faded recognizing the voice of Marcelino Baca. With him were two other men from the St. Charles settlement, John Jurnegan and Jonathan Atwood.

"*¿Cómo estás, Marcelino?*" *Silas said as the men came to a halt next to him.*

"*Silas, the Ute, they have killed my brother," Baca answered.*

"*I'm sorry to hear that. Benito was a good man."*

"*We moved to the San Carlos and thought we would be safe there, but the Ute are still killing people. We did not expect to see anyone out here except those devil Utes, and were surprised that we found you," Baca said.*

"*We figured you for a lone Ute and was gonna take your hair,"* *said Atwood in English, then asked, "You headed to Taos?"*

"*No, Rayado," answered Silas.*

"We are going to the soldier's fort in Taos, Camp Bergwin. The Army should know what is happening with the Ute," said Baca.

"We're headed over Sangre de Cristo Pass and then down to Taos," said Atwood, "You want to ride along with us?"

"I'll go as far as the Huajatollas," said Silas, using the native name for the Spanish Peaks.

"We sure could use another rifle if need be," said Jurnegan.

"I'm sure the three of you are smart enough to make it to Taos in one piece and with your hair," said Silas, "What say we find a place to camp for the night, and have ourselves a hot cup of tea or coffee?" he asked, the danger of making a fire now diminished by the presence of more rifles. He then added, "You have some about you?"

"Yep, we got coffee with us," said Atwood, "More than willing to share."

"That'll suit me fine," said Silas, and turning Rocinante's head back to the south gave her a kick in the flanks and the four men found a place along Apache Creek to make their camp.

Before daybreak the following morning, the men were in the saddle moving south again. There was little conversation, and what there was concerned the Ute and the uncertainty of the future along the Arkansas.

"You reckon there could be trouble with any of the other tribes?" Atwood asked.

"Can't tell for certain," Silas said, "Possible there might be some from the Apache. Most of the plains tribes war on the Ute."

"Getting to the point where I don't trust none of 'em," said Atwood.

"Smart to just keep one's head on straight, nose to the wind and eye on the skyline," Silas said.

They reached Huerfano Butte, and Silas separated from the other three men, he heading south for the Raton Pass and they went west to the Sangre de Cristo Pass.

Four frigid days later, Silas arrived at Rayado; and Baca, Jurnegan and Atwood arrived at Camp Bergwin near Taos. After telling their story, Atwood went on to the Army's Headquarters at Fort Marcy in Santa Fe. From, there word was sent on to Fort Union where the commander began preparations for campaign against the Ute and their Apache allies.

Upon the news reaching Santa Fe, it was not long before it spread throughout the community, and Bill Craigavon, Whit and

August met to discuss the situation. Their plans for the move to El Pueblo would have to be placed on hold, at least until they knew more about the conditions at the mouth of the Fountain, and the fate of Silas Scott.

The three men decided to go to Rayado, and then if necessary, on to the Pueblo in search of Silas. Before the Army's orders arrived at Fort Union, they had passed the fort and arrived at Rayado where they found Silas Scot safe and sound. Silas told them what he had witnessed at El Pueblo, the massacre of its occupants and the abduction of the Sandoval boys and Chepita Miera.

What he did not know, was that the Ute and Apache had returned to the Arkansas and attacked the Huerfano settlement, this time to be driven off by the well-prepared Dick Wootton and his friends.

After this skirmish, the Ute withdrew, their losses in warriors now outweighing their gain in livestock and corn. With the plunder from their raiding, the Mouache Ute and the Jicarilla Apaches returned to the San Louis Valley and still smarting from their losses at the Huerfano Settlement, they made one final attack on the recently founded village of *San Luis de la Culebra.* Then, assured they had stuffiest supplies to make it through the remaining winter and on into spring, they settled down.

***

February 1855 – Big Hoop Moon

Bear Voice pulled his buffalo robe around him to ward off the cold as he moved across the camp to the lodge of his brother Black Dog. Reaching the lodge, he reached out a hand and scratched on the door cover.

"Come," called out Black Dog, letting his visitor know it was all right to enter. Bear pulled the cover aside and stooping, entered the lodge taking a seat to his right close to the fire.

"Bear, are you hungry, there is buffalo stew, if you want some," said Black Dog from the back of the lodge, where he sat attaching steel arrowheads to wooden shafts. Bear looked over at the copper pot that hung over the small fire. He was immediately offended that his brother would offer him food that had been prepared from a vessel made by the Whiteman's medicine. He shook his head, not sure if his brother had meant to offend or

175

had just forgotten Bear would not use anything made by the Whites.

"Thank you, Brother, but I have just eaten. I only wish to share with you news of what has happened."

"What has happened?'

"Little Antelope, and Carries a Lance, have just returned from trading with Little White Man Bent. They say word has come down that the Ute have killed all the Whiteman near the Boiling River!" Bear was excited and it was the first time in years that Black Dog could remember his brother smiling. *"And, the Lakota have killed many of the White walks-a-heap soldiers on the Goose River!"* he added referring to the Grattan fight at Fort Laramie along the Laramie River.

"And, what does this have to do with us?"

"Do you not see? If someone as insignificant as the Ute can wipe out the Whites, think what the People could do."

"I am not fond of the Whites, Bear, but I have no reason to go to war with them. Let the Ute and the whites kill each other. Let the Cuts Throats and the whites kill each other, it does not matter to me."

"You say you have no reason? What of your daughter? Was it not a White dog that sent her to her death?" Bear was now more excited, but this was not the elation of before, it was anger.

"Do not speak of my child," Black Dog warned Bear, *"She was taken by a bad spirit. We will not talk about this!"* With that said, he turned his attention to his work on the arrows and chose to now ignore his brother's presence. In the Cheyenne way, Bear should have taken the hint that the conversations, was over. But Bear sat for a few minutes before he rose and left the lodge.

Bear Voice spent the next few days speaking to anyone who would listen to him about the weakness of the Whites, and how it was time to drive them back to where they had come, back to where the sun rises.

***

By the end of February, a military expedition against the Utes was organized and on the march with orders to; pursue the Indians, rout them out of their mountain hideouts, and subdue them. This had been done the previous year against the Jicarilla Apache, with success. But, many of the Jicarilla that the '54 campaign had failed to subdue took refuge with the Ute, and these were the Apache that had ridden on the raids with Blanco.

The Commander of Fort Union, General Garland, was certain the Army could chastise the Ute as they had done the Jicarilla. Garland sent Colonel Thomas T. Fauntleroy and units of the 1st Dragoons into the field. With them were six companies of New Mexico volunteers under Lt. Colonel Ceran St. Vrain, bringing the force up to five hundred men.

It was a group of these New Mexico Volunteers who rode up to the Craigavon ranch in Rayado. One of the ranch's herders was the first to spot the group of over a dozen mounted men approaching. He sounded the alarm, and the entire ranch was quick to react. Everyone gathered at the main house, the men standing armed at the walls, the women and children safe inside. Mary Craigavon, rifle in hand, took her own place above the front gate with her sons and Silas Scott at her side.

By the time it was determined that the approaching riders were of no threat, Mary also recognized the rider in the front of the others, Tom Craigavon. Mounted on a spirited gray stallion, he stood out from the others. With his long gray hair hanging over the shoulders of his buckskin coat, and his rifle across his lap, he made an impressive sight. Mary smiled at the spectacle her husband made. He was in his element, riding at the head of a group of frontiersmen, looking toward the horizon in search of adventure. That he had returned home almost a year late from when he had promised was of no consequence. He had returned, he would always return.

"Well, I'll be damned," Silas spoke from her side.

"Aren't we all?" Mary said, puzzling Silas.

"You ain't happy to see him?" he asked.

"Of course, I am, Silas, you old fool," She laughed softly, "I'll always be happy to see that scoundrel." With that said, she turned and climbed down the steps to the ground level. She went to the front gate, opened it and stepped out to greet her husband.

Mary stood, her hands resting on her hips, her chin up, her face showing no emotion as Tom and the other riders rode up and stopped a few yards away. Many of the ranch hands had remained at their positions on the wall; but Silas, Bill, James Duncan and Barret Canfield followed Mary out of the gate and stood behind her.

"Can I help you?" Mary finally said, her voice stern and dispassionate, almost cold. This made an obvious difference in the demeanor of Tom. His brow furrowed, and a bit of his bravado faded away, until a smile broke out on Mary's face.

Tom slid from the saddle and approached his wife. The two embraced, Tom squeezing his wife close to him, and then they kissed.

"I have missed you, woman," he said.

"I haven't missed you a bit," she said, joking.

"Maybe you'll feel better when you see what I brought you." He let go of his hold on her but took her hand and led her through riders to the string of horse behind them. There was half-dozen fine mares, and though in their winter coats, Mary could see the horses were strong and well-bred stock, much like the stallion that Tom had been riding.

"And, I'm to be impressed by a few horses?" Mary said.

"This is better stock than we have ever had. They have more Spanish blood, not so much mustang. With that stud, and these mares, we can grow a herd that will bring top dollar."

"And, what of the stock we have now?" Mary raised an eyebrow.

"We'll do what we have always done, select the best and sell off the rest."

"Are these men part of this new venture?" Mary asked looking back at the riders that had arrived with Tom.

"No, they, we are part of the New Mexico volunteers under Ceran. Along with the regular army, there is over five hundred of us headed north to put down the Ute uprising."

"Ahh..," thought Mary. There is always something to lure Tom away. She looked over the men and back to Tom. "How long will you be staying then?" her disappointment evident in the tone of her voice.

"Until tomorrow," he answered. "I had wanted to bring the horses here first."

"That the only reason?" she asked.

"No, of course not, Mary. I know I've been gone too long, but I only want the best for the future, for you."

"Someday, Tom, the future will be here, and you'll have lost the past." She turned, and as she walked away, she added, "Place the horses in the corral, and have your men look for a warm place to sleep inside the walls of the house. We'll have to feed them if you intend taking them off to chase Indians this time of the year. No telling when they'll next get a chance to have a hot meal."

That evening, the houses large room was filled to capacity, the men with Tom and those of the ranch discussing the planned expedition against the Ute.

It was no surprise that Whit was impressed by Tom. Though he had learned so much about the west from Silas, Tom was different, and Whit was certain that there was much that Tom could teach him. He went to Bill Craigavon, and pulling him aside, asked him about his father. Whit had heard many stories about the past, but now he was more interested in Tom Craigavon.

"As you already must have heard, my father has had many adventures. He was a spy down in Mexico during the war and was almost killed. That's where he received the scar on his face. He's fought just about every kind of Indian from Blackfoot to Comanche."

"You ever go with him to fight?"

"I went with my father, Silas and another friend to track down some people who had made it their life's mission to destroy us. My father is not the kind of man you want as an enemy. But, he is completely loyal to those he calls friend, loyal to a fault."

"What do you mean?"

"He can't seem to stay home for very long. It seems that his loyalties are tied stronger to others than his family at times." Bill paused and after some thought added, "If you really want to know my father, talk to Silas. No one knows him better. Silas took him under his wing when my father was just a boy. We better get back to the others so we can figure out what's going to happen next." They moved back to the others as Silas was questioning Tom.

"So, what is Colonel Fauntleroy's plan?" Silas asked.

"The idea is to establish a base of operations out of Fort Massachusetts, on the eastern edge of the San Luis Valley. From there, we can scour the basin and surrounding mountains for hostile camps. Come with me, Silas," Tom asked. "We haven't ridden together in a long time.

"I haven't had a reason to carry a war hawk," said Silas.

"If Silas is going, I'm going too. Anyway, there might be some need of a surgeon," Bill spoke up, surprising his mother who had stood by listening. Mary remained silent, holding her comments until she could be alone with Tom. Only then would she tell her husband what she thought.

"I'd like to go with you too," Whit offered, receiving a look from Silas and Tom; Silas a bit surprised and apprehensive, Tom delighted to have another rifle added to the force."

"Sure, you can come along, Whit," Tom agreed.

"If Whit is to go, I should go too," said August, beginning to master the sound of Whit's name as well as he had his wife's.

"How are the two of you armed?" Tom asked.

"I have a .50 caliber Deringer rifle, and an Aston pistol in .54 caliber," said Whit.

"My rifle is a .54 caliber Tryon. I do not have a pistol, is that a problem?" asked August.

"No, those rifles are sufficient, and we'll scare up a pistol for you, August. You both should have a good knife though."

August pulled out a big butcher knife from his sheath, and Whit produced the knife that had been his grandfather's.

"You seem prepared. What do you think, Silas, are these two up to chasing some Indians?"

"About as ready as any green grass. Looks like I'm gonna have to go along just to keep them from picking up your bad habits." Though said in jest, Silas meant what he has said. He loved Tom as a son, but he had to accept Tom for what he was, a product of his violent *conflicted* past.

"I see you're packin' a new firearm," Silas said, "Where's your Pap's rifle?"

"The main spring broke on my father's rifle while I was at Fort Union. Ceran found this for me from the Army's arsenal." He went to the corner of room and retrieved his new long arm, handing it to Silas to inspect saying, "It's a Harpers Ferry Rifle in .54 caliber. Effective out past 1000 yards," Tom said. "Same arm Jefferson Davis' Rifle Company used during the war."

"A thousand yards, eh? Take's a good eye to see that far out," Silas quipped. "Caplock, too? What happens when you run out of them little nipple huggers?" He asked about the percussion caps needed to fire the rifle.

"I've plenty, and I managed to get a new sidearm too," Tom said, pulling a pistol from a belt holster at his right hip. He handed Silas a new 1849 Colt's pistol. Silas hefted the six-shooter in his hand, the feel of the curved grips easily conforming to his hand.

"Feels alright, how does it shoot?"

"Took a bit to get used to, but it's a big improvement over my old Patterson revolver. You don't have to take these apart to reload." Tom took the pistol from Silas and showed how the pistol was reloaded by setting the hammer at half-cock, freeing the cylinder to rotate in the pistol's frame. "Come on outside and I'll let you give it a try."

Several of the men followed Tom out into the cold, where he set a piece of firewood up as a target. At fifty yards away, Tom aimed the pistol and fired six shots in succession, each hitting the mark. He then reloaded the pistol and handed it to Silas. Silas' first shot was low, kicking up snow and dirt below the target. His second was a bit high and the following four struck the wood.

"Seems to do the job," was all Silas said. As they walked back into the house, again Silas inquired about Tom's old rifle.

"You didn't just abandon that rifle, did you?" he asked.

"No, it's with the packs, and I'll take in before dark."

"Good. That gun deserves a special place, at least by my thinking."

"Silas, I'd never part with that gun. I remember the day when my Uncle Yellow Turtle walked me into the Creek camp, and we got it back from the bastards that killed my folks. It seemed so big to me then, and now it seems it's a part of my own arm. It wasn't an easy decision to put her aside, and this new one doesn't have the same feel to it, but it was time to change."

True to his word, Tom brought his father's Lehigh rifle into the house. He drove two large nails into the wall above the front door and, in the same way his father had done more than forty years earlier in the backwoods of Tennessee, he hung the rifle with care.

The men with Tom were put up in one of the adobe dwellings of the ranchlands, and for the first time in over a year, Tom shared his wife's bed. There was no awkwardness between them; they had passed that very early in their marriage. For the two of them, no amount of time diminished their closeness, their comfort with each other. It was when they lay curled up into each other's arms that Mary decided to speak to her husband about the plans to take Bill, Whit and August with him.

"You know these boys have never been in a fight," she said.

"Bill had his taste of powder a long time ago, and I understand that August fellow was a soldier back in the old country," Tom said.

"How about Whitney?"

"That young fellow has sand," Tom said, a bit of a chuckle accompanying the statement. "He reminds me of..."

"You?" she asked.

"I wasn't going to say that, but, yep, maybe just a little."

"Tom, I'm afraid he is like you, and if he gets the taste of fighting in his blood it will change him and not for the better. He has the girl and the boy to think about."

"Mary, you know a man can't last out here very long if he doesn't know how to fight, and if he hesitates in doing so, he's dead, and he might just take others with him." With his face nestled in her hair, he hugged her tighter, and then softly said, "I'll watch after them. I won't let harm come to my son, or the other two."

"Don't make promises to me, Tom. I can't count on them."

The following morning, the men mounted up and headed north for the five-day journey. They crossed over Raton Pass, and when they had reached the Spanish Peaks they turned west for the Sangre de Cristo Pass. Once in the San Luis Valley, they traveled on to Fort Massachusetts which would be the base of operations at the eastern edge of the valley. With Kit Carson and Silas Scott as guides, Fauntleroy and St. Vrain's men began to scour the basin and surrounding mountains for Ute and Apache camps. The men and horses suffered from intense cold and deep snow throughout the month of February, but they remained relentless. Their determination payed off, as in the second week of March, near Poncha Pass, they came across a village of Ute and Apache lead by Chief Tierra Blanca.

Spreading out, the Army and volunteer force advanced on the camp from two sides hoping to close in like pincers and stop any retreat the Indians would have. Whit and August rode in next to Tom, trying hard to keep up with him, and Silas followed with more of an eye on the two of them than the Ute.

Charging through the camp, Whit's attention was on the fleeing Ute and Apache, and he failed to properly judge the camp equipment and general debris scattered across the ground. His horse managed to successfully leap over one obstacle, but a stack of lodge poles a few feet beyond proved too difficult for the horse's footing and it stumbled. Its front legs folded under and it rolled forward head-first tossing Whit to the ground. Gaining its feet, the horse immediately bolted, leaving Whit in the dust.

For the briefest moment, Whit lost his senses. Shaken, he was barley on his feet when a Ute warrior was rushed at him with a stone war club raised and ready to strike. Whit could see the Warrior coming at him but had no time to react. In the turmoil surrounding him, Whit heard a gunshot. The Ute tumbled and fell dead at his feet causing Whit to fall back as if the Ute's momentum had been transferred into him.

From his position on the ground, Whit saw Silas Scott looking in his direction as he reloaded his rifle. Silas called out over the din of the battle, "Find your rifle and get back in the saddle!"

Whit located his rifle laying a few feet away and rose to retrieve it. As he reached the rifle, he turned his attention to finding his horse. He spotted it in the possession of another Ute, who with the reins in hand was attempting to mount the frightened animal. Whit drew his rifle up to his shoulder, and with the sights on the Ute's chest, pulled the trigger. The Ute spun and fell to the ground, the horse's reins still twisted in his hand. Regaining some of his composure, Whit immediately reloaded his rifle and made his way to the horse and fallen warrior.

Eyes wide with fright, the horse was pulling at the reins in an attempt to get away from the din of the battle, and the smell of blood that overwhelmed its senses. Whit loosened the reins from the dead man's grip and began to sooth the terrified horse long enough to climb into the saddle. By this time, the fighting had moved on and Whit rode to catch up with those routing the Indians.

They followed the fleeing Ute through the rest of the day, taking up the pursuit the next morning at sunup, and continuing on for three days across the length of the valley to the north. Here, at the saddle between the Sangre de Cristo Range, and the Sawatch Range, the Ute were boxed in with only a narrow pass they named *Pou Nchay* as a means of escape. Called Poncha Pass by the white trappers and traders, this north-south passage led to the rugged country of the upper Arkansas River. Only after capturing the war party's pony herd and killing over a dozen warriors, did the Army and Volunteer force break off the chase.

Colonel Fauntleroy ordered the forces back to Fort Massachusetts where they rested for a period of three weeks. Upon arriving at the picket and lodge post, they went into quarters to recuperate. They sat close to the fires, repaired their horse tack, cleaned and oiled their firearms, and mended their clothing. They also had the time to consider the past weeks as the cold and isolation of the fort drained away the exhilaration of the recent victory against the Ute and the Apache.

In one of the fort's log barracks, Whit finally had the time to talk to Silas. He had a mixture of emotions that he was having a hard time justifying. He was still shaken by his brush with death but chasing the warriors and engaging in battle with them had stirred up a feeling that was new to him. There was a rush of blood in his veins, and the pump of air through his lungs that thrilled him. He had no way to explain it, and he could see it had the same effect on some of the others, especially Tom Craigavon, who seemed to thrive by it. Whit admired Silas, and he had to know if Silas felt the same way he did about the killing. He approached Silas who sat close to the fire, taking advantage of its heat and the light it offered.

"Silas, I been meaning to talk to you," he started.

"'Bout what?" Silas said, the dim light causing him to squint and concentrate his attention on the task of cleaning the parts of the disassembled lock from his Henry rifle. He didn't look up at Whit.

"We been so busy, that I just remembered that I never said thank you for saving my skin."

"Weren't for you. I did it for your boy and the gal you're married to," Silas said, his attention still on his cleaning.

"Silas, there's something else," Whit didn't know how to go forward, "Is it right that I don't feel anything bad about killing those men?"

"Sometimes, a man has to do things that aren't acceptable in a civilized world," Silas looked up at Whit. "I guess it all boils down to how you feel about it. I seen men kill for a lot of reasons. Some of them did it without a second thought, like killin' a snake. Others, well, it ate them up with guilt until there was nothing left of them. And, there are those who just downright enjoy inflicting pain on their fellow man. You just have to make your own peace with what you done."

"Have you Silas?" Whit almost pleaded, hoping Silas would validate his own feelings.

"At times," Silas said and returned his attention to the task of cleaning his rifle.

Whit was disappointed in not getting some form of validation from Silas. Talking with August didn't seem to help as August seemed unaffected, and when asked about how he saw things, he answered much the same as Silas, taking his cues from his father-in-law about how to handle fighting Indians. After some brooding, Whit sought out Tom Craigavon.

He found Tom in a neighboring building in conversation with Kit Carson and Ceran St. Vrain. Whit joined the circle of men listening as they talked. Patiently, he put his own questions aside until he could get Tom alone, until then he paid attention to the words the men exchanged.

"The Colonel and I have decided to split up our forces and go into two different directions," Ceran said, "The regular Army will go back toward Poncha Pass and cross over it to the north, while we go east to the other side of the Sangre De Cristos and scour the plains. We'll do much the same as Anza did back in '79." He spoke of Juan Bautista de Anza, Governor of Nuevo México, who in 1779, led a punitive expedition against the Comanche who had been repeatedly raiding New Mexico year after year. Anza traveled north through the San Luis Valley, crossing over Poncha Pass and entering the plains by circling El Capitan Mountain, called James Peak by the Americans. There he followed Fountain Creek from its headwaters southbound, meeting the Comanche heading northward on their way back to their summer hunting grounds in the Black Hills. Anza surprised the Comanche and entered into a running battle back to the south that lasted for several days. About twenty miles south of the Arkansas River, the Spanish and the Comanche fought a final decisive battle, and the Comanche Chief Cuerno Verde, was killed. The mountain and the creek where the battle took place were both named after Cuerno Verde, translated to Green Horn by the Americans.

A point of irony was that in this battle, Anza's eight hundred soldiers were bolstered by Ute and Apache Indians, who now seventy-five years later were the ones who were pursued.

Whit knew little of this story, but many of the others who had spent most of their lives in the Southwest had been schooled in the history of Indian warfare in New Mexico. It was these men like Carson, St. Vrain, Scott and Craigavon, who knew their foe, and knew how to defeat them. The plan was to hound the Indians, not allowing them to settle in one place for long, depriving them of their ability to secure food and shelter. Sooner or later, the Indians would have to yield to the pressure and accept defeat.

"Once we cross over Sangre de Cristo Pass, we'll follow the Huerfano River out onto the plains, sending out scouts in several directions to see what we find. The main group of us will work our way north toward the Arkansas. See to your firearms, your horses and your personal gear, we'll be heading out day after tomorrow." The group began to break up and Whit caught Tom on his way out the door.

"Can I talk to you, Sir?"

"It's Tom, Whit. You call me Tom."

"Thanks. I've just been pondering a few things and would like your advice."

"Sure, let's go over by the fire and we'll talk."

They found a comfortable seat near the fire and Tom asked, "What's on your mind?"

Whit started much in the same way he had with Silas, "You know this is all new to me."

"And, you've taken to it! I've watched you," Tom said.

"Thank you, but I'm not sure about the killin'. I don't know if the way I feel is right."

"Don't give it a lot of thought, Whit. Do what you have to so you can get back to the one's you care about. Do what's needed to protect them whether it's at your front gate or a hundred miles away. Best think of it like killin' a snake." This surprised Whit. Tom had used the same reference as Silas, but the way Silas talked about a snake seemed different. Whit decided he would work through it on his own.

The volunteers under Ceran St. Vrain headed out, crossing the pass between Blanco Mountain the and the Spanish Peaks, then following the Huerfano down onto the plains east of the Sangre de Cristo Mountains to look for Utes. As they reached the lower altitudes, the snow began to disappear, and the site of green grasses and wildflowers began to appear. Early spring made the front range of the mountains appear as a Garden of Eden and reminded the men why they had fallen in love with this country, and why they were determined to live there without the threat of hostile raids by the Indians.

Scouts were sent out in all directions each morning to search for the Ute and Apache camps, but by the last week of April it seemed they would find no sign of them. On the 26th of April, they had reached the southern foot of the Green Horn and St. Vrain sent out Kit Carson, Tom Craigavon and Silas Scott to scout north, south and east of their line of march. Finding no sign by dusk, Tom and Silas returned to the main force, just in sight of the Huerfano Butte.

Plans were being made to go into camp when Carson came galloping with word that he had spotted a large village on the river below the butte. Using the trees along the shallow river course as cover, the entire force was set back into motion and covered the short distance of less than ten miles. When within striking distance, St. Vrain divided his men sending some to circle to the south and come at the camp from that direction and from some from the east.

The camp was taken completely by surprise, the New Mexicans charging in from three different directions. Whit's apprehension seemed to have melted away, replaced by the rush of excitement and the thrill that coursed through his veins. He rode through the camp, firing at any foe that exposed himself to him, not noting if the target had fallen wounded or dead. He fired, reloaded, and then fired again, his aim growing steadier and more precise with each shot.

The Indians fought back as they fled, but the New Mexicans were a superior force and the battle was over in what seemed like a matter of minutes. When the sound of gunfire had ceased, over a dozen Ute and Apache lay dead and as many were captured, the rest had been put to flight. The camp equipment was destroyed, and the horse herd taken.

Satisfied that the plains were secure, the New Mexicans headed back toward Fort Massachusetts to awaited word from Fauntleroy, not knowing the Colonel had met with success only two days later. Guided by the light of a large bonfire, the Army had crept undetected into positions on two sides of a large Ute camp. As the Indians danced around the fire, the soldiers struck with devastating effect. Frightened, the Indians scattered in the opposite direction, the soldiers hard on their heels, charging through the village engaged in a running battle. As the New Mexicans had done, after routing the Indians the Soldiers returned to burn the lodges, food, and other supplies in the village. Almost four dozen Utes had been killed, and their resistance had been broken.

Colonel Fauntleroy rejoined his two forces, and for the next three months engaged in several more skirmishes. By July, the Indians sued for peace, and Fauntleroy returned to Fort Union and the volunteers were mustered out of the service.

The men from Rayado left Fort Union and returned home, and all but Whit seemed to be content. He alone was still restless, even more so than Tom Craigavon. He had grown to love the idea of being a scout. Whit was convinced that he wanted to get back into the service of the Army, though actually enlisting as a soldier was not attractive to him.

Whit reasoned that though the Ute and the Apache had been subdued, there were still other enemies that would eventually have to be dealt with. Since the opening of the Santa Fe Trail in 1821, the Kiowa and Comanche had made travel on the Trail a dangerous venture. It was the duty of the soldiers at Fort Union to make it safe to travel and keep it open for commerce. It was prudent then, to make regular patrols between the Arkansas River and Fort Union. These patrols soon became escorts when the need arose.

The growing numbers of merchants and freighters knew the conditions of the trail, and most organizing their own defense felt they were safe and didn't require escorts. It was here Whit saw one chance of employment. The other possible employment was with the stagecoaches that ran the route from Independence to Santa Fe carrying the mail. Crossing the Cimarron Desert, south of the Arkansas River, often worried the company or postal officials and they requested the Army at Fort Union for help.

The main problem with the Army escorts was they were not organized in the same fashion as the mail coaches. The escort usually consisted of a sergeant and fifteen to twenty men who accompanied the stages between Fort Union and the Arkansas River in both directions. The wagons that accompanied the soldiers were drawn by mules, and this created a drawback. These mules traveled more than six hundred miles, from Fort Union to the Arkansas and back, without relief. They wore down and had trouble keeping up with the mail coaches who had relay stations with fresh animals on the Mora and the Arkansas. It was with the mail coaches that Whit sought a place to feed his sense of adventure. He could also keep in close contact with the Army in case a time came again to take the field against the Indians. He left Rayado promising Maggie that he wouldn't be gone long, just long enough to put aside some money that would provide them security for the future.

The future on the Arkansas was still uncertain. Though the Ute and the Apache had been subdued, their attacks put an end to the settlements on the Arkansas. In the spring Eliseph Doyle, Ben Ryder, Levin Mitchell and others took their families back to New Mexico. Marcelino Baca, stripped of most of his wealth, returned to Greenhorn and then finally back to Rio Colorado in New Mexico. By summer, only two men and their employees remained on the Arkansas; Charles Autobees at his ranch up the Huerfano and William Bent in his stone fort at Big Timber.

At first Silas had thought about returning to his cabin but he was soon given a reason to remain at Rayado. Willow had given birth to a baby boy and both August and Silas had no desire to venture where the mother and her new child might be put in danger, and there was not really much to go back to if it was only the three of them. Whit had left Maggie and Zachery at Rayado, and with no growing settlements on the Arkansas, Bill Craigavon had no reason to relocate either.

So, it was of those who remained in New Mexico, Bill Craigavon seemed the most restless, and the most disappointed. He returned to Santa Fe and the ranch that had been in his wife's family for years. Starting over at the Arkansas had seemed so promising, and now it seemed the area was deserted. He had not given up though, and still talked about it both with his wife and with the rest of his family at Rayado. He reasoned that the troubles in the north were in the past, it was only a matter of time before people would return and start to settle down.

Willow and August gave more thought to their growing family, and most important in their minds was finding a name for the baby boy. They had almost named the child after his grandfather, but Silas protested, suggesting they choose a name that meant something to them as parents. Not being well schooled in the bible, August asked about biblical names and

Silas suggested a few more obscure ones from the Old Testament, Mordecai being his favorite.

"I will not name my child Mordecai," said Willow. "I have always liked the name John. We do not know anyone named John, do we?" Then to her husband she asked, "Is there a version of John in Danish?"

"Yes, Johan," he said. "It means asked from God, I think."

"Close enough," said Silas.

"Then we will call him Johan, Johan Klausen," Willow said.

"No, he will be John. He is not a Dane, he is an American," August said, "We will call him John."

***

CHAPTER NINE
THE PEOPLE AND THE PILGRAMS

July 1856 - Moon of the Ripening Chokeberries

It was inevitable that the influx of whites crossing the land of the Plains tribes would cause problems. It had been agreed upon through treaties that the only whites that would stay were those that were manning the forts and trading posts; but sooner or later, there were those that chose to stay, settling near these posts and trading houses. Since the Grattan massacre, as it was now being called, tensions grew in proportion to the influx of gold seekers. In 1849 alone, some 80,000 immigrants poured into California, a vast number of them coming overland through the hunting grounds of the Plains Tribes.

Also imminent were the conflicts that resulted between the two cultures that were unable to understand each other. Core values of the incoming tide of immigrants and gold seekers, compared to those of the Plains Tribes, were at times completely opposite. Most of the acts of violence, like the Grattan incident, were more a result from a lack of understanding and overreaction by both sides. In the coming years, the conflicts between the two would devour the entire west.

One item that both peoples agreed upon was the value of horses, and like the Mormon cow, horses were the spark that ignited the first true acts of violence between the Whites and the Cheyenne. In the spring of 1856, Cheyenne hunters found four horses straying on the prairie. To the Indians, these were free for the taking as the owner was not around to tend to them. To the owner of these horses, they were considered stolen property. When news about the location of these horses reached military officials, word was sent to the Cheyenne that the stock must be returned, and a reward was even offered to make the return of the animals less painful. Three of the horses were given up, but the owner of the fourth horse identified refused to relinquish it, stating his horse was not one of the original four found. The commanding officer of the army post ordered the arrest of the first four Indians found. The four unfortunate victims of this attempted arrest resisted, two making good their escape, a third named Otter's Tail was killed while fleeing and the fourth, Wolf Fire, was taken into custody, and locked in the soldier's guard house where he soon died. When the two Cheyenne who had escaped reached the village and spread the word of the encounter, the entire camp broke up and fled. In their retreat, they came across an old trapper by the name of Ganier. Ganier, like Wolf Fire, was an innocent, but like Wolf Fire he was killed. The Cheyenne felt some sense of revenge had been achieved.

By the Breeding Moon, August of the Whiteman's calendar, both the Northern and the Southern Cheyenne hoped that tensions had cooled. In an attempt to resume their normal pattern of life, they gathered a sizable war party of two dozen seasoned warriors with the intent to attack Pawnee who were camped on Grand Island in the Platte River near Fort Kearny. Among those in the war party from the Southern bands were Bear Voice, Little Bear, Sitting Hawk, Little Gun, and White Badger.

While the Cheyenne were encamped not far from the Fort, some of the young men left on their own, a violation of the rules that a war party remain together. Approaching up the wagon road to the fort was the mail coach, and the young men decided to wave it down and ask for tobacco.

The motions of these young Cheyenne appeared threatening to the frightened coach driver and he sped past, pulling his pistol and firing at them. In return, the young men fired back with their bows, one arrow striking the coach driver in the arm.

Alarmed by the gunfire, the leaders of the war party mounted their horses and sped to where the young men had encountered the coach. After finding out what had taken place, the young men were driven back to camp, whipped with quirts along the way by the Dog soldiers. As the weather had turned cold and rainy, the Cheyenne were confident that nothing further would happen, and they remained in their camp for that night.

As the sun rose the following morning, one of the Cheyenne scouts rushed into camp raising the alarm. Fifty pony-soldiers from the fort were approaching. As the soldiers neared the camp, a bugle sounded, and they spread out into a long line. With no parlay or warning, they attacked the Cheyenne. In the first few moments of the charge, ten of the Cheyenne were killed, and the rest, caught off guard, retreated across the river, leaving half of their horses and all their belongings behind. The soldiers, satisfied that they had routed the Indians, did not follow them but captured the horses and plundered the belongings.

"We should have stood and fought!" Bear Voice protested, as the remainder of the war party gathered around a fire to lick their wounded pride.

"And, we all would have been killed," said Little Gun, *"There were twice our number, and they are all armed with pistols and rifles. I have a long gun, but like you, most of our war party has only bows."*

"It would have been better to have died than to have been driven from the camp like dogs," Little Bear said. *"It is the fault of Travels Far and his friends for shooting at the coach driver!"*

"Talk of what we should have done is no good," said Eagle Dog, the leader of the war party. *"We must decide what to do next."*

"We must not go home defeated like this," Bear Voice said, his anger growing.

"What would you have us do?" White Badger asked.

"We must replace our horses, we must take scalps!" pressed Bear Voice.

"Seldom do I agree with Bear Voice, but we must take some kind of revenge," said White Badger.

"I took up the pipe to fight the Pawnee. I am uncertain about fighting the Whiteman," said Little Gun.

"That is because you are White in your heart." Bear Voice was being bold to go up against Little Gun, *"The White blood that flows through your veins is weak and makes you a coward."* he added, pushing further than he should have. Though Little Gun was the son of Silas Scott, Little Gun had lived with his mother's people his whole life and never had he been accused of being anything other than a Cheyenne, let alone being a coward. He was slow to anger, and usually a

rational thinker, but Bear Voice's words sparked a rage in him that was instant. He sprang at Bear Voice and if he had not been stopped, he would have taken the man by the throat.

"It is of no good for us to fight amongst ourselves," urged Eagle Dog, *"Let us search out a way to avenge the attack on us."*

When they were one day's march from the soldier's fort, the Cheyenne came across a small wagon train, the last wagon lagging behind the others. This was an opportunity that was seen as a gift to the Cheyenne and they attacked, killing two white men, and a young boy. With the plunder they received from this attack, their revenge was somewhat appeased, but Sitting Hawk protested that Bear Voice had killed the boy.

"I would have taken him and raised him as my own," Sitting Hawk argued, *"I would replace the child that the White's took from me with the Spotted Sickness."*

"There will be others. The boy was too old to be anything other than a slave," said White Badger, *"You need one young enough that can give up his white ways."*

The attack should have been enough to sate the Cheyenne's thirst for revenge, but they had lost too many warriors and were still in a dangerous mood, and the next convenient target presented itself. Three days distance from Fort Kearny, a Mormon wagon train was making its way slowly up the road westward. As they had the previous wagon, the Cheyenne attacked with little warning and less restraint. This time, they killed two grown men, a woman and another child. A second woman was taken prisoner by Porcupine Bull. She fought him off as best as she could, but once Bull cuffed her across the face with the back of his hand, she submitted to his will. Again, Sitting Hawk voiced his discontent that the small boy could not be taken. But he would wait until another opportunity came. He and the others knew there would be other conflicts with the Whites, and there were bound to be prisoners for the taking.

By autumn, the Southern Cheyenne moved down to the Arkansas and Bent's Fort to receive their annuities, the trouble in the north seemed not to have followed them. The depredations committed in the north had been blamed on the Lakota and the Northern Cheyenne, and the Indian agent on the upper Platte,

Thomas Twiss, seemed to be sympathetic. He reported to his superiors about the dispute over the four horses, the killing of Otter's Tail and the death of Wolf Fire while a prisoner. He also spoke of the killing of the old trapper, Ganier, and the attack on the mail coach and the emigrant trains.

A delegation of Cheyenne leaders who spoke to Twiss told him they deeply regretted what had happened, but they had no control of the young warriors who were reacting to the death of their friends at the hands of the soldiers. With the return of the captive Mormon woman, Twiss seemed to be convinced that there would be no more trouble.

The Cheyenne were not as sure they were safe from conflicts with the Army, and after receiving their annuities the Southern Cheyenne joined their northern brothers and gathered on the Solomon River where they spent the winter months. As in the past, there were those in the camps that took advantage of the People's uneasiness. Among these were men like Bear Voice, who constantly argued that the Whites wanted to fight them, reminding those who had lost relitives of their injury and feeding their anger. Thus, Bear Voice and those like him fostered a growing feeling of injury and hostility with a passion to fight back.

Some of the medicine men in the camps purported that their power was so great that they could make certain motions with their hands and the White Soldiers would fall dead. Another said his medicine could cause the soldier's rifle balls to drop to the ground as soon as they left the muzzles. These medicine men may have truly believed their own prophecies and convinced others that it was true, but Bear Voice understood differently. He felt that his medicine worked from the inside of an enemy. Many times, since the death of Little Bird, he had caused harm to come to those he felt had wronged him. He never chose a specific method of this harm, but it seemed those victims of his wrath always had some tragedy befall them.

So it was that the medicine men performed their ceremonies, as did the soldier societies such as the Dog Soldiers, preparing themselves and the People for the coming year when they would go to war against the Whites.

***

SAM J. PISCIOTTA

January 1857 - Moon of Frost on the Lodge

"Can you tell me again about your trip to California?" Azariah Bolt asked his wife's uncle.

"Yes, I can," said George Yellow Hammer, speaking with a pipe clenched between his teeth. "We were gonna' go up to the Oregon Trial and follow it west, but Daniel Five Killer, who's family had moved out here back in '17, you know, with one of the first groups, he talked us out of that. Anyways, Five Killer, he worked for a man named Bent, up the Arkansas River. Five Killer was a hunter fer Bent, and he said everybody else was headin' up the Oregon Trail and that there wasn't no grass, or no game left along it. He says, if'in we were smart we'd go up the Arkansas 'til we hit the Rockies and then head north to the Laramie and then west again to Fort Bridger, and meet up with the Origen Trail there. He said there was plenty of grass and game going that way." The older man paused, took a draw on his pipe and continued with an exhale of blue-gray tobacco smoke, "We then went on over the mountains to California.

"It were hard out there. Too many folks digging for gold and not enough of it to go around you know. Only men getting rich was the ones selling goods; food, clothing an' mining tools. After almost two years, we had found only a bit of color an' we come home, same as half the people that went out there had done."

"What about the gold you said you found on your way out? That's what I want to hear about," Azariah persisted.

"Oh, that was before we made it to Laramie. When we left Bent's place we followed the Arkansas River to the mountains and then about four days north of it, we came on a big village of Arapahos on the South Platte, must have been a thousand of 'em. We steered clear of them Injins, moving off to the west toward the mountains and when we camped, Jimmy Mixedwater, he dipped his gold pan in a stream and worked the gravel a bit. He hadn't worked no more than two pans and brought out flecks of gold and some nuggets mixed with it. We figured they must have been washed downstream from the foothills."

"Did you go back there on your way back home?"

"Nope, we pretty much had enough of prospecting."

"Do you think you could draw a map to where Mixedwater found the gold?"

"Naw, a fellow would just have to make his way north from the Arkansas until you hit the South Platte, then head west." He took another draw on his pipe and with a chuckle added, "You know, they're calling the route we took the Cherokee Trail? Don't that beat all?"

Azariah Bolt had come to the Indian Territories after leaving Georgia and started a new life among the old Cherokee families living there. He had even taken on a new wife, if for no other reason than to have someone to cook for him and warm his bed. The new wife also gave him a family to be a part of, one than was somewhat forgiving when it came to his drinking, and less concerned that he only did enough work to just get by, the rest of the Yellow Hammer family taking up the slack.

Azariah was filled with a mixture of feelings, frustration being the most prevalent. He was by no means content with his life on the Arkansas River near Fort Smith. It was more a matter of biding his time until something better came along, and in the back of his mind were always the thoughts of gold nuggets laying in a creek bed someplace in the Rocky Mountains, waiting for him to snatch them up. So many things had gone wrong for him he thought. He hadn't forgot what had happened to him back in Georgia and vowed to someday go back there and teach them all a lesson, especially Hammond Burchfield. Azariah was determined to be wealthy someday, and if the rumors of gold were true, his chance at obtaining those riches was close at hand. Then he'd show them, he'd show them all.

***

July 1857 - Moon of the Ripening Chokeberries

The Southern bands of the Cheyenne had traveled for about a dozen suns south, separating from the Northern Cheyenne who had gone in the opposite direction. The apprehension of the winter camp had faded somewhat but was still in the mind of everyone. All doubts of an eminent conflict disappeared when the Northern Cheyenne appeared at the heels of the Southern bands. They had left the Solomon River only a few days when they spotted a large force of Soldiers coming in their direction. They also said that the soldiers had followed them and that it was time to stand and make a fight. They had only to choose where they wanted to meet the soldiers in battle.

They found a place that would be to their advantage on the Cherry River, adjacent to a small lake, and set up camp. There the warriors prepared for battle, each performing his own type of medicine; but many trusting in the words of the medicine men, dipped their hands into the lake expecting to hold them up and stop the bullets harmlessly.

In a few days, six companies of the 4th U.S. Cavalry under Colonel E. V. Sumner appeared. Anticipating their arrival, the Cheyenne drew up in a line that stretched across the valley floor placing the river on their left and a bluff on their right. The soldiers, marching in three columns, quickly drew up into line and the order was given to "Draw - Sabers." With no halt in their march, two companies were detached to turn the Indian's flanks while the remaining companies moved forward at a trot until the order "Charge" was given.

The Cheyenne's medicine had prepared them to turn away the Pony Soldier's bullets, but the Long Knives of these Pony-Soldiers was a different subject. Many of the Cheyenne stood and fought, ducking and dodging the swinging blades, four being killed before the entire mass of warriors turned and fled. Their fresh mounts soon out distanced the soldier's worn horses. Behind them, the Cheyenne left their lodges but had the foresight of packing horses and travois with their possessions as a precaution if flight was necessary. The Soldiers followed the retreating bands as far as the river and then marched up its course to Bent's Fort where Sumner confiscated the Cheyenne's annuities for the year, using these for his command, and giving a portion to his Delaware and Pawnee scouts.

Routed by the soldiers, the People moved further south after crossing the Arkansas River and fell in with the Kiowa, Apaches, Comanche and some Arapaho. It was there, that the Cheyenne went into council arguing on what course to take, and by the following spring no real agreement had been reached.

There were, among the People, many who stood up and voiced that peace should be made with the Whiteman, arguing against fighting such an ever growing enemy.

"I was a boy when I saw my first Whiteman," said Little Wolf, *"Like many gathered here I too have lost those I love. But I see a new type of Whiteman coming from where the sun rises. Those of my youth were satisfied to take the skin of the beaver and at times take a wife from among us. They never stayed long, nor did*

they turn up the soil to plant crops. Those who did stay were like Little Whiteman Bent. I do not understand this new breed.

"We are a mighty people, and as far back as the time of our grandfather's we were the power on the land. We took what we wanted, driving others like the Crow and the Comanche out of the Sacred Hills and the hunting grounds of the grassland. I wonder, if the Whites are not much different. They are powerful and they intend to take what they want."

"You speak like an old woman!" Bear Voice spoke up, surprising many gathered in the council. Though Little Wolf was over fifty winters old, and his hair was as white as snow, he was still a respected medicine man and warrior of the people. Little Wolf had a long history with the Whites. While he was just a boy, he was caught attempting to steal horses from Silas Scott. Wolf learned to respect Silas and had grown up to be friends with Tom Craigavon, the two of them fighting next to each other and spending most of their lives as brothers. Though Wolf had lost a wife, children and grandchildren to smallpox brought to the Cheyenne by a White man, he had never found hate in his heart for the Whites. His son, Sitting Hawk, and a grandson, Little Bear, were of a different mind and they had sided with Bear Voice on calling for war. Now, in council, Little Wolf watched these two as Bear Voice went on.

"Yes, the Whites are powerful, but they can be stopped. We have lost too many good warriors to the Whites. Do you not remember Coyote Ear, Yellow Shirt, Carries the Otter, and Black Bear who were cut down by the pony-soldiers with their big knives? I do not forget them. When the grass greens we should go against them."

"Your words are those of one who looks at the world as a mouse," Little Wolf said, *"You see only what is close to the ground. You must also look with the eyes of an eagle, see further then the end of your nose."*

"I believe we must learn to live with them," said Black Kettle, chief of the Council of Forty-four, *"It is useless to fight against them for they will soon cover the whole country. The buffalo are starting to disappear, and if we do not wish to disappear and survive as a people, we must learn to live in peace."*

"Do you believe we truly can? Have you not heard the words of Comanche and the Kiowa?" Bear Voice asked. *"They do not wish peace."*

As it had many times in the past months, the council broke up with no real decisions made. There were too many viewpoints in the large number of men among the Cheyenne, a people that prized their opinion and pride.

Little Wolf sat in the lodge of his apprentice, Carries the Shield who would someday take the position held by Wolf as the band's medicine man. With them was Wolf's son-in-law Crow Eyes, and Black Kettle. Little Wolf and Black Kettle were close to the same age, and both men had a clear vision of what the future might hold for the People.

"There is some truth in what Bear says," Little Wolf said shaking his head. *"His heart is bitter for many reasons. He has always been ambitious and wishes too much for power. When he was my student, I told him that it is not good for the People to have everything they want. These pale-skinned ones have a medicine that is so different from that of the People, that I believe that the two cannot live together without one of them choking. I thought those who relied on the gifts of the Vé'ho'e, would perish. Now I am not sure this is true. We must find a way to live together."*

"You are right, Wolf. But the Great White Father cannot control the men who come to our country, any more than we can control the young men who want war," said Black Kettle.

"Is it that they cannot control them, or that they do not want to control them?" asked Carries the Shield.

Wolf thought about this and looking at Crow Eyes asked, *"What do you think Crow?"*

"They do not think as we do," said Crow Eyes, *"I have lived alongside them, as have you Wolf, and I see that like the People, no two of them is the same. Some would live with us in peace, and others would have us gone from the land."* He paused for a moment and then added, *"I have raised my son to be a good man, a man of the People,"* Crow said, *"And, I have also let him make the decisions of a man. He will soon see his eighteenth winter. He has already made a name for himself as a warrior, and I believe like many of the young men he will not willingly put down the war pipe to take up the plow and plant corn."*

"I will still speak of peace, with both the Whites and the people," said Black Kettle.

"I fear that the People will be torn apart," said Carries the Shield.

RIVER OF SAND

***

March 1858 – Dusty Moon

Fort Smith bustled with not only the normal activity of a military post, but there was a feeling in the air that excited everyone. Word that gold had been discovered in the Rockies along the South Platte River had reached the east, and now the first of the coming tide of gold seekers had arrived in Indian country. The Russell brothers, William, Oliver and Levi, Ethan Beck and a party of other whites and Cherokee from Georgia were making a brief stop to resupply and rendezvous with more Cherokee from the Territory.

Among the prospectors was Eli Thornton, and as he adjusted the panniers on the packsaddle, he had no idea that he was being watched from the shadows. Slowly a figure moved his way to stand close to Thornton, until he was within arm's length.

"Howdy, Eli." The voice so close startled Thornton and brought him around with an impulse to defend himself.

At first, he didn't recognize the man who stood in front of him but seeing past the man's ragged beard saw it was Azariah Bolt.

"Damn, Tiah! Is that you?" Eli stepped back a bit.

"Yep. Didn't ever expect to see me again, did you?" Azariah said, hiding his own surprise at seeing his old friend. Then, he added, "'Course you probably didn't give much thought to me the past few years, did ya?"

"I've thought about you more than once," Eli said. "How you doin'?" he asked, not really out of concern, but curiosity.

"I'm gettin' by. You part of this group headin' out to the gold country?"

"I'm with the Russell brothers, yes."

"You reckon, they'd be willing to take on another man?"

"I don't know..." Eli wasn't sure what to say. He was sure that Azariah was still probably trouble. "You'd have to ask them. I'm not one that could say."

"I might have some information that would be of help to them," Azariah offered. "Can you take me over and introduce me ta them? Kind'a give an old friend a boost, 'specially after the bad hand I got dealt back in Georgia."

201

"You..." Eli started to remind Azariah that he was lucky he had left with his life, but Eli was the kind of person that felt a fellow deserved another chance. "You come with me and I'll take you over to Mr. Russell." Azariah followed Eli to where William Russell was speaking to one of his brothers.

"Excuse me, Mr. Russell," Eli said waiting for the man to acknowledge him.

Russell turned his attention to Eli and spoke, "Eli, by now you should be calling me William. What can I do for you?"

"This is an old acquaintance of mine, Azariah Bolt." Bolt noticed that Eli had not said "old friend." He held out his hand for Russell to shake.

"What can I do for you, Mr. Bolt?" Russell asked.

"Well, Sir, it's more what I might be able to do for you," Bolt said with some cockiness.

"And, what might that be?"

"You see, back in '49 my uncle, George Yellow Hammer, he went with a bunch over to California looking for gold. And, on the way out there, he stopped on the Platte and said he found some color."

"That's interesting Mr. Bolt, but I already know that there is gold to be found on the Platte River."

"That may be, but the Platte is a mighty big river and someone else might just find that gold before you, that is unless you know exactly where to look."

"And, you know exactly where to look? Is that right?"

"You could say that."

"So, Mr. Bolt, what are you asking for this knowledge?" Russell, like Thornton, thought at this point that Bolt was only attempting to take advantage of the gold fever and extract payment for information that was more than likely false.

"Don't want a single dollar. Just want you to let me go with you. Oh, and maybe you could buy me a drink of whiskey to seal the bargain."

"Do you have a horse, Mr. Bolt?" Russell asked.

"I do, and a good rifle too," Bolt answered.

"You go get your horse and rifle, along with whatever personal belongings you need, and meet us at our camp down along the river. We leave before sunup tomorrow morning."

Eli walked away with Azariah, and as they walked, Eli asked him, "When did you get an uncle here-a-bouts?"

"I been taken into a Cherokee family. They treat me real good, like I was born into them."

"Tiah, I'm not gonna say anything to William about what happened back in Georgia."

"I wouldn't expect you to," Azariah said in a tone Eli wasn't sure how to interpret. It could have been a threat, so Eli decided to give Azariah a warning of his own.

"I will keep my peace, but remember this, I owe you nothing, and if you make one step to the side of things, I'll not hesitate to inform on your past, also I'll deal with you myself."

"You may not find it as easy as you think to deal with me. I'm not the same weakling you kicked across the river." Azariah turned and walked away.

The following morning, Azariah showed up at the camp just before dawn and was ready to head west with the prospectors. William Russell introduced him to the others in the party and before the sun had risen above the treetops, the entire party was on the move.

The Russell\Beck party traveled down the Santa Fe Trail, and along the way others joined in making the entire party swell to over one hundred men. All well mounted and armed, they had not fear of trouble with the native people they might meet; in fact they gave little thought to any type of danger. The Cherokee and Delaware in the party who had previous encounters with the plains tribes actually held them in contempt.

Around the campfire at night, some of these members of the "Civilized" tribes told stories about how the plains people were more likely to turn and run rather than face the devastating fire power of their powerful rifles.

"A Cheyenne may be able to fire four or five arrows in the time it takes me to load and fire once," said one Delaware, "but he has to get in close, and I'll be damned if I'll let him get within a hundred yards of me."

So, assured in their safety and visions of riches filling their thoughts, the party traveled westward until they reached Bent's Fort at Big Timbers. This would be the last vestige of civilization they would see before arriving at the foot of the Rocky Mountains almost one hundred miles further west. For some of the party members, this would also be their first introduction to the Cheyenne and Arapaho, a camp of which was situated along the south bank of the Arkansas River, not a mile from the trading post.

Eli Thornton was one of those who, for the first time, saw what the real plains people looked like. Though he had known Native peoples all his life; Cherokee, Creek, Choctaw, and Chickasaw among them, they were more like the whites Eli had known. The few Cheyenne and Arapaho who were at the post to trade were almost a foreign people in their speech and dress. From head to toe, their hair style, to the cut of their moccasins, they were truly a different breed.

Thornton also met a different breed of Whiteman, the old trappers, men who had survived years in the west, knew the territory and the Indians who inhabited it. One of these men, a gray-haired, bearded figure in greasy buckskin pants, a calico shirt and a head covered with a blue bandanna caught Thornton's interest and he went to where the man was talking to some of the other members of the Russell\Beck party, catching the conversation in mid-sentence.

"Yes Sir, you best be on your toes from here on out," the older man said, "No matter what you've heard, no matter what you have experienced, not a one of you is safe out on his own. You keep in a group, you keep to yourselves and you'll pass through alright. If'in you run on to a group of Cheyenne, or other Indians, you treat them with respect, give them a bit of tobacco, coffee or sugar, and they'll leave you alone. You molest just one of them and you've opened up a hornet's nest." He stopped and taking out a pipe filled it with tobacco and then leaned down to the fire pit where a kettle of some undefined meal was simmering. From underneath the blackened kettle he withdrew a live coal with his bare fingers and lifted it up to the pipe in his mouth to light it.

"They can't be all that fierce," one of the group gathering around the old man said, "Hell, we've dealt with Indians before, and they ain't no match for a good rifle."

The movement of the red coal in the old man's hand stopped just shy of the pipe, and he looked at the fellow who had just spoken. With his free hand, he took the pipe from his mouth and used it to point at the man.

"You take my advice; the Indians out here aren't the sod-busters you know about back in the States. Not to say the Cherokee, Delaware and the like, aren't some of the bravest fighters I have ever had the pleasure to stand next to; but I lived among the Cheyenne and count some as close to me as brothers. I wouldn't want to be their enemy an' have them take me alive. There's more than one fool that underestimated them and ended up with his hair hanging on a belt." With this said, he placed the pipe in his mouth, set the coal into its bowl, drew on the stem, and then exhaled letting out a cloud of blue-gray smoke.

As if this was a sign that the conversation was over, those gathered around moved off. Eli, though, stayed and moved closer to the man, addressing him.

"Excuse me Sir, my name is Elijah Thornton, and I wonder if I might have a bit of your time?"

The man looked up at Eli and nodded his head in assent, then said, "Have yourself a set," and pointed to a bench in the shade of the awning along the wall, and asked "What can I do fer you?"

"First, might I ask who you are?"

"Silas Scott," the man said and held out his hand. Eli took it and it was surprisingly firm, obviously hiding a strength that was held in reserve as needed, not to impress.

"It's a pleasure, Mr. Scott. I didn't catch all that you had said, but your advice sounds like it comes from experience. I was wondering..."

"Now, you're gonna ask me if I know where you can find gold," Silas interrupted Eli.

"No, Sir, I'm wondering what the country to the west is like. Is there good soil there? Could a man make a home for himself out here?"

"Son, my advice is to go back where you came from. The land out here belongs to the Indians, and they demand a heavy price if you stay too long."

"You said you live out here, that you've lived with them?"

"That I have. Went up the Missouri with that damned Spaniard, Manuel Lisa back in '07, came back out here on my own hook with friends in the 20's, lived through the war with Mexico, had a Cheyenne wife and have children livin' with them now. But, with all that said, I'd have to take just one wrong step, run into just the wrong Cheyenne warrior, and I'd have a fight on my hands."

"I see. And, what if there is gold in those hills?"

"Then son, you just might have to pay for that gold with your hair."

"Father," the voice of a woman attracted Silas' and Eli's attention. Walking toward them were two women, one was obviously an Indian dressed in Cheyenne style dress, the other wore clothing like a white woman, but without a bonnet framing her face, her hair pulled back into braids held in a bun by hair pins. She had a dark complexion, and Eli thought she might possibly be a mixed breed.

As the two women walked up to Silas, he stood to meet them, and Eli followed suit. The Indian woman spoke with a little hint of an accent, "Father, the package you were waiting for has come from Westport." She held out a small paper-wrapped parcel, slightly bigger than her hand.

Eli was surprised at first that the woman spoke such polished English, sounding so different from the way she looked, but he was more amazed when he had a closer look at the second woman. Her features didn't hold the same look of the Indian woman, and she was unlike any female he had ever seen. Her complexion, though dark, had a honey tone to it, giving her a warm glow. Her almond-shaped eyes were a soft brown, and her lips formed a slight cupid's bow. Eli found himself staring at her longer than was polite.

"Damn, I had mixed feelings about that coming," Silas' voice broke into Eli's daze. "Hand it over and let's take a look at the damned things."

Silas took the parcel, breaking the string that bound it, and tore the brown paper from a small wooden box. He slipped the lid back on the box and revealed four small hard paper boxes, and a hand-written note. Silas handed the note over to his daughter and she read it out loud.

"Dear Mr. Scott,

In response to Dr. William Craigavon's missive of September, last, please find enclosed optics in three different calibers of visual strength. We offer this fine aid for sight, made by the Philadelphia firm of James Queen & Company. These are made from the finest quality coin silver, and we are more than assured that per Dr. Craigavon's reconditions, one of these will aid in improving your eyesight. Please select the proper pair for your use and return the remainder with a remittance of $1.70."

She stopped and waited for Silas to open one of the small boxes and expose a pair of spectacles. He held them in his hand as if they were some foreign object, unknown to man.

"There is more here in the note, but it just says how this Mr. Holt, hopes you are happy with the purchase and that you can count on him in the future," the woman said.

"Try them on, Uncle," said the woman who had caught Eli's admiration. Her voice was mellow and sweet yet tinged with the smoky flavor of a Spanish accent, making her more exotic. Eli's blood warmed, he was now totally captivated by her.

"Hold on until I figure these out," Silas said and then as an afterthought, "Where have my manners gone? Ladies, this is Eli Thornton. Eli, this is my daughter Willow and our good friend, Magdalena Voss."

"It is pleasure to meet you, Mr. Thornton," said Willow.

"My friends call me Eli," he said extending a hand first to Willow and then to Maggie. "Voss", he thought, "What a strange name for such an exotic woman.

Maggie only acknowledged Eli with a slight nod of her head and a smile, feeling a tinge of discomfort in his presence. The touch of his hand in hers gave her gooseflesh and a flush rose to her dark cheeks. Though uncomfortable with the feeling, Maggie was not displeased.

"There you all are," a deep man's voice broke into the introductions and August strode up, a small boy riding his shoulders, another older child walking beside him.

"Ah, Eli, this is my son-in-law August, and that rascal on his Papa's shoulders is my grandson Johnny," Silas said introducing the big Dane to Eli.

August shook Eli's hand and like Silas', it was firm, but had a reserved strength that in August was obvious by his powerful muscles.

"And, who is this?" Eli asked looking at the small child that looked as much Cheyenne as Willow, expecting it to be another of her children.

"That is Zachary, my son," said Maggie, bringing more questions to Eli's mind and adding to the mystery about this woman. He wanted to ask where her husband was, if she did indeed have one, but knew it would be rude.

"¡ Mamá, tío agosto me dio azúcar!" Zachary said holding up a piece of stick candy.

"Do you have some to share with your Grandpa?" Silas asked the boy, and the child held up a bundle of the sweets wrapped with paper. Silas gently waved it off saying, "You save it for me." and winked at the child.

"Now Father, show us your new spectacles," Willow said, and obeying, Silas tried on a pair, squinting as he attempted to look through them.

"Too strong," he said and removed them to try another pair, and then the third and finally the fourth. He repeated the process several times until he found the ones that suited him and gave him the best vision.

"Vell, do you see better?" asked August.

"A bit, but I'll have to be careful as not to break them," Silas said. "It appears that I'll have to send these others back to this Mr. Holt, and I best get that over with before we leave for home."

"Where is home for you, Mr. Scott?" Eli asked.

"Upriver yonder." Silas pointed with a thumb over his shoulder.

"Ve have a ranch, west of here, where the Fountain meets the Arkansas," August offered, receiving a side glance from Silas.

"So, you do live in the territory of the Cheyenne?" Eli questioned.

"I've already told you that. But, you're lookin' for gold and there ain't any where we live."

"I understand that, but if I may, I'd like to visit you before I go back home to Georgia."

"If'n you still have them curly locks of yours after your done diggin' all over the mountains, you're welcome to stop by fer a cup of coffee," Silas commented and as if to dismiss Eli, said, "We'd better get our supplies loaded and head out of here, I want to be half way ta the Apishapa before dark. Anyway, I want to get ahead of these pilgrims before they burn up all the firewood and scare off all the game along the trail." If Eli had known that Silas was lumping him in with these "pilgrims," he showed no sign of it, and took no offence. He did note though, where August had said the location of the ranch was, and thought that someday he would make his way there in hopes of seeing the beautiful Magdalena again.

The Russell\Beck party left the following morning. After discussing the country to the west with Peter Goodall, Charles Bent's number one man, William Russell and John Beck were satisfied that Bolt had been telling the truth about his knowledge of the territory along the South Platte River. With the new information gleaned from Goodall, they decided that rather than following the Santa Fe Trail west, they would turn northwest making an almost straight line for the headwaters of the South Platte some one hundred and seventy miles away.

By May, they had reached the South Platte and began prospecting in the riverbeds, exploring Cherry Creek without success. After twenty days, several of the men became disheartened and decided to return home, leaving the Russell brothers and ten other men behind, including Eli Thornton and Azariah Bolt. Finally, in the first week of July, a small placer deposit was found near the mouth of what was being called Little Dry Creek. This yielded about twenty ounces of gold, worth several hundred dollars. This was the first significant gold discovery.

Each day brought out more gold, but not in the quantities that had been expected. They men finally decided that the gold had to have been washed down from the foothills further west, and slowly moved in that direction with limited success. The amount was enough though, and word of the discovery reached Kansas City by fall. The newspapers picked up the news stating that the gold had been discovered near Pike's Peak, and like a spark to dry tinder, the flood of gold seekers headed west. It made no difference that Pike's Peak, or James Peak as it was more commonly known, was far south of the gold strikes, for the new Argonauts headed west with the slogan, "Pike's Peak or Bust" on their lips.

By the following spring, more discoveries were made further into the mountains, and following the "color", William Russell discovered placer gold deposits in a gulch that was soon named for him. By the coming fall, there were almost one thousand men mining gold in Russell Gulch, and a small town sprang up near its head to serve the miners.

Small towns began to appear along the Front Range, spurred by the mining. One, called St. Charles, sprang up at the confluence of the Platte River and Cherry Creek, and William Russell and his followers, erected their own settlement on the south side of Cherry Creek. To compete with St. Charles, where lots were being sold at an inflated price, Russell offered land free to anyone who was willing to build and live there. He named the little town Auraria, after Auraria, Georgia. It soon grew to over fifty cabins and boasted of having its own post office. St. Charles was soon all but abandoned, until land speculators form Kansas, General W. Larimer and Captain J. Cox, arrived and moved onto the site. They unpacked their wagons, and with the blessing of the Territorial Governor James W. Denver, established the new town of Denver City.

Since the first camp on Cherry Creek, Eli had found the excitement of searching for gold had tarnished. He had made enough to keep himself fed and a roof over his head, even though it was canvas, but the riches he had envisioned eluded him as it did most men in the mining camps. Eli shared the canvas-roofed, log cabin with Azariah, and two other men, in Auraria, and by spring he was coming to the realization that going back to Georgia a rich man was a dream never to be fulfilled. The cost of a farm and slaves to work it were still out of reach for him.

This realization was accompanied by the fact that those making the real money were not the miners. Someone needed to feed all those hungry prospectors, and food prices were high. There was good money to be made, but Eli wasn't sure how to get in on the now growing population of farmers and ranchers moving in to raise potatoes, corn, pumpkins, squash, and wheat, along with cattle and horses.

There might be a possibility, he thought, of land to the south, down along the Arkansas, where Silas Scott had his ranch, and where he could find the woman with the soft brown eyes was.

***

CHAPTER TEN
THE WHITE TIDE

March 1860 - Dusty Moon

The Cache la Poudre, Lodgepole Creek, Pawnee Creek, Clear Creek, Cherry Creek and Box Elder Creek drain the large basin located on the front range of the Rocky Mountains. These waters flow into the South Platte River as it makes it way out on to the Great Plains. Called the Fat River by the Cheyenne, the South Platte and its tributaries were always a source of game during the winter months as they offered water and forage to both man and beast. It was near the headwaters of Cherry Creek, on a ridge of this basin's south edge, where the group of Cheyenne hunters gazed out in surprise, stunned by the haze of smoke that hung low in the cold air, trapped in the bowl-shaped depression.

"*Is that a single village of the Whiteman?*" Red Fox Waiting asked his father.

"Yes," answered Little Gun. "*That is a single village. And there is the village of the Blue Sky People we have been searching for.*" He spoke of the over three hundred lodges of Arapaho who were camped east of Denver City.

"*That is why we have not been able to find game,*" said Little Gun's other son, Turtle Shell. "*They have either killed it all or driven it away.*"

Little Gun was almost sorry he had brought his boys with the hunting party. The presence of so many Whites could be dangerous and neither boy was of warrior age, Turtle being twelve and Fox only ten years old. There was comfort though that the other members of the hunting party were older men, all experienced and reliable.

Below them, Denver City spread out, a scattering of structures, houses, and tents. It was hard for the Cheyenne to calculate how many people there were in the White settlement, but the number of Arapaho lodges meant there were close to one thousand men, women and children of that tribe.

"It has been coming to this for ten winters," Sitting Hawk said, *"The Vé'ho'e promised this land was ours, and we have allowed them to cross it in peace with the promise they were not to stay. But look, there they are."*

"How many times must we allow this?" Bear's Voice asked. *"They have made war on the People many times, attacking and killing our people and we do nothing. Now, see, they have built this...this village, and you know they are here to stay."*

"How can we stop them? Every time we have fought with them, we have lost warriors we cannot replace," said White Bear, speaking of the past half dozen years. The small skirmishes had only built tension with the Whites, and most of the People knew it was a matter of time before war would break out. *"Now it appears that our allies the Blue Sky People are living with the Vé'ho'e! Will they too rise up against us?"*

"No, I do not believe so," said Little Gun, *"They only camp to trade for the powerful things the Vé'ho'e offer; firearms, powder and lead as well as blankets and other things they cannot make themselves."*

"What are the Vé'ho'e here for? Just to trade?" asked Turtle.

"They are driven crazy by the yellow rocks they pull from the earth," said Little Gun, who knew far well the value of gold. *"They will cut into the earth looking for it."*

"Why would they want to search for something that makes them crazy?"

"They are the same as those who are possessed by evil spirits. They are confused and do not know how to live like a human being."

***

The hoarfrost made visible patterns on the cabin's canvas roof as sun light began to fill the small structure. Eli Thornton shivered under his blankets, though he was much warmer this morning than he had been in the past. He was lucky enough to have found two new blankets the previous day, paying eighty dollars in gold dust for each. He knew of men paying more than that for blankets that were worn and contained more holes than wool. From the relative comfort of his pallet, he opened one eye to see if there might be any sign of a fire in the crude fireplace but was disappointed to see nothing but dark ashes. Reluctantly, he threw aside the blankets, shivering from the assault of cold air against his thin clothing. His first action was to pull on his coat and his boots. Then he moved over to the stone hearth and with numbing fingers, took out flint and steel to strike sparks into tinder and start a fire.

Starting with a few small flames, the fire grew as Eli placed larger and larger kindling onto the pile. He heated his hands in the warmth of the growing fire, and when satisfied that he could leave the blaze unattended, he turned to the task of making coffee. Old grounds had been left in the pot as a matter of economy; each and every ounce of flavor had to be extracted from the roasted and ground beans, their value equaling almost that of gold. Green coffee beans sold for up to five dollars a pound. Sugar, at almost a dollar a pound, was a luxury that was done without. But, coffee, that was another story.

The "False Spring" in February had offered a few warm days, but the nights were cold, ice still clung to river and stream banks and the ground remained frozen. Thoughts of giving up and heading south again crossed Eli's mind. He had heard several of the miners talk about the land around the mouth of Fountain Creek, and that some men had already settled there, using the adobe bricks of the old post to build their homes. This was not the only new settlement in the south. Approximately fifty miles south of the Arkansas, a Spaniard, don Miguel Antonio Leon, and a family named Atencio had settled on the north side of the Cucharas River naming the new village La Plaza de los Leones. Other New Mexicans, Pedro Valdez and Felipe Baca, while hauling flour from Mora, New Mexico to the gold fields, traveled through the Purgatore Valley and decided it would be a good place to settle. So, they brought a dozen families to the site and named it el Trinidad. Eli worried that by the time he made it south there might not be any land left to settle.

In the time it took for the coffee to boil, Eli had made his decision. He figured he had enough gold to buy some supplies to see him south. The last time he had held the small, leather bags that contained his dust, flakes and nuggets, he judged it all weighed close to three pounds. At twenty dollars an ounce, that meant he had over nine hundred dollars saved. He smiled to himself, and to reassure the sense of security his hoard gave him, he went to his bed and lifted up the blankets on his low pallet. With his knife, he pried up a board about halfway down the length of the bed. The hole, underneath his bed, where he had thought his gold was safe, sat empty. The five small bags of his past year's labor were gone. His immediate reaction was to turn to where Azariah slept, and only then did he notice that bed was empty.

"That son-of-a-bitch!" Eli's voice woke Hezekiah Cable and Nealy Engel, the other two occupants of the cabin, Cable, almost tumbling from his blankets.

"What the hell you yellin' about?" asked Engel.

"That bastard Bolt, cleaned me out. My gold is gone!"

This prompted the other two to look where they thought their gold was safely hidden, only to find that they too had been robbed.

"Mine's gone!" said Engel.

"Damn, mine too!" said Cable, "And, my Colts pistol is gone!"

"I still have mine," said Eli, and reaching to where he hung the belt and holster, opened the removed the pistol and rotating the cylinder, checked the percussion caps, of the .36 caliber six shooter.

"He didn't take my Walker," Engel said, hefting the heavy .44 caliber pistol, and then added, "Let's go find the bastard." The three men left the cabin and found Bolt had taken the mule and the best one of the saddle horses. They saddled up and started a search of the crooked muddy streets of Auraria, stopping at each of the tent-city's merchant establishments with no success. They then crossed over to Denver City and started the same process. Near mid-day, they came to the store operated by Charles Blake, one of the original Russell\Beck party. Blake had brought with him four wagon loads of merchandise and was honest as well as fair when it came to handling gold dust.

"Sure, I saw Bolt this morning. He was waiting for me when I opened for business," Blake said, "Traded him some supplies for dust."

"He say where he was headed?" Eli asked.

"No, I figured he was headed back to your claim," he paused and added, "I figured you boys were just stocking up."

"He was stockin' up," said Engel, "The bastard cleaned us out!"

"Hell. That's a shame boys. I wish you good luck in finding him."

The three men left the store and standing at the side of the street, they discussed their options. All three wanted to go after Bolt, but they couldn't leave their claim unattended, and at least one of them would have to stay at their dig site. It was decided as Engel and Eli both still had their firearms, they would be the ones to look for Bolt, and Cable would remain behind.

Now, the decision was where to look for their thieving friend. They all agreed that Bolt must have left the mining towns, and would probably head back to the States or Indian Territory. Bolt was also not one to take chances striking out across country and would take a well-traveled road, either the Cherokee Trail south or the newer Smokey Hill Road east. Engel said he would go east along the Smoky Hills road, and Eli was more than happy to go south. Both men knew there was danger to traveling alone, but the desire to catch up with Bolt far surpassed the need for caution.

As he rode south, Eli chided himself, for his thoughts were on Magdalena, and not on finding Azariah Bolt. On the road toward the Arkansas, each group of men he passed had no news of Bolt, and it seemed as if Azariah had disappeared from the face of the earth. It was possible that Bolt hadn't gone south at all, and that heading in that direction was a waste of time. But, there was the chance he would see the beautiful woman with the soft brown eyes and enchanting voice. The sooner Eli made it to Pueblo, the sooner he could confirm whether Azariah had gone that way or not. And, he could also ask about her.

***

Azariah had made over twenty miles along the Smokey Hills Road before the sun started to drop behind the mountains at his back. He had convinced himself that there was little to no chance his partners would miss him until late in the day, and then they would only become concerned about his absence after he failed to return to the cabin that night. It would probably be the following morning before they started to look for him, that is, if they worried about him at all. "Why should they?" he thought. They didn't give a damn about him, and his disappearance would be no more than a slight inconvenience. They'd miss the mule and horse more than him. That is, until they found he had

215

SAM J. PISCIOTTA

cleaned them out. By then, they wouldn't have any idea where he had gone, and he'd be so far away there was little chance they would ever catch up with him.

The security offered by a hidden spring, and a small grove of trees south of the trail, made the perfect place for Azariah to spend the night. He threw caution to the wind and made a small fire where he cooked some bacon and brewed some coffee; these he relished along with one of the biscuits he had purchased from Charles Blake's store. There, in the comfort of this secluded hiding place, he fell asleep with a full stomach and an unfettered conscience.

"You move more than your eyelids and I'll scatter your brainpan!" Azariah's sleep was broken by the sound of Nealy Engel's voice, and the feeling of a cold, hard pistol barrel pressed up against his temple. He opened his eyes and looking up saw Engel's angry face above him.

"Nealy, I..." Bolt started to speak but Engel cut him short by pulling the heavy Colt Walker up and bringing it down hard, striking Bolt across the head with the barrel, knocking him senseless. Engel then pulled Bolt out of his blankets, through the cold ashes of the fire and out onto the frigid ground away from the small camp's equipment.

He then started to go through the bedding and packs searching for the stolen gold. When he found the small bags of dust and nuggets, he turned to look at where Bolt now sat, head in hands, the blood oozing from the laceration on his scalp flowed down his forehead and into his eye.

"You no-good bastard," Engel said, "I can't think of anything lower than stealin' from men you've lived and worked beside. You'd never have made it on your own if we'd not carried you."

"Sure, you carried me," Bolt said, "And, you never let me forget it. You was always remindin' me how I owed you and the others. Well, I deserved better. I worked just as hard as the three of you and never once did any of you say so."

"So, you decided to steal from us?"

"You owed me for the way you treated me," Bolt said and reaching down to his boot top pulled out a slender double-edged knife, called a "toothpick", its ten-inch blade reflecting even in the early morning light.

"You stupid bastard, I was just waiting for a good reason to shot you," Engel said and leveling the big pistol in Bolt's direction pulled the trigger. The Walker's hammer slammed down on the percussion cap, and there was the dull thud, the sound of a misfire. Before Engel could pull back the hammer to the next round in the pistol, Bolt threw the knife, its razor-sharp blade driving deep into Engel's chest. Engel dropped to his knees, a look of shock on his face. He fell back, his life's blood pumping from the wound.

Bolt rose to his feet and took the few steps over to Engel. Reaching down, he easily pulled the knife from the man's body. He wiped the blood on the dead man's chest and replaced in his boot. He rekindled the fire, brewed some coffee and calmly ate another of the biscuits.

When he had finished his coffee, he rose and rummaged through Engel's pockets taking the man's pocket watch, a jack knife, and a pouch of tobacco. Laying on the ground was Engel's Walker Colt, and Bolt picked up the heavy pistol. The Walker was twice as heavy as the pistol Bolt had stolen from Cable, and it carried .44 caliber bullets. Eyeing Engel's boots, but finding them too small, he left them on the dead man's feet. He then turned his attention to packing up camp. When that chore was complete, he headed out on the trail, pulling the pack-mule and Engel's horse behind him. As a caution, he turned south, away from the Smokey Hills Trail.

By mid-day, Bolt decided to rest and started a search for another secure place to stop out of sight. The surrounding terrain was a sea of rolling hills, sparsely covered with pine and cedar trees, but there appeared to be a dip or depression not far from him and Bolt headed in that direction. The depression turned out to be the head of a larger gully that widened out into what was a now a dry stream. Following this, Bolt rode about a quarter of a mile and when satisfied that he was secluded enough as not to draw attention from anyone who may pass by, he built a small fire and cooked some bacon. There beneath the branches of an aged cedar tree, he concentrated on his anticipated meal, failing to notice the six Indians who had ridden silently up to within a few yards.

Blue Crane and his friends had ventured out from the village with the intent of hunting for antelope or possibly deer in the rolling hills to the west. They had been unsuccessful, blaming the weather, lack of grass, or bad medicine. Each one of the young men holding their own suspicions, but all of them grateful to have a chance away from the camp, its older men, and especially the Dog Soldiers who seemed to find fault in every action they took.

"*I am made to think that if the lodges depended on our skill as hunters to survive, we would all starve,*" said Small Belly.

"*You may be a poor hunter, but the rest of us can see tracks where others do not,*" quipped Bobcat.

"*Well, then where are those tracks, Bobcat?*" asked Wolf Horn.

"*You must learn to be patient,*" said Blue Crane, "*There is always something to hunt, you must only keep your eyes open and your mouth shut.*"

"*Look,*" said One Bad Leg, "*There are tracks of the Whiteman's horses. See the marks left by the metal they place on the hooves?*" All six of the young men now spied the tracks that lead from the well-traveled trail off into the broken landscape to the north.

"*Let us follow them,*" Red Arm suggested.

"*They may have the rifles that shoot far,*" said Bobcat, not sure he wanted to encounter a well-armed, Whiteman with a rifle.

"*There are only three horses. That means we are twice the number of the men who made these tracks,*" Red Arm said with confidence.

"*Look, one of these may be a long-eared horse. Two have left round tracks, the other has hooves that are narrower and longer,*" Wolf Horn pointed out the hoof prints left by a mule.

Not waiting for the discussion to continue, Blue Crane kicked his heels to start his horse in the direction that the tracks led. With no further protests from Bobcat, the rest of the young warriors followed their impromptu leader.

The tracks moved down into a drainage that widened out. As if to help them find their prey, the smell of smoke drifted in the air, getting stronger as they rode on until they spotted a single Whiteman squatting near a fire, cooking meat.

They had ridden to within a stone's throw of the man before he realized they were there, and a look of panic crossed his face. This emboldened the young men and they slid from their ponies and strode up to the campfire. Small Belly spoke to the man, not caring if his words were understood or not.

"Thank you, friend, for making a meal to fill our hungry bellies," he said reaching down into the frying pan with his knife to snatch up a piece of the sizzling meat. He placed the hot morsel into his mouth and then spit it out, not liking the taste of bacon. He looked up at the Whiteman, who was now visibly trembling, and added, *"You are a poor cook."*

Wolf Horn saw the man reaching for the leather pouch suspended from his belt and knew that the flap on the pouch covered the handle of a small gun. He had seen these worn by the White pony soldiers and knew that it took time to pull the firearm free. Wolf Horn raised his bow, an arrow ready, its string seated in the nock. The man, seeing this, stopped his reach for the pistol and raised both hands to show he submitted.

By this time, Bobcat, One Bad Leg and Red Arm had started going through the man's possessions, tossing aside anything that did not look of value. Red Arm came across the small pouches of gold dust and nuggets. He tore each of these open to inspect the contents and finding these of no use, tossed them over his shoulder, spreading the gold across the ground.

Blue Crane walked up to the man, and reaching down, unsnapped the holster flap pulling the Colt revolver free. Feeling the weight of it in his hand, he became excited. He now owned a firearm. This would increase his status among the People. He took the belt from around the Whiteman's waist and placing the pistol back in the holster, cinched the leather belt around his own waist.

"There are many things here we could take with us," said Bobcat.

"Yes," said One Bad Leg, *"Kill him, take his scalp and we can go back to camp!"*

Wolf Horn drew back the arrow and was ready to lose it when Blue Crane stopped him saying, *"No, we have been told by the elders that we are not to kill the Whites."*

"Let us take his possessions, and leave him alive then," said Red Arm.

"This is good," said Blue Crane, *"Take what you want and burn the rest, we will leave him unharmed."*

The fire grew higher and hotter, the smoke growing black from the unwanted items that were added to the flames. The last articles to be burned were the tall boots the man was wearing, the sharp knife hidden in one of them saved by Small Belly.

Nothing would be left behind, not a morsel of food, not a stitch of clothing.

"*Look how pale his skin is,*" said One Bad Leg, "*He is the color of a fish's belly!*"

"*See how small his man part is!*" said Bobcat, laughing as he poked at the man's genitals with his bow.

"*I wonder if his blood is as dark as ours,*" said Red Arm, then turning to Blue Crain he added, "*I would have his scalp.*"

"*We have been told not to kill any Whites!*"

"*It would not kill him, unless he is weak. I have seen Whitemn at the trading posts that have no hair on the top of their head, and they were not dead.*"

"*Be careful then,*" said Blue Crane.

Red Arm stepped over to the man and reached out grabbing the Whiteman by the hair. He pulled him off his feet, forcing him face down on the ground. He then placed a knee in the man's back to hold him and again taking a handful of locks, ran his knife around in a circle, half the size of a man's hand, cutting the top of the man's scalp. The man screamed and thrashed about, but Red Arm's weight held him to the ground, and he could not escape. As the Indian gave a final tug, the scalp came free and the man let out one final cry of pain.

The young men rode off with their new valuables, Blue Crane and Wolf Horn each with a pistol, and the other three with the horses and the mule. The remainders of the man's possessions were packed onto the mule. These would be given away as presents when the young Cheyenne Warriors returned to the camp. This generosity would gain them much respect among the People.

Before them, across the grassland, they drove the pale, naked man. When their amusement faded, they casually rode past him, leaving him behind, none of them caring to glance back.

Azariah Bolt stood and watched as the Indians rode away. His face and beard were covered with the blood that had ran down from his wounded head, and his bare feet bled where he had stepped on sharp stones or cactus thorns had pierced his flesh. He shivered, and for the first time since the Indians had ridden up on him, he let his complete fear loose and fell to the ground, curled up in a ball and began to shake. He did not remember falling into the blackness of unconsciousness, but when he woke, it was dark, and he was freezing. He sat up and pulling his legs up against his chest, waited out the night until the sun broke over the horizon.

With the dawn, Bolt awoke and shaking, stood up to look about him, not knowing where he was. He started to walk, picking the direction he was facing with no real destination in mind, driven only by the will to survive.

Azariah Bolt was cold, naked and lost in a hostile world, but in his mind, he was sure of one thing, someday he would get vengeance on those who had stripped him, humiliated him, taken his scalp and left him to die.

***

Five hard days of riding brought Eli to the cluster of shacks, small houses and tents on the Arkansas now called Pueblo. It took less time to ask around about Azariah than it did for Eli to water his horse and decide that the trip had been useless. He was sure now that Bolt had not come this way. His knew that he had a duty to turn back to the north and his two remaining partners. He owed them that and felt that one night's rest would not matter that much. With this in mind, he found lodging in the only hotel, if it could be called that, in Pueblo.

The establishment no more than a tent stretched over a rough-hune wooden-planked floor was operated by Abbott Sager and his wife, Amelia. Sager was off hunting, but Mrs. Sager offered a hot meal and a bed for the night. The bed was one of eight raised pallets in a portioned off section behind the front of the "Hotel" where meals were served.

Amelia Sager offered a plate of beans and elk steak, with biscuits made from bleached flour. As Eli ate, he casually inquired about Silas Scott. Mrs. Sager told him that Silas and August Klausen had a ranch up-stream on the Fountain. More than willing to talk, Mrs. Sager went on telling Eli everything she knew about Silas and his "little tribe" as she called them.

"They're all related up there, Scott and the Craigavons," she said, "The Doctor and his wife are a good sort. Up here from New Mexico, I hear. But I'm not sure about the others. The old man carried himself a squaw for a number of years. That's where the Indian gal comes from, the one married to that German fellow.

And the Mexican gal, her husband is a scout for the Army, and mean as a rattlesnake I hear."

"What's his name?" Eli asked.

"Who? Oh, the Scout? Whitney Voss."

A husband, thought Eli, something he hadn't considered. Now that he knew the woman was married, he had to look at her in a different light.

At dawn the following morning, Eli turned north following the Cherokee Trail, but from the opposite side of the river. He first came across the ranch owned by the Doctor. Passing this by and keeping to the trees, he made his way two miles further upstream to the ranch of Silas Scott.

Under the cover of the barren cottonwoods, Eli sat on his horse and watched the house. It wasn't long before she appeared crossing the open space between the house and what appeared to be a well in the yard. Though at a distance too far for him to see her clearly, Eli imagined her face, and for the briefest moment was tempted to go cross the river, go to the house and speak to her. But, an overwhelming feeling of shame came over him, and he turned his horses' head north and rode away, his heart aching.

***

Irrigation water would soon flow through the ditch from Fountain Creek out into the neat rows plowed into the field that had been cleared of trees by August and Silas. Willow and Maggie worked the rows of freshly turned earth in preparation for sowing the seeds for corn and beans. Produce, such as carrots, would be planted closer to the house and would have been in the ground for almost a month before the corn and beans. Other crops would be added as the season changed, and the threat of frost diminished. Already small weeds were starting to break through the soil and the women carefully hoed the rows.

Zachary and John played games, chasing each other up and down the rows, receiving a warning by the women to be careful where they stepped. Zachary, having the edge on the five-year-old by being twice as old, never took advantage of John, despite his age and size. He loved the other boy as if they were brothers.

"Zachary, that's enough," called Maggie, "It's time for you to help us.

"I will, Mother," Zachary called back in Spanish, *"Come little brother, our mothers need our help,"* he said to John, changing to Cheyenne, the language they spoke mostly to each other. Both boys had been taught to speak the languages of their parents; English, Spanish and Cheyenne, and used these, switching from one to the other with ease.

John was not as much help in the weeding as Zachary, but he helped gather the unwanted foliage and piled it at the side of the plowed rows. With the added help, the weeding was complete by mid-day, and the women and the boys walked from the field to the sod and log house for a noon meal.

They had just reached the porch when Zachary pointed out toward the field and said, "Look." A group of Indians on horseback was approaching, riding directly through the freshly plowed field.

Without a word to each other, both women reacted to the possible threat. Maggie ushered the boys into the house, and Willow grabbed a rifle from just inside the door and stood with the weapon ready to fight if need be. Maggie reappeared, taking a place beside Willow, a double-barreled shotgun in her hands. As the riders grew closer, Willow saw that they were Cheyenne and she lowered the rifle and set it against the cabin wall, still within reach.

"They are of the People," Willow said calmly, though still apprehensive.

"Do you think we are in danger?" Maggie asked.

"I do not know. That will depend on what they want."

"I wish the men were here," Maggie said, thinking of Silas and August. They had left earlier in the day for Dr. Craigavon's ranch a few miles downstream, closer to the cluster of buildings now called Pueblo.

"We will be fine," said Willow, "If we stand our ground." She took a step, and holding her hand above her eyes to shield the sunlight, she smiled and added, "It is my brother."

The riders came up to the house and stopped. At first, they said nothing, looking around as if to search for something in particular, then Small Gun spoke to his sister in Cheyenne.

"My heart is happy to see you sister," said Little Gun.

"And mine to see you brother."

"Where are the men?" he asked.

"Our father and my husband have gone but will be back very soon."

"What of the Mexican woman's man? Where is he?"

"He is with the White Pony-soldiers." When these last words left her mouth, she regretted it as she saw a change come over the faces of some in the group. There must be trouble between the Army and the People, she thought.

"We would have something to eat," Little Gun said, and all the men dismounted. Both Willow and Maggie recognized some of the men, among them Bear Voice. Some of the women's tension dissolved when they noticed the two young boys with the Warriors.

"Sit there and we will bring you food," said Willow pointing to one of the large cottonwood trees close to the house. The men sat on their blankets at the foot of the trees, the branches just starting to bud in the early spring warmth.

Willow and Maggie brought the men dried buffalo meat, coffee and white bread that had been baked that morning in the beehive-shaped adobe horno that sat in the yard beside the house. Behind them, peering from one of the house windows, John and Zachary dared to sneak a view of the Indians, a sight not uncommon to them but still cautiously waiting until their mother's said there was no danger.

"Did you wish to speak to our father?" Willow asked her brother, speaking in English.

"Yes," Little Gun said, "I had wanted him to see his grandsons." He motioned toward the boys and waved them closer to him. They moved to him, sitting at his side. "This is Red Fox Waiting and this is Turtle Shell." Then, to the boys, he said in Cheyenne, *"This is your aunt, Willow Woman."*

"They are good looking boys," Willow turned and motioned to John and Zachary to come out of the house. John went to his mother's side, and taking hold of her skirt folds, half-hid behind her. Zachary stood next to Maggie.

Until this point Bear Voice had paid little attention, but he now saw Little Bird in Zachary's features and now recognized Maggie for whom she was. He chewed on a piece of the dried buffalo and his mind worked on how the knowledge of this child and woman could be an advantage to him.

"This is my son, John," Willow said to Little Gun, "And, this is Zachary, the son of Whitney Voss."

"The one called Sky Eyes?" asked White Badger.

"Yes," answered Maggie in Cheyenne.

"Ahh, I remember you now. You are the one called "Mo'e'ha", Magpie by the People." White Badger recognized Maggie and turning his attention back to Zachary said to the boy, *"You are Yellow Horse, I am your uncle, White Badger."*

"It is good to see you, Uncle," Zachary said, surprising Badger that he spoke the language of the People. Zachary also was surprised, for he had never heard his Cheyenne name, and liked the sound of it.

"I see your mother in you," White Badger commented, not knowing that he had hit a tender subject with Maggie. The boy had only known Maggie as his mother, but there were times that Little Bird had been spoken of, and Zachary had wanted to know more about his Cheyenne Mother. Each time Maggie heard Little Bird's name, she feared that down deep Whit still loved his first wife far more than he ever would love her. Why else did he spend so much time away from her?

"Come, sit with us and eat," said White Badger and motioned for Zachary to come to him.

"We will spend the night," Little Gun said, telling Willow and his companions who offered no objections. Then, he said, *"Fox, Turtle, go set the horses out to graze and watch them."*

"Can I go with them, Momma?" Zachary asked Maggie, warmth returning to her hurt feelings upon hearing him call her Momma.

"Yes, go with them and keep the horses out of the field."

The three boys took off to unsaddle the horses and take them out to graze. They were soon fast friends especially as they were able to talk to one another, and being boys, they could overlook any cultural differences they may have. John, remaining with his mother, seemed not to care that his only playmate had left him, for he was mesmerized at the sight of the Cheyenne. They were so different from his father and Silas, the man he called Grandpa.

It was dusk when August and Silas came home, spying the small camp of Indians as they neared the house. Both men approached, ready for any danger that presented itself, each man his rifle resting across his hips in front of him.

Silas, his glasses perched on the bridge of his nose, could make out the number of Indians sitting around a fire under the cottonwood and spoke their number to August, "Six, of em'."

"It looks like three more out there with the horses," said August.

"Yep, sure does," Silas agreed. They rode forward, straight to the seated Indians, the three horse herders rushing and arriving before them. When within a few yards away, Silas recognized his son, and some of the other Cheyenne in the small group. He was delighted to see Little Gun, and the presence of the others didn't matter. He and August dismounted and let their horses loose to graze on their own.

"Grandpa," said Zachary, calling Silas this out of respect and familiarity. "My Uncle has come to visit!"

Silas now looked closely at each of the other men, all known to him; Little Bear, son of Crow Eyes, Sitting Hawk, son of Little Wolf, White Badger, Whit's brother-in-law, White Bear, a known Dog Soldier, and lastly the troublemaker, Bear Voice. Then, he spied the two boys, and it took a bit for him to recognize them as his grandsons.

"Is that Red Fox and Turtle Shell?" he asked.

"Yes," Little Guns answered. Then, in Cheyenne, he spoke to the boys, *"Do you remember your Grandfather?"*

"I do," said Fox.

"I also remember you," said Turtle.

"This is good," Little Gun smiled, and speaking to August in English, said, "It is good to see you also, August."

"I am happy to see my wife's brother," replied August, "Will you be staying with us long?"

"Only for the night. We must not stay too close to the settlements for long. Not everyone is happy to see Cheyenne near them."

"You are velcome in my home," Said August.

"Zachary, go tell your Ma that we're back, and take care of our horses," Silas said.

"I'd like to stay here," Zachary protested, but in a way that was more a request.

"First the horses and tell your Ma what I said."

"Yes, Sir. Can Fox and Turtle come help me?"

"Sure."

Silas and August sat down with the Cheyenne, and both took out their pipes to smoke while they chatted; all except Bear Voice, who sat somewhat apart from the rest and remained silent.

"What brings you to this neck of the woods?" Silas asked little Gun.

"We had a camp on the Smokey Hills, but game is scarce there, all of it chased away by the miners heading to the mountains. We are now moving down toward Big Timbers. The buffalo are further to the east, so we will go there, trying to avoid contact with the pilgrims."

Silas smiled at his son's use of the word "pilgrims", one that he himself had used many times over the years. "They are a troublesome breed, these newcomers," he said.

"I am worried there will be blood spilled. The week before last, we were up along the South Platte hunting and looking for an Arapaho village we knew was in the area. West of them is the settlement of miners. Father, the miners have built a city like those in the East. I can't say how many of them there are, there were too many buildings. We ran across some Arapaho hunters, and they told us they had been camped there since the summer trading with the Whites, and they even left their women and children there when they went to war against the Utes."

"If they're living in peace with each other, what's your concern?" Silas asked.

"It won't last. Sooner or later, a horse or a cow is going to come up missing, and they'll blame the Arapaho. They'll probably be right, but it will lead to someone getting killed." Little Gun paused, a look of melancholy crossing his face. "It isn't like it used to be, when I was a child, we lived closely with the Whites. I miss those times." This reminiscing brought to mind his childhood friends the Craigavons. "Have you any word on the Craigavon's? It has been a long time since I have seen them," he asked.

"We were just over at Billy's place. He moved his family up here and started a ranch just downstream." Silas thought a moment, and then added, "I wouldn't go by that way though. It would be too much of a temptation to run off some of the horse flesh he has, and you wouldn't want to steal from a friend." Silas looked at the other warriors with his son.

"As I said, Father, we want no trouble."

"That's good," Silas said and smiled at his son.

The sun set and the men talked into the night. To the boys' delight, the Cheyenne soon began to talk about past exploits and the many battles fought against other tribes.

"*Uncle, have the People always had enemies?*" Zachary asked White Badger.

"*Oh, yes, Yellow Claf, from the time when the Great One created the People, we have always had enemies. But, if we did not have enemies, we would not be the powerful people we are now,*" answered White Badger. "*When our grandfathers lived on the other side of the Great Greasy River, the Cree, Wrapped Ones, Assiniboine and Ojibwas often attacked us. We fought back but were weak. It was when we crossed the river into the land of the Arikara, that we traded for guns and horses that we became strong.*

"*For a while, the People lived in earth-lodge villages near Standing Rock, like the Arikara. From there, the People made two hunts each year on Good River and Grand River, at first hunting on the lower courses of these streams, but gradually moving west toward the Sacred Hills. In time, the Good River became our favorite hunting ground. In their tongue, the Vé'ho'e call this river, the 'Cheyenne River', after the People.*

"*The People, with horses and firearms, drove our enemies before us like a fire in dry grass that spreads across the plains.*" He listed those tribes that the Cheyenne had warred against, some they had pushed out of the Black Hills, like the Crow, and the Comanche.

"*I can show you places where the People had fights with Pawnees. North of Bent's Fort is a place we call the Pawnee Hills. It was there that the People annihilated a war party of Pawnees, and between the forks of the Platte are Pawnee Creek and Pawnee Hills, where the People and Arapaho killed other Pawnee war parties.*"

The flames in the fire died down, and the glow from the coals was all that was left when the older men decided it was time to go to bed. The boys would have stayed up all night listening to stories, but Silas told them that they would have to wait for another time. When the sun rose the following morning, the Cheyenne were ready to leave, and White Badger suggested to Silas that he allow Zachary to go with them.

"I can't speak for the boy's father," said Silas.

Maggie, standing close by, spoke up, "I am the boy's mother and I say he will stay here with me."

White Bear seemed more surprised than offended and said no more. Little Gun bid farewell to his father and sister, hugging each and saying that he would miss them. He gave August a firm handshake and joined the rest of the Cheyenne who were already mounted. They moved slowly off to the east and Silas was the last to watch them disappear among the cedar and pinon trees.

The Indians were quiet as they traveled away from Fountain Creek, putting the new White settlement now called Pueblo, behind them. As they made their way, they failed to notice a wagon and team of horses tucked back among the dense stand of piñon trees. This was a relief to the wagon's driver and his young son.

***

Since finding the injured man three days earlier, Abbott Sager and his son Morton had feared they would run into a war party of Indians. The condition of the naked man that they had run across bore evidence that he had been assaulted by savages, especially the patch of missing scalp from the top of his head. Abbott and his son had ventured far to the northeast of the new little town of Pueblo in search of buffalo, hoping to secure enough meat to last into the summer. They had been successful in killing three of the shaggy beasts, but it had taken almost a week to accomplish.

When they first spotted the man, they thought him dead, his body was in such bad shape. His naked flesh had been burned by the sun, and he was covered with blue-black bruises. Only when they turned him over did they realize that he was still breathing, and they loaded him into their wagon. Abbott had dressed the cuts and the man's exposed scalp with bear grease mixed with the resin from cottonwood buds and then bandaged the man's head.

Morton had voiced his fears only once to his father, and these were eased by Abbott's assurance that they would be safe and that it was their Christian duty to help the unfortunate soul. Thus, they intended to bring the man down to the new doctor who lived on the Fountain Creek above Pueblo.

After the massacre at the trading post, the structure stood empty for almost six years, being only a temporary stop for travelers. Many avoided the location, spooked by the restless spirits of those who had died there. As gold seekers moved through, some found the confluence of the Arkansas and the Fountain attractive and soon small shacks and other buildings began to appear.

The doctor had come up from Santa Fe, and along with him a few others who had started ranches and small farms along both streams. Abbott had the notion of setting up a store of sorts, and with his wife and four children, started a modest place that offered some goods. The buffalo meat would not only feed his family but would supplement the supplies offered for sale. He also added a structure that would offer a place for those who needed lodging. It was not much more than four walls with a canvas roof, but it was out of the elements.

It was late in the day when Abbott pulled his wagon to a stop in front of the house owned by Dr. Craigavon. He was met by the doctor's wife and oldest son standing on the porch, each holding a shotgun; Roseanne's nestled easily across the crook of her arm, the eleven-year old Ransom, using all his strength to keep his level.

"Evenin' Mrs. Craigavon," Abbott said.

"Good evening, Mr Sager," she replied, "What brings you out this way?"

"Found a man bad hurt, an' thought the Doctor might be able to help him." Abbott pointed to the bed of the wagon where the man lay. Leaning the shotgun against the wall near the front door, Roseanne Craigavon moved to the wagon and peered over the tailboard at the figure wrapped in blankets. With no reservation, she pulled her skirt up to free her lower legs and climbed into the wagon bed to get a closer look. By this time, all of her children had come out of the house to see what was happening.

"Help me get him inside," Roseanne said, "And I'll send Ransom to fetch my husband. He's not far away, working horses with some of the men." Without being told, Ransom took off in a dead run toward Fountain Creek.

It was not long after the man had been laid on a bed, Bill Craigavon reached the house and came in to examine him.

"What did you use to dress these wounds?" he asked Abbott.

"I used the bear grease salve you gave me for my sore back," Abbott said.

"You may have saved this man's life."

"I didn't do more than the next man."

"You did more than most would have. Right now, we'll treat his injuries and see how well he responds."

Abbott left for home, leaving the man in the doctor's care. Bill and Roseanne began the task of cleaning the man's wounds and dressing them. When this was finished, they left him to rest in the room that Bill used as his surgery.

Bill and Roseanne Craigavon had taken the risk of moving north from Santa Fe and starting life over again along the Arkansas River. For the most part, Bill's practice as a doctor was minimal compared to that of raising horses and cattle; but as time passed, the growing town of Pueblo offered an increase in patients. Though most people relied on self-diagnosis and treated themselves accordingly, there were times, such as broken bones, when Bill's expertise was necessary. Payments for treatments were seldom made in silver or gold, more often in trade, but the Craigavons were happy with their new home.

Bill sat in his chair, searching through the few medical books that he owned, some of these gifts from his mentor, Silas' brother, Father William Scott. As he read, he became excited.

"Rosie," he called to his wife, "I think I found what I was looking for. I remember reading about it when I was at school in Baltimore."

"And, what is that?" she asked.

"There is a reference written here from a Doctor Felix Robertson in '05, about a method to treat scalping."

"How?"

"If the scalped head was left untreated, the exposed bone could eventually become necrotic and separate from the healthy bone, or it could cause an inflammation of the bone and marrow resulting in the victim's death.

"This Dr. Robertson wrote about his father, who learned a technique from another surgeon, a Dr. Vance, in 1777. The senior Robertson treated a scalping victim using Vance's instructions in the art of skull boring. Holes were bored in the skull using a flat pointed straight awl. This instrument is the best to bore through the thick surface of the skull. When the awl was nearly through, the pressure on it is reduced taking care

231

not to bore too deep, only proceeding until a reddish fluid appears on the point of the awl. He placed each about one inch apart, and, as flesh appeared to rise in those holes, he bore more holes between the first. Besides boring holes in the skull, the wound had to be cleaned and dressed at least daily to prevent infection. New skin eventually grew sufficiently to attach to the edge of the uninjured part of the original flesh remaining on the skull. I might be able to help him restore some, or his entire scalp."

"You believe you can do that?" asked Roseanne.

"I'm sure I can. Robertson's patient recovered from the scalping. It takes time, months or even a year, but according to Robertson, hair could even grow back! Apparently, the success rate for this treatment was very good."

"When will you try this?"

"When the man is sufficiently conscious and consents to the procedure."

"That may take some time in itself," Roseanne said, "He is in terrible shape."

"We'll treat this poor soul and bring him back to health. And, with that care he can resume his life."

***

CHAPTER ELEVEN
BIG ELK DOGS

May 1860 – Bright Moon

The herd of horses churned up the placid surface of Fountain Creek as they raced across to the sandy eastern shore, the water turning a muddy brown in their wake. Thirty warm-blooded mares, many with new foals, beat their way out of the water, and up the cut bank onto the cottonwood covered river bottom. The sound of beating hooves, the blowing and whinnying of the horses all mixed with the shouts and whistles of the vaqueros and Whitney Voss, who drove them forward into the large corral.

The corral was made of deadfall and cottonwood limbs woven around upright cedar poles and formed an enclosure almost five feet tall which held the herd in a tight group. The foals listened for their mother's "come close" nicker and stayed near to her flanks in fear of being separated. As the last horse entered the enclosure, Zachary, Silas, August, another vaquero and Ransom Craigavon closed up the opening with more deadfall and tree limbs.

Whit brought his horse to a skidding stop and Zachary ran to his father who leaned forward and scooped the boy up into his arms, setting him across the saddle in front of him.

"Pap, I'm so glad to see you!"

"Missed me, did you?" Whit asked.

"I didn't think you was ever comin' home!" The boy could barely talk, he was so excited. "Do you like the corral we built? Ransom and me helped Federico, Grandpa and Uncle August. We had it done two days ago," said Zachary.

"Hello, Silas," Whit said, looking down at the older man.

"Fine bunch of horse flesh you got here," Silas said as he eyed the horses, taking time to also look over Whit. There had been a change in him. Long gone was the young man with wide-eyed wonder. He had been replaced by an older, hardened plainsman, his blond hair hanging down around his shoulders, his back stiff and a self-assured look in his gray eyes. He was more and more like Tom Craigavon, and like Tom, he now carried a six-shot pistol. Silas silently said a small prayer that Whit had not traded away his love for family for the love of adventure.

"Once we mix them in with that stud of Billy Craigavon's, we'll have us the best stock in the country!" Whit boasted.

"Yep, I'll just bet Billy's stud will love getting a bit of these gals," Silas smiled as he puffed on his pipe.

"Who's the boy?" Whit asked.

"That's Ransom Craigavon, Billy's oldest. Spittin' image of his grandpa. Speaking of, how are Tom and Mary?"

"They're fine. Mary sends her love to you. She wants to know when you'll make it down that way for a visit."

"I don't travel too far away from home much. My backside just can't sit in the saddle more than a day or two anymore."

"Silas, you've outlived many a man, and I expect you'll be around for a good many more years."

"Possible, but I'm on borrowed time, can't complain though. When St. Peter calls, I expect I'll just mosey on over to the other side."

"Hell, Silas, St. Peter don't want you and the devil wouldn't take you for fear of fouling his nest!" Whit laughed while Silas only smiled slightly and puffed on his pipe.

"Let's go on up to the house, I 'spect Maggie and Willow will have supper ready," Silas said.

The reception Whit received was as he had expected. Willow was graciously happy to see him, and Maggie smiled at the very sight of him. When he dismounted, he first gave Willow a friendly hug. Then putting his arms around Maggie, he pulled her up off her feet and squeezed her to the point she begged him to let her down.

"God, it's good to be home," Whit said. He then introduced the vaqueros; Mateo, Santiago and Juan Pablo. The women already knew Federico, who had arrived four days earlier.

"It is good to see you Whit," Willow said, "Come in, and we will feed you and the men." Maggie remained somewhat reserved but was obviously happy to see Whit.

The seven men took up all the room that was available at the table in the little house of Silas, the Klausens, Maggie and

Zachary. The women fixed the boys a plate and sent them outside to eat on the porch, and then fed the men.

When supper had ended, the men went back to the corral to get a better look at the horses, smoke their pipes and discuss the future. Ransom and Zachary were sent the few miles downstream to inform Bill that Whit had arrived with the horses, and it was not long before Bill and the boys returned. After the initial greetings, and introduction to the vaqueros, Bill turned his attention to the horses in the pen.

The mares, a variety of colors but mostly sorrels, had settled down. They had small, short, refined heads, with strong muscular bodies, broad chests and powerful hindquarters. They all stood between fourteen and sixteen hands high. Bill's stud was of the same character but a bit taller at seventeen hands, and more refined, more resembling a thoroughbred.

"They look like fine stock," he said. "It looks like they're a good cross between the American horse and the mustang, just enough thoroughbred blood to warm them and mustang stamina to keep them strong. They'll be perfect for running cattle."

"The Army might be interested in them, too," said Whit. "Them, or maybe the new coach line running along the Republican. He spoke of the Leavenworth Pike's Peak and Express Company that had established a line of coaches up the Republican River, through the heart of Cheyenne and Arapaho hunting grounds. He went on to speak about the quality of the colts and fillies, "Looking at the colts, I didn't see one that stood out for breeding, so I thought we'd geld them all. That is, unless you see something in them I don't."

"Señor Whit, I would like to have one of the foals as part of my pay," Federico said, pointing out the single black filly. "Este pequeño relleno negro me."

"What do mean she speaks to you?" Whit asked.

"Look at the way she looks at me, when she does not think her mother is watching!" Federico laughed, "How can I resist her affection?"

She's yours, Federico," Whit said, "But, it will be some time before she is weaned."

"This I know, Señor Whit. I think I will stay behind to watch her."

"I was hoping to convince you and the others to stay and work here with the horses, and the cattle."

"We'll be needin' more help," Silas offered, deep down knowing that as soon as things settled down, Whit would most likely find a reason to leave.

It was agreed that all but Juan Pablo wanted to stay on as hired hands, and he would be leaving in a few days. With the addition of the other three men to the ranch, it was also decided that another structure would need to be built to house them.

Pleased with himself, Whit could only imagine a prosperous future. He knew all his partners were men to be trusted, especially Silas. Though the man was close to eighty-years old, he was still sharp-minded and tough as rawhide. The investment in the horse herd could only turn a profit.

As the sun began to set, Bill Craigavon and his son left for home, and the vaqueros bedded down under the giant cottonwood near the house. Whit decided to walk down to the horse pen and have a final look before turning in himself. He knew that on his return to the house, Maggie would be waiting for him in her room. Zachary, who normally shared the room, would stay the night with Silas, as had been the habit in the past when Whit came home

Whit walked across the grassy field toward the pen and smiled at the sight of the horses. They had completely calmed down and some were even dozing on their feet. He leaned on the fencing and watched the animals, admiring their condition, and Whit was pleased with what had been accomplished.

As the sun dropped behind the treetops along Fountain creek, the air began to cool slightly, and a chill passed through Whit, raising the hair on the back of his neck. Whit was alarmed, and at almost the same moment the horses also sensed something and began to mill around, the mares nickering and herding their foals to the inside of the group. Whit reached to the holster on his belt, pulled out the Remington pistol, and slowly made his way around the corral. He thumbed back the pistol's hammer, and pointed the barrel slightly upwards, as it was easier to draw down on an adversary then to pull the weapon up.

It seemed as if the light was fading too fast, and out of the corner of his vision, he caught movement in the cottonwoods. A shadow passed by, and he turned in that direction. With his pistol ready, he slowly made his way forward. The shadow appeared again, moving to his right through the trees. He adjusted his path and entered the tree line to intercept what or whoever it was. A slight breeze rustled the leaves in the leafy canopy above him and the chill returned, running down his spine.

"Damn!" he thought, and as to bolster his spirit, he attempted to spit, an act of defiance against anything out there, a sign that he was determined to face whatever foe came against him. And then, he saw it again, this time clearer, the shape he had seen many times before, the woman with long hair that seemed to flow in the breeze. As always, her features weren't clear enough to make out who she was.

Whit took a hesitant step forward and for a moment he was frozen by the feeling of a hand on his shoulder. Drawing on his inner courage, he spun around bringing the pistol down to level it at the perceived threat.

"Whoa there, Son!" Silas said, deflecting the pistol in Whit's outstretched arm. "Careful with the shooter."

"Damn Silas, I didn't hear you come up on me," Whit's heart was pounding in his chest, and he feared Silas could hear it.

"Well, good thing I ain't someone after your hair," Silas said. "You see something out here?"

"Yes, I thought I saw...I mean it looked like a..."

A woman, Silas thought, but dared not say it out loud, but did ask, "What did you see?"

"Nothing. Just the shadows playing tricks on me."

"That happens, but best to be cautious," said Silas, for he had seen specters more than once himself. "We best be getting back to the house," he added.

The two men walked in silence, each of them thinking about the specter that had appeared to them. Whit was almost afraid that Little Bird was haunting him, and not knowing that Silas had seen a similar apparition, worried about his own sanity. Silas wondered why Red Calf Woman would show herself to Whit. That just didn't figure in the way he saw things.

"Silas, do you believe in ghosts?" Whit finally asked

"Don't know, Son. Sometimes there are true mysteries in this world and some of those are not meant to be understood."

Maggie lay awake in her bed, waiting for Whit. As in the past, his infrequent visits made their reunions somewhat awkward, but she had grown used to the fact that Whit came to her bed only for the physical comfort she offered. His passion, his caring for her had diminished. There had been a time when they were first married that a chance for a loving marriage had existed, but that had faded with his wanderlust and the possibly his memory of Little Bird.

When the sun rose in the morning, Maggie realized that Whit had not come to bed. She rose, dressed and went out to the kitchen where Willow was already busy preparing breakfast.

"You have slept in this morning," remarked Willow. "You must have had an exhausting night." She smiled, but that smile soon faded as she saw the tears welling up in Maggie's eyes. "Are you all right?" she asked.

Maggie shook her head, and wiping the tears from her cheeks, said, "I fear that I have lost my husband."

"What do you mean? Did it not go well last night?"

"He did not come to bed last night." Maggie's mood changed from hurt to one of resignation, accepting that she was not truly Whit's wife, merely a convenient caretaker of his son.

"Men have many reasons for not coming to their wife's bed," said Willow, attempting to find some words to comfort her friend.

"No, I have known for a long time now that he has never truly loved me, and I can accept that."

Willow was about to speak again when the door to the house opened and Silas entered followed by August, John, Zachary, Mateo and Juan Pablo. Both women turned their attention to the preparation of breakfast, the men taking seats at the table, August going first to the coffee pot on the stove to pour himself a cup.

"Good morning, Maggie," August said.

"Buenos días señoras," said Mateo, echoed by Juan Pablo.

"Good morning," said Willow

"Buenos días," Maggie said, then replied to August, "Good morning." She didn't look in his direction but kept her eyes on the stove, and opening the cast iron door she retrieved the biscuits Willow had baked. She placed the small hot breads on a plate, their fragrance hinting at the soft interior hidden beneath their firm brown crust.

As soon as she placed the hot bread on the table, Maggie gave a quick look to see who was seated and noticed that Whit was missing. Another glance toward the now closed door was a waste of her effort. She knew that Whit would not be coming through it.

Willow placed a large plate of fried eggs and slices of cured ham in the center of the table next the biscuits and asked if anyone wanted butter or sweet wild strawberry jam. Zachary answered yes and thanked her as she added these to the table. After buttering and adding a spoonful of preserves on to a biscuit, he almost stuffed the entire biscuit into his mouth and tried to speak at the same time.

"Chew and swallow, before you choke!" Maggie scolded him, in a tone that was much harsher than was her normal manner. With a sheepish look on his face, Zachary obeyed. When he had finished, he looked up and spoke, the first to mention Whit, "Pa left this morning without sayin' goodby!" All eyes went to the boy, and then only Willow looked at Maggie.

"Well, I expect he wanted to get a good start to Denver, and talk to those fellows with the coach line," said August, "Took four of the mares and dat fellow Santiago with him."

"When are you thinking about leaving, Juan Pablo?" asked Silas to change the subject.

"I believe I will go first light tomorrow," the young Navajo answered.

"You got kin waiting for you?" Silas questioned.

"Si, Señor. I have a mother and a sister."

"We could use an extra hand here-a-bout, just for a bit. Like we was talkin' yesterday, we need to put up another building to house the help. Maybe you could stay long enough to help with that?"

"I do not know, Señor. I promised I would not be gone for too long, and I do not want to make my mother worry."

"We would pay you extra," August added, "Maybe $5.00 if you stay through the week."

"That is very generous." Juan Pablo answered looking at his friend. "Will you pay Mateo the same?"

"Mateo has already agreed to stay, and we'll be taking care of him for the long run," said Silas.

"Then, yes, I will stay longer."

After breakfast, a site to erect the new quarters for the help was chosen about a dozen yards to the north of the main house with its front planned to face south. Plans were also made to go to the little valley called Fisher's Hole in the Wet Mountains to cut timber for the new structure. There, the men could find pine trees that grew straight and were stronger than the cottonwoods that grew along the Fountain River. Silas and August figured that with the help of Juan Pablo and Mateo, they could remove the wagon box from the running gear and use this bare frame to haul the long timbers back to the ranch.

"It would have been nice if Whit and dat other Mexican would have stayed to help," August complained.

"No good in sayin' how things could have been or should be," said Silas, "We'll have to just get by with what we have. Of course, we could go over and talk to Billy Craigavon, see if he could part with one of his men."

"Ja, that would be good. Have you seen dat fellow what had his hair taken by da Indians?" August said.

"No, ain't had the pleasure. Heard he was a queer one though. Can't say's I blame him. Not sure how I'd behave if'n some buck had lifted my hair!" Silas clucked his tongue and shook his head. "I'll take a ride over there and talk to Billy this afternoon.

True to his word, about midafternoon, Silas saddled up Rocinante and headed downstream to the Craigavon ranch, taking Zachary with him, the boy riding a gentle gelding. As they rode, the boy asked Silas to tell him another story about his past and the "adventures" he had experienced.

"Not too sure I'd used the word adventure, more like misadventure!" Silas laughed. "Any ways, I don't think there's any tales left to tell you about myself."

"How about Uncle Tom? You talk about him all the time, but you never tell about how you met him."

"That story son, is one best left for when you're a bit older." Silas puffed on his pipe, and the memory of having to kill two men to save young Tom Craigavon's life came back to him. He felt no guilt, or remorse over their deaths, in his mind two grown men had no right to attempt the murder of a little boy. As he thought about Tom, another man came to mind and he asked Zachary, "Have I ever told you about Ransom Carter?"

"You mean the man Ransom Craigavon is named after?"

"Yep, one in the same. Well now, he was just a shave of a youngster when I came across him. He looked like a fence rail stood on end with a mop of red hair stuck on top!" Silas chuckled. "His looks were deceivin'. He was as tough as rawhide, but he had a charm about him no gal could resist. I'll believe that kind of talk is best left till you're older. I will tell you about when he was a boy. And, just before I met him, how he survived one of the greatest massacres whatever took place." As they rode Silas recounted the story of Fort Mimms and how Ransom Carter had lived while over five hundred men, women, and children had been killed by the Creek Indians. He told Zachary how Ransom outran the Indians making it to the Alabama River, armed with nothing but a knife given to him by Captain Dixon Baily, who was killed in the massacre.

"Is that the knife that Dr. Craigavon has?" Zachary asked.

"Sure is! Ransom Carter gave it to Billy just before he died, just like Cap'n Baily gave it to him."

"I'd sure like to have a knife like that," Zachary said, almost wishing Silas had one to give him, and the old man took the hint.

"Well, Son, maybe we can find you a good blade someday."

"Really, Grandfather? You mean I could have one of my own?"

"Yep, every boy ought to have more than a jackknife." Silas chuckled.

The two covered the half-dozen miles to the Craigavon ranch in short time, and for those few miles all Zachary could talk about was how he would treasure the knife he anticipated getting from Silas. Silas had to remind him that something as special as a good knife would have to be earned; it wasn't necessarily going to be a gift.

"I'll work hard, Grandfather! I promise."

"We'll see how you do around the horses, and maybe by Christmas time you might just have earned a good blade. I'll have to find you a Sheffield blade, no Green River for my grandson!" Silas smiled, and looking at the boy, thought he probably loved this child as much as his grandchildren by blood.

"Grandfather, why do the Cheyenne call horses, mo'éhno'ha? They don't really look like elk or dogs."

"You got to understand Zach, the first time the People saw a horse they didn't know what to think of it. The way they tell it, they saw the Rees and the Comanche riding them, and figured they were something special, you know, big medicine. The Rees and Comanche were not only riding them but using them to pull travois like a dog. So, they figured horses were some kind of tamed elk, but also something like a dog, so they call 'em big elk dogs."

"Sometimes, I like speaking Cheyenne more than American or Spanish," Zachary said, and he switched to that language, *"I will grow to be a mighty warrior of the People! I will take many scalps with my new knife!"*

Silas reached out and grabbed the reins of Zachary's horse and pulled his and the boy's horse to a stop and said, "A good man doesn't kill or take scalps for sport, Son. Among the Cheyenne and other tribes, a man's worth may be measured by his war deeds, and the number of scalps he takes or horses he steals; but the strongest and best of 'em are the ones who give to others, take care of their kin and those in need. You understand this?"

"Yes Grandfather." Zachary was a bit ashamed of himself, but deep down inside he felt those who were truly respected among the Cheyenne were the warriors, the Dog Soldiers.

As they approached the Craigavon ranch, young Ransom spied them and rode bare-back out to meet them at a speed that seemed reckless.

"Hey Uncle! Hey Zach!" he called out to them, as he came to a halt next to them.

"Hey Ransom!" Zachary said, "Race you to the house," he added, and immediately put his heels to his horse's flanks and sped off. Ransom, accepting the challenge, turned and followed.

Silas took his time covering the last hundred yards, and when he reached the main house both William and Roseanne were on the front porch waiting for him.

"Hello Billy, Rosie," Silas said, tipping his hat.

"Hello Silas, get down and come on in for a cup of coffee," William said, and Silas, easily slid from the saddle like a man less than half his age. He gave Rocinante's reins to Zach and the two boys went off to tend to the horses. Silas stepped up onto the porch and opened his arms wide for Roseanne, who threw her arms around him, letting him give her a firm but gentle hug.

"My, my," Silas said to her, "Don't you just grow prettier each time I see you."

"You'd say that to anything in a skirt!" She protested, though basked in the compliment her old friend paid her.

"What brings you over this way?" William asked as they entered the house and took a seat at the table.

"We were thinkin' about heading up to the Wets and cutting some timber. Gonna put up a building for the vaqueros to stay in, much like you have here for your men. We could use some help and thought about askin' to borrow two of your men. We're a bit short."

"Short, how so?"

"Whit and one of the vaqueros headed up to Denver to deal horses with the coach line folks, that leaves August, me and the two that come up from New Mexico. I would like to leave at least one of them here for safety. You know, keep the wolves away. I think we could cut all we need in a week or so."

"We could use some timber too," William said, "but, like you I have to leave someone here, I could go with you and maybe three of my four men."

"There's also Lazarus," Roseanne said as she placed cups of coffee on the table for the men.

"Lazarus?" Silas asked.

"Rosie is talking about the fellow Abbott Sager found, beaten and scalped. He hasn't spoken since he's come around, and evidently doesn't read or write. Poor wretch seems simple, or has lost part of his mind, but he works hard and understands when spoken to."

"So, how you know his name is Lazarus?" Silas asked.

"We don't, Rosie just has been calling him that."

"But, not to his face," Roseanne added.

"What's he answer to then?"

"I have been calling him Abel, and he seems to respond to it," said William.

"Well, I guess that's better than Cane!" Silas chuckled.

"When you thinking about leaving?"

"Day after tomorrow, need to get the wagon bed off of the running gear."

"We could bring back twice as much wood with two wagons. We'll take ours too."

"That sounds fine, Billy. We'll be here before sunrise."

***

Denver and Auraria had grown since the last time Whit had been in that part of the country. The population of the two towns numbered about three thousand at the first part of the year, but at times hundreds of newcomers would arrive daily. In the past year, brick buildings had begun to appear, a steam sawmill had been established, and a bridge had been built across the Platte on Ferry Street.

Another sign of "civilization" was the construction of a bank, coining and assay business, on the corner of G and McGaa streets. Both Whit and Federico were awed, and at the same time repelled, by the mass of people on the streets. On McGaa Street, the pair of men found the Rocky Mountain News office, a bakery, and several other businesses. Still following McGaa, they found the livery stable of Charles Lawrence.

Lawrence was an amiable man and willing to chat with newcomers, though not to the detriment of his business. As Whit arranged to stable their horses, he inquired about the location of Leavenworth Pike's Peak and Express Company.

"Hell, they went bust last year," said Lawrence "Didn't last but about nine months. So, you're out of luck."

"Hell!" Whit said, "I was looking to do horse trading with Russell."

"You lookin' to sell them horses? I'd make you a fair offer."

"The horses are for sale, but I had wanted to do some long-term business with the stage line," Whit said, a bit of frustration in his voice.

"Well, Russell didn't give it all up. He reorganized with his old partners, Majors and Waddell. Callin' the business the Central Overland California and Pikes Peak Express Company."

"Where they located?"

"Not sure where the office is now, but if you want to sell horses, I'd suggest talking to Mary Cawker at the last stop before comin' into town. Just follow Cherry Creek down about four miles and you'll hit the stage station, place run by her. It's the last stop to change teams before hitting town. Nice sturdy two story house, with a bar downstairs and a tavern on the second floor. You'll get a good price for your horses from her, but if'n you don't like what she offers, come on back and we'll talk. I'm always lookin' for decent horse flesh and I'd give you seventy-five a head." Whit knew the horses would bring more than that amount and thanking Lawrence, he and Federico left.

The short ride back down the Cherokee Trail along Cherry Creek brought Whit and Federico to Mary Cawker's Four Mile House late in the afternoon. They had passed it on the way into

Denver, and Whit remarked that they had wasted their time having to back-track.

Federico commented, "I do not think it was a waste of time, Señor Whit. Did you not notice the señoritas and the cantinas? I would love to have a drink and a warm woman next to me for an hour or two."

"So, would I, my friend, so would I," Whit smiled and the thought of sharing a bed warmed him, and then he thought of Maggie, something that he had not done since leaving Pueblo. He knew he should have felt some shame in the way he left her, but there was something keeping him from being with her. Then the thought of Little Bird pushed Maggie away, and Whit became gloomy. He pondered his depression and decided that maybe a good drunk and a loose woman could drive those thoughts away, no more Maggie no more Little Bird invading his mind.

"Did the fellow at the livery say that there was a cantina here at this coach stop?" Federico asked.

"Yes, he did," said Whit, "And, I do believe we are due for a drink, or two."

The Four Mile House was called so as that was the remaining distance before entering Denver. The two men found Mary Cawker ran a tight operation, and the two-story house, barn and out-buildings were kept in good shape. Just as Lawrence had told Whit, she operated not only a stage station but had a bar downstairs and a tavern that held dances on the second floor. Stages regularly stopped at the house to change horses and to allow passengers to change clothes and freshen up before their arrival in Denver.

The coach company had the contract for the mail, as well as freighting and passenger service, running a tri-weekly from St. Eli, Missouri to Denver, Colorado, making the distance in six and a half days.

Whit found Mary Cawker to be a no nonsense and savvy businesswoman. She looked over the four horses, running her hand over their backs and legs, checking their eyes and teeth. It was obvious she knew what she was doing.

"I don't have much of a need for mares," she said.

"I can bring you some geldings, in just as good shape," Whit told her, "But, I figure you could make out in the long run, resell these or breed 'em. You'll make a good profit either way."

"What are you asking for them?" She turned her attention back to Whit, sizing him up.

"You won't find better horses like these here-a-bouts," Whit smiled at her, attempting to use the charm that had gotten him his way in the past. But, as soon as he tried it, he saw that Mary Cawker was no young girl to be sweet talked, and never had been.

"Name a price," she said.

"I'll take one-eighty-five for each of them."

"I'll give you one-twenty, and that's my top dollar."

"Let's talk. How about one-fifty," Whit counter offered.

"One-twenty. You try to get more, and my next offer will be one hundred." She stood looking Whit straight in the eyes, her face showing no sign of backing down.

Whit smiled again, this time not to charm, but as a goodhearted sign of resignation. He then held out his hand and said, "Done!"

Mary took his hand and shook it, her grip stronger than Whit had expected, and she answered him, "Done Mr. Voss. Take these girls over to that corral on the right side of the barn. Hand them over to my men and when you're done come on up and I'll settle with you."

Whit and Federico led the horses over to the corral and found Mary's employees working with a big-chested gelding. The horse was stubborn, but the man on him seemed to be a good match using just the right amount of force and patience.

"He knows his way around horses," Federico commented to Whit.

"It appears so," Whit replied.

"With Juan Pablo returning to Mora, we could use someone like this hombre."

"Yes, we could. We'll feel him out and see what he's made of. Find out if he has sand," Whit said, not sure yet if he liked the looks of the man.

They waited until the hired hands finished with the gelding and turned it loose with other horses in a separate part of corrals. The man, who had been on the horse, walked over and greeted them.

"Can I help you Gentlemen?" he said as he reached Whit and Federico.

"Name's Voss, Whitney Voss. And, this here is Federico Vigil. We just sold these horses to Mrs. Cawker. She said to bring them out to you."

"Pleasure to meet you. I'm Elijah Thornton, but my friends call me Eli," Eli held out his hand to Whit and Federico. He recognized the name, and as he shook Whit's hand, he tried hard to act natural. Looking the horses over, he said, "These are good lookin' horses, can't be from the mining camps."

"No, we brought them up from Pueblo way. Good strong Spanish blood in these girls," Whit said.

"I can see that," Eli complemented. "Let me take them and give them some water and grain."

"Not too much grain," Federico said, "They have been eating nothing but sweet grass."

Eli took the horses, allowing Whit and Federico to go back up to the station house. As they walked away from the corral, a coach came up the road, kicking up dust and filling the air with a filmy cloud. The driver yelled, "Whoa!" and pulled back on the reins bringing the coach to a stop in the yard, the hooves of the horses digging into the soil. Mrs. Cawker came out to meet the coach, and Eli ran up from the corral.

"Expected you earlier in the day, Allister! You have trouble?" Mrs. Cawker called up to the driver.

"God damned Injins!" swore Allister O'Brien, "I had to damn-near kill my hosses to get away from them."

"What'd they do?"

"Tried to get us to stop, either to beg or steal from us. I couldn't take a chance with the womenfolk onboard!"

"What happened to the missing horse?" Eli asked.

"Broke a leg! I had to unhitch and shoot 'em," O'Brien cussed. "Then, the front right wheel started wobblin'. Liked to shake the whole coach apart, and we had to limp on in here, far behind schedule."

At this point, O'Brien was climbing down from his seat and the passengers were starting to exit the coach. O'Brien seemed not to care about the condition of the passengers, even as the single male passenger was complaining.

"I have never witnessed such utter incompetence!" His nasally voice was shrill for a man, and his mannerisms effeminate. His slight figure was clad in matching jacket, waistcoat and trousers of bright yellow plaid. His black congress style shoes only added to his overall un-masculine appearance. The obvious question that came to mind was, "What was a man like this doing west of St. Louis?"

The attention the man received was quickly diverted to the other passengers who emerged from the coach. One by one, the women looked out and stepped down from the coach into the yard, with no offer of help from the dandy or the driver. Whit was quick to step in and offer a hand, missing the chance with the first lady, but apologizing to her and reaching up to assist the second.

Whit hadn't seen women like these since his last visit to Kansas City. The dress of these damsels made their occupation plain, though they were far superior to their sisters, who plied their trade at the "Hog Ranches" near the military forts. These fair belles, though worse for the wear of traveling in an open coach, still maintained their allure, and Whit received a smile and "Merci, Monsieur." from a raven-haired temptress.

Whit knew enough French to reply, "Vous êtes le bienvenus." And though his pronunciation was rough, it was well received.

"I was afraid that we would not find gentlemen this far from civilization," she said, her accent so flawless that is was impossible to determine if it was not genuine.

Whit felt a flush of warmth and was embarrassed that he could be affected by a woman so easily. He regained his composure and his natural abilities to flatter surfaced. "Well, there aren't many ladies here-a-bouts," he said. "Whitney Voss, Ma'am," he introduced himself as he helped the other two women exit the coach.

"Enchantée. Are all the men in this wilderness as gallant as you?" the first woman asked.

"No Ma'am, there is only one Whitney Voss."

"Ah... I am called Harmonie. We must get to know each other better, Monsieur Voss," she cooed, tilting her head to one side and smiling at Whit.

"I'd like that very much," Whit said.

"The damned wheel hub is cracked!" said O'Brien as he and Eli examined it.

"I can have a new wheel on there and a fresh team ready in a couple hours," Eli said.

"Blast! It'll be dark by then and I'm not gonna do the last few miles in pitch black!" O'Brien cursed again.

"We'll put up the passengers for the night," offered Mrs. Cawker, "Come on in and we'll get you all something to eat too." She turned and led the way followed by the dude, the soiled doves, Whit and Federico. O'Brien drove the coach over to the barn, where the horses were unhitched, watered and fed, after which Eli and the other hired man replaced the damaged wheel.

Mary Cawker set out a good but simple meal for the travelers and offered whiskey at an exaggerated price though that did not stop her guests from drinking into the night.

The dude offered the story behind their journey to Denver, he an entertainer and musician, and the ladies, professional "hostesses."

"Yes Sir, we intend to bring a bit of culture to the wilds of Kansas Territory," his high-pitched words slurred by the amount of whiskey he had consumed. "Let me give you a sample of what we offer," he added and taking a banjo from its case, began to strum and belt out "My Old Kentucky Home," followed by "Listen to the Mocking Bird." After a few minutes this, Whit stood and headed for the fresh air of the outdoors. As he was leaving the room, he caught Harmonie's eye and she rose to follow him out the door and into the clean night air.

Whit made his way toward the barn knowing that Harmonie was only a few steps behind him. He slowed in order to let her come up beside him, and as she did, she slipped her arm in his and pulled him close.

"I would feel better, being close in case there is danger, no?" She again cooed, her voice soft and seductive.

"I'm sorry, Ma'am, but I'm not too sure I could afford...your charms."

"*Tsk-tsk*, Monsieur Voss. There is no need to speak of money between us. That would be..." she paused, "Vulgar."

"So, what did you have in mind?" Whit asked.

"We should find a place where we can..." again she paused, "Commencer les rapports!" Whit was lost in her French, and noticing this she offered, "We will start a conversation, in a special way." She laughed softly.

Though still not understanding her words, Whit knew full well what she meant. Arm and arm, they moved to where stacks of fresh cut grass stood in piles and there, Whit turned to face her, the frustration he had felt for so long was set free and he kissed her. They stood for some time embracing, until she pulled slightly away and spoke.

"Lay down on your back, and then we will start to converse in earnest." She slightly pushed him down, letting him pull her with him. Once nestled in the sweet grass, Harmonie positioned herself over him and they "talked." It was as if the rest of the world had drifted away for Whit, his head spun with the giddy feeling of sex, mixed with the mind numbing of the whiskey.

They walked back to the station house in silence, Harmonie pleased with herself, and Whit feeling the whiskey more and more, his steps a bit uneasy. He stopped to steady himself on a nearby hitching rail and tried to clear his head. Looking out across the semi-darkness, he saw a movement, a shadow of a woman crossing the open area between them and the barn, and a chill ran through him.

The following morning, the repaired coach and its passengers left for Denver and Whit and Federico headed south along the Cherokee Trail for Pueblo. They had made a deal with Eli Thornton, and as soon as Eli knew Mary Cawker had a replacement for him, he would also travel down to Pueblo and start working at the ranch. Whit had no idea how much Eli was looking forward to being near Maggie.

The trip to Fishers Hole, west of Pueblo, had resulted in filling both wagons with long straight timber that could be cut into planks and rough boards for building. Silas and Will Craigavon were satisfied with how fast they had worked, and that there had been no problems. As they approached the Arkansas crossing, Silas separated from the group and his grandson Zachary went with him.

"Where we headed?" Zachary asked.

"We're gonna check on your grandma," Silas said, and they rode to the location of Silas' old cabin.

There was little left of the cabin, the frequent flooding of the river bottom having washed away most of the log structure. Silas clicked his tongue, and commented, "Nothing lasts forever."

From the cabin site, they moved toward the bluff, at the foot of which was the grave of Red Calf Woman. As he approached the spot, he had visited so many times in the past, Silas saw that like the cabin, flood waters had attacked his wife's grave and his heart sunk. As he slipped from the saddle, he felt old, and his chest hurt. The cairn of rocks that had once stood high had been reduced to a little over two feet high, and at one corner the wrapped remains of Red Calf were exposed to the elements.

"Oh, I'm sorry ol' Girl, I should've taken better care of you," Silas said. Turning to his grandson, he said, "Get the blanket from behind my saddle and bring it here."

Zachary brought the sky-blue blanket to Silas, and seeing he was removing the stones from the grave, got down on his knees to help. Silas looked over to him and smiled, but there was sadness in the older man's eyes and something else that the boy couldn't quite make out. There was a venerability in Silas that Zachary had never seen in his grandfather. And, for the first time, Zachary realized how old Silas was.

When all the stones were removed, Silas carefully lifted the wrapped bundle that contained what was left of his wife. The bones held little weight, the flesh long gone, but to Silas it was like the world weighed heavy in his arms. Placing the remains on the new blanket, he folded the wool over and tied it, making a tight bundle. This he lifted and placed on the back of Rocinante, securing it to the saddle.

"You go on ahead, Son. I'll see you back at the ranch. Tell your Ma I'm bringing her mother home with me."

The wagons had made it across the Arkansas, crossed the Fountain at the puertocito, and turned north to follow Fountain Creek upstream. When they reached the Craigavon ranch, Zachary was waiting there, and he told them what Silas had found at the old cabin site. The first wagon was left in the yard, and the men took the second to Silas' and August's place. Along with them went Roseanne Craigavon, and her children, in a Dearborn wagon driven by Azariah Bolt, the man they all called Abel.

When Silas came up to the house, everyone he considered his family was there, including the Craigavons. He fought back the tears that welled up inside him, keeping a brave facade that only his daughter, Willow, could see through. She walked up to him and they embraced, Silas' body quivering with the emotions he battled to hold in check.

"I've brought your mother home with me, Katherine." It was the first time he had used her Christian name in years. "I mean to put her where the wolves won't get at her. Put her where she is safe."

"You pick a spot Papa, and we'll take care of her," Willow said, and she kissed Silas on the cheek before letting go of him and turning to the men. We'll need a shovel."

Silas led Rocinante to a level area void of cedar and pinon trees, not far from the house, and there chose a spot to dig the grave. As August brought the shovel and began to dig, Silas stopped him and took the tool in his own hands. "I'll be needin' to do this myself, Son," he said, and August, with Will Craigavon, kept watch as Silas dug into the rocky soil.

The reburial of Red Calf Woman was completed just before dark, and Silas allowed the others to help stack rocks on the grave, until it was certain that her remains would be safe. August suggested that they should find a piece of sandstone and carve for her a marker. Silas agreed, and said, "I 'spect we should get two chunks of stone, for I'll be layin' next to her pretty soon."

The hired men unloaded the timber from the wagon, and the boys took care of stock. Everyone felt the need to keep busy, even those who had no real connection with Silas. Though not a happy gathering, the women prepared a large evening meal with the intention of feeding everyone.

Azariah Bolt watched those around him. He had allowed them to call him Abel. He had let them believe that he was simple minded, and that he was a mute. The only time he did speak was when he was alone, and sure no one could hear him. At those times, he spoke to himself, mostly ravings about his hatred for Indians and anyone who felt any form of love for Indians. As he talked to himself, he would often run his fingers over the small oval scar on his head where his scalp had been removed. It took all his strength to hold back his disgust at being near any Indian. This included half-breeds such as Willow and her son, and Dr. Craigavon and his children. That day, as he helped unload the wagon, he had no choice but to work alongside these half-breeds and the full-blood Navajo, Juan Pablo. Azariah glared at the young man, and in his mind imagined what it would be like to take the long black hair in his hand and cut the scalp free.

The majority of those at the ranch spent the night; only two of Will Craigavon's men returned to his ranch to watch over and care for the horses there, one of those men being Azariah.

The following morning, the Craigavons, and their men left for home, and Silas and August started to plan out the new quarters for their help. As had been agreed, Juan Pablo headed for his home in New Mexico, his pay in silver dollars secured in his pocket. He had ridden with the Craigavons as far as their ranch and from there he intended to go south along the Fountain Creek, cross near the puertecito and then ford the Arkansas.

As he reached the Fountain Creek crossing, he saw a man on horseback sitting between the two hills that formed the puertecito. He could tell it was a white man by his dress, and the way he sat his horse, so he raised his hand and the greeting was returned. Juan Pablo figured the man was from Pueblo, just west of the hills to the west of the Fountain. When he came out onto the west bank, he pulled up next to the man who smiled at him but said nothing. It was at this moment that he recognized the man called Abel, so he returned the smile and extended his hand which Abel took.

As quick as a snake strike, Azariah pulled the young man toward him, and with his other hand, stabbed Juan Pablo in the neck with his knife. The young man could not call out and had no time to react, dying before he fell to the sandy soil. Azariah slid from his saddle, and kneeling next to the boy, took the knife and scalped him. Searching the body, he found the silver coins. After taking these, and Juan Pablo's rifle, he rolled the body into Fountain Creek and let the water carry it downstream to the Arkansas where it would float away and out of sight.

Azariah tossed Juan Pablo's saddle into the bushes and taking up the horse's reins, led it into Pueblo where he sold it for seventy-five dollars. Horses meant wealth, and he wasn't about to pass up what he thought was owed him by an Indian.

***

SAM J. PISCIOTTA

CHAPTER TWELVE
BLOOD ON THE SAND

May 1860 - Bright Moon

In the early part of the year, Reverend John Chivington was appointed presiding elder of the Rocky Mountain District by the Methodist Church, and in May, he arrived in Denver with his family. He had come to Denver with a reputation of being a man of strong convictions, especially when it came to his contempt for slavery. In Missouri, he had stood against pro-slavery members of his congregation, and at one point ascended the pulpit with a Bible and two pistols in hand. His declaration that, "By the grace of God and these two revolvers, I am going to preach here today," earned him the sobriquet the "Fighting Parson."

He also held strong belief in the superiority of not only himself as a person, but that of all Anglos over any other race, especially the "Godless Heathens," the Indian. Rather than see an opportunity to evangelize or convert the natives, he felt deep down exterminating these human lice was a better solution.

He also held strong aspirations of a loftier position in the territory surpassed his zeal as a preacher. With the growing population, he saw an opportunity to become a leader, a figure of power, possibly Governor, or better yet a place in Washington.

Another figure, seeking his fortune in the gold fields, arrived at about the same time as Chivington. Like Chivington, Silas Soule had deep convictions and was also an abolitionist. Originally from Maine, his family had moved to Kansas, helping found the town of Lawrence, and were active in the Underground Railroad. In 1859, after the execution of famed abolitionist John Brown in 1859, Silas Soule traveled to Harper's Ferry, West Virginia, in an attempt to rescue two of Brown's followers. Though the rescue mission failed, Soule had proved his courage and resourcefulness.

Soule's attitude toward the Native population was somewhat like most Americans who had moved into the gold country, he would try to avoid them if possible, and would prefer not engaging in any conflict. He held what was considered a healthy respect for the Indians, and felt if they left him alone, he would let them be. He looked at most of life as a matter of moral right and wrong.

The ever-growing numbers of inhabitants to the Denver region brought all manner of people, some honest men like Silas Soule, came with good intentions and spirit. Others came with nothing by the basest of human faults, especially greed, and in the case of Azariah Bolt, vengeance. Azariah's character had evolved to the point that he no longer thought out or planned a killing; he simply went ahead and committed it. It was not that he was reckless, for he still held self-preservation as his main priority.

Along with his new sense of bravado, Bolt had put behind him the fear of being caught by Thornton or Cable. He held no fear of either man, or none that he would admit to himself. The only caution he exercised was to change his appearance by allowing his hair to grow down to his shoulders, and shaving his mustache and chin, but leaving heavy sideburns to cover his cheeks down to the corner of his mouth. His head he kept covered with a hat, not wanting the world to see his shameful scar.

Since arriving in Denver, Bolt had honed his skill with a knife, having replaced the Arkansas Toothpick he had lost to the Cheyenne Red Arm. Five men had fallen prey to his stealth and cunning, with each loosing whatever money they had on them. In the case of the two who looked like they might have had some Indian blood in them, he also took their scalps. Azariah now had a bag tied to his belt in which he kept his bloody trophies, and he saw no number of top knots that would end his hunger for revenge.

***

June 1860 – Fattening Up Moon

The ranches of William Craigavon and Silas Scott blended into one, there being no definite boundary, and the mixture of their stock made it virtually one business. The only separation was the pay to the hired hands for each ranch, but the duties of those hands often took them to both operations.

The sale of the horses to the coach line by Whit was well received, and plans to drive more horses north for sale were agreed upon. By the fall there would a better idea of which horses could be culled out for sale. The new foals, whether colts or fillies, could be judged, and those that weren't of the best quality could be sold or gelded.

Whit spent more time around the ranch working with the horses, but it was obvious that he was uneasy. He spent his nights with the hired hands, making it clear that there was no longer a connection between him and Maggie. The only affection he showed was toward Zachary, and this was sparing. At times, he was overly hard on the boy, finding fault and seldom offering praise. Yet, the boy idolized his father

Maggie had become a bit harder, but not bitter. She still loved Zachary as if he were her own child, and Willow as if they were sisters. Silas, she loved as a replacement for her parents and with him she showed what little softness she had left. She would go with Silas to the grave of his wife and there, tend the few Prickly Pear cactus that grew there, the yellow blossoms pleasing him.

The absence of Azariah Bolt had caused little disruption at the Craigavon ranch, as the man had done little to endear himself while there. A search was made of the surrounding area, with no sign of the man. The simultaneous disappearance of a horse and saddle, combined with Bolt's known mental condition, left little doubt that he had wondered off and fallen prey to some tragic misfortune.

Eli Thornton had arrived from Denver, and soon was well-liked and a trusted employee. He was handy not only with the stock, but proved his worth as a carpenter in helping construct the new buildings on both ranches. His work also gave him many chances to be near Maggie, and he never passed up an opportunity to be helpful around the house, especially when Maggie was present.

Planting of the crops had been completed and Eli, August and Silas worked on some of the farm equipment before storing it away. As Eli tightened the bolts of a plow, Silas studied the man. As if he had received a sudden revelation, Silas took his pipe from his mouth and pointing at Eli with the stem, said, "Now I got you! I been turning it around in my head since the day you showed up here. We met back at Fort Smith, what, two years back?" Eli looked up at Silas and wondered what was about to happen.

"Ya Silas, you do not recognize him? I knew who he was right off," said August.

Silas smiled, and said, "Well shit, you can't expect a fellow to remember pilgrim he's met." And then he slapped Eli on the shoulder, and added, "Seems like you kept that head of curly hair didn't you!"

"It appears so, Silas," Eli said. "Surprise you, does it?"

"Not really," Silas said.

"August," called Willow from the house, "I need a hand up here."

"I'll go," Said Eli, "we're done here." He stood and strode off toward the house.

"Young fellow seems eager to please, don't he?" Silas commented.

"Ya, I think he is a good worker," said August, completely missing what Silas was suggesting. Silas was not the only one to notice. Willow had seen that Eli had a habit of always being eager to do work or lend a hand when Maggie was close by. She had thought about mentioning it to her friend but noticed that Maggie didn't seem to care. As Eli didn't seem to be a threat, she had let the idea slip into the back of her mind, replaced by things more important.

Such was the task that Eli offered to help with now. The chimney crane, the iron arm that swung out from the fireplace wall to support pots over the fire, had come loose from where it was anchored. When Eli entered the house, he quickly ran his eyes across the room looking for Maggie and was pleased to see her standing next to Willow.

"Eli, I think the top clamp is broken," Willow told him, "Can you fix it? I need it before I can cook dinner."

"Sure, Mrs. Klausen. Let me take a look." He got down on his knees, and leaning into the fireplace, reached out to test the stability of the crane finding the top clamp didn't appear to be broken, only loose.

"I'll have to mix up some mortar and reset it," he said as he pulled on the clamp, his hand slipping and catching the wrought iron's jagged edge cutting across the palm of his hand. He pulled back the hand in pain but held back the swear words that were in his mind, blood flowing from the open wound. Before Willow could react, Maggie had rushed forward, taking Eli's hand in hers and wrapping a rag around it.

"¡Dios mío!" Maggie said, "You have been badly cut!"

Her concern was a surprise to both Eli and Willow, but Willow smiled. Now she knew that Maggie had noticed Eli's attention, and she wondered where things would go from this point on.

The rest of the year passed with little excitement, save for a visit from Little Gun and his sons in the fall. Little Gun carried the news from the bands. Raids were still being carried out on the Ute and Pawnee, the young men still making names for themselves as warriors and increasing the wealth of the People in horses. The Buffalo were plentiful along the Arkansas, in the south, and along the Republican and Smokey Hills in the north. But, tensions between the Whites and the Cheyenne, Lakota and the Arapaho were growing in the north. Horses, as always, still seemed to be the reason for contention between the Whites and the Indians, as neither could agree on what the term "ownership" meant.

In the south, the Comanche and Kiowa were raiding up from the Texas panhandle to the Solomon River. Clashes with the Army there had increased in proportion to the number of ranches sacked and the number of settlers killed or carried away as prisoners.

The Indian Commissioner Greenwood called the Cheyenne and the Arapaho to hold council and open up new treaty talks at Bent's Fort. These talks were useless as no real agreement could be made without all members of the Council of Forty-four Chiefs. Even if all these had been present, the ratification of the treaty would not be consummated without first consulting with the leaders of the military bands of the Cheyenne: the Kit Foxes, Bowstrings, Elkhorn Scraper Red Shields and of course the Crazy Dog Society, the Dog Soldiers. Black Kettle and White Antelope argued this point, saying the northern chiefs were not present, but Greenwood persisted stating there were time constraints and he had to deal with other tribes. The Arapaho and Cheyenne chiefs, who did sign, agreed on annuities of

$30,000 each year for the next fifteen years. Black Kettle refused to sign.

Near Bent's Fort, the Army had begun to build a new fort calling it Fort Wise, and there was some fear that the presence of more White soldiers would only cause greater problems. But, the band of Little Wolf and Crow Eyes were camped in the Smokey Hills far north of the new fort and there, it was peaceful. Peace seemed so secure south of the Platte River that Whit and Maggie again allowed Zachary to visit White Badger, his Cheyenne uncle. Whit had reservations about letting his son spend time with his wife's people but gave in after his son begged to go.

It was agreed that before the winter snows, Whit, and Silas or August, would make their way out to meet the band and bring Zachary home. In the past, Whit had found one excuse after the other to stay away from the Cheyenne during Zachary's visit, and this disappointed the boy, but the experience of living among the Cheyenne instilled in Zachary a longing for the freedom this lifestyle offered that equaled the wanderlust of his father. More and more he saw himself as Yellow Horse the Cheyenne.

***

August 1861 - Breeding Moon

The new year had brought with it many changes, not only in the west but nationwide. In February, the Big Hoop Moon, the chiefs of the Cheyenne and Arapaho were again gathered to sign another treaty. This time, they assembled at the new Fort Wise. Among them were: Black Kettle, White Antelope, Lean Bear, Little Wolf, Tall Bear, Lone Bear of the Cheyenne, and Left Hand, Little Raven, Storm, Shaved Head and Big Mouth of the Arapahos. Again, Black Kettle had insisted upon gaining approval of the Cheyenne Council of Forty-four, as he was one of only six of its members who had signed this new treaty. It was evident to anyone who knew the Cheyenne that this was basically a serious breach of Cheyenne political. The treaty drove a deeper wedge between the people and their leadership, and the Cheyenne people began to show their dissatisfaction in their leaders. Most of all, signing of the treaty by Chief Lean Bear enraged many of the Dog Soldiers, as he was one of their own.

In the east, that same month, the U. S. Congress approved the establishment of the Colorado Territory, incorporating portions of the New Mexico, Utah and Kansas Territories. Statehood seemed eminent to some, but the Congressional designation of new western states and territories had been bogged down for several years as southern and northern politicians fought over whether slavery would be permitted in the new western regions.

Overshadowing this, Abraham Lincoln the 16th President was sworn in. Disagreements, over tariffs, territorial issues, and slavery between the northern and southern states had already culminated in the secession of South Carolina from the Union, followed by Mississippi, Florida, Alabama, Georgia, Louisiana, and Texas. By June 1861, Arkansas, North Carolina, Virginia, and Tennessee joined the newly established Confederate government led by President Jefferson Davis.

With the outbreak of the war, most of the regular U. S. Troops were removed from the Indian country and sent east to fight. If the Cheyenne had truly desired to go on the war path, the opportunity was at hand. But, other than minor disagreement over a horse or mule now and then, the Cheyenne and Arapaho remained peaceful.

Newly appointed governor of the Territory, William Gilpin, filled the void left by the removed U.S. force, when he signed orders to establish the 1st Regiment of Colorado Volunteers. Recruiters began enlisting men in August of 1861, and Gilpin offered John Chivington the position of chaplain of the new regiment. But the preacher refused it, stating he wanted to fight instead. So, the Governor appointed Chivington as Major in the first Colorado Volunteers. Like Chivington, Silas Soule left civilian life at the outbreak of the Civil War, joining the Regiment and soon earned a commission as a lieutenant in Company K.

Though the Cheyenne and Arapaho had kept a relative peace with the whites, the old habits of raiding the Ute and the Pawnee were still commonplace. The peace along the upper Arkansas had lulled those living at and near Pueblo into a sense of security, and again Zachary could spend time with his Cheyenne family.

The summer had turned long and dry, and game had become scarce along the Arkansas. The People could not wait until the fall when the government annuities would be delivered at Fort

Wise. So, it was decided that hunting parties be sent out past the boundaries of the newly established reservation, and with one of these hunting parties was Zachary.

There were two dozen Cheyenne in this group, and as this was not a war party, it included women and a few small boys. Zachary knew most of the group from his previous time in the camps with White Badger. A good many of the hunters were Dog Soldiers, his uncle among them. Other Dog Soldiers in the group of men were: Bear Voice, Sitting Hawk, and Blue Crane the young man who had taken Azariah Bolt's scalp.

Among the women were Zachary's aunts, Red Willow Woman and Sees Far Woman. Sees Far always made Zachary uneasy when he was around her, for among the People she was considered special, one who had been touched by a sacred spirit. To Zachary, her shabby clothing and unkempt hair gave her the appearance of a crazy person. She would stare at him and babble some incoherent words or chants, and constantly ask Zachary if he had seen Little Bird, never mentioning her by name, but calling her his "true" mother. Zachary made every effort to keep a distance between the woman and himself.

Zachary also tried to keep a distance from Bear Voice, who like Sees Far, seemed to have some form of fascination for him. Sees Far made Zachary uneasy, but Bear Voice could send chills through the boy's blood.

White Badger had taught Zachary how to hunt in the style of the People, both by stealth and by "running" or chasing the desired game. This day the group had come upon a group of six buffalo grazing near a wallow, and there had been no time to sneak up on them. The buffalo broke into a run at the first smell of the hunters. One, a great cow, separated from the rest and was pursued by White Badger, with Zachary close to him, following his every movement as he rode after the shaggy beast. Trailing behind them was Badger's wife, Red Willow Woman, and the packhorse. The other members of the hunting party followed the other five animals and soon Badger, Zachary and Badger's wife Red Willow were separated from the group.

It took almost a mile for White Badger to pull alongside the buffalo and position himself for a shot with his smoothbore Trade Gun. His first shot drove deep into the cow. Her steps faltered, but then she regained her stride and ran on. As she did this, Badger reloaded, first pouring powder directly from the horn down the barrel, and then he spat a lead ball from his mouth, striking the butt of the gun on the pommel of his saddle to seat the lead against the powder. He primed the pan in the same careless way, slapping down the frizzen, and shouldered the gun, fired another shot into the cow. She slowed, took a few more hesitant steps, and finally rolled to a stop on the dusty prairie. Badger circled at safe distance, waiting to see if she would rise to her feet and fight. But he had no need to worry, both gunshots had penetrated the cow's lungs, and within a minute she was dead.

When Badger signaled that all was safe, Red Willow and Zachary rode forward, pulling a pack horse behind them. Red Willow went directly to work on the cow, first removed tongue, then she skillfully cut the hide down the buffalo's spine, laying out the skin on either side of the carcass. She then removed the internal organs, the liver she handed to Badger, who sliced off a chunk and handed it to Zachary. Both Badger and Zachary cut smaller pieces, stuffed them in their mouths and chewed, relishing the rich meat.

The three were so preoccupied with the butchering that they did not notice a dozen warriors of the Wolf People, Pawnee, who had appeared at the crest of the hill overlooking them. If it had not been for an overenthusiastic young warrior among these Pawnee, they could have ridden directly down on the Cheyenne with little trouble. But the war cry that had escaped the young man's lips warned Badger. He quickly brought up his Trade Gun and firing, dropped one of the Pawnees from the saddle. Without looking for the result of his shot, he reloaded, as the remaining Pawnee thunder down the hill, all now screaming.

Badger stood his ground near the buffalo, as arrows and lead flew past him or landed in the ground harmlessly. He calmly reloaded and fired, and as he did so, he warned Zachary to get behind the dead animal, but the boy stood next to his uncle and pulling arrows from his quiver, fired one after another in the direction of the Pawnee. Two more of the Wolf People fell from their saddles, and the remainder wheeled and returned to the top of the hill, where they assessed the situation.

Badger asked Zachary how many arrows he had left, and the boy replied he had only three.

"Hold those back until they are right on us," Badger said, *"We must make every shot count. Show these eaters of dog shit that*

you are not afraid, you are a warrior of the Tsitsistas, a Cheyenne."

The Pawnee had lost three of their warriors to a single Cheyenne man, a boy and a woman. They could not leave the field of battle with this shame. They summoned their courage, and again with war cries escaping their lips, they charged down on three Cheyenne.

Again, Badger stood as if there was nothing to fear. He dared one quick glance at his nephew, and smiled inwardly thankful that if he had to die this day, he would die with a brave young man next to him. If they lived, he would sing of the day he and Yellow Horse defeated a force of enemy four times their size.

Badger raised his trade gun and fired, striking a leading Pawnee in the thigh, and as he reloaded, he watched Zachary fire an arrow, though the targets were too far away. But the boy's aim was good, for he had aimed high allowing for the distance, and his arrow struck a warrior in the chest, sending him to the ground. Badger did not watch where Zachary's second arrow went as he was aiming at another foe. Just as he pulled the trigger the air filled with the war whoops of a dozen Cheyenne and their shots and arrows fell among the Pawnee. Some were killed instantly, the rest turning to flee, but these were easily overtaken. Within minutes, not a single Pawnee survived.

Blue Crane and his friends Red Arm and Small Belly were already off their horses taking scalps and other plunder from the dead. Wolf Horn was just bending down to take a scalp lock from one warrior when Badger stopped him.

"Look at the arrow in that man's chest," he said, *"It is that of my nephew, Yellow Horse. The scalp is his to take."*

Wolf Horn stopped and willingly stepped aside and gave his attention to another dead Pawnee.

Badger called Zachary over to him, *"Yellow Horse, come and take what is yours."*

The boy, his face ashen, came closer and looked from his uncle to the dead man lying at his feet. This was the first dead person that Zachary had seen and the weight of this and the fact that he had caused this death overwhelmed him. He felt faint, and then nausea overcame him, and he lost the raw liver he had just eaten. He wasn't sure if he felt shame or embarrassment, but he hesitated to look at his uncle.

"Do not worry nephew," said Badger, *"There are few Cheyenne that can boast of taking their first scalp at your age. Here, let me show you how it is done."* Badger reached down and taking the Pawnee's roached hair in his hand cut it free, then handed it to the boy, asking, *"Is there any other prize you wish from his man?"*

Only then did Zachary notice the beaded knife sheath and the long knife it held. He shook his head, still not daring to open his mouth, fearful he would vomit again. Pointing at the knife, he waited to see if his uncle would remove it for him. When this did not happen, Zachary reached out with shaking hands, undid the belt holding the knife sheath, and pulled it loose. Sliding the knife from the leather, he saw the markings on the blade, "H. M. SLATER SHEFFIELD."

As he looked down at the knife and bloody trophy in his hands, Zachary was startled by the scream of a woman that split the air. Sees Far stood pointing in his direction. With a maniacal laugh she yelled, *"Look, see his mother stands by his side! She stands by his side and is proud of her warrior son!"*

***

October 1861- Moon When Thin Ice Begins to Form on Rivers

A poorer selection of sites could not have been chosen for the newly built Fort Wise. It was located too close to the river, and the drainage was poor. Far from impressive, the fort consisted of little more than loose stone corrals and crudely constructed buildings with dirt floors.

At the fort, was newly appointed Indian Agent, Samuel G. Colley who had only recently replaced Albert G. Boone, grandson of Daniel Boone. Colley, with his son Dexter, also operated a trading business using John Smith from Pueblo as interpreter.

When Silas and Whit arrived, they found things in a wretched condition, the soldiers looking almost as poorly as the few Cheyenne who had chosen to stay near the fort. Speaking with these Cheyenne, Silas heard rumors that Confederate forces were poised to attack in the west and take all the forts in New Mexico and along the Arkansas River. He did know that representatives from Texas had been courting all the tribes in the south, but with little success.

Another rumor that the Cheyenne passed on to Silas was that the Colleys and Smith were selling government-issued annuities to the Indians. Angered by this, Silas was determined to give Colley a thrashing, but Whit convinced him that a cooler head, when faced with a fort full of soldiers, was more prudent. Silas reluctantly agreed and the two made their way to Bent's where they would stay until Black Dog's band came in with Zachary.

It was three days later that the several bands of Cheyenne and Arapaho arrived and camped nearby. Silas and Whit started their search for Black Dog's people, going from one band to the other. At many of the camps, Silas was well-known, and the offer of Cheyenne hospitality was given freely. He was asked to stay, smoke and eat. These he had to refuse but promised that he would come back at another time.

One offer Silas and Whit did except, was that from Little Wolf. His band set apart from most of the others, and was far smaller, consisting of only a dozen lodges. Little Wolf now lived with his son-in-law, Crow Eyes and Crow Eyes' wife, Meets the Enemy. They were happy to see Silas, and Silas was overjoyed to see them. While Meets the Enemy set out food for the men, Silas and Wolf talked, and smoked.

"There is much discontent among the People," said Wolf, *"The young men do not agree with their chiefs, and the Dog Soldiers are becoming stronger and stronger in their influence among all the bands."*

"Do you see some preparing to go on the war path?" Silas asked.

"It is possible. I have been saying for many years that there would come a day where we could no longer live alongside the Whites. Now, with this new treaty, and the small reservation set by it, there is not enough room for the people, and many are already leaving it to hunt and follow the buffalo."

"The time has come to leave the old ways," Whit said, drawing a look of disbelief from Wolf, and he switched to English.

"You have not lived among us long enough to understand, Sky Eyes. Before the Americans came, before the French, before the time of the horse among the People, we were free to go where we wanted. Our land had no boundaries other than those we set for ourselves. We went where we were led by the buffalo, and if there were those, like the Crow or the Comanche who did not want us in their territory, we pushed them aside. We will not be like the Crow, and the Comanche, we will not step aside."

"Why can't you live with the Whiteman?" Whit asked.

"I have just told you, we have been free for too long to settle down and plow the earth."

"Life was much easier when you were a boy trying to steal my horses!" Silas chuckled, smiling at Wolf.

"Yes, Uncle, life was better then. We did not have to depend on someone else to dole out annuities so that we may eat through the winter."

"It may change for the better, son," Silas said.

"It would be easier to believe that we could drink sand." Wolf paused, took a puff on his pipe, and then smiling said, "Tell me of my brother Tom Craigavon, and of your daughter Willow. I would know about everyone."

Whit left the two old friends and they talked, catching up on friends and family on into the evening. Whit continued his search for Black Dog's lodge, and it was not long before he found it.

Sitting in front of the lodge was Black Dog, White Badger and a few other men. Some, Whit recognized, other were new to him. Among those seated in the group was Bear Voice, and the medicine man met Whit's appearance with a scornful look.

Whit dismounted his horse, and taking a large bundle from where it had been tied to the cantle of his saddle, he approached the seated group, his right hand raised in greeting.

"*Hello White Badger, Black Dog, excuse my interruption of your talk,*" he spoke in Cheyenne, "*I come with gifts and am in search of my son, Yellow Horse.*" He held the blanket-wrapped bundle out in front of him.

"*I see you Sky Eyes,*" said Badger, "*Come sit, we are done with our talking.*" he motioned to a place on the ground near him. As Whit eased himself down next to his brother-in-law, all but Black Dog and one other rose and moved off, Bear Voice casting another look of hatred before turning away.

Whit looked across at the remaining figure, and with surprise saw that it was Zachary. His hair had grown past his shoulders, and his skin had darkened with exposure to the sun. But most of all, he no longer looked like he was eleven years old, but much older.

"Hello Father," Zachary said, a slight smile crossing his face. He rose and went to Whit who stood and the two embraced.

"Damn, I hardly recognized you," Whit said. He looked the boy up and down, and still could not believe the change he saw before him. "You look like you've grew a foot taller in the past three months and put on some muscle too."

"I have done well among my mother's people," Zachary said, his words also more mature than before.

"Sit," Badger said, *"We will eat and talk."* and he called to his wife Red Willow to bring food out for them. As they waited, Whit opened the bundle and pulled out the presents he had brought. For Black Dog and Badger, he had brought each a new blue wool blanket, powder and lead, tobacco and half a dozen German silver conchos. For Red Willow, and Prairie Grass Woman, Whit had brought brass bracelets, several hanks of glass beads, a new looking glass, and some packets of vermillion.

"I thank you for taking my son into your lodge and keeping him safe," Whit said.

"Yellow Horse has been little trouble," said Badger.

"Yes, I am proud of my grandson," said Black Dog.

"I am sure he will have many stories to tell me," said Whit, looking over at his son who sat straight, smiling at his father.

Whit had no idea the depth of change that had occurred in his son. When Black Dog and Badger spoke of their pride in the boy, Whit thought it was only that he had been a good and obedient child. There was no way to know that the boy was long gone, and a budding warrior had taken his place. It was not until they had left the village and were on their way back to Pueblo that Silas asked Whit if Zachary had told him about his stay with the Cheyenne.

"Na, but I figure we have plenty of time to talk about it," said Whit still unsuspecting. Silas held back a bit and let Zachary catch up, so they rode together, slightly behind Whit and just out of earshot.

Silas looked over at Zachary and seeing the knife on the boy's belt remarked, "See you found yourself a knife."

"Yes Grandfather, an English knife like you said I could have. Isn't it wonderful?"

"Sure is. I 'spect you earned it?"

"Oh, yes," Zachary said, not sure if it would displease Silas if he knew how he had earned it. "My uncle, White Badger, gave it to me."

"I see," said Silas, knowing full well the entire story behind the battle with the Pawnee, for Little Wolf had told him. He would now have to think about the event and see if Zachary told his father about the killing of the Pawnee. If the boy didn't, Silas would have to decide if it was his place to tell Whit. His only problem was wondering if he should speak further about it with Zachary first.

***

November 1861 - Hard Faced Moon

News of the war in the east made its way to the west, and the men, like those before them, came to establish themselves as prospectors and miners or providers of goods, liquor, or prostitutes. They also brought their political leanings for the Confederacy or the Union with them. Thought the conflict in the eastern part of the Country seemed far away, the territory was Union in name only and was soon divided between Unionists and Secessionists. Only the actions of the Governor and the establishment of the Colorado Volunteer Army stopped total chaos in Denver.

In the opinion of most of those in the west, the war had already been raging for years in Kansas. Blood had been spilt, but anti-slavery forces prevailed, and Kansas entered the Union as a free state in January. Even though Colorado Territory leaned toward the Union, it was common opinion that the war would sooner or later touch the west. By fall, news about battles in the east had reached the mountains, and sentiments flowed hot following each Northern or Southern victory, especially those as close as Virginia and Missouri. And, what had been rumored, but not expected was the threat from Texas.

On May 13, 1861, career U.S. Army officer, Major Henry Hopkins Sibley, resigned his commission and sided with the Confederacy. A native of Louisiana with southern sympathies, his choice was a simple matter of loyalty to the South. He had served in the west and his knowledge of Union forts there made him an excellent choice for command. Jefferson Davis gave Sibley a commission as Brigadier General and command of a brigade of volunteer cavalry in West Texas. Sibley returned to the west and began consolidating his forces with the goal of invading the north soon after the first of the year.

Word finally reached Colorado Territory that the Confederacy had claimed the southern half of the vast New Mexico Territory as its own, naming it Arizona Territory. It was now obvious that an invasion from the south was imminent, and this placed the operations of the ranches on the Arkansas, and that of the Craigavons at Rayado, in danger.

Silas, William, August and Whit sat at the table in William's home discussing the course of action they would take. The talk contained a lot of speculation of what might happen in the coming months. With the men were Roseanne, Willow, Maggie and some of the children, the boys being the most excited.

"We need to decide what is practical," William said.

"Right, but we need to know what the real threat is," Whit said, "And do our best to make sure it doesn't reach our door!" Silas could see the fire in Whit's eyes, the longing for a conflict he could put his skills as a warrior against. Maggie also saw this old mistress that controlled Whit, and for the first time she was neither jealous nor was she afraid he would leave and not come home. She had ceased to care.

"We can't all leave here," Said William, "Silas and August can hold things together here, and Whit and I will go south, maybe stopping at Fort Garland first, then on to Rayado and if need be Fort Union. If all-out war comes north out of Texas, I'll try to talk as much of the family into coming here as possible."

"You'd have an easier time talking the sun out of the sky, than to get your Ma to leave her home," Silas said.

"I know, but I'll try," William said with a wry smile, "Truth is, I'd feel sorry for any sessish' that thought he was gon'na run her out of her home!"

"It's settled than," said August, "Silas and I vill take care of here!"

"I want to go too!" Zachary said.

"Sorry Son, but this ain't not trip for a boy,"

"Why can't I go?" Zachary asked, his anger growing.

"You don't understand, if it comes down to a real fight there'll be killin' an' that isn't right for a boy to see," Whit said laughing and tasseling his son's hair.

Zachary jerked his head away, and with a look of determination said in Cheyenne, *"I am not a child! I am a warrior of the People, my Mother's People!"*

Whit looked at his son in surprise, and then glanced at Maggie as if she would say something, but she remained silent. Turning back to his son he said, "I don't know where you got this nonsense from, but you'll stay here, and that's the end of it." Whit this, Zachary rushed from the house.

"I'll go with him," said Ransom, "He just needs to blow it off a bit." He followed Zachary out into the yard where they mounted their horses and sped off to be alone, away from the adults.

Zachary pushed his horse harder than was necessary, but Ransom kept up with him until Zachary brought his horse to a sudden stop and jumped off. Ransom stopped, dismounted, and tied both horses to a deadfall, then followed his friend into the woods.

"He just don't want me to go with him is all!" Zachary said, tears streaming down his cheeks.

Ransom stood and waited for his friend to vent, He knew, as boys do, that nothing he could say would help until Zachary reached the point where he almost asked for it.

"He thinks I'm a child, an' I'll just get in the way. I've always been in his way of doin' what he wants! He don't have no room fer me! If he knowed what I done, he'd see I'm more of a man than he thinks."

"What you done?" Ransom asked hesitantly. And Zachary told his friend everything that had happened with the Pawnee.

After Zachary was done, Ransom thought for a bit, surprised and somewhat envious of his friend, but he also felt sympathy for him.

"What you aim ta do?" he finally asked.

"I don't know. I don't think I belong here anymore. I wish they had left me with my mother's people."

***

271

SAM J. PISCIOTTA

CHAPTER THIRTEEN
BROTHER AGAINST BROTHER

February 1862 - Big Hoop Moon

The cold days of winter dragged on for Zachary. It seemed as if they would never end and spring would never come. The walls of the main house slowly began to feel confining, and the ever-presence of the others in the house unbearable. His patience and his gentle, tolerant nature seemed to disappear. Where once he had shown his affection to young John Klausen, he now showed irritation and hostility. And, at seven years old, John could not understand that his once loving "brother" wanted nothing to do with him. Still, he came back to Zachary asking him to play checkers with him.

"Can't you leave me alone?" Zachary almost shouted at the child, causing him to retreat to his mother crying.

"What's gotten into you boy?" Silas asked. "You know better than that."

"He's always bothering me," Zachary protested.

"He's a child," said Maggie.

"Well I got better things to do than keep him occupied," Zachary's words became sarcastic.

"You best remember who you're talkin' to," Silas said, his attitude changing to match the boy's. "Your mother doesn't deserve that kind'a tone."

"She ain't my ma!" Zachary almost spat out the words. As words had left Zachary's mouth, Silas was up from his chair, and the appearance of an old man disappeared, a powerful and angered man in his place. As he moved across the small room toward Zachary, the boy stepped back.

Silas didn't lay a hand on the boy and he kept his voice calm and serious, "A man's words define who he is and what he believes. That woman took you into her heart when she didn't have to. She gave you love when the woman that bore you left you without a second thought. There's no other person in the world that loves you more than she does."

Zachary looked across the room where Maggie stood, and tears welled up in his eyes. Sheepishly he moved over to Maggie, and head down, apologized.

"I didn't mean..." he started to say, but she threw her arms around him and pulled him tightly to her.

"I know, Zach. I know," she said. "Now go bring in some wood for the fire." He turned, pulled on his coat and went out the door.

"I don't understand that boy," Silas said.

"He misses his father," said Maggie, "And, he wanted to go south with him."

"Still no reason to talk to you like that, and where Whit went is no place for a boy even if he has seen killin'."

"What do mean, seen killing?" Maggie asked, and Silas realized he had almost revealed Zachary's experience among the Cheyenne.

"You know, killing of game or a lame horse, is all." But Maggie felt there was more to what had been said. For the time being, she would let it go. The door opened and Zachary and Eli entered each carrying an armful of wood.

"Saw this rascal struggling to carry a whole cord of wood and thought I'd give him a hand," Eli said, and he and the boy took the wood over and stacked it next to the hearth.

"Thank you, Eli," said Maggie, "Want a cup of coffee?"

"Yes, Ma'am," Eli said.

"Well, take off your hat and coat, and sit down with Silas," Maggie said as she retrieved a cup from the shelf and poured a cup of coffee for him, her slight smile noticed by both Eli and Silas.

"Thank you, Zach," Maggie said to the boy, and placed her hand on his shoulder to reassure him that she had forgiven his unkind words. Zachary said nothing but went to the room he shared with John and played checkers with the boy. Though cowed somewhat, Zachary was still deeply unhappy, and in his mind began to make plans for the coming spring. He would share these plans with no one, except his best friend Ransom Craigavon.

***

RIVER OF SAND

March 1862 – The Dusty Moon

In August of the previous year, Ceran St. Vrain and Kit Carson organized the 1st New Mexico Volunteer Infantry Regiment. This regiment, like the Colorado Volunteers, was formed in response to the removal of regular Federal troops in the west. In contrast to the peace along the Arkansas, the decrease in number of regular Federal troops had increased the hostilities of the Apache and Comanche in the southwest. Indian raids began to increase as some tribes took the chance to regain lost territory, while others, their treaty allotments having been disrupted by the war, turned to raiding for subsistence.

Whit and William Craigavon joined the 1st as scouts, and when they arrived at Fort Union, they were pleased to add William's father, Tom, to their ranks. The three soon found themselves far south of Santa Fe, at Fort Craig, near the town of Valverde, in what was now claimed by the Confederates as part of Arizona Territory. Under Kit Carson, they had joined the forces commanded by Colonel Edward Canby. Canby's forces comprised of almost four thousand men, mostly infantry. But only a quarter these men were seasoned soldiers. The remainder consisted of militia, and the New Mexican and Colorado volunteers.

They didn't have long to wait on the Texans. General Henry H. Sibley had left Texas in January and with over three regiments, arrived south of the fort on the 13th of February. Sibley judged the fort too strong to be taken by direct assault and deployed his men with the goal of enticing Canby out into the open for an attack. Failing to draw out the Union forces, Sibley decided to cross the Rio Grande, move up the east bank, and capture the river's ford at Valverde. This would sever Fort Craig's lines of communication to Santa Fe.

Whit, William and Tom had been sent out to scout the position of Sibley's forces and soon returned with news of the troop movements. Tom warned of the advance of Texans toward the ford. Canby immediately dispatched a mixed force of cavalry, infantry, and artillery, the cavalry arriving first to secure the crossing. When the Texans arrived, they were surprised to find Union troops there and took up position in the dry riverbed. As more troops arrived, the battle commenced with the Union forces taking the upper hand at first, but in the fierce fighting that followed, the Texans succeeded in taking the Union artillery and shattering the Union line. His position collapsing, Canby was compelled to order a retreat across the river to the fort.

Falling back to Fort Craig, Canby resumed a defensive position, and though Sibley had won a victory in the field, he still lacked enough forces to successfully attack Fort Craig. Short on rations, he chose to continue north towards Albuquerque and Santa Fe with the goal of re-provisioning his army. Canby, believing he was outnumbered, elected not to pursue, but called on his scouts to flank the Texans and report to Fort Union.

Knowing the country well, the three men were able to outdistance the Texans and made their way north arriving at the garrison in Santa Fe at about the same time as the Texans were taking control of Albuquerque. Warning the small force of Union troops located there, they advised a retreat to Fort Union, and to destroy what ammunition and supplies they could not take with them.

Upon arriving at Fort Union, they found the First Colorado Volunteers under the command of Colonel John P. Slough. They had marched the four hundred miles from Denver in only thirteen days. Already unpopular with his own men, Slough made more enemies by establishing himself as the post commander over Colonel Gabriel Paul by virtue of date of rank. Paul, a career officer, was promoted to colonel a matter of months after Slough was appointed colonel by Governor Gilpin.

The strategic location of Fort Union controlled movement along the Santa Fe Trail and the surrounding region. It also housed a significant arsenal of weapons and large stores of ammunition and supplies. But with the news of that the Confederate forces had already taken Albuquerque, and most likely Santa Fe, Slough made only a brief rest to re-supply, then defying Canby's orders to hold Fort Union at all costs, he headed south to engage the Confederates.

Joined by elements of the 1st and 3d U.S. Cavalry Regiments and New Mexico volunteers, the 1st Colorado followed the Santa Fe Trail, hoping to catch the enemy in Apache Canyon before they crossed over the gap in the Sangre de Cristo Mountains, called Glorieta Pass.

Whit and William traveled with the army, and Tom went on to Rayado, where he would try to convince his wife and family to move north to the ranch at Pueblo.

Slough sent out advance troops, under the command of Major John Chivington, who set up camp east of Glorieta Pass. Whit had gone with Chivington as a scout and guide, while William stayed behind with Slough. Soon after establishing camp, Chivington ordered a detachment from the mounted company, with Whit as guide, to find some actionable intelligence.

Whit was the first to spot a small contingent of Sibley's scouts and these were easily captured. A quick interrogation of these scouts provided enough information on the whereabouts and intentions of the Confederate army. On the morning of March 26th, Sough's troops began movement towards the suspected Confederates.

In the ensuing engagement Union forces took to the high ground, and with well-timed cavalry charges, the Rebels were forced to withdraw. The day ended with the Coloradoans holding the field, having pushed the Texans several miles back to the mouth of Apache Canyon. Taking the next day to reorganize, both Union and Confederate leaders assessed their next moves. Texas Colonel Scurry would attempt to take the higher ground but divided his forces, leaving an entire company to guard the Rebel supplies against looters or a surprise attack.

Slough had also divided his forces, putting Chivington in charge of four hundred men with the task to locate and destroy the enemy supply trains. He also ordered Chivington to be prepared to support the main Union force with a charge on the Confederate's right flank if he heard guns. Again, Whit went with Chivington to act as a scout among the skirmishers who would be sent out first. Among these was a soldier that recognized Whit but went unnoticed by him in the sea of blue greatcoats. Sargent Azariah Bolt had watched Whit and William for days, careful lest the Doctor recognize him, but less cautious around Whit. Azariah would bide his time and in the frenzy of battle would make his move on William, hopefully taking the Doctor's scalp while he still lived. Bolt planned on ask the doctor if he could heal himself. He was slightly disappointed when it was Whit who had been chosen to go with Chivington and not William, but there would be other opportunities, and of course there was other prey among the Rebel trash.

On the morning of March 28th, the Coloradoan's encountered a Texan force moving southeast from Santa Fe. What followed was some of the most intense close quarters combat of the battle. Many of the Texans carried shot guns loaded with several rounds in each barrel, each shot striking several soldiers at a time. The Coloradoans and Texans would trade ground back and forth as a result of several attacks and counterattacks at the center of the battlefield, none proving successful. The fighting was in such close quarters that the combatants at time mingled without knowing it. The Texans, wearing blue coats taken from the Union armories in the south, at times found themselves fighting next to the Coloradoans.

After some time, it became evident to Scurry that the key to victory was possession of an outcropping of high ground on the southeast portion of the battlefield that afforded command of the entire area. The Coloradoans held that position, and Scurry became determined to capture it. As Scurry contemplated how he would secure it from the Coloradoans, a company of fresh Rebel soldiers seemingly appeared from nowhere and flanked the Union right. With the Coloradoans on the high ground focused on the center of the battlefield, the company of Texans drove them from the ridge after intense fighting. These fresh Rebel troops were the company that had been left guarding the supply trains, but upon hearing gunfire, they had moved toward the battle. They helped drive the Union forces back, but had left the vital supplies only lightly guarded.

Meanwhile, Chivington's column of mounted scouts had made their way across the Grand Mesa and had located the Texan's supply train. With only a handful of soldiers guarding it, Chivington ordered an attack. The charge was quick and devastating, the Coloradoans easily defeated the handful of Texans. The Coloradoans destroyed the wagons, set the supplies ablaze, and freed several Union prisoners while capturing many of the Confederates guards.

Whit rode through the destruction of the Rebel camp, and for the first time he had the chance to see the faces of the defeated, the dead and the dying. The adrenalin from the battle had cooled, and he now had time to think. On one hand, these men had invaded from the south, and Whit felt justified in vanquishing them. On the other, this had been different from fighting Indians, these men looked no different than himself, and he was stirred by these conflicting emotions. Among the sounds of the burning wagons, exploding and popping ammunitions, Whit could hear the moaning of some of the wounded, but a shrill cry from behind one of the smoldering wagons drew his attention and he moved toward it.

As he moved around the upturned vehicle, he thought he caught a glimpse of a soldier going around the other side, but on the ground, he found a Texan, lying on his back, holding his hands to his stomach, to stop the flow of blood. He was barely a boy, not much older than Zachary, and Whit knew that he was gut shot and had no chance of surviving. The boy looked up at him and Whit could see the belly wound was not his only injury. The top of his head was bleeding where the scalp had been torn off.

Whit got down from his horse, and removing his canteen, knelt to offer the boy a drink. As he placed the neck of the canteen to the boy's parched lips, the young Rebel went limp and died. Looking around, Whit wasn't sure what to do, but the urge to find the soldier who had just left the boy overcame him. He wondered if it had been one of the boy's comrades who had abandoned him, or was it one of the 1st Coloradoans who had taken a trophy.

He mounted his horse and moved out from behind the wagon looking for the blue-coated figure, but there out in front of him were several men, all looking alike. For the first time in years, Whit felt what was akin to homesickness and Zachary came into his thoughts. He decided as soon as possible he would return to Pueblo and be a better father to his son.

The baggage train was the sum-total of the Confederate resupply, and without it, they were crippled. Its destruction was the decisive blow, crippling the Texans. And, at the end of the day, the Texans were forced to retreat and not only give up Santa Fe, but all of New Mexico. Their march home was long, and they faced starvation the entire length of the journey. Behind them they left the dreams of taking the Colorado gold fields. A Confederate victory in the west had evaporated.

The Coloradoans, flush from victory, turned back toward home. Now that there was no threat from the south, their thoughts, real or perceived, were now on the plain's tribes.

Whit and William returned to Pueblo, and good to his intentions, Whit tried to be closer to his son. For two weeks, he would try to engage Zachary in one thing or another, but the boy remained distant and would not forgive his father for leaving him behind. It was not long before Whit gave up and as in the past found a reason to leave. His leaving, driving another wedge between him and his son, and distancing himself from Maggie.

By late summer, the government annuities or other goods and services promised in the Fort Wise Treaty, were still not delivered. Although the Treaty demanded the Cheyenne and Arapaho remain in the Sand Creek, few of either tribe remained on the arid and inhospitable Sand Creek reservation; instead, they reverted to the old practice of following the buffalo herds, and the encounters with White emigrants increased. To aggravate the tensions among the tribes, the political division over the treaty tore an even bigger hole between the warrior societies and the elders. Hostilities grew to the point where it seemed there would be a total breakdown of the old social order.

With the threat of a Texas invasion from New Mexico resolved, the Colorado Volunteers had returned home. Newly appointed Territorial Governor, John Evans, combined the members of the 1st Colorado Infantry and of C and D Companies of the 2nd Colorado Infantry to form the 1st Colorado Cavalry. The duties of the 1st Cavalry were both to protect Colorado against further incursion from the Confederate forces and if needed, fight the Indians who already inhabited the territory. Command of this unit was given to Colonel John Chivington.

***

September 1862 - Moon of Plums Ripening

Zachary sat on the spotted pony given to him by his uncle, White Badger, looking out on the horse herd grazing along the Cherry River. Next to him were Silas' grandsons, Turtle Shell and Red Fox Waiting. Fox was the same age as Zachary, and Turtle, two years older. At each visit to the Cheyenne, Zachary had become closer to these two boys and was their constant companion. He had spent as much time with them as he could and was now enjoying his last few days with them among the Cheyenne.

"I heard the old men talking about going to the Whiteman's stone lodge after the buffalo hunt," Fox said, speaking of Bent's Fort.

"No, I believe we will stay here on the Cherry River into the winter moons," said his brother.

"I wish we could go to visit our Grandfather," said Fox, *"We could go with Yellow Horse when he returns to Grandfather's lodge."*

"You would not like it there," said Zachary.

"Why would I not? Grandfather has always been good to us, and I would see him before he travels over to the other side. You are lucky to live in his lodge!"

"When will you leave us?" asked Turtle.

"I believe I will not leave," said Zachary.

"That is foolish! Of course, you will leave, my father has said so."

"I do not stay in the lodge of your father, I live in the lodge of White Badger, my Uncle."

"I am made to think you will leave us," Turtle said, *"You have little choice."*

"What do you know? You are not a warrior. You are still a child!" Zachary's words were meant to hurt Turtle, but Turtle, like his grandfather, was slow to anger, and would not take the bait.

"I have been four times with a party to still horses from the Pawnee, and once from the Ute. I returned home with horses that I can call my own. I have ridden as a man in hunt of the buffalo and brought meat to the hungry. I am looked on with favor by the young women. And, when the time comes for me to earn the right to be called a warrior among the People, I will be ready. It will not be by accident."

The words cut Zachary and with little thought he sprang from his horse's back toward the older boy. The few years difference in their age gave Turtle the advantage of not only strength, but agility and speed. The fifteen-year-old used Zachary's momentum against him, and taking the boy by the arms, pulled him forward, throwing him over the neck of his own horse on to the ground.

Zachary looked up from the ground, his face red with rage. The anger made even worst with the laughter of Fox. Turtle slid from his horse and held out a hand to Zachary, helping him to his feet.

"*I know that you have taken a Pawnee scalp,*" Turtle said smoothing over the wounded pride he had caused Zachary. "*I envy you that. But you have much more to learn before you can place yourself above others.*"

"*I will be a Dog Soldier one day, and many of the people will know of my deeds,*" Zachary said, then as his embarrassment cooled, he added, "*You are right Brother, I have much to learn.*"

News seemed to spread across the grassland of the plains, like a fire driven by a strong wind. Word had reached the Cheyenne concerning the battles being fought among the Whiteman, the number of the dead astonishing those who heard, most not believing there could be that many Whites in the world. Those who did believe the numbers, hoped they were true, convinced that if this Whiteman's war continued, soon there would be no Whites left.

Word also reached the Cheyenne of large war parties of the Lakota that had went on the warpath. The Santee Lakota had attacked and killed many Whites in the land where the grandparents of the people had lived, far beyond the Big Muddy River. It was rumored that all the Whites in that area had been killed.

Closer to the territory of the Cheyenne, a second war party of Brule and Yankton Lakota had wiped out an entire village of Pawnee on the Loup Fork of the Moon Shell River. This had caused the alarmed Whites in that area to flee their farms. This bolstered the bravado of some of the more militant among the Cheyenne, and they began once more to talk of taking the war path.

***

When Whit returned to the ranch, he brought with him all the news from Denver, as well as that from the East. Whit would often bring copies of the Rocky Mountain News, and on this occasion, he brought copies of *Harper's Weekly* from March through June. Inside the pages were articles and illustrations of the battles that had raged in the East. They spoke of battles in Kentucky and Tennessee, what was considered the "West" by most folks in the States. There, a major battle had been fought in Corinth, Mississippi and a tragic battle at the Pittsburg

Landing near the Quaker meeting house of Shiloh in Tennessee. As everyone listened, Silas read aloud that over twenty-four thousand soldiers had lost their lives in just two days.

The newspaper was filled with articles about battles elsewhere in the States that had been just as fierce. The news was a litany of battles, Pea Ridge in Arkansas, a second battle at Manassas in Virginia.

Everyone found the news hard to comprehend. Silas commented that when he was with Andy Jackson at Horseshoe Bend, in Alabama, Jackson's whole force wasn't much more than three thousand. The thought of almost ten times that number dying in a single day was hard for anyone to imagine. The numbers astonished Whit. Though he had just fought the Texans in New Mexico, there were only a little over four thousand men under Slough's command, and the thought of ten times that number fighting in one battle made his head spin.

News from other quarters of the country were more of interest to those on the Arkansas. There was reports of an uprising of the Santee Lakota at New Ulm, Minnesota. Like the annuities guaranteed to the Cheyenne, those of the Santee had been slow in coming, if at all. Unlike the Cheyenne, the Lakota had taken out their frustrations on the Lower Lakota Agency's Redwood post, and the surrounding settlements, killing over one hundred men, women and children. The last news received was that the settlers were fleeing the area.

News from south of the Arkansas was not much better, with the defeat of the Texans, the Comanche and Kiowa had begun to raid, and the Texas frontier was in the worst turmoil it had ever seen. Everyone wondered if this unrest would spread to the Cheyenne and Arapaho? How far away was war in Colorado Territory?

A few days later, Whit and Silas traveled out onto the plains seeking the where-a-bouts of Black Dog's band of Cheyenne. At Bent's Fort, they ran onto a group of Cheyenne hunters who told them that the band had moved to the Smokey Hills River and would winter there. This would place them far to the north, and the two men headed in that direction following the Big Sandy River.

As they rode, they talked, and Whit expressed his thoughts on the War between the States, "We can't allow the Country to fall apart over slavery. If the States don't come back together, it won't be long before things go to hell out here."

"I agree with you that the Union needs to be preserved," said Silas, "Never did own another man, but never gave much thought to other than my own freedom. Like amongst the Whites, there's slaves in Cheyenne camps. Usually from another tribe, when a prisoner can't be absorbed into the family so to speak. Not common to sell a slave among the tribes, but not unheard of.

"I do recall a Snake woman taken prisoner by the Lakota who was sold to the Cheyenne. When she wouldn't work, the Cheyenne woman who owned her, beat her so bad she died. I guess slavery is bad no matter what race of people do it. might be a thing worth fighting against."

"Different killin' a Whiteman," Whit said, and this struck Silas with surprise.

"What you mean?" he asked.

"Well, fighting them Texans wasn't like fighting Indians."

"A human life is a human life, Whit. People bleed red no matter what the color their hide is."

"I've seen you kill, Silas. You ever kill a White man?"

"Yes, but I never took to killin' though, White or Red. Whether what I done was right, or wrong, I 'spect I'll pay for it in the end. I never took it lightly."

Whit waited for a while and then asked, "What was it like at Horseshoe?"

"That was a long time ago, Son."

"I know, but was it like fighting the Ute or the Blackfeet?"

"No, men killing men on that scale, is a terrible, terrible thing to be a part of. We were out for revenge as much as we were out to stop the war. The Red Sticks had pretty much killed anyone that they got ahold of. They slaughtered over five hundred people at Fort Mimms. Killed people all up and down the country. On the Duck River in Tennessee, they killed a dear friend of mine, and a woman I admired greatly, Tom Craigavon's Ma and Pa." Silas paused then added, "I don't like thinking about them times, I much prefer thinking about better days."

"Silas, you think there's gon'na be real trouble out here with the Cheyenne?"

"I'm afraid so," Silas shook his head. "It's been comin' for a long time. The nature of a man has a way of causing grief to himself and those around him. Doesn't matter what color your hide is, sooner or later, you'll rub someone the wrong way and he'll try to kill you for it. He believes he's right, and you'll believe he's wrong." Silas paused and then offered another opinion on the possibility of an all-out war with the plain's tribes. "I'm thinking there might not be a big fight. There isn't any cohesion, among any one tribe, let alone among the different tribes. They just don't have a knack fer a united action. Could be something may come from one small group like the Dog Soldiers, but that wouldn't mean all the bands would come together fer a fight."

"You've taught me a lot, Silas, but I can't understand how you see things from two different sides. The Cheyenne, like everyone else, must change with the times, an' if they don't, we'll have to force them."

Silas looked over at Whit, not sure what to say. After all the time with Whit, Silas was still surprised by him. Silas knew Whit had a wanderlust, but he questioned if Whit wanted a confrontation, a war, with the Cheyenne. Did he just want a fight, or did he have some other reason?

They made camp at what appeared to be a recently used village site. The area was littered with the castoff of an Indian village, and the garbage that was left behind. Silas would have preferred to move on a bit further, where to him, the air was a bit fresher, but Whit saw no reason to travel more and wanted to make camp.

They built a fire in a ring of stone that had been left in place by the previous inhabitants and there they settled down for the night. They talked little, as both men had thoughts that kept their minds busy, and there was a feeling between them that made them seek their own council. They both curled up in their blankets, and as the fire started to burn down, their eyes grew heavy, and it wasn't long before both men were asleep.

From a lifetime of living at the edge of death, Silas woke at the sound of movement near the horses. It was dark and the only light was that of the quarter moon, making the surroundings shades of black. Quietly he reached over and nudged Whit who woke with a slight start, but gained his composure when Silas whispered, "Something near the horses, might be some young buck trying to steal them."

Slowly, both men pulled back their blankets. Whit reached for his pistol and slowly rose to stand near his bedding. Silas stood and with his rifle in hand moved cautiously toward the horses. Both men listened to the night, the air now empty of sound except the slight movement of the horses. Whit lost sight of Silas as he melted into the darkness, and Whit strained his eyes to see anything moving that could be a threat. From the corner of his eye he caught a glimpse of what appeared to be more shadow than a real substance, but he raised the pistol and pointed it in that direction. Before he could act, the form of a woman rushed at him as though driven by a strong wind and it seemed to pass through him rather than around him. This left him drained and cold. An old feeling of unrest welled up inside of him. When Silas returned, he found Whit building the fire back up.

"Didn't see any sign," Silas said, "Could have been anything that spooked the horses." He crawled back into his blankets and saw Whit sitting on his bedding and stirring the coals in the fire, so he asked, "You stayin' awake?"

"Yep. It's close enough to dawn that I won't get back to sleep."

"I'm good fer a few more winks," Silas said and rolled onto his side leaving Whit to sit and ponder what he had seen, and why he kept seeing it.

***

The camp was deserted, the lodges torn down and the People moved off to a new site. Sees Far Woman walked through the waste that is always left behind when a village moves on. She was not afraid, for she knew, Little Bird, her sister, was with her. Only a few yards away, Little Bird too, walked through the old campsite, searching for something, her head down. Sees Far heard horses behind her and when she turned to look in that direction, the sky had become deep blue, and the horses were black silhouettes against it. She turned back to look for her sister and found her lost, but there seemed to be the glow of hot coals visible where there had once been a campfire. Sees Far moved toward the glowing embers and from the darkness that surrounded them, the figure of Sky Eyes, Whitney Voss appeared. He came at her and in fear she fell back hitting the ground, only to wake in her own bed, sweat drenching her.

The fear did not leave her and as it intensified, so did her hatred for Whit. Her only comfort was that her nephew, Yellow

Horse, was close by, in the lodge of her brother. the boy seemed to have adopted the ways of the People and with a scalp under his belt at only twelve winters old, he was sure to grow into a great warrior. Thoughts of him warmed her, and the fear seemed to melt away. She envisioned herself as someday sharing a lodge with Yellow Horse, of taking care of him, and in turn, he would care for her. This last though stirring something in Sees Far than she had thought long dead. Something she knew was wrong but thrilled her all that much more.

***

November 1862 - Hard Faced Moon

No sooner had Whit and Silas returned to the ranch with Zachary, then Whit found reason to leave. He had spent the few days traveling from the Cheyenne camp with his son but found the boy moody and unwilling to commit to even the smallest conversations. Most questions put to the boy were answered with either a shrug, or as few words as necessary. Zachary's attitude changed little with the departure of his father, and though respectful, he did little to make himself feel part of the family.

The only one he seemed to still be close with was Ransom Craigavon, and every opportunity he had he would spend with his friend. They would pass hours together, Zachary talking about life among the Cheyenne, and how one day he would never come back from them.

"Come with me," Zachary asked.

"I don't know," said Ransom, "It might be alright fer a week or so, but I like it here."

"You like working like a Digger?" Zachary used the term that applied to those Indians who made their lives farming or digging in the ground for their subsistence.

"Nope, I'm thinking about being a doctor like my Pa."

"You'd have to go away, back to where they have schools for that kind of thing. And, you may never get a chance to come back. You can't pass up livin' with the Cheyenne."

"There'll always be a need fer doctors," Ransom said, "But, even if I go, that won't be for some time, and maybe next summer I could go with you for a bit."

"Do you promise?" Zachary asked.

"Sure Zach, I promise."

***

January 1863 - Moon of Frost on the Lodge

Though the daylight hours started to become longer, the days passed slowly, and the temperatures dropped steadily into February. As was normal for the front range, there a few days when the temperatures were almost pleasant, but they created a false spring that served only as a taste of the warm weather that was still months off. To remind everyone of her power, Mother Nature sent a heaver and deadlier storm. From the north, she sent the cold air out of Canada to descend onto the plains. There she brought moist air up from the south. The marriage of these two forces of nature along the front range of the Rockies brought the heavy snows and strong winds of a blizzard lasting three days that brought all outside activities to a halt.

When the sun finally did appear, it was time to assess the damage done by the storm. The violent winds had driven snow into drifts as high as eight feet, and filled gullies and ravines making them invisible. One drift had completely covered the north side of the ranch house, and exit from the back door of the house was impossible. Where there were spaces between the boards on the barn's walls, snow had been driven in and much of the interior was covered with snow. The milk cow and the horses stabled in the barn were spared, but several animals had fallen into the unseen ravines or froze out in the open. Others had been scattered across the prairie east to the Baculite butte and south toward the Arkansas River.

To make a search for the missing stock, the hired help was divided up into two groups, one under Silas and one under August. Silas, with Eli and two men, and Zachary went south along the Fountain toward the Craigavon ranch, stopping there to check on their welfare. August, with three men, skirted the butte to the east and moved south toward the Arkansas.

Silas had donned his old wolf-skin hat and heavy winter blanket coat. With his gray hair and beard it was hard to tell where the fur from the hat ended and that of Silas began. Clenched in his teeth was his ever-present pipe, the blue-white smoke curling up and drifting away in the clear cold air. On either side of Silas rode Zachary and Eli. Zachary wore a heavy coat but had also wrapped a buffalo robe around himself.

Like Silas, Eli wore a fur cap, his made of badger fur, with ear flaps tied down under his chin. His curly dark beard contrasted the lighter colored fur, and made his face look rounder than it was. Hoarfrost had formed around his mouth, pulling at the hair on his face. Eli ran his hand across his face to clear the icy crystals, and Silas chuckled at the futile effort.

"Don't much care for the cold, do ya?" Silas asked with a chuckle.

"Not so much," Eli said, his breath vaporizing in the air as he spoke. "Guess I'm more partial to summer. Seems I can cool down a lot easier than I can warm up."

"This is cold, but I've seen it colder," Silas said puffing on his pipe. "Why when I was up on the Missouri with that Spanish bastard Lisa, it got so cold words would freeze in midair as we spoke 'em. We'd have ta gather them up and carry them over to the fire to thaw them out, just to have a conversation." He chuckled at his own joke and looked over at Zachary to see if the boy had found humor in the little story. Zachary only pulled the buffalo robe tighter around himself, covering most of his face.

Eli, let out a small laugh, and this made Silas smile broader. Seeing that he had at least one captive in his small audience, he went on to spin another tale.

"I remember a night so cold that when we woke up in the morning we found ourselves surrounded by a passel of Blackfoot. There must have been thirty of 'em, just standing there right among our beds. Hell, I jumped up outa my blankets and was ready fer a fight, but them Blackfoot was all frozen solid. They had left their blankets behind in order to sneak up on us and froze to death right in their tracks." He chuckled. Again, he looked over to Zachary and there was still no sign the boy was amused. The only reaction from Zachary was to kick his heels to his horses' flanks and push out ahead of Silas and Eli to ride alongside of Santiago.

"The boy don't seem to have a sense of humor these days, does he?" Eli said.

"Naw, he has a lot on his mind. I figure his blood is startin' to warm. He'll be thinkin' of gals pretty soon," Silas knew that this was probably only part of the truth. Zachary would be thirteen years old in a few months, but Silas knew it was the absence of Whit in the boy's life that was affecting him more. Eli had a similar notion.

"Don't help none that the boy ain't got a father to turn to," Eli said but quickly added, "Not that you ain't a good substitute as a grandfather."

"No offence taken, Son," Silas said.

"You can tell me if I'm out of line, but it seems to me the boy needs a man close to him, and so does Miss Magdalena." He surprised himself at mentioning Maggie, but it was now out in the open. He had finally broached the subject.

Silas had wondered when Eli would make his feelings for Maggie known. He looked over at Eli, and asked, "You got some intentions toward Maggie?"

"I don't want trouble, Silas, it's just..." he paused as if to build up his courage, "I have noticed her, and I respect her, being a married woman and all. And, I ain't one to come between a man and his wife. But Whit don't seem like much of a husband to me. If she were my wife, I'd treat her like she deserves."

"You spoke with her?" Silas asked.

"No, Sir! I haven't had the nerve to."

"Well now, I can't tell another man what he should do, but I know you won't get what your heart desires just waiting for it to happen. I had a similar situation with my wife. You see my best friend was in love with her and I thought she with him. It wasn't until I talked to her that I found out she wanted me."

"So, you think I should speak to her?"

"I didn't say either way. That's your choice."

They rode on, collecting what stock they found along the way to the Craigavon ranch. When they reached there, they found that it had also lost stock due to the blizzard. William, Ransom and their hired hands joined in the hunt for the cattle and horses that had spread across the plains from both ranches. The hunt continuing until dark when they returned home, driving what few animals they had found in front of them.

Maggie and Willow had a hot meal waiting for the men when they returned, and the mood was one of quiet optimism with the hopes that with the coming warmer weather, more of the lost horses and cattle would be found.

Maggie took special care making sure Zachary was warm and had enough to eat, but as it had been for some time, her care was lost on the boy, and without speaking he went to his bed directly after eating. Having grown accustomed to his mood, she went about cleaning up after the meal with Willow at her side. Willow knew the hurt her friend felt, but could not find the words that would ease the pain.

Eli watched the women as they cleaned the dishes, and seeing Maggie near the coffee pot, went to pour himself a cup. As he did this, he spoke to her, "Thank you for supper. Can't say when I've had a better meal."

She looked over to him and her eyes met his. He smiled and a pleasant flush of warmth came over her, causing her to smile back.

"You men worked extra hard today, and needed a good hot meal," she said.

"I just know that food tastes better when you cook it." Eli had no idea what he was saying, but he saw that it had pleased Maggie. Not wanting to press his luck, he moved back to where the men sat talking. Maggie followed him with her eyes and the disappointment over Zachary seemed to fade a bit.

The next few days warmed up, the sun bright in the clear pale blue sky. With the warmth came a thaw that made the ground muddy, and progress in finding more stock was made difficult. After the search was completed, the losses were felt but the outcome was not as bad as it could have been. Work was also started on repairing the damage done to the barn and the corrals. This is where Eli's skills as a carpenter were of their best use. He and Santiago were replacing the top hinge of the barn door, when Eli spotted Maggie coming toward them, carrying a coffee pot and cups. She was wearing an ill-fitting wool coat and had a scarf over her head and ears to keep the chill away. He could see only a small portion of her face, and the small puffs of her breath in the cold air, as she walked across the yard. Though she was bundled up against the cold, she moved gracefully thought Eli, and he was sure he had never seen a more beautiful woman in his life. For the first time since he had met her at Fort Smith, he wondered how old she was. Surely, she couldn't be much older than twenty, but that didn't seem right, she had to be older.

"You fellows like some hot coffee to warm you up?" she asked.

"Si, Señora, muchas gracias," said Santiago. Both men put down their tools. Maggie handed them the cups and filled each.

"Thank you, Ma'am," said Eli.

"Please, call me Maggie," she said looking up into his eyes.

"I'd like that," he said, "Thank you, Maggie."

"Perdón, while we have stopped our work, I will fetch my gloves from the bunk house," said Santiago, and, taking the cup with him walked off toward the quarters of the hired hands.

"Funny," said Eli, "He just took off his gloves and laid them down when you walked up." He pointed to the gloves laying on the tools. They both felt a bit embarrassed at realizing that Santiago had left them alone on purpose.

"I would guess he had a reason to leave," said Maggie.

"I don't mean to be bold, but I have wanted to talk to you for some time now. I have had feelings for you, and I can't hold back any longer." He feared she would back away, but she remained. "I know you're a married woman, and now that I have told you how I feel, I should probably leave the ranch. I don't want to cause you no trouble."

"I wouldn't like that," she said, "That is, I wouldn't want you to leave."

"What of your husband?"

"He hasn't been a husband to me for a long time. I doubt he would care what would become of me."

"I feel I must be patient, and the first chance fate allows, I'll speak with your husband, and ask if he will release you."

"If you wish. But, don't wait too long Elijah. I see no reason why we could not spend some time getting to know one another better."

"Might it be possible to go riding together, when the weather gets warmer?"

"I'd like that very much, Elijah," she said and with this, she moved closer to him and standing on her tiptoes, she gave him a quick kiss on the lips. This startled and thrilled Eli, and before he could react, she had turned and walked back toward the house.

***

CHAPTER FOURTEEN
A NEW WAR

March 1863 – Dusty Moon

The raid against the Ute had been unsuccessful, and the war party was not looking to go home empty-handed and hungry. The homes of the few White settlers on the Cache la Poudre were easy prey and were looted for any valuables and stock left by the fleeing inhabitants. It was almost too easy thought Wolf Horn, who led the small party of Cheyenne warriors. If war against the White was this effortless, he felt that with just a hundred warriors, he could rid the country of the ve'ho'e.

With no fear of reprisal, the war party moved eastward, slowly making their way to the headwaters of the Republican and the Smokey Hills where buffalo was still to be found and also the camps of the Cheyenne.

The Whites, who had fled from the raid along the Cache la Poudre, mistakenly identified the looters as Lakota, and this is what they reported to the authorities. Thus, eyes were turned toward the north, and the Cheyenne simply made their way home.

***

On the Fountain River, just north of Pueblo, the ranches of William, Silas and August prepared for Spring. March always held the hopes for the last moisture of winter snows, and the coming rains. The early planting of the fields and the yearly birth of foals and calves were on the minds of everyone, except for Eli and Zachary.

Whit had spent the entire winter away from the ranches and Eli was anxious for his return. Until he had the chance to speak with Whit, he would not openly declare his love for Maggie. What he did allow for himself and Maggie, was a ride out together along the river, or up on the mesa to the east. Always in sight of the ranch, they felt it was safe and that they were exercising discretion. During these rides, they spoke honestly about their situation and their growing feelings toward each other.

Though it was cold, and they had to bundle up, they were willing to endure frigid morning air to seek out their favorite place on the Mesa where the sun's rays hit first, melting the frost on the pinons. At this spot, looking out onto the foothills and mountains to the west, they dismounted their horses and stood watching the sunlight reflect off the snow caped peaks of the Wet Mountains and peeking out behind them, the Sangre de Christos.

"Beautiful, isn't it?" Maggie asked.

"Yes, but it pales compared to you," Eli said.

Maggie laughed and said, "I am not a beautiful woman. Your words are flattering, but I am not a silly girl to be talked onto my back with just a few honeyed words. I know you speak them only to win me over."

Eli reached out and placed his hand on her cheek and felt the warmth of her blush as her blood warmed. He leaned down and kissed her, and as their lips parted, he softly said, "To me, you are the most beautiful woman in the world. Yes, I would make love to you with only a single word from your lips. But I am willing to wait, until I deserve that word. Until your husband is willing to divorce you."

"Kiss me again, Eli," she said, and in the cool spring air they embraced, kissed and for a short time the rest of the world faded away and they lost track of time.

Zachary had watched Maggie and Eli ride off toward the mesa, and waiting until they were a good distance away, he went to Willow to ask if fresh meat sounded good for the evening's meal.

"I saw some deer yesterday, down by the river not too far away. Maggie said I could go hunt for one if we needed the meat," he told her, no longer referring to Maggie as Mother.

"If she said it was alright, some venison does sounds good. I'm not sure about you going by yourself though,"

"I was thinking of stopping by and asking Ransom to go with me," he assured her.

"If he'll go with you, then that's fine. Don't be gone all day though."

"I won't," he said, and taking up his bow and quiver, he was out and gone.

His heart pounded in his chest as he rode toward the Craigavon ranch house. For him to go hunting was not unusual, but he lied about Maggie knowing he would go out this morning. He felt that Willow would not worry as much as Maggie, and this would give him the time he needed to disappear.

When he arrived at the ranch house, Ransom was waiting for him at the corral. With Ransom was his younger brother Tobias, and Zachary worried the younger boy would spoil the plans he had made.

"What's he doin' here?' he asked Ransom.

"He wanted to go with us, and I was just tellin' him he couldn't," said Ransom.

"I go huntin' all the time with you and Pa!" the boy protested.

"This time is different," said Ransom, "We'll be gone late, and Ma doesn't like it when you're out after dark."

"But I wanna go!" the boy protested.

"Toby, I promise that next time you can go, and I'll let you shoot my rifle," Ransom promised.

"You mean it?" Tobias asked.

"I swear. But you have to promise not to tell that we'll be gone late."

"I promise." And he jumped down from the fence rail and left the two older boys to talk.

"You ready?" asked Zachary.

"Yep, all saddled up and have my bedroll hidden down by the river."

"Good, let's get."

Both boys were excited, but this was the first time Ransom had taken the opportunity to ask Zachary why he wanted to leave for the Cheyenne now.

"Why didn't you want to wait until your Pa was home to take you?"

"I didn't want to wait until later this year. He might not show up, or I'd have to wait until after planting to get away." What he didn't tell his friend was that this time he didn't intend to come back. He knew that if he had told him, Ransom wouldn't go with him. What he would do when Ransom found out, he had no idea. He would face that when the time came.

"How sure are you that we can find the Cheyenne?"

"My uncle, White Badger, said they'd winter near the little lakes, north of Bent's old trading post. I been there when I was with him."

"What if they ain't there?"

"We'll head further north, toward the Smokey Hills, they call it the Cherry Hills."

"I didn't bring enough food to last more than two days," Ransom said, starting to think practical, and second guessing his decision to follow his friend.

"We'll find the Cheyenne, or something to eat before we need food." And, with this said, he kicked his horse into a gentle lope.

Maggie had returned from her ride rejuvenated with the feeling her life was brighter and the burden of a loveless husband eased. She approached the house with a glow about her and a pleased smile on her lips.

Silas, who sat on the porch sharpening his knife, noticed her smile, and commented, "You look like the cat that's got the cream," he said, grinning.

She knew her happiness couldn't be hidden, and said, "That obvious, is it?"

"Well, I can't say as I've seen you so well pleased for a long time."

She sat down next to him on the porch, and leaning her head on his shoulder said, "Silas, I am happier than I have been in as long as I can remember. He makes me laugh."

"He makes you laugh, eh?" Silas said, "Seems to me there's more to it than that."

"You have always been like a father to me, I trust you and your approval means a lot to me."

"My approval? Don't seem as if you need that from me."

"No, but am I doing the right thing to allow myself love with Eli? Don't I owe something to Whitney?"

"Ahh, Girl, you need to do what is right for you. I believe Whit left you a long time ago."

"Was it my fault? What did I do to drive him away?"

"I don't rightly believe it was something you did or didn't do. Flesh and blood can't compete with a memory."

"You mean Little Bird?"

"Yep."

"Is that the problem I'm having with Zachary too?"

"No, Zachary's problem is with Whit, an he's comin' to that age when he wants to be a man."

"I hate the thought of losing them both."

"I don't think you'll ever lose the boy, and don't fret about the man. You never really had Whit all to yourself."

"I've decided to tell him the next time he shows up," she said and leaned over to kiss Silas on the cheek. She then rose and went into the house where she found Willow starting to prepare the main meal of the day.

"Did you have a nice ride," Willow asked, and received only a sheepish smile as a reply from Maggie.

As the women worked preparing the meal, Johnny came through the main room. Willow, her mother's eye catching the boy's attempt to hide something behind his back as he made for the door, called out to him to stop.

"What are you up to?" she asked.

"Nothin'," he answered, his eyes wide with the fright of being caught red-handed.

"Let me see," Willow ordered, and held out her hand to the boy who slowly produced a folded piece of paper. Inspecting the paper, Willow noticed it was a note addressed to Maggie, and held it out to her. Maggie unfolded the paper and read its contents.

"¡Dios mío! He has run away!" she exclaimed and handed the note to Willow who read it.

"I thought he was only going out to hunt," Willow said, "He told me you knew he was going." She turned to Johnny and asked, "What do you know about this?"

He said, "He told me to give this to Tía, after supper, if you all started to look for him."

"Silas!" Maggie called out. Alarmed by her shout, Silas entered the house, knife in hand.

"What's the matter?" he asked, and Willow handed him the note.

"He says he's goin' with Ransom. I'll head over that way and see if William or Rosie know what's goin' on. Then we'll see if we need to go after those boys."

Maggie turned to Willow, and her friend took her into her arms as Maggie sobbed, "I should have been a better mother to him."

"It's not your fault, he was restless like his father and it was bound to happen."

"I don't know what I'll tell Whitney when he comes home."

"Tell him his son is following in his footsteps."

Silas rode out to the Craigavon house, accompanied by August, Eli, Federico, Mateo, and Santiago. William and Roseanne were surprised by the news, not suspecting that something was amiss. It took little time to discover that Ransom had indeed left with Zachary and had kept it a secret from all except his younger brother Tobias.

"They told me I couldn't say a word," the boy explained, "Ransom said they was just goin' huntin' and they'd be out late."

"By reading Zach's note, he plans on a bit longer," Silas told William and Roseanne. "He says he ain't comin' back."

"It's not like Ransom to go along with something like this," said William.

"I thought the boy had a better head on his shoulders than that too," said Silas.

"Let me and my men saddle up, and we'll see if we can't cut their trail. Which way you think they'll go?" he asked Silas.

"In the past we've taken Zach out towards Bent's and found the Cheyenne there. I reckon if we look somewhere parallel to the river, we might find sign of them."

Before they were ready to leave, Whit rode up, his horse lathered from being run hard. He had arrived home expecting his usual homecoming, only to find that Zachary had run away so he went to the Craigavon ranch. His horse had hardly come to a skidding stop, when he bellowed, "Where's the boy?"

"We don't know yet," said Silas, his voice calm, but stern as his eyes bore into Whit.

"I thought I had left him in good care, Silas, and you and that woman let him run off!"

Silas leaned over the horn of his saddle, removed his pipe from his mouth and pointed the stem at Whit, "You best calm down and think about what comes out of your piehole. There'll be plenty of time to place blame if need be after we find the boys."

The men left the ranch and fanned out across the prairie following the Fountain River, and before they reached the Arkansas, they came across tracks left by the two boys. By this time, the run-a-ways had several hours lead on the men and it was plain that they wouldn't be found before dark. It was also decided that not all the men were needed to follow the obvious trail left by the boys, and only William, Silas, Eli and Whit went on, sending the rest of the men back.

When it became too dark to travel further on the moonless night, the men made camp, with only a fire to cheer them as they had not brought food. They sat discussing the recklessness of the two boys, wondering what made them think it would be safe to run off.

Whit, still filled with rage, felt he had to lash out, "Damned bitch never was much good as a mother to my son," he said.

With this, Eli stood and took a step toward Whit who rose to meet him.

"I'd advise you to choose your words a bit more careful," Eli said, a look of anger about him that no one had seen before.

"I don't see as where you have any say in my voice," Whit edged closer.

"The two of you don't need to do this!" said William, "You can settle things about Maggie latter."

As if Eli's motivation just became evident, Whit said, "So that's what it is! You been sniffin' around my woman."

"I think you gave her up a long time ago," said Eli.

"He's right, Son," said Silas, "You haven't taken care of that gal for a long time. And, as a matter of fact, you've neglected the boy as well."

"You all against me then?" Whit asked.

"No, nobody's agin' you, Whit. Just tellin' you what you already know," said Silas, "We'll stand with you on anything except blamin' someone else for the way the boy is. He's his own person, but there's a lot of you in him, and too, he has his own head about him."

Whit looked at the men in front of him and with some resignation, looked at Eli and said, "I guess you might be right." He stepped back, turned and moved away from the campfire.

Alone in the darkness, Whit looked up into the sky, its blackness pierced by the tiny specks of light. He had never felt as lonely as he did now, lost amid the vastness of the empty night. He wondered why it mattered so much to him that Maggie had found someone else. Why wouldn't she look for comfort elsewhere, he had. He thought about the many times he visited Harmonie in Denver, but this he placed no value on. After all, it was only a diversion and meant nothing. Or so he told himself. His thoughts occupied by his own misery left him vulnerable, and the specter that stalked him appeared in the corner of his vision. As he turned, the shadow seemed to disappear, and he knew that it would always follow him, torment him.

The boys had spent an easy but cold night. After a meal of biscuits and dried beef jerky, they rolled into their blankets and shared a buffalo robe. Before they packed to leave their campsite in the morning, Zachary changed his clothing. He tossed aside his brogans and pants. Then he donned moccasins, leggings and a breechcloth. At the back of his head he tied an eagle feather to his long black hair, and across his shoulders he wore his bow case and quiver. Hanging from his right hand was a quirt made from elk antler, with a beaded wrist loop, and two long strands of thin leather. Ransom watched Zachary as he rode and noticed a change in the way his friend sat on his horse. He seemed to be more fluid in his movements, matching those of his horse. He was surprised at the transformation in his friend that occurred just by the change in what he wore. To him, Zachary now looked every bit a Cheyenne.

The morning air was crisp and clean, invigorating the boys and they rode enjoying the freedom of the open prairie. The carefree attitude tempted the boys to throw caution to the wind and they kicked their heels to their horse's flanks, and they sped recklessly toward the rising sun. Near midday they found a spring close to Chicosa Creek and stopped to rest. As the horses grazed on the sparse grass, the boys talked.

"I could live like this forever," said Zachary.

"It is some, but I kind'a wish I had a piece of my Mam's fresh bread, smothered in chokecherry preserves." Ransom licked his lips thinking of his mother's cooking.

"When we reach the village, my aunt will fix us a great meal, and you'll forget all about bread."

"Zach, why'd you throw away your boots and trousers?" Ransom asked.

"Don't need 'em anymore. Never gonna wear 'em, again."

"Not even when you get back home?"

"I ain't goin' back. My home is with the Cheyenne."

This surprised Ransom, and he asked, "What do you think will happen when our folks find out we left?"

"I don't much care."

"Well, you know I'm gonna go back, don't you?"

"You could stay with me. You don't know what it's like bein' with the Cheyenne. Once you prove yourself, they respect you."

"Prove myself? Like when you killed that Pawnee?" Ransom asked.

"Yep. Just like that."

"Not sure I'm ready to kill someone," Ransom said, and for the following hours the mood was less festive. They followed the low hills on the north side of the river and when they reached the flat expanse, they turned somewhat northeast, where they would find the small lakes that the Cheyenne might be camped near.

Ransom stopped his horse and pointed out small shapes in the distance saying, "That look like a herd of goats?"

Zachary strained his eyes to look for the pronghorn antelope Ransom spoke of and spotting the figures in the distance seemed to wake his hunger, and his stomach growled.

"If we lean down on our horses and go really slow, we might get close enough to get a shot at them with that rifle of yours," he said. Ransom checked the priming in his rifle's pan, and satisfied it was good, they moved slowly toward the herd grazing in the distance, hoping the keen-eyed animals wouldn't be alarmed by their approach.

The small herd was comprised of all females, as it was still early in the year. They were fleet-footed and sharp-eyed. When the boys were within a hundred yards of the antelope, the matriarch of the bunch rose her head and peered in their direction, her nostrils flaring as she sniffed the air. The slightest indication of danger would cause her and her sisters to bolt and race away at lightning speed.

The boys stopped their horses and stood motionless, allowing their mounts to graze as if they were riderless. After a few tense minutes, the dame lowered her head and went back to gnawing on the dry grass. Ransom and Zachary both breathed a sigh of relief, but with little warning, the lead doe bolted, and the entire bunch sprang into a dead run, not directly away from them, but off to the right.

Rising in their saddles the boys looked in the direction opposite their flight to see what had frightened the pronghorn. From the north came a line of men on horseback, and Zachary's first thought was that Silas had tracked them down and would make them return to the ranch. He was about to turn his horse and run, when he saw that it now appeared to be a half-dozen Indians. A new fear arose, and he voiced that fear to Ransom.

"If it's Pawnee, we're dead."

"We can try to outrun 'em," Ransom suggested.

"Yep, might be our only chance. Wait!" said Zachary as he recognized one of the approaching warriors. "They's Cheyenne! I know them! That's Little Bear and Red Arm!" He let out a shrill cry and kicked his horse into a dead run toward the approaching Cheyenne, Ransom following at a discreet distance.

The Cheyenne stopped their own advance and spread out in order to receive an enemy, each readying their weapons. Little Bear, somewhat out in front of the others, held a stone war club in his right hand. Within ten yards, Zachary brought his horse to a skidding stop, almost losing his seat.

With a foolish grin on his face he called out in Cheyenne, *"Hello, brothers! My heart is happy to see you! We thought you might be Wolf People."*

Little Bear tilted his head to one side eyeing the youngster, then spoke, *"I know you. What is Yellow Horse doing so far from the lodge of his father?"* and as he talked, he looked past Zachary at Ransom.

"I have come to live with my mother's people," Zachary said.

"And what of the vé'ho'e, has he come to live with the People?" asked Red Arm.

"I have come to visit my relatives among the People," said Ransom, his Cheyenne not as polished as Zachary's, but suitable enough to be understood.

"And who are these relatives?" asked Red Arm, almost mocking in his tone.

"I have an uncle among the people, Crow Eyes, a great warrior," said Ransom. Though Crow was only a half-brother to his father, and Ransom had met the man but once in his life, he hoped the name would carry some weight.

"Crow Eyes is my father," said Little Bear, *"How is he your uncle?"*

"My father is William Craigavon, *his brother,"* Ransom felt a tightness in his stomach, and he wished he had never talked himself into leaving with Zachary, even if it was only meant to be a visit.

"I have met the son of Pale Eyes Craigavon, he is a medicine man," said Little Bear.

"Yes, my father is a healer," Ransom was still not sure he was safe, so he added, *"He is a healer like his mother, my grandmother. She is called Speaks With Her Hands Woman."*

Little Bear resisted a smile thinking of Mary Craigavon but acknowledged the connection he had with Ransom, *"She is also my grandmother. This makes us brothers. You will ride with us back to the village where you will stay in my lodge."* Ransom and Zachary joined the Cheyenne and they moved off in the direction of the largest of the small lakes that dotted the prairie north of the Arkansas.

"It will be good to live with my mother's people," Zachary said to Red Arm, as they rode side by side, and was disappointed that the Dog Soldier seemed to ignore him.

"Is my uncle in the village that we are going to?" Ransom asked Little Bear.

"No, he has gone with other chiefs to the Whiteman's village, called Wash-eeng-ton, *to speak to the Great White Chief."* said Little Bear, having trouble with the word, but it was plain to Ransom that he meant Washington,

Ransom could not have known that by invitation of President Lincoln, Indian Agent Samuel Colly had taken several chiefs from the Cheyenne, Comanche, Arapaho, Kiowa and Caddo tribes to the Nation's capital. From the Cheyenne were Crow Eyes, War Bonnet, White Antelope, Standing in Water, and Lean Bear. While there, the President would promise the chiefs that everything would be done to help the Indians learn to farm and build settlements. This was providing the Indians quit their nomadic ways and conform to government law. Of the group, Lean Bear was one of the only two Dog Soldiers that would ever advocate for peace.

The boys joined the warriors and they moved in a more purposeful direction. The party of Cheyenne had been out scouting the area to the west and south of their village locating game, and on the lookout for any sign of danger. The group consisted of four Dog Soldiers, and two young men not yet members of that society. Little Bear was the oldest, having seen twenty-four winters. He had his Cheyenne mother's complexion, but his features and curly hair were those of his father, Crow Eyes. Ransom knew some history of his distant cousins among the Cheyenne, those related through his Grandmother Mary Craigavon, and he wasn't sure if he should ask Little Bear about that history. His curiosity getting the better of him, he took a chance when they stopped that evening.

It was a warrior's camp, cold, with no fire. Out in the open, a fire would signal their presence to any enemy, and caution was the best defense. Zachary sought out the younger men in the group, but Ransom moved closer to Little Bear, who seemed to place his bed away from the others.

"Little Bear, will you talk with me?" he asked as he approached.

"What have we to talk about?" Little Bear answered, displaying a detached attitude.

"May I sit?"

"Sit if you must," Little Bear saw that the boy would persist, and he wanted any conversation to end quickly.

"I would know more about my family among the Cheyenne."

"You believe I am the one to tell you this? Speak with your Grandmother."

"She is far away, and you are close."

"What would you know?"

"Tell me of yourself." He appealed to the Cheyenne propensity to talk about themselves.

"I have many war honors, counting coup twice times ten on enemies of the People, and I have taken the lives of those who would do harm to the People, four times."

"Have you a wife and children?"

"No. Some still fear that I have the Whiteman's sickness," Little Bear looked directly at Ransom, and pointed to the pockmark scars on his face.

"Smallpox?" Ransom said in English.

"Yes, small-pox," answered Little Bear

"That would not happen," Ransom said, having learned from his father that only certain carriers of the disease can pass it on.

"When I was six winters old, White Hair Scott brought gifts from Pale Eyes Craigavon to the People. With those gifts were blankets that held the sickness that eats the flesh. Before our Medicine Man, Little Wolf, knew of the danger, many became sick. My mother, brothers and sister were taken. Many others also died. I survived, as did my father.

"There were those who thought Pale Eyes and White Hair did this knowingly, but my father and the Little Wolf argued that White Hair's daughter had been attacked by the sickness and died. White Hair would not kill one of his own children!

"We discovered that the gifts had been sent by an enemy of Pale Eyes, but this did not take away the pain. For this reason, I am a Dog Soldier, and I will defend the People from any enemy, especially the Whiteman. Now, I am done speaking."

Those last words chilled Ransom and he moved to where Zachary sat talking to the others. There Ransom spread out his blanket and curled up under the heavy wool and the buffalo robe he shared with Zachary. He began to shiver and dread the coming night. His apprehension increased as he lay listening to the talk of the warriors. One commented that he had taken a liking to Ransom's rifle, another admired his horse, and one made a comment about his knife.

He knew that Zachary could hear these comments, and he wondered why his friend said nothing in his defense. As fear welled up inside him, he wondered if he was safe among these "defenders" of the People. even with Zachary's presence.

Ransom spent a sleepless night and was almost relieved when in the predawn the Cheyenne began to stir and prepare to leave. He had decided that he would tell Zachary he would not be going on with him. He felt he would rather face the unknown dangers of the open prairie than what seemed an eminent fate with the Cheyenne.

He was about to speak to Zachary when an alarm went up in the small camp. The warriors all leaped to their horses. Little Bear ordered Zachary and Ransom to also mount their horses and prepare for a fight. The warriors milled about for only a moment, then spread out in a line to face this early morning threat. Approaching from the south were four riders, the rising sun casting a pale glow on them.

With the sun at their backs and their superior number, the Cheyenne had the advantage on these men, and in their bravado, some of the young men whooped out war cries and taunts. One of the figures raised his right hand, and Ransom could now easily see it was Silas Scott, his bearded face surrounded by his wolfskin hat. Beside him rode Whitney Voss, Eli Thornton and his father. Ransom wasn't sure if he would be saved, or if he and Zachary had caused these two groups to be drawn into a confrontation. His impulse was to kick his horse into a run and go to his father's side, but something told him to hold back.

One of the younger Cheyenne, named Wolf Horn, could not resist the opportunity to show his bravery and charged at the four men, pulling his horse aside only at the last moment. With a whoop, he turned back and joined his friends, encouraged by their cheers of approval. Little Bear sat quietly on his horse and moved slowly forward followed by the rest of the Cheyenne, Ransom and Zachary. When within a few yards of each other, the two groups stopped, and the expected greetings were exchanged.

"Hello, Little Bear," Silas said in Cheyenne accompanying the words with sign language.

"Hello, White Hair," answered Little Bear.

"I see you have found our lost boys."

Little Bear looked over his shoulder at the boys, and back at Silas as if to say, "So?"

"Our hearts are happy to see them." Silas' words seemed to be wasted. *"Let us sit and smoke,"* Silas offered, and Little Bear dismounted his horse, his pipe bag in hand, followed by both the White men and the rest of the Cheyenne.

They sat there on the open prairie, and Silas produced his pouch of tobacco, holding it up as a sign that Little Bear was to provide a pipe. Little Bear retrieved a short pipe stem and small red stone bowl, and placing them together, handed the pipe over to Silas who filled the bowl with tobacco, placing a bit of charred cloth on top. Striking flint to steel provided a spark onto the char-cloth that glowed hot and offered fire to the pipe. Silas puffed and exhaled the bluish-gray smoke, letting it float up. He then handed the pipe back to Little Bear who took a puff, and as he exhaled, pulled the smoke up over his head in a gesture as if washing.

The pipe was passed around to the others until the tobacco was consumed. This was the only formal part of Cheyenne etiquette performed, and then the conversation began.

"You are hunting?" Silas asked, wondering if this was a small raiding party. They weren't after horses, as they were mounted, not on foot.

"Yes, but we have found only these two," Little Bear referred to the boys.

"Not much to eat there," Silas quipped, "Is your village close by?"

"No, it is two sun's travel from here."

"That is a disappointment. We must return to our lodges, and I would know of your grandfather and father. Are they well?"

"Yes."

"I would also ask of Little Gun. Is he also in the village?'" Silas asked about his son.

"No, he is with the Hairy Rope Band, on the Cherry River."

Silas now turned to the matter at hand, "I am grateful that you have found them. We will take them with us."

"They are of no concern to me," Little Bear said, "They can come or go as they wish."

"As I am poor, I can only offer the tobacco as a gift of my thanks to you and your friends for finding the boys." and he handed over his tobacco pouch to Little Bear.

As a sign that he felt the conversation was over, Little Bear sat speechless for a moment and then rose to his feet. The others followed and all mounted their horses.

"It is good to part as friends," Silas said as he settled into his saddle, but Little Bear didn't reply.

William gave his son a look and Ransom gladly moved his horse next to his father. Whit gave a similar glance to Zachary, but the boy remained with the Indians.

"Zach, time to leave," he finally said, but Zachary refused to move. Agitated, Whit moved over to his son, cutting between him and Red Arm, where he again told his son, "Come, it's time to go home."

"I am going home, to my mother's people." Zachary said in Cheyenne.

"Zachary, come, now!" Whit's anger grew.

"I no longer carry that name, I am Yellow Horse!" the boy was defiant. Whit reached out to grab him by the arm, and in doing so caused the horses to become spooked and they shied away, moving sideways. Red Arm had a hard time controlling his mount, but at the same time he reached for his quirt, intending to strike Whit.

Whit anticipating his movements, released his hold on Zachary, who pulled his horse away. As Red Arm swung the quirt, Whit ducked and let the already unstable Red Arm's momentum carry him sideways. Whit had only to use the lightest effort to toss the young man to the ground. Before Red Arm struck the earth, Whit had pulled his Remington revolver and had it pointed it at the fallen Cheyenne.

"Stop!" yelled Silas, "There ain't no need for bloodshed!"

As if taking his cue, Little Bear also ordered calm, *"This is not the day for war!"* he called out, and though tension was high, the cooler heads prevailed.

"Put that iron back on your belt," Silas ordered. Whit separated from the Indians, and returned his pistol to its holster, and Red Arm remounted his horse, all the time glaring at Whit.

"I ain't leavin' my son," Whit hissed as he holstered the pistol.

Silas lowered his voice so only Whit could hear him, "You'll get us and the boy killed!"

Whit's rage was at the point where he didn't seem to care what happened. He wanted someone to pay for the hurt he felt, and Red Arm seemed to be a suitable target, until Silas laid a hand on his arm. He turned to face Silas and the hatred that Whit felt was visible in his eyes.

Silas looked back at the Cheyenne, and he knew full well that one more wrong move would cause blood to be spilled. He had to defuse the situation and spoke directly to Little Bear.

"It is best that we part as friends. The wind is turning, and I feel the cold."

"Yes, White Hair, the wind is turning cold, and a storm is coming." He turned his horse and moved away, Zachary and the rest of the Cheyenne following him.

Whit watched his son ride away. The pain and hatred growing as the distance between them increased. He turned to follow Silas and the others, staying a distance behind them as they rode toward the west.

"I'm sorry, Pa," Ransom said to William.

"You could have gotten yourself killed," William said, his voice hard, but then he softened, and looking at his son added, "We'll speak of this when we get home. You had your mother worried sick. I expect facing her disappointment will be harder than anything I could say now."

Pushing hard, they traveled west, reaching the Huerfano by dusk where they made an uneasy camp, but one with a fire. The fire added some comfort, but it could not drive away thoughts of the conflict they had avoided.

Whit sat apart from the others, brooding, and they gave him the solitude he needed. They sat close together, sharing the warmth of the fire and talking quietly. After a bit, Eli said, "I ain't never been that close to a fight with Indians."

"Wouldn't have been much of a fight," said Silas, "Quick and bloody though."

"We wouldn't have come out on the winning side?" Eli asked.

"Maybe. We all have firearms, but rifles aren't that handy close in like we were. It would have come to pistols and knives," said William.

"Would have been close," said Silas, "Little Bear is a seasoned warrior, and maybe one or two of the others also. But the younger ones were inexperienced, and that would have been in our favor."

"You've had your share of Indian fighting, haven't you?" Eli asked Silas.

"More than I'd like. You find yourself in a spot like that again, and have time, pick out the one you think is the leader. Take him out first. The others will lose their fight and you might save your scalp."

"Would you have killed Little Bear?" Eli asked Silas.

"If it had come to that. Yes, I would have," Silas said, "And I would have regretted it the rest of my life."

The trip back to the ranches on the Arkansas was a somber one. Whit kept to himself. The others contemplated what could have happened, and what may yet happen. Roseanne was overjoyed to see her son, but angry at what he had done. As William had predicted, her disappointment was punishment to the boy who idolized his mother. His guilt allowed him to willingly accept the loss of his rifle as punishment. He would have to find a way to make amends before the firearm would be his again.

Maggie had suffered in anguish as she waited for the men to come home. When she saw them returning without the boy, her knees buckled, and she almost sank to the ground crying in fear that something terrible had happened to him. Willow was at her side to offer comfort, but neither woman was prepared for the news the men offered. Silas, like a sympathetic father, told Maggie that Zachary was not going to come back. He told her the boy had made his own decision and forcing him to come home would have caused bloodshed.

She looked past Silas to see Whit looking at her. She moved over to him and started to speak, "Whitney, I..."

"Don't give me excuses!" He cut her off, "I trusted you to care for the boy, and you let him run wild. You let him go Injin!" His words were cold and emotionless.

Eli stepped to Maggie's side, and placing his arm around her spoke to Whit in a calm but strong voice, "This woman did more for that boy in a single day than you have his entire life. You blow in with the wind and figure you can just start where you left off, and everyone is supposed to accept it. The boy deserved better. Magdalena deserves better."

Whit looked from one of them to the other, then turned and mounted his horse. He sat for a few moments, as if he were weighing those words. He then finally spoke, "I guess you're right. There is nothing here that belongs to me." He turned his horse and without looking back, rode away.

***

May 1863 - Bright Moon

Buffalo were scarce along the Arkansas and many of the Cheyenne moved further to the north hunting along the Republican River. Those that remained in the south were forced to compete with White hunters, who were shooting buffalo for their hides and tallow. To compound the situation, traders were cheating the Indians, buying the few robes they did have for whiskey.

Zachary had settled into his new life easier than when he was only visiting during the summer months. He had never been happier, and though some of the other boys eyed him with suspicion because of his White blood, most accepted him as a Cheyenne. Thus, he immersed himself in training as a warrior, and soon was as proficient in those skills as any boy his age. He also sought the company of those men who were Dog Soldiers, admiring their bravado and dedication to the tribe.

As a medicine man among the Dog Soldiers, Bear Voice found opportunity to be close to Zachary. Once past the apprehension the boy felt about him, he gained Zachary's confidence. This placed Zachary in a position where Bear Voice could influence him, and at some time in the future use him as a tool.

Sees Far was also pleased that Zachary had come to stay, and though not able to gain Zachary's confidence like Bear Voice, she found ways to make him more comfortable around her. She made him moccasins and leggings, decorating them with quillwork of special designs that were infused with her medicine.

As more Cheyenne and Arapaho gathered along the Republican, rumors reached Governor Evans that Cheyenne were holding councils with leaders of other tribes and were talking of a united effort to drive all whites out of Colorado. With the memory of the New Ulm massacre still fresh in his mind, Evans met with Arapaho leaders warning them that the Army will commence a war of extermination against all tribes if this alliance happened. But his threats, like his fears, were baseless; for other than a few missing head of cattle or horses, there was no impending danger.

The Colorado frontier was now relatively calm. Other than the intertribal conflicts between the Cheyenne and the Utes, and the Arapaho and the Kiowa, there was peace. Even the Lakota and other tribes along the upper Platte appeared to be friendly. It seemed that some troops in Colorado Territory could be released to aid in fighting Confederate bushwhackers in eastern Kansas and Missouri. Chivington and his men would soon have to leave Denver putting aside any thoughts of fighting Indians. This Chivington did not want.

SAM J. PISCIOTTA

CHAPTER FIFTEEN
A LIFE IN TWO WORLDS

APRIL 1863 – MOON OF BUDDING TREES

The room on the second floor of the Cherokee House saloon and hotel suited Whit's purposes. It gave him a central place to stay in Denver that offered easy access to those people he needed to do business with, as well as the whiskey he needed to deaden his senses. The rooms were clean, and here he could entertain Harmonie. With her, he could set loose his desires, and his hunger for the feeling of flesh against flesh. He did not confide in her his deepest thoughts, nor those demons that haunted his dreams. His relationship with her becoming one of companionship, one of solace. Whit also shared was a vague idea of what he intended for the future, his plans on how he would make a life for himself without the ranches on the Fountain.

In turn, Whit's room gave Harmonie a place away from her profession. She looked upon Whit not as a customer, but a diversion. With him she could enjoy sexual congress and no expectation of satisfying a customer. She could be completely selfish. Of course, she was thankful that her beauty and charm allowed her to work in one of the better establishments of Denver. She could demand up to $40 per customer, and limit herself to no more than five customers in a single night. Though one half of this went to the proprietor of the parlor, she earned far more than the girls who worked in the common brothels, or the cribs who could charge as little as 25¢. And, her income was far better than the $5 a week she had earned as a schoolteacher in St. Louis. Like many of her 'sisters', she dreamed of a better life, one more independent, and of course respectable. Unlike other 'soiled doves', she did not hang this future on the hook of having a man to act as her savior.

The arrangement between Whit and Harmonie worked well until the early hours of the morning on the 19th of April.

Harmonie had only just found her place under the blankets with Whit, and before slumber could overtake them, they heard cries, "FIRE! FIRE!" Springing from their bed, they hurriedly put on what clothing they could, and taking up a few possessions, they rushed through the acrid smoke, out of the room, down the stairs and into the street.

Help had already arrived and attempts were being made to extinguish the flames that roared at the back of the hotel, but the dry wooden structure acted like tinder and the growing wind soon caused the fire to grow out of control. The Cherokee House sat in the heart of the business district and within less than two hours, the fire had spread beyond control, and people turned their attention to saving goods from endangered buildings. The banks of Cherry Creek were soon covered with heaps of goods from stores and the household paraphernalia of residents. From Wazee to Magaa streets, and from Cherry Creek to Sixteenth, every wooden structure was destroyed and only those buildings made of brick were spared.

Whit and Harmonie took stock of their situation when the sun finally rose. Harmonie had escaped with her clothing and her purse, losing only a pair of stockings and her shoes. Whit had fled the inferno wearing little but his shirt and trousers, but in his hands had saved his boots, hat and his belt holding his knife and Remington pistol. What he had lost was his bed roll containing the rest of his clothing, and worst of all, his money pouch and his Deringer rifle. Luckily the stable where his horse and saddle were kept, had been spared. He wasn't afoot, and not exactly penniless. Laced into the saddle's rigging, Whit had hidden two Clark- Gruber & CO. ten-dollar gold pieces, but $20 wouldn't last very long in Denver.

Harmonie was no worse for wear and walking barefooted back to her own apartments was a mere inconvenience. Whit saw her safely her there and then took stock of his own situation. It never entered his mind to ask her to put him up, this was not in his character, and if she had offered it would have been an offence to his pride. With limited funds, he would now be forced to find work as soon as possible, and his skills were limited. He could fall back on the trade he had been taught in the wagon yard of his grandfather, but he wasn't willing to submit to the drudgery of a daily job. What he needed was something he was accustomed to. This meant finding someone who would advance him a stake or offer him work more suited to his taste and talents. His thought was to seek out those men he had served with in New Mexico, at Glorieta. He had only to find them, but his first stop would be the stable where his horse and his gold were safely waiting.

The stable was all but deserted, most of the people in the area drawn to the area of the fire. The only other soul there was a young boy who was angry that he had been left to tend to the establishment. As Whit worked the lacing loose on his saddle, two men walked in and went to a stall where their horses were kept. Whit thought he recognized one of them as Elbridge Gerry, an old trapper who had a trading post at the confluence of Crow Creek and the South Platte. The other man didn't look familiar, and Whit held back until he knew these men were no threat. While they saddled their horses. He listened to them as they talked.

"Can't say as I'm sure there may be trouble, but my wife heard from a Ute woman that came into trade with her husband, there's something brewing," said Gerry.

"You put much store in rumors?" the other man asked.

"I've carried me four Indian wives over the past years, and I tell you, Cable, if a woman says there's gonna be trouble, there's gonna be trouble. The Ute may be a problem, but I don't think that jackass Bob North knows shit about what's goin' on with the Cheyenne and 'Rapahos."

"You think it's safe then for us to hunt some buffalo?"

"Sure, as long as we don't trespass on a hunt of the tribes. Try to keep as far away as we can and not be too greedy."

It was at this point that Whit stepped out from the stall where he had been working on his saddle and approached the men.

"Excuse me for my ill manners, but I couldn't help but over-hear your conversation," he started, then waited to judge the two men's attitude about his interruption to their conversation. Satisfied he had not offended them, he continued, "My name is Whitney Voss, and I've had experience amongst Indians, and am a good shot with rifle or pistol. I consider myself trustworthy and am looking for honest work."

"My name is Elbridge Gerry, and this is Hezekiah Cable." Cable reached out and shook Whit's hand.

"You a drinker Mr. Voss?" Gerry asked.

"I will partake when the chance arises, but I'll not allow spirts to master me."

"Good. Never trusted a man who neither drank, nor one who let drink get the better of him. Where do you hale from, Whitney Voss?"

"I was born and raised in Pittsburg but have resided in the west for better than ten years now."

"Been in the gold fields?"

"No, of late I have been involved in ranching," Whit hoped to avoid his recent failures.

"Where at?"

"Down Pueblo way," Whit admitted.

"Pueblo?" asked Hezekiah, "You know a fellow by the name of Elijah Thornton?"

Whit held back a sudden feeling of anger and shame, answering, "Yes, I do."

"Him and me was partners with two other fellows in a mining claim. But he went down to Pueblo awhile back. He's still alive then, and doin' well?"

"Last I saw him, he was alive, and happy." Whit wanted this topic of conversation to end and considered leaving until Gerry spoke up again.

"You say you have experience with Indians, how is that?"

"I've traded with them, fought against them and..." he paused before saying, "I had a Cheyenne wife."

"You claim you're a good shot. What rifle do you carry?"

"I had a Deringer rifle in .50 caliber but only just lost it in the fire."

"Not much good without a rifle, are you?" Gerry sneered, but with a smile.

"I have twenty dollars in gold and I am willing to put that up towards a new rifle, but fear that might not be enough," Whit said.

"You're right there, Son," Said Gerry, but I can fix that. If you turn out to be a man of your word, we'll settle later. If you're not, we'll find that out too, and we'll settle accounts as well. By the looks of you, you're in need of more than a rifle. Lucky you run into someone who has his own store."

"Then I have work with you?" Whit asked.

"That you do, and by Gawd, you'll earn every penny. I take it that that's your horse and saddle over there? If so, the first thing we'll do is get you a good rifle, and then some clothing."

The men left, and Gerry led them to a gun shop on F Street owned by W. S. Hawkins. The Hawkins name was made famous by Samuel and Jacob Hawkins, brothers who had made rifles and repairs from their Laurel Street gun shop in St. Louis. A Hawkins rifle was a prized possession of such men as Charles Bent. But a Hawkins rifle was not what Gerry had in mind for Whit, as they were expensive and being muzzle-loaders, outdated. Hawkins made most of his living doing repairs, selling gun parts and offering firearms made by various others. Upon inspecting the stock on hand in the gun shop, Gerry chose a repaired 1859 Sharps breechloading rifle in .52 caliber, at a price of thirty dollars. Loading the Sharps rifle was much faster than Whit's Deringer. The breech had what was called a falling block, and once the lever on the rifle's underside was pulled down, the breech opened, and a premade paper cartridge could be inserted. Once the breech was closed, the ignition source of either fulminate of mercury wafers or percussion caps were used. Reloading took less than a few seconds.

"That there rifle will be more than you need for buffalo," said Gerry. "Now, let's head to my place and get you some clothes and bedding."

Whit left Denver with Gerry and Cable, and as they rode Cable was the most talkative of the two. Though he was an associate of Thornton, Whit found himself liking the man. He was open and held back little, telling Whit about his life on a farm in Missouri, and then his trip to the gold fields.

"Yep, I was teamed up with Eli and two other fellows, Nealy and Azariah. That bastard Azariah robbed us and we never did hear word of him again. I heard Nealy got himself kilt by Injuns. Sure am glad that Eli is doin' fine, he always treated me well. When he left Denver, he signed over his share of the claim to me. But I lost it in a card game. You said you knew him down in Pueblo? You two work together?

"No, he works on a ranch owned by friends of mine," Whit said, hiding his still tender feelings. He had spent little time thinking about Maggie since leaving Pueblo, but he had made his peace with leaving her. He knew that she deserved better than he had to offer, and listening to Cable talk about the Eli, Whit figured that he was most likely the man she needed.

"Hezekiah, you worked for Gerry long?" Whit asked.

"My friends call me Hez," he said, then answered Whit's question, "Elbridge found me passed out in the street. I had too much to drink and got robbed of what little I had left. He picked me up, cleaned me off and offered me a job. I ain't much good at shootin', but I can skin out a buffalo just as fast as any Injin'!"

With the decline of the fur trade by 1840, trading houses like Fort St. Vrain, Fort Vasquez and Fort Lupton were all abandoned, and Elbridge filled a vacuum they left behind. Using his 1857 trading license, he had set himself up in business. Gerry had fortified his trading post on the South Platte, some calling it Fort Gerry. And by marrying into several tribes, Gerry had also solidified his customer base among those tribes.

It mattered little that one wife was exchanged for another, or as Whit found out, that the trading post had two mistresses. One a Ute and the other a Lakota. Though the two tribes did not get along with each other, these two women had formed a truce and between them took care of Elbridge's half-dozen mixed-breed children, both theirs and those of the various wives.

Once provided with more suitable clothing for his new career, Whit and Hez ventured out onto the plains north of the Platte to hunt for buffalo, bringing in meat and hides to Gerry's trading post. He was not the only provider of hides to Gerry, for the Indians themselves were carrying out their own killing of the buffalo for profit, and the goods the Squaw-man provided.

***

July 1863 – Moon of Ripening Cherries

By midsummer, tensions with the Indians increased in Kansas Territory leading the understaffed commander of Fort Larned, Colonel Leavenworth, to request the War Department release the troops garrisoned at Fort Lyon in Colorado for duties in Kansas Territory. The 1st Colorado, under the command of Lt. Colonel Samuel Tappan, are not in the same military district as Larned and Colonel Chivington orders Tappan to stay where he is posted, stating that the safety of Colorado had priority.

By the middle of July, Indian troubles at Fort Larned increase and a group of Cheyenne, Arapaho, Kiowas and Apache approach the fort demanding whiskey. Tempers ran high, and when refused the spirits, a Cheyenne struck an Osage Army scout guarding the stores. The Osage, with little love for the Cheyenne, promptly shot the Cheyenne, killing him. It took all of Leavenworth's abilities of persuasion to avoid an all-out battle. Again, he makes a request for more troops, and this time Lt. Colonel Tappen sends reinforcements from Fort Lyon, against Chivington's orders. As a result, Chivington removes Tappen from his duties at Fort Lyon and transfers him to Fort Garland in the San Luis Valley.

With trouble brewing in Kansas, Governor Evans decides that it is time to meet with the Cheyenne and the Arapaho again, whether to appeal for peace or demand it was the only question the Governor had in his mind. It would be better if the Indians wouldn't have to be dealt with at all, he thought, but either choice was distasteful to him.

Rather than rely on Robert North to contact these tribes, he turned to Elbridge Gerry who he felt had a good relationship with them. Gerry took Whit and Hez with him, as both men had become his friends and had proven themselves trustworthy. Gerry was impressed not only by Whit's skill with the new Sharps rifle, but also his ability to read "sign", tracks both visible and almost nonexistent of either animal or man.

Whit had confided in Gerry some of his past, but not all the details. He had shared his history, and that of Zachary being lost to the Cheyenne. He had explained how Zachary had been allowed to spend time among his mother's people and that he had honed his own skills of tracking down the location of the Cheyenne in the vastness of the plains. Gerry surmised that two sets of eyes were far more likely to find camps, and three men had a better chance of surviving than one or two.

They first searched along the Republican and then moved down toward the Smokey Hills where they found two camps of the Cheyenne, the first under the leadership of Black Kettle, and a second close by. Though Gerry had no extended relatives among those in this camp, he had acquaintances, as did Whit.

A council was called, and the most important men of the two camps came together to listen to Gerry. Not only was Black Kettle among these, but also White Antelope, Little Wolf and the Dog Soldier Chief, Lean Bear. Of the prominent warriors who accompanied these leaders, some were; Bear Feathers, Bob-

Tailed Wolf, Kingfisher, Standing Bear, and most notably to Whit, Crow Eyes.

Gerry stressed the importance of arranging a meeting with Evans, stating that any form of violence or theft of the Whiteman's stock would be dealt with harshly. The leaders seemed to agree that war should be avoided at any cost. They pledged they would meet with the Governor during the Moon when Plums Ripen, September, at a designated spot on the Chief River, the Republican. They also promised to spread the word to the other bands as well as the Arapaho and convince them to commit to the meeting. Once the arrangements had been agreed to, the three men were treated as guests and were fed, and a lodge to sleep in was erected for them. Gerry and Hez spent the evening with Black Kettle, and Whit followed Crow Eyes to his lodge, accompanied by Little Wolf.

After Crow Eyes' wife, Meets the Enemy Woman, fed the three men they sat and talked, catching up on what had transpired over the past year.

"Tell me of my friend Silas Scott," said Little Wolf, his English better than that of some Whites that Whit knew.

"Silas is well," said Whit, "He lives on the Fountain River just above the Arkansas."

Little Wolf smiled and chuckled slightly, then asked, "Has he ever told you that is where we met?"

"No, he hasn't."

"It was when I was very young, maybe twelve or thirteen winters old. I was with two friends, Antelope and Digger and we found some trappers camped on the Boiling River, the Fountain. We tried to steal their horses and were caught. Silas was one of those trappers, and we thought we would be killed." Whit had always thought that Little Wolf and Silas were close to the same age. Wolf possibly being older, his craggy face etched with exposure to the sun and time. Now he found out that Silas was almost twenty years older. As he sat and listened to Little Wolf about his history with Silas and Tom Craigavon, Whit's admiration was rekindled. He appreciated these men who had been his mentors, and he wondered if he had lost their friendship as he had lost Maggie.

After reminiscing, Little Wolf asked, "What is the mood of the White leaders? Do you think there will be peace?" He had already decided what the outcome of any talks with the Governor would be.

"I think they mean well, but they do not understand the Cheyenne, and might expect what your people cannot give," Whit answered.

"This is true," said Crow Eyes, "No matter how hard one tries, he cannot live in two worlds. I have found because of my mixed blood, I had to choose to live among the Cheyenne, I do not think I could live among the Whites. An eagle cannot be a mouse." This statement gave Whit a chance to ask about Zachary.

"Have either of you seen my son, Zachary?"

"He lives sometimes with his grandfather, at other times with his uncle," said Crow Eyes.

"Is he well?" asked Whit.

"He is growing strong and has found a place among the Dog Soldiers. It is thought that he will join that society one day." Little Wolf switched to Cheyenne to emphasize the importance of what he would say next. *"Yellow Horse is learning to walk the path of the People. White Badger and Bear Voice are teaching him sacred dances. He has seen his fourteenth winter, and it is time for him to seek his spirit guide."*

"What are these 'dances'?" asked Whit.

"He will learn those of the Crazy Dog Men, the Animal dances and the Sun Dance," Little Wolf had become serious, for the the matter of entering manhood for the Cheyenne was not something to be talked about lightly.

"What do mean by the Sun Dance?" Whit asked, for he had only heard about the ritual.

"He may not participate in this ritual," said Crow Eyes.

"You must understand now more than ever," said Wolf, *"The young men symbolize the strength and fortitude of the People. It is important that they be inducted into one of the adult societies so that they are prepared for whatever challenges and problems they may encounter in the future. The members of these societies are regarded as the forebearers of peace, safety, and livelihood of the People. They are responsible for all aspects of life. It is a transition that is vital for them to expect the unexpected*

"So, Zachary will learn these things? He'll search for some animal to guide him?" Until now Whit had held a slight hope that his son would someday come back to him. Now he feared if his son went through these rituals, he would be lost forever.

"Whit, these are things that all men of the People have gone through," said Crow Eyes. "He is young and may not commit himself to some of the more sacred ceremonies."

"If you see him, tell him..." Whit paused, "Tell him that I think of him often."

"It is close to the time when the bands meet for the renewals and healing. It is possible that he will be there," said Little Wolf, not telling Whit that part of this healing would be a Sun Dance. It was not necessary for him to know this, and Zachary was nowhere near the time when he would dance, he would only observe. Zachary would probably go on his vision quest, depending on his advisor, Bear Voice. Little Wolf felt sorry for the boy having Bear Voice to look after him at such an important time, but he had no say in the matter.

Within a few days, Whit left the camp with Gerry and Hez. They sought out a few other bands and made the same request to them, offering to meet with Governor Evans on the Republican River in September. With this mission accomplished, they returned to Denver satisfied that there would be peace. But, as Gerry's Indian wife had predicted, Utes began raiding mountain settlements and struck Medicine Bow Station near Camp Collins. Major Wynkoop had led the 1st Cavalry on an expedition from Camp Weld in Denver but failed to find the Ute war parties. Whit was almost disappointed that he had been out chasing friendly Indians suing for peace when there had been a chance, though a slight one, to fight.

***

August 1863 – Breeding Moon

The sweltering air seemed to suck the very breath from Zachary's lungs. Each time he inhaled, it failed to offer any relief to his burning lungs, dry throat and parched lips. The hill was not very high and offered not even the slightest of breezes to cool his sun-burnt shoulders and back. The view he had to the east was unobstructed for miles, ending only in the far-off horizon where the sun rose. Behind him, out of his sight was the village, and at times he thought he could hear muffled sounds from that direction. He wondered if they were real or the results of his imagination. He had lost track of time as he sat on the low hill overlooking the Bunch of Trees River and wondered if it had been two or three days. He had tried hard to pray as Bear Voice had taught him, but he questioned his self-discipline as it seemed that he spent his time wishing the ordeal was over, rather than he be granted a vision.

He thought now of the heated conversation between Bear Voice and the old healer, Little Wolf. Though Bear Voice was Zachary's teacher, Little Wolf had sought him out to voice his concerns, saying that most young men prepare an entire year for their vision quest.

"You push the boy too far," Little Wolf had said, *"He is not ready."*

"That is not for you to decide," said Bear Voice.

"A vison specifies a spiritual path to be followed by the seeker and establishes the spirit contacts which will guide him for many years. If he is lacking a heartfelt pitifulness, he cannot serve the People."

"I have offered up the prayers that will appease the spirits," Bear retorted.

"You cannot bribe the spirits. The most important thing will be his relationship and dependence on them for his spiritual growth and the welfare of the people."

These words ran through Zachary's head over and over, "For the welfare of the People." He closed his eyes and felt himself falling into a thick fog of fatigue. Around him was a village, the lodges burning, the smell of the smoke stinging his nose. Here and there lay dead Dog Soldiers. He walked through the destruction and could find no one in the suffocating smoke, until there appeared a figure walking toward him, a woman, her long hair blowing in a breeze he could not feel. As she came closer, she reached out her hand to him and as he extended his to take it, he stumbled and fell. When he hit the ground, he found himself back on the hill overlooking the open prairie. His eyes felt as if they had sand in them, and with the sun setting, he looked forward to the coolness of the coming night, relieved that he had made it through another day.

As he blinked his eyes, and they adjusted to the dim light, he saw a lone wolf sitting within a few yards. Its shaggy gray and white coat made him look old. Staring at Zachary, his yellow eyes seemed to hold some secret knowledge. The wolf, as if satisfied that he had sated his curiosity, stood, turned and loped away, its long legs carrying it out of sight.

***

September 1863 – Moon of Plums Ripening

The Governor's escort to the Republican River consisted of a troop of the 1st Colorado Cavalry, and as chief interpreter, Elbridge Gerry. Whit and Hez were also among those who waited for the arrival of Black Kettle and other chiefs, but the Cheyenne didn't show up at the agreed meeting place. After two days, there was still no sign of the Indians, and Evans sent Elbridge, Whit and Hez to locate the bands. They traveled to the Smoky Hill fork where they found the main body of Cheyenne camped, and discovered that the Dog Soldiers were camped there as well. The Dogmen had prevented Black Kettle, White Antelope and Bull Bear from attending the council with Evans.

It was clear the shift in the political power structure of the Cheyenne had changed dramatically. The general dissatisfaction with Black Kettle and the other signers of the treaty in 1861 had grown. Black Kettle, White Antelope, Lean Bear, Little Wolf, Tall Bear, and Left Hand, as well as the Arapaho chiefs Little Raven, Storm, Shave-Head, and Big Mouth were no longer looked upon as leaders who took care of their people. They had signed away all but a tenth of the territory ceded to them in the Laramie Treaty of 1851. Many of the bands of Cheyenne, especially the Dog Soldiers, refused to abide by the constraints of the new treaty and could see no reason to enter new talks. These bands continued to live and hunt in the buffalo-rich lands outside of the reservation, and by doing so increased their chances of conflicts with the ever-increasing number of Whites.

It was also evident that the mere presence of the three Whiteman in the Cheyenne camps was unwelcome. As Elbridge, Whit and Hez prepared to leave, they found themselves surrounded on three sides by ever-growing numbers of young men, some shouting insults at them, others brandishing war clubs. Behind the young men were older, seasoned warriors, and behind them a throng of women and children.

Elbridge looked neither left nor right as they walked to their horses, while both Whit and Hez's gaze went from side to side in anticipation of a coming blow. One young brave standing with the older Cheyenne caught Whit's eye, and seeing past the long hair and Cheyenne clothing, Whit recognized his son. And Zachary, his heart pounding, stood watched his father and the other two men as they were driven out of the village.

Leaving the Cheyenne on the Smokey Hills, the three messengers moved up onto the Republican intent on following it back to where Governor Evans waited. Unexpectedly, they came across the camp of Northern Cheyenne. This camp was larger than the one on the Smokey Hills, and Gerry pointed out different groups of lodges. There were not just Cheyenne, but Lakota and Arapaho.

As the three came close to the camp, a group of warriors rushed out to intercept them and discover their intent. As with all tribes, there was the bravado displayed by the younger warriors in their rushing the White men, riding as close as possible to them, either turning at the last moment or passing within striking distance of an extended arm. Gerry, Whit and Hez held their ground, keeping their hands away from their weapons, and Gerry raised his right hand open-palmed to show he came in peace. Through the group of lodges, Gerry thought he recognized the markings of one lodge in particular, that of Hooked Nose, called Roman Nose by the Whites.

"I come to speak with Hook Nose," Gerry said in Cheyenne and in hand signs.

Without talk the Indians ushered the three into the village. As they rode slowly between the lodges, Gerry quickly informed his companions as to who they were about to meet. He told them that Hook Nose was not a chief, but a well-respected warrior and a leader in battle.

"He's not a Dog Soldier," said Gerry, "But a member of the Crooked Lance Society. He's also pretty superstitious, havin' a bunch of taboos when it comes to what he does and how he lives. He never shakes hands and won't eat anything that has been touched by metal. We're safe with his protection but be careful and expect anything."

They were led to the lodge that Gerry had suspected as that of Roman Nose and hearing the commotion, Roman Nose had exited his lodge and was standing in front to meet them.

"Hooked Nose, my heart is glad to see you," Gerry said in Cheyenne, still seated in his saddle.

"I see you, White Eyes," Roman Nose said, using Gerry's Cheyenne name, *"Come and we will talk."* With this, he sat on a willow back-rest in front of his lodge. Gerry, Whit and Hez, dismounted and seated themselves with the warrior. Many of the inhabitants of the camp were still standing around to listen in on the conversation. Roman Nose dispensed with the customary protocol of welcoming a guest, signaling that he expected the Whites to state their business and leave as soon as possible.

Seeing this as the case, Gerry spoke up, *"I have come with a message from the White leader, Governor Evans. He wishes to meet with the People and the Arapaho to talk of peace. He waits now to hear from them."*

"Tell him that he can wait. The People, the Lakota, the Kiowa and the Arapaho no longer want to talk of peace." Gerry was surprised that Roman Nose did not hold back his feelings for the Whites and gave a side glance to Whit and Hez.

"My heart is on the ground," said Gerry, *"We will tell Governor Evans that there will be no talks."* He made it to his feet followed by Whit and Hez, and they mounted their horses and rode slowly out of the village. When they had passed the last lodge, Gerry spoke to Whit and Hez, "Looks like all the talking is done."

"He has the power to talk for the Cheyenne and the other tribes?" Whit asked.

"Not so much, but what I saw back there tells me that it's not just the Dog Soldiers that are callin' for a war. All four of those tribes are startin' to get together, and blood can be the only outcome.

Evan's was angered over word that the Cheyenne, Arapaho, Lakota and Kiowa refused to talk, and they were disposed to go to war. Upon returning to Denver, Evan's received reports from the new commander of Fort Lyon, Major Scott Anthony, that the Kiowa and Comanche had committed depredations along the Arkansas, and friendly Indians had informed him that Lakota warriors had been roaming the area stirring up other Indians to convince them to start raiding the settlements. Adding to this distressing news, Robert North informed the Governor that he had witnessed a council between leaders of the Cheyenne, Arapaho, Lakota, Kiowa, Comanche and Apache, in which all leaders pledged to wage a large-scale war.

Now sure that there was an all-out uprising coming, Evans wrote William P. Dole, Commissioner of Indian Affairs, stating that he was satisfied with the validity of North's report, and that he deemed it prudent to make whatever arrangement was necessary to prevent war and "ferret out any step in progress of this foul conspiracy among these poor, degraded wretches."

By November, no uprising had materialized, but the situation along the Arkansas continued to degrade. As per the Fort Wise Treaty, the Government finally began construction of the Point of Rocks Indian Agency, with work on an irrigation system, a blacksmith shop and other buildings. All too late, for most of the Cheyenne and Arapaho were nowhere near the Sand Creek Reservation. Agent Colley reported that the depredations that were taking place were a result of starvation. He was convinced that the Indians could not understand that they had no right to what belongs to the White settlers, even if they were starving.

Major Anthony agreed with Colley's assessment of the situation saying that the Government would be compelled to subsist the Indians to a great extent or allow them to starve. His further opinion was that starvation would be the easier way of disposing of the Indians.

***

April 1864 – Moon of the Budding Trees

The winter had been harsh on the majority of those who chose to stay along the Arkansas, but game was more plentiful to the north and the bands that had moved to the Republican and Smokey Hills had faired far better. The spring hunt had been successful, and the confinement and restlessness of winter could be eased with forays against other tribes and taking advantage of what opportunities arose.

One such opportunity presented itself to a dozen Dog Soldiers under the leadership of Little Chief. Leaving their camp on Beaver Creek, they started north with the intent to make a raid against the Crow. Just before coming up to the South Platte, they found four mules grazing on the open prairie. Seeing no one around to lay claim to the animals, Little Chief saw the prospect of a reward from the Whites if the owner of the mules could be found. That same night a ranchman by the name of Ripley came into their camp claiming the mules belonged to him. Little Chief told him that he could have the mules if he would give presents to pay for their trouble. Ripley refused and went to

Camp Sanborn and told the officer in charge, Captain Sanborn that Indians had stolen his mules and he wanted them back.

The following morning, Captain Sanborn sent Second Lieutenant Clark Dunn with twenty of the 1st Colorado Cavalry to find the Dog Soldiers and return the stolen stock. As the Cheyenne were approaching the large grove of trees called Freemont's Orchard, the soldiers came into view and both groups took the defensive posture of spreading out in a line. In anticipation of a conflict, the troopers drew their pistols, and the Indians readied their bows and firearms.

Whoever fired the first shot was unimportant, but what followed that initial shot had repercussions that would destroy the fragile peace. When the two groups broke off, four of the troopers and two of the Dog Soldiers had been wounded. The Indians returned to their camp on Beaver Creek and the Troopers returned to Camp Sanborn, where two of the wounded died from their injuries.

May 1864 – Bright Moon

The killing of the two soldiers under Sanborn's command seemed to add fuel to the fire that soon spread and called for control of the plains. Between the 3rd and the 18th of May, the military and the Cheyenne would clash nine more times. First, on May 3rd, at Cedar Bluffs on the South Platte Road. Maj. Jacob Downing, 1st Colorado Cavalry, and two dozen men attacked a Cheyenne village. Downing claims that over two dozen Indians were killed while he lost but one soldier. One week later, Downing comes across an abandoned village and his soldiers destroy fourteen lodges, and all provisions found there.

The Cheyenne begin a widespread campaign of running off stock and stealing horses and mules, as far east as Fort Larned, in Kansas. On May 16th, Lt. George S. Eayre's, commanding an entire company of 1st Colorado Cavalry and a battery of two mountain howitzers, found the village of Lean Bear located halfway between Fort Larned and Fort Lyon. When Eayre approached the village, he was met by four-hundred warriors.

Lean Bear's people had been camped all winter long near Fort Larned, trading at the fort, and he expected that he would be able to talk to the soldiers. He persuaded his warriors to hold back as he and another chief called Star went out to talk.

Wearing the Peace Medal given to him by President Lincoln, he rode to within a few yards of Eayre and stopped. With no warning, the soldiers opened first and both Lean Bear and Star fell from their horses. The soldiers rode up to them and shot them again while they lay on the ground. The Cheyenne returned fire, killing four of the soldiers, then retreated losing another warrior before the battle was broken off.

The following day, the Cheyenne moved completely away from the vicinity of Fort Larned, along the way collecting stock and provisions from the ranch of John Dodds, Woodward Ranch and the Cole & Center Ranch and Trading Post.

On the 18th of May, the freight train of Jesus Sanchez Alarid traveled along the Santa Fe Trail, its destination St. Joseph, Missouri. Alarid had just crossed into Colorado Territory from New Mexico when over one hundred Cheyenne warriors rushed the wagons. Out-numbered and out-gunned, the New Mexicans surrendered. It was plain that the Cheyenne had been raiding, as some were dressed for war, wearing only a breechcloth, while others wore civilian clothing, some with stove-pipe hats. Others wore soldier blouses, and some had soldiers' hats. The Cheyenne drove off the horses and mules and captured the wagons and provisions. When they rode off, they left the New Mexicans stripped of all clothing, but spared them their lives.

Both Northern and Southern Cheyenne seemed to be at the epicenter of the conflict that was now self-feeding. For every action by either the Indians or the soldiers, the other side found a way to strike back. Carried along with the fever was, Zachary Voss, and he was excited at the prospects of becoming a true warrior. He gave little consideration that one day he may have to choose whether to kill a Whiteman or not. He was satisfied to participate in the raiding, and for the time being, no killing had been done by the small group he followed.

Though he thought himself distant from his old life, he was still tied to those he had left behind. Among the Dog Soldiers he rode with were: Little Bear, Mary Craigavon's grandson, his uncle, Sitting Hawk, and Silas Scott's son, Little Gun, with his sons Turtle and Red Fox Waiting. These last two were only sixteen and fourteen years old, but old enough to start practicing the arts of the warrior in stealing horses from an enemy. Others in his group included; Bear Voice, White Badger,

Small Belly, Wolf Horn, Blue Crane, Polecat, One Leg, and Red Arm who still carried the scalp of Azariah Bolt on his belt.

Along with this core group were several Arapaho and some Lakota who were also Dog Soldiers, making the formidable party number over two dozen. Their intent was to roam from the Smokey Hills River all the way up to the Republican and as close to Denver as possible.

***

CHAPTER SIXTEEN
AN EYE FOR AN EYE

June 1864 – Fattening Up Moon

Isaac Van Wormer built his ranch eighteen miles southeast of Denver on Box Elder Creek. The ranch was successful to the point Van Wormer could afford two hired-hands, Albert Miller and Nathan Hungate. Miller had come to Denver with the gold rush and ended up working for Van Wormer as his talents for livestock surpassed those as a prospector. Hungate, twenty-nine years old, had been in the west only two months. With him, he had brought his wife, Eliza and their daughters; Laura age three and Florence, five months old. The Hungates left Cass County, Nebraska Territory with the offer to work for Van Wormer and eventually have a ranch of their own.

Nathan was optimistic and a good hand, never shying from the work asked of him by Van Wormer, and along with Miller, ran the ranch smoothly. On the 10th of June, Van Wormer told his help that he would be going into Denver for a few days.

"I'm not worried but keep an eye out. I had some trouble with the damn Indians last fall, and a bunch of them have wintered not too far from here. I doubt there'll be any problems, as I pretty much put the fear of God in them the last time they tried to steal from me.

"Albert, you see if you can't find that big heifer and her calf. She's wandered off again. If you don't find her today, head over to the sawmill in the morning and ask Johnson if he's seen her. Nathan, you stay here and finish the work on the roof of your cabin. I would guess Ellen won't mind having you close by."

"She is a bit worried," said Nathan, "But, I've assured her I'll keep her and the girls safe."

"Yep, with that arsenal you have, you could hold off an army," Miller quipped, making fun and at the same time admiring the firearms owned by Nathan. Before coming west, Hungate purchased two fine rifles, an 1860 Henry rifle and an

1864 Warner Springfield carbine. Both firearms used metallic cartridges, the Henry held sixteen .44 caliber rounds in a tube under the barrel that were fed into the rifle's breech by a lever. This allowed the rifle to eject one round and chamber the next by the shooter in one swift motion.

The Warner carbine was a breech-loading, single-shot weapon, chambered in .56 caliber. After each round was fired, a door on top of the carbine's brass breech block was opened, the spent round extracted and a new one inserted. This made the weapon fast and deadly. Along with these two long arms, Nathan also owned a .32 caliber five-shot Smith & Wesson pistol, an 1862 .36 caliber Navy Colt and lastly a small Tipping & Lawden four-shot "pepper box" pistol in .22 caliber. Hungate felt he was adequately armed to handle any situation.

More than once, Nathan had told Eliza to keep the small pepper box pistol handy, adding, "You know what to do if it comes down to it. Don't let yourself or the little-ones fall into the hands of the savages."

His apprehension, like that of other Whites in the area, had been raised by the fear of a complete uprising of the Indians. This was mostly speculation and based on the report from Robert North, the husband of an Arapaho woman who had lived among his wife's people for years. North had gone to Governor Evans the previous fall and said that the Comanche, Apache, Kiowa, the northern band of Arapaho, and all the Cheyenne, with the Lakota, had met. He claimed to have heard them discuss the matter often, and the few of them who opposed it were forced to be quiet and were in danger for their lives. North said the principal chiefs pledged to each other that they would shake hands and be friendly with the whites until they had all the ammunition and guns they needed. The plan was to commence the war at several points in the sparse settlements early in the spring.

***

A combined raiding party of Arapaho, Lakota and Cheyenne Dog Soldiers, numbering over thirty warriors, had gathered on Kiowa Creek southeast of Denver. From this camp, they split up into smaller groups ranging from three to five men per group. The groups fanned out in the general direction of Denver with the intent of raiding the outlying ranches for horses and any other plunder conveniently at hand. These were soft targets with usually only a few men of fighting age, and there was little chance that any killing would take place. The Whites were easily surprised, and easer to evade once their stock was stolen. As a member of one of the raiding parties, Zachary looked forward to the challenge of stealing horses and proving himself, once again, as a Cheyenne. The leader of this small detachment was the formidable White Badger, with Bear Voice and Wolf Horn rounding out the foursome.

The individual groups moved away from the rallying point, toward the ranches, and stage stations, each with the intent of searching out a target. Zachary's group made its way to the southwest and it was not long before White Badger stopped them.

"I smell smoke," he said and pointed in the direction he thought the scent was coming from. They cautiously rode a bit further and dismounted at the bottom of a small hill. Leaving Zachary and Wolf Horn to mind the horses, White Badger and Bear Voice slowly crept up the hill on their bellies and looked over the crest. Below them, they spied three wagons, and eight men. Four mules were tied to one of the wagons, and the rest were out grazing and rolling in the grass. The men were busy preparing a noon meal and their attention was on the fire and the food they were preparing. It seemed as no one was watching the stock.

Returning to Zachary and Wolf Horn, White Badger told the two younger men what they had seen. He explained their plan.

"Ride as fast as you can, yelling and waving your blanket to scare the mules. Pay no attention to the white men. We will be able to run off the stock before they can react. Do not try to engage them, do not even try to count coup," said White badger. He then vaulted onto his horse followed by the other three.

Zachary's heart was beating in his chest as White Badger led them over the hill to a point where the wagons were just visible. Looking at Zachary, he offered one last bit of advice, "Move quickly and keep close to us. We will ride fast and scare away the horses and mules before they know what has happened."

Then he seemed to pass an unspoken message that signaled everyone to kick their horses into a dead run down the slope toward the wagons. Without another word, the four Indians rushed forth waving their blankets and yelling.

As predicted, the White teamsters were caught completely off guard and the raiders were within fifteen or twenty feet before they were seen. They dashed in between the wagons where the mules were. Only then did the teamsters react, running out towards the stampeding mules. Those few white men who had pistols seemed to forget they had them and failed to draw and fire at the Indians. The teamsters could only stand and watch the mules as they bolted away.

Zachary kept yelling long after it was necessary, the excitement completely overwhelming him. He had never felt so alive as he did at that moment. He dared to glance back only to see the white teamsters standing and watching their stock disappear in the distance. If he had his doubts about being one with the Cheyenne before, they were all dispelled. This was the life he wanted to live

They drove the horses and mules on towards where they would meet the other raiders, and it was not long before some of the other groups came in. Everyone was elated at how easy it was to steal the stock from the Whites. Small Belly, Blue Crane, Polecat, One Leg, and Red Arm came in with half a dozen horses. Small belly laughed, saying that stealing the horses was no challenge, but a white woman had come from her cabin, mounted a horse and chased them for several miles before she gave up.

"She was very fearsome," he said, *"I believe she is braver than any white man I've ever seen!"*

"If she rides her man the way she rode her horse she must go through many men!" said Polecat, *"It is a good thing that she did not catch you, she might have ridden you to death!"*

The mood in the camp was joyful and it seemed nothing could spoil it. When the four Arapaho rode into camp, the atmosphere changed. One of them had a bullet wound in his stomach, and Bear Voice went to tend to his injury. There was not a large amount of blood, but the young man's abdomen was beginning to swell, and his pain was intense.

"What happened?" asked Bear Voice.

"We went to the lodges of the white man, Van Wormer, and another man came out of the small lodge with his long gun and shot many times at us. Rain on His Back was hit in the stomach," said one of the Arapaho.

"I can put medicine on his wound to ease the pain, but the bullet has done great damage inside. All I can do for him is to ease his pain so that he may pass on to the other side peaceably," said Bear Voice.

As the last few straggling groups came in with the horses or mules that they had raided, the leaders of the group set to discuss what they would do next. The wounding of one of the party would have been taken as a sign of bad luck and normally this would be the end of the raiding with the members of the party returning to their villages. But Bear Voice saw it in a different way, he felt this was a good chance to stir things up.

As the hours passed, Rain on His Back's pain grew worse, and the man groaned in agony. Throughout the night, his three friends kept vigil next to him, and Bear Voice chanted his incantations and sang his medicine songs. Sometime just before sunrise, the young Arapaho died. All three of his close friends began to wail, their grief soon turned to anger, and they pressed the others to go back to Van Wormer's ranch and exact vengeance on the white man who had killed their friend.

It took little convincing, and with just a few left behind to watch the stolen stock, over two dozen warriors moved to Van Wormer's Ranch on Box Elder Creek. When they were close to the ranch, they divided into two groups advancing on either side of the buildings. Zachary was with the group that would go around to the front of the buildings, and his stomach was tied in knots. This was a different type of excitement then yesterday's raid. He had no idea what would happen, and he feared a conflict with the Whiteman where he would have to make the choice of spilling White blood.

Half of them rushed into the open area in front of the buildings, where they found the Whiteman working on the roof of one of the cabins. As soon as he spied the Indians, he scrambled down the ladder and shut himself up in the building. As the Indians approached, cautiously spreading out, shots rang out from the window of the cabin, striking trees and the ground around the Indians. Taking cover, the Indians fired back but there was no way to get at the man behind the heavy log walls. It did not take long for them to decide that the only way to get him to come out would be to burn him out. More shots rang out from the cabin, and it seemed there was more than one person shooting from the windows. Zachary could hear the different sound that each of the two firearms made. The type of rifles the white man had must've been the those that fired several rounds before needing to be reloaded, as shot after shot came rapidly from his gun. The man fired many bullets, not even one of the Indians was hit. Though well-armed, it appeared the man was not well practiced in the use of his weapons.

It was not long before the fire was started and torches were lit. Once these were burning, they were taken to the back of the cabin and thrown onto the roof. The fresh cut lumber, loaded with pitch, soon caught fire and it was not long before the entire structure started to burn. Smoke began to pour out of the two windows in front of the small cabin and everyone knew the white man had only two choices; stay in the structure and burned to death or come out and fight.

The cabin door burst open and the white man came out firing his is lever action rifle, behind him was a woman carrying two small children, one under each arm. Within a few paces the man was brought down by fire from the Indians, and the woman fell beside him clutching her daughters to her. The Indians rushed in and overpowered the man and wrenched the children from their mother's arms.

What took place next was unlike anything Zachary had ever seen. It was different from what had happened with the Pawnee. The killing of the Pawnee had been more of a battle. This seemed more horrific, more barbaric. The man was wounded and scalped while still alive, and then a rope was tied around his feet by one of the Arapaho who drug him off behind a horse. The other two Arapaho turned their attention to the woman and the two small children. Zachary had to turn away, he could hear the woman's sobs and the cries of the two little girls.

As the rest of the warriors moved off to ransack Van Wormer's house and finally set it ablaze, Zachary moved away from what was taking place in the yard. He hoped no one would notice as he tried to find a place where he could empty his stomach and hide the fear he felt inside.

"You must harden your heart," someone said behind him. *"This is the way of war."* Zachary looked around to see that it was White Badger was speaking to him.

"I did not know it would be like this," said Zachary.

"Sometimes it is necessary. In the next life that man and his family will remember they should let the horses go and not kill the young Arapaho."

"I am not sure I could do such a thing. I do not know if it is in me."

"You have much to learn Yellow Horse, if you are to be a warrior among the People."

When the torture and the killing of the Hungates was over, the raiders moved on, returning to where the herd of horses and mules had been left. These were divided up to the individual groups who returned to their villages, the Arapaho taking their dead comrade, and Nathan Hungate's Henry rifle with them. Most of them seemed to be satisfied that revenge had been taken for the dead Arapaho, but there were a few among the Cheyenne whose blood was still hot, and Bear Voice was quick to see which of these he could agitate, in order to cause more destruction. Through that evening, he fed the fires of hatred and by the following morning it was guaranteed that the first convenient target they came across would be attacked.

***

The rear axle of the wagon broke where it had been weakened by the uneven wear of the wheel, which had long needed proper grease. As the axle gave way, the wagon lurched sideways and the contents of the Yoder family, shifted to the side. The wheel was forced against the wagon bed and the spokes snapped under the sideways pressure. Lavinia and Eleanora, her daughter, were thrown from the wagon, landing in a dusty heap of petticoats, sage brush, and prickly pear cactus.

Lavinia shrieked as she tumbled, and struggled to stop from rolling, finally coming to an unflattering stop on her back, her legs in the air, her skirt and petticoats tossed up over her face. She flailed her arms and legs about, her ample size; both in height and girth, made her seem that much more graceless in her predicament, somewhat like a turtle stuck on its back.

"Esau!" she screamed at her husband, "Esau you fool, help me!"

Her husband, who had been walking with his son next to the oxen, barely stopped the team from dragging the crippled wagon further down the trail. He ran back to aide her. He reached out to help her up, only to have his extended hands slapped away by the woman.

"You simpleton! I could have been killed!" she berated the man, who stood back to one side, allowing her to roll over to her hands and knees, from where she struggled to raise herself, first onto one shaking leg and then the other.

As Esau watched his wife dust herself off, he reached up, removed his hat, and scratched the heavy mop of red hair on his head. Though worried about her condition, he showed little sign of emotion. After years of verbal assaults by the woman, he had learned that almost any show of sentiment would be met by a doubled attack on his character, physical condition, or mental acuity. He had also learned to stay out of reach, or out of range from any object that could be thrown in his direction.

Once she had adjusted her clothing to proper alignment and pulled her bonnet back out of her eyes and square on her head, Lavinia gazed wide-eyed at the crippled wagon some twenty yards away, the broken wheel not far from where she stood. She seemed not to notice, or care about the condition of her daughter. Eleanora had managed to be tossed harmlessly to one side, missing both sage brush and cactus, and now stood beside her mother, who sputtering in her anger tore into Esau again.

"Look what a mess you have made of things!" She pushed Esau aside and made her way to inspect the wagon and its contents.

"If my mother's china has the least little crack in it, I'll take it out of your worthless hide!" She flung the words over her shoulder at her husband, who stood behind her. "Now what do you intend to do?" She turned to look at Esau, who was a good half a foot shorter than his spouse.

He stood afraid to answer or give any form of opinion, but finally called to his son, "George, come give me a hand." The boy, just past ten years old, followed his father to inspect the wagon.

The end of the axle was shattered beyond repair, and the wheel was no better. Parts of the wheel could be reused in building a new wheel, if Esau had the needed wood, and the tools necessary, but even at that, he lacked the expertise. Both axle and wheel would require replacement.

"Well?" Lavinia asked, "What are you going to do?"

"I 'spect I'll have to walk on ahead and try to catch up with the other wagons. See if maybe they have an extra axle an' wheel," he paused. "Don't rightly know what else to do."

"Then you had better get at it," his wife barked, "and don't dally. You get there and get back." As almost an afterthought she added, "Take the boy with you, you'll need the help. Anyway, he's no good to me here."

Esau and George walked slowly to the west following the tracks of the wagons that had outdistanced them two days ago. He held no bitterness in his heart toward those good people, who had decided that Esau and his family were holding them back. Time was precious and the longer it took them to reach Denver, their chances of getting settled before winter diminished.

Esau was surprised that his family had lasted as long as it did with the small train of wagons. He had long ago resigned himself that the day would come when his family would no longer be welcome among them. Each day since they had left Westport, there had been one thing or another caused by Esau's wagon, team or more often, his wife. In truth, it had been more about Lavinia than anything else. She had alienated even the most forgiving among the other families, constantly contriving some reason to complain, stirring up excitement at the slightest trouble, and creating conflict so that she could be a part of what she thought was the solution to the imagined problem.

Each night in the past months, Lavinia had repeated the same complaints over and over. First, she would comment on the condition of her own family blaming either Esau or another member of the wagon train. Her next attack would be directly on Esau himself.

"I am so mortified that we had to leave the safety of Illinois," she would start, "If you hadn't let your brother cheat you out of your portion of the farm, we'd never have had to move out to this God-forsaken wilderness."

In fact, Esau's brother Ezra, had been kind enough to buy Esau's share in the farm left to them by their father. Life as a farmer had never suited Esau and when the War broke out, it initially disrupted the Illinois economy. Like other farmers, Esau and Ezra found no market for what crops they would normally float downriver to New Orleans to sell. Their bank held southern state bonds as backing for the notes they issued, and it failed in the war's first months.

It seemed that an almost herculean effort would be required to save the farm, and Ezra and Esau both knew Esau could not stand up to the challenge, he was not suited to be a farmer. He didn't have the perception for reading the condition of the land, and what action or remedy was needed in the care of crops. More than once a crop had been lost due to his incompetence, and though Esau felt the guilt for these failures, his brother never held him accountable or uttered an unkind word.

The previous fall Esau and Ezra had discussed the buyout, and Ezra gave his younger brother more than what his half of the farm was worth. At first Esau refused the generous offer, but Ezra pressed him into accepting. Deep down Esau knew the farm would be better off in Ezra's hands.

"You'll need the money to start some kind of business in this Denver that you are headed for," he had told Esau. "I hope only the best for you my brother."

At first, Lavinia was pleased to get out from under the shadow of her brother-in-law. The deal had been less than she thought was due her husband, but the burden and the loss would now be Ezra's, not Esau's. She had heard that there were opportunities in the West, and with the discovery of gold, she was sure that she could steer her husband into a lucrative mercantile business in the boom town along what was called Cherry Creek in Colorado Territory.

But everything changed as the War progressed. The federal government's seemingly insatiable demand for military supplies fired Illinois' industrial economy. As the Illinois economy recovered, businesses increasingly turned away from the southern markets linked by rivers and looked toward Chicago and its contacts, via the Great Lakes and Erie Canal, with the northeast.

While the disruption of water transportation temporarily unhinged farm markets, crop prices consistently rose as did the value of agricultural land. The farm, under Ezra's hand, increasingly became a business rather than a self-sufficient way of life, and Ezra became a prosperous man. Lavinia soon became displeased that her husband had sold his "birth-right" for pennies and had no qualms about voicing her opinion. She even pointed out that if he had been an able-bodied man, he might have looked to the Army to ensure an income for his family, the bounty of $450 and wages of $25 a month seeming like an enough incentive.

But Esau was no more suited to be a soldier than he was a farmer, and when spring did arrive, the wagon and team of oxen that he had invested in the previous fall were readied, loaded and Esau took his family west.

Now Esau found himself walking westward, his son George at his side. Esau hoped that if they walked on through the coming night that they might catch up with the other wagons. Neither father nor son spoke as they walked, but Esau felt compelled to reach over and place a hand on the boy's shoulder. Though he never turned the thought of love around in his mind, he carried more for the boy than anyone else. There was a bond there that needed no thought or explanation, and Esau accepted it as his one and only piece of happiness. He looked down at the boy and the lad turned up his face and smiled at his father, an act that was very rare.

As they walked into the wind, it carried away the small clouds of dust their feet kicked up along the trail they followed, and the increasing force of the breeze blew it far behind them. If they had chosen to speak to each other, they would have needed to raise their voices, as their words would have been swept along with the dust. In this way, the wind and the rhythm of their footsteps, lulled them into a mindless plodding down the trail.

Engrossed in their own private thoughts, neither of them heard the single horse and rider come up from behind them. The first sign that they were not alone in the endless rolling prairie was the sharp pain Esau felt that radiated from his back into his chest. He stumbled forward, lost his balance and fell face first into the trail, his hat rolling off and then carried away with the breeze.

George, at first thought his father had stumbled and started to reach for him, then realized that protruding from his father's back was the feathered shaft of an arrow. Frozen, and unable to take another step, he looked from his fallen parent back to where he now heard a Dog Soldier's war cry.

"Pap!" escaped George's lips, as the mounted Cheyenne came closer, the rider and horse both painted with symbols, feathers attached to main and hair. The Indian walked the horse slowly up to George and slid from its back. He knelt and taking a handful of Esau's hair, pulled the dead man's head back. With the other hand he pulled a knife from its sheath at his waist and made a circular cut around the top of Esau's head, pulling free the curly, red scalp.

He stood, tucked the bloody trophy into his belt and then mounted his horse. He pulled the rope reins and spun the pony around, the horse's hooves barely missing the boy. The Cheyenne looked down at George, and then he reached out, taking George by the shirt, lifted the boy up to sit in front of him.

George wasn't sure where the Indian was taking him, he didn't even wonder why he hadn't been killed like his Pa. All he knew now was that they were headed back toward where the wagon had been left. When it came into sight, he saw more Indians throwing things out of the wagon and going through the satchels and boxes. Three of the oxen were dead their bodies filled with feathered shafts, the fourth was bellowing in its agony as arrow after arrow was sunk into its red hide.

Looking around, George saw his sister, Eleanora, sitting on a horse behind one of the Indians. Her bonnet was missing and her hair, usually tied back in a bun, was hanging loose, some strands laying across her face. Beneath the copper colored strands George could see her face was bruised and her lip was split. He also saw that her dress had been torn down the front, exposing her pale breasts. The look in her eyes was that of a frightened animal caught in a snare. Her gaze darted around as if looking for something, some form of rescue from what was happening to her.

George looked for his mother, but he couldn't find her. What he did see was a large pale figure lying on the ground. He realized it was the body of a woman, and that she was naked. But what he could not comprehend is that this was the body of his mother, raped, scalped, and like the oxen, shot with several arrows.

The Indians set the wagon on fire and what was of no value to them was tossed into the blaze or left to lay on the prairie. What had been Lavinia Yoder's treasured possessions, destroyed in the flames. The raiding party turned to head to the east.

Zachary had spared himself watching the rape and torture of the day before, but this day was different. He could not turn his back and move off and spare himself the sight of the fat woman being raped then scalped and killed. When he turned his gaze away from this, he saw Small Belly, Blue Crane and One Leg taking turns raping the girl, when One Leg was done, he had suggested Zachary take a turn. Zachary only shook his head no, but he could not turn his eyes away. Yesterday it seemed surreal to him, today was all too real.

As he rode, he couldn't help but glance at the young girl riding behind One Leg. She didn't seem to be much older than him, and her skin was the palest white Zachary had ever seen. Her hair was a light red that seemed more the color of a rusty nail. Her eyes were vivid blue, almost like sky. But in her eyes, there was no fire, there was no spark, only what reminded him of what he had seen in the eyes of a rabbit or a deer as it was about to die. Her fate would probably be that of slave, given to one of the older Cheyenne women who was without a daughter or sister to help around her lodge. There was a slim chance that she would be taken as a wife, only if one of the young Cheyenne took a liking to her. This of course would depend on her adapting to life among the People.

The boy was a different matter. He seemed simple to Zachary, as if he had no real idea what was happening around him. Zachary knew that the boy might possibly be adopted by someone in the tribe and raised as a Cheyenne. But, like his sister, it would depend on his ability to adapt to the Cheyenne way of life.

The raid on the freighter's wagons had netted forty-nine mules and horses belonging to Daniel's & Brown, the ranch of Thomas J. Darrah had four horses in two mules taken and the cabin burned down. The Ferguson ranch had lost half a dozen mules, and though Mr. Ferguson was not home at the time, his wife Catherine was. She mounted the single horse not taken by the Indians and pursued them for nearly two miles. While the Indians knew she was following, they did not try to molest her but rather kept the horses just out of her reach. Catherine finally gave up and went to a neighbor's house to enlist someone to help her try to recover horses. By this time though, the Indians were able to escape with her stock.

Darrah decided to go to Denver and report his losses, and on the way ran into the freighter's. Together with John Brown, he made it as far as Running Creek, where they found a group of soldiers, commanded by Captain Maynard, preparing their dinner. After dinner the soldiers saddled up and traveled to Box

Elder Creek accompanied by Darrah and Brown. When they were within a mile of the Van Warmer ranch, they discovered the body of Nathan Hungate. Traveling further they found that the buildings had been burnt, and there was no site Mrs. Hungate or her two daughters.

A further search found a note attached to one of the fence posts. A party from Gomer's sawmill stated that Mrs. Hungate and her two children had been killed and the bodies had been taken to the mill. The mutilated bodies of the Hungate family were then taken to Denver where they were placed on display for the public to see. People crowded to look at them, and what horrified most people was the condition of Mrs. Hungate and the two small children. From this time on all the people of Denver were in favor of exterminating all Indians.

The killing of the Hungates, almost within sight of Denver, created panic. The ranches in the area were all abandoned, and everyone fled to Denver. When a rumor began circulating that Indians were advancing on the town, people became alarmed. The doors of the ordinance storehouse were forced open and the people took possession of the arms and ammunition belonging to the United States. There were no troops in Denver except for a handful of soldiers, who, with help of the militia, started to look for Indians but, returned without having accomplished anything.

The Lakota, except for those who were living with the Dog Soldiers, had been peaceful, as they were warned by the government to keep the peace by staying away from any of the hostile Indians. They were also told to keep away from the immigrant road and make no further raids on the Pawnee. Nevertheless, a small party of young Lakota men decided to make a raid on the Pawnee. In the haste to seek out their enemies, they happened to come up on a party of whites who, in the dark, they mistakenly took for Pawnee. They immediately attacked the party of Whites, killing some. Immediately the Army was ordered to hunt down the Lakota and obtain retribution for the killings. This would force the Lakota into being considered hostile.

Governor Evans sent out a circular to friendly Indians calling upon them to come in and camp near the posts. There they would be considered in a safe place, putting themselves under the military protection and watched by the troops. According to the circular the Cheyenne's and Arapaho were to come to Fort

Lyon, while the Kiowa and the Comanche were to go to Fort Larned. Part of the Cheyenne, those living on the Arkansas, were at this time and camped at Salt Springs on Medicine Lodge Creek south of the Arkansas and near Fort Larned.

Though there was a lack of trust, most of the Southern Cheyenne and Arapaho gathered within twenty-five miles of the Fort. The groups of Dog Soldiers that were living among these bands refused and moved to other camps were those of their own making.

As if to emphasize their resistance to making peace, on June 28th the Dog Soldiers raided a wagon train between Julesburg and Fort Laramie, running off all the mules. The same day a coach was attacked on the Arkansas between Fort Larned and Fort Lyon. The following day, General Curtis reported that he was starting with a large force to march along the road from Salina to Fort Larned, with the intent of leaving small garrisons along the way to guard the stage line. From both sides, every possible motive was given to incite the Indians to fight and raid, and they were doing both.

Zachary was with the main camp of the Cheyenne on the Smoky Hill, which contained many Dog Soldiers, and this group soon moved south joining the Cheyenne camp long Ash Creek. Zachary had never seen a camp so large, or so many Indians gathered together in one spot, and he looked forward to the feasting and the dancing that would be held in this vast camp.

This camp however did not contain all the Cheyenne, and within a few days, he went with a small group of warriors further South, crossing the Arkansas above Fort Larned and on Salt Springs, near Medicine Lodge Creek, they found, a small band of Cheyenne, Comanche, and Apache camped.

The Cheyenne remained near Salt Springs until they had held their Medicine Lodge, and then they would move north. At the crossing on the Arkansas they were met by runners from the Lakota camped on the Republican, who notified them that the Indians up there had been making raids on the Overland Stage along the Platte. The Cheyenne moved up to the Republican and began to send out raiding parties of their own.

The war now in progress was chiefly confined to the Platte route, though the Kiowa, Comanche and Apache made a few raids on the Arkansas. Now and then, a small spot party of Cheyenne and Arapaho also strike along the Arkansas Road, but there was far less travel there and fewer ranches. Orders were given by the Army to call back the troops sent to the Arkansas in order to get a force effective for work on the Platte. Between Fort Larned and Fort Lyon, a distance of two hundred and sixty miles, there was only one station, and it was abandoned along with the few ranches about Fort Lyon.

Conditions on the Platte Road were quite different. Here the travel was much heavier, and the road was better protected by garrisons such as Fort Kearney in Nebraska Territory, Fort Cottonwood further up the Platte, and Julesburg above the forks of the Platte. The Overland Mail still ran up the Platte and there were stations every ten or twelve miles. At these stations, there were ranches, and at almost every ranch a store were travelers could sleep and buy goods.

The route was crowded with mail coaches, freight trains, and of course immigrant trains. All the goods imported to Colorado, including supplies of food, were taken up the Platte River Road. And the great freight trains bound for Utah, for the new mines in Montana, and for California and Oregon, also passed up the Platte. Despite the military presence, the Cheyenne and the Lakota began their raiding parties in July.

Cheyenne Dog Soldiers and Lakota warriors consolidated and began their raids along the Republican and Platte River routes. The Platte route, Denver's primary sources supplies, was cut off as warriors continued to move towards unprotected Denver. Though Governor Evans continued to plead with Washington and for help, the Civil War in the East preoccupied General Curtis in the war department.

July 1864 - Moon of the Ripening Chokeberries

On the 17th of July, near Bijou Ranch on South Platte River, the Indians ran off horses belonging to an immigrant train. They killed two men and wounded a third. They also took seventy horses and killed thirty-one head of cattle from the Junction and Murray's Ranches, killing five men. The same day, they attacked the Beaver Ranch where one Whiteman was wounded, the stock of the Godfrey ranch stolen, and at the Washington Ranch, two dozen horses were taken. In response, troops were sent out. They surprised five Indians on Beaver Creek near Murray's Place and recovered one hundred twenty-five head of stolen stock, but the Indians escaped.

Zachary rode with the Cheyenne Dog Soldiers under the leadership of Bull Bear, attacking small settlements in Nebraska, and with them rode Arapaho and Lakota warriors. They raided along the Overland Trail, hitting the ranches, along a sixty mile stretch of the Little Blue River. It was during the raid along the Little Blue River at the Eubank Ranch that Zachary killed his first Whiteman.

North of the ranch, the Dog Soldiers first came upon the men cutting hay in the field. Three men, a teenager, and nine-year-old Ambrose Ascher were caught completely off guard. One of the men was killed instantly, the other two were run down and slain. The teenager turned and using his scythe as a weapon swung it as Zachary rode down on him. Almost without thought Zachary ducked the swing of the long-bladed instrument. Turning in his saddle, he loosed an arrow at the young man, striking him in the chest. Immediately, Zachary brought his horse around and rode back to where the young man lay dying.

Zachary dropped from his horse and walked to the boy's side. Looking down, he could see this young man was not much older than himself. The boy clutched the arrow in his right hand, and with each breath he took, pale blood poured from between his clenched teeth. His pale blue eyes stared up at Zachary, not in fear but in hatred. Zachary thought if this was another time at the ranch on the Arkansas, he could envision himself as the boy on the ground. But he wasn't the one the ground. It was just another immigrant, like so many he had seen in the past months, an enemy to the Cheyenne, to his people. Zachary removed the knife from his belt, and hands slightly shaking, he knelt next to the boy and cut away the scalp. With this simple act, Zachary Voss no longer existed, he was now completely Yellow Horse.

Ambrose Ascher was taken captive, but two small children found in the house were not as fortunate and were killed, and the house set on fire. Within a half-mile of the house, Joseph and Lucinda Eubank, their two babies, Isabel and Will, and the visiting teenage girl, Laura Roper, were out for a walk when they saw the smoke from the house curling into the air and heard screaming from the homestead. Joseph Eubank told his wife to hide in the brush and keep quiet. He then ran towards the house to aid his children. His efforts were futile, and he was brought down before he could act against the raiders.

As the Dog Soldiers were riding away, they heard one of the toddler's crying. Lucinda Eubank, her children, three-year-old Isabel, nine-month-old Will, and sixteen-year-old Laura Roper were taken captive. For a few moments, Zachary pondered why some children were taken as prisoners and others killed. To him, it seemed to depend on the whim of the raiders. He did not think much on this, as he figured it was the way of the Cheyenne and he did not need to know why.

August 1864 - Breeding Moon

For the next two weeks, Zachary rode with the Dog Soldiers, joining other groups and finally meeting up with a larger group under the leadership of Bull Bear. In four successive days, this group of Cheyenne Dog Soldiers made raids along Plum Creek in Nebraska. About two miles west of the Plum Creek stage station on the South side of the Platte River, the Dog Soldiers and Lakota attacked a corralled wagon train. Only one of the whites was killed, as the teamsters immediately retaliated firing their shotguns and killing two of the Cheyenne driving off the rest.

That same day, they attacked two more wagon trains and were far more successful. In the first, they overran the wagons, killing all the men and taking a Mrs. Morton captive. The second wagon train, including six wagons loaded with corn belonging to Mitchell Kelly, was attacked and again all the men were killed save for one young boy, Daniel Marble.

The next day, the Cheyenne attacked the Little Blue Station on the Comstock ranch. Twenty of the Dog Soldiers rode in, calmly pretending to be friendly. Ranch workers became nervous and the Cheyenne suddenly struck, killing some of the men. Several of the survivors fled into the ranch house and began to fire on the warriors as they retreated. On the following day, the Indians returned and finding the station empty, looted and burned the buildings, carrying off the stock.

After leaving the Little Blue Station, they ran off the stock from the Giroux and Dion ranch. They finished out the day by attacking the Kiowa Ranch stage station and burning the buildings there.

This raid caused a panic, and the Army gathered a large force to march against the Indians. They went up the Platte and scouted south to the Republican but found no hostiles. They had no idea there was a huge camp on the Solomon River; Cheyenne, Arapaho and under the leadership of Spotted Tail and Pawnee Killer, Brûlé Lakota. On the Overland Road, the Lakota made their raids east of Fort Kearny, the Cheyenne west, while the attacks of the Arapaho were made on the same road further west and on the South Platte near Denver. These raids were terribly destructive, attacking and burning ranches, wagon trains, coaches, killing many people and running off stock.

For over a month, the Indians completely closed the road. On August 15, the last coach reached Colorado. Coaches from the west gathered at Latham Station on the South Platte and remained, awaiting the opening of the road. About one hundred passengers were gathered there when a rumor arose that the Indians were coming up the Platte to Latham and threw these people into a panic.

The freighters continued their trips for some time, but they had to move in large, strongly armed groups that could defend against small war parties. By the middle of the month, conditions grew so bad that the freighters were forced to corral their wagons and wait for better times. In the meantime, food grew scarce in Denver and prices soared. Flour jumped from nine dollars to sixteen for one hundred pounds, and then to twenty-five dollars. Adding to the shortage of food, a plague of locusts devoured the crops on the South Platte.

On August 18, Governor Evans, sent a telegraph to General Curtis, stating that the Indians were killing people within thirty miles of Denver, and a large war party of Indians were close to the town. The roads were blocked, and what crops there were could not be gathered for fear of Indian attacks. As a result of this, the whole of Colorado Territory was in a state of starvation. Evans requested the Second Colorado Cavalry, then serving in Kansas, to be sent home to protect the Overland Road and the people of the territory.

Governor Evans then issued a second proclamation. In this, he authorized the people of Colorado, "to go in pursuit of the hostile Indians on the plains. Also, to kill and destroy as enemies of the country all such hostile Indians. I hereby empower such citizens to take captive, and hold to their private use and benefit, all the property of said hostile Indians that they may capture."

The result of this proclamation put the friendly Indians at the mercy of any revengeful immigrant who had been attacked by Indians. Any man, who coveted an Indian's horse or property, could shoot him as a hostile, and seize the property as his own lawful prize. The governor also sent telegrams to the secretary of war pleading for the authority to raise a militia under sanctions of the Army. And on August 11, the volunteer regiment was authorized, with guaranteed pay and supplies for the period of one hundred days.

CHAPTER SEVENTEEN
THE HAND OF PEACE OR WAR

August 1864 - Breeding Moon

Zachary watched the captives as they rode along, each of them seated behind a warrior. Mrs. Eubank rode behind Wolf Horn, her bonnet covering her disheveled hair. She had been allowed to take clothing for herself and her two children, who rode one behind Small Belly and one with One Leg. The teenage boy rode behind Polecat, and the girl behind Red Arm. There would've been one more captive, a teenage girl, but she had resisted and been killed and scalped.

As with the Elenora, this teenager attracted Zachary's attention more than the other captives. He wondered if she, could tell that he was half white. He felt confident enough though the towards the middle of the night he rode up next to her and started to talk her.

"Aren't you afraid that you be killed?" He asked.

"If you had intended to kill me, you would've done it as you did Hannah Eubank," she answered.

"The other girl resisted, she fought back. That is why Bear Voice killed her and took her scalp." They rode on for a bit, and then he asked, "What is your name?"

"Laura, Laura Roper." For the first time she turned to him and gave him a good hard look. "And what is your name?"

Without hesitating, he said, "I'm called Yellow Horse."

"You speak good American," she said. Zachary thought he would let the conversation drop and move past her.

They rode on through the next day when they were joined by another group of raiders with extra horses. The captives were then placed on their own mounts, and Zachary watched Laura Roper, noticing how well she rode. He wondered if she might try to escape, but she calmly rode on with the Indians, until they began to cross a deep arroyo. Laura's pony slipped and fell, her saddle shifted, and she was thrown to the ground. As the pony was trying to get up, it kicked Laura in the face breaking her nose. Zachary and Red Arm dropped from their horses and both went to the girl. Zachary helped her off the ground and gave her a piece of cloth to wipe the blood from her face, while Red Arm began to beat the pony with his stone war club, killing it. He then took Laura by the hand and remounting his horse pulled her up behind him again.

They rode through the second night until the next afternoon, having not stopped the entire time. The only thing they had eaten for two days was dried buffalo meat. They finally stopped to eat a hot meal only Wolf Horn shot and killed a turkey. They ordered Mrs. Eubank to clean and cook the bird, which they all shared. They unsaddled their ponies and spread Buffalo robes out and motioned to the captives to lay down and rest. Laura Roper's face was so badly swollen that her eyes were almost closed. Zachary went to Bear Voice and asked him if he would help her with his medicine. Grudgingly, Bear Voice approached her, and taking her chin roughly in his hands he inspected her face. From his parfleche bag, he took the red powder and mixed it with bear grease, and this he spread over her face.

After a rest of only two hours, the Indians decided it was time to remount the horses and move on. Little Belle Eubank began to cry, wanting her mother, and angering One Leg. As she struggled with him, he grabbed her by the hair with one hand and pulling out his knife motioned as if he was going to cut her throat. Surprising everyone, Laura Roper sprang forward and grabbed his arm, surprising both One Leg, and the other warriors.

"You are very brave for a white squaw," said Blue Crane, laughing. *"We should give you your own war honors, and a name befitting a warrior!"* Then he laughed again, along with some of the others. Even One Leg seemed to find some humor in this. Springing into his saddle, he leaned down and took Belle Eubank up, and placed her in front him. Because she had gained new respect, once again a horse was found for Laura to ride. Again Zachary rode up next to her and addressed her, "You are probably right," he said, "I do not think that they will kill you, I don't think they will keep you long either before they give you up." And then he kicked his horse and moved on past her.

They traveled on through the night until the next afternoon when they met a band of over two dozen other Cheyenne and

Arapaho. After greeting each other, they all stopped, and each warrior took out leather bags, and from these they drew out paint, feathers and decorated clothing. Each warrior painted himself, placed feathers in his hair, and put on their regalia. They then all remounted, traveled a short distance and soon came upon a huge camp containing thousands of Indians.

Within half a mile, the warriors started running their horses giving out their war cries in a race towards the camp. Residents of the camp, the women, children and old people came out to greet them, all of them returning shouts and cries, the women sounding their high pitch trilling. The warriors rode into the middle of the camp, and there was a feeling in the air that surpassed any excitement Zachary had ever experienced. But his enthusiasm did not take away his attention to Laura Roper. He watched as Red Arm dropped her amidst a group of Cheyenne women, who jumped on her, pulling her hair, and striking her with their hands. But this lasted only a short time, and one of the woman taking her by the arm pulled her off to a lodge where Zachary knew she would be given a place to rest of something to eat.

The following day, the entire camp packed up and moved to the Solomon River, creating a great village containing thousands of Cheyenne, Arapaho, and Lakota. Zachary spent a few days in the lodges of friends from the raiding. But it was not long until Bear Voice found him and brought him back to his lodge where Sees Far Woman was waiting. She was ecstatic at the sight of him, offering him the comforts of the lodge, and a bowl of buffalo stew. She commented him on his looks, telling him how magnificent he looked, how strong, and virile.

"*All the young women will be looking to you, hoping that you will choose them to lay with,*" she told him, "*you must be careful. Young women have ways of trapping a handsome warrior like yourself. They would not truly love you, they would only want you to be their own so as to gain status among the People. You are too smart for them. You know that no one could appreciate you as I do. I will protect you from these greedy young women.*"

"*I have not seen any of the young women looking at me,*" said Zachary.

"*Ahh, Yellow Horse, I have seen them. Their eyes follow you as you walk through the village. They go to their medicine men asking for love charms to make you want them. My medicine is*

strong, I will protect you. Look, see what I have made for you?"
Then from a parfleche box, she pulled out a finely made war
shirt of soft deer skin. It was decorated with strips of dyed
porcupine quillwork across the shoulders and down the arms.
She held this up for him, smiling. On the chest was a great
medicine circle, also made of dyed porcupine quills, and along
the arms were long strands of leather fringe entwined with locks
of long black hair. Her hair. All of this infused with her special
medicine, that she believed in her mind warded off evil, and
sealed him to her and her only.

"Now you have a fine war shirt befitting one of your status as
a warrior," she said, "wearing this shirt will protect you. The
white man's bullets will fall to the earth before they strike you.
Neither arrow nor lance will pierce the shirt. Here, try it on." And
she helped Zachary slip the leather garment over his head, the
smell of the smoke garment engulfed him.

He would rather have had one of the fine silk shirts many of
the other young man were wearing, but Sees Far Woman would
not touch material made by the Whiteman. He was also still
somewhat uncomfortable around her, but he had to admire the
shirt. It fit him perfectly, and she had tanned the leather soft
and supple. If what she had said was true, that the young
women of the camp were looking at him, he felt now they surely
would look at him. Sees Far Woman had intended to bind him
further to her, but what she had done with the new shirt was to
make him all that more appealing. Zachary knew this, and as
Yellow Horse, he would be more desirable to the young women,
and the envy of many of the young men.

The next day, he donned his new war shirt and moved
through the camp, more aware now of the young women whose
eyes followed him. He stood a bit taller, his stride a bit more
purposeful, and he reveled in this adoration. He moved from one
part of the great village to the other, stopping to speak with
friends from the raids, and others that he had not seen in a
while. He also spent time watching the scalp dances constantly
going on. Camps were filled with plunder taken from captured
wagon trains; warriors were strutting about with lady's silk
cloaks and bonnets and the Indian women were making shirts of
bright colors and stripes, for the young men out of the finest
silk. The different groups had gathered together to celebrate
their victories over the whites, ranging from the Cimarron River

north to the Platte River. One group had even been so bold as to raid the horse herd at Fort Larned.

Not all the groups gathered in this great village had taken part in the raids. Black Kettle, with a large Cheyenne village had been camped with the Kiowa and Comanche's on medicine Lodge Creek on the Salt Plain, and here they held their Sundance and made medicine. These people had been quiet and did not participate in the raids as did those bands along the Platte.

By the end of June, Black Kettle's village had left the Kiowa and the Comanche on Medicine Lodge Creek crossed the Arkansas and headed north towards Smoky Hill. It was here that they met runners from the Lakota camp bringing the news of the raiding that had begun along the Platte. Those with Black Kettle had refrained the raids, wanting no confrontation with the Whites, but some of the young men broke away and headed north to join in on the raids.

The remainder of the Cheyenne from this group under Black Kettle, moved on to the Solomon River joining the other Cheyenne, Lakota, Arapaho, and Dog Soldiers. As large as this village was, there were many in leadership, such as Black Kettle, who still held hope for peace. They knew once this village broke up, and the small bands went their own separate ways for winter, they would be vulnerable to vengeful whites and the Army that could not tell one band of Indians from the other.

Before the camp broke up, the Cheyenne Chiefs received a message from William Bent urging them to make peace with the Whites. Several of the chiefs held council and decided it best to attempt to make peace again. With this in mind, they enlisted the aid of the half-breeds, William Bent's son, George, and Edmond Guerrier to write a letter to Indian Agent Cooley and one to the commander of Fort Lyon, Major Wynkoop.

In these messages, they acknowledged receiving Bent's letter proposing peace. They said that they regretted that the war had been started and that they desired peace. They asked for help in securing a peace that would include the Kiowa, Comanche, Arapaho and Apache. They also offered to hand over White prisoners, in exchange for Cheyenne prisoners being held in Denver.

They also stated that their council had included some Arapaho and Lakota, but that there were still small war parties out, and they were expecting them to return soon. They closed with a final request that Cooley and Wynkoop reply in good faith. The letters were entrusted to two sub-chiefs, Eagle's Head and One Eye who took them to Fort Lyon, One Eye taking his wife with him as a sign that their intentions were peaceful.

To help with the negotiations, the chiefs had purchased the White captives; Laura Roper, little Belle Eubank, Dannie Marple and Connie Eubank, but Mrs. Eubank and the baby had been purchased by a Lakota who would not negotiate for their release and instead took them north with him.

The bands that Black Kettle spoke off continued their raiding and from the point of view of many Whites, there would never be a difference between one Indian and another, what one did the other condoned.

**

The wagon bed was filled with buffalo meat and hides that Whit and Hez collected over the past three days. They looked forward to getting them unloaded at Elbridge Gerry's little trading post. Elbridge was more than pleased with what his two hired hands brought in.

"They're fine looking and hides, even if they are summer weight," he said.

"We figured this would be enough meat to get us through till the weather turns cold," said Eli, "anyway Hez has been a might skittish ever since killing of them folks down on Box Elder Creek."

"It wasn't just them," said Hez, "it's everything that's been happening all up and down the road, from here all way along the Republican and Platte."

"Well, with a scarcity of food down in Denver, more meat would've been better because we got top dollar even for poor bull," Elbridge remarked. "Not sure if you've heard, but the roads closed completely East all the way into Nebraska and Kansas territory."

As they were talking, to Indians approached. Two men, an older woman and a small child. They were Cheyenne that Elbridge recognized as Long Chin and Pushing Ahead. Both men were in their sixties, and Elbridge had known them for a long time.

"*Hello, Long Chin and Pushing Ahead,*" Eldridge said in Cheyenne, "*I am pleased to see you.*"

"Hello, White Eyes," said Long Chin not only speaking but also using hand signs. "We have come to trade." Eldridge looked past the two men eyeing the travois being pulled by the woman's horse. On it were very few items, and it was obvious that the Indians had very little to trade.

"Come, get down from your ponies and we will speak of your trade." Both of the Cheyenne slid down from their saddles, slower than younger men, but still graceful from a lifetime of living on horseback. The woman and the child remained on her horse.

Gerry led them into a small establishment and offered them a seat on a buffalo robe already spread on the floor. Like their movements dismounting their horses, they eased down onto the floor, taking their time. It was obvious that both men were uncomfortable and impatient, wanting to get the business at hand over with so that they could be on their way. They settled, adjusting their blankets tied around their waist, for the day was warm and they required them out of habit, not for warmth. Gerry brought them each a cup of coffee heavily laced with sugar, and they took it, sipping politely at the dark brew.

After a single sip Long Chin spoke up, "We have little time to stay and talk. We have brought you word of a coming danger, and hope that this news will be rewarded with gunpowder and lead."

"And what is this news that you would tell?" asked Eldridge.

"It would be best for you to take your stock away from the river and move off. There are more than ten times one hundred warriors who are raiding up and down the Red Shell River and the Moon Shell River. They are of the People, the Cuts Throats, the Snake and the Blue Sky People. These are all warriors that have no lodges with them, no women, no children. Their warriors are taking scalps. We tell you this White Eyes, because you have always been a friend to us, and we thought to warn you."

"Are you saying that they are heading this way?" asked Eldridge.

"It is as I have told you," said Long Chin.

Eldridge thought for only a short time and going behind the counter took out a few lead bars and two cans of gun powder and gave these to the two Cheyenne whose age showed as they got to their feet. Their movements not quite as graceful as they had been a few minutes before.

"I thank you my friends," said Eldridge, and the three men went back into the yard where the Indians mounted their horses and rode away.

"That was awful fast," said Eli.

"Didn't take them long to get what they wanted," said Eldridge. They looked around trying to decide on what to do next. "They warned me there's a war party of over thousand Indians headin' this way. They said it was made up of Cheyenne, Lakota, Arapaho and Comanche."

"Shit!" swore Hez, "what we gonna do?"

"Well, I'm gonna head down towards Denver and spread the word. People got to know what's coming, be prepared."

"What you want us to do?" Asked Eli.

"Hez, I'm going to ask you to load up my women and kids, get them closer to the soldier camp at Fort Collins, it's closer than Denver. Eli, it's up to you, can you spread the word East and still hang on to your hair?"

"I can do that," said Eli.

"You both watch your hair." Eldridge turned and went to talk to his women, telling them that he would join them as soon as possible but he had to warn the people of Denver about the large war party first. With this said, Eldridge saddled his horse and headed for Denver.

Whit helped Hez finish unloading the buffalo robes from the wagon and then helped Eldridge's family get loaded up. Once Hez was on his way, Whit headed down the road warning any settlers that had not already abandoned their homes and inhabitants of the way stations.

As Whit warned the settlers along the Platte, Eldridge rode over sixty-five miles without stopping to Denver. The settlers along the Platte were warned by Whit, and within two nights Indians appeared all along the river. They found that those settlers who had remained were on their guard, and they left them alone not making many attacks. But at some places they run off the stock and one of these was Eldridge's ranch.

Three days later, Whit made his way back to Denver where he found that Gerry was being hailed as a hero, some calling him the "Paul Revere of the Platte." Eldridge had warned the Governor, thus giving time for troops to be raised and a defense of the city established. "Hell," thought Eli, "I rode damn near twice that distance, and no one is calling me a hero!" He shook it off though and began his search for Hezekiah, finding him in a saloon.

"Thought you give that up," Whit said as he approached Hez.

"Well, I had me a good scare," Hez said, "Comin' down from Collins I run onto half a dozen Cheyenne. I hid out and they passed me by, but damn if'n I didn't 'bout shit my drawers!" Whit laughed, and slapping Hez on the back, ordered himself a glass of whiskey. They retired to a table and discussed what they would do next.

Hez asked, "You hear about these hundred-day volunteers? They's payin' thirteen dollars a month. I figure it's easy and quick money, and hell, we can't get into much trouble in just one hundred days."

"I'm not sure I wanted to join the Army, even if it's just for a little while," said Whit, "Of course, it would depend on who we served under. Wasn't much impressed by some of the fellows I was with down in New Mexico, though there were some that measured up in my mind. I wonder if Silas Soule is still soldiering. I wouldn't mind serving with him."

Looking around the bar, Whit noticed four soldiers from the Colorado Volunteers sitting at a table, and excusing himself from Hez, walked over to them.

"Evenin', who you boys serving under?" he asked.

"We're under Colonel Chivington," answered one of the privates.

"You know if Silas Soule is still in the Army?"

"Yep, got himself promoted to the rank of captain, an' commandin' his own company of the 1st Colorado Cavalry down at Fort Lyon," said the private.

"Thanks. Y'all take care," Whit said, and he turned back to where Hez stood at the bar.

"Them fellows said Silas Soule is down at Fort Lyon," he told Hez, "But that's over two hundred miles away through hostile territory."

"Well, the trail is closed so there ain't no freight wagons or coaches running. Joinin' up with the Volunteers still sounds good to me, better chance of surviving in numbers!"

"I don't know," Whit said, giving a look in the direction of the four soldiers, "Not sure I like the looks of what we'd be servin' with."

"What do you think we should do?"

"Puttin' on a uniform just doesn't sound appealin' to me."

"Well, I have two dollars left, and I say we drink that up while we're thinkin' it over!" Hez said and rose to get them another round of whiskey.

They spent the rest of the night talking and going over possibilities for employment, but when the two dollars was gone, they found themselves in the stable with their horses where they bedded down for the night.

Unknown to them, one of the soldiers had followed them from the saloon, his slouch hat pulled down low to help hide his features. He watched as they went into the stable, and then turned and walked away. He knew both of them and made plans to keep an eye on them, as either one of them could cause him trouble. Whit might not remember him from when he worked at the ranch on the Arkansas as they had not really met, but only seen each other a few times. But Hezekiah was different. No matter what changes the soldier made to his appearance, there was always the chance that Hez would recognize him as Azariah Bolt.

The following morning, Hez and Whit saddled their horses and started looking for work, finding no prospects except a single day's labor helping clear the debris from a building that had burnt down near Cherry Creek. The owner of the building said he couldn't hire both of them, so they drew straws with Whit pulling the short straw and winning the job.

"There's a fellow about two mile downstream that might have some work," the man said to Hez, "Needs some fence work done, but probably won't offer much more than a hot meal in payment."

"Much obliged," said Hez.

"You get done, I'll met you back at the stable this evenin'," said Whit.

"Sure," said Hez and he rode along the Creek. As the buildings became fewer and fewer, Hez's apprehension grew, and as he passed the last structure, he was glad to see soldier on horseback moving down the road in front of him. He kicked his horse into a faster pace to overtake him, the soldier only slightly turning in the saddle and glancing back to see who approached from behind. The closer Hez got to him, he could see the soldier had sergeant strips on his shell jacket.

"I sure am glad to see you," Hez said as he pulled up next to the sergeant, "I feel a lot better riding with someone. You goin' far?"

"Just a bit down the road," the soldier said.

"Hope you don't mind me riding along side."

"Nope, I can use the company." The man's voice seemed familiar to Hez, and he tried hard to place it, but the bushy sideburns and the uniform made it harder to remember who he was. They rode on for a few minutes with Hez telling the soldier about what he had been doing over the past few months, and all the while still trying to figure out where he knew him from.

Finally, he asked, "Do I know you?"

"Don't know, I been around," the soldier said, "might have been up in the gold diggings." It was at that moment that Hez recognized Bolt.

"Azariah?" he said, the realization overcoming him, and before he could pull his pistol from its holster, Bolt reached across and plunged a knife between his ribs. A look of shock crossed Hez's face, and paralyzed with pain and fear, he fell from the saddle onto the road. Bolt dismounted and took the reins of both horses and led them off the trail and out of sight. He then returned and took hold of Hez and drug him to where he had tied the horses.

The knife had slid between Hez's ribs, puncturing his lung. He lay slowly suffocating in his own blood and began to cough up frothy, bright red blood. Staring up, he saw Bolt standing over him, and he tried to understand why he had been stabbed. He had meant no real harm to his one-time partner, he only wanted answers as to why Bolt had stolen from him.

"You'd done fine if you hadn't recognized me," Bolt said, lying. "But, I guess I just couldn't take the chance of you trying to put the law on me." He squatted down next to Hez as he talked, and then he reached out and took Hez's hair in his hand, brought his knife up cut away his scalp.

Hez screamed with the new pain, but this only brought on more coughing and he finally passed out. Bolt had seen enough mutilations performed by the Indians to copy them expertly and he spent the next few minutes making sure that if Hez was found, his death would be blamed on Indians.

When Hez failed to return to the stable that evening, Whit figured he had spent the night at the ranch where Hez was looking for work. When the day and the following night passed, Whit began to worry and decided to head in the direction Hez had taken down Cherry Creek. Once he had left the last building behind him, he had only to travel a short distance before he saw what appeared to be an Indian woman leave the road and head out of sight. His blood chilled at the sight of her and he kicked his horse into a run determined to overtake her.

As he approached the spot where she had left the road and gone out of his sight, he heard and then spotted a flock of crows taking flight. He moved to where they had risen into the air from and found Hezekiah Cable. Whit recognized Hez by his clothing, and though the crows had created substantial damage to the body, it was clear to Whit how his friend had died. He wrapped the body in his own blanket, placed it across the saddle and walked back into town.

When word got out about the killing, there were a few who wanted to put Hez on public display like the Hungates, but Whit refused and took Hez to the area on the east edge of town, called the Mount Prospect Hill, that had been set aside as a graveyard. Whit dug a grave and buried his friend. He then took a plank of wood and with his knife carved; "Hezekiah Cable murdered Sept 9, 1864." This he set at the graves head.

"I don't know what to say, Hez," he spoke looking down at the mound of dirt, "I'm sorry I wasn't there to help when you needed me. I promise you though, I'll get blood for blood." He wiped the dirt from his hands, turned and went back into the city searching out the first saloon he came to.

***

September 1864 – Moon of Plums Ripening

Tensions had increased at Fort Lyon, Maj. Wynkoop's efforts to engage the Indians where and when he could, were fruitless. His meager forces, unable to both secure the Fort and pursue Indians, were exasperated, and his request for more was troops denied. Finally, his situation improved with the arrival of a detachment of soldiers from New Mexico. With the strict shoot-to-kill orders still in effect, he waited word to move against the Cheyenne under either General Curtis who was commander of the Department of the Missouri, Colonel Blunt, or Colonel

Chivington, who he knew was planning a campaign along the Republican.

When three Indians arrived at Fort Lyon, carrying a white flag, the sentry on duty was uncertain whether to fire on the Indians as per the shoot to kill order, or honor the white flag. He chose to give the messengers the benefit of the doubt and presented them to the Major. Wynkoop was completely surprised when Eagle's Head, One Eye and his wife, Big Owl Woman, were presented to him. Like the sentry, he was conflicted between the orders he had to shoot to kill on site, and the boldness of these three bearing letters from the Cheyenne.

The letters had been pinned to the coat worn by One Eye. In this way, if he had been shot before delivering them, they would've still been found and delivered. Wynkoop was impressed by the willingness of the old man to sacrifice his life for the sake of peace and asked him if he was not afraid to die.

Wynkoop was amazed by One Eyes bravery in approaching the fort, but One Eye told the Major, *"I am young no longer, I have been a warrior, I have not been afraid to die when I was young, why should I be afraid when I am old."*

After reading the letter, Wynkoop had a decision to make, he could act on his own, or do nothing. He felt a war was not necessary, and it could be avoided. Though he had no authority to meet with the Indians, there was little time to lose. As the mail had stopped moving, he could not send a request, nor get permission from his commanders in the foreseeable future. He also knew that General Curtis and Colonel Blunt had already taken to the field and Chivington would soon follow with the recently formed third Colorado volunteer. If Wynkoop waited too long, there was a possibility that the Indians would be attacked, and the white captives would be in danger of losing their lives.

Leaving his post garrisoned by the New Mexico detachment, he and a force of one–hundred men left for the Smokey Hill River, three day's march north of Fort Lyon. He also knew his force was small, and vulnerable to attack by the superior numbers of Indians that were present on the plains. Keeping this in mind he brought with him Eagle's Head, One Eye and Big Owl Woman, hoping that the presence of these three Indians would also signal that his intentions were peaceful.

As they neared the Smokey Hill River, Wynkoop's command found themselves facing almost eight-hundred warriors drawn up in a line for battle. Wynkoop halted his troops and sent One Eye on ahead to let them know he had come in peace. One Eye returned and informed Wynkoop to pull his men back and make camp, where Black Kettle and some of the other chiefs would come and talk to him. The soldiers fell back and circled their supply wagons to establish a defensive perimeter. And they waited out a long night anticipating either a fight or parley the next day. The following morning Black Kettle, Bull Bear, White Antelope, Sitting Bear, and the Arapaho chief Niwot approached the camp along with their entourage of sub chiefs to hold a council with "Tall Chief", their name for Wynkoop.

The Major started by reminding the chiefs what had been stated in their letter. He then told them that he had no real authority to make a lasting peace with them and that he answered to a higher authority in Denver. He told them if they would be willing to turn over their prisoners, he would do all in his power to set up a council between them and Governor Evans in Denver. By doing this he seized the opportunity to possibly save the lives of the captives, but at the same time promise no more than he felt he could deliver under what authority he held.

The chiefs began to discuss this amongst themselves, at times appearing to argue. Wynkoop, not speaking the language, had no idea what was being said. One chief suggested that the opportunity to kill this entire white force should be taken advantage of. Another argued that Wynkoop must think them fools to surrender their prisoners without receiving any promises. Then Black Kettle reminded all those present that Wynkoop had been promised safety and that they would not go back on this promise.

Black Kettle, who had paid the highest price for procuring the white captives with his own ponies, stood, took Wynkoop by the hand and spoke.

"He has been told that he should come and go unharmed, he did not close his ears, but with his eyes shut followed on the trail of him whom we had sent as our messenger. It was like coming through a fire for the white men to follow and believe in the words of one of our race, who may have always been branded as unworthy of confidence or belief. Had this white soldier come to us with crooked words, I myself would have despised him, and would've asked whether he thought we were fools, that he could be saying sweet words into our ears and laugh at us when we

believed in them. But he has come with words of truth, and confidence in the pledges of his red brothers, and whatever be the result of these deliberations, he shall return unharmed to his lodge from where he came. It is I, Black Kettle that says this."

The council broke up, and Wynkoop withdrew his troops a little further away and went into camp to await the council's final decision. Another tense night passed, but fears were relieved the next morning when the Arapaho Chief Niwot brought over young Laura Roper. The following morning, Black Kettle appeared with three additional prisoners; Ambrose Usher, Daniel Marble and Isabelle Eubank. The other three prisoners mentioned in the Cheyenne's letter were not with this camp, but with another, and Black Kettle promised to deliver them as soon as it was possible.

Pleased with the outcome, Wynkoop invited Black Kettle, White Antelope and Bull Bear of the Cheyenne, along with the Arapaho chiefs Neva, Bosse and Heaps of Buffalo to accompany him back to Fort Lyon. When Wynkoop reached the post, he sent a dispatch to Governor Evans reporting of the events the past two weeks, then set out for Denver accompanied by the Indians. Just before reaching Denver, he rode ahead to meet with Evans and received a chilly reception. The governor said he had no intention of holding this Council. He reminded Wynkoop that he had just raised the 100-day 3rd Colorado Cavalry at a considerable expense, and he insisted that the Indians were still at war and needed to be punished before any talks occurred. But as the chiefs were already en route to Denver, he agreed to meet with them at Camp Weld in hopes of extracting information about the killing of the Hungate family and the other depredations committed by the Indians.

***

Whit heard news of the impending council Cheyenne at Camp Weld, and decided, like many others, to go and observe talks. He was in search of answers to the many questions he had. Would he somehow find out who had murdered his friend? Would he possibly see his old acquaintance Silas Soule? And, would there be a chance Zachariah was among the Indians present there?

He traveled along the Platte's bank about two miles southwest, the site of Camp Weld. Like many military posts the buildings were positioned around a central square where the volunteer troops could practice their drills curious townspeople could come and watch. The post covered about 30 acres, consisting of officers' quarters, barracks for the soldiers, a mess room, and even a hospital. Running entirely around the enclosure and twenty-five feet from the buildings, was a top rail fence, on the eastern side, just inside the main entrance was the guardhouse.

On the opposite side of the Platte were a few tepees, and Whit could tell by their shape that they were Cheyenne and Arapaho lodges. The thought crossed his mind these Indians must be very brave to camp so close to Denver and at the doorstep of the 3rd Colorado volunteers, now being called "the Bloodless 3rd," by the press and many the people of Denver. Sentiment about the ineffectiveness of the 3rd to bring retribution for the depredations that had been committed by the Indians bordered on complete contempt, some people even jeered at soldiers in the streets.

Whit eyed some of these Hundred-day Volunteers and found them to be a collection of the dregs of humanity gleaned off the streets of Denver. It saddened him to compare them with other soldiers that he knew. He knew that there would be trouble as these men were inexperienced when dealing with the Indians, and the atmosphere of hatred was heavy. He, himself, was holding some resentment over the killing of Hezekiah, and still felt hurt about his wife, Little Bird abandoning him and the selfishness of taking her own life.

He looked for the site where the actual talks would be held, and in his search came across a pleasant surprise, he spotted Thomas Craigavon, Silas Scott and William Craigavon. The sight of these old friends pushed aside any feelings of guilt over his separation from Maggie, and he went to greet them. William, being the first to see him approach, offered a smile and an extended hand.

"Why, hello Whit," William said.

"Hello, Billy," Whit answered, taking his hand and shaking it. He then turned to the other two men and received the same warm welcome from Thomas, but only a handshake from Silas. Even that small gesture was taken as a good sign from the old man.

"It sure is good to see some friendly faces," Whit said.

"It's good to see you, Son," said Thomas, "What brings you to these doin's?"

"Curiosity mostly," Whit said, and then feeling a bit of shame, "And, I was hoping I might find Zachariah among these Cheyenne."

"He ain't here, Whit," Silas said, disappointing Whit.

"I thought it might be a long shot, but worth a chance," Whit said, then asked, "Have you heard any word of him?"

"Last I heard was he was runnin' with the Dog Soldiers," Silas said. "We got that from Crow Eyes."

"When did you see him?" Whit asked.

"He came through Booneville east of Pueblo, along with this peace delegation on their way here. He's with Black Kettle, Little Wolf and the other Chiefs for the talks. That's why we're here. We know these people and feel a need to have an understanding on what's taking place."

Whit shook his head acknowledging the bond between his friends and their Cheyenne brothers. Then he asked, "How is everyone?" not directly asking about Maggie but wanting to know.

"Everyone is fine. Rosie is as pretty as ever, and the children are growing fast. Ransom is turning into quite a man. August and Willow have another child, boy they named Henry. And, it appears we'll have a good harvest this year and the herds are growing bigger," said William. Whit was unsure if William and intentionally avoided speaking about Maggie, and feeling a bit sheepish decided to ask.

"How's Maggie?"

"She's doin' good, Whit," Silas said. "Priest out of Santa Fe stopped by on his way to Denver and married her and Eli last fall. We helped them build a house just upriver from us, and they had themselves a baby boy two months back, named him Joseph." Whit wasn't prepared for what he felt. It was a bit painful to hear Maggie was now happy with a real family of her own, but the pain was tempered by knowing she deserved that happiness.

"You know when the talks are going to start?" Whit asked, changing the subject.

"Supposed to be this morning. We're headed there now," said Thomas, and he pointed in the direction the Indians were now being escorted by a squad of soldiers. The men followed and found a place close enough to the proceedings where they could observe and hear the negotiations.

Present were; Governor Evans, Colonel Chivington, Major Wynkoop, Captain Silas Soule, Agent Colley's son Dexter, interpreter John Smith and Denver Mayor Amos Steck. Representing the Indians were; Heap of Buffalo, Bosse, White Antelope, Black Kettle, Little Wolf, Neva, Knock Knee and Bull Bear, the only Dog Soldier present at the council.

Evans began in an aggressive manner, asking the Indians what they had to say for themselves. Black Kettle responded that he was attempting to collect his bands in compliance of the notice the governor had sent out and that he desired peace. Evans seemed to ignore this and told the Chiefs that he had just raised a new Regiment, and regardless of the good intentions on the part of the Indians, he would act that winter against those who refused to comply with his proclamations. The council soon degenerated into an interview by Evans to gather information about the raids, and which tribes were involved and what alliance had been made. Chivington, asserting his authority, told the Chiefs that they were in the hands of the military and had better make peace. Also, that it was the Army's job to disarm them, and that if the Chiefs were truly interested in peace, they must surrender themselves to Wynkoop at Fort Lyon.

In all, the Camp Weld Council proved to be a failure and indicative of the contradictory relationships between General Curtis and the Colorado authorities. On the day of the Council, General Samuel Curtis had telegrammed Evans stating that he wanted no peace until the Indians suffer more. He felt the idea that the Indians should seek safety at a U.S. military post directly contradicted his plan to keep the Indians starving and on the run throughout the winter months. He closed by reminding Evans that, Fort Lyon was no longer in Chivington's district, it was under his control.

After receiving the telegram, Evans wrote Agent Colley, telling him to make it plain to the Indians that he can promise them nothing; reminding them of his words that they were in the hands of the military. He instructed Cooley to tell them that his meeting with them at Camp Weld was for the purpose of ascertaining their views and not to offer them anything whatsoever.

Wynkoop had made two mistakes in meeting with the Indians on the Smokey Hills, and then taking the Indians to Denver. First, he should have reported to General Curtis, the commanding officer of his district, rather than to Governor Evans and the commander military District of Colorado, Chivington. Second, he should not have subsequently followed Chivington's order to bring the Indians to Fort Lyons thinking that they would be safe from harm, for it was not Chivington's order to give, nor as Wynkoop should have known, his to obey.

In either case, Wynkoop either misunderstood the proper chain of command, or acted out of hopes for a better outcome. Taking Evans and Chivington on their word, Wynkoop instructed Black Kettle and the other chiefs to bring their lodges near Fort Lyon.

***

SAM J. PISCIOTTA

CHAPTER EIGHTEEN
TEARS ON THE WIND

October 1864 – Moon When Thin Ice Begins to Form on the Rivers

There were no guarantees made by either side of the Camp Weld Conference. Governor Evans and Colonel Chivington had avoided an actual declaration of peace. Black Kettle and the other chiefs felt that they had acted in good faith and were now under the protection of the Army, but they could not speak for other groups of Indians who were still against any form of coexistence with the Whites.

Major Wynkoop was uncertain of the council's outcome but felt he had done his best to avoid a war. He returned to Fort Lyon and prepared for the arrival of the Cheyenne and Arapaho. Upon his return to the post, he sent a report to his official superior, General Curtis, detailing his actions and participation in the Smokey Hills and Camp Weld Councils. He would act on his own until he received word from Curtis.

Tom Craigavon and Silas were traveling with the Cheyenne down to the Arkansas and Fort Lyon, in hopes that they could help with any further negotiations. Both men were uneasy about the abilities of Agent Colley to care for the welfare of the Cheyenne and Arapaho. They held some trust in Wynkoop's intentions, but they also knew the true hearts of Governor Evans and Colonel Chivington. On the journey. they spent the evenings with Little Wolf and spoke of their shared past and what the future might bring.

On the third evening, the Indians camped in a grove of cottonwoods, sheltered from the cold wind blowing out of the north. Silas sat by the fire with his pipe clamped between his teeth, clouds of pale-blue smoke curling up around his gray beard and circling about his wolf-skin cap. He pulled a blanket around his shoulders to ward off the cold night, as he listened to Tom and Little Wolf talk.

"What do you think of the words spoken by the Governor?" Little Wolf asked.

"He's pretty riled up, Wolf. Him and that preacher, Chivington, have a taste of bile in their mouth and I fear they aim to spill blood," said Tom.

"There are many among the People who feel the same," said Little Wolf, "It hurts my heart to think that there will be war between us."

"Never gonna be one between you and me, Brother."

Wolf exhaled out a small laugh, then said, "No, never between you and I, but between your people and mine. There will be no turning back."

"There are a lot of folks who want peace, both White and Indian," Tom said, believing it.

"True, but I fear not enough. Men like Evans and Chivington see only one way to live on this land and that is to kill every Indian. There are also those among the People who see no other way than to kill all the Whites." He paused for a moment and added, "My own son, Sitting Hawk, and grandson, Little Bear, are among those who have taken to the War Road. They, and my brother-in-law Crow Horse, have all joined the Crazy Dog Soldiers. The old societies have lost their power among the People, even the Council of Forty-four cannot lead the People away from war."

"What will you do my Brother?" Tom asked.

Little Wolf looked at Tom, the man who had been his friend since they were young, and felt he had no choice but to be honest.

"Tom, I have been a healer most of my life," he said, "I have always sought peace with the Whiteman. But before I was a healer, I was a warrior, and if I must defend the People from the Whites, I will fight."

"I hope it never comes to that, Wolf. I hope to God it never comes to that." Tom said and shook his head.

"You both know you can't stop a prairie fire when the wind is driving it." Silas spoke up.

The three men sat for some time in silence until Silas said he was going to turn in for the night. He was soon followed by Tom, leaving Little Wolf alone by the fire. Little Wolf thought about his life up to this point, weighing the fifty-eight winters he had seen and wondering how he had survived so long when so many had perished. He remembered his wife, Swan, and how beautiful she was before contracting smallpox and dying. He thought of his daughter and grandchildren who had been taken at the same time, and he wondered why in his heart he did not hate the Whiteman. He looked up into the cold night sky and asked his relatives who had gone before him, why the people would have to suffer so badly. He needed answers and decided that he must select a place and seek a vision. He would wait until after the bands went to Fort Lyon, and then he would take the needed time for this quest, knowing that this time of year the nights would be cold and seeking the guidance he needed might mean his death.

Whit, still searching for news about Zachariah, went with the Army back to Fort Lyon and there he offered his services to Major Wynkoop and Captain Silas Soule as a guide and interpreter. Since Zachary's departure to the Cheyenne, and the death of his friend Hez, Whit's feelings for the Cheyenne had grown darker. He did not consciously foster these feelings of enmity, but it seemed that he found more and more reason to believe the Indians needed to be dealt with.

Governor Evans was certain that the Indians had to be dealt with harshly, and in a report to Commissioner Dole, he stated that peace without conquest would be the most barbarous of humanity. Commissioner Dole reproved Evans and told him if any of the Indians wished peace, it was his duty as superintendent of Indian affairs to foster the spirit and to do all that he could for peace.

Chivington, however, was eager to fight, and in a telegraph Major Charlot expressed his frustration with Wynkoop's meddling and the situation in general. He said that the harsh winter months were approaching and recruitment for the 3rd Colorado Regiment was complete. He was certain that the Cheyenne knew this and were afraid they would be punished for their outrages, and this was the only reason some of them now wanted peace. He believed the Indians should make full restitution and then go on to their reservations.

Chivington was sure that any correspondence would be shared with Major General Curtis, and his report would distance himself from Wynkoop. Curtis would deal with the peace-loving Wynkoop. Curtis replied to Chivington telling him that Commissioner Dole was too eager to give presents to the Indians.

He felt it was better to chastise them before giving anything but a little tobacco to talk over. He felt that no peace must be made without his directions. Chivington took this as approval for him to act.

While at Fort Lyon, Whit's friendship with Captain Soule developed. They had known each other from their service in New Mexico, but for the first time, Whit learned about the man. He identified with many of the Captain's convictions concerning abolition, but Soule's feelings about the Indians was a bit more forgiving than Whit's. Soule had a healthy respect for the Indians and felt if they left him alone, he would return the favor.

Where he strayed from the popular feelings of most people was that like Wynkoop he looked for a peaceable solution to the problems being faced in the territory.

"I'm not real comfortable about the kill-on-sight order," he told Whit, "There's more Indians like Black Kettle who want peace."

"I've been around them for a while now," said Whit, "And, though not an expert, I've come to know that they'll never settle down and be farmers. They've went where they want and done what they want for too long. There's too many of them that would just as soon take your scalp as share a campfire with you."

"You're probably right, Whit, but we need to remember who we are. We need to hold on to our humanity."

"Hard to do that when you look at the mutilated and scalped body of a friend," Whit said, thinking of Hez.

"We need to look at life in matters of moral right and wrong, no matter what," replied the Captain.

Soule's strong convictions would be no match for the ignorance shown by Army Headquarters when dealing with the Indians. They thought that punishment had to be dealt out to the tribes at large. What they did not know was that the Indians held enough power to inflict far greater loss of innocent blood on the whites than the whites could inflict on them.

Those Chiefs who had attended the conference at Camp Weld, knew that there were still many bands who did not desire peace, and they understood they did not speak for those bands. Many Whites did not understand this, and they thought one Indian was like another. They did not understand that each

Indian was a nation unto himself, going where he wished, following who he wished.

Zachary had completely turned his back on the White world. While Black Kettle, Little Wolf and the other peace chiefs were in Denver for the conference at Camp Weld, he was in a large village of Cheyenne and Arapaho on the Pawnee Fork about sixty miles from Fort Larned. Two days before the conference, a village of over a thousand warriors confronted Major General James Blunt and his force of four-hundred solders and a troop of Delaware scouts. An advance guard of the soldiers, under Major Scott Anthony, had surprised six hunters not far from the village and immediately attacked. The sound of the gunfire drew other warriors from the village and Anthony's men were in danger of being overrun when Blunt arrived to support him.

The superior number of Indians held off the soldiers giving the women time to take down the lodges and retreat. The skirmish was brief, with only one soldier and two Delaware killed. After the Dog Soldiers lost nine of their number, they withdrew, leading the Army on a two-day chase, finally leaving them in their dust.

Black Kettle and the other Peace-Chiefs made their way back to their camps and then on to Fort Lyon where they turned in their firearms and were issued rations by orders of Major Wynkoop. While this was taking place, General Curtis received Wynkoop's report and reacted by ordering Major Anthony to proceed to Fort Lyon and take command of the post from Wynkoop. Anthony was to investigate the promises made by Wynkoop at Fort Lyon, and the unofficial rumors that Wynkoop had issued stores, goods, or supplies to hostile Indians in direct violation of orders.

Wynkoop was ordered to go to Fort Riley and answer for the unauthorized distribution of food, and his participation in both the Sand Creek and Camp Weld conference. This put him well out of the way. When Major Anthony took command at Fort Lyon, his orders were not to make peace, and yet he had little choice as he found a camp of six-hundred Arapaho within a mile of the post and camps of Cheyenne on Sand Creek.

***

November 1864 – Hard Face Moon

As if to bolster the beliefs of men like Evans and Chivington, raids continued both on the Arkansas and on the Platte. The day after the conference, only thirty-five miles west of Fort Kearny on the Platte Road near Plum Creek Station, an immigrant train was attacked. One civilian was killed and two were wounded. One week later, Dog Soldiers ambushed Captain Thomas Stephenson's troop of the 1st Regiment of Nebraska Militia who were out on scout near Pawnee Ranch, inflicting only two casualties, but proving they could strike at will.

Through the month of October and on to the end of November, fifteen raids were made on ranches, stage stations, and wagon trains by the Dog Soldiers and Lakota. These were mostly along the Platte, with a few taking place near Fort Larned, and one further west at Deer Creek Station in Dakota Territory. Zachary participated in seven of these raids, occurring between Craig Station and Midway Station on the Platte. By the middle of November, at only fourteen years old, Zachary was a seasoned warrior. On his belt were now three scalps, one containing blond locks. Soon he would go through the rituals required to become a Dog Soldier.

Brigadier General P. E. Connor had been ordered by the Secretary of War to give protection to the Overland Stage between Salt Lake and Fort Kearny. Governor Evans had left Denver and gone to Washington to seek more military funding, so Connor contacted Chivington requesting he turn over a portion of his command to fight Indians along the Platte. Chivington suspected Connor's motives, and he refused to provide any Colorado troops. He knew that if Connor were to strike a decisive blow against the warrior bands on the Platte, his own shaky political career would be undermined. To save any hopes of attaining a political office, Chivington knew he must wage a decisive battle against the Indians before his militia's 100-days enlistment expired.

Chivington left Denver without orders to rendezvous with the 3rd Regiment now in camp on Bijou Creek south of Denver. He ordered seven companies of the Colorado 3rd and three Denver companies of the 1st Regiment to march south to Camp Fillmore, near Booneville, on the Arkansas. He also ordered Colonel Shoop to retrieve the remainder of the 100-day troops on the Platte and marched them toward the Arkansas. By moving the 3rd Regiment out of the district, he left Denver unprotected. These movements were all committed under strict secrecy, and with Governor Evans in Washington, there was no one to protest Chivington's movements.

From this time on, General Curtis had no knowledge of Chivington's actions. Chivington would move his troops on toward Fort Lyon commanded by Anthony whose support of an aggressive war of extermination was in line with his. Chivington knew the Cheyenne and the Arapaho gathered near Fort Lyon were easy prey, and with the help of Anthony, he could attack Black Kettle's band at Sand Creek. As there could still be some officers at Fort Lyon who supported Wynkoop, any advance knowledge of the troop movements was kept unknown to that post. Above all, Chivington wanted no chance of Black Kettle being warned.

Whit, Silas Scott, Captain Soule, Lieutenant Cramer and Tom Craigavon sat near the stove, drinking coffee and discussing the change in leadership at the fort. They spoke in low voices, not wanting their opinions about Major Anthony overheard.

"You trust Anthony to keep his word?" Tom asked.

"So far he seems to be honoring Major Wynkoop's promises to Black Kettle and the others," said Soule. "He has promised the Army's protection."

"I'm not sure Black Kettle feels assured," said Silas, "he trusts Wynkoop, but he's not sure about Anthony."

"Major Anthony gave him an American flag to fly above his teepee as a sign that they're friendly," said Lieutenant Cramer, hoping that things wouldn't escalate before Wynkoop could clear matters with General Curtis and return.

"Little Wolf said that Black Kettle and Left Hand will be moving up Sand Creek away from the post to avoid trouble, while Little Raven is going to move his Arapahos down the Arkansas. Raven may just have a better idea of what your new Major is all about," Tom said and sipped at his coffee.

"You think there are Dog Soldiers with Black Kettle and Left Hands camp?" Whit asked.

"No telling," said Tom, "They tend to be everywhere. I'm going to the camp and talk to Little Wolf before they leave. I might have a better idea if there's some hot-heads in the band after that."

"I'd like to go with you," said Whit, "I'd like to get any news on where my boy is."

"Not a problem, Whit," said Tom.

"I'm going over to see William," Silas said, referring to William Bent. "I want to find out what he has to say about this whole foolishness."

The following morning Tom and Whit rode out to the Cheyenne camp to find Little Wolf, and Silas went to Bent's Ranch south of the river. As Tom and Whit were approaching the village, Little Raven's band of Arapahos were already packed and moving off down the Arkansas. Tom and Whit rode past them and into the semicircle of Cheyenne lodges and received furtive glances from those few people who were out in the chilly morning air.

Tom selected an older woman carrying a bundle of kindling, and addressed her in Cheyenne, *"Mother, I would find the lodge of Little Wolf. Can you show it to me?"* The woman scowled back but with an upward motion of her head pointed with her chin toward a lodge with a black bird painted on it, and the two men rode over to it.

Dismounting, Tom went to the lodge's door flap and in the Indian's form of knocking, scratched at the covering, saying *"Hello the lodge."*

"Come in," a muffled voice from inside replied, and Tom motioned to Whit to follow him inside. Removing his fur cap, Tom lifted the cover, and ducking entered the semi-darkness of the lodge. The light was dim inside as the buffalo-hide lodge was darkened from the smoke of frequent fires that were made inside. Tom stooped over and stepped to his right making room for Whit to enter and waited for the lodge's owner to speak, as their eyes adjusted to the light.

"Tom, it is good to see you." The words were spoken in English and the voice was that of Crow Eyes. "And Whit. Welcome. Come sit and eat with us."

Crow Eyes sat at the back of the lodge and next to him was Little Wolf. To their right was Crow Eye's wife, Meets the Enemy, and a small boy that neither Tom nor Whit recognized. Tom and Whit took a seat to the left of Wolf and they were no sooner settled, cross-legged, when bowls of a hot soup were dished out for them. They ate and again waited for the lodge's owner to speak.

"What has brought you two out in the cold this morning? I thought you would be staying at the Fort," said Crow Eyes.

"We come to talk to Wolf before you move up Dry Creek," Tom said, using the Cheyenne name for Sand Creek.

"What would we speak of, my friend, that we have not already discussed?" asked Little Wolf.

"My heart is heavy," said Tom. *"I wonder what you think about the way things are working out."*

"Crow Eyes and I have been talking about this very subject," said Little Wolf.

"Speak truth to me, Brother," Tom said, and Wolf looked at Crow Eyes as if asking him to speak.

"We have talked much about what has happened," Crow Eyes said, *"Black Kettle, White Antelope and Left Hand trust Major Wynkoop. But now Wynkoop has been replaced and he will be leaving in a few days. He had suggested that he could convince General Curtis that we truly want peace. He even suggested that we send our warriors to help the soldiers protect the road along the Arkansas from the Kiowa and Comanche. It is curious that one day the Whiteman wants us not to fight other Indians, and the next he asked us to go to war against them."*

"How do you see Anthony?" Tom asked.

"He has parleyed with the chiefs and the face he shows to us says he is of the same mind as Wynkoop. But Little Wolf and I agree that he would have us move up Dry Creek so that we are close enough to be watched and if Dog Soldiers come to our camp, he will know of it."

"How will he know?"

"He is sending John Smith and Agent Colley's son Dexter to us with rations," Little Wolf said, his words almost in contempt.

"I'm not sure what you mean Wolf," Tom said.

"Smith and Colley are Anthony's eyes and ears," said Crow Eyes. *"I believe he has bought One Eye with a few presents. He will tell all he knows about his own people."*

"Will the rations be enough to get you through the winter?" Tom asked.

"No, we must hunt, but there is no game inside the boundaries of the reservation set by the treaties. The buffalo are far to the east and we will send our young men to hunt there."

"I will see what I can do to help," said Tom.

"I will help also," said Whit. *"I told Captain Soule I would scout for him, but I have not signed papers to obligate me."* Whit's words in Cheyenne were not as polished as Tom's, but they were understood.

"That Big 50 of yours is the right iron for making meat," Tom said in English, referring to Whit's Sharps rifle. "It'll be appreciated. First thing tomorrow we'll go down to Bent's ranch and see if we can get a wagon, and maybe a driver. If the weather holds, we can be back before the snows come," Tom promised.

All four men knew that even a wagon loaded with buffalo meat would only go so far in a village of close to eighty lodges, but it would help and make the difference between starvation and making it through the winter.

"Do you want more to eat?" Crow offered.

"No, thank you," said Tom, knowing full-well that what was in the pot might have to last the lodge for a while.

"Who is the boy?" Tom asked.

"He is called Red Elk," said Crow, *"He has no family, the Pawnee killed his father and his mother died of grief. He has come to live with Meets the Enemy and myself."*

"What of you, Wolf? Do you now live with your son-in-law Crow Eyes?" Tom asked.

"I find a place to lay my blanket when it is needed," answered Wolf.

"What of your son?"

"Sitting Hawk is now a Dog Soldier, as is my grandson, Little Bear." Wolf paused for a moment then added, *"Many have gone on the road to war."*

"Do you know if my son, Yellow Horse is with them?" Whit asked.

"The last time I saw Yellow Horse he was with his uncles, White Badger and Bear Voice," said Crow. *"They are somewhere on the Bunch of Trees or the Moon Shell River."*

This news didn't help Whit feel any better about the welfare of his son. Knowing his was alive was reassuring, but his being with the Dog Soldiers put him in greater danger, and Whit was at a loss as to what he could do.

The following day, the Cheyenne and remaining Arapaho packed up their camp and moved north to Sand Creek. Tom and

Whit rode the few miles to William Bent's ranch on the south side of the Arkansas to arrange for a wagon, a driver and a man to help butcher the buffalo they intended to hunt. Silas Scott, though tempted to go along on the hunt, decided to take advantage of William Bent's hospitality and remain at the ranch. On the same day that Tom and Whit left to hunt, the Colorado 3rd Regiment with three companies of the 1st Colorado arrived at Camp Fillmore east of Pueblo.

The wagon acquired at Bent's ranch, pulled by six mules, moved across the prairie with Tom and Whit riding far out in advance. The two men rode almost a half mile apart in order to search more of the terrain in front of them, returning to the wagon near sunset. There was no sighting of any type of game for the next four days.

Near mid-morning on the fifth day, Whit spotted movement on the horizon, but as the day was overcast and the light dim, the dark figures were hard to make out against the slate gray sky. He hoped it was a small group of buffalo, but as the shapes moved closer, he could see they were men mounted on horseback, and though bundled up against the cold, they were clearly Indians. Whit spun his horse around and at a full run, headed toward Tom until he caught Tom's eye, and signaled by turning his horse into a circle and waving his rifle above his head. Tom, seeing the signal, stood up in his stirrups for a better view and looked past Whit, spying the fast approaching group of riders. Both men turned their horses toward the wagon and kicked them into a dead run.

Thompkins, the teamster from Bent's, pulled the wagon to a stop when Whit and Tom approached in such haste, and without a warning handed the reins to young Juan, the Mexican camp-keeper, seated next to him. He then reached down and took hold of a double-barreled shot gun and checked the priming, making sure it was ready for use.

"We got trouble?" Thompkins yelled, as Tom and Whit reached the wagon.

"Could be," Tom said, "Riders comin' this way and they appear to be Indians."

"Kiowas or Co'manch" Thompkins asked.

"Not sure, but we'll find out pretty quick," Tom said, and both he and Whit dismounted, tied their horses to the wagon and readied their rifles.

When the riders were within fifty yards, they pulled to a stop and two of their number cautiously rode forward.

"They's Arapaho," said Tom, "I recognize that fellow in front with the skunk-skin turban. He's called Flint Striker. I think he's with Little Raven's bunch. It also appears they have women with them."

"We safe then?" asked Thompkins.

"Nothing is ever certain. Just keep that scatter-gun close." Tom moved out away from the wagon and held up an open right hand, signaling peace. Flint and his companion moved in closer and stopped a few yards away.

"*Hello, Flint Striker,*" Tom said in Cheyenne and hand-sign, hoping if one language didn't work the other would.

"*Hello, Tom,*" Flint replied in broken Cheyenne and hand-signs, "*What you do here on prairie?*"

"*We hunt the buffalo for Black Kettle's people.*"

"*We hunt also,*" Flint said, and looking over to the wagon saw that it was empty. "*You no have luck?*" he asked.

"*No. Maybe we should hunt together. Many eyes better than a few.*"

"*This is good,*" said Flint. And with no further discussion, the eight Arapaho joined the White men and the chance of finding game increased as they fanned out across the prairie.

They scouted out further and further east and northeast, not finding buffalo until three days later, when they came across a small herd of the shaggy beasts. It took Tom some effort to persuade the Arapaho to allow him and Whit to shoot the animals calmly, one at a time rather than chase after them Indian style.

The two White men separated, each finding a good spot to sit and set up crossed sticks in the form of an X, on which the barrel of their rifles would rest to steady their aim. The buffalo, if not alarmed, would keep foraging for grass hidden under the snow, unaware that one of their number had been shot but only if that buffalo was taken down with skill. So, one by one, twelve buffalo were soon brought to the ground by well-placed shots from Whit's Big-50 and Tom's Mississippi Rifle.

When the killing was done, the Indians and the wagon moved forward, and the butchering began. The two women showed their expertise in reducing the meat down to manageable sizes, faster than all the men put together. And, at the end of the day, the little party feasted on fresh Buffalo. The mood of the camp was cheerful and there was no mention of the coming winter or the troubles between the Indians and the Whites.

When the Arapaho and the Whites split the next day, both groups were loaded with over three tons of meat. The wagon moved slowly, but the six mules and the hard ground made travel much faster than expected in retracing their path back to Fort Lyon. Six days later, they were within a few miles of Bent's ranch and decided to stop and drop off some of the meat for William. As they approached the ranch, they were surprised to be met by half a dozen soldiers who rode up on them as if they were hostile Indians.

"Where the hell you think you're goin?" demanded a Sargent whose prominent overbite, tiny chin and little close-set eyes made him look almost rat-like.

"And, who are you to be askin'?" said Tom, his hand, resting on the rifle sitting across his lap.

"Sargent Pender," the rat-face trooper stated, as if it carried some weight.

"Is that supposed to mean something to me?"

"Damn right! I got orders that no one is to be moving around. You need to pull that wagon up to the ranch and stay there."

"And, what if I told you I'll do what I want?" Tom asked.

"Then I have orders to shoot," said the Sargent, his voice shaking, and the other five soldiers pulled up their carbines.

Tom leaned forward, and pulled back the hammer on his rifle, then slid his hand around the rifle's wrist, his finger resting on the trigger. He felt confident that he could pull up the rifle and drop the Sargent before he could react. But, that would leave the other five soldiers and Tom wasn't sure if Whit and Thompkins were ready for a fight. He looked the Pender straight in the eyes and spoke, "You may try, but your sorry ass will be the first to get blown out'a the saddle."

"I...I got my orders," Pender stammered.

"From who?" Tom demanded.

"Colonel Chivington."

"Chivington? He's in command of a whole other district!" Tom said.

"He took command of Fort Lyon, and we come down here to fight Injins."

"Shit!" Tom spat and kicking his horse into a walk moved toward the ranch, followed by Whit and the wagon. Inside the ranch house, they found William Bent and Silas Scott, held almost as prisoners.

"William, what's goin' on?" Tom asked.

"They've taken my boy," William said, looking haggard and older than his fifty-five years, but still strong and angry. It was evident that he was frustrated.

"Who?" Tom asked.

"That god-damned preacher, Chivington," Silas said. "He marched in here with his whole regiment the day after Wynkoop left for Kansas. Came in here and put up a guard so no one can leave, did the same with the Fort and John Prower's ranch. He had old Jim Beckwourth with him as a guide, but Jim was all worn out from the march down here from Denver. They wanted me to take his place, an' I told 'em to eat shit."

"When Silas said no, they took my son Robert to show them the way to Black Kettle's camp. They're gonna attack the camp Tom. George, Charlie and Julia are there. My children are there!"

"When did they leave? Can we catch up with them, or maybe warn Black Kettle?"

"They left the day before yesterday," Silas said, "The camp is forty miles away and they're probably already there. God help 'em."

"Why attack Black Kettle?" Whit asked.

"They're out for blood and know Black Kettle's camp is an easy target. Plan on finding Little Raven's camp too if they get a chance."

"What about Anthony's command, He take them with him too?"

"Yes, from what I can tell, over a hundred of 'em went with him."

Five days later most of their questions were answered by the return of Chivington and his regiment. The guard around the ranch was released, allowing Silas, Tom and Whit to go down to Fort Lyon and find out what had happened.

Approaching the fort, the first thing that came into sight was the huge herd of horses captured from the Cheyenne camp. The soldiers were dividing them up, choosing the best of the stock to take back with them to Denver.

They found Captain Soule and Lieutenant Joseph Cramer in their quarters, and it was plain that they were both upset, Soule livid.

"What happened?" Tom asked Captain Soule.

"Colonel Chivington arrived on the 28th and Anthony welcomed him like he's the commander of the district. First thing Chivington does is picket the Fort so no one can slip away and warn the Indians. He orders his men to shoot anyone from the 1st Regiment who attempts to leave.

"Then he ordered Anthony to prepare troops to join the 3rd for an attack on Black Kettle's village, and said after they took the village, he'd head north to attack the Dog Soldiers camped on the Smokey Hills. Anthony agreed without any hesitation.

"As soon as I knew of their movement, I was indignant and went to Lieutenant James Cannon's room, where a number of officers of the 1st and 3rd were congregated. I told them that any man who would take part in what I considered murder, knowing the circumstances as we did, was a low-livered, cowardly son-of-a bitch.

"Joseph, Lieutenant Chauncey Cossett and I then went to Chivington and Anthony, and protested, saying that Black Kettle's people were a camp of prisoners under our protection in accordance with Major Wynkoop's truce. I told them that we had civilians in the camp also: John Smith, Dexter Colley and a teamster, as well as one of our own, Private Louderback, who were distributing rations and trade goods. Chivington said that Major Wynkoop had no authority to make any agreements or promises to the Indians."

Lieutenant Cramer then added, "When Chivington said 'Damn any man in sympathy with the Indians!', I thought Captain Soule would strike the Colonel. It took several of us to calm things down, but Chivington said he'd kill the Captain or any other soldier that disobeyed his orders."

"With Anthony and the rest of the officers backing Chivington, we had little choice but to comply. It was that or mutiny against our own soldiers and Chivington's seven hundred men," Soule said.

"What happened then?" asked Tom.

"We left here about 8:00 PM, most of the men were bolstered by whiskey to keep them warm, and we traveled through the night arriving at the village just before dawn. There were maybe one hundred lodges set up along the big bend of Sand Creek. Even in the dim light, I could see an American flag waving above one of the lodges with a white flag underneath. Chivington didn't hesitate for a moment and he gave the order to attack. They were taken completely by surprise and the 3rd attacked without any organization, even catching some of the 1st in the crossfire.

"By this time, it was plain to see that it would be a rout, and I couldn't discern any sizable resistance from the village. It seemed like most of the Indians retreating were obviously women and children. I thought of placing my Company between the 'Thirdsters' and the village, but it was too late, so I called my Company away, refusing to fight. Joseph and his men followed suit and we were witness to the most unspeakable atrocities." He found it hard to continue, and Lieutenant Cramer told them what he had seen take place.

"I saw John Smith come out into the open holding up his hands and running towards us, when he was shot at by several of the 3rd. I heard the word passed along to shoot him. He then turned back and went to his tent to escape. Private Louderback came out with a white flag, and was served the same as John Smith, the wagon driver the same. I got so mad I swore I would not burn powder, and I did not, and followed Captain Soule. It is no use for me to try to tell you how the fight was managed, only that I think the Officer in Command should be hung, and I know when the truth is known it will cashier him.

"The action taken by Captain Soule and myself were under protest, and I told the Colonel that I thought it murder to jump them friendly Indians. He says in reply that such men as us and Major Wynkoop would be better to leave the U. S. Service, and that we'd then judge what a nice time they had on the trip. I expect Colonel Chivington and Major Downing will do all in their power to have Captain Soule, Lieutenant Cossitt and I dismissed. Well, let them work for what they damn please, I ask no favors of them."

"What of the Cheyenne?" Tom asked.

"They attempted to mount a defense, while the women and children desperately tried to escape, but their weapons were no match for the militia's guns and cannons. Some of the Indians fought when they saw no chance of escape and killed twelve of our men, wounding forty," said the Captain, "It was hard for me to see little children on their knees begging for their lives, only to have their brains beat like dogs. It was the 100-days men who did this noble deed!"

Cramer then added, "It was the most uncivilized act I have ever witnessed. Bucks, women, and children were scalped, fingers cut off to get the rings on them, and this as much with Officers as men, and one of those Officers a Major, and a Lieutenant Colonel cut off ears of all they came across. I saw a squaw ripped open and a child taken from her, little children shot while begging for their lives and all the indignities shown their bodies that was ever heard of. Women were shot while on their knees, with their arms around soldiers begging for their lives. Those men did things that Indians would be ashamed to do. I heard some squaws killed their own children and then themselves, rather than to have them taken prisoners."

Silas, Tom and Whit had all taken part in the battles against Indians, but this was different. They could hardly believe that what they were being told was done by White men.

"How far did the pursuit go?" asked Whit.

"Not far," said Soule, "No more than a mile or so. They did not pursue, instead opting to loot the village and scalp and mutilate the dead. By late afternoon, the Colonel announced that he intended to go after Little Raven's camp and Major Anthony realized that Chivington duped him. Chivington never had intended going north in search of the Dog Soldiers. I believe Major Anthony had regrets about throwing in with Chivington, as he ordered my company to accompany him and escort the wagons carrying the dead and wounded back to the Fort.

"As for the rest of the command under Chivington, he marched them south, toward the Arkansas, and after a few days of wandering along the river, he gave up on finding Little Raven. I believe he knows that as soon as the Dog Soldiers hear about what happened, they'll come down out of the Smokey Hills and bring their vengeance to the Valley. He has no stomach for a real fight. He'll pack up his men and hightail it back to Denver."

"There were survivors, weren't there?" Tom asked.

"I'd estimate that there may be as many as four or five-hundred fled out onto the prairies," said Soule, "and half that number left in the village murdered."

"You think it would do us any good to head up that way?" Whit asked Tom, and Tom looked at him I surprise.

"What the hell for?" Tom said, "There's little chance we'd find anyone alive, and I don't know if I want to go up there and find remains of the people I know, left for the wolves. I'm going to head back to Pueblo and let them know what's happened. I have a feeling this will start an all-out war and there won't be a safe place for anyone, White or Red."

Before leaving Fort Lyon, Chivington dispatched a messenger to Denver with a letter to the Rocky Mountain News boasting that he has decimated the entire Cheyenne Nation and killed many of their chiefs, among them Black Kettle, White Antelope and Little Robe. In an attempt to glorify the militia's expedition, he claims that the village contained from nine hundred to one-thousand warriors. He asserts that over five hundred of these warriors were killed, when in reality, less than two hundred Cheyenne and Arapahos were killed, most of those women, children and elderly.

He then sent a dispatch to General Curtis containing similar lies. And, in an attempt to produce proof that the camp was made of "Hostiles", Chivington closed his report with, "I will state, for the consideration of gentlemen who are opposed to fighting these red scoundrels, that I was shown, by my chief surgeon, the scalp of a white man taken from the lodge of one of the chiefs, which could not have been more than two or three days taken; and I could mention many more things to show how these Indians, who have been drawing government rations at Fort Lyon, are and have been acting."

Both Silas Soule and Joseph Cramer penned letters, reporting the incident to Wynkoop, and General Slough, as well as to friends and family in the East. It was not long before Chivington's exploits came under scrutiny, and an investigation was ordered. While Chivington and his command were on route to Denver, word filtered back that a congressional investigation into his attack was possible. Rumors also started in Denver that anyone who spoke out against the 3rd would be strung up. The Rocky Mountain News took up Chivington's defense and led the threats, publicly warning anyone who joined the investigation "to get their scalps insured before they pass Plum Creek on their way out of town." The paper went on to say that, "Among the brilliant feats of arms in Indian warfare, the recent campaign of our Colorado volunteers will stand in history with few rivals, and none to exceed it in final results." Upon arrival in Denver, the 3rd, waving their bloody trophies, was honored by a cheering crowd, in a parade down Ferry Street. Four days later, the 3rd was mustered out, and Chivington resigned his commission from the Army the following February.

When word of Sand Creek reached Washington, General Halleck, Chief of Staff of the Army, ordered Chivington's conduct investigated, and General Curtis attempted to have him court-martialed. But, as Chivington's term of service had expired and he had resigned his commission, he was beyond the power of the Army.

***

December 1864 – Big Freeze Moon

The inside of the lodge was chilly, and Zachariah had no incentive to leave the comfort and warmth of his bed. The heavy buffalo robes created a cozy cocoon around him that protected him from the cold winter's night. There were times when he had wished that some of the goods made by the Whiteman, such as wool blankets, were allowed in the lodge of Bear Voice and Sees Far, but those items were not only frowned upon, but forbidden. The English blankets were lighter, and in his opinion, warmer. Some of the Lakota and the Northern Cheyenne in the camp had long winter coats made from these blankets and Zachariah was somewhat jealous. He was determined that someday he would confront Bear Voice about the lack of convenience the goods of the Whiteman offered, not only blankets, but firearms. Zachariah wanted a good rifle, and though proficient with a bow, he remembered the guns owned by Silas Scott and August with fondness.

Though the light in the lodge was dim, Zachariah could see his breath when he poked his head out from under the buffalo robe, and he could see that there were only embers left in the firepit in the center of the lodge. He wished Sees Far or Buffalo Cow Woman, would wake and build up a fire to warm the lodge. Only then would he venture out from the protection of the heavy, hairy hides.

As if his thoughts could be read, Buffalo Cow Woman stirred from her own bed near the lodge's door, and in the semi-darkness began to add kindling to the coals. Then with gentle puffs, blew the embers into life and produced a small flame, which she fed with bigger pieces of wood until a good blaze was produced. With this completed, she exited the lodge and adjusted the smoke flaps so the interior of the lodge would not fill with smoke. Zachariah then heard her walk away to either tend to her morning toilet, or possibly go to the lodge of a friend. As was her habit, she would leave preparation of meals to Sees Far, for Bear Voice had long ago found her cooking more to his liking.

The inside of the lodge began to warm and Sees Far rose from her bed and began to prepare a meal. She placed dried pieces of buffalo meat and water into the opening of a buffalo stomach suspended off the ground by four sticks. As the fire grew it warmed stones that Sees Far kept for cooking. When the stones were glowing hot, she used two sticks to remove each stone from the fire to place them in the stomach. The stones caused the water to boil and thus a crude stew was created.

This was another thing Zachariah was not fond of. The cooking of Maggie had been far superior to that of Sees Far, especially her stews of beef, or chicken. Zachary also missed her bread, and when he thought of this his mouth watered. The meals made by Sees Far seemed to always taste the same, but as Bear Voice was satisfied with the bland product of her cooking, that was all that mattered. Zachariah had to be content until he visited the lodge of a friend where he could eat meals cooked in a cast-iron pot.

Zachariah waited for the stew to heat, and Sees Far to wake Bear Voice, but before either happened an alarm rose outside. With no further thought of food or the cold, Zachariah threw back the buffalo robe, and taking up his belt, knife bow and quiver, exited the lodge to find out what the threat might be. Sees Far and Bear Voice followed him, the older man with a robe wrapped around his shoulders.

Coming into the camp were some Cheyenne and Arapaho from Sand Creek, who had been able to catch horses and ride for help. They quickly said that the village on Sand Creek had been attacked the day before, and that were probably more survivors still out on the prairie that needed help. Almost everyone in the

Smoky Hills' camp had friends or relatives at Sand Creek, and the fear and anger over their fate spread. Immediately, a rescue party was arranged with horses loaded down with blankets, buffalo robes and cooked food, and the party headed south to rescue the survivors.

Zachariah went with the rescue party and by mid-day they began to find the refugees in wretched condition; half of them wounded, most on foot, and many children. Few had warm clothing for they had been driven out of their beds at dawn and had no chance to dress. During the previous night, they had all suffered from the bitter cold as there was no wood to be had. The young men and women, some of who were wounded themselves, collected grass and made fires. The severely wounded and the children were placed near the fires and covered with grass to keep them from freezing. And throughout the night, they had kept up constant calls to attract the attention of anyone who might be wondering in the darkness.

Those camped at Sand Creek were from several clans, the camp divided up into groups of lodges, each band with its own chief. Of these clans, Black Kettle's suffered a heavy loss, with few its men escaping. Chief Sand Hills band had few killed as they were camped further down the creek and most of these people escaped before the soldiers could reach them. Yellow Wolf's band lost half of its people, including Yellow Wolf, and his brother Big Man. War Bonnet's band lost half its people. Chief White Antelope's clan lost heavily also. One Eye was killed together with many of his people. Of Left Hand's Arapaho, only five out of the fifty escaped with their lives.

Among the last to make it into the Smokey Hills camp was Black Kettle, his wife who had been wounded several times, George Bent who was wounded having been shot in the hip, and Little Wolf, with Crow Eyes, who in his arms carried the badly wounded Red Elk. Meets the Enemy Woman had been shot down only after she had killed one of the soldiers with a knife, keeping her name in death as she had in life.

At first, the Dog Soldiers and many of the people blamed Black Kettle for what had happened. They believed that the massacre illustrated the foolishness of the peace chiefs' policy of cooperating with the Whites. They believed a more militant position toward the whites was justified by the massacre, and the time had come to pull the other tribes together and strike back.

Soon after the fugitives from Sand Creek reached the Cheyenne camp on the head of the Smokey Hills, a council was held, and it was decided to send a pipe to the Lakota and the Northern Arapaho inviting them to join in a war against the Whites. To begin a war in the dead of winter was an uncommon thing, but the Cheyenne putting aside their mourning, were angry and wanted vengeance. Cheyenne pipe bearers went first to Spotted Tail and Pawnee Killer's bands of Brûlé Lakota on the Solomon River. Then, to the Northern Arapahos camped near the Republican River. The leaders of the Lakota and the Arapaho all smoked the Cheyenne pipe and agreed to join in on the war.

The Dog Soldiers, Southern and Northern Cheyenne, Northern Arapahos, and Lakota united, gathering on Cherry Creek in a great village numbering ten-thousand people, including two-thousand warriors.

While these Indians were gathering, one hundred Cheyenne, unaware of the massacre on Sand Creek, attacked a wagon train near the Plum Creek Station. Soldiers of the 1st Nebraska Cavalry from the station relieved the train and pursued Indians for over fifteen miles to Spring Creek. There, in a small canyon the Indians turned to fight. The soldiers and Cheyenne both dismounted and fought on foot until night fall, with two civilians and one soldier killed, and seven wounded. The Indians, losing three of their own, withdrew. The outcome would have been different if this band had known about Sand Creek. They would have pressed harder and taken as much revenge as possible.

As this one party was only one of many small groups out raiding along the Platte, the Chiefs in the large village waited until all had returned and then held a council in which they decided to make an attack in revenge for Sand Creek.

Black Kettle continued to speak for peace and did not agree to join in on any raiding, but after the slaughter many changed their minds, including the great warrior Roman Nose, and many Arapaho joined the Dog Soldiers to seek revenge on the Whiteman.

***

CHAPTER NINETEEN
THE WAR PIPE

December 1864 – Big Freeze Moon

There was no end to the number of people who wanted to buy Azariah Bolt a glass of whiskey. Like other members of the "Heroes of Sand Creek", he was a celebrity, and the drinks flowed in the Denver bars. He accepted the slaps on the back and the admiration offered with the drinks, but he smiled and hid the contempt he held for everyone. All he had to do in order to draw a crowd was display the collection of his trophies; long haired scalps, severed ears, and most popular was the tobacco pouch he had made from the skin of a small breast. As impressive as these gory tokens of Sand Creek were, Bolt held back other mementos, those taken from White men. With the exception of the scalp taken from Hezekiah Cable, this he claimed he had found in the lodge of Black Kettle.

Hezekiah's locks seemed to enrage the onlookers and at the same time grow admiration for Bolt, as he and his comrades had not only taken revenge for the atrocities committed on the Hungate family, they and more importantly he, had produced proof of the Indian barbarity.

Reports of the massacre had already reached Washington, and General Curtis began to realize that Chivington had lied about the battle. Where Curtis had declared Wynkoop's attempts to make peace with Black Kettle an embarrassment, he knew that Wynkoop may now be his only hope to prevent the government from implicating him in the slaughter of the Cheyenne. To save his own reputation, Curtis orders Wynkoop back to Fort Lyon and to resume his command. In addition, he orders Wynkoop to investigate the Sand Creek battle and interrogate all participants.

Not only in Washington, but across the country, most people saw the massacre as a sickening butchery of women and children. Congress' Joint Committee on the Conduct of War declared, "As to Colonel Chivington, this committee can hardly find fitting terms to describe his conduct. Wearing the uniform of the United States, which should be the emblem of justice and humanity; holding the important position of commander of a military district, and therefore having the honor of the government to that extent in his keeping, he deliberately planned and executed a foul and dastardly massacre which would have disgraced the vilest savage among those who were the victims of his cruelty. Having full knowledge of their friendly character, having himself been instrumental to some extent in placing them in their position of fancied security, he took advantage of their inapprehension and defenseless condition to gratify the worst passions that ever cursed the heart of man. It is thought by some that desire for political preferment prompted him to this cowardly act; that he supposed that by pandering to the inflamed passions of an excited population he could recommend himself to their regard and consideration."

Rumors of the investigation did not bother Bolt, for like Chivington, he was no longer under the authority of the military. And, until the gratitude of the populace of Denver wore thin, he had no need to find a means of living. When the time came, he would look for some form of work that would accommodate his compulsions.

***

Soon after the survivors reached the camps of the Cheyenne on the Smokey Hill and Republican rivers, a small party of warriors set out and attacked a wagon train east of Plum Creek Station on the Platte road, but the whites took refuge in an abandoned ranch house and were soon relieved by Company E, 1st Nebraska Cavalry Veteran Volunteers under command of Capt. S. M. Curran. As the attack took place late in the day, the Cheyenne broke off and withdrew without causing any casualties. In response, Colonel L. L. Livingston, commander of the 1st Nebraska, reported, "December 8, 1864, On this day the Indians struck the overland road at a late hour, by which means, when pursued by our forces, night interfered to stop the pursuit and the majority of them thus escape. I feel convinced that nothing short of an expedition against the encampments of the hostile Sioux and Cheyenne south of the Republican River, which will strike and destroy some large band, will terminate this

394

barbarous warfare. All that is necessary to obtain peace with the Cheyenne and Sioux is to crush some of their large winter encampments out of existence."

January 1865 – Moon of Frost on the Lodge

The war pipe was passed from camp to camp among the Sioux, Cheyenne and Arapaho warriors. The chiefs waited until all the small war parties had returned from the Platte and then held a council. Though the winter moons were not normally a time for war, they decided a large-scale attack against the whites was necessary. They chose Julesburg as their target, though a small Army garrison, Camp Rankin, was located nearby.

In the first days of the Moon of Frost on the Lodge, a party of over one thousand Cheyenne, Lakota and Arapahoe warriors left Cherry Creek and set out in a northwesterly direction for Julesburg. They were accompanied by a number of women with extra ponies on which to bring back plunder. The Brûlé Lakota bands under Spotted Tail and Pawnee Killer led the war party as they were the first to accept the pipe, and as was the custom, they received that position of respect. The Lakota also knew the location of the ranches and stations near Julesburg better than the Cheyenne who seldom visited that area. Following the Lakota chiefs were those of the Cheyenne and Arapahoe. The march disciplined, with the soldier bands thrown out on all four sides of the column to maintain order, and prevent any stragglers, or attempts by young warriors to make a premature attack.

Zachary was excited being a part of such a great force of warriors. Among the vast number of warriors, he saw many that he knew. Just in front of him rode the brothers Charles and George Bent, sons of William. George had been at Sand Creek where he had was wounded. Sneaking back to his father's ranch on the Arkansas, George recuperated and then he, his brother Charles and Charles' mother Yellow Woman left for the camp on the Solomon Fork to join the Dog Soldiers. The Bent brothers were older than Zachary, George twenty-two years old and Charles twenty, but being half-breeds themselves, Zachary found them easy to be around and a bit more tolerant of him then others in the bands.

The war party reached a point in the vicinity of Julesburg some miles south of the Platte late in the evening and set up a camp among the sand hills. Again, the soldier bands were tasked with keeping order, and kept a close watch on the young men preventing them from slipping off on their own. There was also a strict order that the camp remain quiet, so no noise was permitted.

The collection of buildings known as Julesburg Station sat some distance from the South Platte River in the level sandy valley, which was several miles broad, and closed in on the north and south by the low hills and bluffs. Here, the South Platte, called the Fat River by the Cheyenne, was about two-hundred feet wide, dotted with small islands covered with brush. The banks were low and what water there was in the river was less than a foot deep, and frozen over at this time of the year. All the timber in the Platte Valley near Julesburg had been cleared, used either for building or firewood, and wood had to be hauled from Cottonwood Canyon almost one-hundred miles away.

Julesburg Station was important on the stage line. Here the company had a large "home station," with an eating house, a big stable, blacksmith and repair shop, granary and storehouse, and a big corral enclosed by a high wall built of sod. Besides the stage company's property, the Overland Telegraph Company had an office, and there was a large store selling all kinds of goods to travelers and emigrants trains. Altogether, Julesburg Station was quite an impressive place along the Platte, with fifty station hands, stock tenders, drivers, telegraph operator, and the merchant. The station itself was built of cedar logs hauled from Cottonwood Canyon, with the remainder of the buildings built partly of cottonwood logs and partly sod.

Fort Rankin was located opposite the mouth of Lodgepole Creek about a mile upriver from Julesburg. It was built of cottonwood and sod like the buildings of Julesburg but surrounded by a strong stockade and garrisoned by a single company of the 7th Iowa Cavalry.

The Indians realized that if the small company of soldiers knew they were outnumbered, they would stay inside their fortified walls. With this in mind, a plan was made to draw them out into the open where they could be engaged and annihilated. Before daylight, Big Crow, the chief of the Cheyenne Crooked Lance Soldiers, selected eight men, five Cheyenne and three Lakota, to go out and show themselves near the fort. Zachary hoped he would be chosen as one of the five Cheyenne, but knew he was not as experienced as many of the others and was a bit jealous of those who were picked. It was hoped that these warriors would act as bait and draw the soldiers out into the sand hills where the main body of warriors would be concealed.

Zachary was still too excited with the prospect of the coming battle to sleep, so he decided that he would keep watch with Wolf Horn and Red Arm, who as Dog Soldiers, were both watching the camp and waiting for a sign from the decoys on the coming day.

It was a new moon, and though the night was dark, Big Crow and his eight warriors were cautious. There was a small ravine that ran from the hills south of the river across the flat bottom land and ended at the Platte below the post. They followed this ravine, staying under cover of its banks, until they arrived near the fort and there they waited until dawn. As the sky to the east began to lighten, they saw a few men walking about outside the stockade. This was their signal to mount their ponies and ride up out of the ravine. They charged toward the men, not so much as to engage them but to draw out those inside the stockade.

As soon as the Indians were spotted, the men ran for the safety of the fort, but within a few minutes, an officer and sixty cavalry troopers came galloping out of the fort accompanied by some mounted civilians. The fort had a small compliment of soldiers, and it appeared the officer had brought most of his men out to engage the Indians. Big Crow and his men retreated toward the sand hills two or three miles south of the fort, staying just out of the soldier's reach and drawing the troops after them. The soldiers, firing a few shots as they pursued the decoys, pushed their mounts hard and after two miles they were confident of overtaking the Indians.

From where Zachary had spent the night with Red Arm and Wolf Horn, the sound of gunfire was faint. They weren't sure it was time to fight until the unmistakable notes of the soldier's bugle floated out in the cold morning air. Then, they were sure the soldiers were in pursuit of Big Crow.

"Go, spread the word in the camp that it is time to prepare for the battle," said Red Arm, and Wolf Horn and Zachary leaped to their ponies and speeded back into the camp, calling everyone to get ready to fight and mount their horses.

The Indians in the camp began to prepare, painting themselves, putting on war bonnets, and taking covers off their shields. As soon as they were ready, the soldier bands formed the warriors into a column and marched them up behind the sand hills. Here, guarded on all side by the bands of soldiers, they sat waiting on their ponies, excited but restrained. The sound of the gunfire came nearer, and as feared, a body of impatient young men broke out from behind the hills. The plan of drawing out the troops and surrounding them was ruined. As further efforts at a surprise were dashed, the signal was given, and all the warriors rushed out to attack.

The troopers of Captain O'Brien's 7th Iowa Cavalry were sure to overcome their quarry when the first of the hidden multitude of warriors burst from behind the sand hills. Most of the troopers had their sights on Big Crow's men, but the Captain's eyes were constantly scanning to the left and right in his field of vision. He had not expected the vast number of warriors coming out to face his mere sixty troopers and handful of civilians. When the first of the hidden warriors appeared, his instincts alerted him, and he had already decided in his mind to pull back.

"Come About!" He shouted the order, his bugler echoing the command immediately sounding the brassy notes, the short tune cutting above the sound of the galloping horses. The entire troop turned to following their captain. As soon as the troop was heading back toward the fort, O'Brien shouted out the second order, "Rally!" calling on the troopers to return to their formation using the guidon as their point to follow. Normally O'Brien would have called for skirmishers to fall back and cover his retreat, but he knew that any soldiers left behind would be overwhelmed and he had no stomach to sacrifice any of his men needlessly.

The safety of Fort Rankin's palisade was almost three miles away and the trooper's horses had been run hard pursuing Big Crow and his men. Now, the Indians that they had been chasing were turned about, hanging on their rear, and combined with warriors on fresh mounts, were gaining on the White soldiers. The number of warriors grew as the stamina of the Cavalry horses diminished. And, unlike the soldiers, the Indians fought as individuals, so those with the fastest horses caught up with the soldiers first and began to fire on them. Those few troopers and civilians who fell behind were soon overtaken, shot and dropped from their saddles. Half a dozen of the soldiers, resigned to their fate, stopped and dismounted, determined to fight on foot and sell their lives at a cost to the Indians. Their efforts though were useless, and they were overrun before they could put up any resistance.

With many of the lead Indians breaking their pursuit to finish those soldiers and civilians that had been taken down, O'Brien and his remaining force broke through and made it to the safety of Fort Rankin. Of the sixty troopers and a dozen civilians who rode out with the Captain, fourteen soldiers and four civilians had lost their lives, and their bodies were left to the Indians.

At the same time the troopers were starting their way back to the fort, the westbound stage had arrived at the station and the driver and his sole passenger, the Army Paymaster, abandoned the coach. Along with the station hands and the storekeeper, they fled to the fort and arrived there just as O'Brien's men were entering the gate. Safe behind the walls, they helplessly watched as the Indians descended on Julesburg Station.

At first, Zachary circled around the post with many of the warriors but saw no point of wasting his arrows and broke off to follow those who had went to the station. The Indian women came out of the hills with the extra ponies and joined the men in plundering the store, station and warehouse.

Zachary went to the station house and there on the table sat breakfast, hot and waiting for the morning coach passengers. At once, everything else seemed less important and Zachary, along with some others, sat at the table and devoured biscuits, ham, eggs and coffee heavily laced with sugar. The biscuits seemed to melt in his mouth, the fluffy layers and texture reminding him of Maggie's baking. The saltiness of the ham, was slightly bitter but combined with the eggs, was heavenly to him. The food was so delicious that Zachary relished every bite and filled himself to the point where he couldn't eat more, though he wanted too. Taking in so much rich food that he hadn't eaten in a long time, and the long absence of sugar in his diet, increased Zachary's energy, alertness and made him giddy.

Zachary went into the store and looked about to see what might remain. On the floor, someone had dropped a long hunting knife and picking it up Zachary tucked it into his belt. Under the store counter, he found a sky-blue blanket that had been overlooked and he took this too.

The shelves in the store were packed with all sorts of goods, and groceries, including canned goods. Indian women were loading everything they could onto the extra ponies to the point where the little steeds seemed overburdened. Most of the Indians left the canned goods behind, some taking only a few. But scanning the rows of tinned goods, Zachary saw a label that made his already full belly seem in need of more, "CHOICE PEACHES, PACKED BY STEWART, SULLIVAN, & CO." Zachary picked up one of the cans and instantly looked around to find a way to open it.

Coming up beside Zachary, Polecat, seeing the can in his hand asked, *"What is that, Yellow Horse?"*

"This holds fruit from a tree," Zachary answered.

"How do put a tree inside of that?"

"It is not important. What is important is how we can open them," said Zachary.

Polecat took one of the cans, eyed it for a moment, then struck it on the countertop, denting it but doing little more damage. Frustrated by this he set the can on the counter and withdrawing his tomahawk brought it down on the can, ripping it open. The liquid contents of the can shot out and sprayed both young men, but the sweet pieces of fruit were now free for them to eat. Both devoured the peach slices, smiling and laughing almost childlike. Looking back at the canned goods on the shelf, Zachary decided that he would take some of these and placed a few cans inside a canvas bag.

Zachary and Polecat went out into yard, near the coach, where Small Belly and One Leg were hacking at a tin box held closed by a padlock. The Army payroll master had abandoned the box in his flight to the fort. When the lock gave way to the assault, small bundles of green paper were exposed. Zachary knew these were currency, but had no value to his comrades, and Small Belly began to chop the paper up with his tomahawk, and laughing, threw the pieces into the air letting them drift across the valley. Before all the bills could be destroyed, Zachary picked up a handful, not sure why, but thinking sometime in the future they would come in handy.

The Indians spent the rest of the day hauling load after load of plunder and provisions into the hills and driving off the station's herd of cattle, while the soldiers were helpless to interfere. Zachary saw George Bent come out of the express office with a wrapped package, and opening it, pull out a new Army officer's coat, which he put on. Other Indians were wearing shirts, hats and coats found at the station.

Wrapped in the wool blanket and carrying his plunder, Zachary mounted his pony and headed off to join the others in the sand hills where they would begin their march back to the village on Cherry Creek. The euphoria caused by the excitement of the raid, the Whiteman's food and especially the canned fruit, started to fade, the food lying heavy in his stomach. He felt a bit bloated and miserable. He also began to wonder how he would hide his new-found possessions from Bear Voice and Sees Far Woman, and he guiltily looked about, expecting to see his mentor. He knew Bear Voice was among the warriors but had not seen him during the raid. Sees Far had been with the other women, but Zachary had not seen her with the others while the looting was going on, and if she had been there, she would not have taken any of the Whiteman's goods. Then, as if his thoughts of her had conjured her up, she rode up from behind him and not recognizing him wrapped in the blanket, rode on past. A chill ran up his spine, and the rich food he had eaten forced itself out and he emptied his stomach.

The ponies were so heavily loaded that it took three days for the raiders to reach the village on Cherry Creek. The first blow had been dealt to the Whiteman in revenge for Sand Creek, and everyone was starting to feel better. The camps were full of plunder, and that night the young men and women held scalp dances and feasted on the Whiteman's food, which they had never had in such quantities until now; tame beef, bacon, smoked and canned meat, flour, corn meal, shelled corn, sugar, and molasses.

Several days after the war party returned, the entire village moved further north to White Butte Creek between the Fat River and the Red Shield River. There was also more talk of carrying on a great raid along the Fat River, and then move further north to the Powder River and join the Northern Cheyenne and the Ogallala. Black Kettle still led a large faction that remained opposed to war and when they heard of the plans to escalate the fighting, they announced that they would go south of the Arkansas and stay with the Southern Arapaho, Comanche and Kiowas, until peace could be obtained. With eighty lodges, they started south the following day.

The rest of the camp divided up. Most of the women and children, with a few of the men, went due north. The Cheyenne warriors went northwest to raid above Julesburg, while the Lakota went northeast raiding below Julesburg Station and finally the Arapaho party set off directly north to raid near Julesburg Station.

In the following days, the Indians raided between Julesburg and Denver, attacking; Gartrell's Ranch, Godfrey's Ranch, Lillian Springs Ranch, Harlow's Ranch, Spring Hill Station, Bulcer's Ranch, and Buffalo Spring Ranch. They struck: the American Ranch, Valley Station, Dennison's Ranch, Moore's Ranch, and Wisconsin Ranch, each twice. They started the Big Hoop Moon by returning to Julesburg Station, sacking it again and this time burning the buildings. Eighteen Whites lost their lives, only three being soldiers. Ten people were unaccounted for, three of these being a rancher named Morrison, his wife and child. This number of casualties could have been greater if the Indians would not have concentrated on looting and destroying property and stealing livestock. They had taken over two-thousand head of cattle alone.

Since the raid on Julesburg, Zachary had managed to lose himself among the vast camps, staying in one lodge or another, all in the attempt to keep his whereabouts unknown to Bear Voice and Sees Far Woman. He wanted to distance himself from them. But he knew sooner or later, they would find him and coerce him to come "home". He had been successful avoiding them for weeks, spending his nights wrapped in the sky-blue English blanket, and enjoying the Whiteman's food cooked by his hosts. He also took part in the raids along the Platte Valley, riding with the Bent brothers and his comrades; Small Belly, Wolf Horn, Blue Crane, Polecat, One Leg, and Red Arm.

It was during the first raid on Moore's Ranch that Zachary found himself a group that included Bear Voice. The older man seemed matter of fact about them being together, until after the raid. They were riding along, only two miles from the ranch, when Bear Voice came up next to Zachary and began to talk to him.

"Your Aunt has been worried about you," he said. *"She feared you had been injured or even killed by the Whiteman. I told her that this must be true, for you would not cause her distress, and worry by staying away so long."* His sarcasm evident. *"I told her*

that you would not be so disrespectful and unthankful for her care."

"*Uncle, I...*" Zachary started to speak but was stopped by Bear Voice who reached over and grabbed his forearm with a vice-like grip.

"*Have you lost all respect for those who have taken you into their lodge?*" Bear Voice almost hissed, his words cutting into Zachary like the fingernails he sank into Zachary's arm, drawing blood.

He continued to berate his nephew, "*I do not know who you are! Look! What is this you have wrapped around you?*" He pulled at the blue blanket. "*Have you taken up the Whiteman's medicine? You must be cleansed! Discard that filth, NOW!*" and with this, he tore at the blanket, ripping it from Zachary's grip and threw to the ground.

"*I was cold Uncle, and I only took it...*" again Bear Voice stopped him, this time striking him across the face with his quart.

"*You will stay by my side until we return to the camp. Then I will perform my medicine to cleanse you. You will also go into the holy lodge and sweat.*"

Zachary was about to protest, but a cry went up from the warriors in front of the party and they kicked their horses into a run. On the road were nine White men, who seeing the Indians, attempted to flee but were quickly overcome. A short fight broke out, and many of the Whites were knocked from their horses and killed. Some fought but most were taken without a struggle, these men were completely terrified, only one of them showing the least bit of bravery.

The Indians began to pull the clothing off these men and beat them with their war clubs and strike them with their bows. As Blue Crane was going through the saddlebags and valises of the men, he found four scalps with long black hair, one having a dragon fly fetish tied into its locks, another a peculiar little shell.

"*Eyeee!*" he shouted, "*I know who this belonged to!*" referring to the scalp with the small quilled fetish, "*I have seen it worn by Tangled Horn's daughter. She was killed at Dry Creek!*"

"*And this one, with the shell. I know that it belonged to White Leaf!*" exclaimed Polecat.

When the Indians discovered that these men were veterans of Sand Creek, the blows became more intense and deadly. Two of men were scalped while still alive, and lay on the ground, one begging for his life. No one took pity on him, and several of the warriors took turns exacting their own savage revenge on him with a final blow from the stone war club of Bear Voice. As was the custom of the Cheyenne, the bodies of these nine men were mutilated, and small trophies such as severed fingers taken along with their scalps. Zachary, still reeling from the scolding of Bear Voice, stood by and watched. Any thoughts of taking out revenge on these men was lost in his own humiliation.

After the raids during the Moon of Frost on the Lodge, many of the Cheyenne went north to join Red Cloud on the Powder River. In their wake many of the homesteads in the South Platte River valley were left burning. These fires light the night sky, the whole valley illuminated by the flames of burning ranches and stage stations. As these fires burned out, darkness fell on the valley, but this was truly only the beginning of the darkness that would fall on the entire West.

***

February 1865 – Big Hoop Moon

Soon after Sand Creek, Colonel James H. Ford of the Colorado 2nd Regiment took command of Fort Riley by order of General Curtis, and at the same time Curtis ordered Colonel Thomas Moonlight to take command of Denver's Military District, replacing Chivington. Captain Silas Soule was scheduled to muster out but was convinced by Colonel Moonlight to reenlist in the Veteran's Regiment, and the Colonel appointed Silas as Assistant Provost Marshal in Denver. Among Soule's first duties was to investigate reports that the stock captured at Sand Creek, along with much of the stock procured from local ranchers to be put in service of the 3rd Regiment, was unaccounted for. Accusations ran rampant that many 3rd Regiment officers and soldiers, as well as some 1st Regiment men, had either kept the stock for themselves or sold it.

At the same time, Wynkoop arrived back at Fort Lyon and immediately initiated his own investigation on Sand Creek. He wasted little time, in sending a report that detailed the true events of the massacre severely criticizing Chivington and calling him an "inhuman monster." Although Chivington was officially no longer under military authority, the Army ordered a special military commission to gather evidence and call witnesses in its own investigation. The War Department and the House of Representatives, along with the existing Joint Special Committee of Congress, also began an inquiry. Fearing that he would be left holding the bag for the massacre at Sand Creek, Major Scott Anthony resigned his commission and mustered out of the army. He, too, was now immune from a military court-martial.

Raids escalated in reprisal to the massacre at Sand Creek, and Chivington's actions had caused more harm than good. Denver City was still divided into two factions, the first, comprised of most citizens, were beginning to realize that Chivington's claim of killing over five-hundred warriors was an outright lie. The other side, consisting in part of the "Bloody Thirdsters", were staunch supporters of Chivington and believed that Wynkoop, Soule and Lieutenant Colonel Samuel Tappan were the architects of a conspiracy to ruin their hero.

In Washington, the Committee on the Conduct of the War took testimony from Governor Evans, Jesse Leavenworth, John Smith, Anthony Scott, other Denver officials, Samuel Colley and several other soldiers. Colonel Moonlight convened his military investigation into Sand Creek, and appointed officers of the Colorado 1st Regiment, who were not present at Sand Creek, to lead it. He appointed Samuel Tappan, Captain Edward Jacobs and Captains George Stilwell. He chose Tappan, Chivington's most enthusiastic critic, as ranking officer to preside over the hearings.

From February through May, the commission took testimony in both Denver and Fort Lyon, from soldiers, officers and civilians. Tappan emphasized that the proceeding was not a trial but a hearing to collect facts, to investigate the charges against the 3rd Regiment, fix responsibility and insure justice. In a bid to salvage his political career, Chivington testifies, enlisting the services of Denver Attorney, Major Jacob Downing, himself a key officer who led in the attack at Sand Creek. Chivington was also allowed to present evidence and his own witnesses, as well as cross-examine witnesses introduced by the Army. On the eve of the hearings, Chivington publicly announced that he would personally pay five-hundred dollars to anyone who killed an Indian or and White who sympathized with Indians.

With a few exceptions, the evidence and testimony given was against Chivington, and offered by officers and soldiers of the 1st

Regiment. That offered by those who testified from the 3rd Regiment contradicted their own earlier claims. They swore that very few women and children were killed, and no scalping, mutilating and other atrocities took place.

The most damning testimony against Chivington was given by Major Wynkoop, Lieutenant Cramer and Captain Soule. Chivington and Downing, in cross-examining the witnesses, severely rebuked Cramer and Soule while they were on the stand attempting to deflect the mounting evidence against Chivington.

April 1865 - Moon of Budding Trees

Throughout February, March and April, Soule received anonymous death threats and three unsuccessful attempts were made to assassinate him. In a conversation with Whit, Soule confided that he believed if he was killed, Chivington would attack his character in order to discredit his testimony in the hearing.

"That will not happen," said Whit, "You have too many friends and supporters."

"It may be, but you'll remember Chivington has put a five-hundred dollars bounty on any Indian or those who sympathize with them." He paused, then added, "I'll not live in fear of cowards when I am doing what is right," said Silas, "Anyway, I have my Hersa and a new home to lighten up my life." He spoke of his new bride Hersa Coberly, who had become his wife, April 1st.

"I'd still be on my guard."

"Though I don't feel it necessary, I will keep myself armed." He pointed to the holstered Remington revolver hanging on a peg near the door. "I wear that now, more than before, for my wife's sake."

"As Provost Marshal, you should be armed at all times anyway," said Whit.

"True, but there are times when duty should be put aside. Like tonight." He smiled at Whit.

"Are you sure you and Hersa wouldn't like some company at the theater tonight?"

"No, Whit. You have better things to do than spend the evening with us. Anyway, I want to spend as much time alone with my new bride as can be spared from my duties."

It was close to midnight when Azariah Bolt slammed an empty whiskey glass down on the table and looked at the two men he sat with. They were as broke as he was, so his gaze scanned the saloon searching for a likely admirer of either the 3rd or Chivington, that would buy him another drink. When the hearings began, the offer of free drinks didn't disappear, but slowed. The saloon was all but empty, so Bolt turned his attention back to his companions.

"Shit! What's a man got to do get a drink around here, kill someone?" he complained.

"Probably not a bad idea," said Private Charles Squier, of the 2nd Colorado Cavalry, meaning it in jest.

"And, just who do you suggest?" Bolt asked seriously.

"OH, shit, any In'jin would do," replied Private William Morrow, joking like his companion. "You think the Colonel's offer of five-hundred dollars is good?" He added, more serious.

"There ain't a savage close enough to fill the bill," Bolt said, but we might be able to find ourselves someone on the street who'll spot us a few dollars." Bolt's meaning of the word "spot" was for someone to hand over their money at either knife or gun point. "Let's get out of here," he told them, and standing up from the table, walked out onto Lawrence Street.

Even at this late hour, there were people on the street, too many in Bolt's opinion. It would have been better if there were only one or two, one of those being the convenient target of their planned assault. They hadn't walked far when Bolt saw Silas and Hersa Soule walking down the opposite side of the street, on their way home from the theater. He reached over and took hold of Squier's arm, pulling him to a stop and into the shadows.

"Look there, boys. There's your five-hundred dollars walking as pretty as you please down the street." He pointed at Soule.

"Gawd Damn! Let's get 'em!" Squier said, reaching for his pistol.

"Hold on you idiot! We need to take him when there's no witnesses." Bolt thought for a moment and a plan formed in his mind. "He's headed home and will turn on G Street. As soon as he rounds the corner, we fire a few shots in the air. Whoever is left on the street will run for cover, and if I judge that son-of-a-bitch right, he'll do his duty as Provost and come back to see what the trouble is." He smiled, pleased with his ability to conceive such a plot so quickly.

Just as Bolt had predicted, Silas and Hersa turned at G Street. As they disappeared around the corner, he, Morrow and Squier stepped out into the street and pulling their pistols, fired a few rounds. Immediately they moved toward where Silas Soule would come back to investigate the disturbance.

Bound by his duty, Silas Soule appeared faster than expected, and though Morrow and Squier both took shots at him, they missed, their aim rushed and poor. Silas had enough time to pull his own pistol from its holster, and fired a single round at his assailants, his shot striking Squier in the arm. A well-aimed shot from Bolt's pistol, entered Soule's cheek, passing up through his brain, killing him instantly. Squier had lost the grip on his pistol, and he as he reached down to retrieve it, Bolt was grabbing him to pull him away.

The shots, rather than clear the few people from the street, had attracted attention, and the curious began to come out to find what had happened, as the three assassins fled down the street.

Whit was among the mourners who attended the services and burial for Captain Silas Soule, along with Lieutenant Cramer, Major Anthony, Governor Evans and a large contingency of the 1st Regiment. The entire ceremony conducted at St. John's Church, the procession and the gravesite were full of military honors, as befitting a true hero. Each was filled with the most prominent citizen of Denver City, officiated by Reverends Kehler and Hitchings. The eulogy given by Hitchings, was inspiring.

"It is of Captain Soule as a soldier that I may say something without fear of encroaching upon that sacred private memory that belongs alone to his widow, his mother and his friends," he started. "I am told he was a good soldier, and how much does that short objective involve? It implies that he had no fear of work, of fatigue, of suffering, of danger, of death. And was it not so? Did he not at the midnight hour, go out to discharge his duty as commander of the Provost Guard of this city? Did he not go when he had every reason to believe that the alarm which called him out was only to decoy him into danger? Did he not go when he knew positively that his life was threatened with deadly intent? Did he not go, feeling so certain that his doom was sealed, that he took farewell of his young wife, telling her what she must do in case he returned no more alive?

"Yes, and there is the spirit of the soldier, and the good soldier, too; he did his duty in the midst of danger, did his duty in the face of death, and fell by the assassin's hand."

The earth had barely been placed on Soule's grave when rumors began to be passed around that Chivington was behind the assassination. Chivington himself fueled these rumors by going in front of the commissioners and immediately accusing the Captain of being involved in a conspiracy with Agent Sam Colley and trader John Smith to profit from the war with the Cheyenne. Chivington also alleged that Silas Soule was a coward, a drunk and an outright thief.

His claims aroused more anger than support and they were dismissed as a transparent ploy to draw attention away from the truth of what had taken place at Sand Creek. On the 30th of May, all three government investigations into the massacre were complete and transcripts submitted to the War Department. One report stating that, "From the suckling babe to the old warrior, all who were overtaken were deliberately murdered. Not content with killing women and children, who were incapable of offering any resistance, the soldiers indulged in acts of barbarity of the most revolting character...It is difficult to believe that beings in the form of men, and disgracing the uniform of United States soldiers...could commit...such acts of cruelty and barbarity."

Although all three government investigations resulted in the severe censure of Chivington and Anthony, no legal action was taken against them as both had mustered out of the service. Governor Evans, however, blistered by criticism, would pay a high price.

The condemnation of the massacre at Sand Creek had little effect on the people of the territories, or the Indians who continued to raid from Fort Kearney in Nebraska Territory all the way to Bridger's Pass Station in the Dakota Territory. What would soon make a marked difference were the events that were unfolding in the East. In April, General Robert E. Lee surrendered his Confederate forces at Appomattox Court House in Virginia. Five days later, President Lincoln was assassinated by John W. Booth.

With the end of the war in the East, Federal troops could be redirected to the West to quell the uprising. And, newly appointed President Andrew Johnson felt the Indians were warlike and easily instigated by real or imaginary grievances. Johnson's policy concerning the Plains Indians was that they needed to be relocated to reservations remote from the traveled routes between the Mississippi and the Pacific.

One slight action by Johnson, in connection with Sand Creek, was to direct Secretary of State William Henry Seward to send a letter advising Governor Evans that his resignation from the office of Governor of the Territory of Colorado would be acceptable, and that circumstances with the public interest made it desirable that this resignation should reach the President without delay.

***

Magdalena smiled as she looked down on Joseph as he slept next to Willow's son Henry, on the patch-quilt. The breeze blew gently through the leaves of the giant cottonwood above her and the sleeping children. Thoughts of Whit hadn't entered her mind in months, and she was more content now than she had ever been. There was nothing more she felt was needed to make her life perfect. News of the unrest along the Platte and Republican Rivers to the north seemed as far away to her as the moon. Here, along Fountain Creek, life was slow and peaceful. The ranch had prospered, and Eli and August had become as close as brothers, working day after day to care for it and their little families.

Silas Scott had grown somewhat melancholy since his return from Bent's Ranch the previous fall. He seemed to spend more time at his wife's grave. Maggie understood the pain he had felt, but he seemed to have accepted what had happened, and was now resigned to look to the future. His greatest joy was playing with his new grandson, Henry.

***

CHAPTER TWENTY
THE POWDER RIVER

June 1865 – Fattening Up Moon

The groups of Southern Cheyenne and Arapaho moved further north to the Cheyenne River near the Black Hills. While they camped there, they received word that Northern Cheyenne and Red Cloud's Teton Sioux were in camps along the Powder River where there was plenty of timber, good grass and buffalo. Among the runners who brought this information south were some Northern Cheyenne. This was the first time that Zachary had seen one of these people.

Their dress was different than that of their southern brethren. The Southern Cheyenne had more contact with the whites, they wore more garments made of cloth, even some articles taken from the whites. The Northern Cheyenne were more in line with what Bear Voice had preached was proper. They wore buffalo robes and buckskin leggings, and wrapped their braids in buckskin strips died red. In their hair, they wore crow feathers cropped at the tips. Zachary thought they had a look about them that seemed less tame, less "civilized" than the Southern Cheyenne. He was in awe of them, and when Bear Voice mentioned his approval, Zachary had to agree.

"They also keep all the old ways," Bear Voice added. *"They know how to respect them. It will be good to camp with them."* He was correct in some respects. During the almost forty years that the Northern and Southern Cheyenne stayed apart, and the Northern Cheyenne lived close to the Sioux, they grew more like them in habit and appearance. Their exposure to the Siouan language also affected their speech in as much as some of them were hard to understand.

Bear did not mention, or he ignored, that many of the Northern Cheyenne carried firearms, metal knives and tomahawks. This did not go unnoticed by Zachary, and he felt that if his uncle approved of these Northerners, then maybe he could take his knife out of hiding and use it more. He would wait though, until the time was right.

The move to the Powder River was uneventful, and when they arrived there was much feasting and dancing. On the second night after their arrival, Crow horse thieves took advantage of the distraction these celebrations caused, discovering a huge herd of horses left to graze unattended. Nine of these Absaroka snuck into the vast herd under the cover of darkness and culled out over two dozen horses without being detected and then drove the horses toward the Tongue River. Their theft might have gone unnoticed if one of them had not dropped his bow and quiver. In the darkness he wasn't able to find them, so he left an unmistakable clue.

The following morning, herders found the Crow bow and quiver and small parties of warriors mounted up to track them down. The best horses had been kept close to the village in log corrals, and these were the mounts of the pursuers. Zachary joined one of these groups, and as his horse was a strong red roan, he was able to keep up with the other warriors. They were the first group to catch up with the fleeing Crow. The horses stolen were not of the best quality. Some of them played out before the Crows could all escape, and four of the nine were overtaken. The fight was short as the Crow had only bows and arrows and were easily routed. The remaining five Crow made their escape, so Zachary and the other warriors withdrew, content with the retrieval of most of the horses and four Crow scalps.

After the Lakota, Cheyenne and Arapaho congregated in the Powder River country, they intensified their raids along the Bozeman Trial, harassing the miners and other travelers. The area had been designated as Indian Territory in the Fort Laramie Treaty in 1851, and though roads through it had been agreed upon, these same roads were viewed as a threat by the Indians.

For three weeks, the scalps of the Absaroka were carried in dances held throughout the nights, the northern bands dancing almost continuously accompanied by the beating of the drums. It was thought by some that the drums frightened away any game in the vicinity, especially the buffalo, and it was soon found that the herds had drifted southeast toward the Little Powder River. The bands moved, following the buffalo, and the drumming was called to an end.

The camp moved every few days to take advantage of the greening grass, spending most of their time along the Tongue River; the Cheyenne setting their camps in circles, the Lakota pitching their lodges in small groups strung out along the river.

Along the Tongue River, Zachary experienced Indian life as it had been before the Whites came. He was exposed to many ancient customs, ceremonies, and dances. All the Soldier societies of both the Cheyenne and the Lakota were present and each held its own rituals and feasts. As the days passed in favor of the People and their allies, the chiefs held councils. The ponies had grown fat, and the spring weather would soon give way to summer when it would be time to commit to another grand raid. It was decided that small groups of warriors would go back to the Platte. These small groups would collect information and determine the best place to strike.

The camps kept moving south, slowly following the Tongue back to the Powder River by end of the Fattening Up Moon. It was from there that the small parties were sent out, and again Zachary was chosen to be among them.

Bear Voice said his special prayers to call on his medicine to protect Zachary and himself in the coming raids. He was careful to watch Zachary, keeping him in sight as much as possible, but Zachary found ways to slip away for a few hours of freedom each day. He left his camp of Southern Cheyenne and moved among the lodges of their Northern kinsmen. On day in his haste, he rounded a lodge and ran into a woman carrying wood, knocking her down and scattering the wood she had in her arms.

Stopping, he apologized and started to help her pick up the wood. It was then he looked up and realized that the woman was white. She was filthy and her clothing was tattered. She bore evidence of being beaten; a black eye and a split lip, as well as bruises along her bare arms. This alone would not have given him pause, but he recognized her. It was Eleanora Yoder. Never expecting to see her again, his first reaction was that of shock, and then pity welled up inside of him and he was tempted to reach out to the poor girl. He started to ask her if she remembered him but thought better, not wanting to bring up the memory of how she came to be among the People.

"Are you all right?" he asked her. She answered only by the nod of her head and downward cast eyes. Zachary could hold back no longer and he reached for her hand. She pulled back at

first, but then allowed his touch, as if resigning herself to whatever he had planned for her.

"I will not hurt you," Zachary said, taking her hand softly in his and lifting her chin to bring her face up where he could see it. The pale skin that he remembered had browned from exposure to the sun, and her face was framed with her dirty and unkempt, copper-colored hair. Her eyes stood out, contrasted by the bruised flesh. As Zachary peered into them, they began to well up and tears started to flow down her cheeks. He felt a trembling in her hand and could see that her whole, thin body was shaking with fear.

"I will not harm you," he said again. *"Let me help you carry this wood to your lodge."*

"I...I...can manage," she said, pulling back her hand from his, her fear now mixed with shame at her appearance and the determination to survive the life fate had given her.

"I am called Yellow Horse. Where is your lodge?" Zachary asked.

Eleanora pointed to a lodge a few yards away and bent down to pick up the remaining kindling.

"I have told you my name," Zachary said, not asking hers to avoid being impolite. This puzzled Eleanora, and looking up at him, she spoke.

"I have no name in the tongue of the People, I am only called Girl. Horn Scrapper Woman also calls me Bitch Dog."

"You speak the words of the People well for someone who has no name," Zachary said, admiring her skill with a language that she had not known a year ago. Eleanora either ignored the compliment or did not perceive it as one, and taking up the last of the wood, started off in the direction of the lodge she had pointed out, Zachary following.

"There you are, you lazy bitch!" A tall woman, with a quart in her hand, came striding toward Eleanora. Zachary thought that this must be the Horn Scrapper Woman, that the girl had spoken about. Before he had caught up with Eleanora, the woman had struck her across the shoulders twice and was about to land a third blow when Zachary spoke up.

"Mother," he said using the polite term, *"It is my fault that this girl is slow in coming to you."*

"The fault lies with her," the woman said, *"She should not be wasting time by speaking to whoever comes along. She is worthless."*

"If she is trouble, why do you not give her away or sell her?"

The woman paused for a moment and saw a chance to not only rid herself of the difficult White girl, but possibly gain something of value.

"I would, but I am old and in need of help," she said in a weak voice, acting frail. Thinking that this young man had an interest in the girl, she added, *"If someone were to offer me something of value, like one of the Whiteman's cooking pots, I might give her away."*

"I understand, Mother. But I do not have the things of the Whiteman, or I would make you a trade so that your life would be better." Having said this, Zachary turned and walked away. As he walked, he wondered why the girl had such an effect on him. He owed her nothing, and she was not all that pretty compared to the Cheyenne girls. But there was something about her that made him want to help.

Even if he had something to trade for the girl, he had no idea what he would do with her. He was not of an age where he could keep a wife, and if we were, would this girl make him a good one. Coupled with these thoughts, what would the reaction of Bear Voice and Sees Far Woman be? Surely, they wouldn't agree, so he tried to put thoughts of her out of his head.

Horn Scrapper Woman and Eleanora watched as Zachary walked away, the girl wondering why this young man had shown any interest in her, and the old woman irritated because he had wasted her time. She turned on the girl and struck her again with the quart.

"I would cut your throat and be rid of you if I did not need your help!" she scolded, and Eleanora could only take the blows, the long thin leather strands of the quart cutting into her arms as she shielded her face.

The group that Zachary was in numbered about one hundred warriors, and a few women. This included Bear Voice, who as a medicine man, had been chosen to tell the warriors how to paint themselves in order to prevent injuries and achieve success in battle. Looks Far Woman was one of the three women who would tend the camp, and Zachary cringed at the thought of her fawning over him in front of the other warriors.

Zachary knew he was being watched constantly by both his aunt and uncle and could sense their animosity they felt when he rode alongside another of the raiders, George Bent. Bent, like Zachary, being a half breed himself, understood what living in two worlds meant. Zachary confided in him that he was confused, and Bent assured him that he was not alone and that he felt the same at times. To take Zachary's mind off his own situation, Bent relayed a bit of his most recent past, much to Zachary's delight.

George told him that when the war between the States broke out, he was in St. Louis and immediately joined the Missouri State Guard with the Confederate Army. He told Zachary of the battles he had been in at Wilson's Creek, Pea Ridge, and Corinth, Mississippi. He explained how he had been captured and spent a short time in Gratiot Street Prison before his guardian, Robert Campbell, paid to have him paroled on condition that he swear an oath of allegiance to the United States. Once freed, George came home to the west, but he found the pro-Union sympathy among those in Colorado Territory intolerable and soon joined his mother's people, identifying more with them.

He assured Zachary that a time would come when he would no longer be confused as to which world he belonged. Zachary did his best to convince Bent that he had already made that decision, but there were times he missed his life on the ranch. He wondered too, if his father missed him.

Another concern of Zachary's that he confided to Bent was the question of Eleanora Yost. It had occurred to Zachary that he might have been rash in thinking to take her as a wife, but he also felt that it was somehow the thing to do. Bent offered little advice, only saying that things like that tended to work themselves out, but he did offer to give Zachary a cast-iron pot if he ran across one that was no longer needed by a Whiteman. Zachary thanked him, but almost hoped the pot never materialized.

The war party moved to the south and struck the North Platte Road about thirty miles below a bridge that had once been used for a stage line, but now only saw some emigrant traffic headed west. There was a small garrison of U. S. troops in the abandoned stage station, protecting the bridge. The horses and mules of the garrison were left out to graze, and Zachary's group easily ran off the stock belonging to the soldiers.

Happy with the ease in taking the horses from the Pony Soldiers, they decided to go into camp for the night. But, no sooner had the party made camp, then one of their scouts came in with word that there was a wagon train coming up the river road, guarded by a troop of cavalry. A second target offered to them so soon could not be passed up, and plans were made to attack the wagons the following day.

At dawn, like they had done at the bridge, the warriors swept down and ran off the herd, escaping without a single casualty. In all, they had captured over two-hundred and fifty fine mounts, most branded with U. S. On the way home, the horses and mules were divided up among the warriors, and Bear Voice was given the choice of any horse that he wanted. They believed that his instructions on how to paint themselves had saved them from being wounded or killed.

Along with the strike at the bridge, the raiders attacked isolated outposts, stagecoach stations, and wagon trains almost daily, reaching as far south as the South Platte River near Julesburg, Colorado.

When Colonel Thomas Moonlight learned of the attacks, he sent soldiers out to investigate. They found three stage stations abandoned, and all the civilian employees eighty miles west of Fort Helleck, holed up at Sulfur Spring Station. The soldiers returned the civilians to the stations and left a detachment at each to protect them. The Indians re-raided the stations and ran off most of the stock, leaving both civilians and soldiers on foot.

The Platte River bridge was a key crossing point on the North Platte River for wagon trains of emigrants traveling the Oregon and Bozeman Trails. It was decided that the bridge would be the perfect place to start the great raid and the group headed back to the main village on Lodgepole Creek, a branch of the Powder.

July 1865 – Moon of the Ripening Chokeberries

With the success of these forays, councils were held, and they approved that the great raid should begin with a strike the Platte River Bridge. Over three thousand Cheyenne and Lakota warriors were sent to descend on the Platte near the bridge and the small garrison of only one hundred and twenty men.

This was the largest war party Zachary had ever seen, and the war leaders included; Red Cloud, Old Man Afraid Of His Horses and his son Young Man Afraid Of His Horses, Roman Nose, Dull Knife, Crazy Horse, and others. The march was perfectly organized with the undisciplined young men held in check the Dog Soldiers.

Upon arriving a few miles away from the bridge, the Indians advanced on foot, leading their horses to avoid throwing up dust. Hidden behind the hills, the main force waited while a group of ten trusted warriors tried to induce soldiers out of the stockade, hoping they would cross the bridge and chase them to where they could be trapped. Enticed by the chance to rout a smaller Indian force, a twenty-five men detachment of the 11th Kansas Cavalry crossed the Platte Bridge at a walk, then formed into a column of fours and rode west along the north bank at a trot to drive off the decoys. Behind them, a thirty-man contingent of the 3rd U.S. Volunteer Infantry and a 11th Ohio Volunteer Cavalry escort, crossed the bridge on foot as a support force. They formed a skirmish line after they observed young warriors appear on the horizon. With the ambush spoiled, warriors rushed from behind the hills to cut off the troopers of the 11th.

The officer leading these troopers wheeled his detachment into two lines and charged the first group of Indians, but soon found himself heavily outnumbered. He then ordered a retreat to the bridge by breaking through the Cheyenne who had circled to his rear. Simultaneously, another large force of Lakota rushed the bridge from the south. The skirmish line at the bridge held the Lakota at bay with volley fire until twenty-one of the twenty-six troopers fought their way through. All were wounded to some extent, and five were killed, including the officer who was wounded in the hip and shot in the forehead with an arrow while trying to aid one of his wounded soldiers.

While the battle was raging at the bridge, a detachment of soldiers with five wagons was spotted within five miles of the bridge and a force of Cheyenne and Lakota went to meet them. The soldiers corralled the wagons and piled cargo underneath them to form a breastwork. Armed with Spencer repeating rifles, they held off the Indians for almost an hour. When they ran out of ammunition, the Indians overwhelmed them, killing all twenty-two.

During the attack, the Indians had cut the telegraph wire to Fort Laramie and destroyed a thousand feet of the line before the soldiers thought to request reinforcements. Soldiers were sent out to make the needed repair, but the Indians drove off the detail of soldiers, killing one trooper. Two Shoshone scouts were then paid to take a message to the next telegraph station east, requesting reinforcements. By the time they had made their way through the hostiles and relief arrived, the battle was over, and the Indians had gone.

The day following the battle, the Indians broke off into smaller groups, some stayed along the Oregon Trail to keep raiding, but the majority returned to the villages along the Powder River. It was time for the summer buffalo hunts to begin and the villages would need the meat the herds would provide.

When Zachary returned with the warriors, he looked for the Northern Cheyenne lodge where he would find Eleanora but could not locate it. The small band that Horn Scrapper Woman belonged to had moved off and no one could tell him where. He had thought about the red-haired girl and he wanted her to know this. At fifteen winters old, he had already experienced the awakening of his sexual desires. But, this was different. She had stirred something in him that he hadn't felt before. The warmth that flowed through him was accompanied by a pain, an ache in his chest. No Cheyenne girl had created this feeling, and Zachary knew some day he would find her again and do his best to hold on to her.

August 1865 – Breeding Moon

Though he had been exposed to them for several weeks, the Pawnee still seemed foreign to Whit. They had been enemies of the Cheyenne and other plains tribes for long before the memories of their grandfathers. Their animosity toward their traditional enemies went so far as not calling them by their different names. They called the Lakota, Cheyenne, Arapaho, Comanche and Kiowa collectively as "cahriksuupiiru", or enemy. It was not so much their appearance, they dressed similarly to other Plains Indians. Nor the vast number of earrings and nose rings they wore. But the men's hairstyle was unique, their head was shaven except for a scalp lock, combed erect and curved backward. It was also their attitude which Whit could not quite place into perspective. They had a reputation for their endurance and courage, being brave to a fault, charging headlong at their enemies.

The two Pawnee who rode with Whit were scouts for the Army, employed in much the same way as he was. These warriors were members of Captain Frank North's command, who they admired greatly, considering him their equal in battle. As for Whit, they seemed to tolerate him, not so much as passing judgment, but considering him just another White man compared to Frank North.

In response to the raiding, Major General Dodge had ordered a punitive campaign against the Lakota, Cheyenne and Arapaho. He chose Brigadier General Patrick Connor to lead the expedition into the Powder River Country. Dodge's directives to Connor were to "make a vigorous war upon the Indians and punish them so that they will be forced to keep the peace."

Connor intended to advance into the Powder River Country in three columns. The first column, personally accompanied by Connor, would move along the Powder, with the intent of establishing a fort near the Bozeman Trail. The second column would march from Omaha, Nebraska and follow the Loup River westward into the Black Hills. The last column would head north from Fort Laramie and traverse the country west of the Black Hills. The plan was for all three columns to unite at the new post near the Powder River. And, no sooner had the post been built than it was named Fort Connor.

Having worked at various jobs that had thrown him in contact with the troops stationed at the various posts, Whit had signed on as a scout. He possessed accurate and extensive knowledge of the country, as well as a natural aptitude for finding his way anywhere, and soon became known to the Army officers. From the time he had spent with Silas Scott and Tom Craigavon, he had learned well the craft of a plainsman. It could never be said of him that he was lost. As he traveled through new territory, he made mental notes of all its features, and they remain so impressed upon his memory that on a second visit, the surroundings seemed like familiar ground.

Whit's mission this day was to carry dispatches between General Connor and Captain North. He could have made this journey alone, but the two Pawnee were intent on joining their comrades. Whit had no objections with their company, even though both Pawnee spoke little, and he only recently picked up a few words of their language.

Whit and the Pawnee caught up with North near the Crazy Woman's Fork of the Powder, and Whit handed over the dispatch bag. While waiting to see if the Captain would send a reply, one of North's Pawnee spotted a small group of Cheyenne warriors, and North ordered pursuit. Living up to his reputation, North outdistanced his men, and the retreating warriors turned on him. North's horse was struck by several arrows and went down, and the Captain took cover behind it. Using the animal as a barricade, he began to fight off his attackers. His position looked dire, until Whit rode up and joined him in the fight. Several Pawnees arrived, and the small party beat off the Cheyenne, who quickly fled.

While waiting for the full party of Pawnee scouts to catch up, North took the time to read the dispatch from Connor. The orders were only a repeat of those already in force. North was to ferret out any hostiles he found.

"You have a message to send back?" Whit asked.

North looked in the direction the Cheyenne had fled and considered if the incident was worth reporting at this time. "No," he said, "Not until I have something real to report. You want to stick around until something happens?" he asked Whit.

"I think I'd like that, Captain," Whit said, "I've been a bit bored lately."

"Well, we'll see if we can't change that for you."

They waited until the full force of the Pawnee Scouts arrived, bringing their number to forty-five. North was supplied with a new mount and the entire force moved out, following the trail of the Cheyenne. The tracks left by the Cheyenne indicated that there were over two dozen horses carrying riders, with another forty head of horses and mules being driven along. There was also sign of a single travois, possibly carrying a wounded warrior.

For the next two days, the scouts followed the trail north, catching up with the Indians after midnight. The Cheyenne had made camp and North thought it best to let his own men rest until dawn, when they would attack.

When the sun was starting to peek over the horizon, four Cheyenne warriors and a woman were seen already in the saddle and moving as if to gather the horses and mules. A few of the Pawnees scouts disguised to appear like Cheyenne or Sioux, showed themselves at the top of a hill and signaled with their blankets, *"We are friends. Come close."* Convinced that these were friends, the Cheyenne rode forward without suspecting danger. When the woman, and the four men riding with her, came closer to the hill, the full body of Pawnees came over the top and charged. The woman and her four companions were overtaken, and all killed.

The rest of the Cheyenne were taken by surprise and overwhelmed by the Pawnee who killed the twenty-seven men, women and children, sparing none. Witnessing the killing of the women and children, Whit went to North and expressed his concern.

"I understand your feelings, Whit. But you must understand the mind of the Indian. The Pawnee and the Cheyenne have been deadly enemies for long before we were out here, and the Cheyenne would treat them in a like manner. We both have seen what they do to White women and children, have we not?" Whit did understand, but it still repulsed him.

While he stood next to North, one of the Pawnee came up to them and showed the scalp of the woman who had been killed first.

"This is the hair of Yellow Woman, the wife of Little White Man, William Bent," the Pawnee said.

"How is it that you know this?" asked North.

"I have seen her with him. She was his second wife," the Pawnee answered.

Whit knew just enough of the Pawnee language to understand what had just been said. He addressed the Pawnee, *"Take me to the woman."* And the Pawnee lead Whit and North back to where her body lay.

"That's Yellow Woman," Whit said. I met her down at William's ranch at Big Timbers.

"What the hell is she doing way up here?" North asked."

"My guess is she went back to her people after Sand Creek." Whit shook his head. "I'm gonna bury her."

"You'll have a hard time finding a shovel," North said.

"Don't need one, the cottonwoods over there will do for her," Whit said pointing to the few trees along the river. "Can you ask your Pawnee not to molest the body?"

"That I can guarantee."

Whit wrapped the woman's body in a blanket and tied it tight, and then in the crouch in the largest tree he found he placed her body. As he climbed down from the tree, he caught a movement in the corner of his eye and pulling his pistol turned to face whatever danger confronted him.

He could not swear what he saw, but thought he spied another woman disappear around one of the trees. He moved forward, and as he walked, he knew in his mind that he would find no one if he looked further. He holstered his pistol, mounted his horse and went back to where North's men were rounding up the horses and mules, many with government brands showing they had been captured in the recent battles at Red Buttes and Platte Bridge Station.

Whit, along with North and his Pawnee, returned to General Connor and joined the General on a march northward from the new Fort Connor. The General had taken on the old mountain man, Jim Bridger, as head scout and Whit didn't mind playing second fiddle to the famous and seasoned frontiersman.

"Old Gabe," as he was called, had been in the mountains since the Ashley days, trapping on the upper Missouri River with the likes of Jed Smith, Tom Kirkpatrick and Hugh Glass. Bridger was agile, rawboned and had a powerful frame, standing over six feet tall. And even at almost sixty years old, he stood straight as an arrow. His gray eyes were sharp, his expression mild and his manners agreeable. He reminded Whit so much of Silas Scott, possessing many of the same qualities, especially a remarkable sense of humor. When Bridger would tell a tall tale, he would relate it in such a serious manner as to fool even the most skeptical into believing.

Though aimable, he was all business when it came to the work he was being paid for. He and Whit were scouting to the west of the main column when Bridger spotted what he thought looked like smoke in the far distance. While he waited, keeping watch, Whit returned to the main column and reported the possible sign of an Indian village to the General. Connor sent out Whit, Frank North and two Pawnee to find the village.

From where Bridger waited, the four went on in the direction of the Tongue River. Before nightfall, they found a village about thirty miles away from the main column where Wolf Creek entered the Tongue. The village was a band of Arapaho led by Black Bear and Medicine Man. Connor quickly collected his most mobile soldiers, consisting of about two-hundred troopers, two howitzers, North, thirty of his Pawnee, and forty Omaha and Winnebago Scouts.

Marching through the night, they reached the village about eight the next morning. The howitzers were quickly moved into position, pointing down on the village. Luckily for Connor, most of the Arapaho warriors were not present, having left for a raid on the Crow along the Big Horn River. In the village were about five hundred people, mostly old men, women, and children.

The troops and the scouts waited for the first shots from the cannons, then they rushed in, catching the Indians unprepared. Whit went through the village firing on any warriors who came into his sight. As had happened on the Tongue River, there was a great deal of indiscriminate firing in the melee and women and children were killed as well as warriors. But the Arapaho put up a stiff resistance, the women fighting alongside the men, and every bit as capable as combatants.

Whit spied a woman in a long buckskin dress, raise and fire an old North West trade gun. As he aimed his pistol at her, she turned to look in his direction, as if frozen where she stood, her doe-like eyes fixed on him. He hesitated, and in that moment of indecision, the woman dropped the empty gun, turned and ran.

Whit quickly regained his composure, and along with the soldiers and their allied Indians, pressed forward, driving the Arapaho out of the village and up Wolf Creek. At some point, a few able warriors turned and put up an effective defense, retreating slowly up the creek while covering the flight of the women and children. The resistance was fierce enough to stop the advance of the small number of soldiers that had pursued the Indians, as most of the soldiers remained in the village to loot and burn the tipis.

With Connor were only thirty troopers, the two scouts, Whit and North, as well as fifteen of the Pawnee. The Arapaho counterattacked and the soldiers, their horses spent, were forced to retreat to the village. There the soldiers finished their work of destruction, while being harassed by the Indians from a distance.

By midday, the soldiers abandoned the destroyed village, North and the Pawnee leading and driving before them more than five-hundred captured horses. Along with the captured loot, eight women and thirteen children were taken prisoner. The Arapaho continued to trail the soldiers, persistent in their attacks, but failed to re-capture any of the horses. Eventually giving up, they returned to treat their wounded and mourn their dead.

Connor rejoined his main force and then marched north toward the Tongue River. On the day after the battle, Connor halted the column. Prior to the engagement, he had strictly forbidden looting. He now had all the plunder collected from the occupation of the village and ordered it burned. He then released the women and children that had been captured.

This battle was the only significant engagement of the entire expedition but considered a success as a fort had been established on the Bozeman Trail. Not so successful was the attempt to further a survey of the trail and make improvements to it. This expedition was turned back in the face of the Indian attacks, and Connor began to lose many of his Volunteer force. The regiments under his command contained a great number of Civil War volunteers whose terms of enlistment were up, and they were mustered out of service.

In all, the campaign only caused the Lakota, Cheyenne and Arapaho to be more resolute in their opposition to the Whites, and fighting in the Powder River Country grew into what would be called Red Cloud's War. The combined forces of these three tribes forced the closing of the Bozeman Trail from the North Platte River to the gold fields in Montana.

***

October 1865 – Moon When Thin Ice begins to form on Rivers

While General Connor was preparing his forces north of the Platte, Colonel James H. Ford, the commander of the troops along the Arkansas River, was gathering a force of almost seven thousand soldiers at Fort Larned. He was intent on attacking the Indians along the Cimarron, but Colonel Henry Leavenworth, who was the agent for the Kiowa, Comanche and Apache, convinced him to hold off his campaign until talks could be held with these tribes. Leavenworth was certain that a war could be avoided, and he convinced representatives from these tribes to meet on the Little Arkansas. With help from William Bent, and Silas Scott, the Southern Cheyenne and the Arapaho made a similar agreement. The president appointed a commission to negotiate the new treaty, headed by Major General John Sanborn and including; Major General William Harney, Colonel Leavenworth, Kit Carson, William Bent, Silas Scott and others.

When all were assembled, Sanborn began by addressing Black Kettle and apologizing for Sand Creek. He then offered to give three hundred and twenty acres to each chief and one hundred and sixty acres to each woman or child who had lost parents in the massacre. All the rest of the land that had been part of the treaty in 1861 as Cheyenne Territory was to be ceded to the government.

Silas had argued prior to the council that the land that was offered already belonged to the Cheyenne. But his protests were dismissed as a matter of what was best to obtain peace. And as Silas predicted, Black Kettle, speaking for the Cheyenne, refused the offer.

"There are only eighty lodges of my people here." He spoke of the Southern Cheyenne. *"The rest, more than four hundred lodges, are north of the Fat River. There are also only one hundred and ninety lodges of our brothers the Southern Arapaho, here, and three hundred and ninety lodges of them are also in the north. I do not wish to make agreements about the land for I know it will cause trouble when those in the north return. I have always been friendly to the Whites but since the killing of my People on Dry Creek, I find it hard to trust the Whiteman.*

"Look," he said, and he had his wife, Medicine Woman, brought in and she showed where she had been wounded at Sand Creek. *"Even after she lay on the ground, wounded, the soldiers shot again and again into her body. Nine times she was shot."*

When Black Kettle was done speaking, Little Raven got up and spoke for the Arapaho. *"You offer my people land north of the Fat River, but this land you have already given to the Sioux. And, the land you offer south of the Meat River, you have already given to the Comanche and the Kiowa. If my people accept these lands and move onto them, we will at once be at odds with the tribes to whom the land rightfully belongs."*

The debate was useless, and the chiefs present were finally persuaded to sign the new treaty in hopes that some peace could be achieved. Though only a sixth of the Cheyenne were represented, the Southern Cheyenne gave up all their lands between the Arkansas and the Platte Rivers. They were still permitted to hunt in that region, but agreed to settle on a reservation established for them south of the Arkansas River. They were not to go within ten miles of any main traveled road, post, or station without permission. The Arapaho also agreed to the stipulation of this new treaty.

As part of the treaty, the U.S. government admitted guilt for Sand Creek Massacre and agreed to pay reparations to Cheyenne families who lost relatives and property caused by the actions of the troops. Signing the treaty for the Cheyenne were; Black Kettle, Seven Bulls, Little Robe, Black Whiteman, Eagle Head, and Bull That Hears. Signing for the Arapahos were; Little Raven, Storm, Big Mouth, Spotted Wolf, Black Man, Chief In Everything and Haversack.

With two blankets, a sack of coffee and sugar in hand, Silas went through the Cheyenne camp and found the lodge of Crow Eyes. The half-breed son of Mary Craigavon looked older than his forty plus years, and though glad to see Silas, there was no longer the warm feeling of seeing an old friend. He greeted Silas politely, offering a place to sit in the lodge.

"My heart is sad for you," Silas said in Cheyenne, *"And, for all the People."*

"There is no need for pity," Crow Eyes said in English, "It was inevitable that someday there would be more White men than Cheyenne. The troubles in the north have only just began, and when the rest of the Southern Cheyenne bands return in the winter, I am afraid things will become worse."

"I wish we could go back to the days before all this," Silas said.

Crow Eyes gave a short laugh, and said, "Silas, remember what we have been taught, only the earth and sky last forever."

Silas looked around the lodge and its poor furnishings, and asked, "Where is Meets the Enemy?"

"She fell at Sand Creek."

"Oh, Crow, I am sorry. What of Little Wolf, I had been expecting to see him at the talks?"

"He refuses to witness what he calls, 'Drinking from a river of sand'."

"He is here, in the camp?"

"Yes, he shares this lodge with me and Red Elk. Between the boy and I, we get by."

There was a rustling of the door flap, and Little Wolf came into the lodge, followed by the boy, Red Elk. Little Wolf's back was bent with the weight of years and the sorrow of his people. His hair had turned gray, and his body had grown thin, almost frail looking. When he looked up, he noticed Silas and it was if new life had burst in him.

"Aw, Silas Scott! It is good to see you, my friend." He moved over and took a seat next to Silas, reaching out and clasping his hand.

"I am happy to see you too, my little horse thief!" Silas said, recalling the first time they had met.

Little Wolf smiled, remembering how as a boy, he and his friends had tried to steal Silas' horses. The memory was bittersweet, as it was the first time Little Wolf had seen a White man, and from that day his life had changed.

"I have brought you some gifts," Silas said, pointing to the blankets, coffee and sugar.

"That is kind my friend," he said and then noting that Crow Eyes had not offered their guest anything to eat, turned to Red Elk and instructed the boy to offer Silas some dried buffalo. Silas took only a small piece, as the parfleche bag seemed to be light.

"Things haven't turned out too good, have they?" Silas said.

"No, they have not," said Wolf, "But the sun has not set yet for the People."

"I hope you are right," Silas shook his head. Wolf looked at Silas and then remembered that Silas must be over eighty years old. "You have seen many winters haven't you Silas?"

"A few," Silas answered, "But, I have Willow and her husband to look after me at the ranch." Then he laughed, and added, "You'll find this strange, but the ranch sits pretty much where I met you for the first time!"

"I remember. You were terrifying to a young boy on his first horse raid." He let out a small laugh.

"You know Wolf, there will always be a place for you in my home, for as long as I live."

"I am grateful for the offer, but I believe I will end my days as I have lived those before, in the freedom of the plains."

Silas understood, and asked, "Do you know the where-a-bouts for my son?"

"Little Gun rides with the Dog Soldiers, As does my son, Little Bear. They are in the north, near the Powder River, but I believe they will return south before winter sets in," said Crow Eyes.

"I see," Silas' eyes began to mist, and before he allowed tears to fall, he said, "Please tell him that I ask about him, and that there is a place in my heart for him no matter what."

"I will do this," said Wolf, and the three men sat and chatted until the sun set. When the hours grew late, they all slept in the lodge, more like family than friends.

In December, most of the Southern Cheyenne returned from the Powder River country, and though they were unhappy with the new treaty, most of them accepted it as binding. The Dog Soldiers however, refused to accept as it had ceded their land between the Republican and the Smokey Hill. The war on the Plains was far from over.

***

SAM J. PISCIOTTA

CHAPTER TWENTY-ONE
THE MEDICINE LODGE AND THE WASHITA

April 1866 – Moon of Budding Trees

Efforts to convince more of the Cheyenne bands to sign off on the Treaty of the Little Arkansas were pursued by Indian Agent Wynkoop, with little success. Zachary stood by, curious as another council with Wynkoop was held near Fort Dodge. He had come in with Big Head and Rock Forehead's Dog soldiers and watched as both of these leaders refused to sign the new treaty. Not achieving this first goal, Wynkoop asked the Dog Soldier' permission for the building of a railroad through their country along the Smoky Hill Road. This, the Dogs Soldiers also refused.

These talks would have been considered a failure by most, but Wynkoop did manage to secure the freedom of a White captive, Mary Fletcher. Mary was taken by Sand Hill's band of Cheyenne during a raid near Fort Halleck, in August, and Sand Hill had traded the girl off to John Smith who then turned her over to Wynkoop. Tensions seemed to cool, and a small party of Cheyenne even moved up closer to the Fort.

Trading became brisk and it seemed as if it had become business as usual. A trader, Tom Boggs, heard that a Cheyenne Dog Soldier, White Beaver, had in his possession ten one-hundred-dollar bills. White Beaver had kept these pretty pieces of paper since the raid at Julesburg, and Boggs engaged the Cheyenne into making a trade, the ten one-hundred-dollar bills for eleven crisp one dollar-bills. When White Beaver showed the money to Zachary, his friend explained that he had been cheated.

With Zachary and three other warriors, White Beaver took after Boggs, who barely outdistanced the angry warrior, taking refuge in the fort. His anger still hot, White Beaver and his companions started back to their camp. On their way, they ran across Boggs' young son a few miles from the fort. White Beaver, acting on a Cheyenne's idea that revenge on a member of the guilty party's family was the same as exacting revenge on that man himself, killed Boggs' son.

This killing caused little excitement, and there remained an uneasy calm throughout the west, with only a few minor incidents. In May, the overland Stage and Telegraph Office at Deer Creek Station lost two mules and nine steers, driven off by Indians. The following month, six cattle and a colt were stolen from the ranch of William T. Wilds in Lincoln County, Kansas.

In August, Wynkoop held another council on the Smokey Hill with eight Cheyenne Chiefs, who in exchange for six hundred ponies, supplies, and the return of two Cheyenne children taken at Sand Creek, promised to hold their young warriors in check. The month had not passed though, when Roman Nose and Spotted Horse began to threaten violence unless the Smoky Hills country was abandoned by the Whites.

As if to emphasize their refusal of any new treaty, Dog Soldiers attacked two freight trains within two days of each other, running off over one hundred oxen, and either destroying or taking the provisions of both trains. Only a single teamster was killed, but the message was clear, the peace was fragile.

The real end to peace occurred the last week of December. Oglala chief, Red Cloud, had been negotiating with the army out of Fort Laramie, complaining about emigrants settling in Sioux territory. When he was unable to reach agreement with the Government negotiators, he no longer held back the war parties who then attacked emigrants and Army patrols. These hit and run tactics were more than the military could deal with, relief always arriving too late to engage the Indians.

Lakota, Northern Cheyenne and Northern Arapaho executed the well-proven tactic of luring overconfident soldiers into a trap near Fort Phil Kearney. This time, there was no mistakes and those Indians who made up the trap exercised self-discipline. The Indians had been harassing woodcutters from the Fort, and Captain W. J. Fetterman with a column of eighty men, were assigned to protect them. When a group of warriors attacked the woodcutters, Fetterman could not pass up the chance at a fight. He disobeyed orders, that under no circumstance was he to engage or pursue Indians. He especially was forbidden to cross Lodge Trail Ridge in pursuit of Indians. Fetterman was desperate to prove his superiority in battle against Indians, once proclaiming, "give me eighty men and I can ride through the whole Sioux Nation." He gave the orders to follow the Indian decoys and crossed over Lodge Trail Ridge, where he and his entire command fell into the trap. Later that day, their stripped and mutilated bodies were found by a relief patrol. The Indians soon called this fight the Battle of the Hundred in the Hand.

***

February 1867 – Big Hoop Moon

The kitchen at the Scott Ranch had grown to be the gathering place for the men to discuss business. On this frigid morning, Silas, Eli, August, and William Craigavon with his son Ransom, sat enjoying hot coffee and a special treat of a cobbler made from the last of the dried apples covered with a biscuit crust.

"I could get spoiled pretty easy if you made this more often," Silas said to Willow.

"If I fed this to you every day, I couldn't get you out of the house to do much of anything!" she teased back.

"Well, it sure is better than the pie my Ma makes," said Ransom, receiving a playful cuffing from his father.

"You had best not let her hear you talk like that or you'll be eating hard bread and water," William said.

"We should get back to discussing our agreement for the coming year," August said, attempting to bring the conversation away from his wife's cooking to the reason they were gathered.

"Do you think we really need to have a written contract?" Eli asked William, "We're all friends and there ain't one of you I wouldn't trust with my life, let alone my business."

"It's not a matter of trust. It's a matter of lawyers. Now-a-days more than ever," said William. "Something happens to any one of us, we need to know that some slick-talking fellow with a law book in his hand doesn't take what we've built and toss our loved ones out in the cold."

"I'm still not sure I like this place called the Scott Ranch," Silas said, "It ain't mine, it belongs to August and Eli."

"We've done that to make it easier, and it sounds better than the Klausen & Thornton Ranch," Eli half kidded.

"Ja, it is better. Anyways, our names are on the papers as partners with you," August said, "Vithout you, there vould be no ranch here any vay."

"That's fine with me then. Just don't make me sit here and listen to you read the whole damn thing again," Silas sniffed, and then asked for another helping of cobbler.

"We are all in agreement then?" asked William, and each of the men said yes. In turn they each placed their signature on the paper, and the partnership between the Craigavon and Scott Ranches was officially formed. Each ranch would maintain its own boundaries, but the operations of the two would be joint, offering an amount of insurance if one venture or another failed.

"That's done and I'd toast with a good whiskey, but I don't think my Maggie would appreciate imbibing this early in the day," Eli said.

"Be good enough if I just had me another helping of that apple pudding," Silas suggested.

"We have one last thing to discuss," said William, "You all know that Charles Goodnight and his partner Oliver Loving brought two thousand head of cattle up from Texas last year and made over $12,000. They sold the majority to the Army at Fort Sumner. They then drove the rest to Denver making a healthy profit.

"It's not too late for us to consider it this year. I still believe we could make an agreement with Goodnight & Loving to purchase and bring cattle up here to raise on the two ranches. We can buy cattle for as little as eight dollars a head and if we fatten them up here first, we can sell them for twenty-eight to thirty dollars."

"You've been talking about us going down to Texas to bring the cattle back ourselves. I'm not sure about leaving our families alone, Billy," Eli said.

"That's a valid concern, but we'll leave enough hands here to make sure things stay safe, and there hasn't been any trouble to speak of for the past year."

"That's true for down here along the Arkansas, but trouble is brewing up north in Montana Territory. You know what happened up at Fort Kearny not over a month ago. It was in the Chieftain newspaper. The Lakota killed over a hundred soldiers under Fetterman. And, there's talk of closing the Bozeman Road," said Eli.

"True, but that's up north, and it doesn't seem that the Cheyenne or Arapaho in the south were involved. For the most part, I think the ranches will be safe. We'll not take all the vaqueros with us. We can hire some down there."

"You best give it more thought," Silas said.

"Why, you see something we don't?" William asked.

"No, don't see no sign, but I feel there's big trouble brewing," Silas said, then suggested, "I'd make all your plans for next year, feel out Goodnight and look at the pasture land near Rayado for wintering the cattle as an option rather than pay that pirate Dick Wootton ten cents a head to pass over Raton Pass. Just because things have been quiet down our way, you all know when something gets pushed, something else pushes back. And, the Indians don't like being pushed."

"Do the rest of you feel this way?" William asked.

"It vould be good to know if trouble was coming," said August.

"I tend to lean toward the cautious side too," added Eli, "Is there any way we could get a feeling if the Cheyenne or Arapaho along the Arkansas are planning something when the grass greens up?"

"I'll send a letter to William Bent, down at Big Timbers. If there are any hints of trouble, he might have news." He paused, then said, "I would guess unless we hear to the contrary, the tribes aren't planning war in the spring."

It took little time for news to reach the upper Arkansas, and the partners learned that there had been trouble in both the Dakota Territory and near Fort Larned in Kansas. Close to Fort Laramie, employees of the telegraph company were killed, and a detachment of soldiers out of Fort Reno had been attacked.

Word from some of the traders who had been in the Indian camps through the winter confirmed that the bands between the Smoky Hills and the Arkansas were waiting for their ponies to fatten up. Though there had not been much unrest in the south, General William Tecumseh Sherman, Commander of the Military Division of Missouri was convinced that, the killings along the Smoky Hill the previous summer and the annihilation of Fetterman's men in December meant that the Cheyenne, Arapaho and the Lakota must be exterminated as they would not settle down. General Hancock was ordered to take his command into the field.

Hancock had in his force; eleven companies of the 7th Cavalry, under the command of Civil War hero Lieutenant

Colonel George Armstrong Custer, seven companies of the 37th Infantry, and a battery of the 4th Artillery. This brought the expedition's number to fourteen-hundred soldiers.

News that Hancock was headed from Fort Larned made the Cheyenne uneasy, and they viewed the movement of so many troops as a declaration of war. As soon as the bands came together war parties were made up and raids began. All thoughts of leaving the ranches on the Arkansas unmanned for a trip to Texas was postponed by William, August and Eli.

***

June 1867 – Fattening Up Moon

Zachary sat on a willow backrest in the shade, smoking a pipe and talking with his friends. The past four moons among the People, had been more exciting than his first four years with them. It had started during the moon of Budding Trees, when General Hancock approached the combined village of Cheyenne and Lakota about thirty-five miles west of Fort Larned. There were over two-hundred and fifty lodges, half of these belonging to Dog Soldiers.

"I will tell my children and my grandchildren about the day, on Red Arm Creek, when Hooked Nose stood in front of the Soldier Chief and almost killed him." Small Belly spoke of Roman Nose and Hancock.

"The white Soldier Chief should have listened to Tall Bull when he warned him not to come too close to the village," said Wolf Horn. *"Hooked Nose wanted to kill him right there in front of his men. It is good that the women and children were getting away while the chiefs were talking with the soldiers."*

"I was there, and I remember when the Soldier Chief asked Hooked Nose why the women were leaving, Hooked Nose told him women and children were more timid than men. He said the warriors of the People were not afraid. He asked if the Soldier Chief had heard what had happened on Dry Creek to Black Kettle's people. Then told him that he and his pony-soldiers looked just like those who had killed women and children there," said Blue Crane.

"It was then that Hooked Nose told Bull Bear to go back to the line of warriors because he was going to kill the Soldier Chief," said Wolf Horn boasted.

"It might have been a bad day if Bull Bear had not stopped Hooked Nose," said Zachary, "The big guns were aimed at the village and many would have been killed."

"It is of no matter. We slipped away and left the White Soldiers in our dust," Wolf Horn.

"Yes, but we lost all the lodges and belongings left behind," said Zachary.

"You still think like a White man sometimes, Yellow Horse. Lodges can be replaced, there are more buffalo than there are stars in the sky!" Blue Crane laughed.

Zachary laughed also, and he and his friends talked of the more than five dozen raids that had been made over the past four moons.

"I believe it is a bad thing that the Wolf People are now wearing the blue coats of the White Soldiers, and have the firearms that shoot many times without having to be reloaded," Pole Cat spoke of the Pawnee scouts armed with Spencer repeating carbines.

"We must have firearms like those," said Zachary, "Some of our warriors already have these, or ones similar."

"Bear Voice would not approve." Wolf Horn knew he was touching a subject that at times frustrated Zachary.

"He will have to change someday," Zachary said, "If he does not, he will be left behind like many of the old men." What his friends didn't know was that Zachary intended to procure a rifle the first chance he had. In the raids he had participated in, he had not killed a soldier, and as such hadn't the chance to take a firearm. During the period of relative peace, when he was around some of the White traders, he found they only offered the English or Belgium Trade Guns, and these were not what he wanted. He still had in his possession the paper money that he had taken at Julesburg, and knew it was more than what he needed. The firearm he coveted was either the 1860 Henry, or the Spencer carbine. Both of these employed mantellic cartridges, and once loaded would fire several shots before needing to be reloaded. If he could not find one in trade, he would wait for a chance to take one in battle. Would Bear Voice object? Of course, but sooner or later Zachary knew he would have to face the man and take control of his own life.

Zachary would be patient. He had learned this well. Bear Voice had protested when Zachary first revealed he had the steel knife and he intended to keep it. At first, his uncle went into his usual tirade against anything made by the White man's medicine. He eventually gave in, but as was his way, he turned his wrath on someone weaker. This day it was his wife Buffalo Cow Woman. With no warning, he began to beat her with his quart, raising angry red welts on her back and arms. Sees Far was wise enough to stay off to one side, and out of reach. She knew that if Bear Voice took his rage out on Buffalo Cow, then she might be safe, especially if she stayed out of sight. So, she slunk away with a twisted smile on her face.

This had been a small victory for Zachary, but he was not finished in his battle for independence from Bear Voice. He intended to find a rifle and use it in combat. He reasoned that if he had stayed at the ranch on the Arkansas, he would have had a one of his own by now. It was only right that he owned a real weapon of war.

There was also the matter of the red-haired girl, with the pail eyes. He would also be patient in his hope that she was still with the Northern Cheyenne, and that someday he would see her again.

***

July 1867 – Moon of the Ripening Chokeberries

On June 1st, Whit, armed with a new Henry repeating rifle, left Fort Hays, Kansas scouting for Lieutenant Colonel George Custer and eleven hundred men of the 7th Cavalry. Custer had been ordered to quell the Indian uprisings which were threatening the area. And though Custer had a certain charm, Whit wasn't fond of his commander, finding him arrogant and a braggart. The less time he spent in the presence of Custer, the better he liked it. He did take a liking to the commander of H Company, Captain Frederick William Benteen. Like Benteen's men, Whit found the officer courageous and honorable. Whit respected and trusted Benteen.

After the 7th patrolled north to Fort McPherson on the Platte River, they headed south to the forks of the Republican River, arriving in July. There, while scouting ahead of the column, Whit spied what he thought were smoke signals, but no hostiles were found and the column moved on. Custer, having received no word from General Sherman as expected, moved his troops toward Fort Sedgwick. Upon his arrival at Riverside Station, about forty miles to the west of Sedgwick, he telegraphed Sherman for orders. A return message informed him that a patrol under Lieutenant Lyman S. Kidder had been sent out to intercept him with orders. Concerned for their safety, Custer left immediately and headed back south, sending out scouts ahead of the column in search of Kidder.

Twenty-five-year-old Lieutenant Lyman S. Kidder, of Company M, 2nd Cavalry, had been ordered to find Custer and give him the messages from General Sherman. With an Indian Guide named Red Bead, he led his ten-man patrol to where Custer and his men were believed to be encamped on the forks of the Republican River. Upon reaching Custer's campsite on the evening of July 1st, he found it abandoned. He had no way of knowing that Custer had left the area, scouting further south rather than northwest. As darkness began to fall, the Lieutenant mistook a trail of the supply wagons that Custer had sent to Fort Wallace for that of Custer's and followed the wrong path.

By noon the following day, Kidder reached Beaver Creek, a tributary of the Republican, where his detachment was discovered by a group of Lakota and Cheyenne. As the warriors approached Kidder and his troops, the soldiers veered off to the southeast, making for the valley of Beaver Creek. As they reached the ridge above the creek, some of the soldiers were shot down. The rest of them made it to a defensive position in a small gully about fifty yards north of the creek where they would make their stand.

The Lakota dismounted and crept up on foot, while the Cheyenne circled around the gully and came in from that direction. Zachary moved through the grass, his bow and several arrows in his left hand, and an arrow ready to be set into place in his right. He felt he must be directly on top of the soldiers. His heart was beating so fiercely in his chest he feared they would hear it. The first war cry almost startled him, and he paused before rising to his feet, nocking the arrow as he rose. With a practiced motion, he loosed one arrow after another, as bullets from the defending soldiers whizzed past. He heard shouting from the Whites and more war cries, one so close it surprised him when he realized it was his own yell.

When he had no further arrows, Zachary pulled his knife from its rawhide sheath and dove at a blue-coated figure. The man swung his carbine, but misjudged Zachary's speed and the swing went wild, missing him. Zachary's judgement was unflawed and using his weight he knocked the soldier over. Falling forward with the soldier, Zachary held on to him with his left hand. Once on top of the soldier he plunged the knife up under the man's ribs.

The man let out a grunt, but there was defiance in his eyes, and he reached up and placed his hand on Zachary's throat. He had dirty blond hair and a mustache and goatee that curved around his mouth, his lips were drawn back exposing clenched teeth. His face was a ruddy sun-burnt red, and rather than scream in pain, he shouted, "DAMN YOU! YOU SON-OF-A-BITCH!"

Zachary felt the man's grip tightening on his throat and was afraid that he may pass out. He pulled the knife from the soldier's ribs and plunged it in again, and again, until blood began to spurt from the blond-man's mouth. With a final scream of defiance, the man released his grip on Zachary and went limp, his pale eyes staring up into the clear sky. Zachary fell to one side, struggling to regain his breath, and found it hard to swallow. The fighting went on around him and it seemed as if no one noticed him or the dead trooper.

When he could finally stand, the killing was over, and though the soldiers fought valiantly, Kidder and all his men were hopelessly outnumbered. Zachary stood over the body of the trooper and thought how brave the man was to have fought so hard until his last breath. He had looked Zachary straight in the eyes and for this reason, Zachary did not take the man's scalp, nor did he cut the body in any fashion. Out of respect, he lay the man out on his back and folded the dead man's arms across his chest. What Zachary did take was the man's carbine, a Spencer carbine. For this, he thanked the dead soldier.

On July 12th, Whit and two other scouts came upon the decomposed bodies of Kidder and his party in the ravine. The bodies had been badly mutilated, and all had been scalped except the Indian guide and a single blond-haired trooper. When Custer and the rest of the company arrived, the Lieutenant

Colonel ordered the unidentifiable remains buried on the spot in a common grave.

Throughout the rest of July and on into August, Custer's campaign on the Republican and the Smokey Hill proved to be a dismal failure. He was unsuccessful in striking the Indians and couldn't protect the lines of travel along the roads. The soldiers were easily avoided when they were in large numbers, and they moved slowly with their baggage and wagons. Only the small details of troopers were engaged. The Indians continued their raids and sparred with the soldiers over a dozen times resulting in few casualties on either side.

Adding to the Army's frustration of not being able to chastise the Indians, a cholera epidemic broke out. And, fearing for the safety of his wife, Libbey, Custer left his command at Fort Wallace, traveling to her at Fort Harker. This contributed to the list of Custer's unfavorable actions, and General Hancock charged him with leave without permission. In mid-September 1867, Lieutenant Colonel George Armstrong Custer was court martialled on seven charges, including; deserting his command, ordering deserters to be shot, damaging army horses, failing to pursue Indians attacking his escort and not recovering bodies of soldiers killed by Indians. He was found guilty of five of the charges and specifications against him. The result of the verdict by the court was for Custer to be suspended from rank and command for one year and forfeit his pay for the same time. With Custer gone, Whit stayed attached to the 7th Cavalry, and it seemed to him the attitude of the soldiers was better without Custer.

The ability to control the west and keep travel safe kept slipping away. The Northern Cheyenne, under their leader, Turkey Leg, became so bold as to take out a culvert under the railroad tracks and derail a Union pacific freight train before dawn on August 6th. As many of the trains crew that could be found were killed, and the boxcars looted. Bolts of calico and silk, sacks of flour, sugar and coffee, were loaded on to the Cheyenne ponies, and a few of the boxcars were set on fire. When daylight came, goods from the boxcars were found strewn across the prairie.

After packing up as much of the goods as they could carry, the Cheyenne headed south toward the Republican where they came upon a band of Lakota. On hearing of the plunder that still littered the prairie, the Lakota and a few of the Cheyenne decided to go back to the wreckage for a second load. Believing there was little danger, they brought with them women and children.

Unknown to the Indians, word of the derailment had spread all along the telegraph line, and Major Frank North loaded sixty of his Pawnee scouts onto a special train and sped toward the site, arriving just before the Indian's return. Armed with their Spencer carbines, the Pawnee drove the Cheyenne and the Lakota back, capturing a single woman and a small boy.

More raids occurred in Kansas and Nebraska, while south of the Arkansas only a few took place. So it was, the Government made an appeal to the Indians for an affirmation of peace with another treaty. With the intent to negotiate a lasting peace in mind, a council with the Cheyenne, Arapaho, Kiowa, Comanche, Kiowa Apache, and the U.S. commissioners was pursued. A site along Medicine Lodge Creek was chosen as it provided a somewhat neutral territory. For a month prior to the meeting the Indian Bureau assembled a vast amount of material near Medicine Lodge to give as presents to the Indians. These stores included coffee, sugar, flour, dried fruits, arms and ammunition, and a herd of cattle.

Carefully chosen from both military men and civilians, the Peace Commission arrived in Kansas. Generals Terry, Harney, Sanborn, and Auger represented the army, while Commissioner Taylor upheld the interests of the Indian Bureau. Senator Henderson, of Missouri, represented congress and Col. Samuel F. Tappan stood for the nation at large.

In late October, the tribes began to gather at Medicine Lodge Creek, the Cheyenne Dog Soldiers under Tall Bull the last to appear. Standing with some of the officers from the 7th Cavalry, Whit watched as the Dog Soldiers arrived. They crossed the creek on one front and emerged from the woods, and then formed up in a battle line. They fired their guns into the air, all the while singing and yelling. They were dressed in their finest clothes and painted. Whit looked out on the warriors, hoping to catch a glimpse of his son, but the two-hundred Dog Soldiers all looked so much alike to him, that it was hopeless. He thought there was still a chance Zachary might be among the throng of Cheyenne present, and believed he might be drawn to the negotiations, so he went to look for him there.

George Bent acted as interpreter for the Indians, and the negotiations in his opinion marked the beginning of the end of the Cheyenne as free independent warriors and hunters. The tribes agreed to allow the construction and operation of railroads in the Platte and Smoky Hill valleys, to abandon attacks on white travelers, wagon trains, and settlements, and to "never kill or scalp white men, nor attempt to do them any harm." The tribes also agreed to cede lands in Colorado Territory and Kansas for a reservation in Indian Territory bounded by the Cimarron and Arkansas Rivers. Legal title of the land, however, remained with Congress. Fourteen Cheyenne leaders signed the treaty, including Black Kettle, Wolf Robe, Tall Bull, Bull Bear, White Horse, and Whirlwind.

Whit payed little attention to the talks. As they proceeded, he looked from face to face of those gathered and his frustration grew, not being able to find Zachary. But, hidden among those gathered with the Cheyenne warriors, Zachary watched his father. Something inside made him want to go to Whit, to talk to him, but he had no idea what he would say. When the talks were over, he turned and walked away with the rest of the Cheyenne.

***

August 1868 – Breeding Moon

After the signing of the Medicine Lodge Treaty, the Cheyenne were required to move south to the new reservation in Indian Territory. They were persuaded to give up their traditional territory for one with little arable land and away from the buffalo, their main source of meat. They upheld months of fragile peace, until the end of March the following year when war parties of Southern Cheyenne and allied Arapaho, Kiowa, Comanche, Northern Cheyenne, Brulé and Oglala Lakota, and Pawnee warriors attacked white settlements in western Kansas, southeast Colorado, and northwest Texas. First, horses owned by Frank Schernerhorn, in Lincoln County, Kansas disappeared. Then, in April, eighteen horses were stolen near Fort Wallace. And in the first four days of June, twenty-one raids were committed.

The month of August brought about raids north of Fort Harker, along the Solomon and Saline Rivers. A force of over two-hundred warriors attacked killing fifteen settlers, wounding others, and taking female captives. Half a dozen houses were plundered and burned. Two days later, the Indians attacked in seven different locations, along the Solomon and the Saline as well as the Pawnee Fork on the Cimarron. Five more homes were burned, and fifteen more civilians were killed.

During the winter, and the months leading up to these raids, Zachary had thought many times about returning to the White world. Food had become scarce, and worst of all he had become bored. The thought of going on a raid excited him and when the opportunity to go out against the Pawnee arose, he was more than ready. When the war party left Walnut Creek, Zachary carried his Spencer in a buckskin sheath slung across his back. Bear Voice had gone into a tirade when Zachary showed up with the firearm, but when his rage had cooled, See Far showed him the sheath, decorated with her special symbols. She convinced him that if he were to use his medicine, he could place a protective shield around the Spencer that would protect them from harm. Zachary was then allowed to keep the carbine, and only remove it during battle. All other times, the "Medicine Stick" of the White man was to remain covered and hidden.

It was while the war party was traveling north that it ran across the first White ranch. The decision was made that it would be far easier to take from the whites that were close at hand, rather than risk the journey farther north to fight the Pawnee. To Zachary, it mattered little. He was content so long as he was kept active and didn't have to spend his time with Bear Voice and Sees Far Woman badgering him.

The decision to raid the Whites gave Zachary an unexpected surprise. Near Fort Dodge, they attacked the camp of a lime contractor, and though they only ran off two horses, they found several rifles and ammunition. To Zachary's delight, there were several boxes of .56-50 cartridges. As his was the only weapon that the ammunition would fit, he was the beneficiary of all the boxes. Now he could load seven rounds through the butt of the carbine, and with a simple downward pull of the trigger guard, he could reload after each shot.

***

Raids occurred the same day, August 13th, along the Republican, the Pawnee Fork of the Cimarron, and back on the Saline River. Whit was scouting for Company H of the 7th

Cavalry under Captain Benteen when they engaged a party of Dog Soldiers raiding a ranch. Benteen ordered a charge into a force of what appeared to be about fifty warriors. To his surprise, there were more than two-hundred Cheyenne in the raiding party. Caught off guard by the sudden appearance of soldiers, the Indians retreated, and H Company pursued them, engaging them throughout the day without respite or rest until dark.

Whit fought alongside the soldiers, taking careful aim with his Henry. Not only did he want to conserve his ammunition, but since the Medicine Lodge Treaty, he had wondered if the next Indian he shot could possibly be his own son. Each time he pulled the trigger, a small part of him ached.

That day, he knew one Cheyenne had fallen from his marksmanship. When the skirmish ended, he personally examined the Cheyenne he had slain and three others who had been killed by the soldiers. None of the them looked even remotely like Zachary. He had no way of knowing Zachary was miles away, but he felt something like grief for those laying on the ground. His mood was broken though, when two white women who had been taken a few days earlier were found safe. Whit was relieved, his apprehension returned the following day when he was involved in another skirmish with the Cheyenne. This time, four Indians were killed, and several wounded. Again, Zachary was not among the dead.

The audacity of the Dog Soldiers seemed to intensify throughout the remainder of August and September with a raid happening almost every day. The Army sent out elements of the 7th, 5th, and 10th Cavalry as well as the 3rd Infantry to quell what appeared to be a total uprising on the plains, but the Indians fought back at every chance. On the Arikara Fork of the Republican River, Colonel George A. Forsyth and a company of fifty scouts, found themselves surrounded by a combined force of Cheyenne and Lakota Dog Soldiers from September 17th until the 25th. The scouts took refuge on a small island in the river and held off the Indians until they were relieved by the 10th Cavalry. During the engagement, the scouts lost six killed, and suffered fifteen wounded. The Dog Soldiers faired far worse, and among those killed was Roman Nose.

More raids followed through the months of October and November, with wagon trains, ranches and even Fort Zarah attacked. So, General Philip Sheridan devised a plan of punitive reprisals. He decided his troops would respond by striking the Indians in their winter camps. While difficult, a winter campaign offered decisive results. By destroying the hostile's shelter, food, and livestock, the warriors and their women and children would at the mercy of the Army and the elements. They would be forced to surrender. To help with this campaign, Sheridan fought to get his "Golden Boy" reinstated. He brought back Lt. Col. George Armstrong Custer early from his court-martial and gave him the mission. Sheridan trusted only Custer with such a deed, and in November 1868 Custer returned to his regiment under special orders from Sheridan.

***

November 1868 – Hard Faced Moon

Black Kettle's camp joined other Southern Cheyenne, Arapahoe, Kiowa, Comanche, and Kiowa Apache bands on the Lodgepole River. As many still blamed him for what had happened at Sand Creek, his village was the westernmost of a series of camps that ran fifteen miles along the river. There were almost a dozen miles between his and the rest of the camps. Black Kettle's camp was comprised of one-hundred Cheyenne, and a few Arapaho and Lakota lodges, clustered on the south side of the river, and contained about two-hundred and fifty-men, women and children.

Downriver from Black Kettle's camp where the Washita looped northward in a large oxbow, were the one-hundred and fifty Arapaho lodges making up the camp of Little Raven. At the bottom of the loop was a large Southern Cheyenne camp under Medicine Arrows, and nearby was another smaller Cheyenne camp consisting of the followers of Old Whirlwind. These two Cheyenne villages were west of a small Kiowa camp headed by Kicking Bird. Further downriver were other camps of Comanches and Kiowa Apache. Overall, there was a total of about six-thousand Indians in winter camp along the upper Washita River.

Along with Little Robe of the Cheyenne, and Big Mouth and Spotted Wolf of the Arapaho, Black Kettle went to Fort Cobb to visit the post trader, Bill Griffenstein. Griffenstein had sent a message urging Black Kettle to come to talk with Colonel William B. Hazen, who commanded the fort, about making peace. The four chiefs met with Hazen and Black Kettle spoke of his concerns.

"My people, when south of the Meat River, do not wish to return to the north side because they feared trouble there, but we are continually told that we had better go there, as they would be rewarded for so doing." He spoke of the annuities that had been given to the Cheyenne at Fort Larned and Fort Dodge, north of the Arkansas, both posts outside the agreed upon reservation for his people.

Black Kettle continued, asking if he might move his people south to Fort Cobb, saying, *"The People do not fight at all this side of the Meat River, but north of the Meat River there is almost always war. North of the Meat River, not long ago, some the young men were fired upon by the soldiers and then the fight began. I have always done my best to keep my young men quiet, but some will not listen, and since the fighting began, I have not been able to keep them all at home. But we all want peace, and I would be glad to move all my people down this way. I could then keep them all quietly near camp. My camp is now on the Lodge Pole River, east of the Antelope Hills, and I have there about one-hundred and eighty lodges. I speak only for my own people; I cannot speak nor control the Cheyenne north of the Meat River."*

Colonel Hazen told Black Kettle and the other chiefs that he had no authority to make any arrangement with them and advised them to go back to their winter camp. On the following day, Black Kettle and the other chiefs left Fort Cobb with food supplied to them by Griffenstein. Traveling through storm conditions in snow over a foot deep, it would take them five long days to reach their villages on the Washita.

***

The winter storms along the plains of the Indian Territory could easily turn in to blizzards without warning. The sub-zero temperatures had the ability to kill those unprepared, and the intense winds churned up the snow making visibility completely obscured to the point where a person couldn't see their hand in front of their face.

Braced against the cold, Custer left Camp Supply with eleven companies of the 7th US Cavalry on November 23. Whit had discarded his old blanket coat replacing it with one of the double-breasted great coats the soldiers wore. It was made of

447

heavy blue wool, and it went down to the tops of his boots. The sleeves had cuffs that could be turned down for added protection to his hands, and the standup collar kept his neck warm. Attached to the coat was a cape that hung down past his elbows, and there was a split from the waist down the back seam, to allow for riding horseback. On his head, he wore a buffalo fur cap that covered his ears, and on his hands, mittens of the same material. Even dressed this way against the elements, he was cold.

After two days of travel in the bitter cold, the first sign of hostile Indians was found by Whit and an advanced patrol under Major Joel Elliott. A trail of over one hundred horses led toward the Washita River. Custer was convinced that he was headed in the right direction and decided to follow the tracks. The march south was drastically hampered due to a snowstorm with powerful winds and blowing snow, and soon the trail they followed was obliterated. Custer ordered patrols out, including Whit and the Osage scouts. By the morning of November 26th, the trail was discovered, and Custer immediately organized a pursuit with his command, leaving all his supply wagons behind with only a light guard. He pressed his troops forward, and they followed this new trail the rest of the day without break until nightfall. Then, the Lieutenant Colonel allowed only a brief rest, sending Major Elliott and his men on ahead, not wanting the Indians he pursued to get away. When there was sufficient moonlight to continue, the men were ordered back in the saddle and near nine o'clock that night the main body of the 7th caught up with Major Elliott's command, confident that they were near an Indian camp.

Custer with two Osage scouts as guides, took point and soon came across a winter camp on the Washita. He immediately made plans to surround the camp. During the remainder of the night, Custer divided his forces into four equal detachments, each moving into position to surround the encampment so that at first daylight, they could simultaneously converge on the village. Custer led the largest contingent, Major Joel Elliott and Captains William Thompson and Edward Myers led the others northeast and southwest. Whit wondered about the plan, for they were going to attack an unknown amount of Cheyenne, over unknown terrain. The valley in front of them was covered by eighteen inches of new snow, topped with a layer of ice. Ice also reached from bank to bank on the Washita. Just before dawn, the order was passed along lines for the men to remove their great coats and prepare to charge the village.

Whit could barely feel his frozen feet in his boots, and the hoar frost caused by his breath had frozen the hair of his mustache and beard so that when he moved his jaw or mouth, he felt ice breaking. Every breath he inhaled stung his lungs with icy needles. Knowing that with his mittens on he would have no control of his pistols, he had placed them inside his jacket. Now, his hands trembled, and the cold steel of his revolver burned in his grip. To warm them, he placed his hand and pistol between his arm and body. As he sat shivering, in the frigid predawn, the old apprehension of coming across Zachary during the battle returned. He pushed the thoughts away and concentrated on the job at hand. He looked to his right where Captain Benteen and Company H waited in the long line of those assigned to Major Elliott and was comforted by the thought he would be fighting in the company of good men. The sky in the east was just showing a slight glow of the coming dawn when a single gunshot pierced the frigid air and the sharp notes from a bugle called "CHARGE!"

From atop a knoll south of the camp, Custer watched as the soldiers drove into the village. Behind him, the regimental band played "Garry Owen", but only got halfway through the first stanza before their instruments froze up. The early morning frost and smoke from the gunfire obscured some of his view, but he could see the Cheyenne being driven from their lodges.

***

Little Wolf, wrapped in his blanket and covered by a buffalo robe, lay in the darkness of the lodge. He had spent a restless night, having had a disturbing dream. He envisioned himself running on all fours as a member of a pack of wolves, his limbs and body covered with thick gray fur. The pack pushed over the snow-covered ground in pursuit of a large elk, nipping at its hind legs. The wapiti finally stopped and spun around, turning on the wolves. Little Wolf and the rest of the pack soon encircled it, and each took a snap when the chance was offered. But the elk kicked with its hind hooves, striking those behind him, and with swings of his mighty rack, he impaled or broke the bones of others.

Little Wolf watched as the wolves and their puppies, were killed, their bodies lying in the blood-soaked snow. The elk turned on him, and sweeping his head upward caught Little Wolf with its antlers and threw him high into the air. He landed hard in the snow, wounded on the side of his head. He lay, mourning the little ones which had been scattered and killed by the powerful elk. With a start, he woke, drenched with sweat. He knew that this dream foretold the coming of some great disaster and wondered if the conversations of the previous evening had been the seed of it.

Upon returning from Fort Cobb, Black Kettle had held a council in his lodge, prompted by the events that had occurred over the past week. Three days prior, a group of one-hundred and fifty warriors, some from Black Kettles camp, had returned from raids on the White settlements in the Smokey Hill River country. These raids had disappointed Black Kettle, but there was little he could do to hold back the young men from his camp, let alone those of Medicine Arrows, Little Robe, and Old Whirlwind's camps.

The following evening, a party of Kiowa, returning from raiding the Utes, passed through Black Kettle's camp on their way to their own village. They told Black Kettle, and the others in the camp, that as they had passed near the Canadian River, they had seen a trail made by many horses and wagons leading toward the camps. The Cheyenne placed little value in this information, knowing that the White soldiers would never travel so far south in such wintry conditions. The Kiowa left for their own village further east along the river, convinced that they had done their part in warning the Cheyenne.

Black Kettle spoke with the principal men of his village about what he had learned at Fort Cobb about Sheridan's war plans, and the warning from the Kiowa. the discussion lasting into the early morning hours. It was finally decided that after the new snow cleared, they would send out runners to see if there were really soldiers in the area, and to talk with them. They wanted to dispel any misunderstandings and make it clear that Black Kettle's people wanted peace. They also decided it would be wise to move camp downriver, closer to the other Indian camps.

Black Kettle's wife, Medicine Woman, had been angry at her husband and the others. She felt it would have been wiser to have moved the camp that night and stood outside the lodge for a long time before resigning herself to her husband's decision.

Little Wolf had not voiced his opinion in the council, knowing that even as a medicine man, his words would have little weight that night. So, he had gone to his lodge, fell asleep and had his dream. Now, in the predawn, he heard the barking of a dog and felt the thunder of horses' hooves beating against the frozen ground, followed by gunfire and the shouts from outside, "Pony-Soldiers! Pony-Soldiers!"

The noise also woke Crow Eyes who asked, *"What is happening?"*

"The White soldiers are attacking. Get your gun," Wolf told him, and rising from his bed picked up his own firearm and exited the lodge to face the enemy.

People were running in every direction, most of them in their bare feet, some hardly clothed at all. Women and children screamed, and warriors shouted in the din and mist of the morning air. Wolf saw blue-coated troopers riding in between the lodges, firing their pistols at anyone who came into sight, so he raised his rifle and fired, knocking a soldier from the saddle.

At almost the same instant, there was a flash of bright light and Wolf's head was filled with pain. He fell back and lay in the snow looking into the morning sky, and thought, *"I go now. I go to the place of my grandfathers."* He blinked as blood flowed into his eyes and the world around him started to fade away. His last vision was that of Crow Eyes looking down on him, and then all was black.

Zachary rolled over in his bedding, and opening his eyes could see his own breath in the dim light inside the tipi. He could hear someone moving in their bedding and then saw the dark outline of Sees Far going to the firepit, and with gentle puffs of air from her mouth, bringing the coals to life. She then added kindling and a small blaze lit up the inside of the lodge. Soon, a good fire was going, and Zachary could feel the warmth chasing away the chill in the air.

"I sure could use a cup of coffee with sugar," Zachary said in English, completely confusing Sees Far.

"Did you speak to me?" she asked, her voice hushed least she wake Bear Voice.

"No, I said nothing," Zachary replied, knowing that this would play on her mind and she would think she was hearing spirits, and he laughed to himself.

He rose, and wrapped in a buffalo robe, went outside, and walked some distance from the lodge before relieving himself. Though it was bitterly cold, Zachary felt exhilarated, and ready to meet the day. He would go back inside and eat something, but only to appease Sees Far. Then, he would go in search of a friend's lodge where he knew he would be able to find coffee with sugar. "Sometimes Bear Voice and Sees Far have no idea what they are missing," he thought. As he walked back to the lodge, he thought he heard something, but it was far away, and he could not tell what the noise was.

It was almost an hour later that Zachary made his way through the camp of Old Whirlwind, to where Small Belly's lodge was. Small Belly had married the chief's niece the year before, her name being Falcon Woman, and Zachary found her to be very pretty. He often teased his friend that she was too beautiful for him.

"Ah," Small Belly would reply, *"She did not marry me for my looks, but for my powers in the buffalo robes! She has said more than once, that I should change my name to Buffalo Penis!"* He would then laugh.

Falcon Woman made delicious, plump fried bread, and she would sprinkle sugar on them when it was available. Zachary's mouth watered as he thought of these. Though still not as good as Maggie's biscuits, they were outstanding. When he reached the lodge, he scratched on the outside.

Small Belly, with almost uncanny foresight, called out, *"It that a hungry dog scratching at my lodge door? Or is it that Yellow Horse who eats like a starving dog?"*

"It is I, Spider who is at your door!" Zachary said, the word vé'ho'e, spider, in Cheyenne, also meaning trickster and lately Whiteman.

"I had better hide my wife!" Small Belly joked, and laughing invited his friend inside. As Zachary had hoped, Falcon had a small kettle of coffee brewing over the fire and she was making small patties of dough from white flour and water. Soon there would be fried bread ready and Zachary was elated. The two friends sat and ate, enjoying each other's company while the sun slowly climbed into the cold winter sky.

Small Belly was in the middle of telling a story when the sounds of a commotion arose outside. Both men went out and found a warrior they knew from the Kiowa camp had come riding in, shouting a warning that soldiers were in the camp of Black Kettle.

"Warriors! Come, take up you weapons! Come Fight!" he called out.

Small Belly darted back into his lodge to retrieve his bow and arrows, while Zachary ran back to his lodge, where he found Bear Voice mounted and ready for battle impatiently waiting on him, and holding the reins of Zachary's horse. Sees Far stood holding Zachary's headdress in one hand and a seashell containing black paint in the other. Zachary quickly dipped his fingers in the paint and drew three lines down the side of his face, after that he placed the headdress on, and vaulted to his horse's back. Sees Far then handed up his carbine. Tossing the rifle's sheath to one side, he kicked his heels into his horse's sides and prompted it into a run.

Soon the warriors from the Southern Cheyenne camp under Medicine Arrows and Old Whirlwind joined those from the Kiowa and Arapaho camps headed upriver. Black Kettle's camp was almost ten miles away, and as the warriors converged in that direction, the sound of gunfire became more evident.

The Arapaho were the first to spot Pony Soldiers, only twenty in number and they turned in their direction. The Troopers dismounted and tied their horses together, forming a tight semi-circle defensive formation. They fought fiercely but there were too few of them, and as soon as the Cheyenne and Kiowa arrived the fight lasted a very short time.

The soldiers were stripped of their clothing, scalped, and the calves of their legs slashed. Many warriors also cut hands or fingers and feet from the dead troopers, and as a final insult, their heads were battered in, and some of them completely removed.

When this short battle was finished, the warriors moved on to the site of Black Kettle's camp and found that it was destroyed. Piles of supplies, possessions and lodge covers were burning. Scattered around the burning camp were the bodies of sixty men women and children, among them Black Kettle and his wife, Medicine Woman. Some of the survivors who had hidden along the river told the warriors that the pony-soldiers had left some time ago and had taken over fifty women and children hostages with them. Before the whites had left, they culled out two hundred horses from the herd at the camp, to be used by their prisoners and carry away what plunder they deemed of value. To the shock of the warriors, in the fields near the camp were the carcasses of the remaining eight hundred ponies which the soldiers had killed.

***

The march back to Camp Supply was slow and hindered by the Cheyenne prisoners. Whit questioned Benteen as to why prisoners had been taken at all, and the Captain only replied that Custer was using them as a shield. If there was to be a pursuit from the Indians, they would think twice before putting their own women and children in danger. But more on Benteen's mind was the fact that Custer had abandoned Major Joel Elliott and his twenty men. Elliott had separated from the three companies he led, apparently without Custer's approval. Elliott, yelling "Here's for a brevet or a coffin!", led his small band in pursuit of a group of fleeing Cheyenne and they were not seen again.

When Benteen questioned Custer's abrupt withdrawal without determining the fate of Elliott and the missing troopers, he was disregarded, and the entire command rode off with the band playing "I Will Be Glad to Get Out of the Wilderness".

***

CHAPTER TWENTY-TWO
THE TAKEN

April 1869 – Moon of Budding Trees

The ponies were sleek and fat after feasting on the new grass. Their boney frames of just a few weeks earlier were now only a memory. The buffalo had also thrived on the fresh grass, shed their winter coats, and when the horses and the buffalo flourished, so did the Cheyenne.

Many of the bands had gathered, and of the councils held throughout the winter and early spring, there was little talk of war. But, with the death of Black Kettle on Lodgepole Creek, there had been no one to speak about peace either. It had been four moons since any conflicts with the Whites had taken place, but it was accepted that as soon as the horses were fat, the lodges full of meat, and the warriors became restless, the time to go against the Whiteman would come.

Zachary thought little of fighting, he had proven himself a warrior many times and even bore the scars of a warrior. Now, he had reached his nineteenth summer, and guided by Bear Voice and Sees Far Woman, he had become a model Cheyenne. Unlike them, he did not seek notice, he was happy to do what was right for the People. Many times, Bear Voice had suggested that he think about becoming his apprentice.

"There is no one greater among the People than a Holy Man," Bear Voice would say. *"With my help, you would be respected, you would have power."*

"I am not worthy of such power," Zachary would answer. He did not dare say what he really thought. Bear Voice was a poor medicine man, and everything he prayed for was either selfish, evil, or to make himself look important.

Zachary would often remember the words of Little Wolf, telling him that if a man used his medicine for the wrong reason, evil would come back to him, or to the People.

"Think," Wolf would say, *"Why are you doing this? Is it to impress someone? Are you trying to prove how brave you are? Or, are you thinking of the People?"* But Wolf was not his teacher, Bear Voice was.

Zachary wondered what had happened to Little Wolf. He knew the Medicine Man had been on the Lodgepole River along with Black Kettle, but he had not heard if Wolf had been killed along with the Peace Chief. Some had said that Wolf's medicine was so powerful that he had stood in front of Custer's 7th Cavalry that winter day and the soldiers could not see him and rode past. Others said he had turned into a gray wolf and now followed the buffalo herds. Zachary found it hard to believe these things and decided that if it was meant for him to know the truth, it would be revealed to him.

This day, he was looking for a place to hide himself from Bear Voice and Sees Far. The old man had again begun to badger him about what he thought he should do.

"The time is coming close for the Medicine Lodge to be built, and for a special few to hang from the tree," Bear Voice said. *"You should think about committing to dance next summer."* Committing to the Sun Dance was a great responsibility, and without the right frame of mind and proper guidance of a Holy Man, it could be a great danger. Zachary had seen this. Those who had low, self-centered reasons for doing it, quickly found the sacrifice during the Sundance impossible to bear. It had become an awful and ugly experience rather than a beautiful, strong one. Zachary knew that even with a year's preparation of praying and sweat baths, he would not be able to focus on what would be considered for the good of the people. He would be doing it under pressure from Bear Voice.

He needed some diversion, something to take his mind off his uncle, and he decided to look among the lodges of some of the newest arrivals to join the camp. There he might find someone who he hadn't seen in a while, a friend or even a young girl that he could flirt with.

As he walked through the camp of the newcomers, he spied a woman that looked familiar walking away from him and out of sight behind a lodge. She wore a long buckskin dress, with fringe that flowed as she walked, and her loose hair hung down her back, shining in the sun like the wing of a raven. Zachary quickened his pace in order to catch up with her and as he rounded the lodge, he ran directly into another woman coming in his direction.

"Oh, I am sorry," he stammered.

"Do you make it a habit of running into people?" she asked, *"I have not seen you in many winters and here you are trying to run over me again."*

Zachary couldn't believe that in front of him stood the red-haired girl, Eleanora Yoder. She had changed. Gone was the skinny, mousey white girl. In her place was a strong, mature woman. Her hair was still a coppery shade of red, but now it was clean and brushed. Her pale skin had darkened to a honey tone from exposure to the sun, and her vivid blue eyes held a clarity that reflected self-confidence.

"I..I..," Zachary stammered, *"I am surprised that you remember me."*

She laughed, and smiling replied, *"Oh I could never forget you. The last time I saw you I thought you may come back and buy me from the wretched, old buffalo cow."*

"I had thought about that, but I was, and still am a poor man, with only a few horses," Zachary said.

"Ah, but I am made to understand that you are an accomplished warrior."

"How do you know of my deeds?"

"The young women talk about all the young men, especially those who are brave in battle, or handsome to look at." Zachary missed the veiled compliment.

"How is it that you come to be among the Southern People?"

"I was traded to an Arapahoe, an old man who had no one to care for him. He was a good hunter, and kind to me. So, I kept a lodge for him and warmed his bed."

Zachary was disappointed that she had a husband, but asked, *"You are happy with this man?"*

"Yes, but he was injured while hunting buffalo four days ago. He has many things broken inside and the medicine man said he will not be with us long."

"I am sorry for your trouble." Knowing it was not proper, he had to know what she would do when her husband died, so asked, *"What will become of you?"*

"I believe that I will find another husband, one who is not so old," she smiled, and with a grace he had never seen in her, stepped around him and walked away. He thought to call after

her, and realized that even after so many years, he still did not know her name.

"What are you called?" he asked.

She stopped for only a moment and over her shoulder she replied, *"I am called Red Wolf Woman."* Then, she resumed her steps and was gone.

Zachary had thought of her many times over the past years, wondering what had become of her, and now he knew her name, and that she was close by. She would also be available.

How would he go about arranging to take her as his wife? When her husband died, the lodge and everything in it would be given away. Not having relatives of her own, she would be left with nothing. It would be a simple matter of him just taking her in. The real problem would be Bear Voice and Sees Far. Zachary knew they would not approve, and Zachary felt Sees Far might be crazy enough to kill Red Wolf. He would have to trap Sees Far into accepting Red Wolf.

As he walked back to the lodge of Bear Voice and Sees Far, Zachary plotted his next moves. He had always been compliant with their wishes, and seldom complained, and Sees Far had never ceased to please him, constantly fawning over him, though she was also jealous. She had a way of persuading the young women to stay away by either working her evil brand of medicine or intimidating them with veiled threats of her powers. She had merely to wait until some young girl had fallen sick or had a hard time during her moon cycle. Sees Far would then spread the rumor that the girl had offended her in some way and the illness was a result of her powerful medicine.

When reaching the lodge, he took a seat against a willow backrest, and waited for Sees. It was not long before she appeared, and as she did, Zachary dropped his head and appeared disturbed.

"Are you sick, Yellow Horse?" she asked dropping to her knees and placing a hand on his cheek to feel for a fever.

"No," Zachary said, *"I am troubled and do not know what I should do."*

"Tell me what troubles you and I will make it well," she said, overly worried in her eccentric way.

"I do not believe I can talk of it with you. It has to do with a dream that I had. I am made to think I should speak with Bear Voice."

"Oh, I can help with dreams!" she became excited.

"I am not sure. In the dream a buffalo cow spoke to me."

"My buffalo medicine is strong," she lied, never having possessed such power.

"Do you believe I should do whatever I am told by such a vision?"

"Oh, yes. You must obey the voices of the buffalo spirits. Without question."

"Would you help me follow her instructions?"

"Of course! This I swear! Look I will make medicine with my own blood." With these words she pulled the razor-sharp flint blade from its sheath at her waist, and sitting back, mumbled some incoherent chant, her eyes rolling back in her head, her body shaking. She took the knife and drew it across her forearms drawing a stream of blood. Zachary had seen her do this very thing many times and he knew that her witch's medicine would hold her to whatever he convinced her into promising.

She regained her composure and with a maniacal smile she asked, *"What did the buffalo spirit ask of you?"*

"She told me that there was a sacred wolf, a red wolf among the people. She said I must find this red wolf and protect it, if I did not, harm would come to those I loved, you and Bear Voice. Will you help me prevent this?"

"I have told you, that I will help you!"

"This is good," Zachary paused, then said, *"She told me that I must find the Red Wolf and take her for my wife. My heart is happy that you will do whatever it takes to help me find this Red Wolf. And as long as she is safe, you and Bear Voice will be safe."*

Sees Far looked as if Zachary had slapped her. The blood drained from her face and she felt faint. She had just agreed to help Yellow Horse find a bride, and the welfare of this bride was tied to her own safety. She was trapped. Of course, what was the chance of there being a Red Wolf close at hand?

***

May 1869 – Bright Moon

The sun beat down on the shale bluffs west of Fountain River, and the men sitting on their horses atop the bluffs looked longingly at the coolness that the shade of the cottonwoods offered below them. The Fountain snaked its way from its source in the north, along the grass covered river bottom to Pueblo where it entered the Arkansas River. As leader of the ten brigands, Azariah Bolt was satisfied at what he saw below him on the east bank of the river. The ranches that he remembered were still in operation and he had no doubts that Craigavon and Klausen, still owned them. As Bolt had promised his confederates, stretching across the grass covered river bottom and prairie, there were over two hundred head of horses and mules.

With the Indian troubles from the Dakotas to New Mexico, the Army needed good mounts, horses that could not only keep up with the Indian ponies but outlast them. At the $75 a head the Army would pay for green-broke horses, there was a fortune grazing along the river. The only question was how many ranch hands there were, and how much trouble it would be to run off as many horses as possible.

Bolt looked over at the men with him; ex-Confederate soldiers, Army deserters, renegades, outcast Indians and mixed breeds. Each man has some reason to be on the wrong side of the law, and their only bond with each other was that of safety in numbers.

"Chatto, go down and get a good look at both ranches. Don't go as far down stream as Pueblo. Don't be seen, and don't get caught!" Bolt ordered the snub-nosed Mexican, who instantly spurred his horse and rode off to the north before crossing the flat land between the hills and the river.

"The rest of you find a place out of sight and make camp. No fire! Do you understand that?" A few of them nodded their heads, the rest sat silent in their saddles. "Go!" Bolt ordered and they moved off to the west away from the river. Bolt looked back across the bottom land and scratched his chin as he pondered his next move. He made the decision that he would ride downstream and see how the town of Pueblo had changed.

He circled to the west and came at Pueblo following the Arkansas River. The town had grown to over two hundred permanent residents. There was a mixture of small houses, shacks made of adobe or planed wood planks. When he passed the old site of the fort, there were only a few weather-worn adobe bricks outlining where it had once stood, most of the bricks had been reused to build houses and other buildings.

Riding through the town, he found a grist mill, several grocery and merchandise stores and hotels. One with a sign that read "Sager's Restaurant and Hotel" made Bolt smile. He remembered Abbot Sager. He was the man who had found him when he had been scalped by the Cheyenne. Bolt rode up to the hitching rail outside the establishment and walked in to find a modest interior, with several tables and chairs to accommodate travelers. As he stood looking over the room, Amelia Sager came in from the kitchen.

"Oh my, I didn't hear anyone come in," she said.

"Sorry, Ma'am. Might I get a bite to eat?" Bolt said, showing a yellow-toothed smile, but not removing his hat like a gentlemen.

"It's a bit late for breakfast, but I have some cured ham and could fry up some eggs to go with it."

"That would be mighty nice of you, Ma'am," Bolt said again, and moved over to take a seat at one of the tables. In a few minutes, Amelia returned with a plate of eggs, a ham steak and a slice of fresh white bread, placing it on the table in front of Bolt.

"I thought you might like some coffee also," she said and set a steaming cup next to the plate. "Traveling through?" she asked, her curiosity getting the better of her.

"Why, yes, "Bolt said, sopping up the rich yellow egg yolk with a piece of the bread and shoving it into his mouth.

"New here, I see?" she said prying more information from the man.

"No, I been through here some time back. Things have changed a bit since then."

"Oh yes!" Amelia said. "We've grown to be a nice town. We have a courthouse, and a telegraph office. Line runs all the way to Denver and Santa Fe."

"That's some, it is," Bolt replied between bites of food.

"There's also a stagecoach line running up to Denver and east down the Arkansas route. Only takes the stage twenty-four hours to get from here to Denver!"

"It that a fact?" Bolt said.

"Yes, and we have a newspaper. Comes out every week, and there's an apothecary owned by Doctor Beshoar, he owns the paper too!"

"What happened to the doctor named Craigavon, he still live here-a-bouts?"

"Oh yes, Doctor and Missus Craigavon still have their ranch north of town, and he has an office above the general store owned by Mr. Thatcher. You know Dr. Craigavon?"

"In a way. He treated me years ago, you could say he made me the man I am today." He took another bite and as he chewed, he continued to talk. "I sure would like to pay my respects."

"What a pity. You'd have to wait until he returned from Texas."

"Texas?" What would make him go down that way?"

"He, Eli Thornton and August Klausen from the Scott Ranch, have made an agreement with Mr. Goodnight and they are bringing cattle up here from Texas," she said. Her intention at the beginning of their conversation had been to learn as much about the strange man as she could, yet she had ended up giving him all the information he needed.

"That is a shame," Bolt said, "I hear there's been some Injun trouble here-a-bouts," Bolt said matter-of-factly.

"Oh, we haven't had any trouble around here. Most of it has been up Nebraska way. And even up that way, it's been quiet since the first of the year."

"Well, I'm headed south to Santa Fe," Bolt said, swallowing the last bit of his meal, gulping down the remains of his coffee, and wiping his dirty lips with his shirt sleeve. He stood, reached into his vest pocket, pulled out a twenty-five-cent piece and handed it to her, taking her hand in both of his. "Will this cover the cost of the meal?" he asked. Amelia, surprised that he had taken her hand as he did, felt a chill rush through her body, and without looking at the coin, only nodded yes.

Bolt smiled again, and she could see flecks of his meal still clinging to his mustache and mutton chops. She wasn't sure if it was her imagination or the feeling of cold that had just washed over her, but she swore she could smell his foul breath. Her stomach turned. He released his hold on her and walked out into the street where he remounted his horse and rode south, out of town.

Daylight was just streaking the eastern sky with wisps of yellow and red clouds, when Bolt and his men crossed over the Fountain River. Chatto had spent most of the previous day watching both the Craigavon and the Scott ranches. While the Craigavon ranch had a few hands about, the other though ran by Thornton and Klausen, sat all but deserted. It appeared that

462

there was only one ranch hand and two women there, and as the two ranches stood several miles apart, Bolt figured he and his men could move all the horses off with little interference.

Smoke was coming from the chimney of the ranch house, and light shown through the glass-paned window. The raiders had already started to quietly gather the herd and move them off when Bolt, Chatto and one of the Indian renegades dismounted their horses at the front of the house. Bolt could smell the odor of biscuits baking, and that combined with the expectation of encountering the two dark-haired women caused his mouth to water.

"Who's there?" A voice came from out of the twilight. It was the single ranch hand who had just left the bunkhouse to come up for breakfast at the house.

His question was answered by an arrow that sank into his chest, followed by a second shaft, fired by the Indian. The man dropped to the ground, and all was silent again. As the Indian scalped the ranch hand, Bolt spoke, "Look in the barn and see what stock is there. If there are horses, put saddles on two of them, and bring them up to the house." Then he turned, and with Chatto, stepped onto the porch and through the door.

Magdalena was standing at the stove cooking bacon, and though she heard the door open thought it was the ranch hand and greeted him over her shoulder, "Good morning Seth. Breakfast will be ready in a few moments. Coffee's done though, help yourself."

"Why thank you kindly," Bolt said, and Magdalena turned to see the two men standing in front of her, Chatto coming her way. Instinctively she took hold of the only item she could reach and flung the pan of bacon at the Mexican, the hot grease splashing across his upraised arm, and scalding him. With the speed of a rattle snake, he brought his other arm around and with a closed fist struck her in the face, knocking her to the floor. He then reached for his knife with the intent to kill her.

"Leave her be!" Bolt ordered, "I want her alive." And he reached down slightly lifting her and noticed that she was unconscious. "Find the other woman and bring her out here, unharmed," he added, and Chatto moved down the short hallway to the back rooms. He opened the first door and found a child cowering in the corner. He went on the next room and as he opened its door Willow came at him, a knife in her hand, slashing at his face.

"¡Hijo de puta!" he hissed, and letting her own momentum pull her forward he took her by the hair and tossed her to the floor. As Willow tried to rise, Chatto kicked her in the ribs and she fell back, the wind knocked from her lungs. Chatto kicked her knife away and then pulled her by the hair, out into the kitchen.

"This zorra damn near cut me!" He said to Bolt as he tossed her over in the direction of Magdalena.

Anyone else here?" Bolt asked.

"There is a cachorro in the other room," Chatto said pointing with a movement of his head.

"Get the child and bring him here," Bolt said and then turned his attention to Willow who now held Magdalena in her lap. He stared at her and tilting his head slightly said, "I had forgotten how black your hair was. As black as your heart, I would expect."

"Who are you and what do you want?" Willow asked.

"You don't remember me? Well that's alright. We'll get reacquainted over the next few days." As he spoke these last words Chatto brought out the little boy, who when released ran to Magdalena and Willow crying, "Mama! Mama!"

"Whose child is this?" Bolt asked.

"Her's," said Willow referring to Magdalena.

"There anyone else around?"

"No, only the ranch hand," she answered.

"Where's the old man that used to live here?" he spoke of Silas.

"He went south to New Mexico."

"He's lucky he can still sit a saddle, isn't he?" Bolt snickered.

"He'll be sitting a saddle long after you're in the ground," Willow mocked.

Bolt dismissed the comment and over his shoulder he ordered Chatto, "Search the rooms again and take whatever you think might have value." Then he took a seat at the table where the two women and child were still in his sight. He eyed them for a moment and then pulled his pistol from its holster and lay it on the table close to his hand, and said, "Come here boy."

Joseph was trembling with fear, and looked to Willow, as if asking what to do.

"Don't hurt the child," Willow said, her words more a threat than a plea.

"He'll be fine. Come here boy!" his voice was more forceful, and Willow urged Jospeh to stand and go to Bolt. As he came within reach Bolt picked him up and placed him on his lap.

"The Mexican bitch said there was coffee," Bolt said to Willow, "Pour me a cup and if the biscuits are ready, I'll have me some of them too."

Willow rose, only now realizing that she was wearing nothing but her chemise, and she went to retrieve a shawl that hung by the door.

"Careful now woman," Bolt warned her, "Don't get no ideas."

Willow wrapped the shawl around her, and made her way to the stove, where she took the biscuits out and set them on the table in front of Bolt.

"The coffee?" he reminded her, and she brought a cup to him.

Chatto returned and showed Bolt the few items that he had found, that were worth stealing; silver hairbrushes, silver clad hand mirrors, and the few pieces of jewelry that belonged to the two women. There was also a double-barreled shot gun and a holstered Colt pistol, on a belt with a sheathed hunting knife.

Magdalena started to stir, and Willow went back to her side again holding her. There was already the sign of bruising on her chin where Chatto had struck her and as she became more aware, she felt the pain in her jaw. She looked up at Willow and then over to where Bolt sat, eating the hot biscuits and holding her son on his lap. She attempted to get up, but she became dizzy and sat back down.

"What do you want?" she asked Bolt.

"Just a friendly visit with old friends." He paused and then said, "Oh, I might just relieve you of a few horses." He looked directly at Willow and said, "Go put on some clothes, and remember I have this here little whelp on my lap." Willow left and returned wearing a cotton day-dress.

"You don't wear buckskins no more, Squaw?" Bolt chuckled.

The Indian returned with the horses, and Bolt ordered the women out of the house and into the saddles, he handed Joseph up to Magdalena who held him close to her. Then he and Chatto mounted their own horses, but before they rode away Bolt ordered the Indian to stay behind. He was to first cut the telegraph wire that ran north out of Pueblo. Then, when the sun was well up, return to the ranch and set the buildings on fire. Bolt then reached into his saddle bag and drew out a small buckskin pouch, with Cheyenne style quillwork on it, and tossed it to the ground. He and Chatto then led the women off to the east, catching up with the rest of the raiders and the horse herd.

Magdalena and Willow rode next to one another, and when she felt no one could hear, Magdalena, speaking in Cheyenne, hoping no one would understand that language, asked *"Where is Henry?"*

"When it all began I had him slip out the window. I told him to hide down by the corral. I told him that he was not to come out until everything was all over and then go to the Craigavons.*"* Both women worried about the child, he like Joseph, was only five years old. His Mother had placed a great burden on him, but she knew he was strong and would endure.

The horses were driven northeast and by the time the sun was completely up, the herd was more than twenty miles away from the ranch. Bolt intended to push them on through the day and into the night to put as much distance from the ranch as possible. He believed that his subterfuge of leaving the Cheyenne bag at the ranch would convince anyone that Indians has stolen the horses and carried off the women. He was also betting that with the telegraph wire down, not much in the form of a pursuit would be organized, at least not until late in the day.

Clothed in nothing but his nightshirt, Henry watched from his hiding place behind the pile of fence posts. He saw the Indian move over to the body of Seth Cooper and was lucky that distance saved him from witnessing what the Indian was doing to the body. Henry knew it must be Seth laying on the ground, as he recognized the vest the Indian pulled from the body and put on.

He was scared, but his mother had told him to be brave and he was trying hard not to cry, even when he saw the Indian set fire to the buildings. He knew he should wait, but that overwhelming fear was pushing him to run. He started to rise but noticed a woman standing in the yard looking in his direction. Her hair was unbound, and flowing in the breeze, and she had on a buckskin dress, much like the one's his mother owned, but seldom wore, preferring the lighter cotton dresses like Magdalena. So, Henry waited for what seemed an eternity after the Indian mounted his horse and sped away, and the woman disappeared around the burning house. Only then did he come out from hiding and headed toward the Craigavon Ranch. He walked down the road, his bare feet kicking up dust.

He had gone less than a mile when he heard horses coming in his direction and fearing it was more Indians, he looked for a place to hide, starting to run from the road toward the cottonwoods along the river. As he ran, he could hear a horse coming up behind him and when he thought he would be run down, the horse came up next to him and the rider reached down and scooped him up off the ground. His first instinct was to fight back, and he beat at his captor with his tiny fists.

"Hold on, Son," the man said, "It's me, Ben Logan, from the Craigavon Ranch." Henry looked at the man and recognizing him threw his arms around the cowboy's neck.

Ben gently pulled the boy away and asked, "We saw smoke and were headed over to your place to see what was going on. You alright?"

"They burned the house," Henry said, sobbing.

"Who?"

"Indians."

Ben turned to one of the men with him and holding out the boy to him said, "Ramon, take the child back to the ranch and tell the Missus, we think Indians have raided the Scott place. Then meet us there and I'll figure out what we'll do next." Turning to the others he said, "Pull your pistols out and be ready." They spurred their horses in the direction of the smoke rising into the hot summer sky.

The trio of cowboys rode directly into the courtyard between the burning buildings, where Logan dismounted and examined the body of Seth Cooper. Bolt's henchman had done his job well, and the body bore all the signs associated with the desecration of an enemies' body by the Cheyenne.

"Shit," was all Logan could utter. He returned to his horse, pulled his canvas raincoat from his saddle cantle and placed it over the ranch man's mutilated form. A quick search of the area offered no sign of the women or Joseph. It was obvious that they had been taken.

"Good sign that we haven't found their bodies," one of the cowboys, said.

"Yep. At least there's hope they're alive, Bob," Logan said. "They'll probably take the boy to raise, but let's hope we can catch up with them before they use the women. The trail is plain, and they don't have that much of a head start. Ride into town and see how many men you can talk into gong with us. We need at least a dozen and can't take everyone from the ranch for this. Tell them to bring rations and plenty of ammunition."

Bob Goodman wheeled his horse around and sped off toward Pueblo in search of men to enlist in the pursuit, while Logan and the other cowboy dug a hasty grave for Seth Cooper, then returned to the Craigavon ranch where they informed Roseanne Craigavon about what had found.

"Are you sure there is no sign of Willow or Magdalena?" Roseanne asked.

"I am," Logan said.

"Then spare nothing in getting them back, Ben. Take extra mounts and drive them into the ground if you have too."

"Yes Ma'am."

"Tell the men I am offering a reward of one-hundred dollars for the safe return of those women and the child."

On the third day out from the ranch, Chatto caught up with the horse herd and rode straight for Bolt. He had been tasked with watching the back trail to spot any form of pursuit, and he convinced Bolt that if anyone was on their trail, they were left far behind. The horses had been separated into smaller groups on the first day, but now they had all joined together, and were headed toward the northeast, then on to Fort McPherson where it was rumored that General Eugene Carr was preparing a campaign against the Indians. The horses had already been driven close to one hundred miles, and now that Chatto reported that there seemed to be no one following them, Bolt decided to slow the pace down and let the horses rest.

He also decided to give the men a chance to recoup. The stops for the last few days had been short, and meals had been hasty, consisting of jerky. Now Bolt felt it was safe enough to make a real camp, and have the women cook a decent meal. He would also relieve himself of the frustration that was pent up inside of him. But which woman would he take first? He had thought long and hard about what he would like to do to each of the women, especially Magdalena, who he felt was the better looking. It was not that he didn't find Willow attractive, for even with the pock marks on her face, she had a stately bearing about her that made her desirable. But Willow was a half-breed, and in his mind, she was still an Indian.

He decided on Magdalena, and when he was finished with her, he planned to turn her over to his men and then, add her long black hair to his collection of scalps. Then he would take Willow and make his time with her last for days.

With camp being made, guards were set to watch the horse herd, supplies were unpacked, and the women were ordered to make the evening meal. A bottle of whiskey was soon being passed around and the men began to relax, their minds on a hot meal and the anticipation of when Bolt would let them have the women. As they worked, Willow and Magdalena talked, speaking in Cheyenne, and keeping their voices low so as not to be heard.

"Maggie, we need to get away," Willow said as she cut bacon and laid it into a frying pan.

"I know, but I fear for Joseph," said Magdalena as she looked over to where Bolt sat, holding the child. Her stomach churned at the thought of his hands on her son, and she swore that if he hurt the boy, she would kill him.

"Tonight," said Willow, *"They'll all be crazy with the whisky, and we can slip out in the dark."*

"No, you go and bring back help. I do not think I can chance Joseph getting hurt."

"We will see," said Willow, and as carefully as she could, she hid the knife in the folds of her dress.

The mood in the camp became lighter and the men began to laugh and joke as they ate their meal and a second bottle of liquor was passed from hand to hand. The women sat watching, as they ate their own meal. Bolt ate, but kept Joseph close to him, talking to the boy and asking him questions about life on the ranch.

"You get pretty lonesome all by yourself, with no other kids around?" he asked.

"No, I got Henry to play with, and when John comes back from Texas, he'll play with me too," the boy answered.

"And who is Henry?"

"He's Aunt Willow's boy. Him and me are the same age."

"Why wasn't Henry with you when we came to the ranch?"

"I don't know, he was there when I went to bed, but I didn't see him when you showed up."

Bolt looked over at the women and rising walked over to them, and squatting on his heels in front of Willow, he said, "You told me there wasn't anyone else at the ranch, and the boy just said you had a boy of your own there. That right?"

Willow stared back at him not speaking, and Bolt backhanded her. She had little time to react to the blow before he was on her, taking hold of her hair in one hand and pulling his knife out with the other.

"You lying bitch! I'm gonna cut out your tongue!" he yelled. He brought the blade close to her face, and in the struggle, his hat fell from his head.

As quick as his insane rage had risen, it quelled. He released her and pulled himself up, his eyes bulging out, a maniacal look across his face. He picked his hat up from the ground and glancing around saw the astonished looks by those around him. No one in the company had ever seen him without a hat and the terribly scared scalp, with its wisps of white hair made him look even more frightening.

He returned his knife to its sheath, and then smoothing his greasy locks over the scar, placed his hat back on. Looking at Willow, he said, "It was your people done this to me, you know."

Willow felt her blood run cold. She had known before that he was dangerous, but she feared a crazy man more than just an evil man. She edged her way up into a sitting position next to Magdalena, her friend placing an arm around her as if to protect her. With no more said, Bolt turned and walked out of the camp.

Magdalena whispered to Willow and spoke to her, "There's no question now. You need to leave as soon as possible. Did you see the look in his eyes? He is going to kill you."

"I can't leave you and Joseph," Willow said, "Please come with me. I fear for you with that man."

"Alright, we'll go together," said Magdalena.

As the end of the whiskey was reached, the camp soon quieted. The silence broken only by the sound of someone snoring. When the women thought they might slip away, Bolt came back into the camp circle and walking over to where the women lay reached down and picked Joseph up into his arms. He carried the boy over to his own blankets and there he tied a rope around the boy's neck, and the other end he wrapped around one of his hands. Satisfied with this insurance, he rolled into his blanket and soon was adding his own snoring to that of the others.

Magdalena wept, her thoughts of Joseph being in Bolt's possession frightening her. She turned to Willow and said, "Go. Go and bring back help."

"I can't," Willow said.

"Please, for God's sake! You may be our only hope."

They embraced and Willow slipped from under the blanket they shared and into the darkness.

Though she had spent the past years on the ranch, life growing up in a Cheyenne camp had taught her many skills that were engrained in her very nature. With skill, she slipped up behind one of the nightguards, and easily slid the butcher knife across his throat. She then took his serape, his smoothbore escopeta, and shooting pouch. Now well armed, she chose two horses from the herd and lead them out away from the camp. At what she considered a safe distance, she mounted one horse, and leading the second moved off into the darkness.

As the predawn sky began to lighten, the body of the horse guard was found, and Willow's absence noted. Bolt became furious and dragging Joseph by the hair strode over to Magdalena and threw the child at her feet. She instinctively pulled the child to her and put herself between him and Bolt.

"So, the Injun slut left you and the brat," he spit the words at her, his face red with rage. "Well, it don't matter whose fault it is, you're going to pay the price." He stepped closer, and reaching out grabbed the top of her dress and pulled her forward. She resisted and the cotton material tore, exposing her chemise. Again, he reached out and grabbed at her clothing catching the top of the undergarment and ripped it away. Magdalena brought one arm up to cover herself but retained her hold on Joseph intent on protecting him before herself.

Bolt reached around taking hold of the boy, and with his free hand backhanded Magdalena knocking her to the ground. He lifted the boy off the ground with a single hand, and as if the child weighed less than a feather pillow, tossed him toward Chatto.

"Hold on to the boy, and if she fights me in the least, cut his throat," Bolt ordered the Mexican. He then turned his attention back to Magdalena, and almost threw himself on her. He pulled at her clothing, this time stripping her completely to the waist, and with his threat on Joseph's life in her mind, Magdalena lay helpless as he lifted her skirt, and forced her legs apart.

She closed her eyes praying that if she could not see what was soon to happen it would make it somehow bearable. She then attempted to fill her mind with thoughts of her child, of Eli, of anything but the violation she would soon suffer.

Word had spread quickly about the obduction of Willow, Magdalena and Joseph. It brought thirty riders to the Craigavon ranch, and each man had come prepared for an extended search. The trail of the stolen horses was easy to follow until the herd was divided into separate groups. The decision was made that most of the posse would stay on the trial of a single group, while a set of two men would follow each of the others. It was surmised that that the separate groups would most likely rejoin at some point.

The men paced themselves, attempting to save the strength of their horses, and changed mounts often with the spares they had brought with them. Ben Logan, as the chosen leader of the party, had a hard time disciplining himself, as the urge to speed ahead was strong. He hoped that the decision to follow a single bunch of the horse thieves had not been a mistake. Not finding sign of the women was a good thing in Logan's mind. It meant that they were probably still alive.

On the morning of the fourth day, all the horse thieves had seemed to have rejoined into one band, as did the posse, and soon after mid-day a single figure was spotted coming in their direction. They spurred their horses forward and soon came up on the lone rider and found it to be Willow Klausen.

She told the men that it was not Indians who had stolen the horse herd and kidnapped her and Magdalena. She said it was the man who William Craigavon had treated for being scalped years ago. The man they had known as Abel or Lazarus.

"The men he is with are calling him Bolt though," she added.

"It don't matter what his name is, we need to catch up with them as soon as we can," Logan said. "We'll send you back with a few of the men, Missus Klausen."

"You'll find them faster if I show you the way," Willow said, and though fatigued, she was determined to turn around and lead the ranchmen back in rescue of Magdalena and Joseph.

The posse doubled their speed, now pushing their mounts to their limits and by late in the day they neared the spot where the renegades had been camped. There was no sign of the horse herd, and as the ranchmen came upon the camp, they were astonished and horrified by what they discovered.

There was no doubt about who had committed the atrocity that lay before them. The bodies of the raiders lay about the campsite, arrows protruding from their lifeless and mutilated bodies. Each man had been scalped and stripped. Most brutally treated was what had once been Azariah Bolt. From the trail of blood behind him, it appeared that he had suffered greatly, and after he had crawled several yards, his scared skull, void of a scalp, had been caved in with a stone war club.

Neither Magdalena nor Joseph were found among the dead, and the hope of rescue that had been high earlier in the day, faded with the new evidence of their captivity by the Cheyenne. The discovery of Magdalena's torn dress caused the most concern. The thought of her at the hands the Cheyenne had caused dread before, but now that physical evidence of her possibly being violated arose pity and fear for her. Following the fleeing Cheyenne was a far more daunting task, as they didn't leave the site of the killings in one or two groups but fanning out to the north and east and south, a few riders and horse in each direction.

"You think they saw us coming, and scattered?" Bob Goodman asked.

"Possible," said Logan, "Either way, there's no way we can figure which way they took Missus Thornton and the boy."

"You're right," added Willow, "But, if two or three of you are willing, we can go forward in hopes of finding any Cheyenne camp. I believe I can talk our way in, with a chance of not being harmed. My brother is still out there with one of the bands, and we might use that to our advantage."

Ben Logan looked at Willow and then at his friend Bob Goodman, not sure why he would go along with what was more than likely suicide, then he told Willow, "I guess, I'll throw in with you."

"Well shit!" exclaimed Bob, "I guess I can't let you go by yourself. Count me in."

The rest of the posse turned back toward home to carry the word of what had taken place, and with the intent of spreading the news via telegraph both north to Denver and east to Kansas about Magdalena and Joseph's abduction.

***

CHAPTER TWEENTY-THREE
THE WOMAN

May 1865 – Bright Moon

Near dawn, a haze on the skyline offered a clue as to where a village of Cheyenne might be, and Willow, Ben Logan and Bob Goodman headed in that direction. They had followed the tracks made by one of the groups of horses stolen first by Azariah Bolt, and then by what they believed were Cheyenne. The coolness of the previous night disappeared as soon as the sun rose, and the air was clean and still.

"What do we do if they aren't there?" Bob asked.

"We will see if we can find out where they were taken," said Willow, "I wish we had something to trade for them."

"We could always tell them they can keep the horses they stole," joked Ben half-heartedly, and for a moment Bob thought he was serious, but Willow smiled at the thought.

"We'll just have to do what's necessary. We have a better chance among the Cheyenne than we would have had with that filth that took Maggie and me from our home. I can only hope that he didn't die too quickly."

Ben looked over at the woman, and though he had known her for several years, he had never witnessed this side of her. He wondered if it was the Cheyenne part of her that wanted this sort of revenge, or if every woman would feel that same way about her abductor. Either way, he was glad she was on his side.

They were about five miles away when they became certain a village was ahead of them. The horse herd was visible first and the lodges beyond that. The open, somewhat flat prairie offered no concealment and their approach would be discovered long before they were close.

Willow untied the ribbon she had in her hair and let it flow down the sides of her face, to look more Cheyenne. She almost wished she had been wearing either a buckskin dress or at least a cloth dress cut in the Cheyenne style. She prayed that she had done the right thing coming after Magdalena, and hoped that she had not led the two men with her to their death.

It was not long before a group of mounted warriors were speeding toward them, the Indian horses kicking up dust behind them, billowing into the still morning air. Willow and the two men stopped and waited as the warriors, yelling war cries and taunts rode down on them and circled around them, the dust cloud adding to the confusion, and their intimidation.

Both of the ranchmen kept their hands away from their rifles, and Willow held up her right hand, attempting to speak above the shouts of the Cheyenne warriors.

"I am Willow Woman, of the Hairy Rope Band of the People. I have come in search of my brother," she almost had to scream to be heard, and spoke also in hand sign, *"I have come looking for family!"* A single warrior brought his horse to a skidding stop next to her and leaned in, his face painted and fierce. He frightened Willow. She held back the urge to break free of the group, she only repeated what she had just said.

Bob noticed the blazed face horse the Indian was riding and as quiet as possible brought it to Ben's attention, "That the mouse dun mare Elis has been workin'."

"Why do you bring these White dogs with you?" the warrior asked as the other warriors brought their horses to a stop and corralled the three.

"They are friends to my family, and have protected me," Willow said.

"Tell me why I should not kill them?" he asked.

"Because they have come in peace and you would respect that," she appealed to his honor. *"They have come with me to find my brother."*

"And what is your brother called?"

"Little Gun. He has two sons, Turtle Shell and Red Fox Waiting."

"Why do you look for him here?" asked the first warrior.

"We followed the horses taken three sun's back," Willow said, pointing to the dun mare the Indian rode.

"We found some horses on the prairie, they seemed to belong to no one. Do these men claim the horses?"

"The horses were stolen by White wolves. It is a good thing that they are dead." She avoided laying claim to the stock, for the moment.

The warrior gave her words some consideration and thought it better that the conversation should be continued in the presence of the village's leader and elders.

"I am called Little Whirlwind, come," he said, *"Follow me into the camp and we will speak to Shoulder Blade, who is our chief."* With this, he kicked his heels to the dun's ribs and the entire group leaped into a trot to the village.

Their arrival, though expected, seemed to cause an uproar, the rest of the village coming out to see what the excitement was about. As they entered the circle of tipis, barking dogs followed at the heels of their horses and they were surrounded by the people shouting.

Little Whirlwind led them to the lodge of Shoulder Blade, where the older man was standing as if expecting them. They dismounted and the Chief greeted them.

Whirlwind sat with the chief, and Willow sat to the side and a bit behind the two cowboys. She quickly told Ben and Bob that it would be better if she spoke as if she were translating for them, and it would be better if she acted subservient to them.

Shoulder Blade ignored the regular formalities and asked Willow directly what they wanted.

"We have come as friends of the People, and I am one of them."

"Which band do you belong to?' He asked.

"My mother was of the Hairy Rope Band."

"You speak for these men?"

"Yes, they come following horses stolen from them and my husband."

"They are either brave or foolish!" Shoulder Blade smirked. *"How is it that you come here to my village seeking these horses?"*

"We tracked the thieves, White wolves, to where they were killed by warriors of the People."

"These wolves you speak of had many scalps in their possession. Some were short haired, but most were long, and it was plain that they were taken from either our People or from another People." He thought, then asked, *"Has Willow of the Hairy Rope band come looking for the horses or her brother?"*

"I come looking for my brother." Willow paused and felt at this point honesty would be the best choice. *"We were also in search of a woman that was with the scalp takers, a Mexican woman with a small child."*

"We have no Mexican woman or her child."

"We would ask of you any word concerning this woman. The only gifts we would have to offer are the stolen horses." And with this said, she smiled.

Shoulder Blade's eyes widened a bit and he let out a laugh, surprising everyone.

"I had my doubts that you were a woman of the People, Willow, but only a woman of our kind would be brave enough to offer that which has already been taken. Come, we will eat, and I will spread word around the camp to find word of your brother and the Mexican woman."

A young boy was sent to ask among those warriors who had taken part in the raid on Bolt's men what had happened to Maggie, and if any of them knew the whereabouts of Little Gun. It was not long before the boy returned with one of the raiders called Many Kills.

"I know of this man," said Many Kills, *"He is in Tall Bull's camp."*

"And what of the Mexican Woman?" asked Shoulder Blade.

"She and her child were taken by Yellow Horse to Tall Bull's camp."

***

The inside of the lodge was stifling, even with the sides rolled up to allow any slight breeze to flow in. Maggie wasn't sure where the village she was in was located, but she knew it was far from home. She also had some feeling of safety, though the Cheyenne woman sitting across from her and Joseph glared at her and her son. The woman was clearly deranged, for she sat rocking back and forth, mumbling some incoherent gibberish under her breath.

It had been three days since the horse thieves led by Bolt had been attacked and she had been taken by the Cheyenne. She relived the experience over and over in her mind. Bolt had knocked her to the ground and ripped her clothing. As he lowered himself onto her, the expression on his face changed from maniacal to one of surprise, and then pain. Screaming, he had rolled off to one side and reached back to where an arrow protruded from his bare buttock. The shaft quivered with every move he made, and as he screamed louder, the entire campsite became filled with shouts, screams and Cheyenne war cries.

Chatto released his grip on Joseph, and the boy immediately ran to Maggie. Ignoring her own nakedness, she held the boy close to her, trying to protect him, as she watched the butchering of Bolts men. Some of the marauders begged for their lives, and were killed without mercy. A few attempted to fight back, but were quickly overpowered and suffered the same fate as their companions.

Bolt tried to escape, but hampered by the arrow, hobbled, dragging one leg behind him. With a chilling howl, a Cheyenne wearing a Dog Soldier headdress, caught him, striking him in mid-back with a stone war club. Bolt arched backwards with the blow and then stumbled forward, falling onto the ground, gasping for breath as blood spurted from his mouth. Slowly, he dragged himself a few more feet before the warrior placed a foot on the back of his neck and forced his face into the ground.

Bolt struggled for only a moment before falling limp. The Warrior, with the intent to scalp him, reached down for a hand full of hair and was surprised to find only the scared flesh with a few wisps of thin white hair where a scalp should have been. He rolled Bolt over on to his back, and the White man's eyes were wide with fear, almost bulging from their sockets. With a cry of disgust, the Cheyenne drew his knife across Bolt's throat. As Bolts eyes narrowed and glazed over, the warrior brought the war club down again crushing his skull.

Noticing a leather bag attached to Bolt's loosened belt, the warrior reached down and opened it finding the scalps that Bolt had collected over the years. The Cheyenne almost trembled with rage, and turning, looked in Maggie's direction. He strode toward her, with the intent to take out his vengeance on who he perceived to be Bolt's woman and child but was stopped by a hand on his arm from another warrior. This man, splattered with blood, spoke to him.

Maggie understood the hastily spoken words, *"Stop! This woman is my mother!"* With shock, Maggie realized that the bloodied warrior was Zachary.

Now, she awaited what fate might bring. Zachary had placed her and Joseph on a horse and led them to a small camp not far away. From the spoils taken from the renegades, he supplied her with a long-tailed shirt to cover her nakedness, and blankets for her and Joseph. He also offered her dried buffalo meat. She attempted to talk to him several times, but he seemed he no longer understood English nor Spanish. She tried Cheyenne, but it was evident he was reluctant to speak with her.

Leaving the small warrior's camp, the party of Cheyenne moved on, some splitting off with a portion of the captured horses. Zachary's group traveled on to a large village near the Republican River. It was when they reached the camp that Zachary finally spoke to Maggie.

"You will stay with my family," he said, his words spoken hesitantly in English. "I will show you where." He led her and Joseph to a lodge where there were two women, one a red head, both scraping a buffalo hide staked out on the ground. As Zachary approached the women, the red head stood, and joyful to see him, rushed to his side. Maggie noticed the young woman was obviously white.

"Yellow Horse! You have come home!" she said and threw her arms around him in a very un-Cheyenne manner. Maggie's gaze went from the embracing couple to the other woman still sitting next to the buffalo hide and noted her scowling with disapproval.

Maggie listened closely, the Cheyenne language she had learned coming back to her now. Zachary spoke to the red-haired woman.

"This is my White mother. The one I have spoken to you about, called Magpie by the People." He pointed to Maggie. *"I have brought her here to keep her safe. Be kind to her."* She turned and smiling at Maggie walked over and threw her arms around Maggie, hugging with genuine affection.

"It is good to meet you, Yellow Horse's mother. I am called Red Wolf Woman," she said in perfect English.

Maggie was stunned, and stammering said, "It is good to meet you. My name is Magdalena Thornton, and this is my son Joseph."

The girl looked down at the boy and smiling placed a hand on his cheek, saying, "He looks hungry, and so do you. Come, I will feed you." She then led Maggie and Joseph into the tipi and there fed them and showed them the place where they would be sleeping.

"This is your home now," she told Maggie.

"I must get word to my people and let them know where I am," Maggie told her.

"This is your home now," is all the girl said. She then turned, and going through a parflesh box, pulled out a cotton dress cut in the style of the Cheyenne and handed it to Maggie. "Here," she said, "you may change into this and I will bring you water to wash." She started to leave but stopped, and pointing toward the Cheyenne woman outside the lodge added, "That one is called Sees Far Woman. Take care around her, she is a witch." Then she left to fetch fresh water from the creek for Maggie to bathe.

Zachary returned later that day, and in the evening, an older Cheyenne man also came to the lodge. Maggie found out from Red Wolf that this man was called Bear Voice and was the uncle of Zachary's Cheyenne mother. She also told her that Sees Far was the same woman's sister. Red Wolf warned her about Bear Voice also, telling her that the man hated Whites, and was dangerous.

"Why does he not hate you?" Maggie asked.

"Oh, he hates me, as does Sees Far, but Yellow Horse has convinced them both that bad medicine will come to them if they harm me." She giggled. "Yellow Horse and I often speak in English to confuse and annoy them. Do not worry I will keep you safe as I don't believe in the old witch's medicine."

"Red Wolf, you speak English so well. How long have you been with these people?"

"I was taken five winters, years ago, when my parents were killed. The Cheyenne took me as a slave. Then an older man took me as his wife. When he died, I became the wife of Yellow Horse."

"Do you remember your White name?"

"Yes, it was...Eleanora Yoder." Red Wolf had not spoken this name in a long time, and it felt foreign to her.

"Eleanora, I have family I must get back to. Tell Zachary, I must get back to my husband."

"You should not think about that now. Think only that you are safe."

Maggie sat back and listened to the men talking and learned that they would be leaving in the morning on another raid. So, the following day she found herself alone with Red Wolf and the insane woman, Sees Far, who she knew was a danger to her and her child.

Inspired by Tall Bull, the Dog Soldiers descended on the settlements along the Solomon River, and in the early evening hours on May 30th, the first victims fell along Spillman Creek. Eskild Lauritzen, his wife Stine, and Otto Peterson were quickly killed, then stripped and scalped. The Cheyenne next approached the neighboring home of the Christensen's, but the occupants were well-armed and ready. They fought off the raiders who soon moved on. Traveling downstream, the Cheyenne came upon Fred Meigheroff, George Weichel, and George's wife, Maria, who fled south along Spillman Creek, fending off the Dog Soldiers. But after two miles, they ran out of ammunition. The men were quickly killed, and twenty-year-old Maria was taken captive.

The Healy homestead, along the Saline River, was the next target. At the homestead were: Mister and Missus Noon, Mister Whalen, Bridget Kine and her daughter, and Susanna Alderdice with her four children. When shots were heard, the Noons and Whalen mounted horses and fled the house, leaving Susanna, Bridget and the children behind. The women, with their children tried to escape along the Saline River. Bridget, holding her two-month-old child, waded the river and hid in the brush. Susanna, with her four children, could not keep up and soon fell behind. Exhausted, she sat on the ground clutching eight-month-old Alice and two-year-old Frank in her arms. John Daily, five, and Willis, four, stood hugging their mother.

The Indians came upon them and immediately pulled the three older children away from Susanna. They shot John with four bullets and put five arrows into Frank, then bashed him against the ground. They shot four-year-old Willis with five arrows and two bullets, then speared him in the back. They attempted to tear Alice from Susanna's arms, but she held on tightly to her last child, and the two were taken as prisoners. In all, thirteen civilians were killed in the raid.

At the end of the day, the Cheyenne camped south of the Saline not knowing that within two miles was the camp of Company G, 7th Cavalry, under Lieutenant Edward Law. The officer and his men had no knowledge of the raid until the following morning, and when they found the raider's trail, they followed it but came up empty. Before the day was out though, they found Bridget Kine and her daughter, and miraculously, young Willis Alderdice still alive.

***

June 1869 – Fattening Up Moon

"You really should let that hole in your back heal a bit more," William told Whit.

"I feel fine," Whit insisted.

"It's only been ten, days Whit. I'm not sure how well the stiches will hold," the Doctor warned.

"I trust your work, anyway, Carr is leaving tomorrow and I aim to go with him."

"You've done enough," Eli said, "You don't owe anyone."

"Eli, I owe Maggie, I owe her for the grief I caused, and I'll get her back to you no matter what."

"Well, we had better make sure we have plenty of ammunition," said Eli, "Oh, did you hear if we go, we're under a new chief of scouts?"

"No, who is it?"

"A fellow named Bill Cody, been hunting buffalo and scouting for the Army."

"Well, it don't matter none who I ride under, as long as they don't get in my way."

The following day, June 9th, Major Eugene A. Carr and eight companies of 5th Cavalry, and one hundred and fifty Pawnee scouts under Major Frank North, left Fort McPhersons with orders to clear the Republican country of hostiles. William F. "Buffalo Bill" Cody, his long hair hanging about his shoulders from under a broad-brimmed hat, rode next to Carr. Whit and Eli rode with the rest of the scouts, with William Craigavon riding next to Dr. Tesson, the military surgeon.

Scouting parties were sent out, both under Cody and North, and the following day one of those under Cody was attacked by Cheyenne with the loss of Army stock driven off by the Indians. On the 11th, flankers of the cavalry were fired upon but there were no casualties. On the 12th, ten more civilians were killed along the Solomon River, and a group of Indians were spotted and pursued, but they outdistanced the soldiers and there was no engagement. The Indians seemed to appear, strike and disappear at will throughout the rest of June and on into the first week of July. Their path of destruction led west toward the Republican River, with Carr and his 5th Cavalry on their heels

***

July 1869 – Moon of the Ripening Chokeberries

Word spread through the camp that there were soldiers camped where Cherry Creek flowed into the Chief River, just downstream from the village. Zachary hurried to paint himself and donned his headdress, making himself ready for war. Red Wolf stood outside the lodge holding the reins to his horse, and nearby, Sees Far glared at her with hatred, seething inside but also fearful of the fiery-haired woman's medicine. She vowed that if any harm befell Zachary, she would first kill Red Wolf, then the Mexican woman who usurped her as Zachary's mother. Lastly, she would kill the child, and only then would she cut short her own hair and fingers in a sign of mourning for "her son".

Bear Voice sat on his horse scowling at everything before him. He had grown to hate almost everyone gathered around him. He had even lost all fondness for Zachary. The boy had refused to follow in his footsteps, and he had taken as his own those items of war that were made by the Whiteman's medicine, the steel knife and the carbine. Finally, he had taken a White women as a wife. This all had built to the point where he considered killing his onetime pupil, no matter what the outcome. The idea came to him after a dream that plagued his thoughts. He had seen Zachary transform from the virile young Dog Soldier into the image of his White father, Whitney Voss, the man he hated more than any other.

Three troops of Pony Soldiers were met out in the open and though the odds were evenly matched, Howling Magpie, Shave Head, and Little Man fell to the bullets of Pawnee Scouts. The soldiers turned and retreated, followed by some of the Cheyenne and a few of the Lakota, the others returning to the village with the bodies of their fallen comrades. Within a few miles, the Indians realized that the Soldiers were only an advance party, and a much larger force of Calvary with wagons was not far away.

When the warriors returned to the village, it was decided to move. The Dog Soldiers, under Tall Bull, with a number of

Lakota, moved toward White Butte in the south. As they moved, Zachary finally spoke more with Maggie.

"I am sorry you have come to be in this state," he said in Cheyenne, "I can do little but protect you."

"You could take us to one of the soldier houses, or a trading post," Maggie said, speaking of either a fort or a stage station.

"They would not let me get close enough to talk. It would be just as dangerous for you as it would for me. For now, do not find yourself alone with Sees Far. She is crazy, and there is no telling what she might do. Trust only Red Wolf and myself."

Maggie took his words to heart, and that evening when they camped, she and Joseph accompanied Red Wolf when she went to visit with some of the other women in the camp. The midsummer air was stifling, and the women sat in the shade of a lodge with its sides rolled up for ventilation. They spoke of the things that women anywhere talked about; domestic duties, their men, and other women in the camp. All were careful not to mention Sees Far, not wishing to bring bad medicine down on themselves.

While they sat and talked, Maggie looked out at another lodge, that of Tall Bull. Outside of the lodge were what appeared to be two White women, both haggard, filthy and clearly abused, one sobbing uncontrollably. Maggie stood and walked over to them and knelt next to them. She knew full well that she was taking a chance of being rebuked by whoever held these women captive, but she was compelled to offer some comfort.

"My name is Maggie Thornton," she said, "Is there anything I can do for you?"

The woman who was weeping answered, "There is nothing you can do for me. They have killed my baby. They killed her because she was crying. She wouldn't stop crying." She looked down at her swollen belly and added, "And when my new child is born, what will they do to it?" She sobbed, shaking her head.

"Can you tell me your name?" Maggie asked, but the woman didn't answer, and the other woman seemed not to understand, only speaking in words that sounded somewhat like August's Dutch. Maggie was at a loss. She was about to speak further when Red Wolf came to her and pulled her gently to her feet.

"You should not interfere. These women belong to Tall Bull, and if he or his wife see you with them, there will be trouble," Wolf said.

"But look at them," Maggie pleaded, "We must do something."

"We cannot. Not without putting ourselves in danger. Come, we must go now."

"Do you know who those women are?"
I do not know their names, but from talking to the other women, they have been Tall Bull's for the past six weeks."

"The one woman said they have killed her child!" Maggie said.

"Yes, Tall Bull strangled the child three days after taking the woman. The child would not stop crying."

"How can anyone do that sort of thing?"

"I have found that there are some things that are not meant to be understood. It is just the way it is, in both the White world and that of the People."

It then occurred to Maggie that Zachary had been living the life of a Cheyenne for years, raiding with them, becoming a warrior. Hesitantly, she asked, "Has Zachary, Yellow Horse, committed this type of horror?"

"My husband does not have it in him, that part of his heart is different than most men."

"I can only imagine the misery of those two women, they cannot even console each other as they do not speak the same language."

As the village moved, Maggie watched those around her, noting the different people. A warrior rode past, and behind him two young men, one a teen, the other close to Zachary's age. As the warrior turned in his saddle to speak to one of them, Maggie saw his face bore the scars of smallpox, and she recognized that he was Willow's brother.

"Pistol," she called out to him, and startled by hearing his name in English he pulled back on his reins and moved over to Maggie. "Do you remember me?" she asked.

"Yes, you are Magdalena. How do you find yourself here among the Cheyenne?"

Maggie related what had happened to her and Willow, and Pistol became concerned about his sister.

"You have no idea what became of my sister?"

"No, I am sorry. All I am sure of is that she left in the night, and the following morning one of the retches was found with his throat cut."

"That sounds like the thing my sister would do."

"I am sure she safely made it and will send someone to look for me. But I need your help. Will you take me to one of the stage stations or military posts?"

"Do you not understand that there is a war between the Whites and the Cheyenne? I would be throwing away my life. I cannot help, Magdalena. Will your son not take you to one of these places."

"No, he feels the same way you do."

"It is possible you may find a chance on your own," he said. And, after a pause he asked, "How is my father?"

"Silas is well. He speaks of you often and would have you and his grandsons by his side."

"I would wish to see him also. That would only be possible when this war is finished. You and I will speak more when we camp." He kicked his heels to his horse and sped off to catch up with his sons.

The Cheyenne, and Lakota, reached White Bluff Creek on the rolling prairie and spent an uneventful night. The following day like those before, was hot and windy, and the village settled into a familiar routine. In the late afternoon, a warrior came rushing through camp shouting, *"People are Coming!"* but very few paid much attention. Then, the sound of a bugle split the air, followed by gun fire. Soldiers and Pawnee scouts began to pour over the hills.

Many of the Indians had horses tied up in camp, and they mounted them, taking up the women and children behind them. There was total chaos as the Soldiers and the Pawnee came at the village from three sides. Those people who were left on foot either fled south, the only direction there were no soldiers, or toward the bluffs in search of hiding places. At a distance, Maggie saw Pistol and his sons racing southward, the oldest boy with a young woman behind him on his horse.

Maggie stood transfixed in the confusion, until she felt Red Wolf's hand on her arm, and the girl yelled above the bedlam, "Get Joseph and follow me!"

As Maggie turned to find her son, she saw Sees Far, a knife in her hand, holding Joseph and pulling the child's head back to expose his throat. Looking for the first thing she could use as a weapon, Maggie took up a piece of firewood and swung as hard as she could, at the same time calling out Sees Far's name. The woman looked up just as the wooden cudgel caught her in the face, and she fell to the ground, releasing her grip on the boy. Maggie took up her son and ran in the direction Red Wolf had fled. As she ran, she heard chilling war cries and looking over her shoulder saw Pawnees coming through the village, killing everyone in their path.

***

Whit, pistol in hand, charged through the village, taking careful aim, but not looking back to note if his shots had any effect. North's Pawnee Scouts seemed to be everywhere, and if not for their distinct hair style, they could have been easily shot as one of the Indians of the camp. When his first pistol was empty, Whit retuned it to his holster, and as he drew the second from his belt, he was struck from the side. A Cheyenne took him from the saddle, both men falling to the ground. To avoid the hooves of his panicked horse, Whit rolled away, ending on his hands and knees. He lost the grip on his pistol, and he without thought, reached for his knife and drew the long blade from its sheath after he gained his feet.

No sooner was he upright than he was tackled by the Indian who had unhorsed him. As they tumbled over each other, the Indian's face came into clear view and Whit recognized Bear Voice. The Medicine man struggled to stab Whit with the obsidian-bladed knife he held in one hand as he clawed at Whit with the other. Whit held on to Bear Voice's knife wielding arm, keeping the deadly blade away from his face as he tried to bring his own knife around to strike Bear Voice. His attempt was clumsy, and he only managed to cut Bear Voice's forearm. The Indian screamed and pulled away, separating himself from Whit.

Both men gained their feet and began to circle each other, unconcerned with the battle that raged on around them. The painful cut to Bear Voice's arm served only to enrage him more and like his namesake, Bear Voice made a grunt and then with a roar, he sprang. Whit, in turn met him with his own charge and again the men locked in a struggle to overpower each other. Bear Voice pulled Whit's left arm up and leaning in took hold of the arm with his teeth, biting deep and pulling free a piece of flesh. He smiled, spiting the bloody fragment into Whit's face.

Momentarily blinded Whit pushed his opponent away, loosening his grip. Bear Voice then took the opportunity to swing his knife out at Whit, cutting through the material of his vest and shirt, leaving a deep laceration. There was no pain at first, the blade's edge being so sharp. But within moments, it felt as if a hot iron had been drawn across his chest. The sensation of the pain and the feeling of blood flowing down his stomach, stunned Whit, but his instinct to survive gave him a burst of energy. With a roar of his own, he leaped at Bear Voice, bringing his knife up and sinking it under the man's ribs.

Bear Voice, caught off-guard by his overconfidence, could only look in shock as Whit pulled him close, their faces only inches apart. He opened his mouth as if to speak and then went limp, and Whit let him fall to the ground. The once arrogant medicine man now lay face down in the dust at Whit's feet. Only then did Whit take the time to look at his own wounds. His arm throbbed from the bite, and the cut across his chest stung. He pulled his bandanna from around his neck, and wrapped it around his arm, not sure how to treat his chest.

As his mind was occupied with this, he looked around and saw that some of the Pawnee, or maybe the soldiers, had set a few of the lodges on fire and smoke was filling the air. The acrid fumes filled his lungs, causing him to cough and bring more pain to his chest. Through the gray-black clouds of the smoke he saw a movement, a dark form taking shape. It was a familiar form, one that he had seen so many times over the years, that of Little Bird. She was partially obscured by the smoke as she came closer. Whit smiled at the thought that she was coming to him and wondered if he died now, would they be reunited?

He took a hesitant step forward as the smoke parted around her and the woman's features became clearer. There, standing before him was Sees Far Woman. Her leather dress old, worn and tattered. Her hair disheveled, her face bloody. Whit's heart fell and he questioned, if he was dead, and he in hell?

Sees Far had a distant look in her eyes, as if she could not see Whit. But as her gaze fell on the prone body of Bear Voice she changed. With a slight tilt of her head, she started a low moan that grew in intensity to a wild shriek. Her vacant eyes now blazing with hatred and vengeance, she ran toward Whit. Before he could react, she leaped upon him, knocking him down. He rolled on to his stomach to gain his feet, but she was on top of him, pinning him to the ground. Again, and again she drove a knife into his back, the pain so terrible that Whit could not draw enough breath to cry out.

As his consciousness started to fade, he felt her weight disappear and someone turned him over. Through his fading vision he saw the painted face of a Cheyenne Dog Soldier, the long feathers of his headdress quivering with the movement of his head. Whit, resigned to his fate, closed his eyes not fearing death. His only regret is that he was not able to save Maggie and her child. He wondered if, in the afterlife, he would know whether they had been rescued or not. Then, he let the weakness he felt pull him into the dark abyss.

With the end of the fighting, the Soldiers and the Pawnee scouts began a thorough search of each of the standing lodges in the village. As a Pawnee scout stooped to enter one of the hide structures, he took a step back and looking around motioned to the only white man he saw, William Craigavon, to come to the lodge.

William moved over and peering into the semidarkness saw a woman cowering in the darkness of the lodge. She was obviously a White woman. Bending over to enter the lodge, he slowly moved to her, and she drew back in fear. She had probably thought the Pawnee who found her was a Cheyenne who had come to kill her and was still not sure who William was.

"You're safe now," he said in a calm voice, but she didn't respond.

"Nein! Nein! Nein!" she cried, tears running down her checks. William surmised that she didn't speak English and she was most likely the missing Weichel woman, who only understood German.

Drawing on what little German he knew from his reading, William said, "Ich din doctor." He then carefully moved closer and held out his hand. Hesitantly, she took it and allowed him to escort her out of the lodge. It was when they entered the light that William saw how terribly she had been treated. She was thin and frail, having been beaten, and he found blood soaking the side of her tattered dress. She permitted his inspection of her and as he touched the spot where he found a hole in the material, she flinched in pain. She had been shot, but the bullet had been reflected by her ribs.

RIVER OF SAND

He scooped her up in his arms and carried her out of the village to where she would be safe, and he could treat her wound. He soon found Doctor Tesson and informed him he believed the woman was Maria Weichell. At the same time, a Sargent found them and said that Carr was requesting a surgeon. Doctor Tesson and William, still carrying Maria, followed the trooper and found Carr and several soldiers gathered outside the lodge of Tall Bull.

The emaciated body of Susanna Alderdice had been found in the lodge. Her frail form bruised, her face bearing marks of a hatchet, and her stomach showed signs of pregnancy. Carr asked if anything could be done to make the poor woman more presentable, and the two doctors quietly discussed what they could do. As William already had a patient, Tesson offered to bathe the body, closed the wounds, and brushed her hair for burial.

The battle had moved out of the camp and there were a number of Cheyenne still fighting from a ravine. Carr gave orders that his camp was to be organized, and the wagon train called in. It was soon found that the only casualty suffered by the 5th Cavalry was a scratch from an arrow on the forehead of a trooper. As Tesson was occupied, William, with the aid of two Army orderlies, set up a spot where he could treat Maria, making her as comfortable as possible, until the ambulance wagon could be brought up.

Leaving Maria in the care of the orderly, William's services as a surgeon were no longer needed and he turned his attention to looking for his friends, Whit and Eli, who he had been separated from during the battle. It took little time to find Eli, who was talking to Frank and Luther North. Eli hadn't been able to find his wife or son among the dead in the village and had just been asking North if any of the Pawnee scouts might have seen them.

"I'm sorry, but there hasn't been any sign of them. Maybe Whit has found them and taken them toward the wagons," Frank suggested. With some hope both William and Eli started back to where the wagons would arrive making a second search through the village on their way. When they reached the wagons, there was no sign of Maggie, Joseph or Whit.

"I need to go through the village and look again," said Eli, determined to make a third search, and a fourth and fifth if necessary.

And as they turned toward the lodges, a storm broke out, lightning piercing the growing darkness, and hail fell from the sky as if signaling the end of the battle. Throughout the remainder of the night, troopers and Pawnee scouts straggled in through the raging storm.

An honor guard was established to guard the body of Susanna Alderdice for burial the next day. The first guard detail was posted during the height of the storm, to stand a two-hour watch. When the first relief guard detail arrived, those on post refused to leave. This reoccurred as each relief detail arrived. Each honor guard stayed throughout the night until a funeral could be held.

The storm of the previous night turned into mist by reveille at five o'clock the next morning, and Carr sent out a detachment to determine if there were any Indians in the vicinity, while other units went through the Indians camp to count the bodies and collect any stray horses.

As the morning warmed, the mist lifted and the body of Susanna Alderdice, wrapped in a buffalo robe and a lodge skin, was placed in a deep grave. In Susanna's honor, a passage from the bible was read, three rifle volleys were fired, all followed by taps. Once the grave was filled and the sod placed over it, a wooden headboard with her name was placed over it.

When the ceremony was over, a torch was put to the Indian property, their clothing, provisions, and lodges, and the command moved out. The Army's horses were worn so badly that returning to Fort McPherson was impossible, so Carr turned his command toward Fort Sedgwick. It was there, that Eli, and William Craigavon parted from the Army. They returned to the Arkansas with the sad news that they had not only been unsuccessful in finding Maggie and Joseph, but that Whitney Voss was now lost.

***

August 1869 – Breeding Moon

The travois bounced along the prairie, every jolt sending a flash of pain through Whit's chest and back. He found it hard to raise his head and his only view was that of the vacant prairie. He had no knowledge of how long he had been traveling in this condition, as time seemed to blend into small pieces of consciousness, and then he would drift back into the blackness and find himself in a dreamworld. At times, he had no idea if what he saw was real or a dream. The only thing he was sure of was the pain he felt.

During one spell of awareness, he felt a hand on his shoulder and looking over he saw Little Bird walking next to him. She smiled and spoke to the travois, "You will be fine," she said, "We are taking you home."

"I'm ready," he replied, thinking that he was dead, and they were headed to the other side, the world beyond, were there was no pain, no sorrow, no regrets.

***

"Indians!" The warning split the air, and Ben Logan beat on the steel triangle that hung from the front porch of the main house. The front door opened, and Eli, August and Silas came out, rifles in hand. The rest of the ranch hands soon joined them, and they took up a defensive posture in front of the house. The riders, obviously Indians, slowly came closer to the ranch house. There were only three of them and one of the horses was dragging a travois.

"My eyes aren't what they use to be," said Silas, "But, there only appears to be one buck."

"You're right," said Eli, "The other two look like..." He words broke off and he broke into a run toward the riders. "Maggie!" he called out. Maggie reined up her horse and leaping out of the saddle ran to meet Eli, and they embraced holding each other.

"Papa!" Eli heard and looked over to where Joseph sat in front of the Indian.

Eli looked at the Indian and Maggie said to him, "It's Zachary, he brought us home."

"I don't quite understand," said Eli.

"We have come a long way, and I'll explain to you later. Right now, we need to call Doctor Craigavon. His skills are needed for Whitney."

"Whitney? We thought him lost at Summit Springs! We looked everywhere for him."

"You were there?" she asked.

"Yes, William and myself. We were with the Army."

"We saw only Pawnee," she said.

"Who is this," he asked looking at the girl with red hair.

"My name is..." she paused, "My name is Eleanora. Eleanora Voss, I'm Zachary's wife."

"Come on up to the house," Eli said, "There's a lot of people that'll be happy to meet you."

They moved toward the house and when they reached the yard Willow rushed out to take her friend in her arms.

"I have missed you so very much, Sister," she said through tears.

"And I have missed you," Maggie said.

Whit was carried into the house and placed in one of the bedrooms while one of the cowboys was sent for William Craigavon. Before Maggie entered the house, she stopped in front of Silas, who smiled at her and said, "I sure did miss your biscuits, gal."

She smiled and with tears streaming down her checks, she placed her arms around him and gave him a kiss on the cheek.

***

September 1869 – Moon of Plums Ripening

Though it took a while, Zachary and Eleanora slowly adjusted to life outside of a Cheyenne camp. It helped Eleanora having Maggie and Willow as surrogate mothers, and she was soon comfortable back in the White world. Zachary found life on the ranch a bit more challenging, but he had matured during this time away, and saw things in the light of a man. He was happy to rekindle his friendship with Ransom Craigavon and the two became close friends again.

Whitney Voss healed under the care of William Craigavon, and Maggie's watchful eye. He and Maggie found they could still be friends, and their shared past, a part of that friendship. Eli found no threat in Whit, and with the agreement of Silas and August, offered him a place at the ranch. Whit was grateful, but he felt that once he was healed, he would move on, knowing that he always had a place to hang his hat if needed.

Silas was content with the life he had been dealt. Maggie told him that she had spoken to Pistol and that he had asked about his father. She also told him that the last time she had seen him and his sons, they were alive.

"It appears that Turtle Shell has a woman of his own too," she added.

"Well, that means there's a bit of me in my grandson, and maybe someday I'll get to meet my great-grandchildren."

For the present, Silas was content with the single grandchild he had with him, and Henry loved his grandfather in return. Everyone in the extended family looked to Silas as their mentor, and father.

He sat in the kitchen with Zachary, time having taken its toll on the old man, and he seemed to spend more time talking about the past. Since returning home, Zachary seemed more eager to hear about Silas' life and adventures. But at times it seemed as if his "Grandfather" was a bit confused. This day was one of those.

He watched as Silas moved around the kitchen, speaking one moment of the things that were at hand for that day, and the next moment as if he were years in the past.

"You need to take care of the graves over yonder, under the piñons. Make sure that nothing grows up to cover the markers." He moved to the stove and with a rag retrieved the coffee pot.

"Do you need some help?" Zachary asked.

"No. I can fend for myself." He motioned Zachary back with a shake of his head. He moved slowly to the table and poured hot coffee into a tin cup. He then eased down into the chair. It creaked as if it would fall apart under his frail weight.

Zachary couldn't remember when this strong vibrant man had grown old. When had those powerful hands become the boney appendages now covered with paper thin skin? They shook as he lifted the steaming cup to his lips. Zachary feared he would burn himself, but he only blew on hot liquid and then set the cup back down on the table as another thought flickered through his mind.

"I wonder where Red Calf has gone off to." He spoke of his dead wife. "I can't wait all day. Do you know where she could have gone? She was going to fix me biscuits."

"I don't know, Grandpa," Zachary said, "She'll probably be back soon." He sometimes confused Willow with her mother, and it was plain that he sometimes lost understanding of time passing. Red Calf had passed away over thirty years ago.

"You promised me that you would bury him with his best suit on! Don't let me down! Remember, put that silver ring on his hand. The one Red Calf bought him when they went ta Santa Fe. And have Willie say the words over his grave!" Silas exclaimed speaking of his long-gone brother, Father William Scott. Zach knew he was speaking about himself.

"I won't forget the ring." He couldn't figure what more to say. How do you answer a man who talks about himself in the third person?

Then with a clarity of mind that came and went, he said, "I sure would like some fiddle music played during my buryin'."

"I'm sure we could find someone in town that knows how to play one."

"That would be fine, Zachary," Silas said. "There's something else, I'd like, find a good piece of stone and have my name put on it, with the year I was born, seventeen hundred and seventy-nine. Didn't know I was that old, did you?" He smiled and let out a little laugh. "Let's see, on Christmas day, that makes me pushing...ninety-years on this side of the sod!" He clucked his tongue and laughed again. "I wonder if I'll see 1879. You can place that fer the year I go under." He laughed even harder.

"Grandpa, it sounds like you're planning on leaving us." Zachary was concerned.

"No, Son, I'm just being practical. Now, did you saddle up Rocinante like I asked? I want to take a ride out to the north end and get a good look at the geldings. I'd like to pick one out. Rocinante is getting a bit long in the tooth and I'm thinking about letting her spend the rest of her days without carrying this old hoss around. You goin' with me?"

"Sure, you can tell me mores stories as we ride," Zachary said.

Before they left Silas took out his pipe, filled the bowl with tobacco, and then smiled, saying with a smirk, "Ain't no campfire to grab a coal from!"

I'll get you a light from the stove, Grandpa," Zachary said, and taking up the broom, pulled a straw free and stuck it into the stove to set it alight. He held it up to Silas' pipe and he drew on the pipe until a blue-gray cloud of smoke rose.

"That's good, but not the same as a campfire coal," Silas said, and Zachary understood, having seen his grandfather pull a coal from the fire with his bare fingers many times.

As they started out the door, Silas took up his old Henry rifle and shooting bag, and Zachary strapped on a belt with a holstered pistol. They both moved out the door into the yard where Silas' old horse was tied next to Zachary's yellow dun.

Silas went first to the horse's head and let her nuzzle him a bit, and he patted her heck speaking softly to her, only words that she could hear. With some effort, Silas pulled himself up into the saddle, and placed the rifle across his lap as he had done countless times. Though old, Silas sat ramrod straight in the saddle. He adjusted his seating, gave Rocinante "Get up," and with a slight tug on the reins, they left the yard.

The two moved away from the house toward the Fountain River and swung north to where the horses were grazing on the late summer's grasses, a mile or so from the ranch house. There were several geldings among the mares, and Silas and Zachary discussed each one's qualities. Silas dismissed each horse for one slight reason or another, until they came to a buckskin gelding that stood about sixteen hands high. Silas smiled, and with his pipe in hand used it to point out the horse.

"That one will do," he said. "Throw a rope on him, and let's take him back to the corral where you can start working him."

Roping the buckskin was easier said than done, the horse speeding off at a good clip, his head and tail held high. Zachary did manage it though, and once the lariat was snuggly around its neck it resisted for only a short time, then followed Zachary and Silas back to the corral. There, the young man began the slow process of saddle breaking the horse. He used the knowledge he had learned among the Cheyenne and combined it with the tactics of the vaqueros who worked on the ranch. Eli and Whit watching were surprised at the horse's speed and stamina, as well as Zachary's skill.

"He's a stubborn one," Eli said.

"You talking about the horse or Zach?" Whit joked.

"Both I guess," Eli said with a chuckle.

Whit looked at Silas as the old man sat on the fence rail, puffing on his pipe, and watching Zachary.

"That's a lot of horse, Silas." He said, questioning if Silas would be able to handle it, but not daring to say this out loud.

Silas pulled his pipe from between his teeth and without taking his eyes off the Zachary, said, "You know I have always admired President Jefferson. He had a lot of good things to say and one of them comes to mind. 'There is a ripeness of time for death, regarding others as well as ourselves, when it is reasonable, we should drop off, and make room for another growth. When we have lived our generation out, we should not wish to encroach on another,' Been thinkin' a lot about that lately."

"Don't make room too soon my friend," Whit said, patting Silas on the shoulder.

"I think that horse should be the boy's. You know, time is like sand. Sometimes it slips through your fingers," he smiled.

***

Author's Note

At least fifty-two Dog Soldiers died fighting at Summit Springs, as well as many women and children, with seventeen prisoners being captured. Some known Dog Soldiers killed at Summit Springs were: Tall Bull, Brave Bear, Two Crows, Kills Many Bulls, Lone Bear, Black Moon, Powder Face, White Rock and Big Gip. Wolf with Plenty Hair staked himself to the Dog Rope and fought to the end, the last of the Cheyenne Dog Soldiers to die pinned to a Dog Rope.

In the "Life of George Bent", written from his letters to George E. Hyde, Bent says of Summit Springs, "With the destruction of Tall Bull's village, and the consequent breaking up of the Dog Soldiers as a band, some going to the Northern Cheyennes and others to the south, the power of this famous society was broken and never since have they been a factor in the wars of the Cheyenne tribe."

SAM J. PISCIOTTA

Other books by Sam J. Pisciotta

The Cold Rider
Children of the Wolf
Stray Dogs on the Mountain
Dogs of the Winter Star
The Stoney Mountains

Please visit your favorite retailer, Amazon, Barnes & Nobel or
Join other readers at "Books by Sam J. Pisciotta" on
Face Book:
https://www.facebook.com/StrayDogsOnTheMountain

www.ingramcontent.com/pod-product-compliance
Lightning Source LLC
Chambersburg PA
CBHW080856020726
47502CB00008B/2259